GALLOWS

AND OTHER TALES

OF SUSPICION AND OBSESSION

John Arden

ORIGINAL WRITING

978-1-907179-19-8

A CIP catalogue for this book is available from the National Library.

Published by Original Writing Ltd., Dublin, 2009.

Printed by Cahills, Dublin.

Dysdayne I sawé with Dyssymulacyon,

Standynge in sadde communicacion.

But there was poyntynge and noddyinge with the hede,

And many wordés sayde in secret wyse ...

I dempte and drede theyr talkynge was not good.

[John Skelton, *The Bowge of Courte,* c. 1498]

Contents

Part 1 : Ireland

Part 2 : London

Part 3 : Yorkshire

To my son Finn

*who came to make a film of me as I was finishing these
stories, having assured me he'd neither bother me nor create
interference.*

"I am a fly on the wall," said he.

"What the fly sees, I shall see.

Just as it comes and nothing more.

You at work on your PC.

Please, just look toward the door –

No, you'll have to turn your face,

Wrong light, wrong posture & wrong place."

Oh this fly is no mere lazy gazer:

He must direct, he must command:

He beckons with imperative hand.

No fly at all, he's a serjeant-major.

PART 1:

IRELAND

GALLOWS

THEN

King Billy the Dutchman was dead less than a year, but his penal sanctions against popery were very much alive. The protestants of Ireland had begun to believe they were cocks-of-the-walk forever. A damned curious specimen of this interloping tribe was Dr Azariah Brude of Galway city, a physician more feared than respected, more respected than admired, not known to be loved by anyone. He had arrived in the country in 1649 from the rain-blown, desolate uplands of Dentdale in Yorkshire, surgeon's assistant with Cromwell's army, still in his teens and vividly good-looking; he was briefly desired (but not necessarily attained) by a flock of susceptible women. On his travels through the war he had crammed his saddlebags with loot: cash, bullion, jewelry. More unusually, he'd laid hands upon a batch of learned books. It was thought that much of this learning might be heterodox, if not in fact unlawful. However, over the years he proved himself well able to splint broken bones, apply leeches, inhibit the flux, and so forth. He set up a practice in a mouldy old three-storied house on New Tower Street, close inside the south-east wall of the city. He never married: uninformed rumours as to his voluptuous private habits were fantastical and scabrous.

By the time he was in his seventies his blond beauty was reduced to a desolation of trenches and pits, purple blotches, broken teeth. His breath constantly stank, which was odd for a medical man. Many of his patients left him and he had outlived most of the others. He made no obvious effort to find new ones. He devoted himself (so he said) to experiment and philosophical research, whatever that might signify: at all events it seemed to mean that he rarely asked colleagues or neighbours to drink or dine with him, and when he did come out of doors it was nearly always after dark. At times he would sit in the

back-parlour gloom of a tavern in Kirwan's Lane, something of
a thieves' kitchen, where he would swill smuggled brandy and
show his perilous teeth at whomever dared approach him. Now
and again he had a companion in his bouts, a swart, sweating, thick-gutted fellow, an ex-papist from somewhere behind
Oughterard, whom he called his amanuensis. This man had an
instinct for curative herbs, maybe poisons, who could say? He
was known as "the Goose" Cloherty: if he'd ever been christened with a regular first name, he kept it to himself. A doubtful, lopsided sort of creature, as rebarbative as his aged master;
he'd had land (the story went), hill-pasture and meagre cattle
west of the lake; he'd lost every acre of it to the greed of "his
own", his gombeen kith-and-kin. He now made it his business
to show unthinking loyalty: Brude's shadow (as it were) from
the shadows of Kirwan's Lane, a man who did nothing, said
nothing, went nowhere, except upon command.

So when it came to the assizes and the doctor must face trial
for the very terrible murders alleged beneath his roof, the whole
city was astonished to find this Cloherty in the witness box, less
like a goose than an angry cockatoo, screaming out great gulps
of rancid evidence (Queen's Evidence, for a free pardon), swearing his employer's life away, hour after hour of butchery and
rut, until even the judge could bear to hear no more: he sprang
from the bench to throw up his breakfast, while the jurymen
begged for an adjournment.

Cloherty told the court, in surprisingly good English, that
for years Azariah Brude had roamed the wilder parts of Connacht in search of boys and girls, aged between eleven and thirteen, to bring them home to Galway as "medical neophytes"
for the laboratory at the top of his house: complex experiment
was carried out there, extra hands were always needed. Cloherty arranged things with the parents, impoverished mountainy
folk, papists who had no English, only too glad to see a son
or daughter carried off to learn a trade; the children in effect
being bought holus-bolus, to fulfil the doctor's needs and no
recriminations. Cloherty tried hard to persuade the court that

he personally did not witness these needs in all their horror: he would be sent upon errands to Ennis or Ballinasloe, and when he returned the "neophyte" would be gone and a replacement must be sought for.

He did concede that yes, he had once or twice been dismayed to see the doctor lay a young one on his working-slab, stripped and strapped down, he (Cloherty) having been instructed to prepare certain queer little blades, trays, buckets, jars. To scrub them and boil them out with salt. Blood, he described, dung, piss. Spilt seed and vomit. Offal. No, he'd told no-one; for had he not truly believed that Azariah Brude was a humane philosopher who had fed him when he was in dire straits, and whose scientific applications could cause no hurt?

But he went on to testify that a mutilated female corpse, found sunk among the reeds of the lake near Menlo, had been left there by himself, and moreover was one of several: he could not altogether remember how many. The doctor would just say to him, "'twas another unhappy accident, be a good man, tidy things up." When he (Cloherty) heard that this girl's body was discovered, he went straight to the mayor to offer his evidence: he had come at last to apprehend he had been working for an ogre. His conscience stormed in his breast like a fusilier's bomb-ball.

The landlord of the Kirwan's Lane dramshop stepped up to tell the court how Azariah Brude, one Hallowe'en drunker than usual, made a brag and a boast as to the first stage of his experiments, and how the second momentous stage was all but ready to epiphanize, when he surely would reveal, precisely and exactly, in what manner the soul was domiciled in the flesh, and whether it or the flesh made pleasure and made pain, during life, during death, swift or slow - in short, the enormous question, where in fact was God when His little people shrieked for Him?

Brude's defence was absurd. He bent pathetically in the dock, mumbling "innocent, innocent." He denied everything, said the children in his house were legitimate servants and Mr Cloherty was in charge of them ... they fetched, cleaned and carried ... frequently ran away: it was possible that Mr Cloherty was harsh with them ... he himself, God knew it, being too old and infirm to oversee everything ... why, 'twas even possible that Mr Cloherty, oh God! maybe 'twas Cloherty who had ...

And then he began to shout: of course it was Cloherty! Why, the bloody-minded wretch could never have understood the proper function of his service, which was at all times -of course it was - to ensure the good health of the children, body, brain and spirit, as soon as the experiments were completed. For of course the experiments were radical. In the name of God, how could they not be, when corporal, terrestial immortality was at issue? He himself was innocent, innocent! there were sound professional reasons for all the strange instruments in the garret, even the whips and the manacles and the glass retorts with lewd pictures so carefully engraved on their bellies; if he thought the jurymen would understand, he could explain ... And he did so explain, bawling out pedagogical formulae at incomprehensible length.

The jurymen may have hoped for him to be innocent; for were they not twelve good protestants, doubtless feeling now and again that the occasional dead papist, child or adult, could only improve the security of the realm? But the prosecutor was adamant that if a devil-possessed and secret murderer were to seem to be acquitted just because he was a protestant, the realm would have no security. "Riot, rebellion, arson and rapine." The judge said the same, pointing out that in any case Brude's religion was quite out of window: the man had arrived in Ireland an extreme sectarian, and today he adhered to an hotchpotch of occultist quackery - when did anyone ever see him in church?

Thus prompted: a verdict of "guilty". All the catholics of the county knew he was guilty. Protestants, disturbed, disquieted, did not know what to think. (Some few of them nonetheless remained robust in his defence.)

So he came to the gallows at the far northern corner of the wide play-field beyond the main gate of the city. He cried from the hangman's cart, in a huge, ugly voice, "They bring me to a place called the place of a skull, which is called in Hebrew Golgotha ... Father," he bellowed, "forgive them, for they know not what they do!" The hostile crowd groaned and jeered at the blasphemy; stones were hurled, gobbets of filth. The midwinter dawn was darkened by a miserable small snowstorm that drove under hatbrims, into shawls, between the buttons of capes and jackets: all the more convenient for a few reckless men, pope-hating fanatics perhaps, or more probably well-bribed freebooters, who had gathered to attempt an escape. Somehow, between cart and scaffold (and no-one saw it clearly), the militiamen of the gallows-guard were taken flat aback, the hangman was thrown to the ground, Brude's bonds were suddenly cut, a horse was pulled toward him in a flurry of swords and cudgels, he flung himself across the saddle and started off at a jerk and a trot and a stumble up the slope of Bohermore, the great road out of town. But the Goose Cloherty was too quick for him: he led a score of furious catholics, men, women and children, round in a half-circle to intercept the frightened animal. Brude wrenched at the reins and turned its head away from his enemies (and also, decisively, from his friends) toward the city gate, through the gate, into the streets. His way was obstructed by a waggon and a pile of casks left carelessly outside a beershop: instead of being able to ride straight down the town to the fort-bridge and away into Connemara, he was forced to turn left and then to the right and so into New Tower Street. "Innocent, innocent!", he cried. Immediately behind him, well in advance of the rest of the mob and gasping to keep up with the horse, came Cloherty, an almost superhuman burst of speed. The stones were slippery with freezing snow, the beast lost its footing, the doctor was shot from the saddle - crash! into the muck of his very own doorstep. God's judgement? Not quite yet.

For he picked himself up, astonishingly vigorous for an old man after such a shock, he plunged into the house (left unlocked ever since his arrest, and thoroughly ransacked), he staggered up the narrow spiral stair to the top of the building, and from there he doubtless hoped to - to do what? scramble the gables to

safety? jump off to his self-destruction? Impossible to say, because the Goose Cloherty was into the garret behind him, grap-
pling with him, screaming with rage. The doctor, on his knees
beside the fireplace, snatched blindly at a species of trivet that
used to hold a crucible and now lay there broken. He struck
out with the fractured iron and jammed its point into Cloherty's
temple ...

It cannot have been more than a minute, two minutes at most,
before the rest of the wild-eyed herd of vengeful tatterdemalions
came surging into the garret, at least a dozen, maybe five-and-
twenty, and many more upon staircase and street; they were
breathless and implacable (men, women, children), they would
have torn the doctor to pieces ... But O Queen of Heaven! what
drastic slaughtermen had been there before them? For in the
middle of the room, an improvised gallows: and there they
saw hanging the cadaver of Cloherty (all awash with blood and
brains from the great hole in his head); and beside it, the man of
learning, Azariah Brude, as dead as his companion but so newly
strangled that even yet he jerked and kicked and twitched, extruding horrid secretions, breeches fallen down around his ankles, tongue and eyeballs a-bulge in his purple face - the two
of them strung together from one of those dreadful hooks that
the doctor years before had taken such care to screw into his
roofbeams. And no sign at all of any sort of hangman: and
nowhere, so it seemed, where any such a person could have hidden himself.

There was a bit of a ballad made, in very rough English, a tongue
as a rule ignored by the rural poets; but this one was anxious to
thumb his grubby nose at his betters and to see to it that they'd
understand him: -

Come all ye sweet-lipped maidens and a warning take of me
And all ye yellow-haired lovely boys that do inhabit by the strand
    of the sea:
Is it physic y're after traipsing all the way down to town for to
    cure your itching hide?
Beware of the doctors of Galway, sure one's dead but the rest
    are alive.
And they say the one that's dead might walk.
Ah sure, that's only talk?

Aire! *he'll tear out your tripes!*

Beyond that, God knows, the whole story was forgotten.

*

Now

Three hundred years later, exact to the year and the day of Brude's death (though nobody in Galway or anywhere else is likely to be aware of it): the play-field is now Eyre Square, while New Tower Street is St Augustine Street and has in it the public library, the dole office, a café or two, a charity shop, the Department of Agriculture (local branch), a citizens' advice bureau, and the western studio of the national broadcaster, Radio Telefis Eireann. At 7.30 a.m., in wet and dreary weather, a well-known political personage arrives at the studio in his ministerial Mercedes. He is here to be interviewed live on the Morning Ireland radio programme: the delicate issue of Irish neutrality and military non-alignment, and how the devil does it cohere when the Pentagon has Shannon airport as a stopover for its troop-carriers on their way to the Iraq war, just about to begin? He has been in Connemara for a recreative weekend, and could easily have talked to the anchorman over the phone from his hotel bed; but he prides himself on being "a hands-on class of an operator", he gets his professional kicks from the businesslike atmosphere of an honest-to-God studio, microphones, earphones, red lights, green lights, switches, an early girl with a cup of coffee, a sycophantic producer, a sound-engineer slithering about like an eel.

On this occasion, the producer is in Dublin with the anchorman, and the early girl seems in charge of everything. She fits the minister up with a vast set of earphones, positions him in front of the mike and asks him to say a few words to be checked by the sound-man.

"Testing testing, two three four, vote number one for Fianna Fáil, six seven eight nine, no World Cup without Roy Keane, so there y'are, m'dear, and how's y'r father?".

"That's grand, minister; clear as a bell. Now, can y'hear the Dublin studio? They should be talking about unmarried mothers, another three minutes and y're on."

"I can hear. Will he give me the intro?"

"He will. And you'll see the green light when y're on air. It'll be just for the fifteen minutes, and then the Cavan hospital item: the clock's straight in front of you if you want to keep an eye."

"Thank you, thank you, all as it should be ... Jasus, m'dear, han't I done this a hundred times? ... Aha."

He listens shrewdly to the anchorman signing-off the unmarried mothers and "over to our Galway studio for a ministerial exposition of what we are encouraged to hope will be a definitive reassessment of policy ..."

"Minister," booms the anchorman abruptly, right into his ear (so it seems): "We have a denial from the Department of Defence that American military aircraft are using Shannon, we have an admission from the Department of Transport that the go-ahead has been given as from one friendly government to another for the occasional use of Shannon by American armed forces, we have a statement by the Taoiseach that Ireland plays no part in any military alliance, and a parallel statement by the Minister of Defence that neutrality is impossible in the War Against Terror. Can you reconcile the contradictions?"

Slowly and shrewdly the minister begins to hedge, with his well-tried preliminary: "Let's be absolutely clear, David – ", and on without hesitation into a thick, soft cloud of truth suppressed and falsehood suggested. The early girl, watching him through the glass panel, sees a wide self-satisfied smile upon his fat face as he hears himself dodge the obstacles with his usual deftness.

She too is smiling, contemptuously perhaps, but she's beyond his field of vision. Then, all of a sudden, no smile any more and her face changes colour. A light has flickered on her instrument panel: the producer in Dublin is calling her, he's frantic, "Get a grip on it, Deirdre, for godsake! what the fuck are you up to out there?"

"I'm not up to anything," she says flatly. "And let you know I don't respond to that class of language. The minister's as clear as a bell; I have him in me earphones."

"Deirdre, I'm sorry: he is not repeat not as clear as a bell! Interference, intrusion, where does it come from? what is it? what the fuck is it?"

For out there in Dublin he can make nothing of it, a muddle of unwanted voice in a weird old-fashioned Irish, words broken up, phrases unfinished, a moan and a whine and a species of mewing, driving in across the interview, fit to set anyone's teeth on edge, yet obviously the minister cannot be aware of it: somewhere behind the cacophony his garrulous obfuscation can just be detected rumbling on and on, faded away to pretty near damn-all. Through the glass the producer can see the anchorman, untroubled at the microphone, putting questions as weightily as always, no problem, no sense of interruption.

The producer's assistant bends toward her boss, tense with anxiety: "There's calls coming in from all over the shop, nobody out there can hear anything of the minister: David's questions fair enough, but every time the bogus ould bugger attempts to reply, he's drowned in all this -- this -- God, but what is it? it's hideous!"

Hideous indeed. Even now, when it is also, some would say, beautiful: the cacophony has dispersed and given way to a small, thin, Gaelic song. As it were from the throat of a far-distant child among rocks on a green hillside; but excruciating as a needle in your eardrum.

My mammy's cow was red and white, my daddy's dog was black
the man peeped and he crept round the whitewashed gable wall
all a-stoop with a sack on his twisted black back
with a stick and a stick and a spike on the end of his stick –

And overlaying the song, another voice, not quite singing not quite speaking, growing in volume; if the first was male, then this one is female and immeasurably plaintive. "Wicked he said I am, greasy girl of the popery kin, to be punished, he said, hurt – "

A third voice, a boy's, in agonized crescendo. "Wicked he said I am and to be punished, punished, hurt; for being as I am a popery boy, I'm after mitching from mass since all of these three weeks – "

The fourth voice, younger and slighter, full of tears, a boy. "We were filthy, he said. We smelt bad, the other one said. Only that we were fit, they said, for penance and woe in an upper room, they said, wouldn't they tread us down into the bog – "

More of them, voice upon sliding voice; and all the listeners, all over the country, who willy-nilly hear the voices, seem to discern a picture, a ghastly dream-vision that strikes at their hearts – as it were a similitude of a dead grey thorn tree, a bunch of rotten toadstool deep among its roots, and indescribable coagulations crawling up and down the withered bark; and over against it, looming near as tall as the tree, two huge unaccountable tormentors. Ah! how they punish. How the one will be a quiet relentless seeker, as he probes for confirmation of the appalling hypotheses posed by his red-soaked teeth and finger-nails, their sucking, their stroking, their scraping and rending of flesh. How the other will seem a wobbly wet satchel of a man, full-to-burst with black lust and unslakable fury at all the wrongs imposed upon "his own" by his own, long ago, somewhere, where? How it feels to have penance and woe. And then, how it feels to have those moments of kindness and fondling, a feeding with sweetmeats ... until all of a sudden the very worst pain that a poor small creature could conceivably imagine.

While the minister throughout hears only the anchorman,

" -- I must ask you again, minister, are you able to give a figure for the number of American military aircraft landed at Shannon since – "

and the anchorman hears only the minister,

" -- ah now, upon the matter of numbers, I am able to state that the figures presented by certain aggressive lobby-groups are speculative and seriously exaggerated – "

and the public at large hears only the wild crying of the children's desperate tale blown along the airwaves like the smoke of a burning house. "Pierced," wail the voices, "nailed, scourged, thorns in the tangle of hair, rainstorm torrent of blood forced out through the ribs: how can they be forgiven, for they well knew what they did?"

And once again, the high-pitched slender thread of intolerable song: --

You forgot, you'd never thought, in tongue never told, in ink never written,shall you like ourselves be long long forgotten: or shall you now remember?

At which point a most violent eruption of noise, a trample of feet, a crunching as of bones under a great iron wheel - after that, no more words, but a mew, and a grunt, and a choking finality.

No sooner has the programme ended than a swarm of irate enquiries comes buzzing through the producer's telephone, not only from his superiors but left, right and centre from members of the baffled audience. And the anchorman loses his cool: "Bloody well incapable of cutting the interview off, were you? Made a total eedjit of me. All you needed to do was to cue me to say what I always bloody say, 'Apologies for the difficulty in getting through to fucking Galway, so let's go straight to Cavan for a bunch of whingeing health-executives,' -- why the bloody hell couldn't you do it?"

The producer flaps his hands in helpless distress. "Oh don't you see, man? it could not be done! D'you tell me you didn't hear it? Nightmare. Phantasmagoria. Impossible to tear the ears away and you didn't hear it?"

An unproven conjecture: if the present-day RTE premises do occupy the site of Azariah Brude's house, the studio on an upper floor would be at the same approximate level as the garret of the original dwelling. Which may seem to account for the nature of the voices, but how to explain the oddity of their distribution? -- why did neither the minister nor the early girl hear them, nor the anchorman in Dublin, while the producer, his assistant, and listeners all over the country, received them full throttle like a blast of foul air from an abruptly unblocked drain? Should we suppose that as Brude's so-called laboratory was little other than a den for the perversion of science, its toxic emanations three centuries later perverted technology, made nonsense of rational sequence, and incidentally garbled the message?

Ah yes, but what message? Perhaps we should also suppose that those insistent little wraiths, having reached out so fearfully from the bleak bogland of the Further World to ensure that their butchers did not escape the rope, were thereafter compelled to re-create (who knows how often?) their anguish and illogical guilt, pleading to all living souls of Middle Earth who might hear them, for pardon, comprehension, commemoration. And thus, once commemorated, for conclusive oblivion. But nobody heard. Until one day there were radio-waves and thousands were able to hear.

Ah yes, but to comprehend? Nobody ...

The producer's assistant did have a notion, vague enough, to be sure, and she tried to follow it up. At university she had studied the historical varieties of the Irish language and of the people who spoke them, and she now made deductions. She got hold of some facts about the old house and its owner, and a bit of what he perpetrated, or was said to have perpetrated; but the records were no better than a patchwork, she had to guess what she could not find stated ... The producer himself was so disagreeably affected by the experience, that when she told him what she'd uncovered, he said he never wanted to endure another word about it, never. Hallucinatory nonsense, he said, a fluke, a freak, leave it alone. Thoroughly discouraged, she left it alone.

The minister, having learned of the disappearance of his measured words (and they had disappeared: the routine record of the interview was a duff tape, quite blank), dictated an indignant letter to the broadcasting authority. Despite his notorious self-conceit, he might not have been altogether annoyed to read a splenetic article on the state of RTE which appeared a few days later in a national newspaper: --

... another example of the station's incompetence: Morning Ireland was lately afflicted with a cross between a bad acid trip and a third-rate gothic playscript apparently on the run from Raidio Na Gaeltachta. It was perhaps no great loss that an interview with the most evasive of the current pack of dodgy ministers was cast away behind the vocalized mayhem. Or is it possible the whole thing was an exercise in the New Satire? -- warplanes at Shannon and paedophiliac massacre (if that's what we were hearing, it really wasn't at all clear) do carry a certain criminal resonance when placed in juxtaposition.

The Free Travel

He always declared that he was the only Swiss citizen ever known to come to Ireland as an asylum-seeker, and what's more, he was successful: he was granted the status of political refugee; he never ceased to be grateful for it. (Of course it was a long time ago, the early 1960s, and in those days the Irish were actually proud of the succour their state provided for harassed and persecuted strangers.) By 2002, he had become markedly elderly, older in appearance than his calendar years, an abrupt little fellow of wire spectacles, grey goatee beard and Tyrolean hat with a cord for a hatband. In the cord he wore a cock's tail-feather, curly and tawny and half-an-inch too long. He was known among his neighbours in County Mayo as Mr Higgins, Cathal Higgins, or even Charlie: odd for a man with such a strong Teutonic accent, but rather more convenient for day-to-day intercourse than his birth-name, Karl Heugen, which he kept for official purposes.

Now and again he found the chance to insist upon what he called the proper and historical nomenclature: "Ó hUigínn," he would pronounce, with careful attention to the shapes of the vowels and consonants. "That is how it was, and if all of us spoke our beautiful Irish as fluent as were our forebears, that is how it would be."

Forebears? But of course. For in the seventeenth century, during the Thirty Years War, there had been, he would explain, a mercenary captain called Eoin (or was it Éamonn?) Ó hUigínn, a Mayo man in point of fact – cut off in misfortunate battle from the main body of the emperor's army, he blundered through the winter into a deep Alpine valley, and never came out of it. The war had devoured so many of the men of the valley, that when a hard-pressed young widow-woman stumbled over this blood-boltered Gael half-dead in the snow behind her barn, she reacted with immediate practicality – fed him, healed his wounds, bedded him and married him. Nor did his descendants forget their progenitor. Which is why, more than three centuries later, Herr Heugen chose Ireland, and Mayo in Ireland, as his place of political refuge – when he was, as he would explain, a young and perhaps over-zealous financial journalist in unexpected difficulties – difficulties which most certainly were political, as he constantly reiterated – *by no means* some dodgy business with the Zürich police. Anyone who asserted otherwise was collaborating with the slanders that those same police and their newspaper hangers-on had spread so maliciously to cover up their own malpractice. And he had *not* chosen Ireland out of foolish romanticism, but because he believed that his ancestor's nation owed him hospitality in his hour of need while he owed the nation an hereditary duty of service. Whenever he said so, he assumed a formal deportment, miming, as it were, elaborate robes of office as though he saw himself a judge upon the bench or an ecclesiastic at the high altar; he was never a light-hearted man.

And yet he was a married man, and he had married in Ireland, and his wife (when he first met her) was without doubt light-hearted. She was Anastasia Quigley, a quietly merry assistant librarian who had come to Castlebar, the county town, from a sparse, devout parish along the far western seacoast. She had come to look out for herself after years of docile girlhood as the daughter of the local post-office. She had never given anybody any trouble; nonetheless, as her people discovered, she was not really docile at all. At the age of twenty-five she announced her engagement to this clearly impoverished foreigner, refusing any sort of family discussion. She knew they were all shocked and enraged by her wilfulness: nonetheless the wedding took place. At least this queer husband was a catholic. By the turn of the century he and Anastasia had enjoyed almost two decades of quiet companionship, but alas, no children: he was not the kind of man to be an easy-going father and in domestic matters (as she saw it) she tried not to *burden him*.

She had fallen in love with him in a surge of romantic delight, and it really did seem that she'd stayed with him all these years for much the same reason. Except that it was no longer a surge; it was more a profound undertow to a relationship that on the surface was largely made up of irritation, remonstrances, snaps, snarls and slamming doors. Both the romance and the irritation derived from the same source, the circumstances of Herr Heugen's exile from Switzerland. As editor of an outspoken weekly newsletter, he had been suspect for some time in Zürich business circles. One day he took delivery of a mysterious brown-paper envelope: red-hot anonymous scandal, fifty-three pages of hint and implication, deliciously louche transactions between an eminent banker and his even more eminent pan-European clients, businessmen, military men, politicos. Heugen at once plunged into a torrent of excited research. He did not scruple to try bribery and even a shot of blackmail. He found what he wanted to find and he printed it, all of it, with an overplus of perilous detail. In so doing, he allegedly violated an entire complex of unique Swiss laws upon the ins and outs of financial confidentiality. So gross a violation indeed, that the defalcations of the banker seemed of no account compared with the criminality of the journalist who exposed him. A progressively spiteful enquiry by a team of government agents convinced the rash young daredevil he had only one option: to get out of the country before they laid hands on his passport. Which he did, "double damn-quick!" With this powerful quasi-American phrase, accompanied by a cockcrow of infectious, self-congratulatory laughter and the thump of his overdue books onto the desk of the Castlebar library, he quite suddenly won his wife. He talked to her in the library, and then in a coffee-shop, and then most presumptuously in his own flat, like no-one she'd ever met, and he did talk a great deal. All his years in Castlebar, he too had met no-one to hear him so intently and with such undiminished interest.

"The accusations, gracious lady, for reasons of Finance Ministry reputation, were so *trumped-up* – do I make myself clear? of course I do, aha, I might have guessed it, you are swift to comprehend! – so trumped-up and so inaccurate, political pressure, grease upon policemen's palms, that attempts to extradite must fail as unproven, even if it were possible extradition from Ireland for such a type of foreign law, *not* theft, gracious lady, *not* fraud, but for pure Swiss technicality, do you see? You will take another sugar biscuit, please. Therefore, I do consider that I am, and after so long a time, safe ... that is, unless ... *ach Gott*, I must tell you, unless ... "

For his reminiscences carried a price: severe neurotic reaction whenever he'd told her, as he thought, too much; deadly fear lest the Swiss police should after all find a way to get hold of him; even greater fear that the Irish government might be watching him so closely that the slightest glitch in his public conduct could bring instant deportation; and an overriding obsession that somehow somebody (never mind who) would get at his poor little driblets of money in his many different bank accounts at home and abroad and freeze it or confiscate it and utterly destroy him. For an expert in the theory of financial operation, he had proved himself most *in*expert at its practice. It is possible he had been too honest. At times he would venture a mildly blasphemous joke about it: "'He saved others: himself he cannot save.' I am my own *Jesus-Christus* and even less effective." He had not the courage to seek Irish citizenship, although he admitted he yearned for it: the Almighty alone should know what dire questions an application might prompt. Indeed he believed himself "bloody damn lucky" to have scrambled into the country when he did: in this vile new millennium, with all the filthy racist fuss about asylum-seekers, he wouldn't have stood a chance.

Unfortunately for his peace of mind, Anastasia had by degrees grown aware of the horrors of the world outside the public library: the Heugen/Higgins tales of corruption in high places incited her, during her lunch-hours, to dip into all sorts of books that at one time she would never have thought of taking down from the shelves. Paradoxically, her husband seemed unable to recognize his own responsibility for what he saw as her new greed for lurid and sensational information – it could only serve to lead her the Almighty alone should know where, he would expostulate – again and again the fruit of her reading made him gasp with apprehension.

This new public consciousness of hers was also in part due to the shock of the The IRA bomb on Remembrance Day at Enniskillen in 1987, the fourth year of their marriage. Her family ideology, generally speaking, was unquestioned Gaelic-Catholic nationalism; but the fact remained that her maternal great-grandfather had been torpedoed and drowned in the first World War as a stoker on a British battleship. He was a genuine Irish patriot who had nobly gone to sea for what he had been told would be the "freedom of small nations," and she could not shut her mind to it, could not permit the heroisms and griefs of that inordinate slaughter to remain the sole property of prot-estants. Even though she had felt an angry warmth on behalf of the Republican hunger-strikers in Long Kesh, and had wept as a teenager for the innocents of Bloody Sunday, she refused absolutely to accept Enniskillen. And thereafter she found one vicious contradiction after another, in Ireland and out of it, that she knew she must refuse to accept. She began going to politi-cal meetings and writing letters to the press. Mr Higgins was horrified. In *The Irish Times*, her name and address, *Jesus-Christus!* She even took part in marches and pickets. His horror increased: surely here if anywhere, could be a most fatal dangerous glitch! did she intend to destroy him? At first, she paid heed and moderated her activism. But then something else would inevitably crop up, which she must not allow to be passed by in silence. He would remonstrate, she would ignore him, he would rail and rage and weep, oh to be sure she was sorry, and of course of course she loved him, but what else could she do?

And then: one dark afternoon of the autumn of 2002, wet weather, windy weather, black weather, the annual "filling-up of the western lakes," brought the first intimations of gratuitous calamity and an end to all their quiet.

The prologue to the day's events had promised no sort of ill-consequence. A week before his sixty-sixth birthday, Mr

Higgins received his senior citizen's free-travel pass from the Department of Social Welfare. This made him very happy; the more so when he read among the small print that his wife could accompany him gratis, even though she was barely forty-five with a respectable livelihood as administrative officer (newly promoted) to the entire county library – *his* livelihood as much as hers, for otherwise he earned nothing but the odd fee from a freelance article for *The Sunday Business Post*, or from the language-grinds he provided in season to schoolchildren faced with the Leaving Cert. He had applied for a state pension but the state was slow to respond. "They have their reasons," he would mutter darkly, "*Swiss* reasons, through the Interpol; do not think I do not know." He and Anastasia were therefore a prudent couple, miserly (not to put a tooth in it) with their cash. Consider their choice of dwelling: long before the marriage, Mr Higgins had been renting three rooms, cramped and sunless, on the top floor of a plug-ugly, cement-rendered, decrepit old skull of a house (built before the Famine for an official of the Castlebar workhouse, and it looked like it). He brought his wife to live there; there they still were, and moreover with no car.

However, they did manage to make regular little holiday excursions, untroubled expeditions to enjoy the landscapes and monuments of Ireland, a weekend at a time, a couple of nights in a cheap B&B, not too far from Castlebar because of the cost of the buses or trains. And now, with this brand-new sensation of the Free Travel, gorgeous, exhilarating – why, they'd be able to cover the whole country! Anastasia could scarcely contain herself; her most intense personal joy was to take photographs in as many different places as were possible for her to reach, and then to paste them into topographical albums: "A hot day beside Loch Corrib," or "Ourselves on the Inishbofin ferry," or "Drumshanbo in thick mist: Nancy in woolly hat, Cat under umbrella," and so forth. While she made her pictures, Mr Higgins would fill a notebook with pedantic expositions of history and archaeology: "Stone circle incomplete, probably originally contained twelve so-called menhirs, but Dr Wilde expressed doubts, while Raftery does not so much as mention the anomaly; c.f. Duval on Celtic migrations."

The weather was doubtful for a trip to the Rock of Cashel; but Anastasia had been told that to see it at its best, there should be sunshine and rainbow thrown against purple stormcloud, which indeed was the expectation for this particular weekend. Neither of them had ever ventured so far south before. It would be good to say they were not disappointed ...

Anastasia said simply, "I'm wet, let's find a pub," while Mr Higgins could only growl, "Most profoundly pissed-off, profound," repeating it several times with idiomatic variation and plaintive crescendo. The rain was incessant, the view of the rock from the plain was baffled by ground-level cloud, and in any case the spectacular ancient buildings were closed to visitors, off-season, renovations in progress, the Office of Public Works at its most uncooperative. The next day, Saturday, was rather less wet; they caught a bus to Birr to look at the Great Telescope; but that too was undergoing renovation, and was not to be seen. By the evening the rain was as heavy as ever. They found a B&B and decided to go home the next day; but next day was Sunday, and the exiguous Sunday bus service would carry them no further than Athlone; so a second night in the B&B, and a bus to Athlone right upon Monday lunchtime.

They arrived in the early afternoon and had to wait a couple of hours for the next bus to Castlebar. It was due in from Dublin at four o'clock and the timetable said it would leave at twenty minutes past. The bus station was some way from the town centre; they had a long walk in the rain before they found a restaurant that was cheap enough for them and yet not too squalid.

"Pissed-off, pissed-off, pissed-off profound! This fried egg is *leather*. And now, observe outside! it not only rains, it snows. *Jesus-Christus, Sakrament*."

"O Cat, please do not swear, even in whispers. It makes me think you think it's *my* fault. *I* didn't create the weather, *I* didn't cook the food. D'you want to complain to the manager?"

"Complain? How can we complain? No no, my dear Nancy, no! for if we do, we shall be *noticed*."

"All right, so. A glitch. Then we'd best set out for the bus, if it comes in when it says it does we can go on board and stay dry. Up you get, you poor old soldier, march."

Nearly half-an-hour late, the bus swept into the station yard through a ragged veil of flying sleet. It flung up the puddle-water like a sea-horse in a baroque fresco. It stopped with a vicious jerk. It sat throbbing in its open bay while the driver shouted, "Twenty minutes! I'm leaving dead on the minute, I wait for nobody." A slow file of passengers, hunched, huddled, and bowed down with all manner of bags and brollies, caps and scarves, haversacks, walking-sticks, staggered lopsidedly down the slippery metal steps onto the concrete and into the wind. A dreadful sight. The Higginses had left the waiting-room and stood shivering in the middle of a small queue of new passengers, jostling to get on board as quickly as possible.

They were not to be indulged. As soon as all those who wanted to get off had got off, leaving the bus about half full, the driver came stamping down the steps, cashbox and ticket-machine under his arm. A dissatisfied short thick man, bald, with a bulbous nose and the sort of grey beard round his jowl that was only one remove from neglected stubble. It resembled a fragment of coconut matting, bleached. He shut the pivoted door behind him. The queue began to murmur, voices of protest to point out the foul weather, but no good: "Ah no not at all," he growled, "y're not to get on yet, have ye no sense at all o'regulation procedure?" He strode away in surly silence for some twelve paces, totally ignoring the pleas of an infirm old lady who was struggling to pull a heavy suitcase from the luggage boot. Mr Higgins, with a courtly little lift of his hat, immediately went to assist her; Anastasia commiserated with her upon the man's rudeness. Then the latter suddenly bethought himself and came stamping back again, kicking up slush with his toecaps, unlocked the bus and stormed in. He had forgotten his briefcase, full of route-papers and whatever else, a serious matter of security, no doubt. He grabbed it from beside his seat and twisted himself round to come down again. He was cursing under his breath, and he skidded on the bottom step. He nearly fell full length. He seemed to hurt a muscle somehow as he pulled himself upright; he continued to curse, aloud now and very brutally; once more he stamped off toward the station office; and this time he forgot to shut the door.

The queue waited miserably. It was enlarged by several of the passengers from Dublin who had only disembarked for a leak or a cup of tea and would now resume their seats, but felt they mustn't. Anastasia said, "I don't know why we're still stood here. Sure the door's open, look at it, let's get on, are we all in a state of petrifaction or what?" Nobody took her up on this. Those ahead of her in the queue clustered protectively together, blocking any move she might make toward the door. She gave an unexpected burst of the gay laughter of her girlish days, quite enchanting to Mr Higgins, a brief recall of rapturous dalliance. The queue was less enchanted. A stooping, clerkly man responded without looking at her: "He said, no. The regulations. They have a right to keep control."

A woman beside him, hard-jawed, henna-haired, bosomed like a kitchen dresser, completed his thought: "It's the likes o' these that create the trouble, forcing forward all disorderly, never holding to their own proper place."

Anastasia grew angry. She laughed again, and there was no gaiety. She caught Mr Higgins by the hand and towed him round in a semi-circle despite his bleating protests, a swift decisive movement to outflank the head of the queue: under the nose of the hennaed woman, into the bus, into an empty pair of seats. Her action was a startler. The logjam was broken. The intimidated passengers (not so much cowardly as simply too cold to initiate any action themselves) began to swarm up the steps in a flurry. At which point, the driver returned.

He forced himself forward (*all disorderly* indeed) into the bus before any of the others, saw immediately the pair of Higginses sitting there so smugly up near the front, he assailed both them and the rain-sodden swarmers with furious words. "Who in th'name of God let yez onto this bus? There's nobody clambers aboard here till *I* give the word, nobody, d'y'hear? and all of the rest of yez, get offa this doorway; when I get out me tickets and cash and let y'know I'm good an' ready, that's the time for yez to clamber, not before, d'y'hear me, not a minute before." He bent over Mr Higgins so closely that one grey beard almost hooked itself to its opposite, as it were a species of human Velcro; Mr Higgins reared himself up at him, his livid face mottled with resentment; they might have been an asymmetrical mirror-image of one another. Anastasia madly thought of a bookjacket she'd noticed in a library stack ("Fantasy/Horror/ Sci-Fi"): an uncanny pair of doppelgangers: *The Day He Met Himself,* some such title ...

The driver hadn't finished. "Ye're not fucking permitted into a seat without a ticket," he snarled. Shudder and shock all round at his crudity; he took no notice. "Y'cannot fucking *show* a ticket till *I'm* here to check it, so offa this bus this minute and find y'r fucking station up the arsehole o' th'fucking queue."

Something way beyond rational annoyance was stirring the man up, that was clear; was it perhaps the Tyrolean hat and silly feather, or Anastasia's pretty chain that looped her glasses to her neck? At all events, she was so shocked she couldn't speak. To her astonishment, Mr Higgins *did* speak, and moreover with considerable force. "You are exceeding rude, I shall not stomach it. Myself and my lady, be assured, require no ticket. Observe please, observe! here is my pass, 'senior citizen', I travel without payment, it is my privilege, my toil of years deserves respect, and here in my land of Ireland is a government to give it me. So therefore, here I am, here I shall sit."

"Let him sit, he has a right to it." A gratuitous cry of support from an old woman on the other side of the aisle. "An' *you'll* be expecting the same class of right in a year or two's time, me bucko; oh I can see the snow-white of what's left of *your* hair, so I can, so I can."

She cackled away in virtuous derision, while a number of other passengers, emboldened by her boldness, chipped in with variations, "Ah sure let him sit -- they should *all* be let aboard – not the man's fault he's a foreigner – at least he's not a blackie – treat us like cattle, how are ya? – no no 'tis not good enough – public transport jacks-in-office, who the divel do they think they are?" etcetera.

The driver recognized defeat. He shrugged dismissively, he let them sit, he spat out a final defiance: "Ha, the free travel, is it? Be the same token, a bloody asylum-seeker, don't tell me he's not old enough to know better; if I had me own way there'd be no free pass issued to none o'them, not to none o'them at all, at their age it's not worth the fucking candle. Exterminate the pack of 'em, begod that Dr Shipman beyond in Manchester, be-god he was a man o'good sense if ever a medical man was, ha. Exterminate, ha." He turned his back on all of them, plonked himself down in his seat, and with the worst possible grace began to check the queue's tickets and admit them to the bus.

He drove to Castlebar with exaggerated care, sounding his horn at every corner, refusing to let anyone overtake him until the very last minute. When the Higginses got out, he was already out before them, bowing and scraping like a lackey on the pavement, with his old woolly cap clutched against his chest. They coldly ignored him, but Anastasia did feel that this preposterous piece of parody had managed to trump the trick. She wished she could have thought of something really witty and cutting; in default, it was probably best to walk swiftly away without comment.

The next day she said they should send a complaint to the management of Bus Éireann. "'Tis silly enough to be sure," she declared, "but I really would feel I'd let down the other passengers, if we allowed ourselves to neglect it. The buses are a public service, Cat, a much bigger issue than that awful lunch at Athlone; surely you can see it? You're a democrat, you always say so." Mr Higgins, already repenting his outspokenness, did his best to dissuade her. But in the end she was too strong for him. He only submitted on condition he should write the letter himself. Thus, he suggested, he could keep it toned down; no reason to attack the man personally.

"I'd say you've got every reason. What he said was disgusting."

"Your rigidity will ruin me. I shall write what I must write. Go to hell."

He was in no mind to call her "Nancy", his name for her of love and amusement. Today she was one of those other variants of Anastasia which he never mouthed aloud but kept shamefully clasped to his secret heart: "Stasi" when he despised her for her beady-eyed surveillance of his weaknesses, "Nazi" when she imposed her outrageous will upon him, chivvying him to accede to her vulgar public yearnings. That reckless affair in Zürich was the last time in his life he would ever be a public person; *Herr Gott!* but he had learned his lesson. For what good had he done? Swiss banks were as corrupt as ever, and he himself was a man on the run ... So his letter consisted of little more than a formal protest against passengers kept out of a bus at a halting place; why could they not be allowed on board as soon as it came in? He briefly mentioned the driver's scorn for the holders of free passes, but added that he wished "no harm to the individual, who no doubt had had a most trying drive from Dublin through filthy weather." He went off to his bed then in dudgeon and depression. Anastasia opened the letter and added a postscript over her own signature:

> Trying drive or not, he very clearly said that old people should be exterminated. Also asylum-seekers. He shouted at us that we should go into an a---hole. My husband has poor health; if he collapses (as well he might) I shall take legal advice.

She scuttled out to post it; she said no word to Mr Higgins of her additional sentences. Within a fortnight they had a reply, addressed to both of them, a polite restatement of the company's rule that a driver must never leave his vehicle open and unattended, and if by mistake he should do so, then passengers who have illegitimately embarked must obey his instruction to disembark. On the other hand (and here the Bus Éireann spokesperson became seriously apologetic), there was absolutely no excuse for the kind of language, racialist, discriminatory, obscene, alleged to have been used. The employee in question had been reprimanded. Severely. The company took a grave view. Nor did the company in any way endorse the employee's erroneous opinions on the free pass situation. If Mr Higgins had not had a free pass, the company would gladly have forwarded him a voucher for another journey to Athlone. And so on and so forth, humble pie, creep and crawl. Anastasia laughed for triumphant glee; but Mr Higgins was worried. He had not written anything specific about "language", so *she* must have done so behind his back. He said nothing about it, but he knew that she knew he would prefer her not to play such tricks. But then, maybe the driver was a notorious foul-mouth? and if so, would the reprimand quench him? Suppose he drove on the Castlebar service all the time? Scope there for all sorts of funny trouble.

An intelligent premonition. A month later, on a Saturday evening, when the town was packed with pre-Christmas shoppers, Mr Higgins was all but run down in the dusk. A bus came pounding round a narrow corner at what (he was sure) was far more than the legal speed, and down a street where he had never seen a bus before. It was certainly not the normal route. He was the only one of a crowd of people on that piece of pavement to be actually caught stepping off to cross the street when the bus made its violent turn. He leaped backward, caught his heel on the curb, sprawled painfully; a young fellow picked him up and helped him straighten his clothes and gather his spilt parcels back into his stringbag. He was not exactly damaged, but he did need a drink. He went into a pub and bought one, a most unusual extravagance. He was almost sure, not quite sure – but it was as though he had the man's image burnt onto his retina – was not the driver that damned greybeard from Athlone? Just a glimpse, as he fell, but *Jesus-Christus* he was all but certain.

Shortly after the New Year, he was listening to the Joe Duffy programme on the radio; listeners (identified only by their first names) were calling in about the threatened economic downturn and revived unemployment; suddenly a man's voice, hoarse and querulous, a voice that he knew, was all but certain that he knew, introduced merely as "Seámus," made a quick verbal leapfrog from loss of jobs to rancid xenophobia: "Isn't it a fact, Joe, root o'th'matter, now; all these damned asylum-seekers with every benefit in the world and the new cars and the council houses, matter-a-damn they're not supposed to be allowed work here at all – oh they do, Joe, they do, ha'n't yez heard o' th'black economy, wha'? Why 'tis not more than a month since, a feller on my bus, sure he stuck out the tongue at me to tell me I couldn't – " He was cut short by an acid rebuke for racism and irrelevance, but he'd said what he had said and Mr Higgins had heard him. Anastasia had not heard; she was busy up and down the flat with odds and ends, she said the radio reception seemed to be very bad, whatever the man had uttered had been lost to her among the atmospherics. Several times Mr Higgins saw, or thought he saw, or was all but certain he thought he saw, this Seámus yet again with his bleached-doormat beard at the wheel of a bus, passing him far too closely, showering him with wet from the gutters, hurling the vehicle right up to the very edge of a pedestrian crossing when Mr Higgins was in the middle of it. On more than one of these occasions, Anastasia was with him, but she insisted she'd noticed nothing out of the way, nor had she recognized the driver.

He often watched football or hurling on television. Anastasia sometimes watched with him. It was odd that she never saw a puffed-out grey-bearded face – not even the briefest glimpse – somewhere in the quick shots of the yelling spectators. *He* saw it, was certain he saw it, he assured her he was certain. She looked at him sideways and made no comment.

Another sort of television, Monday night, the Questions & Answers programme: the camera panned over the studio audience during a heated debate about pensions and old age. Mr Higgins cried to his wife, "Nancy, Nancy, look there! Third face in second row, is it not him? See the beard, see the great nose, see!" But she was just going into the kitchen alcove to bring out the tea and biscuits, she was sorry, she hadn't had her eye on the screen. (The fact was, she *had* had her eye on the screen and had not seen the man. Had he been there at all? If not, what on earth was Cat up to?)

"I said I am sorry, Cat, and please does it really matter?"

"Oh but of course it matters! I am so sure I saw him clap his hands and cheer, when that right-wing dinosaur idiot on the panel proclaimed that all the pensions, free passes, medical cards, should never be given unless many proven years of public service and evenso with the most strict means-test!

"Part and parcel of what, Cat? Will you tell me what are you talking about?"

"Part and parcel of all of it. Oh I knew they would not let me stay here all these years uninterrupted. I said it would come, it has come." He went off to his bed.

There was to be a great demonstration in Dublin against George W. Bush's invasion of Iraq. The invasion had been provisionally, and most weirdly, announced for the 17th of March, St Patrick's Day, as though (declared Anastasia) the craven support given to Bush by the Irish government had deliberately to be underlined ... Why, the Taoiseach would be in Washington, actually handing a bowl of tributary shamrock to the American President the very morning the bombs began to fall: incongruous humiliation, at which she could only howl and guffaw and spring like a clockwork spider from one end of the flat to the other. Mr Higgins wept. "How can I tell," he sobbed, "how degraded I am by this war? impossible for me to analyse my abhorrence! – am I the more outraged that Bush – with his Blair and the base Spaniard Aznar, what d'you call them, his two hand-guns, his dirty-faced ghillies? – that he is thus to *aggress* like the war-criminals of Nürnberg, so rightly condemned at Nürnberg, yet it was *not* right, never *is* right, to take men's lives by gallows-rope, whoever, whatever, *Gott* so many contradictions! or now my new outrage that I am morally badgered to break all my rules and swagger in streets with a placard? Which oh which is worse? O Nancy what am I to do?"

"You do what you like," she cried. "No-one is badgering you. Never ever have you been badgered, you silly old soldier, not by *me* at all events. *I* shall go to Dublin, *I* shall march, yes I shall carry a placard, if you come I shall love you for it, if you don't come I shall not despise you, I know who you are and why."

"And yet it is the first time since I am in Ireland that this land of my origins has colluded with aggression, unprecedented outrage, incongruous humiliation – "

"O Cat, that's just what *I* said, we're totally in agreement, so. You must say it to everyone."

"They look to expect at least twenty thousand; in a crowd so great it is possible I will not be noticed, will not be deported. O Nancy I am so outraged, *Jesus-Christus,* I will take the risk. I daresay, if they fight with the Guards, I can cower. Do you not think?"

She could not remember him so brave, no never before.

There was a special bus hired from a private company to bring people from Castlebar to the demonstration. They would have to pay a moderate fare. Mr Higgins, of course, could have used his travel pass on the railway or Bus Éireann: why did he not? Because: "Firstly, the trains at the week's end are subject to intolerable delay. Secondly, dearest Nancy, I am now so nervous in regard to any public bus to Dublin, the Almighty alone should know who is driving it. So what to do, but travel private?"

He and Anastasia were among the first to arrive at the rendezvous in the carpark, carrying their small banner rolled up; it was an old bedsheet fixed on two canes to be carried between them, lettered with black and red waterproof markers –

WARPLANES OUT OF SHANNON !
NO BLOOD FOR OIL !!

Gracious Heaven! how could it be? but it was beyond all possible doubt: the driver of the bus was the man Seámus and none other, bottle-nose, pot-belly, abrasive threadbare beard and abominable sneer. Mr Higgins stood and goggled in stupefaction. Anastasia had to laugh, there was such starling-on-a-fruitbush impudence about the creature's posture as he stood by the steps and held out his hand for the tickets, that really he could *not* be taken seriously.

She had to ask him: "Are you moonlighting? Or you're no longer with Bus Éireann?"

"Thanks to you and your gentleman here, *no longer* is the fucking word," he growled. "Who were *they* to reprimand me? I told 'em what to do with their fucking reprimand, so here I am, yeh? And o' course not a word o'support from y'r men at the union, bastards. Oh well may they preen themselves on their sodding anti-racism, when an Irishman in good standing gets the cards for telling the truth ... Sure, the wages here is better but the hours three times worse. Have a good day." He turned away from her. Then suddenly he swung round again, his hand momentarily on Mr Higgins's forearm to check him as he followed her up the steps. A hoarse ferocious whisper, from the busman's throat or the surrounding sky? whichever, it was inaudible to anyone else: "And you too have a good day. And then another and another, as many as y'fucking like, and *I'll* be there too, don't mistake it."

It was as though Mr Higgins had a dagger of ice thrust in beneath his fifth rib. He opened his mouth and shut it, twice. At last he could speak; he put a fearful, breathless question, "What do you want with me?"

"Just so you never stop remembering me, that's all ... Or maybe till I crash the bus and fire you through the windscreen."

This was possibly a joke. Anastasia might have recognized it as one and even made peace on the strength of it. But Anastasia had not heard it, and when her husband told her about it, she told him it had never been said, and would he please get rid, for God's sake, of this silly obsession, it would only destroy him, oh did he not realize? So he fretted and muttered all the way to Dublin.

No further aggravation from the driver during the journey. When they unloaded in a back street of the city centre, he was not to be seen; he'd no doubt (after his surly fashion) gone round the offside of the bus to avoid having to help passengers with placards and so forth from the luggage boot.

An enormous demonstration, unprecedented, incalculable. "Far more than twenty thousand," (Anastasia's implausible cry) "no, at least half a million!" Mr Higgins, in the deepest gloom for having fetched himself there in the first place, muttered only that crowds in streets were impossible to assess (how would he know, so? he'd never come out before, let him leave the assessments to the regulars; Anastasia was displeased with him). The march set off from Parnell Square, down into O'Connell Street. O'Connell Street was already brim-full of demonstrators who had not been able to get through to the preliminary speeches and music, and who were now obstructing the progress of those who had. The Garda Síochána changed its plan: both sides of the street were to be used by the marchers instead of the eastern lane only. There was a great deal of scurrying about of fluorescent yellow jackets (march-stewards as well as Guards), jamming up of banners, shouting of contradictory instructions over loud-hailers. A brief but total blockage in front of the Rotunda was caused by a species of gigantic handcart laden with drummers, dragged along by a dozen young women, almost unmanageable on the turn. In the course of this confusion, the Higgins's banner had to be taken down; Anastasia being so pushed by the crowd that she was no longer within reach of her husband. She just had time to throw her end of the cloth on its cane over peoples' heads for him to grasp and roll up; and then she lost sight of him. Both of them were quite short, and easily became invisible amongst all the placards and leprechaun toppers (fun hats for sportive crowds, and today did seem to be .....sportive.) She thought he was one of those diverted by the stewards down the other side of the street; she yelled out to him as he disappeared, "We'll meet up by the Bank of Ireland!" Had he heard her? Probably not.

But when she reached the Bank of Ireland, there indeed she saw him. And dear God, how she wished that she didn't.

On a traffic island at the junction of College Green and Grafton Street, there he was in the thick of a furious physical struggle against – O dear God, he was fighting the bus driver! With his right hand her husband had apparently seized one corner of a placard the man was holding; he was violently attempting to wrest it from his grasp. In his left hand he had their own rolled-up banner; he was beating his antagonist ineffectually over the head with it. Both of them were yelling filthy words at one another, incoherently, inexplicably. The passing marchers gaped to see them, but no-one seemed concerned to interfere until Anastasia sprang onto the traffic island and flung her arms round Mr Higgins's neck. Half-strangled, he let go his hold on the driver's placard; the driver fell over backwards; the placard shot out of his hand onto the tarmac. A Guard came running up to them. Anastasia grinned at him fatuously: "It's all right, Garda, no problem, sure they're after misconstruing 'emselves, a pair of old men and over-excited; all finished, all gone, that's all that it is, we go home." The bus driver muttered something deprecatory on the lines of "ah not at all, sure 'tis nothing to do wi'me, Garda, no desire o'mine, not at all," reaching for the placard, scrambling shamefacedly to his feet. The Guard blinked and frowned and saw no reason to deploy his power: both parties to the scuffle were off in opposite directions. He stood there for a few moments to make sure of the fact; shrugged his shoulders; rambled across the road to keep an eye on somebody else.

In the ten seconds that it lay on the ground, Anastasia had just been able to snatch one swift glance at what was scrawled on the wretched placard:

JEW'S control Two-third of Worlds' Wealth

Jew's control Bush/Blair, BBC, RTE

SaVE saddam AND palestine FROM israeli'S now !

NO WAR !!

"Cat," she said, as levelly as she could, "No more of that bus. We go home by the train. I think we'd better go home now. We've made our mark on the march, old soldier, no need to stay any longer. Plenty of time to get to the station and have a good dinner in the restaurant there, and then we can catch the train."

"I knew it, I knew it," he was croaking as he allowed her to lead him away, and speedily, along Dame Street. "He's all that I thought he was, absolute Fascismus, a Stasi-Gestapo, a Nazi, I saw him with that placard and arguing with stewards, and they would not take it from him. He's here because of *me*, you know."

"No he's not, so don't be silly. He's here because he's a racist and he thinks this horrid war gives him a great chance to defame Jews; why should you think he thought of *you* when he fixed his intention to come here? O Cat, it makes no sense."

"That bank-director in Zürich, didn't I tell you, I exposed his corruptions, Dr Schwarzloch his name? he wanted me, *wants* me, in prison or dead. He'd do anything, send anyone, to get me there. *And* he was anti-Semite, still is of course, and plus, *plus*, as they say, his bank is nowadays exposed as having stolen Jews' money in the war, millions: of course of course he makes his move toward *me*."

He would not allow her to persuade him otherwise or in any way to comfort him. She fetched him home easily enough, but she was in great distress of mind. The next day was Sunday and he spent all of it in bed, his head under the duvet. He scarcely spoke a word to her. He pushed aside the food she brought him.

Monday morning, he was up before daylight. He went quietly out of the house with his hat and his walking-stick and in several layers of clothes, an old Alpine cloak worn over all of them. Anastasia was fast asleep when he departed: she had to deduce his garments from those he left behind in the wardrobe. The weather was cold but not as cold as all that. Where *could* he be off to? Hill-climbing? It was absurd, it was frightening, it might be very dangerous: she decided not to go to work, and in the early afternoon, after useless enquiries among people she knew in the town, she took herself to the Guards. They told her a man could enjoy a long walk without needing to be reported as a Missing Person. If indeed, as she insisted, Mr Higgins was a little deranged, then perhaps a long walk was the very best thing to help him pull himself together. They did, rather casually, promise to keep a sharp eye.

For two weeks, three weeks, nothing was heard of him. The Gardaí at last condescended to post him as Missing; but that brought them no nearer finding him. And then, some twenty miles away, out beyond Westport, below the slope of the holy mountain Croaghpatrick, a grimly suggestive discovery. A farmer was driving a tractor along a bog-road through the greeny-brown emptiness of dead bracken and heather and gorse; into the corner of his eye came a flutter of cloth blowing out into the wind from where it was caught up on the bushes, portions of clothing, a shirt or two, a cardigan, a ragged Aran sweater, boots (in a bog-hole), socks, trousers, long-johns and – most notable of all – a great torn mantle of a thick grey tweed-like material. It was so unusual a class of litter to be found in such a place that he climbed down from his tractor and began to gather it up. There was a double-breasted jacket that might have belonged to a townsman's best suit; it was all rotten with the rain, but he could tell there were things in the pockets. Loose change, a handkerchief, a ballpoint pen and a small wallet. In the wallet were three twenty-euro notes, an almost illegible draft of a letter (the ink half-dissolved by wet) addressed to "Mrs Anas ... of ... stlebar", and a laminated free-travel pass made out in the name of Karl Heugen.

No walking-stick was found, and if Mr Higgins's hat had at one time lain abandoned with the rest of his clothes, it had long since blown away. At all events, it was never discovered.

The Guards sent the letter to Dublin to be analyzed, whence they sent it to England, where with great difficulty and all sorts of sophisticated laboratory contrivance an expert in the end was able to make out most of it. There were gaps where the writing could not be recovered but the general sense seemed clear enough.

My beautiful Nancy,

I could not bid goodbye because had I tried ...But he is nonetheless after me and I must fly from him. Even after so many years, your old soldier is still a refugee ... absolutely not possible return to Castl ... How ... abandon the only true love of my heart? But bring you into my own private peril? ... dreadful task for myself alone. I make my way first to the haunt of the <u>Patron of my Ancestral Land</u>. Perhaps from his mountain, where I sit and write these ... accrue the wisdom ... what to do next ... never be free, never. Even here he still follows, <u>again again flight?</u> or ...

It took another five days for an elaborate police search to find the stark naked body of Mr Higgins, nearly three miles away from his clothes. It lay submerged in a flooded turf-digging, ten blackened toes sticking out from black water at one end of the trench. The skin was scored and bloodied as though he had forced himself, or had been forced by someone else, through briars or gorse or possibly barbed wire. His spectacles and walking-stick were found on the edge of the trench. The spectacles were broken.

Anastasia identified the corpse in the mortuary, without any
show of emotion. She had not expected, she told the Guards,
to hear that he was still alive. She had done all the crying she
had to do. Now she must sit down and think out just how it
had happened and why. An inquest, in due course, brought in
a verdict of accidental death. Cause of the accidental death:
exposure leading to heart-failure. Despite the curious expressions in the letter, there seemed no serious evidence of foul play.
The funeral was quiet. Many of her relatives forbore to come:
the original row over her insubordinate marriage still rankled.
Moreover, despite the inquest, the circumstances of Mr Higgins's demise were thought to be equivocal and "unpleasant".

Toward the end of the year, almost twelve months to the day
of that unchancy excursion to Cashel, Anastasia decided to visit
Dublin for a professional conference. She would use a private
bus service. The fare was considerably cheaper than on the
public routes. Now that Cat was no longer there to fetch her
along on his free pass, this was of some importance. She had
no thought of the bleached-doormat man; no, not today: it was
not at all the same company as the outfit that had been hired for
the anti-war march, no.

Yet there he was, without a doubt of it, scowling over the
steering wheel.

She supposed he had a right to change his employers. Or
maybe they'd changed *him*. Neither he nor she gave any sign of
recognition, nor did they the following evening when it so happened (and why wouldn't it?) he was the driver for the return
journey. She took her seat at the back, opened her briefcase
and set herself to study some papers from the conference, about
librarians' duties in Sweden.

It was dark when they passed through Longford; her eyes
were tired with trying to read and annotate some very boring
prose in the dim electric light, so she put away her spectacles
and her documents and nodded off to sleep. She was vaguely
aware, as the journey progressed, that many people got off and
nobody got on. She awoke for a moment at Ballaghaderreen to

see what she took to be the last of them leaving the bus. In fact, apart from herself, there was one other still aboard, a school-boy of fourteen who crouched curled-up in his seat a little way down the aisle, his head so low as to be invisible to Anastasia. He was making a short journey between Frenchpark and Swin-ford to visit his aunt; it was the week of the half-term holiday. He too was asleep, or more or less asleep.

Her own sleep reclaimed her. She was swayed back and fro by the rocking of the bus. Aware of the harsh motion even in the depth of her slumber, she dreamed of atrocity. Her husband on a mountain side, bleeding and swooping and crying like a curlew through the snow; he was carrying a sort of halberd, with blood all over the blade, and now he was half-dressed in raggedy horse-soldier's gear and now he was stark naked. He cried her name and came at her, his weapon poised to kill ...

The schoolboy, whose name was Rory McConn, was never exactly certain what happened shortly before arrival at Swin-ford, not even certain of what he had seen, particularly as Garda interrogation at his hospital bedside served only to confuse him. He was pulling himself up in the bus seat, he told them, recog-nizing the outskirts of his destination, looking into his sports bag for a raincoat (the night was coming in wet), when suddenly "this woman, from the back o' the bus, isn't she lepping down the bus, like, with a screech offa her like a – like a fire-engine, know what I mean?" He remembered her as short, in a black suit, with short straight dark hair, and a white, white face a bit like his aunt's but prettier, "foxier, know what I mean? like I'd seen her behind me when I got on? Like, then she was sleeping, like an angel's-face, angel?" The face, though, when she leaped forward, was all distorted and "dreadful, you'd not think it the same one." *Dreadful*: he repeated the word and shuddered at the memory. He said he thought he saw her spring onto the driver from the side. "I saw a giant rat once on the jacket of one o' them horror books, like its teeth were – like thumbtacks the size of y'r fist. Okay. Rat." He said she had seemed to spread herself all over the driver, and he saw her two feet, heels upward in long boots, thrusting out into the air "above the platform where you get onto the bus, know what I mean? Two of 'em, kicking like upward, she'd no balance, it was all a great lep and a flight." At that point the bus had swerved off the road into a tree. The driver, Seámus Connaughton of Westport, originally from Drumcondra, aged 56 (according to the newspapers), was hurled through the windscreen with Anastasia hanging onto his shoulders as it might be a screaming haversack; according to the newspapers, they died instantly. Young Rory was bowled down the aisle, lacerated, stunned, his arm broken. The Guards who went to see him came away little the wiser as to what it was all about.

Maybe Anastasia had intended suicide? maybe murder? maybe both together? Or maybe neither. Maybe no more than a *display* that outran itself. When her briefcase was looked into, it was apparent that her various notes in the margins of the Swedish report included one that had nothing to do with libraries:

sit here in silence, all the way to C'bar? did so yesterday
yesterday was morning, today's getting <u>dark</u>
Cat says I MUST. he says. ~~don't want to hear him~~ says it in the
<u>dark</u> &

MOLLY CONCANNON
& THE FELONIOUS WIDOW

The imminent arrival in Ireland of a war-making American
president was not comfortable for the more senior officers of
the Garda Síochána. (Rank-and-file were in general complacent, greedy fingers already twitching for the rustle of their
overtime banknotes.) Inspector 'Bat' Masterson made his own
views very clear to all within range, which is to say those gardaí
currently on duty in Ballykillard police station and maybe the
small picket of anti-war demonstrators chanting in the street
outside: the inspector had a voice like a low-flying helicopter,
it rattled every window in the building. "Why cannot the oil-
mongering omadhaun choke himself into hospital on another
of his pretzels, instead of distressing us in our own cosy home?
Ah the fuck with it."

Ballykillard, a town of middling but fiercely asserted importance, has a cathedral and a college of the national university,
as well as a fictional name: tactless in regard to its law-enforce-
ment personnel to identify it more precisely. Although it is neither Sligo, nor Galway, nor Tralee, and certainly not Limerick,
it does (like them) lie a little inland from the west coast and it
delights in a very busy summer. By the same token, a police
station at the height of the season in such a locality can also be
very busy – the guards' ears, as well as their telephones, never
done ringing with all the clatter and crack and cacophony of
tourist-events, arts festivals, sports fixtures, irregular buskers,
traffic-jams and traffic-accidents, public carelessness, public incompetence, public incontinence, drunkenness, joyriding and
gratuitous ruffianism, to say nothing of outright crime. Black
injustice (brooded Masterson) to add the absurdity of this presidential visit: one night and no more the man would be spending
in a country-house hotel a few miles from Shannon airport, and
then a so-called conference for just an hour, or maybe two, with

a shabby gang of Euro grandees, their incipient disaffection only slightly moderated by the assured subservience of the Irish taoiseach as titular host. Who could truly *confer* at so brief a meeting? with time for little more than the president's acceptance of tributary courtesies after the style of an ancient Pharaoh, plus a few of his sanguine platitudes as to the next stage of his war, already in its second year. Then the photo-ops for electoral purposes against an indigenous green landscape. Then just possibly a quick walkabout, gift-wrapped by bodyguards, to greet a select handful of 'characteristic' Irish countryfolk, in fact some of the staff of the hotel, gardeners and such, as indigenous as the landscape: by no means Romanian waiters or management trainees from Belarus. Then to meet the press, extruding equal quantities of his arrogance and charm. And then *off* with him at-once at-once and the whole of his strutting cortège! – would he even be aware in which country he'd spent nearly half of a whole weekend, as his looming monster of a jumbo-jet roared out into the Saturday sunset like a dragon-harnessed chariot, legendary, overpowering, a vision of incalculable threat?

"For the protection," Masterson growled to the sergeant he kept by him to be growled at, "of this international corner-boy, I am required to detach myself and two-thirds of my available force to travel to Shannon two days before his arrival, to co-ordinate ourselves with the Shannon gardaí and all the special detachments coming in from all over the country *and* with a battalion of the army moreover, with armoured cars moreover, God between us and all harm! thereafter to place ourselves at the whim and disposal of the United States Secret Service where every man, every woman, holsters a gun beneath their oxter and loaded moreover every hour of the day and night. And as for those same nights, it's highly probable that the Wednesday, Thursday, Friday we'll be sleeping in shifts in a barn. If we don't have to do it on bales of bloody straw, 'twill be a miracle."

"Yessir."

"What d'ye mean, 'yessir'? *You* won't be coming. *Your* job to stay here and keep tabs on whatever inspector they send out as a locum in lieu of meself; he'll know bugger-all about the town or the station or the filing bloody system and you'll even have to show him the officers' jakes. During the continued indisposition of Superintendent Coffey, he'll be effectively in charge: I mean *you'll* be, but he mustn't know it. D'ye hear me now?"

"Yessir, yessir. But." Sergeant Duff felt he had no choice but to nag. The whole affair stank of fuckup. "But sir, you'll excuse me sir, there's an urgent great rake of ongoing this-and-that in the office that'll likely need a senior officer's authority. I mean, for an instance, this business of the laptop dancers in the club on the West Strand Road: didn't you tell me you wanted to handle it personally? but if we should hear from the DPP – " (which is to say, the Director of Public Prosecutions) " – while you're away below at Shannon, is this locum you speak of to be let make a decision? It could be embarrassing, sir, if we're forced to drop the case without your own input and that's a fact ...Or should I maybe stash the papers till after the ...Excuse me, sir, but d'ye expect it to get *heavy* below there at Shannon? I mean, is there a likelihood reinforcements'll be called for? If they are, are they mine, so; or this locum's you speak of? Who's to choose who to send, d'ye know what I mean?"

"Oh dear God, Duff, how the divel should *I* know? ... It is presumed that the demonstrations will indeed, as you put it, be heavy. Garda headquarters is under pressure from government to accept the probability of a national crisis of public disorder. This comes (d'ye hear me now?) through the American embassy and what they call their Proactive Intelligence Programme. We are to act on 'the understanding,' and I quote (more or less), 'of an immediate danger that concealed al-Qaeda echelons will infiltrate legitimate freespeech manifestations with a toxic virus of anti-American prejudice. So no group or individual of potentially terrorist, or even freespeech, coloration is to be let approach within two miles of the presidential person, while he himself must not be let see, hear, or smell, anything that contradicts his own acknowledged leadership of every portion of freeworld freespeech all over the globe.' Not so much a direct order as a definitive inference: and we damn well have to obey it. This is, after all, that same Intelligence Programme that

brought about the invasions of Afghanistan and Iraq entirely to
eliminate these crafty al-Qaedas, and now begod they tell us we
have them in Ireland."

He was, he thought, at the end of his enjoyable tirade; he was
beginning his usual snap-snarl conclusion, "Off you go, Duff:
do your job," when he was piercingly interrupted. A crescendo
of women's voices came up the stairs and along the corridor,
as though the picketeers outside had outrageously invaded the
premises. A young garda stuck his head round the inspector's
door with the look and the bleat of a driven sheep: "O sir, O
sir, I can't scarcely deal with'em; they demand you go to talk
to them, sir; say they'll sit all day in the Enquiries if you don't;
say they have the legality and the right by the United Nations to
ensure 'tis imple-*mented.*"

"What? what? what's this that y'tell me?" Scarlet-faced Bat
was up from his desk, out into the corridor, firing his questions
as he strode. "Those hebdomadal viragoes with their placards
from the pavement, is it? I thought I'd made it clear they could
demonstrate to their hearts' content out there but on no account, no, to be let in! Who was it failed to block 'em? You or
that fool Docherty?"

"'Tis not the ones from the picket, sir; though they do seem
to be known to them. I think, sir, that some of 'em may well
be known to *you.* It seems they have a demand, sir, we should
arrest the American president."

The exasperated Bat jerked to a halt at the top of the stairs.
He said, "Arrest?" He said it again. He thought he had never
in all his life been so astounded. No way could he face these
women until he'd revolved it in his mind entirely. One foot in
the air, poised over the first step down, and his hand slapping
the banister: thirty seconds at least, he hovered. "Ah," he said,
"arrest. Well, maybe we should. Something of the sort, at all
events. It very well may be they have, you might say, an entitle-
ment." With a short bark of laughter he trod softly downstairs,
the young garda deferentially behind him.

There were four of them in the foyer, two young, one not so
young and one positively aged; the latter wore a tam-o'-shanter

and a sweeping shawl in what the inspector took to be a criss-cross black-and-white Palestinian pattern. The two young ones held a banner between them. It was bundled in on itself but the folds revealed significant words and bits of words: –

WAR CRIM LS OUT NOW PLANES SHAN   ON

AR EST & PROSEC   BUSH/BL/ RBER   I

CAR   NG-NOT KILL NG

The not-so-young woman, sallow-skinned in a Muslim head-scarf, dark glasses and a hand-propelled wheelchair, rolled forcefully forward and thrust a sheaf of typescript into the inspector's hand. "The British," she proclaimed with an exotic middle-eastern lilt, "were induced to arrest Pinochet. Milosevic is on trial before an international court. Kissinger dares not travel. All sorts in Rwanda, priests, nuns, politicos, are facing their own consequences. You have a duty – no, a right – as an Irish individual and a lawkeeper, to help us pursue justice against this current war-criminal, here in our sovereign country next week. Do we need to say which war? which crime? when, where, why? It's all written down, read it, we have carefully specified. So."

A voice cried "Guantánamo!," another, "Abu Ghraib!," another one, "Fallujah, coming up!," and finally, the aged woman, braids of snow-white hair trailing like serpents over her shoulders: "Presidential election, coming up! And nobody's fault but our own if there's four more years."

Bat's smile was extraordinarily winning. "I'll tell you what we'll do, ladies: you roll up your banner and leave it in the corner there, and then we'll all go into the inner office and I'll give you the forms to fill in." (Open-mouthed and sceptical surprise.) "You have an information against this American citizen, as I understand, you'll lodge it with me, and I'll put it at once through the proper procedures. Mind you, if he does require to be arrested, it should be Shannon, or maybe Ennis, where the business will need to be done. The best *I* can arrange for you is forward it and see what happens." (Provisional murmurs of appreciation.) "This way, ladies, this way, here we are."

To Sergeant Duff over his shoulder, out of the corner of the mouth: "Defused. And that's how to do it and how you always should learn how to do it. Off you go."

Duff went.

And then he very suddenly came back, full of a flurry of nervous words, just as the inspector was gathering up the completed forms. "Not now, Duff, not now! Don't y'see I'm nearly finished with'em? Any interruption, they'll be here until midnight."

"But sir – "

"Oh be quiet ... Now ladies, this way out, here we go, mind the step. Docherty, you! pay attention! a hand with this wheelchair onto the ramp. We did have the ramp installed in accordance with enlightened practice, ladies; but I'm afraid they're after leaving us one step at the top to get onto it ... There we go and thank you, thank you very much now, God bless ... All right, Duff, what th'divel is it?" The inspector held his head bent sideways, to peer round the edge of the door-jamb, making sure that the delegation was thoroughly off the premises, a *delighted* delegation, they had actually signed some theoretically-effective notifications. Something else was disturbing the sergeant.

"Sir, 'tis that woman that writes the poetry, the Galway guards had her in one time for trafficking asylum-seekers, sure 'twas nothing but a mistake; and then again there was a question there of a sudden death, was it suspicious or not? at all events, they were damn glad above there in Galway to see the back of her, so they tell me ... What is it her name is? Concannon, that's her. We were warned to keep an eye on her, if you remember?"

"Oh God I remember it well. Who does *she* want to arrest? An EU prime minister? Britain? Italy? Poland? Any one of 'em highly suitable."

"I'd say, sir, she has nothing to do with the agitations against the war, it seems 'tis a personal matter she's here to expostulate, though she caught sight from the carpark of the old one in the long shawl and thought fit to take an umbrage, by coincidence I daresay. I judged it best they shouldn't mingle; I diverted her into an interview room, so."

"The old one? Ah you mean Mrs Vandaleur? I'd have you know, Sergeant, Éilís Vandaleur is a most distinguished artist, a credit to the town, a notable executant of symbolical gouache, she exhibits in half the galleries of Dublin. Her late husband made documentary films upon the fauna and flora of Ireland which have been sold to TV channels all over the world. It's just as well you kept her clear of Molly Concannon. Molly Concannon is a potential bloody bogslide overhanging my head, though in Ballykillard as yet no subversion reported of her; what the fuck does she want?"

"If I was able to take her meaning, sir, I'd say 'twas at least in part on the subject of Mrs Vandaleur herself, but I'm afraid she is far from coherent."

As usual.

Molly Concannon was a small excitable personage between fifty and sixty years old, of some literary reputation and well able to put backs up, public authorities no less than fellow writers. She maintained queer private grudges as though they were Mafia feuds. She had very little money; her poetry and stories were not as well known as perhaps they should have been; she had moved during the past few years from one place to another up and down the western counties: everywhere she settled, she laid herself open (so it seemed) to some sort of slight that set her off once again on her travels. Her countenance was strangely attractive, the look of a quick sharp tabby-cat sidling around your ankles, expecting to be stroked but only too ready with its claws.

Today in the interview room she was furiously assailing the reputation of Mrs Vandaleur, insisting to the inspector that a woman of such negligent lack of principle was bound to be the only one originally responsible for the whole shameful transaction; 'twas a wonder, so it was, that the guards had never been able in all these mortal years to have taken the measure o'th'ould bitch, a bloody wonder.

"Transaction, Ms Concannon?"

"What else would you call it, when the scheming sneaking trollop gets his key into her greasy padlock in her very own house the very first time he meets her there? Don't you tell me she didn't manipulate the entire situation! Dammit, he's no more than seventeen, fifteen, oh bother it, I'm not sure, but does it matter exactly? And what in God's name am I going to tell his mother?"

"Key? Padlock? Trollop? Mrs Vandaleur is seventy if she's a day. Are you out of your mind, madam?" Bat's good manners were coming asunder; he tried to smooth it over with a gulp and a cough. "Beg y'r pardon. Can we please have some precision as to who is who and who's his mother? For heaven's sake, take it slowly ... So start please from the start. Hold your breath now, one two three ... "

Molly's story, as it eventually emerged, was one of alarm for the virtue and well-being of a young nephew. He had been staying with her in her cottage a little way out of town. It appeared that a week ago the lad had failed to get Molly's permission to go to Éilís Vandaleur's studio for one of her artistic *at homes*. (Molly had been working hard to keep him under control, following the practice of the girls' school where she used to teach: boys required a different method, as indeed she understood in a vague sort of way, but what on earth would it be? she didn't know.) He had not returned to the cottage that night or the following morning, or any morning after that. He was now a Missing Person, and the Vandaleur was notorious. Molly had never met her, but she nerved herself to go and see her, to challenge her, to make a song and a dance. Whereupon Éilís had offered an opinion, a most casual opinion, that young Roddy was "drifting away on the wings of youthful lust with Róisín O'Grady, to be sure she and he had eyes for no-one else during the music, can you blame them?"

An immediate search of Roddy's backpack, left behind him in the cottage, made it clear that Róisín O'Grady was no stranger to his heart, or indeed by now to his body. It was of course just possible that the molten images in her letters (addressed to him in Dublin long before his arrival at his guileless aunt's front door) were fantastical wish-fulfilment rather than firm predictions of expert and fleshly experience: just possible, but Molly doubted it. Molly knew all about dream-poetry as contrasted with fact-poetry, she had written more than enough of both. She was outraged, not so much at a young fellow's carnal excitement in the promised arms of a dirty young strap (rather older than young, though; for if Roddy was fifteen, this Róisín must at least be twenty, internal evidence of her letters, Molly was *not* to be deceived), but because it was apparent, humiliatingly apparent, that her nephew had only come to Ballykillard because he knew that his slut would be here; sweetly-professed devotion to a long-neglected maiden aunt was a subterfuge and unexpectedly cruel.

And then there was the curious nature of the slut's phraseology. She seemed to be writing as an adept of some dark mystery, weaving authentic magic spells in addition to holding him 'spellbound' as a standard convention of sex-play. Now Molly, during her student days in Galway, had toyed (deplorable recollection) with a foolish little witch-cult, she had danced naked within a stone circle in the wilds of Iar-Connacht, she had led her pixilated coven to seize poultry and tear off their poor wee heads, smearing blood upon breast and belly. Oh long, long ago indeed, long put behind her and earnestly repented during the subsequent stage of her life, her *ultramontane catholic* phase (intense and debilitating) which of course she had also outgrown ... Oh, but it *had* happened! and she knew all the signs when she saw it all over again.

"That bitch," she informed the inspector, "is endeavouring to steal his soul. She has carried him away, she'll abandon him surely, she will leave him in despair, he will kill himself, I know it! Oh God what do I tell his mother? Oh God but I want them found, I want her arrested, I want, I want – Oh God!"

"Arrested, very good; and charged, even better. Charge her with what?"

"Is it not obvious? My nephew is a minor. So it's rape, it's paedophilia, it's all manner of perversion if she truly has him bewitched! do you not understand? in those letters she calls herself Medea, she calls herself Gráinne, she calls herself bloody Calypso, Delilah if you don't mind: mythological exploitation! Oh Christ, man, don't you see how she drives the unfortunate child out of his wits?"

"Child. Now you're sure that your nephew would indeed be underage? Because if he is not, I can't see that it's a police matter at all at all, Ms Concannon. No."

"I told you he was only fifteen. D'you not listen to a word that's told you?"

"Indeed I do. You did say fifteen. You also said seventeen. Which?"

"Will you bloody well find 'em and then you'll find out. That Vandaleur is responsible entirely. Pull her in and give her the third bloody degree. Don't I tell you that she – "

"She may very well be able to give us some information. I'll enquire. In the meantime, the boy's mother. Would *she* perhaps know where he is?"

"Of course she would not, my eedjit of a sister on her holliers in Switzerland, such nonsense! and her wretched pansy husband gone to buggery all over the world. Not that I know a damn thing of their affairs, didn't poor Roddy only come to me the week before last for the first time in all these years, and I really truly thought he was here to look me up from what else but a sense of affection?"

She burst into tears and the inspector had a hard time easing her out of the building.

After a disconcerting visit to Éilís Vandaleur's hospitable house with its picturesque transients, poets, painters, musicians, most of them young and vivacious, and all of them inclined to make fun, the inspector found as it were the erotic spoor of Róisín, sent a patrol car to run her to earth in the arms of disingenuous Roddy in a youth hostel twenty miles down the coast, established the boy's age as definitely seventeen, and reported back to Molly Concannon. "She seems on the whole a respectable class of a girl, an art-student, what else? I asked her was she a witch? and she laughed at me and said yes she was of course. It is a matter of fact that her father is a circuit-court judge, so anything you'd want to say that might reflect upon her character or religious practices, well – you should maybe say it in private ... I do understand, Ms Concannon, that as his only adult relative at present in the jurisdiction, you felt you had to declare the young feller missing, and I'd say that for once you did right. After all, there might well have been a genuine tragedy. He'll be on your doorstep once again when the girl throws him out; but I doubt if it's an issue of suicide, and not at all for the Garda Síochána. Good day t'you, so."

*

The following Saturday, as Inspector Masterson drove away with his family from evening mass at the cathedral, he almost drove over Molly Concannon. She was scurrying across the uneven surface of the carpark, head down behind her umbrella against a blustering squall of rain, looking at nothing above the puddles, trying (as she trotted) to keep her feet out of them. The inspector stopped his car with a scream from the brakes and a curse out of his mouth and a concert of squawks from his wife and three children; he jumped down to see was the bloody woman hurt. She was halfway fallen over, upon one knee in the wet, and her umbrella had blown itself inside-out. No, she informed him, she was not at all injured; and indeed if she had been, let the inspector be under no mistake, the full force of her lawyers would have been fired at his head, stupid head!

Ignoring the vitriol, which he had up to a point deserved, he went on to ask her as nicely as possible, how was the business with the nephew?

"What, what? Nephew? Business?" She seemed not to recall much about it, gesticulating vaguely with her umbrella to wave away the whole story as of basic unimportance. "Oh, that," she continued. "Silly boy turned up again, penniless of course, so he hadn't any choice, had he? *She* wasn't going to subsidize him. He had the nerve to introduce her to me. She has very protuberant eyes, which I've always believed a bad sign: greedy, a predator. At all events, she gave me a little picture; she had made it especially for me, so she said. Collage of cut paper in primary colours. Romantical-allegorical, a species of small-scale throwback to Louis le Brocquy's tapestry designs, dislocated nudes doing God knows what on a hillside above the ocean. I told her I appreciated her generosity, but I wasn't to be mollified about Roddy's deceitful behaviour, and in any case her art'd be better with less of the Vandaleur nonsense inflaming her subject-matter. Off she went with a flea in her ear and silly Roddy hasn't spoken to me since. His mother comes home tomorrow and thank God for it, wouldn't you agree? And isn't all of it a load of nonsense? Whoever *wants* to be a maiden aunt? Degrading occupation and not a morsel of gratitude." She changed subject and tone with a manic intensity. "Oh but I have to tell you! Serendipitous coincidence: I have been vouchsafed an astonishing revelation. Look at that!"

She pulled a printed paper out of her mackintosh pocket, the programme of an academic function or some such, with the crest of the university at its head; but she flourished it too swiftly for Bat to read it. "There you are, Inspector, ah, Inspector Thing? – sorry I've forgotten your name – *my* name, there you are, right in the middle of the Sunday events as bold as a cat in the moonlight! Don't you see, a two-day seminar on *Gaelic Transferences in Anglo-Irish Literature,* and I've a full forty-five minutes at the height of the second day to expound upon 'W.B.Yeats and the Catholic Spiritual Dimension of his supposed Pagan Mythologies.' What they call Yeats's Occultism has been thoroughly misunderstood; up to me to set the record straight; it's tomorrow evening as ever is and isn't it wonderful!"

"What, that old Yeats was a catholic? First I ever heard of it."

"No no and of course he wasn't! Which is, don't you see, the whole point of my paper? Spirituality is now intellectually rehabilitated, the fire of the future! No no, but what's so wonderful is that at last they have recognized *me*! D'you know,

I'm after insinuating meself into the hearts and fucking minds of these snot-nosed bloody colleges year upon year with ne'er a blue hint of response: and at last and at last they have sent me an invitation. Ah sure, 'tis the new man here in charge of the English Department, he is NOT bound by the crippling preju- dice that has informed all those others who at different times have had occasion to consider my name, and let me tell you, in- spector, from the evidence of the papers read today, they damn well *need* a name like mine - "

Bat made his excuses, not too discourteously (he hoped), but his family was beginning to be crabby. He did after a fashion congratulate Molly in a couple of hearty words; but Molly was so high with her "astonishing revelation" that he could have bid her goodbye in Serbo-Croat and she wouldn't have noticed. As he cautiously edged his wheels onto the street (the rain was now heavy and people were hastening all over the place), he heard her triumphantly ululate, a boast and a brag of how she'd sat up all night and every night from the start of the week to finish the paper and now that she had it to rights the whole sodding world would know her name, such insights she had discovered, such unparalleled profundities, every scholar at the seminar would be dumbstruck.

Had she been drinking? She had. Was she proposing to drive? She was. The inspector had no intention of turning back to interfere with her. If there were guards out on duty on the way to her cottage, let *them* pull her in if they thought fit. He himself was going home, absolutely the opposite direction.

*

It was as though Krakatoa had erupted through the floor of the garda station. It began first thing in the morning, the Thursday before the presidential visit, when Éilís Vandaleur turned up with less than half her entourage: the lady in the wheelchair but no banner and no young ones, *they* were off to Shannnon to block roads and drag down fences, leaving the not-so-able-bodied to pursue the legalities – a progress-report, sergeant, please, and at once: what had been done to arrest this huge war-criminal? Polite but insistent as a probing swordblade was the venerable Éilís, while her friend (who described herself as "a hate-Saddam Iraqi exile, even more hatred for Anglo-American oilfield-imperialism and forcible occupation of my country") was more than insistent, she was angrily hectoring; she broke into militant song, Arabic, harsh-toned, extremely loud. Sergeant Duff did his best to fend them off and quieten things down, but without success.

He felt compelled in the end to send for Inspector Lambeg, Bat Masterson's temporary replacement, who had not been endearing himself to the odds and sods of garda remnants left behind for the week by Masterson. Bat had told Lambeg nothing about Éilís Vandaleur and the war-crime prosecution. This may have been because Bat thought it a frivolous issue, or because Bat knew something of his locum and wanted to surprise him, or even out of sheer mischief. Maybe a bit of all three. In any case, it was all there in the records of outstanding business, if the locum had taken the trouble properly to look them through; but he hadn't; he was headstrong and pragmatical, he preferred (as Bat suspected) to find his own way and not to be dependent upon other men's groundwork. Seán Lambeg was a northerner from up near the Border, censorious all his life of what he regarded as the slovenly habits of the greater part of Ireland. He believed himself an honest man and looked upon anyone born in Greater Dublin or south of the Royal Canal as incorrigibly devious. He severely distrusted artistic people of any age or brand, being assured that their talents only led them into moral obliquity. He had seen too many foul examples of drunkenness, drug-taking and unbridled lechery in and around cultural festivals; he had small tolerance of such occasions and no tolerance at all of any sort of public crowd assembled for whatever purpose. He flagrantly asserted that the Papal Visit of 1979 did more damage to the good order of the Catholic Church than anything since Martin Luther, "and I speak as a damn good catholic who looks at what he sees."

So when Éilís Vandaleur explained to him what she had come for, it was all he could do to prevent himself tossing her into a cell forthwith. Perhaps her friend Badr-al-Budur, singing in the wheelchair, gave him pause. ("Go very very carefully with a woman of disability," he told himself. "A piece of porcelain, desperately fragile, God knows what she could sue you for, if you crack her or crash her or knock the wee curlicues off her. Moreover, this one's foreign.") White-faced and breathing heavily, he managed to control himself. His words were quite thick with strangulated passion. He said, "Please be silent. Stop talking. Stop singing. I will tell you what is to be done." He said, "It is impossible that the American president be arrested in Ireland. He has honoured our small country by coming here at all. He has waged victorious war to topple an atrocious tyrant. And now he continues to wage the War Against Terror. All aspects of terror should be abhorrent to a religious, calm people such as we the Irish purport ourselves to be." He said, "That's my opinion. It is also, I believe, the fundamental premiss of the Irish Constitution. Therefore, as a law-enforcer, I am committed to abide by it." His fists were clenched and his left arm exhibited a slight but persistent jerk.

Éilís and Badr-al-Budur gaped at him. They had scarcely expected total support from the Garda Síochána, but they did think (after the cordiality of Bat Masterson) that there was under way a genuine legal process not to be dismissed as "impossible." Éilís fixed her withered features into a mask of the utmost stubbornness. "A legal process," she reiterated. "*Process.* Inspector Masterson stated he would put the papers through."

"Inspector Masterson is not here. *I* am in charge. *I* decide what is or is not to go through." Sergeant Duff, at his elbow, was trying to intervene. Lambeg ignored him. "A religious, calm people, I said. But subject none the less to intermittent and violent disruption, which of course Inspector Masterson has gone to Shannon to prevent. You, madam, represent the same phenomenon here. You are not to be countenanced."

Before they could remonstrate further, the sergeant cut them short with a wink and a cough from behind the inspector. He whispered into the latter's ear, slipping a sheaf of documents onto the desktop right under his eye ...

"Ah," said the inspector. "I am not glad to read of it, but if it is so, then it's so. Inspector Masterson, it appears, acting in my opinion with less than professional prudence, has in fact submitted your request – "

"No: our *demand*. In response to criminality, we have an absolute right to make demands upon the Garda Síochána."

" – your request to the proper authorities by way of the proper channels. I will, in the course of the morning, try to find what has happened to it. In the meantime, vacate the premises. Now, if you please. This minute. Or I shall book you for obstruction."

Hard to say whether the two women would have submitted to the man's insolence, but they had barely had time to glance at one another in disgust before Molly Concannon was into the lobby like a burst from a punctured boiler.

She went straight for Éilís Vandaleur, as though acting out a scene from a sensational melodrama with the wide-eyed gardaí as audience. An *obscene* sensational melodrama: her very first words were, "I have you, I have you, you geriatric terrorist cunt, and what's *she* doing behind you in her wheelchair with her burqa (is it?) *baroqued* all around her head-and-hair like a bloody Blessed Virgin gone rotten?" This was no more than a mere sideswipe at the flabbergasted Badr-al-Budur, for at once she swung back upon Éilís, plunging into realms of unfathomable accusation, no longer specifically related to the corruption of young Roddy (once again with his mother in Dublin), although inspired in the broadest terms by the goings-on in the Vandaleur studio: extraordinarily, Molly seemed to have been spending time there as a guest rather than an intruder. Several guards had to come in to prise the women apart and to keep them apart. Female guards in the end, for the males were non-plussed – two *ould wans* raging and hollering and tearing at each other's clothes like archaic tinkers' mots – had they indeed been tinkers' mots, the guards would have wrestled them to the floor and banged the handcuffs on, and no mistake. But with educated ladies, however eccentric, some discretion must obtain.

Even Inspector Lambeg was aware of the way it would look. He decided to take statements on tape, first from Molly, then from Éilís, separately. Badr-al-Budur demanded to speak as well, although it seemed she had no real knowledge of Molly and was baffled by her arbitrary attack. Lambeg's lunchtime was long gone before he was finished. He sent the women, care-fully segregated, off to their homes, having darkly informed them he would not charge any of them with anything, not yet; but breach of the public-order legislation might well have taken place and he would forward relevant papers to the DPP. (Or maybe he wouldn't, he was thinking as they left: unwise to bequeath loose ends for Masterson to mishandle.) He ordered the three tapes to be taken to his office and a recorder found for each of them, even if it meant – as it did mean – sending out to the electrical shop across the road for a loan of two of the ar-ticles upon a promise of departmental disbursement: essential police resources were a joke in Ballykillard, but not one to be laughed at. Or at least not by the likes of Lambeg ... He would play the tapes alternately and try to make some sense of their infuriating contradictions.

Through most of the rest of the day he sat at his desk in a state of the deepest depression, listening, rewinding, listening, fast-forwarding, listening again. The conglomerated volubility made a queer enough story; he had no notion what to do with it. There was an indeterminate thread of subversion, conceivably of the utmost urgency -- at least if one were to accept the gigan-tic allegations of Concannon, but on the other hand Vandaleur mocked and scoffed to such a degree that the inspector's receptivity was tilted as it were off-balance. It was as though his very brains ran down through his hair like the boy in the fairytale with a hatful of butter on a very hot day – it was hopeless, and yet, and yet – he was afraid to ignore it. He had not thought, when he came to this impossible town, that within a mere three days he would be longing for that eedjit Bat … He certainly was not going to consult Sergeant Duff.

It was already past sunset when his cry for a fourth tape-recorder was with difficulty obeyed, and at once he set about to re-record bits and scraps of the three interviews: a rough-edit to construct a factitious dialogue from disparate but concurrent narratives. And then he played it to himself from start to finish, occasionally stopping it while he entered brief comments of his own into a notebook. To be sure, an unorthodox way to handle evidence, but then the evidence was not evidence in any orthodox sense of the word. What emerged was still almost unmanageably verbose. Here are a few excerpts: -

CONCANNON:

No! I am charging her with incipient terrorism, meaning nothing less than murder, you must listen and then you'll hear! To begin with, 'twas a letter, oh yes she sent me a class of an irregular letter, elaborate Italianate calligraphy on the back of would-you-believe a scrap of red-and-silver gift-wrapping paper, pretending some shape of apology in regard to my nephew, oh yes she had the grace to admit that her attitude had been far from correct, but young people will be young people and she'd had no intent in the world to insult. Would I please to accept her utmost regrets et-patati-et-patata, and she was having a modest little open-house festival kind of thing the next week, that's to say this week, last night in point of fact, and I'd indeed be very welcome. Well. What the hell else to do but to take it as meant and to go? So I went.

I thought, I had always thought she was a West Brit, historically insufferable, by way of being a protestant – family of damned planters, Trinity College and letters to Churchill during the war to tell him how many Hun submarines they could sniff along the Kerry coast? No no, it seems not: but as catholic as they come, maiden name O'Carolan (no less), great-niece (no less) of a martyr of 1916 – if it wasn't MacDonagh then maybe Mac Diarmada, can't quite recollect which – in any case does it matter? The point is, she is lofty; and nothing about her to despise. Highly cultured and I was in her house.

Well.

Let me leave aside the poetry-reading, and the music, all o'that. Let me leave aside some of the young ones, smoking God knows what in the garden in the moonlight just beyond her french windows. And let me very clearly leave aside the casual way she put me off when I asked her would she care to have me read some of my paper upon Yeats and the transferences, know what I mean? Didn't I tell y'all about it in the carpark? I did not: 'twas the other feller ... She said, "Later, we'll do it later." Meaning "never", didn't I know it? don't I have the experience? ha'n't I heard it time without end, and the spite and the despising?

VANDALEUR:

There was no question whatever of anybody putting her down in regard to her scholarship. Indeed, I'd heard from more than one at that seminar that her insights into Yeats were very considerable, well worth our attention, particularly her tendentious dovetailing of the more obscure Yeats images into the conceits of Patrick Kavanagh, which had startled not a few of 'em; but by "later" I did mean later, the night was young, we had an agenda. At least, I'd hoped we had an agenda, but already, even apart from this dysfunctional Concannon, things began to break up, like an old wooden jetty in a roaring high tide. Such as I've seen on the Connemara coast, impossible to hold together. 'Twas a day, or rather an evening, no an accursed long dark night, wherein everything happened at once.

CONCANNON:

She announced to all and sundry that she was "going on the air." I thought for a minute she was so drunk she wished to levitate in the fashion of that guru-feller, whatever his name is? For how the shite should I have known that she kept above stairs a radio transmitter, as illegal as a poteen-still, and there and then she was about to make an utterly blatant broadcast? – pirate radio, if you please, without the shred of a government licence, and every soul in that house involved in her lawbreaking, that's to say if we didn't incontinent run out to notify the guards, and yet in God's name what decent Irish creature would venture without forethought to play the informer? Such things are not done, are never done, ever; or at least when I was a girl were entirely unconscionable. I was caught in a trap, so. Well beyond the bloody mark, even worse than the cannabis, which at least had been kept to the garden, so I asked her about the penalties. D'you know, she'd the brass neck to stand there and laugh at me!

VANDALEUR:

Penalties. I did more than tell her, I told every one of my guests in that house. I had this small transmitter; I announced it. I always announce it with utter transparency: it being what I call my Free Speech Women's FM, whereby for the past eighteen years I have at irregular intervals entertained and instructed and irritated the good and the bad within the very small limit of two to three miles radius. Concannon's wee house, I daresay, would be outside that limit, so she'd never have heard me nor for that matter heard of me in the little time she's lived here.

Of course I have no licence – why should we not as free citizens be as entitled to utter thoughts, dreams or music over the airwaves, as it were in the open street – but a licence would impose whatever restrictions the government might choose to inflict – as for instance before the peace process no chitchat with Republicans – as for instance before this or that referendum no news as to overseas abortion clinics – as for instance which of the county councillors beats his wife and which of 'em rapes the aupair and which carries home the brown-paper cash-bag for rezoning of land for a developer – every word of it available (if you care to hang about in the rain) on the pavement between the Allied Irish Bank and Tesco's, but Free Speech Women's Radio gives it all in the one earful, you never need get up from your sofa.

At which point, Inspector, be very clear as to one thing; your guards cannot prosecute me unless certified by the Irish State Broadcasting Commissioners (or whatever they call themselves these days), and unless they can contrive my disclosure red-handed, with the mike on and pulsing out the sound into the ether. Is it catch me? They haven't yet. Begod they've never bothered. What? to crush one old widow-woman? no better than tearing a beetle. So they lack the brutality of an American fast-food chain, so live-and-let-live and why bother?

from LAMBEG's notebook:

Nonetheless, this Mrs V., so exceedingly high-falutin, has admitted her activity was illegal. And something should surely be done. Not entirely discreet for me, upon temporary assignment, to try to force Inspector Masterson's hand. If the superintendent were in good health, it might be another matter. I have made a cursory exploration of possible penalties.

VANDALEUR:

Penalties. I told everyone: "This house is a criminal enterprise. The householder, that's me, is liable for two years' gaol or a thirty thousand euro fine; aiders and abettors, that's you, can get yourselves six months' gaol. I tell you that, so that you can't tell me I enveigled you hither. Are you game for it?"

CONCANNON:

And then, this damned hypocrisy to assert herself a Women's Radio. 'Twas on the tip of her tongue to turn all the men out of the house, which as a democrat I could not tolerate.

VANDALEUR:

I merely said to my gentlemen friends, as I've often said before, they were not to invade the transmitting room, which is to say my spare bedroom, unless invited; and who could say that I might not invite? I turned nobody out of the house. In the end she turned herself out, huff and puff, yelp and skelp, contempt and derision, damn glad to see the back of her. And she missed the chance to read us her Yeats paper; upon air, had she chosen to be patient. Let alone some of her poetry, for which she'd been dropping her hints the great part of the evening.

from LAMBEG's notebook:

However, it does not appear to have been the issue of gender that caused Ms Concannon to march out.

CONCANNON:

Two years, or thirty thousand, and six months for every-one else? Now she may have laughed, oh yes: but I saw young people there, wide-eyed and the colour of butter-milk, not daring to ask to leave lest she – lest she what? Made mock of 'em? Reviled them? Or just glanced with contempt. To wilfully ask mere children to risk their living and their liberty was felon-setting of the deepest dye. So I cried out, "Fucking felon-setter!" and I left.

VANDALEUR:

*But oh before that, there'd been more, and much more.
At every interruption throughout the entire evening (and
Christ, there were enough of 'em!), her creepy-crawly
mystic Yeats, her spiritual fanatic Kavanagh, came scrambling across my studio to addle her every utterance.*

CONCANNON:

*And I look to the law, I have always looked to the law,
I am neither a murderer nor a terrorist-trafficker, whatever you may have in your files.*

from LAMBEG's notebook:

Memo: to Sergeant Duff. Check the files. Do it directly.
Don't ramble from your own memory of what rumours you may
have of this woman. I want facts.

CONCANNON:

*Long before I left, I had sensed something deadly sick.
A constant stream of outlandish people, most of them
blatantly unknown to the Widow Vandaleur or indeed
to anyone else, drifting in through the unlocked front
door, with demand upon demand as though they took
her for – for the matron of a Victorian workhouse suddenly converted to soft-hearted liberalism, ridiculous –
soft-hearted? Soft-bloody-headed! Did she know where
it was all coming from? If she didn't, Inspector, let me*

tell you that I did (or at least I do this morning), and a good thing if you did as well, because like it or not, you're going to have to take action.

VANDALEUR:

You seem to forget, Inspector, I came here for another purpose altogether, the wee Concannon is an absolute irrelevance, but –

ARAB *woman:*

She is irrelevant, insulting irrelevant, and what does she do but deliberately attempt to divert myself and Ms Vandaleur and indeed yourself from the business in hand. Inspector, how much longer before you are able to trace our requisition for a war-crime prosecution? It surely should not be more remote than a finger-run of clicks on your computer? Click-click? Click-click-click?

from LAMBEG's notebook:

Can she really be a Mrs O'Rourke? That idiot Docherty must have muddled her first name at all events – "Baddledrabadoor" -- ? God knows ... At all events, she slammed her wheelchair to and fro round the interview room, making the noises of a chicken-run: she might have been forty years old, she behaved like a child of seven. I did try to explain the chock-a-block condition of the garda com-puter system. Of course in vain. These ignorant civilians appear to imagine our resources are infinite. Why, of course they would need to be infinite, if (as such people aver) we exist for no other

purpose but to record and collate every doing, every word, every
thought, of all the populace, the better to control and suppress? –
oh would it were true, were true ...

VANDALEUR:

*So, Inspector, let me run you through the lunatic pro-
cession that surely by sheer coincidence came in on me
from ten o'clock onwards. "All Welcome!", as I'd written it on my notice in the public library; very nearly for
the first time in so many years it seemed that the public
had actually read it, and moreover had taken it literally.
Lord help me, I was drowned in it! As soon as one of
my music people started to play into the mike or to sing,
or my chatterboxes let loose to embroider the airwaves,
amn't I called down the stairs for yet another emergency?
and what can poor Treasa do but clip on a CD of that
passionate Algerian lovesong woman, and trust we won't
bore our half-dozen listeners silly with inconsistency,
jump-starts, sudden silences, sudden fragments of unan-
nounced melody, eedjits shouting out from below ...*

from LAMBEG's notebook:

Treasa? Unexplained; but a young Vandaleur kinswoman
(so I deduce); student? Helps with the technicalities of illegal
transmissions?

Memo: to Sergeant Duff .Run a check. Get a surname, get
an address. We might need to bring her in.

VANDALEUR:

First, my dear Iraqi friend comes trundling in on her wheels, with that husband of hers from the university, what's his name? Caoimhín Ó Ruairc? if not Caoimhín he's Micheál, quiet little chappy, never a word to a sparrow, translates Arabic poems into Irish, very many of 'em her poems, I've tried fifty times to get him and her to come and read 'em over the radio but they always ran shy of me. He's an academic, of course, she's a refugee, very conscious, both of 'em, of my illegality, they have to be careful. Cowardly, if you like. But then, all the actions against Bush and his filthy war: and suddenly she's as brave as a wildcat. So I'm not so surprised at her unheralded arrival and I offer her the mike to elaborate upon war-crimes – you are making some effort to trace my depositions, Inspector? I damn well hope you are! – but Godsake it's not the war she wants to talk about at all, nor is it poetry, but wheelchair access in the local law courts, though what she's been doing there I haven't the least idea -   At all events she cuts right across a discussion we were having on air about the human rights of the Guantánamo prisoners -   Of course wheelchair access is human rights, but -   Of course I'm not a slave to consistency and context, but -   I think she could have waited. At all events, she sets the evening off upon a note of cross-purposes, which -   And then, next.

ARAB woman:

Burqa my arse! She knew very well that what I wear is a khimar; and if she did not know, it would have been no great ordeal of politeness to enquire. I don't scuttle around making coarse-grained comical blunders with this and that in the Irish language – although so many a

time, many, this husband, this pedant of mine, so vexes
me with his linguistic pieties that I must take a laugh at
them and I do, and I bloody well scream: but then he and
I are ineradicably me and him and nobody's aware of our
discordances, nobody ...

from LAMBEG's notebook:

I'm aware. It's on the tape. I don't think she was loosened
by drink, far too early in the day (and she remains, I take it, a
Muslim): quite simply, sheer excitement, of an alarming and near-
savage variety. How far would this excitement be religious?

Memo to self: run a check on her. When there's time. Maybe I
should make time, could be urgent: I'm a bundle of nerves.

CONCANNON:

Workhouse matron or not, she cut her Islamic friend
most ruthlessly short over the question of the wheelchairs
– poet, how are ya? We've only the husband's word for it,
to my mind not good enough. How dare she call herself a
poet? I'm a poet. And I write in Irish as well as English,
I need no husband to translate for me, so there. What I
mean to tell ya is this: this vaunted Free Speech Radio
was not so delectably free if you weren't eye to eye with
her highness. And the same all along all the evening.

VANDALEUR:

And then next. A tall rakish woman from the countryside of the Gaeltacht whom I hadn't seen in years, Deirdre is she called? But the surname I don't remember. In she comes, appreciating not at all that I'm in the midst of an open house, asking – no: appealing, supplicating, begging - for a close personal talk, a woman-to-woman confessional of her scarifying private affairs, and would not be put off – how could I put her off? the tears seeping out of her eyelids without her even knowing it; when I offered her a tissue, she stared at it blankly. She'd brought a bottle of wine to grease, as she put it, the wheels of her grief.

CONCANNON:

All I wanted to do was to make a representation as to the subterranean Islamic tendencies and the anti-Semitic corollaries so dangerously implicit in the current political shitehouse. Ever since Eleventh September I have this dream of that catastrophe, recurrent, absolute terror, how against my will they stripped me and tied me up oh so tight to spreadeagle me across the nose of the hi-jacked plane, all the passengers hopelessly screaming through mile upon mile of sky. And so into the inferno. And then falling, falling, falling ... To begin with, I only dreamed it once or twice in three months, and then suddenly once a week, but lately every night it awakes me hopelessly screaming, God forgive me, 'tis a warning! for I have not yet heeded the dreadful Message we were sent on that dreadful dreadful day: sure I'm only after beginning to understand what it meant.

But she ignored me altogether and took this – this bean-pole of a culchie-woman all a-quake with some vulgar emotion – straight off into an inner room, her scullery, can you believe it? Total discourtesy, absolute seclusion and none of us (to begin with) could tell where she hid.

VANDALEUR:

It seems it had at long last been borne in upon poor Deirdre that her saloon-bar hetero husband was in fact homosexual, all their married life he'd been lifting men's shirt-tails. And when she found out, he reared up at her and called her "lesbian". Did she not understand, he bellowed, she was turning into a man before his very eyes, after licking the flesh of women year after year and fingering them inside-out? and the whole of his family believed him. Only for the chance of one word with me, whom she hadn't seen since she was a girl, she'd have run stark mad, oh she would have, and taken her own life. So she said and I knew it true. So what to do? I could not suggest that we put it on the radio, altogether far too raw – though maybe in a few months' time –

CONCANNON:

I discovered that the scullery keyhole allowed me to hear, so I heard. I called to her through the keyhole to put it on her radio, whatever it was! "No privacy in midst of Free Speech," I called out. She ignored me

VANDALEUR:

So Deirdre and I drank and murmured together until she was drunk enough to fall asleep on a sofa and then I went up and took over once again from Treasa. After which –

CONCANNON:

After which, out of Africa, something (as always) new – except it wasn't bloody new, hadn't we heard it all before, hadn't it thoroughly fucked me up with you lot already? - illegal immigrants, criminal traffickers, hideous histories, agent-provocateurs, and what business was it of hers? Did she ask me to advise her, knowing (as she could have found out) that I was the only one in her house there with a serious experience? She did not.

VANDALEUR:

A whole clutter, cluster, gallimaufry of asylum-seekers, one after the other, in the hall of the house, to importunate my help and advice. Three families, all at once, such wonderful bounteous young women, in their beads and their braided wigs and raiment like the orchids in a hothouse, each one with a babe in a pushchair or wrapped in a shawl below her shoulder-blades, and a toddler or two toddling, and decorous gentle husbands slipping along behind. From the Congo, from Angola, from the Ivory Coast: who would dare force them back into such regions of ruin? Who would dare? The Department of Justice dares. For they'd all three been officially issued with forewarnings of deportation, they were terrified and

floundering with their insufficient English, for the sake of
heaven what sort of letter must they write to the Minister
and would I see it was written correctly?

CONCANNON:

As for gentle, ho ho but well I know how these victims
very likely will have hefted their own bloodthirsty guns,
ho ho and used them – how else does a messed-up mas-
sacre end but with the flight overseas of the perpetrators?
Inspector, here's a felonious widow who bare-facedly col-
ludes with out-and-out criminals, for immigrants mouth-
ing falsehoods are surely nothing less – how can she be so
positive they're telling her the truth? For of course she's
not positive, she has other fish to fry; Inspector, have you
guessed what breed of fish? Silly man, you have not.

Have you considered – you have not – what propor-
tion of Africa is today under Muslim hegemony? Even
Christian Africans may consciously or unconsciously be
serving the purposes of such as al-Qaeda: will you lis-
ten to me, Inspector? Even before Eleventh September,
that Grand Climacteric, awful and unique, whereafter
all is changed, changed utterly in the twinkling of an eye
–Will you look at the bombs at the American embassies,
Nairobi and – and the other place? –I am begging you,
will you not look?

*

from LAMBEG's notebook:

I have heard them talk it out and talk it out and talk it out and
now I must go to the keyboard with it. For either this Concannon
is as mad as she seems or intuitively she's onto something so big

*that neither myself, nor Masterson when he returns, are up to the
mark for it. It's a class of a carry-on to be passed holus-bolus to
the top of Special Branch, but if – before that happens – my own
small deductions should illuminate the pattern that Special Branch
shall unravel – MY deductions, not Masterson's, and he'll be back
give-or-take in seventy-two hours, so I haven't got long – as I say,
IF? ... Oh then to whom the kudos?*

*Let me establish what I think Concannon's been getting at. Her
continuing 'verbal,' as she uttered it, is per-se impossible. But a
paraphrase of the overall run of her intolerable loquacity (salted
with highlights of direct quotes) will perhaps be of some help: here
we go: -*

The Vandaleur Free Speech is a **cover for an entire network of subversion,** astonishingly unexplored by garda or army intelligence,
linked by radio-waves with Islamist terrorism. It would seem it is
not linked with Republican ditto, at any rate not yet, even though
the Arab woman's husband is a specialist in the Irish language. But
this strange omission serves but to emphasize the immediate probability of **the main and most frightening fact.**

Concannon, having herself been involved not long ago with similar
phenomena – i.e. illegal Kurds, according to the files – claims now
to have been overwhelmed by what she calls her Serendipitous
Coincidence at a university seminar. Her car (she implies by way
of metaphor) had broken down as it were on the road to Damascus,
and out of the blue she's been offered a lift. She finally sees, as she
has never seen before, the essential preserved virtue of the culture
of Ireland **so wrapped, swaddled, and hugged** in "transcendental"
spiritual imagery – Catholic, she says, though prior to the Council
of Trent – as to be unable to accommodate any further ingredients
**without swelling and choking and in the upshot bursting, like the
frog in the fable who had wished to be a bull.** Is this, she asks,
no more than a retrograde re-adoption of the **ould bigotry** of her
catholic phase? Not at all, she replies to herself, 'tis a gathering
together of all the threads of her hitherto disordered life, a weaving
upon a loom of suddenly clarified vision – this is not quite a quote,

dammit I'm writing unconsciously in the wretched woman's style: unwise.

Therefore she sees these Africans, from the veritable Heart of Darkness, called up to run in harness with the Dupes of Irish Pacifism who tomorrow intend to devastate the heart-stirring visit of the American president and his call for us all to play our part in the War on Terror. The War *of* Terror, as she says, has already been declared upon us.

Therefore she foresees small farmers throughout the western counties (whence less than sixty years ago it was confidently asserted that the purest red blood of the nation was pumped) **badgered, harassed, demoralized and rendered impotent** by indiscriminate calumnies and psycho-sociological questionnaires relating to homosexual vice.

Therefore she nearly saw the irremediable immersion of a simple young Irish lad into a complexity of sex-games associated with the occult.

Therefore she stores in her memory a CD of an Algerian singer played last night over V's radio whenever there was a gap in the programming.

Therefore she heard, last night on V's radio, the whingeing narrative of a German guest-worker who claims he has been ripped-off by an Irish building contractor, arbitrary wages well below standard, no safety-gear, no access for the union and all of it in collusion with a manpower agency in Düsseldorf and the employment authority in Dublin. Because he is an EU citizen, his grievance is a pre-planned **stalking-horse for Islamist guest-workers (guests? oh ha ha, be easy now, sit, will I wet y'a cup o'tay?)** from Bosnia and Turkey.

Therefore she heard, last night on V's radio, an inexplicable rash of queer incidents involving summer-season buskers in the town. An

antipodean didgeridooster [street-musician from Sydney. Memo to Duff: bring him in] cheerfully informs listeners that he has sold, from his pitch at the rear of the court house, consignments of hash to – **would you believe it, Inspector?** – young lawyers of both sexes; far worse, to surreptitious gardaí, allegedly on witness-duty, not even concerned to entrap him. At the same time, a trio of ecstatic 20-year-old Poles of **no sort of talent at all** explain into the microphone how they go out daily from their tent on the river-bank (two boys and one girl in the same small tent) to gyrate half-naked in the market-place with painted faces, gloves on their hands and semi-obscene gestures. They call it a mime-show. They inform the passers-by they need cash for their holiday in Ireland and they wouldn't have come here if they hadn't been told that the natives would pay up out of sheer good nature, which astonishingly has proved to be the case. [or if not the natives, the tourists – jack-asses. Memo to Duff: take a look into that tent.]

This land is ripe for takeover: would you seek any harder evidence?

That's more than enough of her statement for tonight. But as she says, upon ourselves the War of Terror is already declared ... etc. ... etc... etc. ...

*

The above being but a sample of what he transcribed onto the station's sole word-processor, and worked upon far into the night, deleting, rephrasing, cutting and pasting, alternating fonts to add emphasis. It was possible he was about to display himself as the greatest gump in all the world, but -   Round about two in the morning, or half-past, or a quarter to three, he staggered from his chair, bid a surly goodnight to the desk-sergeant of the graveyard watch, and made for his hotel through a drizzle of warm rain.

No more than four hours' sleepless dreams and muscular twitches, stretched out on an unwelcoming bed: and there he was, back again! evacuated (with some difficulty) as to his bowels, washed, shaved and showered, thrusting upstairs into office and chair, clicking on the computer, calling sharply for his cup of tea, staring hard and relentless with a drear northern honesty at everything he had written. Was it a fool's game after all, or did it make appalling sense? If there was even the ghost of a chance it might make sense, then action must be taken – decisive action, here and now! – and before the arrival at Shannon of U.S. Air Force One, gracious heaven, this very evening! Was it conceivable that the life of the Leader of the Free World depended entirely upon Lambeg's insight and initiative? For if there *was* a subliminal plot (now you see it, now you don't), why should it not have its kaleidoscopic epicentre in the ignorantly festive and newly-painted streets of inconsiderable Ballykillard, among tourists and tourist-exploiters, the frivolous and the furtive, the half-wits of Ireland and the riff-raff of the globe?

To start with, Concannon could not in fact be mad. The Inspector was in such agreement with her diagnosis of the huge danger that threatened the world, that he was unable to dismiss the sound balance of her intellect. Of course, she was eccentric. (Some would say St John the Divine had been even more eccentric, yet had he not correctly predicted the pouring-out of the vials upon the Eve of Armageddon, under which dire showerbath all humanity even now was slipping and sliding? The book of *Revelation* was the inspector's regular bedside choice, last night in the hotel more poignantly than ever.) And of course, she had undergone a very swift conversion from her previous views and adventures as recorded in garda files – notably in regard to asylum-seekers and the statutes controlling them – but she herself had made sidelong reference to St Paul: the apostle was surely proof that such conversions can take place.

He sent abruptly for Sergeant Duff. "Bring me a form of application for a search warrant, and let me know who in this town is the right man to sign it for me without, I say *without*, any farting about. Get on with it."

When the form was brought to him he filled in the names of Vandaleur, Éilís and O'Rourke, Budroulador, the latter name chiming vaguely with an ancient memory of a Dublin Christmas panto, *Aladdin*, was it? a unique family treat at the age of, he guessed, seven. He wrote, as the reason for search, "Suspicion of subversive conspiracy: Offences Against the State Act." Once the form was endorsed (and that did not take long, for the entire law-and-order establishment was especially alerted on this very special day), he ordered out every available plain-clothed and uniformed officer, more women than men, but not so many of either, inasmuch as Inspector Masterson had skimmed the curds and left the whey – at all events, they piled into cars and vans to recklessly launch themselves into the early streets of Ballykillard with formidable howling of sirens. Lambeg proclaimed, "I want the Yanks to sit up and take note, I want sound, I want fury, I want all the media we can grab," amd sound and fury were certainly there. Alas the media at such short notice were no more than a youth with camera from the local weekly freesheet, and a hungover stringer for *The Irish Examiner*. No TV, which was galling. When at search-and-arrest in Dublin, Lambeg had always made sure of TV.

It would be untrue to say that the house-searches turned up nothing.

So many vast boxes and bags, of tapes audio and visual, of CDs and DVDs, of books and journals and typescripts (relating to war, to civil rights, to freedom of speech, to justice and injustice, law and disorder, all over the world), were fetched from Mrs Vandaleur's that the inspector reckoned it would take months to collate their contents, let alone find proof of conspiracy. But if there *were* conspirators, whose schemes required documents, they'd be rendered – at least for that period of time – powerless to act. There was also a confusion of electronic parts, said by the garda technical man to be a transmitter, unlicensed. Plus – ha, a *crucial* plus! - minute quantities of substances, probably illegal and quite openly left about on the shelves of the bathroom. These would suffice as a basis for indictment while the major malfeasance was investigated. It was unfortunate that Mrs

Vandaleur was not at home when the raid took place. Indeed no-one was at home, and a scandalized neighbour had to be conscripted to bear witness that all was done according to the proprieties. Where *was* the old lady, then? The neighbour said she thought she had gone to the garda station: was it insolence or innocence? Inspector Lambeg rang the front desk, bellowed for Sergeant Duff – "Duff! if she comes to you, don't let her out again! She's up to something, depend upon it."

Badr-al-Budur's house had her husband in it, a furious fiery presence, objurgations rattling out of him the full run of his teeth in preposterously inventive Irish that went far beyond the inspector's linguistic capacity. She herself was in the passage, grey-faced, silent, terrified, but stubbornly trundling from doorway to doorway, somehow contriving to place her wheelchair wherever a garda wanted to go; until at last one of the female officers ran her, as it were, off the road into the downstairs toilet and kept her there by the strength of two strong arms. A multitude of documents to be bagged or boxed, and most of them in Arabic. Until they could be translated, they were ipso-facto suspicious; their proprietor must be held for questioning. Getting her into a vehicle was a difficulty. None of the garda cars or vans being adapted to take a wheelchair, Micheál Ó Ruairc refused pointblank to drive his wife into arrest in their own car (which was so adapted); eventually a taxi with special accommodation was found in the Yellow Pages and rung for; and all the people of the street came out of their houses to stand around and glower. It was a middle-class tree-lined avenue, spectators' concern was muted and not abusive, but the atmosphere was glacial. Were they disgusted by the guards' macho display, shocked by its sudden proximity, or horrified that a terrorist had been uncovered in their midst? Lambeg could not decide. He would have preferred a bit of a mob throwing bottles at his officers – at least you'd have the right to *do* them with your truncheons.

Not a word out of Badr-al-Budur all the way to the station. Micheál had been brusquely forbidden to get into the taxi with her. Lambeg insisted she travel in handcuffs, clipped to the arm

of the wheelchair. Her horror at this monstrosity of behaviour
seemed to crackle inside the cab like an electrical short-circuit;
the driver became conscious of it, an unpleasantness to his head,
as it might have been a passenger smoking – he turned and he
saw, he said "Ah no, no good." Lambeg beside him told him,
"Shut the fuck up." At the station they rolled her into a cell and
left her to stew.

And then, at the station, arrived Mrs Vandaleur. She had
travelled there on foot by unfrequented laneways and the path
across the park, tip-tap-tapping with her silver-handled walk-
ing-cane; she allowed no-one to talk (neither Duff nor Lambeg
nor anyone else) until she had had her say. "Arrest?" she que-
ried softly, but so firmly she brought Lambeg to a dead stop as
he started out to read her her rights. "By all means, Inspector,
but that is *not* why I came here; and you will please deal with
my enquiry before any business of your own, bearing in mind
that I forewarned you of it yesterday. We laid an information as
to the international crimes of this American who calls himself
'president:' is *he* to be arrested or is he not? You assured me
that you would by now have traced the progress of our indictment. He will be in Ireland in a matter of hours. Delay would
be unconscionable, and so would prevarication. Yes or no?"

Lambeg began to swear. Reminding himself too late of Mrs
Vandaleur's age and gender, he swallowed his further words of
sex and excretion, choked upon some heaven-defying blasphe-
mies, and managed very painfully to bite his tongue. Sergeant
Duff did his best. "In considering the lady's question, sir, I rang
Dublin, the DPP's Office: I did find something out." He whispered into Lambeg's ear.

Lambeg listened impatiently, swung away in his angry intol-
erance, bethought himself and swung back again, leaning toward the old lady as though to spit in her eye. "We have found
out, Mrs Vandaleur, that you came to the wrong shop. Your
complaint, or indictment, or information, whatever, is invalid.
It should either have been delivered directly to Shannon to Superintendent Scanlon if that's where he is this week, or more

correctly via the Office of the Attorney-General, Dublin. We have not the authority to process such a claim in Ballykillard."

"Nonsense. If I had come here to tell you that I had been notified that the bank-robber who'd killed that security man in Cork was hiding in a house in – ah – Waterford, say? – do you tell me you could take no action?"

"Absolutely different. You are a very foolish woman even to think it equivalent. A murder in Cork is – "

" – is exactly the same as a murder – or mass-murder – in the Near East, the Far East, Latin America. If the perpetrators are anywhere in Ireland, 'tis your job to see they are dealt with."

Another, and prolonged, burst of sotto-voce from the sergeant.

Lambeg, for all the world like an actor giving ear to the prompter: "Aha ... And furthermore, as it seems ... Dublin. There was yesterday an attempt in the High Court. By another party altogether. To obtain a warrant for the arrest of the Commander-in-Chief of the United States. The applicant was informed that the court had not – yes, Duff? yes? – that's to say, had no jurisdiction. There you are."

Again the inspector swung away, ordering Duff from the side of his mouth, "Book her. Illegal substances. Lock her up pending further enquiries. And don't let her within six feet of meself, twelve feet, or begod there'll be no murder done in Cork or anywhere else only here on this – this – godammit, d'y'call it a *floor?*" The plastic tiles of the lobby had been swabbed not a quarter of an hour ago, they were dangerously slippery, the inspector's foot skidded, he all but sprawled his length as he stalked out.

He had made himself believe he'd interrogate the two women himself, inducing them to part with the most wonderful admissions. But their expressed personalities during and after arrest had affected him most disagreeably: he was not sure that he would be able to control his rage in front of them. Uncontrolled, he might very well miss some important angles, he might wreck his career instead of flying it to the heights; why, he might even -   By God he might find himself in extremely serious trouble, and very shortly, if -   Protocols to be observed, proprieties, formalities -   How *could* he have allowed his rush of adrenalin to cause him to forget the immediate need to -   If Dublin this minute were not briefed in comprehensive detail, the senior men of Special Branch would infallibly have his life. Special Branch in Ballykillard was represented by no more than a pair of idle nondescripts, a detective-sergeant, a detective-garda, and both of them away with Bat Masterton. So therefore, and at once, Dublin. He must calm himself, slow himself down, sit (for Godsake) to the computer, and e-mail an intelligible report.

He had only just finished the preliminary outline when the media flooded upon him. The very press and TV creatures he had notified at dawn and who had failed to respond (largely because their key personalities were all at Shannon looking for riots, which of course he should have foreseen) had at length received his messages and were sending to the garda station whatever rag-tag and bobtail they were able to pull together. Lambeg's adrenalin came surging again red-hot through his glandular secretions, of course he had to meet them, had to hold an ad-hoc press conference, had to –

Not an occasion to be proud of.

He had scarcely begun when an apparent schoolgirl, grandly announcing herself as *The Irish Times*, thought fit to enquire why Superintendent Coffey had known nothing of the morning's doings.

"The superintendent's indisposed. I am effectively in charge. I am – "

"The superintendent seems to think otherwise. I spoke on the phone to him twenty minutes ago, Inspector. He said – "

"Never mind what I said then." For Superintendent Coffey, tall, hunched and haggard, his livid face streaming with sweat, was suddenly in their midst, swathed in scarves and a great overcoat, leaning on a cudgel-like stick. "I have only the one thing to say now. *No comment*. If this is a press conference, it was not called by me, it is premature, it is over. My apologies for the mistake, but (as you see) I am not too well. In point of fact, arisen from my bed. Good-morning and good-bye to all concerned, and thank you for your trouble." He stood supported by a fierce little woman, his wife. Full of hatred for the journalists and contempt for this jumped-up Lambeg, she clutched the arm of the superintendent; she was dutifully silent but shot her eyes from left to right like a komodo dragon at bay. After a few feeble protests, the media dispersed. "Ave atque Vale," intoned Mr Coffey to their departing backs. To Lambeg he added, "Though I doubt if a single one of 'em knows what it means. As for you, Inspector: bad. Very bad. I do believe, Inspector, you have meddled and muddled, made a plate of shit-soup for your dinner, to say nothing of mine. Into your office, so: let's hear just exactly what you've done." His phrases were hoarse and breathless, interrupted by the hawking of phlegm behind a paisley-pattern handkerchief. His wife clutched him all the more firmly as he slowly ascended the stair.

After fifteen minutes in Lambeg's office of Lambeg's resentful explanations, the superintendent wheezed and coughed and slapped his bony hand on the desk: "Al-Qaeda fuck-all and the evidence against 'em is absolute fuck-all – " (Mrs Coffey jabbing a sharp elbow into his forearm, he reconsidered his vocabulary.) " – absolutely nugatory. Sheer hysteria. Add to which, you've spelt Mrs Ó Ruairc's christian name all wrong, even if she's *not* a Christian, and the warrant'd be thrown out on behest of the defence in any court you care to name. Damnable carelessness. Add to which, it so happens I know both of these ladies on highly cordial terms and so does Mrs Coffey. They are ornaments to the town, cultural treasures, one might say; admittedly neither of them could be called a reliable aid to the growth of the national economy, but – but – whenever was the economy the only idol to be worshipped?"

Lambeg too could be abusive toward the economy, but he retained a keen sense of priorities – "Sir, I would have thought that the national *security* might deserve perhaps a smahan of worship – "

"At this moment, Inspector, per diem, the national security is expending four thousand euros apiece upon three thousand five hundred guards, including the full thousand of the riot squad, plus two thousand soldiers no less, one third of all our force – countrywide, man, countrywide! – to lodge themselves below there at Shannon, and messing – that's all they're damn well doing – they're messing! I *refuse* to have messing in my streets of Ballykillard, I refuse to condone it at the thick-fingered hands of a muttoner the likes of you. So here and now you let 'em go, Mrs Vandaleur, Mrs Ó Ruairc, both of 'em with the fulsome apology, on your *knees*, dammit, d'y'hear me! Here and now."

Lambeg would have tried to object, but the superintendent hobbled over to the window and hauled up the venetian blind. "Be so good as to look at that, will ya, and tell me how many more by midday if we don't send the two of 'em home. I have said, there is to be no *messing!*" In his fluster the inspector had failed to notice an alarming new phenomenon. Immediately beneath him the weekly anti-war picket had been chanting as usual upon the pavement, but now it was reinforced by unprecedented adherents, men for a change as well as women, it spilled over into the middle of the street, its noise was redoubled. Poster-portraits of the 'Leader of the Free World' galumphing like King Kong vied with hastily-improvised placards to flourish in the sunshine like yachts at a regatta: –

FREE THE BALLYKILLARD 2

JAIL THE COLLABORATING POLITICIANS

Preserve Irish Neutrality: OBEY THE

CONSTITUTION, Articles 28, 29

AM-BUSH   AM-BUSH   TOTE HIM HOME TO TEXAS

Eager journalists, deprived of their press-conference, interviewed and photographed such demonstrators as took their fancy. Lambeg ran to the head of the stair, calling down for Sergeant Duff, ordering exemplary arrests and (if need be) a baton-charge. The superintendent shut him up before any more harm could be done, but –"Of a certainty, Inspector, Mrs Ó Ruairc emerging from our premises, her wheelchair carefully guided by the revered Mrs Vandaleur, and Mr Ó Ruairc beside her, with a pair of solicitors to make sure they get home untroubled, will be there upon TV for all the world to enjoy: if not the one o'clock News, then of a certainty at six. Thanks indeed to your initiative in sending for the cameras."

"This is not what I intended, sir, and you know very well it is not. I believe I shall be justified when my report reaches Special Branch."

"That," said Mrs Coffey, suddenly and devastatingly putting in her oar, "will remain to be seen. If you're after using the appliances of Masterton's e-mail, divel a word will have got through to Dublin: 'tis notorious, the technology's banjaxed. Had you taken the trouble to ask, you'd have been told."

Once the ladies were released, the overplus of demonstrators shed away from the garda station, only to reconsolidate higher up the town where High Street widened out into Windmill Market, the regular place for public meetings. One such was already scheduled: local activists who had decided (for whatever reason) not to join the multitudes at Shannon were to be addressed by local notables, trade-unionists, town councillors, a Dáil deputy, a poet, an enlightened cleric. There were men and women of all stripes (except Progressive Democrat and maybe not Fine Gael) – Sinn Féin and the Greens, Labour and the Socialist Workers, even a lone oddball from Fianna Fáil courageously inveighing against his own party leader. Ballykillard on the whole was strong for the anti-war cause. A couple of gardaí lounged inconspicuously at the side of the crowd, relaxed and indifferent until Lambeg in a patrol car emerged from behind the Post Office. The inspector took a look; he called the two men over for an exasperated rebuke.

Little though he liked the business, he did not see how he could put a stop to it. Mr Coffey had retired once again, so it seemed, to his sickbed, but that was where they'd thought he was earlier and he wasn't ... The inspector wanted no more embarrassment. But on the other hand –"Give me the handset. Easy Dog One to – to – Maverick, hello Maverick? Are you there, answer, over to you. Maverick!"

'Maverick' stuttered a reply, his sound-quality breaking up; he was several seconds too slow for the inspector.

"Keep alive there at the desk, can't you? Get me Duff, I want Duff ... Ah, Sergeant, where have you been? An unnecessary crowd: it needs to be controlled, bear in mind Dublin, last year, the Mayday riot, scandalous laxity by the officers in charge! Th'ould Vandaleur's here already, looks like she's intending to speak, and begod they have the other one loosing her wheelchair out of a car. Jasus, man, d'y'hear them cheering? As many as you can, to the Windmill Market, *now*! riot-shields and helmets in the vehicle, d'y'hear me, Duff? y're not to put 'em on till y're given the word. Be prepared though the minute you get here to confiscate these damned amplifiers: the noise is beyond all measure."

The good sense of Sergeant Duff, who somehow failed to hear the inspector's more excited instructions, ensured that the meeting did not mutate into a free fight. In fact there was no need to confiscate the amplifiers, their decibels were courteously abated by the young man in charge of them, and none of the speakers incited any violence. However, the whole affair with its music as well as speeches, and recitations of satirical verse, lasted well into mid-afternoon. By the time Inspector Lambeg thought it safe to dismiss his posse, an approximate eighty percent of the available Garda Siochána had been excluded from all other duties for the best part of two hours.

*

At the end of those two hours, just as Lambeg from his car watched the final placard-trailing stragglers wander off in their various directions, Molly Concannon was sitting in *her* car in a parking-lot just opposite the garda station. She crossed herself, grinned, and stepped down onto the tarmac. In the distance, along Wolfe Tone Street, the end of town furthest away from the Windmill Market, she could hear high-pitched sirens and see the scarlet flash of what might be a fire-engine. And was that an ambulance? ah, she hoped not, but even if it *were*, she refused to be blamed for it. "As they sow, so shall they reap," she muttered, heaving a heavy jerrycan out of the boot.

She repeated the phrase over and over, a species of invigorating mantra, as she shifted herself sideways, heading across the street toward the entrance of the garda station. The jerrycan weighed her down and distorted her walk. A passer-by, a small penpushing kind of man with a grey moustache and rimless glasses, offered to help her carry it. "No no," she carolled gaily. "As they sow, so shall they reap."

"Quite so, madam," said the man, giving her a curious look. He watched her in her little black beret and knitted poncho of grey wool. Bright red stockings and sharp little white shoes, how they swerved among the traffic. He wondered if she might be drunk.

His name was Ignatius Spelman, an insurance agent, only a small man and really quite timid: but when he saw what she was about to do – what indeed she was already doing – he instantly dropped his briefcase and ran after her to prevent her – over the street through the traffic, not a thought for his own safety: he hadn't had *time* to think. He jumped forward to avoid a bus and backwards for an articulated truck, he was too late to stop her pouring petrol all over the threshold, too late to catch hold of her before she half-emptied the jerrycan into the lobby and then hurled it, still spilling, across the floortiles toward the enquiries desk. In fact the desk was empty, the guard on duty having gone for a piss (he'd called in vain for a replacement). The building lay as it were abandoned, stripped of elementary security by Lambeg's uptown crowd-control. Molly stepped back to the open doorway, she fumbled with a matchbox, Ignatius Spelman threw himself at her from behind. He swept his arms around her, but her own arms were outstretched too far for him to reach her hands. She struck a match and tossed it; ineffectual; she struck another and then another as she struggled with the small man. The third match caught fire and kept it, it shot like an arrow straight into a puddle of petrol – a streak of flame from threshold into lobby – a whole bundle of flame over the lobby floor – a *whoosh* like the belch of a cyclops as the residue in the fallen jerrycan exploded against the door to the interior offices.

She had done what she came to do. She broke away from Ignatius Spelman, whipped round at him and kicked him with horrid precision dead-centre in the genitalia. Her shoe was pointed, his agony was extreme, he fell backwards to the pavement, and Molly ran straight for her car. Once again she dodged the traffic, once again she cried her mantra, or at any rate a portion of it – "So they shall they reap," she shrieked, "Oh ho ho shall reap, shall reap, shall reap!"

Such guards as were in the building tumbled out of it at a side door. Those in the lead were just able to catch a glimpse of Molly's unwholesome small Fiat, all rust and daubed patches of mismatched green paint, as it spun wildly out of the carpark and so onto the road out of town. Near the spot where she had parked, they found a sizeable piece of cardboard scuttering in the wind. It might have been the torn-off side of a box from a supermarket. On it, in the rotund scribbles of a red felt-tip marker, was a message of contumelious accusation, apparently written at speed, but before the fire was lit: it must have been tossed from the car as it drove away: –

I am told this by astonishing REVELATION upon the road (as it were) to Damascus:

The WAR of TERROR having been declared AGAINST ALL CHRISTENDOM, we have no alternative but to BATTLE as Best We Can !

I Battle because MY CONSCIENCE Battles. Our enemies are Within as much as Without. Already I exposed

Machinations of the FELONIOUS WIDOW !!

Already I Took Action against her, & "she shall reap".

Now is the time for Action against those who had her held in a <u>Just & Legal Custody</u> and treacherously LET HER GO !!!

[Heard it on the 1 pm News, car radio, an utter OUTRAGE. Whoever says <u>not</u>, is Apologist for TERROR.] Hypocrites and Cynics, you shall BURN !!!!

When Inspector Lambeg was shown this inscription, he at once realized who had written it: 'Road to Damascus,' and 'Felonious Widow', the giveaway phrases. He ordered all cars out to find Concannon and bring her in, he ordered roadblocks, he ordered a check on Mrs Vandaleur's house. (He did have a notion that something about a house-on-fire had already been put out on police radio: he'd been so heavily wrapped up with events in the Windmill Market, he hadn't been able to take much notice).

Molly Concannon knew well she had done wrong. Of course she believed her conscience was telling her she had done right, of course she was scared of the consequence and desperately anxious to avoid it. Whether it was worse to have set her fire at the garda station or at Mrs Vandaleur's house was an academic question. Quite simply she was glad to have hit both. "Oh ho ho shall reap, shall reap!"

She was careful not to drive in the direction of her own cottage, she had a crazy plan to entangle the police in a web of country roads and bohereens and sheeptracks – she recollected one of those films where heroines on the run in a stolen car contrive to bring their pursuers, one after another, into wild collision, piling into rivers, up trees, over gates. Once before she had fled across country with cops on her tail – her nonsensical involvement with that asylum-seeker protection gang – wrong-headed compassion, so totally wrong! she should never have messed with such dangerous do-gooders, the ruin of the country – why, Éilís Vandaleur might be one of them herself or at least she'd more than likely have had them in her house, or would have done before today, before she, Molly Concannon had torched the wicked place, "Oh ho she shall reap!"

She drove for an hour without awareness of anyone following her, until she found herself at the dead end of a narrow lane leading nowhere but into a field near the edge of the sea. A steep little bank at the far side of the field dropped down onto the empty strand, rocks and shingle and streaks of seaweed left behind by the spring tides at their height. Molly thought the tide was as nearly full as it would get at this time of the year. It rolled its great waves up the shingle, boisterous and noisy under a stiff breeze from the west. On either side of the bay there were high cliffs and higher mountains behind them. Half-a-mile away to the right, just where the cliffs began, a cluster of old cottages was strewn up the slope between strand and hillside-proper; beyond them a 'holiday village', white bungalows with thatched roofs, even more cottage-like than the cottages. There was a neat whitewashed church, practically on the strand itself, at the inner end of a stone pier that gave shelter to the moorings of a few pleasure-craft, sailing-dinghies, ketches, a púcán or two ... It was very pretty, very quiet, almost a delusion, Molly thought. Had no-one in that sweet, apathetical place the slightest idea of the Great Horror that strove to encompass the world?

The bohereen gave her no room to turn, so she reversed, clumsily enough, scratching and scraping against thorn hedges, bumping over banks of nettles, until she found a tarred road that might lead to the village, a rough road, too much loose gravel, too many potholes. A minute's erratic drive and she stopped between church and pier. Despite the wind, the sunshine was bright and warm, holiday people lounged on the low harbour wall, or sat with drinks outside a little pub. Nobody worried, nobody seemed afraid. Molly watched them in despair. At length she bestirred herself, got out of the car, went into the little church. She stepped back again, startled: a simple and whitewashed interior (she guessed it could be dated before the Great Famine), its intimate space was quite shockingly overpowered by brilliant coloured glass in the three tall lancets of the east window – she guessed early twentieth-century work, she guessed Harry Clarke. If it was indeed by that notable Irish master, it was surely his masterpiece, and it filled her with dread. The window seemed wholly a-flame, yellow, orange, scarlet, black smoke above and purple sea-waves below. Panic-stricken miniature mortals twisted about in the foreground as though whirled by a hurtling wind, a sinuous and flame-like Blessed Virgin shone through the flames in serpentine vestments of un-believably vivid blue – was she putting the fire out or could she (oh lacerating thought) in fact be the arsonist?

It took Molly some time to force herself up to the altar rails, to study the window more closely. She was shaking all over, her eyes and ears were playing tricks. The flames in the picture roared and crackled and surged, the frightened people waved their arms at her, and waved what looked like oars, how was it they were in boats? – worst of all, the Mother of God stared down at her and *grinned* at her, sharp teeth in the mouth of a she-wolf ... She could no longer look at the window. In-stead, she found herself reading a carved plaque on the adjacent wall. The letters swam up and down but very slowly she made it out. It told of a fire aboard a ship, in this very bay, a night of deadly storm more than a hundred-and-fifty years ago. There was gunpowder in the cargo, hideous danger for the fishermen who rowed out to help. And yet all the sailors were saved and the ship towed away, to blow itself up well clear of church and houses; women on the strand said they had seen the Blessed Virgin holding her hand out as a tow-rope in the midst (so they said) of the flame and smoke.

At last Molly was able to turn and sit down in a pew. Her sight and hearing seemed to have stabilized. She tried to say some prayers, gave up the attempt, she could not concentrate upon the concept of any sort of God or God's Mother, good or bad. She got up and put money in the slot for a candle, set the candle in the grill near the altar rails and lit it, she told herself that the quavering of its flame should carry her prayers aloft to *somewhere* (always supposing she had prayers, but she hadn't any, had she?).

She did not find the candle-business the soothing ritual it always used to be. After all, during the last two hours she had experienced a surplus of flame.

She left the church and trotted anxiously to the edge of the pier. She could not help but imagine the diabolic power of a blazing great sailing-vessel driven straight up the bay toward her in the grasp of irresistible tempest. She herself, all her life, had swept like a driven ship, or so she seemed to see herself, on and on, round and round, and turning at all adventure which-ever way the wind had turned. No hand upon her helm, not even this morning ... For no logical reason, something stuck in her mind from the night before last. How the Vandaleur in her studio stood bolt upright, unbearably pompous, leaning on her silver-handled stick, and pronounced to all and sundry, "Iraq did not throw down the Twin Towers of New York, Iraq did not hold any Weapons of Mass Destruction; if the pretext for war is a lie, then the war is a crime; if the war is a crime, then the peace cannot prosper. These victors have no integrity to reshape a wasted realm." Molly had heard this, had grimly refused it an answer, had done her best to forget it – irrelevant, contradictory, an argument quite doused by her Astonishing Revelation.

But she had not forgotten it.

If the Virgin in the window, seeming so calm, could suddenly grin and snarl with incendiary malice, was it not possible that the Revelation might likewise hide two faces within the one same hood?

Dreadful doubt. Had she really burned the house of a wom-an who laid out an argument? did nothing but *lay out an argu-ment?* an argument which should have been answered – by a poet? by a scholar? by Molly Concannon? – but was not. Could it even be that the argument would brook no effective answer? That the Vandaleur was *right?*

Dreadful doubt. Oh yes she'd done it. Burned to ashes, or merely spoiled, black and reeking from the firefighters' hoses, a private house, a police station: what good, at all? and *why?* Without knowing what she learned, she'd learned the language of the enemy and now she had given the most raucous, cruellest voice to it. Was a jerrycan of petrol better or worse than a hijacked plane? (Could the Mother of God indeed have pretended in jest to hurl a fireship against a fishing-village, only to laugh and excuse it as an Act of God, well-deserved by the hypocritical inhabitants?)

Dreadful doubt.

And by that thought she recommenced her walking. Not any more at a trot but -   One step away from the sea and then stop. Two steps, and stop. Three steps. Stop, and stop.

There she was, at her car. The sun slid behind the shoulder of the mountain to the north-west; it was suddenly chill; the loungers by the harbour had recommenced their own walking, the drinkers outside the pub had gone indoors ... She opened the door of the car, was about to step in, when a whirring and grinding of swift wheels on an ill surface, two garda cars, no, three! were swooping down toward her from the direction of Ballykillard. As soon as she saw them, they saw her: sirens began to howl. Holiday people stopped walking and turned to stare, the drinkers in the pub came out again. A priest in a black cassock cropped up behind the church. Molly stood petrified. The cop-cars skidded to a halt; uniformed men, some of them with sub-machine guns, sprang out and took positions. She had seen something much like this before and survived it, but today it was not the same thing. Why, she had been, if only in error, the Conscience of the Nation upon two fragile legs! never never could she allow this wicked and turncoat gendarmerie (the Irish embodiment, were they or weren't they? of the Axis of Evil) to overmaster her and compel her surrender. She recognized Inspector Lambeg; she heard him shout incomprehensible words through a loud-hailer; she waited till he finished and then she shouted back. "I have petrol in the boot," she yelled, and the wind from the sea carried her words, "I have splashed it all over the inside of the car, I have my matchbox in my hand." (None of which was true except the matchbox, but how would they know?) "So stand yourselves away," she yelled, "if you don't

want the Blessed Virgin to damn well have to *tow* you away –
oh God there's no need for us to burn you."

She jumped into the driving-seat and swung her car onto the
pier, just wide enough for her wheels but no rail or protective
wall. Lambeg and his men came after her, very cautiously on
foot, not at all sure how to handle it. At the pier's end, where
only a dwarf lighthouse stood between herself and the deep
channel, Molly drew up with the engine still running. She stuck
her head out of window. At the top of her voice she threw a
question along the wind: "Which way do I go? Will you tell
me? Why won't you fucking tell me? Either way the Suicide
Bomber: if I was right, and I reverse, I light the petrol. If I was
wrong, then I go forward, and I drown, do *you* drown with me,
so? You do not.

> Eeney meeney miney mo
> Catch an A-rab by the toe,
> Let her holler but never let go,
> G-o-d spells TERROR – !"

Her last word, "terror," was not so much a word as a shuddering exhalation; she flung the car into gear straight forward; *clang-bang!* as she bashed a front wing against the base
of the lighthouse; then an instant reversal and back she came
bucketing toward Lambeg. Then forward again, then back.
Forward. Back. A deadly seesaw. A switch of the wheel, she'd
be into the tide; a flick of a match and she'd turn herself into a
flamethrower.

The inspector muttered instructions, tentative, fussy, to the
armed officers. He moved them indecisively, by soft words and
hand-signals, here and there, up the pier, dodging the car on
all-fours as it jerked this way and that, in behind the lighthouse,
all very tentative, guns on the safety-catch and pointing downwards, nothing must be done to startle the suspect ... 'Suspect',
indeed! such mealy-mouthed nonsense. He ground his teeth
at this need to – what would they call it? – to *downplay* the
exigency when his strained nerves cried out for a violent and

butcherly wrap-up like the last five minutes of a certain style of gangster movie. Not one of today's disasters that had *not* been the fault of that abominable Masterson, he furiously assured himself, oh if he just had the bloody man in front of him! what would he not tell him?

Even as he snarled at the very idea of Masterson, Masterson without warning was alive inside his ear, a clattering quack-quack-quack on the mobile phone, impossible to interrupt. "Hello there, Seán, I thought I maybe ought to get in touch with you from Shannon as a change from the presidential doings – I'm after hearing some strange accounts of what-the-hell-is-it going on above there in Ballykillard? Mr Coffey in a dreadful state, and you know he's in dreadful health, man; you should never have involved the poor ould bugger, *dreadful.* And petrol bombs all over the town? Have y'all taken leave of your wits? Now Seán, don't explain, don't even *attempt* to explain, I'm on me way back directly. And I can, because nothing's happening, there's no riots here, no mayhem, al-Qaeda's taken a holiday, the CIA had a nightmare and determined to exor-*cise* it by criminal waste of our time and the nation's finances, that's all. Mind you, 'twould have been good to have seen a half-million demonstrators, some sense of purpose left in the country, why not? But I daresay they'd too much sense to try to affront a president when they knew they couldn't get near him be the space of miles and he'd never be told about 'em anyway, I daresay if I'd been a civilian I'd ha' thought so too. God but it's sad. Now lookit, Seán, be aisy, aisy, do nothing you don't have to, I'll be back with you in no time, let me pull it all together, find a handle on what's happened – "

Finally Lambeg was able to get a word in. "No," he breathed into the mobile. "No, you must not talk to me. Not another syllable," forcing his voice as low as he could, an intense angry growl like the waves on the shingle no more than a few yards away. "I am at the very heart of a most delicate operation. Jesus Christ, man, there are lives at stake, lives." He rang off. Molly Concannon's car continued its desperate bouncing – backward, forward, backward, forward – on the uneven granite flagstones of the pier. How long could she keep it up, or by what possible means could anyone put a stop to it? Lambeg for the first time noticed the priest in the middle distance. Maybe here was the chance? Persuasions from a man of God, the spiritual element, car broken down on the road to Damascus and so forth ... He beckoned urgently; he worked his mouth with grotesque silent emphasis, suitable (he hoped) for lip-reading. But the man of God preferred to cast his eyes sideways and to slip away sideways, out of sight round the corner of the church.

PART 2:

LONDON

A Masque of Blackness

Ben Jonson laboured hard to remove the taint of his association with the conspirators by aiding the Council. He was by no means the only recusant-sympathiser to do so. But the question of who knew what on these occasions would never be fully resolved, in view of the catastrophe which enveloped the major players.

[from *The Gunpowder Plot*, by Antonia Fraser, 1996]

*

"Merciful Lord Jesus! oh but a most virulent dream, bane and bale and all the bleakness of new-furrowed trepidation, I wonder I did not die before I woke."

The poet Jonson usually called himself the best young poet in England: which might have been true, if you forgot about John Donne. He had lately been scorning the world (his usual resource when his plays had not been liked, or he had not been able to write one, or the generosity of some patron or other had inexplicably stopped short); which is to say he was huddled deep down in his bed with another man's wife. His landlord's wife in point of fact. Her name was Mrs Townsend, and his outcries now hauled her from complacent deep sleep. She propped herself on her elbow to look at him across the bolster, her sly little features puckered with consternation. The fiercely setting sun broke in through the gable-window, shining slantwise down the Strand from behind the tower of St Clement Danes and straight into his eyes; he rubbed them with his nubbly great knuckles, trying to collect himself, uncertain of what he'd said, and wishing he hadn't.

"Why, you dream all the time," says she. "Did y'not tell me, 'tis your function? 'No poets without dreams dammit are worthy the name!' -- how often have I heard it? So why must you wake me? After all your plunging venery from dinner-time till past five o'clock, d'you think I need no sleep? Else I shall nod at the supper board and my husband be forced to know why; moreover, your horrid noise'll fetch him up from his shop and then we are both put to shame."

She bestows upon him her crooked, captivating smile, so she loves him; but she is without question vexed, and he must move now to mollify her; except that he rarely goes so far as to mollify anyone: it is (he would say) a feeble expedient, improper for a man of principle. "Nay sweetheart, nay chuck, nay nay delicious Winifred, I know more of your husband than that. I know that he knows, and takes delight through a chink to *observe* what he knows, now and again, on and off – not today, but he breathes like a bullock, *and* I have heard him at it. So have you but you kept it close."

Whereat he reproaches himself, for dammit she gasps with affectation of shock; or maybe with shock unqualified? Had she never an inkling he was all this time alert to that curious carry-on, the ambiguities of the Townsend marriage? Harsh embarrassment; and he too should have kept it damned well close ... Let him turn all the harshness to laughter. He whips back the sheet and smacks a pink peach of a buttock, she squalls in protest like a kitten with a sore throat, bawdy roughhouse commencing much as usual, but no! she can't keep it up. She tries to laugh, he tries, their voices fail. She thinks again of his bad dream.

"What was it?" she asks; it stabs at her he did not tell her immediately.

Nor does he wish to tell her now. "Oh nothing; 'twas no worse a dream than usual. Oh, I dreamed I was once again in gaol."

"And why was that so virulent? You've been there three times and now you're here. Did y'not tell me, 'twas a trick to be proud of? Twice for the strength of your pen in naughty plays, and once (in between) for the manslaughter of a violent knave of a player. Did you not tell me he gave out his lines in your comedy 'with such malice as to turn 'em from gold-dust into bird-droppings'? Your own words, Mr Jonson, as a playwright of principle. So why would you fear prison a fourth time?"

Rather than answer her, he prefers to hark back to the man-slaughter, which was, he insists, no such thing but a regular duello, an honourable passage of arms, no different from when he was a soldier and fought a Spaniard hand-to-hand in the Low Country wars, for which he was commended and made corporal; whereas in London, godswounds, had he not had the luck to be literate he'd have hanged and goddammit. But she reminds him that his third and most recent imprisonment had all but concluded with cropped ears and slit noses for himself and his two fellow-poets: confederates in a criminal libel against the new king's lousy Scotchmen, notoriously infesting the city. A punishment (she supposes) most frightful, had it happened. She touches his nostrils with quick gentle fingertips, she tickles his ears, she wonders aloud could she endure to lie naked with a mutilated man.

His pock-mottled countenance is rigid and saturnine, he fixes his gaze on the rafters. "Why would you not endure it?" he grouches through set teeth. "You do not distaste to lie naked with a papist, which many would believe to be no less abhorrent, mutilation of the spirit rather than the flesh. I think Mr Townsend may think in such terms, which gives him a relish to his wormlike secret pleasures, yes?"

At this, she surprises herself with the force of her anger, railing at him that all of a sudden he has dredged up religion to undo what small happiness she can get from his company, and why all of a sudden does he reverse his known opinions? Why make his avowed popery seem a sort of degradation, when heretofore 'twas his boisterous excuse for self-pride? She herself is no romanist (far from it), but she has at all times respected Ben's conversion – "An act of your devoted conscience: as such, to be praised. So why d'you think fit to give scorn? Scorn the world if you will, Benjamin, but never your own Christ: for thus you *do* mutilate, both your spirit and the very look of you. See yourself in your looking glass, how ugly you are become and all in an instant? O Benjamin, tell me why. Dear heart, what is the matter?"

Adulteress she may have been, and promiscuous for all he knew of it, but she was nevertheless capable of a sweet, sincere affection. By laborious kindness she would wheedle the sour Ben out of his subterranean rages, even at their most complex when he himself could neither account for them nor unravel the contradictions. This afternoon, ungraciously, he preferred to ignore the wheedling, to dismiss the kindness, to loathe and yet to wallow in the darkness of his own mood. Dared he consider what might have caused it? As for example the heavy drinking he had pursued all that morning before he came home to his garret? – aggravated by a professional rebuff from the gang of snot-nosed pissabeds who disposed the season's work at the Globe (as for example R.Burbage, and by God, W.Shakescene into the bargain: there'd been words in the taproom and bad blood not three hours since, though the hypocrites alleged themselves his sturdy compañeros, fellow-linkmen of the Muse). No. It was none of this. It was deeper, far more drastic, it was a week old already and festering in his very spleen; he scarce had the courage to admit it, let alone to confront it and –

O God, what to do next? Do. He had to *do*. And of course he dreamed of prison, and of course he knew full well that prison was not the worst. He flung an arm out of bed, groping for the neck of the flask of canary he'd left on the floorboards: one deep swig, two, and he swilled the bottle empty.

Merciful Lord Jesus, *he was in danger of his life!* Whichever way in his panic he might try to twist the business, black Nemesis bestrode the causeway! whilst the deadly Grey Sisters, with but one eye and one tooth between the three of them, crept implacably through the grey fields that bordered his path, snuffling about and about, first on one side then on the other, hemming him in, searching the reek of his sweat ...

Most dangerous to talk of it to anyone, *anyone*; even greater peril to shut it inside him ... No man of sense should ever trust his mistress. But the contrariness, the spits and spites and quirks, of Ben's unregulated mistress seemed a hundred times safer than the dire rectitude of his unsmiling wife. (And besides, he had not seen his wife for a matter of months. Not since the day that he last came out of gaol – in the very midst of all his friends, shaking his hand, congratulating, she had told him what she thought of his "antics provocative"; he'd turned upon his heel and walked away from her, direct.)

So he clutched the startled Winifred tight against his hairy chest and gabbled into her ear, unstoppable, phrase upon drunken phrase, with the speed and insistence of a millrace. At first in frantic English, all but incomprehensible, and then (from whatever weird blockage in his brain) he rushed into Latin. Winifred knew no Latin; he knew she knew no Latin ... He finished as abruptly as he'd begun, with a great wail of "Mea culpa, mea maxima culpa!"

She jerked from his embrace, rolled out of the disordered bedclothes, sat herself exhausted on the edge of the bed, feet on the floor, head turned away from him. In a small, dangerous voice, she posed him the one small question: "Ben, what is *wildfire*?"

His peremptory response was no response at all. "Wildfire? Did I say wildfire? Did you hear me say wildfire? I cannot have said wildfire." He thanked God she was not looking at his face.

"Oh but you did. While you were sleeping. And again you did, just now. It must have been part of your dream. So what is it?"

"God, but you're a fool," he snarled, "puddling your hands in a man's dreams like some whoreson grub of a gardener stirring shit for his manure. I'm putting on my breeches and I'm off."

"Ah woe," (with a great gulp of apprehensive distress) "this is not usual!" And then she was off before him, her clothes gathered up in her arms, pattering naked as fast as she could go, down the steep garret-stairs to her marital bedchamber; careless if anyone heard her, servants or husband.

*

Mr Justification Townsend was a well-regarded craftsman with customers in the highest reaches of the realm. He carved ivory and bone and varieties of shell, combs, costly knicknacks, decorative curlicues for the furniture-makers to insert into table-tops, and so forth. A jab of hunger had just given him its usual pleasurable warning that he must very soon stop work for the supper-hour, leave his journeymen to their bread and cold bacon, and himself sit down inside to a great bowl of mutton broth. He was a man of regular appetite who could not bear heedless timekeeping. So he frowned for an instant with a click of his tongue when his lubberly poet of a lodger stumbled down the stairs and made towards the street. He blinked at him through a hole he had been drilling in a sliver of mother-of-pearl. "Ah, there you are, friend Jonson, as you set yourself free after many an hour above stairs at your usual studies. Shall you sup with us tonight, sir?"

"No sir, I've men to meet." (a swerve of the legs and a belch) "Business to settle."

"Men? Your good wife being, so to speak, absent, does not drive you toward women? A warm fellow like yourself? And not yet thirty? Why, the Lord knoweth that the loins are for use and for His praise: oh at your age you should not lie fallow."

"Thirty-two," grunted the poet. "And I'm late." He pushed clumsily past the shop-counter and out into the sultry dusk. He was not always so curt and churlish, even in drink: Mr Townsend wondered had something gone wrong up aloft there with the temper of Mrs Townsend? If so, he must soften her. He could not bear discordance among his people.

He could hear her moving about in the house-place behind the shop, snapping at the maid to lay the supper for all and sundry, herself and himself and the apprentices. He must speak to her, now, before the meal was served and everyone crowded in to eat it, he must speak to her in private. He left his workbench and entered the house-place, sent the girl back into the kitchen with a flick of his testy fingers, whispered, "Now, sweetheart, now, so what is all this sulk between you and young Jonson? His mood since this morning has manifestly worsened and 'twas bad enough then. Is there a quarrel? I hope not. You have both of you always contrived to acquire heaven's grace by the worshipful attainment of – of corporal harmony, so to speak. If Jonson is in grace, Win, you are in grace, and I am in Christ's bosom also by the abundant good grace of your heart's love. Is not that what we've always agreed?"

If she had snapped at the maid she did not snap at *him*, but spoke quietly and darkly, sitting on a stool with head bent and hands in her lap upon her snow-white spread of apron. "Dear husband, is it not true that my lord Cecil sent word to you of especial and cordial praise for the ivory-work you wrought for him?"

"Why, yes, Win, indeed he did. Although I must remind you he is now made Earl of Salisbury and must needs be so styled, even in seclusion betwixt us twain. His praise, chuck, indeed: so what of it?"

"You told me at the time you believed you stood high in his favour."

"Why yes, Win, assuredly. Insofar as a great man's favour is ever assured ... I hope you don't wish to ask me in some wise to presume upon that favour? because, sweetheart, if so, I am scarcely persuaded that – "

She looked up at him now, a strong clear gaze from her steady grey pupils, no expression save a certain discomforting intentness. "I would wish you as soon as maybe to bring me to my lord. I have that to impart to him, alone, which if you fail to make possible you will weep for all your life. No, do not ask; I cannot tell you. Through the years we have been married I have begged you for no such a boon. That I do so tonight is a sign of its very great import. Justy, do you trust me? Ah Justy, shall you help?"

He thought he saw the glint of recent tears on her cheekbones, but as she was always so careful of expensive candle-light and had only the one taper aflame on the dresser behind her, he could not be sure. And he knew he could not ask her, he could not ask anything: by his curious collaboration with her wantonness, indeed by his hidden *control* of her wantonness, he had abandoned a husband's right to put questions and expect answers. He it was, after all, who had found this ill-conditioned Jonson, threadbare and in debt and upon bad terms with all the playhouses, even after achievement of fame; had found him of a winter's morning half-dressed in a muddy laneway, cast out of a Bankside bagnio, beating furiously at the locked door; had recognized him for the very poet whose work but a few years ago (*All the Men in Good Humours*, was it not?) had caused him to laugh so extremely; had timidly ventured to say so and to offer him whatever might be needed. For Justification, despite his name and his adherence to an outlandish Bohemian sect, was no common puritan: he refused to abominate the drama. Nay he was devoted to it, believing as he did in a God with all the instincts of a skilled stage-manager, who would arbitrarily present His elect with all-of-a-sudden "Glories", something like the transformation scenes of a new-fangled court-masque with the movable backcloths and wings. Correctly understood, these quasi-transfigurations would illuminate a bright new path for the wandering spirit. The sight of an admired poet making a beast of himself in the open street had been just such a Glory; to bring him home and let him live there rent free (or almost free) was a very bright new path, and most generously had Justification learned to follow it.

His encouragement of his Winifred into the arms of the poet had arisen quite easily and naturally. Nor was it the dotage of age; he was not much more than fifty. His incapacity for carnal intercourse was due to a malignant fever that had all but made away with him in the very first weeks of marriage. He had sorrowed that his wife had had to sorrow for her barren bed; he had hoped that maybe Jonson might have given her a child (though sadly this had not yet happened). Nonetheless, he had found his impotence astonishingly gratified by an entire new sensuality, the delight of seeing, hearing, knowing and imagining the deeds of love as accomplished by those whom he loved. He did now and then peep at a keyhole, he did now and then crouch upon a staircase to give ear, he did now and then rummage in a freshly-vacated bed to sniff for whatever his greedy nostrils might detect. It is true that by such dealings he felt himself contrariwise all shrunken and small.

So this night it was very true that his Winifred's demand had diminished him to the size of Tom Thumb. Was his well-settled world to turn outrageously upside-down? What horror was about to erupt that compelled her to compel him to risk all his credit with the king's chief minister? Did he dare go to this nobleman with such an unaccountable petition? Or to put it handy-dandy, could he ever dare *not* to go?

*

It might have been two days later that Ben Jonson decided he really ought to find his way home. He had drunk himself quite out-of-pocket, and very nearly out of his mind, in a succession of unfamiliar pothouses where no-one (he hoped) might recognize him, neither theatre-men nor the *others*; he'd awoken God knew where but probably in some corner of Wapping. There was muck all over his clothes and a horse-mill at work in his head. And what was worse, he had been harried and racked by a repeat of his dream, more vivid, more prolonged than before, and unmercifully detailed. Gaol yet again in the dream, of course, after hideous interrogation and a bench of croaking judges (every man of them unjust) and hangman's men like wolves at prey who flung themselves onto him to rope him to the hurdle to be dragged through the streets until -   And what was worse, far worse: this time a prologue to the dream. Even as he dreamed this prologue, he knew that it was no dream but a memory-within-sleep. It had happened, truly happened, in his tangible waking life, not seven days earlier. Memory and dream together made prophetic proclamation: inevitable, infallible, *This* will lead to *That*.

Memory, more or less thus: –

not seven days earlier and nigh upon sunset, he meets the man Catesby in the middle of the Strand, not a furlong beyond Townsend's, gallant gentleman Robin Catesby, one whom (were he a player) you could cast as Achilles or Sir Lancelot, keen and shapely as a heron on a river-bank, swift as a greyhound and as eager to bite, one who (had he been born earlier) might have rounded the world with Drake – ah no, never any of that, this rodomonte of a Catesby would thirty times more likely have captained a Spanish galleon and repelled the old queen's pirates like the protestant ruffians they were – for not only a catholic but a wild warrior catholic whose religion was his own leaping blood and so they meet: not a furlong beyond Townsend's, and Catesby laughing and roaring with his hat on the back of his head and the fluttering lacework of his wide-collared shirt flung open half-way down to his waist – "Aha, Ben! Ah, rare Ben Jonson! Word-maker, sword-wielder, battler upon stage and page! Ben, you shall eat with me, this instant, sir, and no refusal. I've been out all afternoon seeking my guests in the highways and byways like the man in the Gospel; by the Blood, but you're one of us and there are fellows you must meet, sturdy compañeros, they all know who you are, they're all of 'em men for good strong acts and scenes, and you shall know **them!** over ham roast and beef boiled, salmon stewed with fennel, pigeons and partridges snug under piecrust. Come!" And he brings him forthwith into the midst of the **others.**

Down perilous steep steps into the dark entry of The Irish Boy tavern – as ever the steaming haunt of sharp-set recusant heroes – the second-floor back filled like a vision of the Miraculous Draught of Fishes with a thronging platoon of devoted swords – haggard-featured strenuous young men, glowing eyeballs and glittering teeth, thrust-ing the hot food into their maws, swearing and brandish-ing their knives – every oath a damned piety, old-fangled

– "By'r Lady!", "By Lord Jesus His pitiful Bowels!", "By the Holy Rood of Walsingham!", "By the Thorn of old Glastonbury!", "By the Bread!", "By the Wounds!", "By the Father in Rome!" And many a man there with a knowledge of more than he speaks.

Greeting Ben indeed with the hysteric last-ditch warmth of Leonidas and his Three Hundred but an hour before the barbarians should arrive. Passionate curses, and what use are they, hey? that the laws against the Faith are augmented not lessened after two years of this new king – for had not this king promised everything? Release from fines, from distraint, from arbitrary arrest, from torture upon suspicion? Liberty for clergy? In short, toleration unprecedented? Had he not promised, and Salisbury in his name? And everything renegued upon.

Each detail exact, yet the whole of it hyperbolized, like the action of a grotesque antimasque, sordid parody of the lyrical main plot: these were men of his day-today memory and yet at the same time the creatures of a dream of terror and yet their essential was truth. And yet not quite: why, for example, this ancient priest all a-totter, with blood creeping out of his nostrils and his mouth, forcing the wafer of sacrament between Ben's horrified lips? *He* without doubt was a creature of dream, *he* had never been at The Irish Boy last week, but he *had* been with Ben in the question-cells of Newgate seven years ago in the old queen's time, after which they ripped him asunder at Tyburn, as Ben well knew. Each detail exact? Yet nobody's sleep is exact. As he very well knew.

Dear Lord, but the king's promises have been talked about often enough, everywhere, surely today such ex-

citement is superfluous ... 'Fore God, though, there is **Something Else!** *nay, what occult demon, what Lamia, what Scylla in her fearsome coils, lies crouched among the crowded tables, seen by all (save Ben himself), spoken of by none?*

Oh but leave the demon aside, there is to be sure a solid personage whom nobody sees, but everyone seems to speak of, in whispers and never directly to Ben. They call him Guido, they call him Guy, or Mr G.F., or the Soldado, or the Capitán, until suddenly a grey-bearded man (older than the rest of them), with an angry red face like a night-watchman's brazier, leans fiercely across the table, oversetting a gravy-jug, and bellows, "No no! it won't do, his name is Jonson and tonight he's not here, don't any of you forget it, the bloody man's my serving-man, and that's all he bloody is!" – his accent northern, a Mr Percy (so it seems): a veritable raging Hotspur, but why?

And then once again into dream, and there it was: –

oh to be sure here it is, as relentless, as powerful, as from This into That, as from Thames into Tide. Until they drag him through the streets upon his hurdle, bouncing and crashing and scattering the detritus of the street, shite, garbage, puddle-water, until –

He scrambled in disgust from the palliasse where he sprawled, and asked at random where was the door; the bully of the house took hold of him and angrily thrust him through it. Ah yes, it *was* Wapping. For there at a half-mile distance, looming up beyond the end of the street, were the four capped turrets of the murderous Tower. A squalid stinking street, and alleyways leading down to the river. Without doubt a great place to get knocked on the head, even at high noon in strong sunshine. Ships' crimps with knuckledusters looked out to kidnap sailor-men. He'd lost his hat. The sunshine hurt. He felt lucky to be still alive.

He would have walked to St Katherine's Wharf and taken a boat to the Temple (supposing the tide was right to pass the bridge); but he didn't have the fare. So now he must walk all the way and it was hot and he'd lost his hat and the city stank and he wanted to vomit. He did vomit, against a hitching-post in East Smithfield and again at St Paul's into the porch of the south transept. His uncertain feet found Ludgate Hill, and so along Fleet Street blindly, and so under the timbered roof of Temple Bar. Even nearer to Townsend's than The Irish Boy in the opposite direction: but O God how many yards, miles, continents and oceans from the security of the bosom of his mistress? Had he shattered all those hours of prolonged delicious trust (*guilty* trust and he had to admit it), had he wrought complete shipwreck with one crapulous dream and an idiot blurting of words? – why, he could not remember even what the words had been. But they had driven her from his bed like a sparrow from the hands of the birdcatcher. So what would she say to him to-day? Anything, or nothing, and which would be worse?

Hard by the Bar was a modest alehouse, the Elephant and Castle (little brother, as it were, of the great hostelry south of the river), set back from the street behind a shallow strip of pavement; with earthenware jars planted with majoram and sage, and a neat little bench and table. At this time of day it was shaded and cool, to be enjoyed at their leisure by two sombre men, square-shouldered, their narrow-brimmed hats very straight upon cropped heads, thick walking-sticks ready to their grasp. They stood up as Ben approached and moved easily to intercept him.

"Mr Jonson? Yes, of course you are. His lordship, Mr Jonson, would much like to talk to you. We have a boat ready. Come."

"Lordship? Who? What? You're blocking my path. Dammit man, stand aside, what d'you play at? Footpads, dammit – NO!"

His hand reaching for his sword-hilt had been violently hit by a walking-stick; extraordinarily savage and painful, the damned knob of it must have been loaded with lead. Was his wrist broken? Probably not, but –

"You ask who is his lordship? Very well: Earl of Salisbury, secretary of state. He's in his closet at Whitehall Palace waiting for us, we ought not to *keep* him waiting ... No sir, we can *not* say why ... It seems he would be glad of your opinion upon something. Theatrical matters, perhaps? At all events, no refusal. Come."

*

The way through the palace to the Earl of Salisbury's closet was so discreet as to be almost a secret passage. From one narrow entry into another, through the butt-end of a tumultuous kitchen all a-smoke with broiling fish, down into a basement among heaps of coal and firewood, up what seemed to the thickset Ben to be the tightest spiral staircase in the world: at the top, a small doorway with a soldier posed in front of it, an ill-favoured pistoleer who chewed tobacco and spat into a brass basin laid out for him in a wall-niche. He nodded to the poet's escorts, a friendly, slovenly sort of nod: "Let him leave his sword with me," he said. "You're to sit him inside to wait. *He's* waited all morning, now he's had to go the king. He's not best pleased."

They brought Ben past the soldier into a small square dark-panelled room. There were stools and a table; a decanter of wine on the table. They pointedly removed it and replaced it with a carafe of unsweetened lemon-water. There were biscuits, apples and nuts; they told him he could eat if he so desired. The pair of them sat down in the window embrasure with their backs turned; they talked in low tones to each other; when Ben asked them a question, they pretended not to hear him. It was, after a fashion, polite, but downright intimidating.

At long last a pretty jingle from a bell attached to the cornice, and Ben caught offguard with a half-devoured apple in his hand. He'd had trouble eating it comfortably: perhaps his wrist *was* broken. Still holding the fragment of fruit, and holding the one wrist in the other, he rose dazedly from his chair and lurched, rather than walked, through a door thrown suddenly open for him, and so (without escort) into a sunlit apartment rather too well-windowed to be effectively called "a closet". But that was what it was, and there at his great desk sat the smiling hunchbacked earl, a cunning little creature surely, but not just at present an obvious portent of doom. Unless you knew better; and Ben, with his curdling conscience, felt uneasily that he *did* know better. This was grim.

"Shall you sit, Mr Jonson?" So he sat. The earl was genial, in a vague sort of way: he began to discuss the hot weather and its effect on the palace drains, together with other inconveniences of the palace, structural and logistical. (The view from the earl's apparently splendid window, Mr Jonson might notice, was of a small dusty yard full of fluttering laundry.) So it seemed that His Majesty was thinking of rebuilding the great hall, all the better for theatrical occasions – speaking of which, Mr Jonson had perhaps never been asked how serene (or perhaps otherwise) had been his late collaboration with Mr Inigo Jones and the latter's new-hatched Italianism, the moveable scenes in that same great hall for the Twelfth Night masque which Their Majesties – specifically, *Her* Majesty – had so graciously commended?

Which was all very fair and forthcoming, and had to be received as though it were honestly meant. Ben had once before met the secretary of state face-to-face. In hope of patronage he'd been persuaded to present him with some verses; it was possible the flattery still held good. At all events, a few humble expressions of gratitude for the bloody man's condescension: Ben appropriately stammered them out, mendaciously asserting that Mr Jones as stage-carpenter, stage-tailor, stage-candlestick-maker, was a soul of fire, a Tubal Cain, an absolute Vulcan ... Any amount of verbal pastrycookery could legitimately be whipped up, if another such commission for a royal entertainment were truly in prospect: why, it *might* after all be honestly meant. But if so, why stir the question of that intolerable praise-grabber Jones after so long an interval – a whole half-year since Twelfth Night – and why, why the agony in his wrist?

"On the other hand," ruminated the earl, now not quite so genial, "you had no sooner been applauded and paid for *The Masque of Blackness* by the highest auditory in the realm, than you wilfully washed out your entire credit with that auditory: barefaced to the public theatre, you supplied a low comedy crammed with defamatory quips."

"The quips were not *my* quips, m'lord – how should *I* insult the Scots? – my own grandfather a Scot, a Johnstone of Annandale – proud, m'lord, of his memory, proud."

"You did not write the quips, yet you went into prison for them."

"I had not *resisted* the quips: so y'see, m'lord, loyalty, my professional loyalty to my two fellow-poets, poet Chapman, poet Marston – "

"Aha. Loyalty. Let us keep that word in mind ... It occurs to me, Mr Jonson, that – ah – that – "He broke off, he seemed abstracted. "Now," he said. "Yes." He paused again and squinted sideways at a paper on his desk as though uncertain of the next item. And then, without looking up and without even a shadow of geniality: "Tell me, Mr Jonson, *wildfire*. What does it mean and where did you hear it?"

If gratitude but a minute since had been modestly stammered, what verb might be found for the spluttering shattered utterance that marked the poet's whey-faced dread? He sprang upright, gesturing hopelessly; the piece of apple shot from his fingers onto Salisbury's desk. Salisbury tactfully hooded his eyes. "Take your time, Mr Jonson, stand away a few paces, if you please ... Now, nobody believes you are aught but an honest man. But even an honest man has a difficulty, now and again, with the truth. You know what I am talking about, but you don't know how *much* I know, yes? Well then, shall we see? Let us remind ourselves of your landlord." (As he spoke, he prodded the apple with the point of a penknife, edging it away from his papers so that it dropped into his gilded leather wastebucket.) "With his own hands the excellent Townsend wrought all the ivory inlay upon the desk here, take a look, exquisite, intricate. *My* notion as to subject-matter, rather than his: I fancy his religion would have preferred something less – ah – less - Take a look."

Ben's eyesight was swimming all over the place, but he did his best to focus it. (Essential he gave no further sign of guilty concealment, although already had he not issued a score of such signs, the last one appallingly blatant? Merciful Lord Jesus: an *apple-core*.) He saw tiny delineations of a series of Ovidian rapes, Danaë, Leda, Europa, Daphne, Semele, Proserpine, exquisite and intricate and also remarkably sinister. Old Townsend had clearly enjoyed himself in his own scalp-crawling way with all this cruelly copulating nudity; his religion had enjoyed itself too. Crookbacked clever Salisbury did not know the half of it ... Or did he? For he now began to speak of Winifred. Merciful Jesus, what ailed the man, he should be so damnably roundabout?

"I long nourished, without meeting her, a warmth toward Mrs Townsend, for the sake of her good man's craft-mastery. It seems that you and she have been – as it were – playfellows together, and therefore my warmth for her necessarily spills over toward you. It seems that you have puzzled her. *Wildfire,* Mr Jonson? And rather than explain it to her, you let her go hurtling downstairs, after which you yourself avoided her and stayed out of doors two nights and a day-and-a-half."

"Ah no, m'lord, no: that is not how it was, or rather that *is* how it was but not at all by interpretation the identical event." The earl gave a clap of his hands. A satirical applause for Ben's floundering? If so, it only muddled him worse. "M'lord, if I may make clear from the commencement, the hooks of the intolerable dilemma upon which I – " His panic-struck, fatuous phrases faltered on his tongue, for in a corner of the room the tapestries had shifted aside, by God there was a door in the panelling behind, and there in the doorway stood Winifred. She was as pale and rigid as a statue of the Magdalene in a church of catholic Flanders; her dress grey, her bonnet white, her hands at her bosom fiddling with the cross on her necklace. Ben knew that her husband had carved it from what he said was the horn of a unicorn. Two bright front teeth, with that darling gap between them, bit nervously into her lower lip; she looked anywhere but at Ben.

"Wildfire, dear lady?" The earl was smooth toward her, almost obsequious. "No mistake, you heard it? In his sleep, as you tell me? Tell again, and what else you heard that gave it such significance as to force you to force your good man to convey you hither."

A curious mix of reluctance and determination, she replied slow and heavy as though each phrase had to be pushed out by the next one behind it. "My lord. As I said. Mr Jonson was in great trouble of mind. His thoughts were a jumble. As is common with sleep-talk. As is common. He cried 'Wildfire!' many times. All amidst a strange medley. Wherein he seemed to attempt to make affidavit upon oath. 'I aver and affirm,' he cried (it was as though he had a bone in his throat), 'that I did but rejoin the ancient church of our crucified Lord and His blessed Mother, for my love of Their love and Their sacrifice, so how should the king be, nay and the queen? be – ' Then 'hoisted', he cried. Or 'blasted', 'basted', 'wasted'? I could not tell. Then he cried that all the parliament men were rotten rascals every one but nonetheless should not be – " She paused; needing to show perhaps that she'd gone on long enough and was worn out with it.

"Dear lady, not be *what*?"

"'Hoisted'? Or the other. Whatever he meant. His voice was all of a blur. But 'king', 'queen', 'parliament'? And it filled him with horror and terror. And then he ran into a strange language. Latin? And in the midst of the Latin, 'wildfire.'"

"Dear lady, my gratitude: you have done the state much service by your courageous coming-forth. Before I return you into the care of your proper husband, shall you speak to Mr Jonson?"

She swung on her feet, turning for the first time toward Ben, then turning away, then thrusting her face into her hands and swaying as though she would fall. Salisbury was all solicitude. He sprang up and led her to a pile of cushions in the corner, where he sat her down like a sick child, stroking her hands and fetching her a glass of aqua-vitae from a cupboard behind the tapestry. But even as she drank it, he insisted she spoke to Ben; he curtly ordered Ben to keep his mouth shut.

She took a great breath and stared hard into Ben's eyes: "They accuse me, your eyes accuse me, bloodshot. But how *can* I have betrayed you? for 'tis you that have betrayed yourself. O Jonson, blundering fool, stupid tall soldier, mooncalf of a playmaker, *I* cannot guess into what drainhole or cesspit you went out from me and tossed yourself, but you can never of your own will have sought to be thus heaving and writhing above your boots, above your knees in it. Knees? No, your silly ballstones, and all the hair of your itchy fork, and thereupon higher, you foul clown, to the very neck. Is it muck? blood? or is it pitch, to be flaring up wildfire as soon as the torch shall be put to it?" He did not even try to answer her; he shook his hurt right hand at her, helpless, hapless, all askew, like that wounded-soldier beggarman who sat day-by-day in the porch of St Dunstan's – all that was lacking was a tin pannikin for small coins. When she saw this, and saw how his wide-open eyes were filled with his own death, she was up onto her feet in a despair. Had she lost his love for ever? "O Benjamin, by your terror I was so terrified, what else could I do but this? Dearest Benjamin, as *I* did, you too must confide in my lord: he is very kind. All I seek, my poor sweet poet, is to save you from your – "

"Don't touch him!", snapped the earl, thrusting between them as she began to move forward. "Mrs Townsend, it is time for you to go. And not a word, not one word of our discourse to that nosey-parker husband of yours, or I'll hang him. I am sure you'll contrive very prettily to mislead him. I am sure you often have." He took her by the elbow, lifted the tapestry, moved her gently but firmly out of the room. The door shut behind her with a well-oiled click.

"Now, Mr Jonson, before I call in soldiers to put manacles on your wrists – " ("Dear Christ, not the *wrist!*", an agonized parenthesis) "Before I call in soldiers, you have this one chance: tell me first, yes or no, when she said 'affidavit upon oath,' have you in fact taken an oath? Because, if you have, it is broke open in your sleep, you need not consider yourself bound. Yes or no?"

With a great belch, or hiccough, or retch: "Dear Christ, m'lord, no."

"And she is correct, is she not, to conclude you never sought to struggle so deep in the mire? I asked you to think upon loyalty. Is your loyalty at this present to the peaceable honest folk of this peaceable kingdom, sir, whatever their religion, or do you stick fast by the roarers in The Irish Boy? Oh yes and we know you were there, don't attempt to deny it, and all of 'em your old friends there, were they not, were they not? or were there some you did not know? Well, sir? D'you mean to answer me? Names, I want names!" He struts barking round and round the stupefied Ben, high heels a-clack on his polished parquet like a volley of gunfire; this is fury whipped-up in an instant and all the more frightening for its speed. It is also absurd: his twisted, livid face scarce reaches the playwright's breast. Has he forgotten that this playwright is a contriver of comedy? For absurdly and unexpectedly a silent spark in the playwright's brain: "Why could not a man from this exigent draw out a confrontation of two figures in a laughable farce? supposing, that's to say, he might survive sufficient long for it."

"Ah, so you grin, sir. Indeed, I've heard it said, you'd rather lose a friend than a jest. Believe me, I *am* your friend; though what may be the jest, God knows. D'you balk then at giving me names? So instead, I'll give *you* the names, at least of the men whom you knew. Catesby, you've drunk with him for years; the brothers Wright; the brothers Winter – both? you're sure there were two?"

Distracted by comedy, Ben loses immediate prudence: he falls in, like a numbskull, with his interrogator's rattling chatter. "No," he says, "no, not two, just the one of 'em, the elder."

"Young Tom, then, elsewhere? On his travels again? yes ... What about Percy?"

"I never knew any Percy."

"But he was there?"

"I – ah – I – I think I heard the name. I didn't know him so I cannot say."

"Any priests, any Jesuits? ... Wake up, man, find your wits. You know a Jesuit when you see one, I daresay?"

Ben is wary, as who would not be for such a question? But positive he'd seen no Jesuit. "No, m'lord, I don't." He could venture a moment of play. "Do not Jesuits go ever in disguise? I saw nobody there disguised, neither false beards nor eye-patches, nothing."

An irritated pause. A change of rhythm. Weary indulgence of the poet's whims. "Pray attempt, Mr Jonson, to reply without foolery. What *do* you suppose was the purpose of that supper-party? If I were to inform you that you sat upon the fringe of a blood-soaked carpet of conspiracy, would you agree? For *if* you agree, you will assuredly confide in me, because you're as well aware as I am that all romanists are not conspirators. There are bigots and damned idiots who will always think different; nonetheless *I'm* aware, *you're* aware, the *King's Majesty* is well aware. And as for the *Queen* – "

Here was an acute hint; and a pause to follow it, even more acute. The eccentric Queen Anne was reputed a secret papist. For Twelfth Night in Ben's masque she had put on blackface and danced like a fairy-woman, gleeful and mischievous. He adored her ... Upon her mention, he made up his mind. He must needs be bold. Yes, and in her defence. If some would say "cowardly", even "treacherous" – very well, a' God's name, let them say! He knew that already he had acted the coward, huddling himself in bed, and his mistress to his shame had found him out. (How had he ever thought her sly? today she'd been as direct as a slap in the face.) Very well then, no more huddling: he was the best poet in England, he was nobody's gull!

"My lord, I shall be bold, for I am nobody's gull. You ask me the purpose of the party? Upon my entry, I took it for no more than a revel of good fellowship, called together to rail against government, against your augmented repression of the Faith: m'lord, so bitterly hated, and you cannot deny it. Nor deny that we the English will incorrigibly add to our meat the free relish of expostulation at every turn of public affairs: we can name it (if you will) the conscience of the commonwealth."

"It is also named sedition."

"At *your* font, m'lord, not mine ... But then I came to see that in fact this strange supper was no such a thing; in fact it was a species of *test*. 'One of us,' Robin Catesby had hailed me; and he now wished to see, was it true? I make it a point of honour never to allow myself to be put to the test. For who has the right to assess me, save only Almighty God? So in such and such a company, at such an attempt, I roll myself up hedgehog-wise, I watch and I listen. Which I did, and so I saw that all those raucous objurgations, which no-one there present could wisely dispute, were set up exactly for guests like myself. Set up to pose a question which incontinent should furnish its own baleful answer, thus: –

If this hurt hath been done to us, by what deed can we overturn it?

By naught save a hurt far greater, to be perpetrated ruthless and fell.

"When it was observed that I evaded the implied question and showed myself too stubborn to be led toward any such thing, Catesby and his close compañeros began to withdraw from me; they continued indeed to fill my cup, replenish my plate, congratulate my poetry, but the test had been failed. I was no longer needed in the room, their conversation toward me became perfunctory. Whereas others, who (like myself) had been invited at hazard, were treated to sedulous whispers, in alcoves, upon the stair-head, nay in the very privy."

"The *privy?*" A goggle of incredulity.

"Aye, m'lord, the house-of-office, down below there in the yard. Taken short after a surfeit of syllabub, I ran for relief; as I sat, there came two of these gentlemen, pretty well soused, to piss into the sink-hole adjacent. Hoarse-voiced and furtive, the one was instructing the other of this *wildfire* – I had heard already *wildfire* on several tongues in the room above – and then of the king, and the queen. As though king and queen already were dead. My beautiful queen, for whom I made my *Masque of Blackness* for her to dance in her beauty like an Ethiop angel. As though dead. They talked of a new model parliament. Its counsels to be subject to His Holiness the Pope. As though parliament in-toto were already dead."

Salisbury stood very still at the far end of the room. His voice was still and deadly. "Already dead. Dead how? Did you hear?"

"Alack no, m'lord. Unless by *wildfire* should be denoted – "

"Unless. And thereafter you went home?"

"My stomach was disordered. And I had not liked the company. To be frank, m'lord, I took fright. For if there *is* conspiracy, these men are fanatic toward it, beyond anything done in the last hundred years it must *destroy* the Faith without remedy, through all of England destroy it. Who knows, maybe for ever? Against their intent, assuredly. But they are caught in their own trap ... M'lord, save the queen! M'lord, save the king! I say moreover, save Catesby. If we can."

He had been gazing upward as he spoke at the fretted plaster of the earl's ceiling: until he shot out his last sentence directly at the earl. He saw something in the earl's eye that brought him to a sudden stop. O God! let him recollect where he was! If destruction of the Faith without remedy should take place, would

not this protestant statesman have *desired* it to take place? ...
He quaked from head to toe; and then he threw the vile notion
away, over his shoulder (as it were) like a pinch of spilt salt. He
must not over-Machiavel the intricacy of these perils. Easy,
Ben, be gentle. The bloody man's as scared as you are, no wonder he glares like a felon in a cage.

Glaring indeed, and his voice leaping up till it all but cracked:
"Save *Catesby*, can I have heard you? From the scaffold, is that
what you mean? Or are we theological and think he can be
saved from his tigerish imaginings that shall lead him direct to
hell and all his gang behind him? Save *yourself*, were a better
thought: for as things stand this hot afternoon, you bear much
the appearance of an interrupted and most guilty accomplice."
(No scope here for easiness, nor gentleness; none at all.) "O
young man, 'twould have been far otherwise had you come to
me of your own volition. Tcha! but you must loiter till your
strumpet gives you up. Save Catesby? Of course you can't."
(The earl was contorted with scorn, every limb and his working
mouth, and the foam at the corners of his mouth.) "I myself at
such a task would doubt my own ability. And yet we must try.
If the two of us together attempt it, 'tis conceivable we might
succeed ... Save, you say. Safety." (He was suddenly smooth
again, an anxious and considerate mentor.) "And here is how
we do it. You, sir, shall cling to him, as ivy to the oak, while I
cling to *you*, but less observably. You shall seem to suck into
yourself every fume of his poisonous pipe-smoke, you shall relish it and smack your lips, you shall hold it in your lungs until
you find the private chance to exhale it hugger-mugger into my
nostrils."

His hand was on Ben's arm, caressing, insinuating. His other
hand stroked the back of Ben's hand. Merciful Lord Jesus, was
this the way these great men secured their creatures? Ben could
think only of the first time he and Winifred had discovered the
warmth between them; the recollection made him mad. "Hey,
my lord, go fetch! a' God's name, would you have me lie in my
friend's bosom to enact some damned Iscariot, do I appear to
you such a species of serpent? More to the point, to the damned

point, how d'you suppose I'd appear unto *him?* Remember, he took note of my demeanour at The Irish Boy, impossible he'd believe me if I came to him tomorrow full of lust for his secret device."

"Very well, let there be no lust. But go to him nonetheless – no, stay! not tomorrow, let it lie a full week that he may wonder has he lost you for ever -- and then to him slowly, in a melancholy disapproval. In order that he may think that you work to *dissuade* him."

"Dissuade him from what? I have told you I don't know – "

"Yes you do, or at least you've begun to know: Godsake, man, he calls it "wildfire"! And so if you seem to abominate the very notion, there is a chance he'll think it needful to expound it you entirely, the better to convince you of its virtue. For the very fact you come to him – after, as I say, some tremulous delay – shall not this fact signify the snake-eyed fascination he holds over you? and above all, the fascination of his "secret device"? For he, sir, is the serpent, not you. Tcha, you know damned well with what intensity you have been fascinated. Else why d'you roar in your sleep?"

"Never you mind my sleep, m'lord." Ben was stung, which caused him to extend his dangerous boldness into positive truculence. He even wished (if he could) to anger the earl, for why should all the pain be upon one side? With his wrist damn near swollen to the thickness of a siege-cannon's arse. "I shall sleep sound enough, once I prove to myself and you that I am nobody's gull. I began life a bricklayer's apprentice: so I will, if you permit me, set out the steps of argument upon the ends of my fingers, one two three; as they taught me to reckon every brick-course, length and heighth, one brick at a time, and thus to determine the mensuration of the wall."

Salisbury groaned at the man's pedantry; but if there was no other way to make a contented spy of him, it would have to be endured. He stood and waited.

"First, my lord, thumb." Left hand (the uninjured one) was extended, fist closed, almost against the earl's nose. Thumb stuck out, upwards. "My father was a minister of the English protestant church as established almost Geneva-wise by sundry zealous guardians of the child-king Edward Sixth. He went to prison, lost his living, lost his estate, when Queen Mary reclaimed the kingdom for Rome. He died before I was born, so I never knew face-to-face what manner of man it was who'd walk steadfast into martyrdom for the sake of John Calvin, nor yet why John Calvin with all his severities should arouse such strange fervency, a passion indeed of love, among the careless and indolent English, for that's what we are and always were. Never mind the Johnstones of Annandale ...

"Index finger." Ben stuck it out, pointing it rudely toward the earl's eye. "In her widowhood my mother remained severe, not so much for religion as for general prudence, having one stubborn child to rear in her lonely poverty, a great gawk of a disorderly boy: what else could she do but find another husband? She wished me to study, but she compelled herself to force me to work and draw wages; *he* was a master-bricklayer, my trade was predestined. Oh the hatred for those bricks, how it brewed within my spirit! My world was a very desert of burnt clay and lumpish mortar. My few books were the sweet wells of that desert, the Latin language its whispering palm trees.

"Second finger." Ben stuck it out. "I went for a soldier. Why? To succour the Calvinist Dutch with all their severities, as my father would have hoped, had he seen me from wherever he is? No sir, not at all. But to learn to kill men and thereby (as I thought) to become a man myself. And yet I found the sword no less dreary than the trowel. At least with the laying of bricks, noble buildings could be erected; by warfare is nothing built but all the world trampled down into mud and into blood. In that mud I have walked upon corpses as though they were paving-stones.

"Ring finger, item four. I became a player, became a playwright, I created a pretended life, a world of my own construction upon which all my bile was expended. And because I am bilious, I have been most painfully purged. Thrice into prison (which was two times more than my father), where my martyrdom was for no religion but the fervency of a poet's utterance. To die for it, though? I think not."

He thrust out his whole hand, palm towards the earl, five fingers spread as though to tear the earl's face from his skull. "Pinkie finger, little titch. I met a priest in the prison and I bathed in his lovely fervency. A man whom they took day by day to be tortured and who awaited Tyburn Tree and the slicing of his flesh. Oh far beyond poetry, the love for Christ of such a man. And (above all) beyond the scorn that I felt when I saw how my poems and my plays were received – to be sure, they were applauded, but applauded by fools; and when they were hissed, then too often by men of undeniable discernment, or worse, worse, enchanting women, alas my wit offended them, they filled their mouths with spittle. So here was this religion, old religion, true religion, I'd never thought of it before. And if I were indeed to die for it, 'twould carry me to heaven. No?

"And yet you say, and I see, nay I'd already *seen* it, a week since, a week, that even such a heavenly cause can dig its own damned stairway direct down to hell. And as they dig, they'll assure each other they're no less than the new-guise Maccabees, to run like lions through the cities of Judah roaring for their prey, to seek out the wicked, to burn up all those that vex the Lord's people, to restore His holy temple which the heathen hath profaned. My lord, they are formidable, they are bent upon utter disaster; and yet they can be undercut.

"For which, with all five fingers, I do beg you, Earl of Salisbury, as the mover and arbiter of government, to relieve the king's catholic subjects before it is too late. I beg you, I entreat, I implore. Nay nay, sir, I offer a bargain. Repeal these cruel laws and I'll give you every name I can uncover."

From the earl, but a cold answer, and filled with contempt: "How well you know your scripture, you unconscionable rogue. But if you're so presumptuous as to talk to me of Maccabees, I too can rummage up the ancient history. I'd say the Romans were more your playfield than Holy Writ. Did y'not write a ponderosity, *Sejanus: his Fall*, five interminable acts? and he fell in all reality, no more than one performance and not a dozen of spectators left in the house at the end? Your theme was ill-chosen: the tale of an enormous minister who overrides his sovereign's prerogative is not fit for these days, these sidelong, suspicious days. Yet amongst all the old senatorials there might still be a scope for a – for a handy young ink-puddler who can see his advantage? What could we not make of a clear-sighted anatomy of a nightmare flux of evil, wriggling, twisting, slippery and vivid? Read your Sallust, read your Plutarch, discover the vile plot of the malcontent Catiline. Find Cicero in your book and read of *him*, who uncovered the conspiracy by the day-and-night sifting of the informations that came to him: one of which, and not the least, was the pillow-talk of the paramour of a clear-sighted adulteress. Mr Jonson, you will apprehend that Cicero *saved the state*."

"Which is why I'm so unconscionable as to speak to you of a bargain. Cicero's task is yours, but believe me that mine is the same, yet far far the harder for I add to it the saving of catholics. Intolerable dilemma: I told you I was upon hooks."

"And you presume that the king's government will chaffer and haggle? – with conspiracy, with treason -- with *massacre*, for I'm sure it is? You presume that I ask you for names? Ask? Damn your blood, I do not ask: I demand, I insist, I *require*. I already know the names you know, I want the ones you don't know. As for a start, the mysterious Guido, G.F.? whom so carefully you have not mentioned. So who *is* he? Never mind. What I do mind, and incontinent, is how widespread is this secret device? How many men, how many places, how long shall it take to ferment?" He is shouting, showering spittle, a vehement upsurge of explosive prodigality. "Man, you discover *that* for me – why, I'll give you every papist in the land, live-alive-oh like lobsters in Billingsgate. Dear Christ, this is no bargain, but 'tis noblesse-oblige, the unstinted liberality of the conjoined crowns of England and Scotland, Jacobus Rex his magnanimous gratitude!" Voice drops once again to caress and a lingering insinuation: "I do believe you don't believe me. For how the devil can a man of wit put trust in a politic statesman, hey? ... Let me therefore confide in you certain matters of state to which very few indeed are made privy. You say you were a soldier, you fought against the Spaniards. Would you happily do so a second time?"

"Not happily, no. I thought I'd made that clear."

"So you had. Mud and blood. Well sir, all but next door to your ill-omened naughty haunt of The Irish Boy is a great house called Somerset House. For many weeks last year I sat there in wearisome discourse betwixt three or four blockheads of honest English noblemen and four or five sagacious Spaniards. Throughout difficulties unbelievable, we constructed a treaty of peace. I daresay you've heard of it."

"Of course I have heard of it. Everyone has heard of it."

"Why, everyone has indeed. And your Catesbys and your Winters all a-stir like brainless gogmagogs to tear it to pieces." Energetic persuasion, but no more shouting. "Did you know that it's not nine months that Tom Winter was in Madrid, prowling the land for all those hidalgos, priests, inquisitors or conquistadors who hate our new treaty and might therefore re-kindle the war? – I tell you in confidence there are many too many of them, this peace is exceeding precarious. And as for the war: Godsake, wasn't it waged for a full generation and more than a generation, ever since those masterless corsairs, Hawkins and Drake, fetched African blacks to the Spanish Main to sell them as slaves, and when told foreign trade was prohibited, de-manded their market at the mouth of the cannon? Time, Mr Jonson, high time, *beyond* time, that we shut the useless blood-shed down ... And yet here are your good friends, sir, pretend-ing themselves the authentic representatives of the catholics of England, imploring the Spaniards to send troops into England tomorrow or the next day, hurly-burly, another Armada. While asserting 'tis the only way for those same catholics to achieve their – their freedom? No, no, not their freedom: their *suprem-acy,* Mr Jonson. Did you know this, Mr Jonson? All of it? Any of it? ... No. So now you are most privileged."

Privileged or not, Ben was ingenuously shocked. Spanish invasion? What, the jovial Tom Winter, *inviting* such catas-trophe? He was the more shocked because the earl had indeed seemed to confide in him. Ridiculous, humiliating, to allow himself to feel so flattered. Undeniably, he felt flattered ... Let him nail it into his brain: he was nobody's gull.

A thin specious smile from the earl, a shifting of books on the desk to prepare it for the next item of business. "So, Mr Jonson, I shall waste no more of your time. Do me the grace to think hard upon all I have said to you. Loyalty. Safety. And what you choose to call our 'bargain' ... May I, as you take your leave, suggest you ask la belle Townsend to put a cold compress on that unpleasantly swollen wrist?"

He pulled a bell-rope; the soldier from the stairhead came in and beckoned to Ben; uncertainly, Ben followed him out.

"He don't believe me," muttered the earl to himself, once he was securely alone. "He wants to believe me. He'll do it. Or some of it at all events. At all events, I have him." He opened a notebook, found a page headed "B.J.", wrote "Bricklayer" in apposition. Then he wrote "WILDFIRE" three times, and brooded over it.

Ben, trudging painfully toward Temple Bar, hatless and bothered by flies, was also brooding. Bargain? Had it indeed been agreed? He wanted to believe it but he could not believe it. At least he wore no manacles. He was Salisbury's man now, against men that he'd enjoyed to call his friends. No: he had not enjoyed it. Their acquaintance had always troubled him. Friends do not entrap you into drainholes and cesspits. Politic statesmen often do; but if you know it, you're aware of it and can take your own proper precautions ...

*

Mr Townsend, of course, was on heat for an explanation. Ben must hastily employ every iota of his fictive skill. So he told him, in the shop, in front of his wife and workpeople, that Mrs Townsend had been accosted in the street by – ah yes – a malefactor who had been in prison with himself (Benjamin Jonson) and who now sought to exploit the circumstance, to secure (by some crafty cozenage) the embezzlement of certain moneys held in trust by – by – ah, by the ledger-clerk of the Globe in regard to next season's performances at court, and would she sound it out with him (Benjamin Jonson)? Which in her puzzled innocence she did; whereat he (Benjamin Jonson) saw immediately a deep and dark imbroglio. The plot could be profound and aimed at the royal finances. Therefore, he (Benjamin Jonson) had recommended her, in secrecy, to make it known to some great officer of state, and it so happened she remembered that her husband had worked for Salisbury. He (Benjamin Jonson) had been fetched up to Whitehall to corroborate her story: Mrs Townsend was a woman in a hundred.

He told Mrs Townsend, in whispers in the back kitchen while she wrapped him a sling for his right arm, that there was no explanation he could safely give her of anything that she'd heard or seen. She was right, he had been most desperately befouled. Thanks to herself, and to her – to her "ambiguity", some would say; he'd prefer to say "courage" – there was a chance he could bring himself out clean from the business. In the end. Meantime, if she wished to continue their – their intercourse in all its forms, he would happily concur. If not, then – If not, he would, if he could, hope – If not, that is to say most *utterly* not and no remedy, then best to bid farewell, here and now, foot of the stairs, he'd go back into the shop, pay her husband what he owed him, and shog off. (He said this in blind forgetfulness that all his money had gone from him in the snuggeries of Wapping, two nights and a day-and-a-half.)

She saw that he was weeping. She kissed away his tears. Thereby everything might very likely be just as it was before. Except that it wouldn't be, and both of them knew it: a chill at their two hearts, not to be spoken of.

*

As for the kind of service Ben was now upon notice to provide for the earl, he strongly suspected it was the earl's own private service, rather than a true civic duty to the king, to say nothing of the English people. The difficulty was: how to seem to provide it and at the same time withhold it at discretion? The honest servant in such a case would be the rogue who might best deceive his master. Could it be done? Maybe not. Except maybe a few non-committal enquiries, among obviously innocent people. At all events, he was not about to mingle himself, not just yet, with the unpredictable forked-lightning of The Irish Boy. Especially not with Catesby. On the other hand, one of the others - He had a clue of his own he was anxious to follow: how had "Guido" so outrageously been named as "Jonson" by the man Percy, right into Ben Jonson's own beard? Was it deliberate? A password of sorts they thought he might reply to? The incident had caught like a fish-hook in his memory, so much so that he'd taken care to give no hint of it to Salisbury. And at all events, he was not about to mingle himself with Percy. On the other hand, if as it were by an accidental encounter –

It being probable that Percy had some connection with the Earl of Northumberland (also a Percy; they were all of 'em in a clan), Northumberland House at Charing Cross was the bastion or outwork he ought first to reconnoitre. Less of a bastion than a huge citadel, a brand-new palazzo with the builders still at work, it was thronged like a market-place with people and horses and carriages in-and-out and all day long. Across the street, at the corner of St Martin's Lane, was a little cookshop used by hangers-on of the Royal Mews. Ben took to frequenting this noisome establishment, now for breakfast, now for dinner, over several successive weeks. A leisurely watch indeed, but he had his other businesses (a' God's name, he had plays to write!), nor was he in any great haste to make awkward discoveries. He put on his poorest clothes for these visits, he'd trimmed his beard to stubble, he looked as much like a horseboy or a falconer's knave as anyone. He no longer needed a sling to his right arm; and with a dirty old brim pulled down over his eyes, he felt sure he would not be known. (At The Irish Boy that time he'd been jet-

ting it in crimson velvet, with a green-and-blue peacock feather
to embellish a poetical sombrero: the last of his £.s.d. as belat-
edly paid to him for *The Masque of Blackness*, dammit.)

In the fourth week of his watch, he struck lucky.

Emerging from the great gateway of the palazzo: Percy, un-
mistakeable, flushed face and bristling whiskers, he sauntered
hand-on-elbow with a tall wolfish soldier-like rascal, red-haired,
sharp-bearded, dressed (it might be) as a confidential servant –

But what sort of servant would wear such a great sword and
walk so like a ruffian? Watch 'em, Ben. Dodge 'em. These are
your lads. Which way?

Toward Westminster, slowly. The weather had gone bad, no
wind, muggy warmth, a nasty drizzling rain and a thick sodden
vapour of three-parts coal-smoke; it was turning into night and
vision was blurred. Easy to tail two men. Not so easy for the
two to see the one man on their tail.

All the way past Westminster Hall into the entry of a narrow, deserted passage that led down to the river close to the
parliament buildings. The latter being a rain-streaked huddle of this and of that, an old royal chapel now the House of
Commons, a superannuated dining-hall or some such, now the
House of Lords, all mixed up with dwelling-houses, sheds and
pokey back yards. Percy and his red-bearded man stopped under the shelter of a low doorway in a blank wall. Ben slipped
in behind a buttress, no more than five yards from the pair. The
rain had grown from drizzle to downpour; footsteps were hard
to hear, so he hadn't been heard; but voices were hard to hear
too – although if these two beauties were daft enough to have a
conversation out-of-doors in such weather, it would be mortal
misfortune if he couldn't pick up any of it.

What he did pick up was confusing, because Percy spoke
loudly and very fast in a whooping Northumbrian patois, while
Redbeard (who was also a northerner) spat his words indistinctly
from a half-shut mouth. He kept trying to quieten Percy, apparently out of habit, not expecting to be heeded. "Whisht!" he'd
hiss. "Eh, do think on. Our affairs aren't *their* affairs: keep
it close." Percy called him "Jonson", when he remembered; at

other times he called him "Capitán", and then "Guido", and once (in a spurt of sarcastic vexation), "Mr Fox". The vexation seemed due to a boat not arriving where it should have arrived, at the mooring-stairs down the end of the passage. Percy was blaming Redbeard for the mistake. While Redbeard, with angry ferocity, refused the name of "Fox", and also "Guido". Percy gave an apologetic cluck, but continued to dispute: should they wait for the boat, or not? Which explained why they were standing in the rain, but not why the servant sounded more authoritative than his employer.

At last: "There y'are!" Redbeard was dourly jubilant. He stepped out from the porch and pointed across the black water: a lantern swung up and down to the strokes of oars, in a boat's stern fifty yards away and coming nearer. "I told you an hour after dark. If you think best to make it half an hour, you can look for a half-hour's wait. Wet wait and all. Let's just hope the casks are well-enough caulked."

The boat swirled on and off the steps, a man in the bow leapt out to tie up, another man, holding the lantern aloft, came scrambling past the oarsmen to jump ashore after him. "Come on, come on," he panted. "We need a hand, they're whoreson heavy! Speedy, me lads, *sharp!* or this pox-rotted cunt-crack of a cockboat'll be missed and fucking looked-for." Four oarsmen altogether, cloaks, scarves and woollen caps, and all in an urgent hurry. Percy and his man had their own dark-lantern up and shining. Ben glided backwards like a cockroach along the wall, for the way they moved, they'd all be on top of him. As he shifted, he heard another of the newcomers call to "Jack Jonson" to receive what was rolled towards him, "Handsomely, matey, no damned staggering: Godsake Jack, don't let it get staved!"

(The coincidence of name, then, was merely coincidence ... thank God.)

They were barrels, a dozen of them, hoisted awkwardly from between the thwarts of the boat. Three men with a rope-knot to lift each barrel onto the quay, one man after another to trundle it the few paces to the doorway where Percy and Redbeard had been sheltering. Percy unlocked the door and went in ahead of the barrels (into what appeared to be a yard); he pointed the beam of his dark-lantern to show the way. Hard-breathing haste and no more talking, until Redbeard had trundled the last of the load. He swung round upon the man who'd been scolding him: "Sithee here, I tell'ee once an' not ever again: there's no tarry matloe tells *me* not to stagger nor stave. I've humped more casks in-and-out of the magazine than you've had plumduff on the bosun's birthday. So watch it or you're dead." This was louder than his previous whisperings, and spoken with full assurance that no-one would dare contradict. But the scolding man did dare; he swung forward with his fist clenched, only to be knocked off-balance and backwards by his colleague with the boat-lantern, who swore at him greasily, caught Redbeard by the arm, and changed tone in a breathless panic. He gasped into Redbeard's ear a whirlwind of florid verbosity – low-voiced, yet scarcely so low as to hide the fact that his apology, mitigation, explanation or whatever, was all in Spanish.

(Not that the fellow looked like a Spaniard, and his curses had been sheer slum-London. Clearly an egregious foul-mouth, he was much the same shape as his own tub-shaped cockboat, pale and blond in the lantern-light, unhandy with his movements, dexterous enough with his words.)

The altercation done with, there was a chinkety-clink as of coins from hand to hand, and the five of them scrambled back aboard. Redbeard capped matters with general rebuke, half-humorous but caustic. "Aye an' you'd best make sure the next lot comes in a bigger bottom. Twelve at a time's less use nor a costive bowel-pipe." No reply beyond a few more grumbling oaths, their lantern was dowsed, the boat shoved off with speed. Percy and Redbeard went in through the door and shut it behind them. The rain had given over; there was even a glimpse of the moon. Ben, for the first time, noticed a writing daubed on the door.

THESE PREMYSSES ARE A PRYVACEY
+
ALL TRESPASSE THEREBY FORBID

A scrap of parchment was nailed underneath: –

as giv'n under my hande:
Thos. Percy, Gent. (tennant trimestrialle)

Paintwork was old; parchment seemed fairly fresh.

*

In his garret, among his books (Mrs Townsend at her household business downstairs) Ben strove to refurbish his recollections of Catiline. It was years since he had read the narrative
of that fiasco of a plot, one of so many throughout history from
David's Absalom to Elizabeth's Essex. What was there about it
that Salisbury should have harped so strongly? Was it no more
than the importance of Cicero, with whom a great nowadays
statesman might well be sufficient vain as to compare himself?
Or a quirk in the tale more integral, a clue Ben must find and
take note of? *Turn the pages, ponder the translation, check it
against the original Latin, brood upon it, brood.*

The very nature, perhaps, of Catiline's design?
How he gathered together a host of violent, lawless men, out-
cast relics of a discredited dispensation – Sulla's rapacious army
disbanded all over Italy, with no civil war to fight, no loot, no
extortion, until Catiline should show them the way.
How he kept some of them out there, to seize and hold the
countryside, while others he brought into Rome, to stir and
command the rabblement of the city.

How his friends among the gentry, their funds in the hands of the money-lenders, their properties ruinously mortgaged, saw no hope without the abolition of government and the wiping of all bad debts

Their task: to assassinate the consuls and senators, and to oversee the rabblement who must riot in every quarter.

And how, in sundry private store-rooms, this Catiline laid up great heaps of flax and sulphur, watched over day and night by the men who would whirl them through the streets and pitchfork them into arches and porches and the open fronts of shops, and all upon one command set them flaming to the heavens of the gods – *Wildfire!* How thus in one short hour the whole of Rome would be ablaze beyond remedy.

If Salisbury believed that similarities today were in urgent preparation, well might he want to know how widespread, and where and what, was "wildfire" ... Similarities indeed: if for Sulla and his civil war, you understood popery, Mary Tudor, Mary Stuart, the fires of Smithfield; if for the ruined gentry you understood those who had intrigued with the Earl of Essex and lost their chances when he lost his head; if for consuls and senators, you understood king and parliament, and queen.

Flax? sulphur? Or should one say gunpowder? Catiline would have said gunpowder, had the bloody stuff been invented ... Casks. To be caulked against the wet. And how many more boatloads to come? For that matter, how many more private store-rooms? everywhere, anywhere, all over London?

Ben supposed he might drift up to Whitehall and put it loosely to the Secretary of State that Mr Percy rented premises where he'd taken delivery of casks, no less than twelve. Oh yes, and that his servant had at least three names and understood Spanish. This might secure a search and examination of the two of them, but if they were as stout to their martyrdom as so many papists had shown themselves, the crucial question of "widespread" would not even be touched. Besides, would they know the answer, even should the rackmaster drag at their joints with all the strength he could muster? If the conspirators kept as close as good sense said they ought to, no-one would know anything beyond his own task, except for- Except for whom? Catesby? Only if he were chief. What reason to think he was? He was the man who had the task of fetching-in gulls to sumptuous suppers, a plausible, glittering swaggerer; why, he too might be somebody's gull.

Ben feared that a word with Salisbury at this debateable stage could wash out all his credit with the bloody man. Was it not nailed into his brain that he was already suspect, released upon probation? If he could not be more than tentative, let him think upon manacles and keep well away from Whitehall. Better for the time being to find a quiet tavern, maybe even find some poets and such, oh yes and their little doxies, cozen a drink, enjoy talk that would not be exclusively upon black looming counsels of state. Sweeten old Justification with a few more lies about embezzlement at the Globe, borrow a few shillings on the strength of them, buy a new plume for the sombrero, find a quiet tavern – The Mermaid? There were weeks when he was never out of The Mermaid, but of late there had been unpleasantness. Courage therefore! for today must be the day to mend friendships, forget perils, procrastinate! Merciful Lord Jesus, were these thunderclouds to sit on top of him for ever?

The Mermaid lay in a narrow street between Cheapside and the river, a place for skilful conversation and now and again music, always provided the parlour was neither too full nor too loud. Unfortunately this evening it was both. Some actors from the Fortune playhouse made a grudging place for Ben at their table. His ugly behaviour the last time he'd been with them was not quite forgotten: even if he *was* the best poet in England, it was a fool's trick to have said so here. But this evening there was ugliness from a quite different quarter. A fat, sweaty, fair-haired creature, of a pallid physiognomy like underdone pie-crust, sat at a chess-board with the poet Marston and seemed to be balked at every move, for at every move he cursed and swore with rotten emphasis, heavy-breathed, low-voiced, but audible right through the noisy room; the sickening bubble of a toad in a quack's urinal. Marston at length could take no more of it. He conceded the game abruptly and dragged his stool across to sit by Ben. (He was a circumspect and sidelong smirker, younger than Ben and not nearly so bulky. They used to be venomous enemies. Partially reconciled, they had suffered together in gaol; they were friends now, more or less.)

Marston began, without preface: "That pursy, stinking fartbag: a fool's trick even to acknowledge him. Why could I not have kept close?"

"I've seen him before, I think I have, think ... But not here. Who is he? Is he a sailorman?"

Marston tapped his nose and sank his voice significantly. "He's pretty nigh anything his masters would want him to be. And who are his masters? Aha, Ben, there's the question. Some would say Northumberland, some would say Northampton, I think most men'd make a guess at Salisbury. At all events, a secret creeper. Best to keep well away from him ... Thanks to our guardian Muses, the dirty bugger is voiding the room. Shall we ask the potboy to fumigate?"

Once he was quite sure that Fartbag had made a definitive exit, Ben bent his mouth to Marston's ear. "You know more than I do. How do you know?"

"He hung around us in the stone jug. Or he hung around *me* in the jug. Our masterly partner George Chapman, maggoty-brained seesaw of a good poet, bad poet, eternal entangler of syntax, had let it be known that in our three-handed comedy, *I* was the sole progenitor of the dung-pellets flung at the Scotch. So Fartbag didn't bother to trouble George, nor did he trouble you – By-the-by, did I ever truly thank you for your volunteer march alongside of us into durance vile? 'Twas noble of you, Ben: you're a man. And moreover you'll dine out on it for the rest of your life."

"Enough o' that. Think upon Fartbag. In the gaol? That's not where *I* saw him. I do believe I saw him upon the riverbank, somewhere, in the dark, in the rain ... So what did he do in the gaol?"

"Ran messages in-and-out for a highwayman or two and a gaggle of cutpurses, who curiously favoured his society. I came to suspect that he'd picked up a word about *me*, that I might be enveigled into all manner of incrimination. Such being his trade, I've since been told. Could he have hoped to get me condemned as a jackal of Walter Raleigh's? If that was his sling-shot, he missed."

"He has a name?"

"Probably several. The one I heard was something muffled, from out of the caves of Tartarus. Crypt, Cryptic? I don't know. Oh yes, *Crippet*. Sam Crippet and he lives in Redriff. Don't tell me you long for his friendship? Or maybe you'll put him a play. We could both put him in a play. Get George to put him a play. He deserves it."

*

All that night Ben sat hunched in his writing-chair, brooding and scribbling. When Winifred tapped softly at the garret door and peeped in, one look at his face sent her tiptoe down the stairs again, biting her lip with an anxious frustration. In the morning she saw him set out for the boat-stairs, narrow-eyed, angry, resolute, but as nervous as a bullcalf in the shambles. She wished she might speak to him but his demeanour was scaring her; she stepped back into the kitchen and let him go.

Despite all his careful thought of the previous day, he was on his way to Whitehall.

Upon arrival he demanded the Earl of Salisbury. This time he did not have long to wait.

The earl was abrupt and unfriendly. "You should have been here at least a week ago. I expect a certain diligence. Well, sir, have you news for me? Expound."

"There's very little point, m'lord, in my bringing you news when it's already been served to you by Mr Samuel Crippet. Been *made* for you by Mr Crippet. I'm sorry, m'lord, but I do prefer to know that whatever I might discover has not been laid out on a-purpose I'm about to discover it."

The earl's great-browed head, like the head of a monstrous viper nestled deep in his huge ruff, seemed to sink even deeper into the folds of starched linen. He sat in silence, staring. Then, so very quietly that Ben could barely hear him, he enquired, "Did I not request you to spread your nets for the whereabouts, the general dimensions, and above all, the names of this treason? The name Crippet is not one of them. I have never heard the name Crippet. *You* have never heard it ... So, sir: the names you *have* heard?"

"Ah, my lord, names." Ben took out a notebook and made a pedantic performance of consulting it. "As a preliminary I have endeavoured to investigate an anonymous priest, a foreigner. It was intimated to me, through an intermediary, that the chaplain of the Venetian ambassador could produce this evasive divine, who in turn might be able to barter information in return for a species of safe-conduct. However, I have had no further word." (He turned a page.) "There is a persistent rumour, no less evasive, that at least a half-thousand of the catholic gentry throughout the realm are ceasing, or have ceased, to profess their erstwhile romanism. As you ask me, 'dimensions?', I would guess, m'lord, exceeding small." (Another page.) "Oh yes, m'lord, the matter of the man 'Guido'. Here we are. It does seem there is such a fellow, he's said to be somebody's servant, he is often called – ah – often, Jonson."

"You say *what?*"

Ben ventured a feeble smile, apologetic, deprecatory. "Whereas his real name, m'lord, it so appears, is Mr Fox."

Salisbury was far from smiling. "Fox? Mr Fox? And you, I suppose, are Brother Rabbit? Or is there to be a new and papistical volume of Foxe's *Book of Martyrs*? Not before time, would you say? Well, *I'd* say, yet again, do you dare presume to break your fusty jokes with me, sir? Good God but I've a mind to – Your intelligence is perfectly useless. I wonder you find the face to bring it here. I wonder do you *know* that it's useless? If I was sure that that was so, I would – No! you are not worth it."

Ben shuffled his feet without speaking. If indeed he was not worth it, it was on account of Mr Crippet. With that name at the back of his throat, he now knew he would not be proceeded against openly: it was obvious that Salisbury did not dare. On the other hand, the chance of a dark-night dagger, or a suddenly lethal scrimmage in a taproom, must not be ignored. Nail into your brain, Ben, the wicked death of marvellous Marlowe: he too may have ventured to break jokes in the wrong company, maybe even the *same* company ... Courage: the bloody man has made up his mind.

"I have made up my mind. There is nothing you can tell me I want or need to know and I do not want to see you again. In the name of God, Mr Jonson, take yourself off and – and oh! write a play, a silly piddling play, if that's all you're fit for. Just so long as *I* don't have to go to your damned playhouse for it: *off.*"

With a towering display of arrogant scorn, extraordinary from one of such small stature, the secretary of state strode over to his own door and flung it violently open with his own hand, small-boned, long-fingered, trembling with disdain – Ben was not even worth the attention of a lackey. (If there had ever been any chance that the word "bargain" had meant what it said, that chance was null and void, but anyone of any sense would have known that from the beginning.)

*

Winifred said, "I cannot any longer endure to lie in love-bed with a man's dreams instead of his body. Too hurtful, too mysterious, too empty; and too much of being fetched away by Death. Benjamin, d'y'ever think of yourself as the bent-backed old scythe-bearer? grey flaking bones, scant relics of scrawny hair. Last night I did dream that that's what you were. Alas, I'd say 'tis time you found another lodging. I shall say so to my husband, he'll say so too, his fears are unmaking him. Yesterday in his new clumsiness he snapped an ebony bookmark into two weary fragments e'en as he poised his hand to engrave the final touch. Christ's blessing, dearest Benjamin, but – Finished."

*

Ben said (as he trudged the town, great bag upon his shoulders, looking about him for somewhere else to live), "Not drunk, nor am I crapulous, but 'fore God! how I hate myself. 'Fore God, I am nobody's gull. Except Catesby's gull, Salisbury's, Winifred's. Yet none of the three gained what they sought, and even so I do not triumph. 'Tis true that *I* sought nothing, save some fashion of a safe deliverance, and life at my ease. Thus I have gained nothing save shame in the face of all three. For this though, I can be thankful: I *have* kept it close; not one of the three knows of my betrayal of each of the others."

Close. So very close, all of it, this boundlessly burgeoning plot, that a man must surely wonder, would anyone ever know the entirety? as for instance, if Crippet worked for Salisbury and Fox worked for Crippet and Percy worked for Fox and maybe Catesby worked for Percy – then whose conspiracy *was* it that Ben had been expected to infiltrate? Was Crippet under orders to ensure that the plot would spread so wide as to allow Salisbury to – to do what? To terrify the king with it and thereby to lift up his own power once-for-all above every great man in the land? To terrify the nation and enrage it once-for-all against the catholics; by extension, against Spain? Men said already that the treaty of peace was ill-balanced in favour of Spain: if Spaniards were to apprehend the cancellation of that treaty following tumult throughout England, might they not be induced to accept as a *counter*-balance the extinction of the English catholics? And at the same time, to suppress all opposition to the treaty amongst their own irreconcilables?

Ben no longer thought that his thoughts held too much Machiavel. Nothing was now as it had seemed. His task as intelligencer was not as it had seemed. Salisbury did not need to hear news of the plot, he had that already from Crippet, but Crippet was not to be trusted; so Ben (all unwittingly) had been sent to bring news of how filthily far had Crippet's fingers been probing, of how turgidly, how erectile, had the plot changed its shape beneath their insistent stroking – pah! this was a male whore in the sweaty depth of Christ Jesus's codpiece, why Machiavel himself would have shat his Florentine breeches in disgust for the very thought of it.

"'Fore God, I am nobody's gull. And being nobody's gull, why 'tis best altogether to forget all about it." Or try to forget about it. Pretend to forget about it.

And to set about writing a play, silly play, piddling, of course. But for poor old gawky out-of-elbows Ben, what else was his bloody-fool function? Moreover, he had a new subject. Lucius Sergius Catiline, notorious historical conspiracy, most epical historical tragedy, five acts well-builded with expense of the utmost scholarship, and maybe even profitable. Consider it, would it serve? Catiline, year 62 before Christ, was destroyed by the cunning of Cicero: in Act Five, inevitable, no other way to construct it. (Though 'tis true that the vexatious W.S. killed his insipid Caesar in Act Three; but it broke the back of the play, as Ben had never ceased to point out.) Now the cunning of our new Cicero, year after Christ 1605, had probably reached no further than Act Two. Would it not be prudent to wait at least until Act Four before jabbing pen into inkpot?

Watch the shape of it, keep close, by no means draw attention, observe carefully from the living fact what was or was not inevitable. A playwright's picture of Catiline, if traced from the features of Catesby, must needs be affected by the *future* of Catesby. Blood-boltered future? scragged neck, bowels burnt, bollocks and tool torn off – Mental agony was twisting the playwright round and around on his feet, a kite on a short string in the middle of London Bridge. "Dear Christ, should I not forewarn him, at least let him know about Crippet? Ah no, for forewarning would serve no sort of purpose.

"*Item:* 'twould but augment my chance to be exposed as a state spy; if government ha'n't killed me already, Mr Fox'll be given the job.

"*Item:* 'twould not put an end to the 'wildfire'. Plans would be changed to throw Crippet off the scent, and that's all. So I, the forewarner, would have cleared a new road for the fire-raiser, the hoister, the waster, the baster, the blaster, goddamit! And that's all.

"*Item:* in any case, Crippet by now'll be told to shog-off same as me, neither of us useful any more; worthy Cicero will have trepanned someone else.

"Oh the entanglements, the pitiless strangulations! when all that a man yearns for is to get himself a table and to sit at it and write.

"Or would it not be prudent to lay up Catiline on the shelf, pro-tempore, until next year, no longer than that? or maybe the year after? or two years maybe, three? More cowardice, some would say, but what sort of action in such an exigent would be brave? To write about these horrors will not prevent any of them ... Heaven help me, the weight of this bag! all of my latter-day life in it, all my immediate books, every paper I've scrawled since Candlemas, and I cannot afford a porter."

In the meantime, what of the notion, sketched out upon one of those papers, for a pertinent plot about gulls? At first thought, half-a-year ago, he had called it *Mr Fox*. Coincidence, or crawling augury? He sweated under the burden of his bag and the burden of his overmastering guilt, and none the less he shuddered ... But if the tale were set in – say, Italy? – say Venice? a likely city, spilling over with gold and cozenage – as now seemed only prudent, then the names should be Italianized. (Marston and Chapman being nailed into his brain, as also the stone bloody jug: pish-tush, what gulls they had been; how blindly exultant, in the instant of writing, at the sharp topicalities of their City of London comedy!) For certain 'twould be safer to call this new notion *Volpone*. Probably not so safe as entirely to evade notice: so there he was, brave! a little bit brave, brave enough at all events to satisfy himself.

Those mud-wits at the Globe were speaking of performance toward the end of November, whatever shape of a script he might offer them (always supposing he accepted their disgraceful cheat of a fee). Which would indicate commencement of rehearsals upon – he fumbled in his bag for his almanack and pricked off the dates -- rehearsals, at a venture then, fourth or fifth of the month: could he possibly furnish five full acts to that date, with naught to be rewrit or transposed?

"Merciful Lord Jesus, whoever can be certain of any such a thing so far ahead?"

*.

     ... Catiline came on, not with the face
Of any man, but of a public ruin.
His countenance was a civil war itself.
And all his host had standing in their looks
The paleness of the death that was to come ...
They knew not what a crime their valour was.

     [from *Catiline his Conspiracy,* by Ben Jonson,]

DREADFULLY ATTENDED

Upon a cold autumnal morning in the early 1880s, detective officers of the newly-formed Special (Irish) Branch at Scotland Yard sat down to interrogate a certain Jack Nee, alias Aeneas Harrington. They took him, not quite accurately, to be "a warehouse clerk masquerading as a renegade divinity student." They felt sure he was a member of a revolutionary secret society, but could only prove it through the testimony of a particular accomplice whom they could not afford to reveal; so they needed to secure a confession. Once they had it, they'd doubtless be enabled to charge the man Nee with conspiracy to commit murder by means of a dynamite bomb, or, alternatively, a revolving pistol. Although apparently well-educated and perhaps a gentleman (which in itself was a worry for the detectives), the young fellow had become so inarticulate as almost to have lost the ability for rational, connected speech. Could he write? Yes, he could. They found him pen-and-ink and a quire of paper, and left him to it. This is what they got.

* * * * * *

Ruin of a pen nib Police nib a ruinruin If it makes blots, you can't blame me. Blame for murder, *if there was* not blots I'm only doing my best All my life nothing but <u>only my best</u>
So. Why am I here? I was not a dynamitard for the Freedom of Ireland

I was not a Fenian conspiracy
not quite an Irishman, even C of E, without doubt. Born to
serve my Queen and Country until
until I found how I was <u>most dreadfully attended</u>

Hamlet Shakespeare
All my *familiars* (and MY DEAR DEAD BROTHER one of
'em)
crying **"Hamlet Revenge!"**
For why did the great ship *Carausius* enormous inordinate man-
of-war. **Capsize** on her maiden voyage? why? **capsize** with all
hands nearly all? why?
Don't tell me, "not relevant." For I'll prove to yoube patient.
Relevant

> They say that twenty-five
> Came floating up alive
> Five hundred and at least thirteen
> Drank their death in the deep dark green.

Familiars. Soaking wet, dead-white flesh and matted hair
gleaming with salt water, tarpaulin jackets dripping water
all over the root of my cognition, they've been with me all
these years. 513. There are faces I don't know, most of
'em I don't know; but one, two, three, at least, that I do
know. shall I say which is worse, know, or unknow? be
patient. <u>Since the explosion</u>, I'm never quite sure of

I never murdered anybody   nobody was murdered

except ONE, you tell me who? you tell me why? you tell
me who did it

which of you was <u>the bloody hand</u>?

Having put.
Having put

myself at last <u>in balance,</u> even as I put that GREAT QUESTION (no, I expect no answer) – why, I think I can now make consistent sentences, clauses even. <u>Since the explosion,</u> for the first time. Soon I will even talk? So here we are, truly at the start, behind the start, of the STATEMENT you want me to write. Dream, it begins with, rather than memory.

Nearly a score of years ago the great ship went to the bottom: and now we must imagine rather *more* than a score of years ago ...

So. The well-known countenance from coins and from postage stamps, Victoria our emblematic Queen, little older than forty: and suddenly she's a lusty widow all but stifled in her huge palaces by such a multitude of frock coats, hissing at her, scratching, endeavouring to coerce her (grey-whiskered thistles run to seed upon a dunghill, wouldn't you suppose, and herself in the midst of them, one wide-eyed sunflower?) – she could find, so it has seemed, no way to console herself, to protect herself, to poultice her soul indeed, but by drapes of night-black taffeta from head to foot of her sweet plump body, and by rebarbative silence in the face of all the world – the next world as well, such was her grief she would not even talk to God.

(No, I'm not rambling. Nor do I try to scandalize a posse of loyal thief-takers with infantile leze-majesty. It is true that since the explosion, the progress of my brain has now and then strayed, most discomfortably, let me tell you, into culs-de-sac and cubby-holes, but this is not one of them. For this is how it was, this is the Statement. Gentlemen, be pleased to follow it in patience. I thank you.)

Who could tell what curious pictures fled like tadpoles through her weed-choked mind? Sometimes, one might guess, she dreamed of her Albert's lordly nakedness, as she had possessed it on their wedding night. Not a style of brooding she cared to extend. Yet whenever she would turn to a less distressing fantasy, all she could conjure up behind her closed eyelids was a vision of men-of-war, ironclad men-of-war, as formidably uncouth as this new American *Monitor* ship she'd been reading about, now she saw a fleet of them, now a lone patrol, fighting the great waves with threshing canvas and streams of dark smoke from their funnels. To a poor queen in her grief, this was strangely voluptuous, as voluptuous indeed as overt erotic memories, but somehow without their pain. Under cover of all the shawls her ladies would pile upon her as they observed her occasional trembling, her fingers would wander deliciously across her lap and between her thighs as the great ships surged and rolled. (Now that she no longer ventured out of doors, except occasionally and almost furtively into a summer-house in the privy garden, she had left off her crinolines, her layers of proper petticoats: the loose draperies of mourning-cloth were all that she wore, and underneath them nothing but the quiver of her skin.)

And then suddenly, one fine summer morning, it seemed that the battleships had made a meaning for her; her response was immediate, it quite startled the watchful attendants. She poked herself up from her robes like a parrot among the ferns of an aviary, and demanded Lord Palmerston. A rakish though aged nobleman, he was nevertheless Prime Minister. Her husband had hated him. She herself was repelled by him. Or had always believed she was repelled. Her husband being in heaven, maybe watching her, maybe not – in her less despairing moments, she thought not – she felt wildly, abruptly, at large: why would she not try the old scoundrel for herself, uninfluenced by another's opinion?

He came carefully and tentatively, having heard a new rumour that his sovereign lady could be sinking little by little into impenetrable mental derangement. The first words she spoke to him appeared to confirm the rumour. "Lord Palmerston," she croaked plaintively, "it is very hot, even in the shade of the summer-house, and we suppose it will be necessary to spread awnings over the decks of the ironclad battleships lest the sun render the armour plating unendurable for the sailors' bare feet. Particularly in tropical waters."

"Ironclads, ma'am? Aha … Your Royal Navy has only the one, the screw frigate *Warrior*. For modern requirements, we find the steam gunboats more expedient, paddle or screw. Cheaper, too."

"Only the one ironclad and a whole empire to protect? In God's name, Lord Palmerston, what *has* your damned government been doing?"

She had never, ever, been known to curse and swear. His surprise was so great he could hardly speak. And it seemed she had nothing more to say to him: what could he do but bow and reverse himself down the summer-house steps like a posturing head-waiter, lungs wheezing, old bones creaking; and so, without a word, take his leave?

Victoria was hurt and indignant. A tawny-whiskered old debauchee, with a long-standing notoriety for all manner of fornication, and he'd given her nothing! no response whatsoever to the warm ardour of her dream of ships. Did he take her for a fool? Oh alas, indeed he did; and alas alas, he was running the country. So who else was there for her to talk to? She thought she had heard of a name …

In his special train, on the way back to London, Lord Palmerston morosely told himself that someone had been getting at her: as like as not from inside his own cabinet. He was well aware of zealots who seemed to believe that forthcoming war with the French (due very shortly, and so far he agreed with the premiss) compelled us to furnish a whole new line-of-battle fleet for the genius of the next Nelson to monkey around with regardless (and there he did not agree). Unproven, unfathomable expense! and was the queen off her head or what on earth had made her swear at him? – even if no more than a "damn." Within his own circles he was foul-mouthed in all conscience, but this fruity little pop-eyed dollymop in her slovenly heap of indecipherable garments had truly, truly shocked him. And yet she was of the age and ripeness of all the women he liked best and who had consistently and so easily fallen to his naughtiness.

And yet again, it might be prudent to re-examine the Naval Estimates. "For fuck's sake," he told himself, as the train pulled into Paddington.

The name that Victoria thought she remembered was Harrington. Which is – was – *my* name, *other* name, as I think you've found out? Let me tell you, he was my grandfather. Captain Sir Rollo Harrington, KCB, RN, and an undefeated widower. He had earned his knighthood in the Russian war for a very dreadful action he instigated and led against the batteries of a Baltic port. He ordered cannon mounted upon turntables on a great raft, protected only by an improvised breastwork, the whole contraption poled inshore where no vessel large enough to carry such guns might venture without running aground. Every man aboard the raft was killed or hideously wounded before the Czar's batteries could be silenced. But they *were* silenced, and my grandfather (to be sure, a grotesque relic of the disasters of war) received his honour from Victoria and that's what she thought she remembered. Indeed, how could she forget? – the hook for a left hand, the zigzag furrow gouged out of the right-side cheekbone and jaw, the glass eye and brazen nose, and the left boot with its high heel and sole two inches thick. That much she had seen. What went on beneath his clothes was seen by nobody save the medical man and also, I believe, his personal servant; but I'd guess it was very dreadful. As children, we would speculate. We shuddered in pride and horror. And we knew he never stinted to cry and to call, in season and out, for big guns upon iron steamships with enough armour to save men's lives. And that too was what Victoria thought she remembered.

He was invalided out of active service at the same time that they made him knight. From then on he had to rely upon the rents from his estates in Ireland to eke out his meagre half-pay; a most doubtful reliance, for the tenants were too poor to find the money and when he tried to evict them his agent was shot at. He lived like a hermit in a set of rooms in Bloomsbury, working day and night at an engineer's drawing-board, attempting all on his own to design the new-model man-of-war that he knew the British nation required. (The British nation didn't know it, not then: but in the end they would, oh yes.) He had first to design what he called his "draughtsman's jury-rig," a system of pulleys and brackets that enabled a one-handed man to do a two-handed job – he was ingenious and indefatigable, you might wonder did his family not help?

Well, I myself was but an infant, still in petticoats to let me piddle and so forth without rotting a good pair of pantaloons; we had our maids to mop the floor. Palinurus, my elder brother by four years, was already at boarding school, he would go to sea as a midshipman when sufficiently grown. No other brothers. Two or three sisters, kept to be married. I can't be bothered to remember their names. And then: my father, the righteous Hakluyt Harrington Esquire, "Papa," so my mother would have wished us to call him; he preferred "Sir," and enforced his harsh preference with a rod. Ah that dark sharp unsmiling wedge-faced pedant of a lofty Englishman in tall hat and black frock coat, as close-furled and upright as his own black umbrella. There is no doubt that he helped my grandfather. Indeed he was *driven* by the need to help my grandfather – oh no, not money, the old man would have refused that – but within the halls of government, up and down the Whitehall staircases, picking his way in all weathers through the scaffolding and decorators' débris of the barely-completed Houses of Parliament. He was what they call a Clerk in the Admiralty office, which means, oh you know what it means, decidedly *not* a shabby-genteel pen-pusher but a gentleman of consequence who might one day have a seat upon the Board, even become Controller, even First Lord if his politics should be found appropriate.

Oh, how I yearned to call him "Papa."

My grandfather continually memorialized ministers and their officials with elaborate specifications of his new-model design and the arguments for its adoption. My father (who may have been secretly ashamed that he served the Navy from an office rather than a quarterdeck – did he suspect himself of cowardice? or had some cruel schoolfellow said something, years ago, to bring tears to a young Hakluyt scarcely in his teens and Grandpapa already with a glorious name for his exploits at Navarino?) – my father, I say, followed him up with viva-voce lobbying, as often as his duties gave him time. Which was indeed very often, as those duties necessarily led him through the dens of his superiors. Thus he rarely passed their desks without a brisk little crackle of advocacy, which of course they found vexatious. But he knew his daily business so well that they had to rely upon him and they had to respect him, and so could not dismiss his enthusiasm for his father's enthusiasm – alas though, they could laugh at it.

The more government laughed at the cranks and the quirks of the Harringtons, the more frenzied the Harringtons became, each in his own way – Grandpapa like a crippled old sea-lion floundering up and down the narrow iceberg of his working-room, from one end of the drawing-board to the other, thrusting his ink-bow so deep into the paper that he'd tear it in long strips and so be compelled to start a whole new sheet – my father with a stream of augmenting applications to great men and their secretaries, unmanageably prolix (and angry with it, which was worse), a six-foot-six black beetle clashing its mandibles in the doorways of his patrons, that's to say potential patrons, because none of them had promised him more than to think about whatever it was that Sir Rollo was up to, the "old hero" as they would call my grandfather, yet a heroism regarded as little more than laudable imbecility.

Somebody told the joke to Albert; and that prince, so I believe, having no sense of humour, sent for my grandfather and even went so far as to examine his drawings and approve of his notions. But Albert and Palmerston were as amenable with one another as a dachshund and a fox-terrier jammed together into a sack: it was not possible for the prince to recommend my grandfather's notions, or indeed anybody's notions, with any hope of success until maybe a change of government, and so he told Grandpapa; and Grandpapa set him down as a weed and a wet and an article of damned German gimcrack – severely unjust, all the more so in that the prince went on to tell the queen about Sir Rollo, and the queen thereupon determined to have a sharp word with her prime minister – but then poor Albert died and all for a time passed into oblivion.

For a time, maybe for ever, had it not been for the queen's queer dreams.

So. In the midst of her black mourning, despite her black mourning – no! I truly think, *because of* her black mourning – Victoria, all a-sweat and a-tremble, sends for Grandpapa and sends for my father and at the same time sends again for Palmerston, all three of 'em (as I imagine it) to arrive at her summer house at twelve o'clock noon precisely; and she has a mahogany table set up beside her basket-chair for Grandpapa to spread his plans, a mahogany writing-desk with an ink-stand for my father to take notes. She even has a folding chair for Palmerston's skinny old buttocks: in her presence, an unheard-of privilege, but (as she says to him, perhaps unkindly), "You are no longer young, my lord; you shake, you should sit, for we need you to pay attention."

And then, "We might start with Mr – ah? – Hakluyt, he being the nearest to our own age, nearest to dear Albert's age had dear Albert condescended to live: you shall, Mr Hakluyt, explain to the prime minister, for his edification and ours, exactly why you are reputed to promote the eccentricities of your valiant father with such astonishing dedication – even to the extent of stunting your brilliant prospects?"

Or something on those lines. At all events, my father was taken aback.

But he plucked up heart, cleared his throat, stared hard above the queen's head at the blue sky through the fretwork of the verandah, and made his defence of Sir Rollo's proposal. Interminable prosing, I cannot imagine it otherwise, but a discourse nonetheless of irrefragable conviction: not so much the ship-building technicalities as the strategic necessity of such a design, bearing in mind current developments of the American civil war and some dangerously new-shaped ironclads recently launched in France. Even if we were not to go to war with the French (here Palmerston gulped and grunted), even if we were not to intervene against President Lincoln, or for that matter President Davis (here Palmerston shot his false teeth quite horridly in and out of his mouth), a strong force of strong battleships would surely preserve us from *needing* to go to war: in short, a deterrent to all potential enemies ... A few further sentences of geographical analysis, statistical comparison and financial assessment, and my father abruptly fell silent. Had he maybe said too much? After all, it was the prime minister's function to advise the crown upon such affairs ... and the prime minister appeared to be choking.

The queen's smile was like a gash in the wrappings of an Egyptian mummy – God alone knew what lay inside it. She turned it onto Palmerston for fully sixty seconds ... and then toward my grandfather she bent her head in its rustling veils, gently and almost submissively. "Sir Rollo, we see your drawings. Pray point to the significant features and show how they fit your son's appreciation of national policy. Not so very different from Lord Palmerston's, if Lord Palmerston would only admit it. We do hate a shifty prevaricator ... Now sir, we are all ears."

Every line-of-battle ship in the fleet (explained my grandfather, jerking his words out in a hoarse blare as he lurched backwards and forwards on his crutch-handled stick) was obsolete, except for *Warrior*. And *Warrior*, for all her quality, was at best a traditional frigate with exclusively broadside armament. Turrets, by contrast, were nowadays essential. Bear in mind his own Baltic turntables, hugely successful: how much more so had he been provided with no mere raft but a shallow-draught steamship of all-steel construction, armour-plated from below the waterline upwards? But the problem today: assuming that turrets in principle were agreed, then how to *deploy* them, keep them clear of the working of the sails? Shallowness of draught was not now in question: this design, *here,* was for fleet actions in blue water, it must carry the full sail of a four-masted barque, which was to say considerably more than an orthodox ship-of-the-line. And in two revolving turrets, four great rifled breech-loaders of at least 15-inch calibre, on an open-sided turret-deck, each turret with a 135-degree field of fire to port and to starboard. Above the turret-deck, the weather-deck, a species of gantry the full length of the ship for handling the sails, steering, commanding. "In principle, ma'am, milord, nothing on turret-deck but turrets; on weather-deck, nothing but conning-tower, masts, the arrangement of the masts, *here*, is unique; masts and funnels, both, must of course penetrate both decks, as shown *here*, ma'am, and *here*, to a larger scale. I am persuaded it will work."

Palmerston, transfixed by the eye of Victoria, looks at Grandpapa, recoils (not for the first time) from Grandpapa's devastated face, looks at Grandpapa's plans, swivels rapidly to look at my father. "Young man, I am not quite sure I entirely understand your financial projection. The price of steel fluctuates, I am informed; and how do you propose to move it from Sheffield to the shipyard? Railway?"

"By rail to Hull, milord, and thence by sea to the yard at Chatham."

"No. By rail to Liverpool. Build at Birkenhead. Much cheaper; that's to say, if we do have to consider it. Much."

My father's eyes suddenly shoot fire, as though flint-and-steel were at work inside them: the prime minister is taking him seriously! But it wouldn't do to register triumph, no no, no! a man must be cool, must demonstrate scepticism, must beat the old fox at his own snarling game – "You contemplate awarding a contract to private companies, milord? Surely it is usual for a prototype to be built in a royal yard, is it not?"

"I was not aware, sir, we were here to discuss anything at all *usual*. Her Majesty brought you (did you not, ma'am?) to impress me with a spice of the *un*-usual. Very well, I am impressed; I may say, reluctantly. And because I am impressed, I am going to put some questions. Your permission, ma'am?"

Victoria scarified him with another of her black-widow grins. He bore up against it manfully.

"Sir Rollo, " he began, "is your ironclad to be a sailing vessel with steam to assist, or a steamship with occasional sails? I detect an unresolved duality."

"Not at all. Upon a long voyage with favourable wind, a full set of sails provides swift passage without consumption of coal or replenishment of coal, a matter of economics: I should have thought government would appreciate that. In adverse weather, on the other hand, or the complex manoeuvres of battle, the power of the engines will be sovereign, the captain shall steer where he wishes. Are you answered, milord?"

"H'm ... Very possibly. Not being a sailorman, can't say."

Grandpapa whistled angrily between his five broken teeth and my father bit his lip till it bled, while Milord ran on and on with all manner of objection until –

"Why, look at your proportions: can you seriously contend it resembles any possible ship-shape available to human eyes? seriously contend you can sail it right-side-up?"

But my grandfather was perfectly stubborn in his confidence of the ship's stability, my father no less so in his parallel assurance of the genius of Sir Rollo. Father and son, bass and baritone, they harangued the prime minister in vehement stichomythia, one unanswerable argument overlapping the next, until the queen had had enough; she waved her pudgy fingers to signal "Stop."

She leaned back among her cushions, eyes closed, a long pause and then – Did she speak from a hypnotic trance? her voice such a new and unnatural singsong: "Sir Rollo, I have dreamed your great ship, which is more, a great deal more, than to say I have dreamed *of* your ship. Creating it as surely as your own brain created it. They may abuse the vessel's majesty as that of a crude and bristling monster, but are not all the deeds of these days no less monstrous and crude – indeed cruel? Such a very strange circumstance and Lord Palmerston shall pay for it with a vastly augmented set of estimates. Shall you not, my lord?"

Old Palmerston was too weary to furnish any more objections. Whether or no this damned ironclad would finally set sail, he would surely not still be in charge upon that day? Dear God, he hoped not. He couldn't bear it any longer.

*

So. Is it possible, detectives, that you have believed this farrago?
– that a widow-woman's dreams can cause an elderly inventor
(by *sympathetic magnetism* or some other intellectual pinch-
beck) actually to invent without his even guessing whence his
inspiration comes? A mutilated cripple of an elderly inventor?
irascible and stubborn and thoroughly domineering over the
anguished sense of duty of his conscientious son? guilt-grieved
son? yet a son so devoured by secret ambition that his entrails,
if exposed, must have appeared like shreds of gristle spat out
on the edge of your plate? Furthermore, the tale is told to you
by a probable felon who would never have remembered any of
its intricacies from his own childish experience; it can only be
elaborate hearsay, but from whom did I hear it? No, I can't answer that, it's long past and gone, memory fails and be damned
to you.

But if you protest that the tale is incredible, you still have to
solve the fundamental puzzle: how else, except through the invisible power of dreams, mournful, amorous, tragic and bereft,
can so perilous an experiment have been seriously undertaken?
– money allotted and approved by parliamentary committee;
contractors' commissions drawn-up, signed and countersigned;
steel, timber, glass, rope, all bespoke and honestly delivered;
a shipyard selected with its slips and dry dock and travelling-
cranes, and a reliable supply of workmen at government wage-
scales? – a whole series of complex decisions and (in sum) quite
irrational, as was to be shown, as *is* to be shown.

The approved yard was indeed Birkenhead: so my grandfather went to live in a dismal tall town-house in Liverpool; my
father stayed there often, leaving me and my sisters (however
many, four, five? who's interested?) in London under the care of
my mother. A good woman, I have been told, but drawn as it
were in pastel, faint colours and uncertain perspective.

All the time that *Carausius* was building, men who claimed
to be expert in naval architecture kept travelling to Birkenhead
and thence back to London, to offices in Whitehall and lobbies

in the Palace of Westminster and newspapers in the City, all with the same message – that the ship would be weirdly top-heavy. Her crew, they insisted, could count themselves lucky if they were carried past the Holyhead lighthouse undrowned. Of course they were right, God knows how right they were! So how was it that the work was allowed to continue night and day, without debate, without interruption?

Not hard to find answers. The Harringtons would not accept that the others could possibly be right: professional rivalry, they said, malice very nearly amounting to treason; they did concede that in many cases it was no more than sheer stupidity. This forthright self-confidence appeared to convince government. In any case government (and government's contractors and the contractors' employees) simply could not afford pessimism. Far too much at stake, cash, jobs and reputation; inconceivable there could be doubt when the Harringtons, in whom the nation had deliberately placed its trust, denounced even the mildest "ha-h'm?" with the ferocity of Old Testament prophets. Palmerston turned his back from the start: he diverted all questions concerning *Carausius* to the Admiralty or the Treasury and (as a matter of recorded fact) was never known to speak of the ship or its builders, in public or private, to anyone ever again.

A little after my eighth birthday my mother fetched me and my sisters down to Birkenhead for the ceremony of the launch. I suppose it was a splendid occasion. It was certainly cold enough, grey and gusty mid-October. The prime minister, we were told, was ill and unable to be present. I too was ill, after the long, jolting train journey; miserably wishing that *I* was unable to be present, the more so that my mother had been invited to name the ship and was making a feeble fuss of it, all mock-modesty and prunes and prisms. The royal duke who *was* present seemed a guffawing jackass – even to me, so much in awe of his feathered cocked-hat and waxed batswing whiskers. My brother Palinurus arrived at the last minute, smart as paint, shockingly enviable, in the uniform of a *Britannia* cadet: he had a few years to go before he was made midshipman, but

Grandpapa had whispered that a "special circumstance" might be invoked to put him to sea sooner – he must swear to tell nobody, so of course he told me.

(Whenever he was at home – alas not very often, what with boarding school and now the training ship – Palinurus considered himself to be under a chivalric duty to protect me from Father, with whose magisterial presence he had never been impressed. He used to laugh at me that I was so timid and took the man at face value. To be sure, he was barely twelve but sometimes he seemed a complete adult. Even so, he and I were very close.)

No sooner were we all assembled in the distinguished-persons' box, with the grim black prow of *Carausius* towering above us swathed in bunting, than my mother decided to enter one of her swoons. "Oh no," she mewed feebly, to swing the bottle and utter the ship's blessing was more than she dared deal with, considering her state of health (pregnant yet again, I'd guess in hindsight). Problem, whom to substitute? No, not the royal duke: Grandpapa was adamant, it had to be a female: a matter of nautical good luck. But it should *not* be his grand-daughters, he had found them out years ago as sly little brats who deserved no favours. My father, glaring with rage at this futile delay, swung his arm round in a half-circle. A most odd spontaneity; from him, quite unprecedented; but it worked. His hand stayed and oscillated half-way round to his backbone, fingers pointing off to the right and a little below. Whom did they point at?

Why, the prettiest little girl you can imagine, bare feet, black ringlets, plaid shawl and red petticoat. Her name was Kitty Furey. And what a surprise! all these years afterwards, in Scotland Yard you know the name, *of course* you do, you manipulating bastards! Why, she'd be alive today and you know she'd be alive if it wasn't for you and your – what shall I call 'em? your putrescent Sons of Belial from the Charnel of Tophet will do to be going on with, I'll deal with all o'that later. Immeasurable evil.

So. Kitty Furey. A year or two younger than me, and ah how my heart came springing all a-flower and childish-foolish, just to see her there astride her father's shoulders in the special enclosure for the men who'd built the ship, their treat today to witness their good work at last afloat, with beef and beer to follow for the whole gang upon long trestles in the sail-loft the far side of the slips ... So. My father sent for her: she came up the steps terrified, clutching her own father's hand, he seemingly bewildered, she suddenly aware of the horrifying countenance of the "old hero." Who smiled at her and spoke to her, tenderly enough, "My dear, you will not be frightened. All you have do, my little dear, and it's a noble role, an honour for you and your daddy, for you and the entire yard, is to take hold of the wine bottle, here, swing it on its chain, like so: and smash it against the ram. As it goes from your hand, you call out – no, I'll call it out, I am your fugleman, I'll call it very slowly and you'll call it out along-o'-me." All the ladies and some of the gentlemen bent over little Kitty and cooed; her father, relieved that he now understood the situation, dabbed at her tears with his neckerchief and whispered into her ear. He was an engine-wright, Irish, from Inchicore upon an outskirt of Dublin (as I was later to discover, oh dear God! how many times since then have I *known* his dread presence and given ear to his cries), his name was Paschal Furey, he had something the look of a questing badger and his hair was black and flat as an Apache's. Kitty managed to let loose the beginnings of a smile, upon which my grandfather laid his hand over hers and together they swung the bottle: and immediately the crash of the bottle and applause from the hundreds of spectators, drowning out their two voices, harsh and loud, sweet and soft, one upon the other: "I name this ship *Carausius*: may God bless her and all who shall sail in her."

And so the great ironclad was launched.

Why *Carausius*? When I asked my father, I was irritably told I ought not to concern myself with notions beyond my age; when Palinurus asked him, the reason for the irritation became clear. He told Palinurus (who repeated it in private to

me), that "*Carausius* for a man-of-war is not at all fortunate;
it was picked by First Lord, who is superficially well-read but
nonetheless ignorant. He'd been skimming through Gibbon, he
found a Roman admiral, more of a pirate than a responsible officer, who thrust himself up to be an emperor of sorts; he took
note that the fellow's fleet was based in the ports of Britain, so
he thought it appropriate. He did not take note that Carausius
came to a bad end ... Of course, as rational Christians, we
do not believe in omens." Palinurus told me that Grandpapa
strongly resented not having been asked to provide a name of
his own choice for his own ship; and who was to say that *he*
did not believe in omens? – men who had fought in very bloody
battles often did.

I sometimes think my father in his heart believed in omens,
why else should he take such pains to erect himself as proud as
Hamlet, "not a whit, we defy augury!" – oh he did defy it, I
can assure you, wanton and inexplicable, for did he not name
his beloved elder son, his sailor-son indeed, after the unlucky
old salt in Vergil, Palinurus the helmsman, so pathetically lost
at sea? ... And if we're talking of omens, what about the death
of Palmerston, the very day, the very hour, of the launch? –
the telegram only reaching us once the ceremony was over and
we stepped off the Mersey ferry. If that was not significant of
something more than somewhat awry, then coincidences have
no meaning.

Two circumstances of the launch which I haven't mentioned
and must mention.

First. *Carausius* appeared to me a most monstrously ugly
construction. Not only ugly but sinister. True, I knew nothing
of ships beyond the paintings and engravings that hung in our
house in Belgravia, I should say the fringe of Belgravia, no better than Ebury Street, but -   The hull was somehow "out of
drawing", both scanty and bulky at the selfsame time, and ver-
tical girders, extensions of the main frame which would carry
the weather-deck, were sticking at all angles into the air like
grave-markers in a paupers' burial ground. True, I had been
told how the upper-works would radically change the silhou-

ette, and were not to be built until they'd floated the ship into dock, but –

Second.   Alongside the royal duke I noticed a youngish, plump, florid-faced little naval officer with what Palinurus said was a commander's insignia. He seemed to be laughing a lot in an intimate sort of way with Grandpapa, and my father was uncharacteristically deferential towards him. Palinurus found out (I don't know how) that he was a cousin of the royal duke, who was a cousin of the queen, and he bore a German title – Baron von Scharhorn – even though (tactfully dropping the "von") he was to all intents and purposes a regular Englishman in Her Majesty's service. I've more to say about Baron Scharhorn, much more, far too much – as you know, so be patient.

At long last I was not only into trousers but actually at a boarding school. Palinurus would write to me every fortnight, a newsletter from the juvenile underbelly of the Royal Navy: God, how I treasured his scurrilous screeds. I did my best to reply, but our basilisk of a headmaster read all outgoing letters; impossible for me frankly to narrate the full toll of the birchings and bullyings, though I yearned for my brother's consolation. (He himself often used to bully me when we were at home together, an odd contradiction; but it needs to be noted. You *must* understand me and him. I was such a lonely little boy: Palinurus was the only one who ever loved me, the only one I ever loved.)

Palinurus soon understood, and so did I, because he told me, that toward the Harringtons and all their works, the new prime minister was even less sanguine than the old. And then his government fell and the next one was even worse. Our family as a result became steeped in professional gloom, and so it continued for about a year. The fitting-out and arming of *Carausius* had not exactly come to a halt, but the shipyard's activities might have been tied up in nets or smothered in glue, such sluggishness prevailed, and every excuse in the world for delay and obstruction. Most of the time nowadays my grandfather was back in London, there seemed so little for him to supervise on Merseyside.

One evening, when Palinurus was away at his training ship and I was home for half-term holiday, I very boldly took it into my head to take pattern by my brother and do my own bit of spying. This was because Sir Rollo had come over from Bloomsbury to dine at his son's table, a most unusual event; and before my mother had been able to recollect herself sufficiently to banish me and my sisters from the front hall, I'd heard some highly exciting words – "Council of War." My mind upon the villainies of the third Napoleon (like so many minds at the time), I naturally assumed that the French had opened fire against our fleet in Spithead or some such treachery, and the secret plan for England's revenge was to be hatched beneath our very own roof. So I waited until Nurse, being assured that all children were asleep, was occupied in her own little lair with her cosy private supper. In bare feet and nightshirt I crept from the night nursery through the schoolroom and down the flights of stairs, fifty-seven separate steps, until I crouched under an occasional table in the hall by the dining-room door. Breathless with the sensuality of fear, I observed my mother and two or three ladies come out and go up to the drawing room: I knew that the gentlemen were now left to their port and walnuts, and no interruption from servants: now was the hour! and I crouched.

The door was not quite shut. My head down by the skirting-board, I could peep through the crack unseen. I crept forward and peeped. I saw Father; I saw Grandpapa; I saw the backs of a pair of heads, one bald, one grey with a thicket of beard all around his ears; I also saw Baron Scharhorn, in civilian evening dress, flourishing a nutcracker and talking very fast. "If the PM, my dear Sir Rollo, is already alive to it, there is really no excuse for your pessimism – all change! we are on the move! *hoppla!* – you don't believe me, no. But don't you see, with this new government I am by the way of being a confidential go-between from the Palace to Number 10 and vice-versa, oh I know it's always said that HM don't trouble herself about public affairs any longer, not true, all that's true is she don't allow anyone to make public the public affairs she chooses to poke at and prod, I know 'cos I've seen her at it, very impressive sight, I can tell you."

"Yes yes – Frederick my friend – I think we're well aware of it – I think we can picture it." My grandfather's words tonight are unusually bitter, slowed down by deep suckings and sluicings of wine through the appalling gaps where his incisors should have been. "The issue is – Whigs – they gave the approval to the Birkenhead contract. How therefore can – Tories – do other than repudiate? Such being – Fred, my young friend – such being – the inherent malignity of the alternating millstones of political life, from which you – as a sprig of the crown are necessarily – quarantined, and which the boy here, as a civil servant, quite fails to take seriously. Hakluyt, I've told you before: as to politics, you're disingenuous, in point of fact a noodle. I don't want a bloody noodle, I want you fighting for me, hard."

"Which I do, sir, and have done, at the risk of my career," retorts my father, with an edge to his voice. "At the same time, this sprig of the crown is far more of an adept politician than you or I. I've seen him at it, an impressive sight." He is exasperated, and doubly so, at his own father's bloody-mindedness and the know-it-all conceit of the baron. "Scharhorn, I would ask you to be explicit, to be specific, and to refrain, if you will, from the fluidity of trivial gossip. Too much of it already: it makes the heart sick. Be assured, sir, that no-one at this table will talk out of school." Baldhead and Greybeard grunt their guarantees.

The baron chuckles. "Explicit? Specific? Not like you, my dear Hak, to deprecate evasion; it's mother's milk to the civil service, no? But if you wish me to speak as from the quarter-deck, I will." Greybeard and Baldhead begin to laugh, then they realize that the Harringtons are not laughing, and so shut their traps. The baron is no longer humorous: "Good God, sirs, will you listen! I have sweated like a stoker to get them to see *Carausius* for what she is, fons-et-origo of the new navy, the whole world turned upside-down and nothing as-it-was will be ever again: whether you like it when you see it is none of my business. But let me tell you, I predicted it and therefore had no choice but to help to carry it out." Uncomfortable solemnity. I'm not sure I recall it correctly, I'm not even sure I'm not making it up. Though I do know that that's how it was. More or less. Only afterwards did my brother help me to guess what it meant. "Sir Rollo, this ship of yours is not for Liberals, nor for Tories, but the security of empire. You knew that, you had forgotten that others might also know it. Politics upon both sides now dictate immediate funds for a new deepwater fleet, scientifically reconceived. It is already begun! with cunning and good luck, with my own two ears *and* my own small voice alert at every crux, I am certain it will be finished. And oh, let me add, it is not beyond probability that Mr Hakluyt Harrington will very shortly be promoted – word to the wise, Hak, what'd you say to First Secretary to the Controller, and seat on the Board, h'm?"

A burst of appreciative murmuring, glasses banged on the table, somebody claps his hands. I can't quite distinguish who's saying what. In the midst of it, Baron Scharhorn, his voice higher than anyone's, carries on in triumphant crescendo: "All work upon *Carausius* recommences at full speed. O gentlemen, I have their pledge."

One great smack of a fist on the mahogany. Then a space of chuckling quiet, nuts crack, wine goes down. Then my grandfather, grating and sceptical: "My request to command? Where's their pledge upon that? Do I get to be captain of my own ship or do I not? They wouldn't let me name her; I have not forgotten. A mistake, young Fred, to imagine I ever forget anything."

"Ah, command. There is doubt as to your physical condition, of course." (The first gathering rumble of an outright roar from Grandpapa, which the baron easily checks by raising his voice and ignoring it.) "But I said to 'em, 'Absurdity.' I said, 'If he's fit to stride up and down all day long for years and years in front of a drawing-board, then he's fit for the bridge of a battleship.' I said it twice and let it lie. HM has passed the word that she desires it as much as you do. I expect you'll get it."

"Not that anyone else is likely to want it." My father is still exasperated. "Sniping and croaking is not going to stop, y'know. Unbelievable, the persistence of this nonsense about 'top-heavy.' It emanates from Second Lord, who claims he is never listened to and therefore croaks at everything."

"Unfortunately, Harrington, they do listen, that's to say some of them, enough to be a damned nuisance, I'm flapping at 'em all day long, blowflies!" – huff-and-puff from Greybeard.

Baldhead follows him up. "Only way to choke it is to show 'em the Old Hero on the bridge of the Old Hero's ship. Vulgar and theatrical, damned inevitable, what?"

Says the baron, "I'd go further. I'd pick up upon something you put to me last year, Sir Rollo. Would you fetch your own grandson aboard as a midshipman?"

My father, shocked and angry, interrupts before Grandpapa can answer. "Palinurus? Out of the question. He's far too young; he won't have completed his *Britannia* training; entirely irregular; I'm astonished you should even think of it."

The baron is sly. "Oh it can be fiddled," says he. "I can fiddle it. By way of Windsor. The point is, Harrington, like it or not – Sir Rollo as captain marks our confidence in the ship, Palinurus as ship's younker marks *your* confidence, no less important than ours – or don't you think?"

I don't know whether he did think or he didn't, not just then. (Although soon we would *all* of us know it: how Palinurus, apple of his eye, was to be so much less a son, so much more a political token – "confidence"? it was as though they'd stamped the bloody word on every button of my hapless brother's uniform.) At any rate, just then I'd been eavesdropping so earnestly that I quite failed to recognize the heavy feet of Nurse as she pounded downstairs. I was grabbed by the tail of my nightshirt, pulled away and driven skyward in a hailstorm of affronted reproach.

So who were the prime begetters of this murderous catastrophe of a new-model ironclad? My father of course, his friend Scharhorn of course – after, of course, my grandfather. And at the outset, Victoria Regina: was she dupe, was she dreamer? Left to herself, she'd never have known a stout ship from a stupid, all she wanted was men she could trust. So I'd say, dupe. Yet again, at other times, I'd incline to say the dupes were her three trustworthy gentlemen.

So. The ship's trials, from Mersey into the Irish Sea and round Land's End to Devonport, were pronounced both efficient and successful. The vessel remained the property of her builders until completion of trials and formal acceptance by the Admiralty. Thus the trial-crew contained no more than a skeleton complement of Royal Navy personnel, with my grandfather already in command on a semi-official basis, while the rest were civilians, shipwrights, dockyard engineers, and such. The engines gave no more trouble than is usual with new machinery (which is not say they gave none).

Acceptance and commissioning were to take place in Plymouth Sound, whereby Admiralty Experiment *Carausius* would mutate into HMS *Carausius*, as embroidered on the hat ribbons of the ratings. We all went down for the ceremony, just as we had all attended the launch. It was a very different sort of affair.

The ship was at anchor offshore; so we must voyage out to her in miniature steamers, picket-boats, a midshipman in charge of each one. Palinurus (who had been aboard throughout the trials) was actually entrusted with the boat to which we were assigned; there was a petty officer beside him to keep a sharp eye. The eye was not needed. My brother handled the trip without apparent fault; we were all so very proud of him that even our father, upon arrival, smiled abruptly and clapped him on the back. Palinurus had grown several inches in the past few months, he seemed much more than a few months older, and his new uniform hung on him with the negligent elegance (so I thought) of a true naval veteran's.

The ceremony was conducted by a very distinguished admiral with a beard like a battleflag. He spoke to Father most respectfully and treated Grandpapa as a remarkable equal rather than a subordinate. But I don't think he liked the ship. *I* did not like the ship: even though the lines of seamen in white ducks, the marine band in a blaze of brass and pipeclay, and all the officers with gleaming swords, made a very jolly sight (you'd have thought) for a small boy.

My disquiet had begun before we even got aboard. As the picket-boat circled round to find the correct approach to the gangway, we had a series of views of the fully-built *Carausius*, bow, beam and stern. I felt the same inexpressible horror at her shape that had gripped me upon the moment of the launch. They'd painted her in the conventional man-of-war colours, black hull, white upper-works, yellow funnels and masts – as a rule a very decent demarcation of structural elements. But in this case the evident disproportion of those elements was made even odder by the emphasis of paint. My youngest sister squawked out loud, "Oh jiminy, it's a floating gas-works!" The only sensible thing I'd ever heard the little minx utter, although Nurse immediately slapped her for making use of an expletive. I shivered, unaccountably.

It's occurred to me since, that painting *Carausius* was much the same thing as putting Grandpapa into dress-uniform: ship and man, they were both distorted out of all reasonable expectation, and nothing conventional could hope to cover it up.

Another thing. Awnings had been spread above the weather-deck to give shade to the important guests, for it was a sweltering hot midsummer day, with no more than the lightest breeze. And yet I felt a mortal chill; beneath the awnings it was not just a question of mere shade from the sun, there seemed a malignant gloom that I could not endure in my thin summer blouse and cotton trousers. I shivered.

I was crying when I said good-bye to Palinurus, which embarrassed him and turned him away. Maybe he wanted to cry too, but I'd say not. This ship was his whole new life. He was now grown part-and-parcel into his profession. I made sure I had lost him for ever. Our fates were forked.

As soon as the ritual was over, we were ushered to the gangway for the shore-boats. No indulgent fag-end of hospitality, even to family: my grandfather was under orders for the Mediterranean, the ship must be made ready to sail with the morning tide. On the way down, I could not but notice, accidentally, incidentally, an awkward little episode on the turret-deck. A choleric officer, a lieutenant I'd guess, stood at bay beside a hatchway, confronting a group of civilian workmen who appeared to have thrust themselves up from below to make some sort of complaint, all coal-dust and smears of oil – and one of them, I was sure of it! I knew him, I'd seen him before – was it not Furey, the black-avised engine-wright? – and how was it he was still aboard? Father had told me that *Carausius* was now absolutely in the hands of the Navy. Was something not quite right with her, that these men were kept busy? Busy – and I'd say, unhappy at their situation. I ventured to ask Father: he snubbed me as he always did. And this time Palinurus was not in the picket-boat, so I couldn't ask *him*, could I?

I would also have liked to ask, where was Commander Rt. Hon. the Lord Scharhorn, RN? He had surely done as much if not more than anyone else to send *Carausius* to sea: I was surprised not to see him on her quarterdeck that afternoon, to hear his infectious chuckle, to watch his fingers tweak and fidget at his long flaxen side-whiskers. I can tell you now where he was – I made it a point, did I not? years later, to find all I could about him – he was at sea off the Zanzibar coast, captain of a 12-gun steam sloop, rounding up the dhows of Arab slave-merchants and destroying their seaports, commencing a reputation that would owe little to his court or cabinet connections. A sparky intellectual mariner, a credit to the service, damn him to hell.

Damn him to hell, that he was a whole hemisphere away from Plymouth when *Carausius* weighed anchor next morning, oh he never had the chance to look upon his handiwork or take a last sight of the hundreds of men and boys aboard her – what in God's name would he have said, though, had he stood with my father and family (and a number of grave-faced officers) on Plymouth Hoe without our breakfast to watch the great ironclad sail away to Gibraltar? if he had seen what we saw? if he had listened to what was said?

For the wind had vastly increased and shifted to the south-west; no mere jaunt for the Old Hero to bring her easily out of the Sound, so the naval men were telling one another. I heard them and I saw the troublesome dark waves trolling in through the gap of the long bay. A boatswain's pipe blew somewhere on the ship's deck out there (its clear note whipped into our ears by the gathering gale), seamen lined the side, up came the anchor, bright flags rose and fell in such sequences as befitted the start of a maiden voyage. A young officer beside me lent me his tel-escope to see if I could make out my grandfather on the bridge – indeed I could, there he strutted, propped upon his stick as rigid as a flagstaff. He seemed to be looking towards us, he raised a hand in salute and then immediately swung away, stumping crookedly across the bridge, all urgency and emergency and alarm. The wind whipped into our ears the clang of his engine-room bells. Huge gouts of black smoke came pouring out of the funnels. *Carausius* surged forward, with some smaller sails (jibs, I think, staysails, and such) taut in the wind to stabilize her as the waves came towering onto her beam.

It did not seem that the ship was doing whatever should have been done, there was a dreadful tossing roll-and-pitch, she pointed herself this way, she pointed herself that way: I could see her two propellers standing clear of the sea as the ugly brutish prow went plunging down into it, throwing sheaves of white water the height of the weather-deck. The young officer snatched back his spyglass without so much as a "thank'ee." "God!" he cried, or one of them cried, or all of them – "Screws scarcely turning, have his engines foundered? look at that – aye, aye, he's making sail, but has he the time for it? – God, he has not!" We saw a scramble of sailors up the rungs affixed to the tripod masts (a unique notion of Grandpapa's; he didn't want clusters of shrouds to balk the scope of his turrets), we saw the men strung out along the highest yards, swaying in the violent air like starlings on a telegraph-line as they let loose a number of sails – top-gallants, I believe, upper-topsails perhaps, but at any rate well-selected sails, according to the officers behind me; they were in no doubt that the Old Hero knew his seamanship. He did find the time, but only just. He pulled *Carausius* round by her very muzzle, as a man on a contrary horse will haul the reins till the beast obeys him: I don't know how near he was to tearing her bottom out on the rocks of the lee shore, but heart-in-mouth he escaped it, and found his crafty zig-zag course through that deadly damned inlet until he'd reached the open ocean, fair and clear.

That's what the officers were saying, or some of them, smacking their hands together in delight at Grandpapa's skill. But as they watched *Carausius* struggle, turret deck as full as a mill-race, turrets quite buried in the wash, there was a shift of opinion. The young officer, very serious, still peering through his telescope, spoke quietly from a sideways mouth: "If he can't trust his engines to get him out of Plymouth in a middling beam-sea, when *can* he trust 'em?"

An old captain next to him gave a snort of agreement. "*Psha!* and top-heavy: just look at the way she rolls! A moment's error taking in sail and she'd roll herself right over. By God, sir, I'm glad they didn't put *me* on her bridge, I'd not dare lie down to sleep for the length of the commission."

So that day there was no shipwreck, although shipwreck was most direly predicted; and my father heard the prediction (my mother and sisters as well, if it comes to that, though they didn't have the wit to understand); I think he knew for the first time what he had done. *I* heard something break like a death-rattle in his throat, it was altogether beastly and I was sick.

*

My grandfather, being an Old Hero, every inch of a KCB, was far too stubborn, far too sure of himself to put back into Plymouth for an overhaul of his engines. He had shipyard men with him, of experience and cunning, and he trusted them to make things right long before he came up with the Mediterranean Fleet. Maybe they did, maybe they didn't, maybe they couldn't. At all events they were still on board when *Carausius* took her station, widely patrolling between the French naval ports of Toulon and Algerian Oran, on the watch for Napoleon's tricks.

They say she must have been under a full press of canvas, somewhere off the coast of Sardinia – had the engines failed again? – when the storm struck, an hour after midnight, and in less than a minute *Carausius* turned turtle. If there wasn't time to shorten sail, they had certainly no chance to launch the boats. Old Sir Rollo drowned, young Mr Palinurus drowned, nearly all of 'em bloody well drowned. I can't tell you in detail *how* they drowned: nobody saw it, nobody told. (Except the men of a Maltese fishing boat, and they were two miles away and the moon all but lost behind mountains of cloud.) As for what people may have thought of it in England – why, the best I can do is quote a shabby bit of ballad sung and sold at the time down the Ratcliffe Highway. I got the words by heart as soon as I came across them. To the tune of 'The Cruel Sea Captain' –

Half my face and a hand and a foot, sir, was blown away in the Rooshian war:
In my sore pain I did envision a ship of war such as never before.
With steam and sail and guns of thunder and decked ashigh as a castle tower,
They set me on her rolling quarterdeck and said, "She's now in your hand and power."

I sent to the wheel my brave little grandson, for him to learn his sailoring trade.
I said to him to fear no tempest, we'd the fairest weather that ever God made.
I said to him to fear no tempest, our steam would drive through the tallest wave.
I could not know it would drive us nowhere: but the gale would roll us into watery grave.

And who shall bear the guilt and the burden, who set
me to sail the ocean-main
With five hundred souls on board of a nightmare that
leaked from the blood of my gangrene loin?
I know who shall bear the guilt and the burden. It was
my own son in his carriage and pair:
He told their lordships, "You must build this ship, sirs,
or old Dad will die of his life's despair."

So there you are, all you women bereft who weep and
cry and can never console,
Your men did die for the pride of these great ones:
yourlives unto them are but maggots in a hole.

*

The guilt and the burden, indeed. There was of course a tri-
bunal of enquiry. Its report laid most of the blame upon my
grandfather, he being dead and unable to answer. It also blamed
my father, but modified its strictures in the light of his "family tragedy". He was not dismissed from his post, nor did he
resign. He simply *withdrew* from his work at the Admiralty,
he withdrew from his wife, he withdrew from his children, he
did not take his own life, as his friends for a time had feared
– indeed he continued to eat and sleep (at least it was thought
that he slept), but always in a small dark room that used to
be his dressing-room, and he very very rarely came out of it.
He had long been devout, but now he positively tunnelled into
the Bible and books of divinity; he kept sending for clergymen.
When he did come downstairs, we saw him as grey-faced as my
mother, but with none of her careworn gauntness – instead he
grew heavy-jowled and lardy, and began to stoop – moreover he
seemed not to shave for days at a time, he who had always been
so finical and well-trimmed. His manservant gave notice, and
was not replaced.

Of course we were all put into unrelieved black mourning; my mother swore she would never wear anything else and neither should my sisters or myself.

Every night I wept for Palinurus: even at school, where always they'd made me a mock and a scorn and shot out their lips at me, and still did. Whenever they could, they'd pull my spectacles off my ears and throw them out of reach, even trample them under foot.

In my dreams I would see Palinurus, his gleaming young body deep, deep, under water, caught by the wrist in coils of rope from the deck of the wreck, swaying like seaweed among the bodies of the drowned, while fishes and sea-beasts flowed inquisitively to and fro, nuzzling the corpses, caressing them, nibbling, and -   I'd see Grandpapa's corpse afloat over the bridge, head downwards; he seemed somehow fastened by his queer-shaped boot to the spokes of the wheel, as though even in death he would steer his great ironclad to safety, and -   I'd see the face of Paschal Furey through the bars of an engine-room grating, his mouth wide, wide open in agony, I'd see shoals of tiny sprats come swimming in and out of it, and –

Familiars. As I've told you, they're still here.

Nobody blamed Scharhorn.

My father died when I was thirteen (the age of Palinurus when *he* died). During his last illness, he sent for me to his room; he had never done so before. He had a yellow-faced pursy cleric sitting in silence at his bed's foot, like a turnkey keeping watch on a prison visit. I must sit further up, close beside Father's pillow, and try not to vomit at the sickroom stench. He said to me (that's to say, Father said, not the parson, though I wondered, even then, was the parson not invisibly prompting him?), he said, "Boy, you are aware of -   You recognize the burden, without prevarication, of guilt? For assuredly it is here, boy, if only because of -   You know how I insisted upon the building of the ship, how I -   You know how it is said that I sent them to their deaths, how I -   " I hated him, I'd feared him for years, but now I was beginning to pity him; I sat tongue-tied. And amazed: for abruptly he skidded away from the peril to his soul, to argue the point as to *Carausius* being top-heavy. She could *not* have been top-heavy, he fretted. Was it not apparent that the low freeboard of the turret-deck and the weight of the armament located the centre-of-gravity both safely and practically? So if not flaws in the design, then what the French call *sabotage*: the logic was apparent – apparent – apparent – I knew this must be nonsense, I knew he was to blame, and I knew that he knew it.

At last he came back to his reason for my presence. "You are aware, boy, so I need not tell you, that atonement must be made."

And I believed him. I saw that he too had had his *familiars*. For that alone I might have been filled with a schoolboy's uncritical compassion – if only he had uttered one word as to my brother (or indeed as to Grandpapa, or to any other of the drowned five hundred) – one word, that's to say, of understanding that each one of them was a strange and separate creature with his own name and peculiar face ... Palinurus had a face like a Siamese cat; and he used to say that mine was the muzzle of a dormouse. And then he'd chase me.

My father kept insisting that now he was about to die, I had a duty to do what he would have done, had my grandfather not driven him into the Admiralty. I was to complete my studies at school and then go to Cambridge, and then I was to enter holy orders. Until he knew for certain that I was destined for the Church, he would not, could not, die at peace with God. I became aware, at this point, that the clergyman had commenced a sotto-voce counterpoint to my father's exhortations. Between the pair of them I broke down into unstoppable floods of tears (being no more than a child, for God's sake) and I swore, and swore again, that I'd go where they were pushing me, indeed where I was pulled by my God my beloved Saviour, and so forth.

Why wouldn't I? I believed them.

Ah heaven, and then! in the very paroxysms of his ultimate fever, my father had to *go for* my grandfather, like a liquored-up rough in a gin-palace. He called him "that virulent witchdoc-

tor," he called him "the old bugger," in desperate self-pity he
was pleading that he'd had no choice, that my grandfather had
driven him to ensure that the noxious ironclad would be driven
into being at the Admiralty, "driven," was the word he kept repeating, driven – driven – driven – driven -   Until the parson
took fright and rang for the nurse in attendance, who bustled
us both out of the room.

But I had sworn it and sworn it again, and being the kind of
child I was, what could I do but keep to it?

Not germane what I did at school. Cambridge, a slightly different picture. I had money from my father's will, also the rents
of the Irish estates – if and when anyone could collect them. I
was able to buy books. Religious books of course. But then I
found writings upon all sorts of hidden liberties, Paine's *Rights
of Man*, Wollstonecraft's ditto of women – I salted Foxe's *Martyrs* and the *39 Articles* with a acrid strain of Shelley and the
disgraceful Earl of Rochester – I was amazed, I believed everything I read as I read it, never mind the contradictions. But I
kept it to myself. I was living like a dormouse, in a dream. As
for my family: who *were* they, that I should confide in them?
My mother might have given me her blessing, perhaps; but after Father's death, she blessed nobody, only cursed. Never in
violent words; but the spirit of her speech, and indeed of her
silence, conveyed only the one thing: she had been punished
(and for nothing) by her God, so therefore in return she would
punish all and sundry and if God didn't like it, He had only
Himself to thank.

So let me bring you at once to my first spiritual employment,
as a deacon not yet made priest, in a Forest Hill parish, everybody comfortably off, every house a compact band-box of bad
taste and English complacency. Atonement, in such surround-
ings? I tried once; yes, over roast mutton at the rectory, in reply
to a bit of chit-chat about the army's disaster in the war against
the Zulus. "All those men dead," I cried, "and who shall shoulder the fault?" I went on like the ballad, about "women bereft" and "the pride of the great ones" and so forth, useless.
There was a pointed lack of response, indeed a dead stop to

the conversation, until somebody said it was of course awfully sad. Somebody else said that when a man joins the army (or the navy, as it might be) he knows what he's contracted for, death or mutilation necessarily in the balance against food, pay and glory: it wasn't sad at all, it was the way the world worked. And if it didn't work that way, how would quiet Christian people, loyal subjects of the queen's empire, expect to sit down to such an excellent dinner? I apologized, after a fashion, and the matter was dropped.

But not forgotten: I was now marked, I was known to be "unsound". The bishop recommended a transfer. He knew a vicar who might be glad of me, in a parish of notorious squalor, riverbank slums on the margin of the Thames between Bermondsey and Rotherhithe, where hardly anyone came to church; and if they did, as like as not they'd be sailors just paid-off and so drunk they thought the building was a music-hall – why, I've known 'em call out for "some o' them little judies, prancing and dancing, bare-arsed like nanny-goats, fetch 'em aloft, why don't yer?" in the very middle of the General Confession. The vicar was an inept zealot, he was there to destroy Sin, and at the same time keep Sinners out of the clutches of the Methodists; in neither aspiration was he successful. I trotted obediently at his heels, as he stalked into taverns and opium cellars and miserable little whorehouses, bawling the Word of God at the denizens. He took care to stalk out again before anyone could try to argue with him, or for that matter kick him in the stones.

I never saw him speak as a separate living creature to any other strange, separate creature, sailorman, strumpet, or poppy-john. Not that *I* was inclined for such a performance, at least not on the subject of Sin. I cannot but confess I was sinking very low into troughs of hypocrisy. I soon found, if I took off my clerical collar and replaced it with a grimy muffler, I might privately find acceptance in all sorts of despicable haunts. People took me for a reporter from *The Bermondsey Tattler* or *The Southwark Sporting Flash*, looking for stories of corrupt shipowners, or slum-landlords, or varieties of vice, and then they'd talk to me easily enough, and drink with me – and there were girls there moreover who'd now and then –

(Ah Jesus, what to say, how to write it, am I ludicrous? Not pleasant to have to heave up my private memories to the police, to be jeered at, very likely, and called a liar. But I insist it is germane: be patient, I'll cringe but I'll show you.)

When I was at school, at about the time of my father's death, I was most memorably jeered at, by boys who demanded to know did I "pollute myself" and how often? I was in fact too timid to have attempted such a business: I dreaded going blind or going mad or going to hell. Yet of course in the end I succumbed to the temptation (as *they* had succumbed); to tell truth, from then on the wretched habit never ceased, up to and including my pious existence in Forest Hill ... And even now that I walked amongst nothing *but* temptation, temptation no longer toward exclusively solitary vice – why, I was slipping and falling at least once a week – yet timidity still caught me by the crotch. I would confine myself to "sticky fingers", or "the mouth-music", as these girls call their back-alley diversions – and always so brief and furtive that I scarce was aware it had happened.

I insist, though, it was not *false pretences*. I really did write for newspapers, I did have some short pieces published, anonymous and unpaid, modest exposures of social abuse, I tried to make them vivid by the slang and back-talk of real life – I knew better than to be proud of them, the editors only took them as "fillers". But at the same time, there *were* false pretences: as a deacon I was a degenerate fraud and for months I didn't know how long before I was caught out; and even if I wasn't, what should I do, where should I go, did I dare to continue to pray? Forest Hill had been no good. Rotherhithe and Bermondsey were no good. Maybe God was no good, and I'd been stumbling all these months down the wrong bloody passage.

And throughout all these months Palinurus clung to my skull like a cat-faced limpet, laughing softly but continuously reproachful. Nor could I rid myself of the terrifying notion that this foul (and dangerous) waterfront was the only place for me to be; if I could not abide here as a Messenger of God, then – in

some other capacity – as a – oh I didn't know what -   As a
man who must seek and find his own way to earn a living in
such a degraded place, as a serious, professional writer, perhaps?
and stay here and endure, until -   Until I could dream that I
had done what I was constantly promising my poor brother (or
his wraith) that I would do. Even if I must reconsider the very
nature of atonement. For should not justice, retribution, chastisement, nay REVENGE, be incorporate in my sworn duty? I
began to think, "one of these days." I began to think, "yes."

I put my lying collar in a little package and posted it to the
vicar. A little letter to the bishop, saying it had all been a mistake. Another little letter to my mother, to let her know I needed
no more of Papa's legacy, she should divide it among the girls,
and please would she not trouble herself to discover what had
become of me. I crossed the water to shake off enquirers. In a
horrid court off the East India Dock Road I explored and rented
a basement room in the name of Jack Nee (I'd been nicknamed
"Nee" at school, short for Acneas and intended to hurt, the very
sound of it a sneer and a whine). I tried to grow a beard, a red-
dish one, scanty, a bad fit to my face, but -   I think I really did
expect to be able to become a realistic dissector of crime and
folly upon the model of Monsieur Zola, writing from the very
midst of society's garbage heap, pouring out my soul in form of
fiction or poetry – but an author, even an impoverished hermit-
crab author, needs spare time. As you'll see, I never had any.

Today, in this cold tiled cell of yours, I do have time, and
leisure – which is why at last I can indulge myself in the voluptuous delight of literary composition – I apologize if it makes this
Statement more prolix than what you're used to – but I sit in the
shadow of the gallows, and surely I may be excused.

So. I'd got rid of all my investments. I had to go and look
for a job.

I found one quite quickly, in Gaverick Street, the Isle of Dogs,
hard by the entry to the Millwall Docks. I saw a card in the
steamy window of a cookshop:

WANTED !

a YouNg MAN, hoNNest, to <u>start up Ledjers</u> for cash aNd keeP same,

all Neet & KERRECTaPPly withiN – good wage

It was obvious that this foetid grease-hole was by no means brand-new, so I thought it odd there should be a need to pioneer an account-book. In fact, not so odd. The owner had no skill with figures, which hadn't hitherto been a difficulty: she cooked, and her husband (one Plaistow) had looked after the profit. Until all of a sudden they put him into prison, and his attorney informed her that the ledgers were a fraud, Mr Plaistow for years had been robbing his wife's business, losing her money every weekend at fan-tan with the Chinamen, it was damn near catastrophe – she *must* get a competent clerk to sort her out smartly, or else Queer Street. My spectacles suggested to her I might indeed be such a clerk, though there was something out of order about my haircut and clothes – had I perhaps run from the bogeys, after raiding the till of my last boss? – if so, I'd come to the wrong shop, "liver-an'-lights, boy, there'll be no more o' that!" I tried to reassure her with God knows what kind of a story, but she laughed, cut me short, and took me on. She was quite artless. And she liked my big round eyes. As it happened, I liked hers.

She was – is – a tall, sinewy woman of colour, about thirty years old, her parents were a Cardiff barmaid and a ship's cook from Caribbean Montserrat. She is properly Mrs Grace Plaistow, colloquially Miss "Gravy" O'Clara. (As you're very well aware. But you want me to write what I found and when I found it, no?) She explains O'Clara by the fact that the Montserrat blacks are descended from Irish convicts quite as much as from African slaves. Political convicts, I'd guess, Oliver Cromwell's deported victims? The absent Mr Plaistow was – is – a local cockney, sometime cabin-steward on a Harwich packet. He fell down a companion-ladder in a squall, when carrying a tureen full of soup from the galley. "Broke his leg," says his wife drily, "scalded his bollocks, no he'd never do much fucking ever after." He decided he'd prefer to earn his living on dry land. I gather he was also a crimp and a pimp and a bit of a fence and that's why they've gaoled him, over above the embezzlement. I never met the man; you needn't bother to interrogate me about him.

So. I started work and immediately discovered that Gravy not only needed me to write up all transactions, customers' bills, change and tips, as well as outgoing moneys to butchers, grocers, bakers and so forth, and explain the ledgers to her, page by page, every night when she'd put up the shutters. I was also an auxiliary waiter in a grubby ankle-length apron, slipping and sliding on the sawdusted floor-flags, balancing pagodas of loaded plates, fried potatoes, fried fish, chops, sausages, faggots, eggs, bread; cabbage and gravy everywhere; wide trays loaded down with mugs of beer; a sodden napkin to wipe table-tops, a crooked smile to receive insults – furthermore (she insisted on it) a set of brass knuckles in the pocket of the apron, just in case.

So. I started work and worked for about a month until a certain Saturday night (on Saturdays the place stayed open until two in the morning). Gravy came into the stuffy hole we called a counting-house, and bent herself close over me as I bent over the desk. She looked wisely at the ledger, nodded her head as though she understood it, and told me she'd decided that my Saturdays were not to be like other days: I needn't think to be off-duty once accounts were approved and cash locked away in the safe. It was not at all a good idea (she implied) that on my way back to the East India Dock Road I should drop to the cobbles from sheer weariness, or fall prey to roving garrotters. Instead, let me strip off my apron, wash myself if I'd a mind to, take a quick looksee round the premises to make sure all was as it ought to be, and then upstairs after her, chop-chop.

Bemused (and very tired) I did as she said. I found her in her attic room close under the rafters – snug whitewashed walls and rose-patterned curtains – her skinny flesh already writhing, joyful and snug, in her deep creaky feather-bed. I then must strip off rather more than an apron, I must writhe in there with her, I must share her late-night toddy when the slavey carried it up ... Sunday morning, she didn't open until half-past nine at the earliest: so we could lie there, she said, entwined, to take our pleasure as seemed sweetest; the same slavey would bring a tray of breakfast.

Who in God's name was I, that I should be consecrated (as it were) substitute husband to a slippery-limbed bawd I hadn't known any longer than a month? I tried to tell myself I was appalled, for in my mind I was still a virgin, more or less. The little dirtinesses of Rotherhithe didn't seem to count. Foolish, however, to pretend that my imagination (long before Rotherhithe) had not been invaded by a swarm of venereal longings, idealized epical pictures, both beauteous and deliciously impure. They went far to prepare me for Gravy. They were indeed *realized* by Gravy. She held out her arms to me, I swam into her like a fish through a sluice-gate.

I discovered that night that what she really enjoys, above and beyond her serpentine varieties of fucking, is the talk it leads into – she's unbelievably garrulous, and will chatter endlessly about Ireland and the Irish. Of course she's never been there. Neither have I. But I'd incautiously admitted that the Nees (as much as to say, the Harringtons) are in fact an Irish family – quite as Irish, if it comes to that, as any Montserrat O'Clara. Nonsensical fiddlesticks the gist of her conversation, leprechauns, colleens, thatched cabins and pigs – God knows where she picked it up – I humoured her. But then –

Oh but she's a plausible, soothing, insinuating bitch. I plunged (it seemed) for hours through the swamp of her reeking sheets, her reeking irresistible sheets; I lay beside her, ecstatic and exhausted, in the drab November dawn; all night we had murmured and chattered and cried together; and I realized I had told her the story of my life.

Mind you, in the vaguest terms, no names, no dates, and oh no, I was not so careless as to give away my own true name to her, nor my sometime churchwork, but -   I didn't know in any case how much of it she'd really listened to or taken seriously:

maybe my love for Palinurus, she's grossly sentimental. And of course superstitious, so when she heard that I was thronged by importunate *familiars*, when she heard me cry REVENGE in the midst of ithyphallic delirium, why, then, she must have understood - Because she crowed with laughter and proclaimed that revenge was "tip-top", that this sweet Saturday night-riding with her "little ginger honeybun" (as she called me) was no more than her own choice revenge against the abject and deceitful Plaistow - But exactly how and why I should connect myself to naval calamity nearly twenty years old, that didn't altogether logically cohere in her mind - Which is to say, she exerted no effort to *make* it logical. She just knew I was a haunted spirit (like many a sailorman, so she said, though of course I was a landlubber). It gave her a sensual thrill, the silly biddy. Why, she quoted Scripture, applying a Psalm to my predicament (number 102, *a Prayer of the Afflicted*) with her hand inside my thigh: "The voice of your groaning, is that what I hear, boy? bones that shall cleave to your skin, a pelican of the wilderness, an owl of the desert and do you watch from your glittering wide eyes, a sparrow on the house top, alone? Is that you, boy, your voice, the voice of a groan in the wilderness? Liver-an'-lights, how it throbs in my blood."

I was startled to hear she'd even flipped the pages of a Bible, never mind made a point of approximately *learning* them. It gave me quite a turn. Alas, but it also emboldened me to inform her with a smirk that I recognized the chapter and verse; and thereupon I let slip (like a damfool owl indeed) how I'd lived for more than a year in a clergy house across the river, fooling about as a vicar's dogsbody

Her response was more startling than any knowledge of the Psalms. Spitting and hissing, she shot away from me sideways across the breadth of her big bed. She crouched there naked upon all fours and glared at me in the half-light. She clambered out for the bedside candle, struck a match and lit it. She jerked away the bedclothes and lowered the candle to my face. Hot wax was dripping all along my bare body as she moved the flame deliberately from face to feet. I gasped at the sting of it, but did not dare protest. Deliberately, she studied me. At length she gave a nod, as though she'd come to a conclusion. She banged the candlestick down on her side-table and took a grip of both my wrists. She's as tough and as wiry as a race-horse, you don't need me to inform you: your own handcuffs would have been no stronger.

"Oho," says she, harsh and hard, clenching me fast, "a preacher-man. Now we are told. Oh but you *wouldn't* have told, if *I* hadn't put -   So you look for what was it? – oh, chastisement, revenge – was it justice as well, justice?" She rambled on for a long time, much of it with madhouse gestures and a queer West Indian jargon as though she exorcised me by some heathenish ritual. She must suddenly have perceived that my cry for revenge was no mere maudlin boast or erotic joke or fragment of nightmare. No, she saw it now as a real and hideous prospect, contaminated somehow with my turncoat duplicity, first a recruit to Holy Church, and then a deserter *from* Holy Church and doubtless a scorner of the Bible. I had grown a most perilous aura, she sensed a "drumbeat, dead silent" that troubled the air all around us, it must be bred from what she termed the Curse and Pallor of my Cods, just look at 'em down there, dead white among the carroty bristles! – "danger-signal," she grated, "like the gunfire of a ship in fog," she'd a right to be frightened.

Slap upon the word "gunfire" she gave my forearms a cruel twist to throw me off the bed. "Put your duds on this minute," she ordered. "Button it, cover it up. Tonight I'm alone and I think. Tomorrow we maybe talk. No no, you don't touch me." Can you credit? – after no more than half a night of it, I was so much in thrall that I stood there and the tears drove in rills down my cheeks, I was pleading, but no good. I was pleading, I was trembling, I couldn't imagine what had gone wrong. Bit by bit I dressed myself. I slunk out of the room and down her rickety stairs, found a broom and began to sweep the floor – if I worked, I might contain matters – as a matter of routine, I'd to set to rights the eating-room before the waterfront public came bawling for its breakfast.

Throughout most of that strange Sunday she had not one word for me, black or white; I paid attention to my work as conscientiously as I could, under an imprecise darkling thundercloud of - God, how could I know what brand of anathema or why? Late in the afternoon, however, as I went the round of the tables filling cruets, she came suddenly stalking up to me on her strenuous long legs; she caught me by the arm and jerked me out into the kitchen, in front of all the grinning customers, *through* the kitchen in front of her slavey and her scullion, both of 'em grinning, and so into the counting-house.

Now I have called Gravy a bawd, which is to say that there was always a small crop of harlots at her tables, to catch the customers as they ate, or take a bite and a sup themselves before going out on the street. Did she expect a percentage of their earnings? - none of your business; they're decent little pieces for the most part, I don't like to see them molested by peelers, bluebottles, crushers, rozzers, filth. (Ah no, it won't hurt you to know what we think.) You can guess I'd had no more time to get to know any of these doxies than to begin to write a book, so it was a surprise to discover in the gloom of the counting-house that one of them was waiting for me – an ominous narrow-faced girl I'd seen now and again at a table next the door, with a pot of porter and a slice of pork pie. Contemptuous and unforthcoming, she would sit and survey the company, like a police agent at a socialist meeting. She was known as Irish Kate, sometimes Biting Kate, more often Stonecold Kate; she'd no observable friends among the other tarts. I remember she was dressed that day in yellow-and-black striped print, her long black hair pinned raggedly behind her head, the ends of it hanging loose all the way down her back. She'd slung a coarse brown shawl round her shoulders and across one bare arm. The colours of a dusty wasp; I was as wary of her as though she *were* a wasp.

Nonetheless, from the very first time I'd seen her – and served her indeed with her pie – she'd stuck in my mind like a bone in the gullet. Whenever she came to the cookshop I could scarce

look away from her. She was by no means pretty; you *could* say
she was beautiful; but charming? never in all this world.

She perched upon a high stool kicking her legs in her labour-
er's boots, a scornful flurry of patchwork petticoats. Gravy said
to her, "Here is a man who's no good for me, not any more. I've
told you what I know of him. Just a chance, girl, he'll be good
for *you*. If not, you can throw him away."

She might have been talking of a sack of rotten potatoes reluctantly offered for sale ... But next moment a run of words,
filtered out of Holy Writ – "All my pleasure gone, girl, the fears
are in the way, the grasshopper a burden, desire is failed, failed.
Golden bowl broken, the pitcher at the fountain. *He* was the
pitcher, look at him, all in a puddle, and never no more." El-
egaic, melancholic, as she picked her way out of the counting-
house; even then with such a sway of her lithe hinderparts that
the blood of my loins ran a lava-flow all over again – but no!
never no more ... I was alone and shut in with the enigmatic
Kate. Who looked at me, grunted, looked away and then looked
again with a critical distaste.

"Get rid o'them gig-lamps," she ordered. I was curious
enough to make no argument: I took off my spectacles and put
them in my pocket.

She growled, "That's better. Now I can see your face. Without that scrub of a beard I'd see even more of it, but do I want?"
(What the devil was this? Did she think she was hiring a horseboy?) "What do they call yeh? Jack is it? ... Oh begod, don't
answer if you haven't a mind to. Sure I'm only here as a good
turn to Gravy. She's after proclaiming you're a class of an Irishman. Only for I know she's the heart of the roll, I'd not give yeh
so much as a whisper. Jasus, I've heard yeh talk, you're no more
Irish than the Duke of Toffee. Nee? That's a Limerick name?
How am I to know 'tis yours?"

I was becoming exasperated, red in the face, my hands were
shaking. "You can't," I told her. "Because it isn't. But you call
me by it or you call me nothing. I've a right to play games if I
want to."

Her answer to that was deep in her throat and sombre, with her head turned away. "Boy, this is no game: take the wrong card, the whole deck's the Queen of Spades."

I didn't know what she meant, beyond self-indulgent melodrama, so I ignored it. "As for Irish," I snapped, "if I tell you I'm Irish, I am. There's more than one kind."

"Ha!" she cries: "Gentry ... Maybe once you were. Not today, or else why are you here?"

I shrugged and snorted and shook my head. I was going into no details: already I'd told far too much to Gravy. But somehow this girl seemed to be satisfied. I had the feeling she'd been testing me, God alone knew what for.

For she then began to speak in a rational, practical manner, that suggested she might after all be a creature of good sense. She explained that even though Gravy wanted nothing more to do with me, it was nobody's plan that I should starve. There was a possible job for me, which she (Kate) might be able to help me to. A ship's chandler over at Blackwall was in need of a "walking clerk", it was possible I might suit: if I'd be patient for a day or two she'd let me know could he give me a start. He'd require a recommendation and Kate would be able to see to it. I thought it odd that he should rely on a dockside judy for such matters, but everything was bloody odd ... In any event I could write it all out, in the pages of my novel, whenever it might be that I really would sit down to write ... One of these days ...

She said, "Now don't yeh go looking for any jobs any place else, before I've seen you about this one. Sure I'll see you. Gravy's after telling me where you live. One o' these days ... I'll be there."

*

Testily, Gravy called me to abandon the counting-house and take myself bloody well home. It was dark already and pouring wet. Fretful people with drink in them were shoving and splashing through the puddles, wrapped in threadbare greatcoats or with sacks over their heads. Loaded drays came rumbling past, driv-

187

ers cursing and cracking whips to threaten the foot-passengers
(Sunday at the docks is not much of a day of rest): indeed it was
quite dangerous for me to dodge my way forward. I thought I
might be happy to be ground into mash underneath one of those
great waggon-wheels ...

Depression was augmented by the loneliness and damp of
my basement. I scratched a fire together to boil a kettle and
of course it wouldn't boil. I lay down on the bed to wait for
it and to think. All I could think about was the nakedness of
Gravy. No good. My lack of her was akin to my lifelong lack
of Palinurus, and moreover to my grandfather's lack of his hand
– he'd grumble that it often seemed to him the hand was still
there and not the hook, he had to bang it on the table-top to be
sure. And then he'd cry aloud, and groan, "Even years after the
sawbones, years."

The kettle boiled; I got up; I sat to table to brew some tea and
to drink it. I lit a candle in last Friday's empty porter bottle,
I opened the stiff-backed account-book where I strove to write
my novel, I put a point on a pencil, and did my best to point my
brain. Toward a vigour of truthful story-telling, except that –
The only story I could summon up was the nakedness of Gravy.
No good, no damned good. Unless, that's to say, I could perhaps turn it into -   I knew there were publishers for that sort
of stuff, but I didn't know how to find them, and I was afraid (if
I made enquiries) I'd be in trouble with the police.

I was always very timid as regards the police. I'd like you to
take note of that.

Even so, I sat for a couple of hours and I did write some
scraps – not prose narrative but snatches of doggerel verse – I
called them my *Wraiths* – mostly, they went into the fire as soon
as written, one or two of them will be in this Statement and
why not? I cut myself some bread and cheese and nibbled as I
worked. Ah God, but the cat-face of Palinurus was there, creeping quietly, insistently, between me and the words on the paper,
destroying my concentration and my nerve so that I-   Ah
God, and *who was this?* – a clatter of hobnailed feet on the area
steps, I could see through the dirt on my window a cloak or a

hood, was it? swooping down toward my door in the dark to knock with clenched fist, more of a thump than a knock, angry, repeated, determined I should open. I don't need to tell you, I was scared – in such a quarter of the city there's always the fear after nightfall – tenants learn to be very careful to lock, bolt and chain – I called out, and my voice cracked: "Who?"

"Who the fuck d'ye think? 'Tis meself and you're *you!* Willya open up the door for fucksake, I'm after running through a waterspout and I'm drenched to me death."

I turned the key, pulled the bolt, took off the chain. She came in so quickly she very nearly *fell* in, dragging the shawl from her head as she stumbled across the threshold.

"Jaze, boy, don't tell me that's the best fire you have."

"Good enough till you shook your water all over it. You've all but put it out. Lay your shawl on the end of the bed for goodness sake, and sit down."

"Jaze, I'm as cold as a frog. Have yeh e'er a cup o' gin?"

"Porter."

"Porter, if it has to be."

I grubbed for a pair of bottles from my basket under the bed and went to work with a corkscrew. Kate swilled in great gulps with barely a pause for breath. "Shlauncha," she belched - I took it for an Irish drinking cry and repeated it, and she laughed. But she left off laughing almost at once, and began slowly to circle the room, examining my meagre possessions with a surprising degree of attention.

"D'yeh see now," says she, "I've to fix a things clear: not at all able to concen-*trate* them at Gravy's. Them greasy wee looderamauns she keeps in her kitchen had their ears out for anything I'd ask. Like, for an instance, who you are?"

She was leaning against the head of the bed, looking at a picture-frame I'd nailed to the wall there, with three separate pictures stuck into it. There was a photograph of Palinurus in his midshipman's uniform; there was an engraving from *The Illustrated London News* of the Mersey estuary and the *Carausius* steaming away for her trials; there was a crude coloured woodcut that I'd found in a Rotherhithe pawnbroker's, the *Carausius* capsizing under a black and scarlet storm-sky, amid huge waves of greeny-purple bespeckled with the heads and arms of drowning men in their last agony.

She held her own head away from me, slipped down from the bed, and went to crouch over the fire, shivering – I supposed with cold, but maybe not.

"The ship's name?" she asked abruptly. Her face was hidden in her veils of thick black hair.

"*Carausius*."

"Ah-aah," – she slumped down into a long, deep, exhausted sigh. Then suddenly straightened up to thrust the poker into the bars of the grate like a swordsman making his kill. "And the captain's name?"

"Harrington." Despite myself, I said it with a sob, but she didn't seem to notice.

"He was all torn to pieces in the war, his face like a graveyard, he held things with a hook?"

"Yes."

"He used his hook to steady the bottle when I gave that bloody ship the blessing."

Gracious Heaven: she was Kitty Furey, and her father had –

"My daddy sailed with the ship, he and his gang had to nurse the bloody engines, he'd told all of 'em before the trials there was a rake of new devices in the workings of the valves that couldn't be relied on, whatever good reports they tried to get outa him. He did his best for 'em and they drowned him, and I live with him every night. Jasus Mary, he was a lovely man."

She went on to tell how her mother, upon the loss of the ship, had taken Kitty back to Dublin and had died within the year from a growth in her womb, a visitation (said her father's kin) to make the mark of her depth of sorrow – and the mark of her sin that she should have been a protestant, and that she and the papist Paschal had been married in no church, nowhere. And thereafter, who should care for Kitty? sure no-one but the parish clergy, who put her into the nuns, where they whipped her and called her a little bastard and preached at her till she fled

... Before she'd ceased to be a child, she must whore herself or starve.

She had another question for me: "Was Harrington your father?"

"Grandfather."

"They say he made the ship. All out of his own head. And begod he made the corpses. But he cannot ha' been the *only* one. And I do not have their names!" Her voice was soaring up in a great wail of tortured grief. "Oh no, 'tis not true that *I* was the one to drown the men, just because I spoke the blessing, they'd no right to accuse me, they'd no right to accuse me the whole of me life and punish me with their canes and O Christ such a little small creature!"

I had not liked her when I met her at Gravy's, I did not like her even now, but I couldn't prevent myself saying it: "I was at the launch; I stood behind my grandfather. Ah Kitty, when I saw you on the shoulders of your father, I knew you were the loveliest living thing in all the world."

I put my arms around her and we clung. Then she pushed me away with some strength. "No fucking," and she meant it. "When I do it, I get paid and I'm going *out* to get paid, any minute now I'm off. I'm glad, though, I've found who you are."

She went to my table and cut herself some bread and cheese. She devoured it in thick wedges. She looked at me queerly. "Gravy says you have a class of a *contortion* in connection with the Son of God. She says, just the same as meself ... Harrington. That sounds to be English."

The change of tack vexed me, it vexed me unduly. "There's English and there's Anglo-Irish, they sound to be the same, but never. Anglo-Irish is a deadly heritage, a man wears it like the skin of a corpse. Don't ask me ever again."

How the devil had our closeness, only moments before, led me so quickly into rash admission? Last night all over again, the throes of Gravy's lechery, my hapless admissions to *her*. My few wits were by now half-addled, but I could see that "heritage" puzzled her, her eye was cocked, her mouth twisted.

I could not leave it unexplained, even though-   Admission turned into confession, my cheeks were suffused with shame – yes, the Harringtons for two centuries had been notoriously callous landlords, their estates had become *my* estates, I'd neglected them outrageously and then (to soothe my conscience, could she believe?) *I threw them away* – into the neat embroidered purses of my simpering greedy sisters – hundreds of acres, maybe thousands of people; would those consequential bitches give a damn for any one of them? Eviction, starvation, emigration, coffin-ships to America – the whole beastly narrative, we recited it in counterpoint, Kitty condemnatory, myself almost chokingly contrite.

We both ran out of breath and stood staring. "Ah," she said, "away wi't yeh. You were wrong and you know you were wrong. Let's get it right, so. Gravy says, you have a graw for Revenge, whichever way yeh take the word: ah Christ the word is one thing, the thing itself's altogether another. Christ, boy, but y' *do*, doncha?"

I couldn't speak, I was in such trouble: with her, with my legacy, with my *familiars*, and – as she'd said – with the Son of God.

She paused and then went on with her mouth full "Oh but y' do, though. You told Gravy as much in your sleep. She don't have the trick to help you, but *I* do. Jaze, boy, doncha see it yet? You 'n' me, we're on the same long road." I inferred that had it not been for her faint, forlorn hope of Revenge, her spirit long ago would have choked in her violated body. And yet *where* Revenge? She knew nothing, didn't know *how*? didn't know *who*? –

> *of KF and her Long Road: a Wraith*
> No, she had not so much as one single name
> "Queen of Spades"? this was no game
> So what to do, what could be done?
> And there I was, I was the one.

Ah yes! in all of my trouble, I did know a name, in all of my shame I was rash enough to give it her. "Scharhorn. A rear-admiral. More than anyone in England he made sure that that ship was built." (For had not Palinurus every night through wind and water come gurgling to tell me so? so therefore I told *her.*) "Lord Frederick Scharhorn, mark the name, mark it. Oh but it's no great hope, you're never going to get at him."

"Where is he then?"

"The Mediterranean. I read about these things. Constantly, the newspapers."

"He'd not be there for ever, swimming about on his sodding flagship. One day he'd be home again and then we can – "

She broke off, and looked away. I suppose we understood each other. I was not quite so sure that I understood *myself.* However, that could wait; indeed it would *have* to wait, for too much was happening too soon. I was all at once terrified and excited all together.

(The identical feeling when I'd eavesdropped as a child upon the dinner-party for Scharhorn. : And a year or two earlier than that – was I six? maybe seven? – when my sisters had incited me to steal tarts from Cook's personal cupboard. I was in such a state of exultant panic, and so anxious for their good opinion, that I quite forgot to cover my tracks. I was caught almost immediately, red-handed with contraband jam. Oh the girls escaped scot-free; while the lashing my father gave me would have sent him to the penitentiary, had I not been his own sinful child. In his righteous Christian rage he assailed me as "thief, liar, hypocrite! – why, many an adult murderer might well be more easily pardoned.")

She was holding my right hand clasped tight in her hard little hands. She stood away from me as she did so, as though to prevent another embrace. But her handgrasp was strong, warm and most nervously intimate.

A few more words before she went: "Tonight's Sunday. Be Wednesday morning, you'll be ready for the new work, so you will? Sure be then I'll have told him you're the man he needs to have. And I'll call for yeh Wednesday to fetch yeh."

She pulled her shawl over her hair and hurried away into the streaming rain, her boots on the area-steps sounding out like a tinsmith's hammer.

Such a desperately early hour on the Wednesday, half-past four! and my fire refused to kindle. Fierce as a fusilier, she dragged me out, into frost, into fog, toward the all-night coffee-stall at the corner of Saracen Street where at least the water was boiling, whatever the taste of the drink. As we made haste to swallow it, and to crunch a few biscuits, she was urgently whispering profanity, exhortation, instruction –

"Scharhorn, rear-admiral! We strap ourselves tight to that name, boy; like them fucking savage bitches had us strapped up to be caned in the nuns'-house, fucking *tight*. Sure, y'was never amongst the nuns, don't I know it? – Mr Harrington-Nee, little small gent of a protestant in his gig-lamps, untouchable ... In the meantime, this new boss of yours, one of these days if he thinks well o' yeh, he'll likely put it up to yeh to make him a class of a promise, which you won't want to make, maybe. But if for sure y'want this Scharhorn, then you'll need the promise: *I'll* need it ... No more to say, Jack: 'tis time we went. Better run."

She led me off again at a pretty smart gallop to a warehouse and yard off the Blackwall Way. On a board above the waggon-entry was a florid inscription in green and gold : -

FRANCIS X. McGURRELL & Associates
Ship's Chandlery, Nautical Fixings
London   Cork   New York

A burly middle-aged boyo in a whitey-brown billycock had arrived just ahead of us and was hauling the gates open. Kitty said, "There's your man," and shoved me toward him. Then she scurried away without apparent recognition between him and her: I thought it odd. (By the way, from now on, to me she was always "Kitty", no more "Kate", whether Stonecold or Biting. However much she glowered and snarled, she was my darling from Birkenhead, six years old and no older – that mischievous nervous little patch of a dragonfly child and you and your hyenas have ensnared her and made an end of her, ah. The gorge rises, the tears burn, vitriol in my eye-sockets, how're yours?)

The man McGurrell seemed to know all about me, he greeted me abruptly, he told me my duties and at once sent me out to see what I could make of them. He was beady-eyed, red-faced and slack-mouthed, with muddy-grey mutton-chop whiskers and a prominent gold tooth. He hung a prominent gold watch-chain across his well-filled chequered waistcoat, and he tilted his hat on his bald skull at all hours, indoors and out. The work he demanded was easy enough to learn, though it needed nerve and a good deal of tact. I had to interview ship's stewards and sometimes ship's captains to discuss their requirements and secure their money. The warehouse supplied all manner of seagoing stores, food, liquor, sailors' slops, hard-weather gear, paint, oil, medicines; every possible attempt was made by purchasers to avoid full payment. I still had Gravy's knuckleduster, and once or twice I nearly had to use it.

It was not long before my fellow-clerks let me understand that McGurrell was a congenital smuggler. He received consignments from abroad of the goods that he dealt in, and I would be put in charge of their unloading from the ships and their carriage to the warehouse. It was pointed out to me, in a sidelong sort of way, that our documents for Customs and Excise were quite often faked: up to me to make sure that the official who handled them was fair-and-square in my employer's pocket. D'you know, I grew good at it? D'you know, I think it possible I have a criminal mind? Perhaps my father passed it on to me? – after all, he was able to deceive not only himself but also the Admiralty.

Every day I must walk miles around the various docks, and often late into the night, seeking this ship or that in a tangle of moorings. The darker it got, and the colder, the more infested the place became with those swarms of dead drowned men, among mooring-ropes and piles of casks, and dinghies on the black water, and all up and down the ships' rigging. I had a fearful sense of crescendo, a building to a climax, which indeed I could endure, if only it came soon. To wait for it was deadly; you may be sure it took a toll.

I saw nothing of Kitty; I didn't know whether I ought to expect her or not – but I kept thinking she might wish me to tell her about the job, in particular McGurrell's uncomfortable habit (developed after I'd been with him a week or two) of buttonholing me in a corner of the warehouse and subjecting me to his beery confidences about the unhappy state of affairs in Ireland and what could or should be done about it. I bore in mind Kitty's warning of some sort of "promise", and would therefore agree with him on all accounts, expressing a cautious enthusiasm, now and then winking or tapping my nose as though to show I knew more than was actually being said. His main theme was the skill and the wiliness of Parnell; but how (he used to ask) could even such a hero prevail from the soft, deep cushions of parliament, without others, no less wily, to act for him *outside* parliament in any bloody way they knew how? "'No man,' says Mr Parnell, 'sets a bound to the march of a nation' – know what I mean, Jack? 'tis a powerful sentiment. But look at it this way – no man should set a bound to the man who sets no bounds. No, we cannot have the Chief *spancelled* like a mountainy goat and withheld from the right straight road by anglo-saxon shibboleths and futile legalities. Whaddya say, Jack? am I right? y're a feller with the education, am I right or am I wrong?"

As the winter gathered over us, sleet, snow and storms of hail, these conversations grew away from obscure, dubious hint, toward a more positive statement, but never so far as actually to incriminate. (He didn't mention the 'Invincibles', who'd slashed to death in a Dublin park two of Gladstone's grandees, thus engulfing Parnell in a maelstrom of political offal. He didn't mention, I didn't ask, but I gleaned as it were an inkling of approval for those murders.) He was certainly up to something; he was drawing me into it. Which is where, I supposed, Kitty had arranged for me to be. Terror and excitement, day and night in my brain there were cymbals clashing and clanging – had she left me alone as another of her *tests?*

On an early December morning of intermittent and premature blizzard, the traffic of the river almost at a standstill, McGurrell sent me with his horse and cart to an American steam-packet in the Royal Albert Dock, the *George A. Custer* of Boston. She carried a batch of patent medicines of peculiar Yankee potency, much in demand by McGurrell's customers: many a skipper would give such cure-alls his absolute trust, as good for anything from piles to a broken leg. I had a letter for the ship's second officer, a Mr Slattery. He read it and frowned, looking me over with some suspicion – "Face like a Limey, voice like a Limey ... Say, feller, how long since you was last in Ireland, huh?"

"I never was," says I. "Is that a crime?" An honourable declaration, delivered straight from the shoulder, no sign of embarrassment (at least, I hoped not).

His brow cleared, he muttered, "Okay. I reckon if Francey McGurrell opines that y're genuwine, not for me to second-guess him. Okay, come see what we got." He led me to an open hatchway. Below in the hold was a pile of small packing-cases – three dozen of them, each twice the size of a sizeable portmanteau. They were to be hauled up a few at a time in a cargo net and lowered (very carefully) to the wharf, where McGurrell's carter and his boy would load them for the warehouse. One of them was marked with a tiny dab of red paint; as it came up in the net, Mr Slattery leaned over and tapped it casually with the back of his knuckles. "This hyar's the one," says he, out of the corner of his mouth, turning aside as he spoke – to squirt tobacco juice over the rail, and to hide his words from an apprentice who was shovelling frozen snow from the deck.

With the last of the boxes hoisted out, and the necessary papers signed, I handed Mr Slattery the padlocked wallet of U.S.

dollars which apparently were due to him. He opened it with a key from his watch-chain, counted the coins, squirted again, and again spoke obliquely, casually: "This hyar's for your boss." He slipped me an envelope, unsealed, the flap tucked in. "It's secret but it don't pretend to be; read it if you've a mind to. It's kinda coded, so there ain't no looseness, neither for you nor the posse, okay?" He trudged away out of the wind toward the deckhouse, a hunched little crab of a man in his pea-jacket and pilot-cap; he never gave me another glance ... I did read the letter, while I waited for Customs: it was a typewritten list of prices and delivery dates of various quantities of bourbon whisky, sugar, tobacco, and Stetson's felt hats, under the printed heading of Jas. McElligott, Incorporated Export Factor, Boston. There were added scribbles on the envelope in indelible pencil, and some very dirty fingerprints.

Customs made no difficulty; documents were stamped and exchanged; the cart rattled on to Blackwall Way. When McGurrell cast his eye over the boxes, he refrained from comment, didn't look twice at the one with the red spot; he had his hand out for the letter, a twitching hand; he read it through carefully, two or three times; his face cleared and he breathed more easily. He said to me, "Fair enough. Fair enough, Jack, so. You're after seeing Mr Slattery, is that a fact?" He was studying the scribbles. He said, "Aha, he lets me know where we are, Jack. And that's grand ... Into me inner office: keep it quiet." Once inside the inner office, with the door carefully shut, he stoops to put the letter away in his safe, and then brings up his head toward me, like a big drooling dog about to lick.

"Y'know, Jack," says he, "I'd say at this stage it's high time that I – eh – that I *inducted* you, so. Know what I mean? Y'see, I'm what they call the Centre of a Circle that should be all of nine men, ready and willing to give their lives, but -   To tell truth, Jack, I don't have the numbers and New York'll tear out me windpipe if I have to let 'em know the job can't be done, know what I mean? So what d'you say?"

I told him I would say whatever was best for – for the Cause. I assumed a great deal here, because he had never in fact mentioned any Cause to me, *as such*. But the assumption was clearly justified; he smiled, patted my shoulder, crouched down again by the safe, picking and poking till he laid hands on a small black book. He held it out to me and I saw it was a New Testament (Douai version), upon which, there and then, I was hurriedly and furtively sworn-in, as a Member in Good Standing of the London Docks Circle of the Fenian Brotherhood, the Irish Republican Brotherhood, the Irish Revolutionary Brotherhood, three names for the one thing, a model (if I liked) of the Holy Trinity or I could call it maybe the national shamrock. The oath encompassed my lifetime allegiance to "the Irish Republic, now virtually established." I had no scruples about swearing this, I couldn't see that an Irish Republic would be other than an excellent idea, but in truth I was swearing for my own vengeance and for Kitty's vengeance; if this Brotherhood could help us achieve it, well and good. If not ... who could say?

(D'you think I should have been rather more impressed? surprised? disquieted? No, for don't you see? I had heard of these Fenians for years – ever since, as a child in the night-nursery, I'd lain quivering with fear of the Irish-American hobgoblins conjured-up by Palinurus, himself just about old enough to read Father's newspapers and misrepresent their contents. A frenzy of malignant shadows in the dark months after Hallowe'en, and now – would you believe? – here it was, so very easily a new graft to my adult life, and moreover a quite *natural* development, when you consider the state of the nation and the state of my flesh and my conscience, this feverish phantasma, this quicksand of unresolved grief.)

The affairs of a continental-style revolutionary secret society seemed rather to depress McGurrell than exalt his spirits: maybe he'd been a Hibernian Carbonaro somewhat too long, and without sufficient sign of success. However, he braced himself, and wiped off the spittle from his blubbery lips.

"Aha, there we are," he stammers. "So I've to give you a good welcome. 'Cayde Meela Falcha!' – the hundred thousand welcomes, as we say in the Republic, now – now what, Jack? – *Republic, what*?" These last two words very sharp and artful.

I'm as sharp as he is and no less nervous. "Now virtually established?" – I stammer it back at him, and he laughs. An oily unconvincing laugh. We shake hands. "Good," says he, "grand. I'd say there's no harm in letting you know what's to be done and how you'll do it. Sure 'tis well you're here this morning, for begod there's great quantities of work. There's a box in the consignment you brought me in just now: bottles o'this snake-oil laid in the top of it and underneath we ought to find – Sure, why don't we wait till the lads is all gone home? Work a bit of overtime for me, why doncha? In the meanwhile, have the boxes stacked in there behind the tarpaulins, know where I mean? I'd say Mr Slattery showed you the red spot, so he did? – just make sure y'leave it on top."

So I left it on top; and the pair of us hove it down by the light of a dark lantern, well on in the middle of the night. McGurrell set to work at the screws that fastened the lid – they were thickly greased and yielded easily to his screwdriver – inside, as he'd said, was a layer of small bottles of Dr Darius K. Plugstreet's Old Cherokee Remedy, neatly packed in straw. None of them broken. We lifted them all out and laid them on a shelf. Below them, more straw, and below the straw a half-dozen roughly rectangular packages, rather larger and heavier than standard-size building bricks. They were wrapped in oiled canvas and tied with sailors' twine. Wedges of cottonwaste were stuffed in between them to prevent jolting. McGurrell told me to open one of them – "Untie it, don't cut, we'll need to fasten it up again just as secure. And for godsake don't drop the bugger, carefully with it, you damfool, careful!" He had swiftly walked away round the far side of a pillar. You can imagine, I was indeed careful …

I found a contrivance of polished brass, a square box with a dial, and a pointed nozzle. I made nothing of it, until McGurrell (behind his pillar) said, "Didja never hear the term, now, 'an infernal machine'? Because that's what you're holding and if y'want to blow your hand off, you'll mess wi'them titchy turn-cocks at the side. Mind you, 'tis no more than what they call the deeton-*ayt*or with a slick clockwork timing device, it needs its nose jammed-up into a clump o'dynamite before it'll do the real business. These yokes is the first batch to be sent, so they tell me. They're after working 'em up for us in a factory in Pittsburg, begod them Yanks is clever. The dynamite we have already. We store it separate of course ... Pack that up again, put it back, we're not going to use it tonight."

I asked him when we *would* use it; I asked him what for. He looked at me narrowly with an appearance of wisdom. But he could say nothing except that it depended on New York, New York would give us the word, New York had a plan "to bring this empire to its knees" – with dynamite, under the instruction of trained experts in dynamite, who'd be taking ship for London as soon as New York had them organized. Why, it might be as early as Easter, supposing the London Circles could report themselves ready for them with the intelligence and personnel they would need upon arrival. (He seemed to imply that few of the London Circles were entirely up to strength.)

I asked, was it really necessary to cool our heels for New York, now that the – the devices were delivered?

I feared he'd fall dead of a seizure. Did I not understand that the Brotherhood was most strictly disciplined? men had been bloody well "put off the walk" for taking matters into their own hands! let me not be such an eedjit as to abandon insurrectionary science in favour of cutthroat adventure, these matters could not be, must not be, *never were* bloody well fudged ... Whereupon he sent me home to my bed.

The very next night I had a visit from Kitty. No coincidence: she knew all about the *George A. Custer* and wanted urgently to hear how matters had gone with McGurrell. Moreover, she had news of her own. I told her mine first: she clapped her hands and danced like a dragonfly backwards and forwards between hearthstone and door, throwing her arms around me and kissing me with away-to-hell wantonness – I'd never thought she would *kiss* – and neither had she, for she stepped back all of a sudden, screwed up her mouth, shook her head in disgust, and snapped some swear-words at herself. Toward *me* she snapped, "No fucking."

Then she growled that all we needed was to find where he kept his dynamite. There were people she could talk to who would know and might let slip. As she stepped into the candle-light, I saw a sorry black eye and a swollen mouth; I asked her how, and she barked a short laugh. Then she told me her own news – *news from the fleet!* she proclaimed it like a town-crier announcing Trafalgar. She'd lately "had doings with a savage old cockster," ship's corporal aboard HMS *Devastation*. He took pleasure, so he did, in giving her his fist and the flat of his angry hand; and all the time he rummaged her didn't he clatter away non-stop, continuous belly-ache against senior officers? "*Devastation's* berthed in the Medway, out of Malta," says he, "and neither prize-money nor glory." He could inform her first-hand there was a rake of ships at Malta just now ending their tour of duty – "take for a fucking example," says he, "that ponce of a shirt-lifter Scharhorn," who'd surely be on his way home, to wallow in undeserved glory "against the gippos," says he. "Like a dung-beetle in a crock of butter," says he. No mention of dates or ports of arrival; but nonetheless, cried Kitty, 'twas something! – we must watch, wait, be on heat to shaft McGurrell. If those Skirmishers were to get here before Scharhorn, we'd be the ones to be shafted. It made her mad to think of it. "Jaze," she said, "we can't have that."

She was far too far ahead of herself. What on earth, for example, were Skirmishers?

It seemed they were the experts from New York. A type of superior Fenian, front-line fighters for the Cause, while McGurrell was little more than a storekeeper or caretaker.

She knew one hell of a lot, this Kitty. Would she, by any chance, be a Skirmisher herself?

"Jaze, boy, I'm not even sworn – you'd never suppose they'd offer a strap the likes o' me an honourable oath for to serve the Republic? ... Notwithstanding, I have me uses, and begod they do use me; they tell me this, they tell me that; begod they trust me better than most of their own. An' that, boy, is the way that I can use *them*. Believe it."

I put it to her we were dealing in stark luck and coincidence and where in God's name would it lead us? She began to protest, but I continued to lay it out to her as logically as I could: if we really believed we could accomplish the murder of Scharhorn, we would need him in a place where we could reach him. If by means of an infernal machine, we would need more than dynamite and detonators, for somehow they must be fixed up together, and *I* couldn't do it; could *she*? Or failing that, would she shoot? would she – ?

Understand: *this was the first time the word of Murder came up between us.*

I had chosen it most purposefully, for I wanted no mistakes. We were both of us gabbling together when I uttered it. Our eyes met, we stared hard; and then, upon the notion of shooting, we both of us fell silent. Kitty's eyes were remarkable: a very pale blue-grey, not at all in concordance with the rich shiny black of her hair. And tonight they were brighter than the knife-sharp new moon that turned the snow on my area railings into strips of silver braid ... I put forward my hands, she put forward hers, we touched finger-tips, we trembled.

So: she had said "no fucking," but within two minutes, in that sour basement, on my narrow iron bedstead, we – It was not at all the same as with Gravy, this was more like the confirmation of a contract; she couldn't read, she couldn't write, so she signed it (so to speak) between her legs. I wouldn't call it powerful or frantic, or a two-backed ravening beast; more a matter of soft small cries between us, gentle probing and stroking, and our arms round one another in the carnality of mutual compassion. Oh my beloved child.

Afterwards, we came back to where we were. Meditatively she said we must have one o'them machines, we were as good as any Skirmishers any day, let them that had wronged her, *and* their house, *and* their home, be blown to the moon complete – for her, all the life in all the world was exploded when *Carau-*

sius went down – so of course it was the machine we must have, explode them, explode, or we'd make no true end to the tale. She was so quiet the way she said it, unbelievably *cruel*. As to fixing a machine from bits and pieces, ah sure until Scharhorn arrived, all this was but dream-it-an'-guess. We would wait, so. In peace and quiet: no, we would not fuck a second time. She wept, and was determined.

*

Weeks went by. Months. Nothing happened. The usual hard work and the dreary lop-and-lap of my unwearying *familiars* in the coils of my innermost ear. Kitty held herself aloof, just calling in on me now and again so we could tell each other how nothing was happening. (And that's all that we did: we *told*.) I noticed she was growing ever more tetchy and somehow cack-handed, the strain of waiting oppressed her: once or twice she was in liquor. No good. I myself felt I was flaking away like plaster from a mouldy old wall. If something didn't turn up, and pretty swiftly – At last, upon a morning of the first week in March, something did.

I was in the steward's cuddy of a timber-ship from Riga, and I came across the previous Tuesday's *Times*: the Russian skipper, a man of culture, always read the best available local newspaper in every port, it helped him learn the languages. I'd had no chance for quite a while to read *any* newspaper, best or worst. The claims of McGurrell's business just then were exorbitant, and I had to keep him cordial.

I skimmed the column-headings, greedy for news, until the bottom of page 4. Ah! I skimmed no longer – no, I read it slowly, I read it again, and again.

NOTABLE NAVAL VISIT

From our City of London Correspondent

HMS *Scaramouche*, erstwhile flagship of the Mediterranean gunboat squadron, celebrated for successful actions against Arabi Pasha's rebels in the Nile delta, has happily returned to home waters and will berth at Tower Wharf from the evening of the 16th of March. The gallant commander of the squadron (his term of duty now concluded), Rear-Admiral the Lord Scharhorn VC, will be on board and will receive the Freedom of the City for his services to Imperial Commerce, in a ceremony at Mansion House on the 17th of March, to be followed by a buffet luncheon. The *Scaramouche* is to be thrown open to the public between the hours of two o'clock and five, on the 18th, 19th and 20th, and should prove a splendid cynosure for all those Londoners who follow the national triumphs of naval engineering equally with those of bluejacket heroism. The ship is a high-speed gunboat of the very latest model, designed in accordance with the abundant experience of Lord Scharhorn himself – screw-driven, barquentine-rigged, and armed with the most up-to-date quick-firing breech-loaders and a pair of Gatling guns for riverine work. Our readers will not need reminding of Lord Scharhorn's family connection to Her Majesty: it is particularly gratifying that an officer of royal blood should play such a prominent part in the perilous affairs of empire – (*etc, etc.*)

I had to do: what could I do? no no, what *must* I do? Impossible to pretend to ignore it: cries in my ear-holes, wailings in my gut, my right hand shook as with a palsy. Ah Christ, my bowels were water. Nothing was at all clear. Yet everything most balefully imminent. "Hamlet, revenge"? – O cursed spite! (wasn't that how he answered the call?) he'd to set things right, and he did, or he *tried* – he was me and I was him, and no error.

It was early in the day, a brisk blue-sky morning of rasping wind that blew grit all about the streets, into eyes and mouths, maddening – I did not expect Kitty tonight or tomorrow – not even before the weekend – essential I talk to her now, now, at once! I knew where she lived, but she'd never let me go there – "Glasshouse Fields," she'd once told me. "Only if you *have* to,

between Cable Street and the Highway, over against the Marlinspike, a rotten door that used to be yaller, and I'm up in the
three-pair back, and I never want to see yeh there, never." My
familiars seemed to seize me and urge me forward, I ran and
I ran, I was led by Paschal Furey, he swooped above my head
with a herring-gull screech, and all around me drowning men
flapped along the pavement like seals. For once, I didn't see
Palinurus, but of course he was there, he always was.

The Marlinspike is one of the nastiest pubs in London, and
the yellow-doored tenement beside it no better. At this hour
of the morning (ugly thought) would she have a man with her?
– I'd no idea of her times and seasons. I lurched up the stairs
through a reek of vomit and urine to the top of the last flight; I
found a door there in comparatively good repair, a card nailed
to the woodwork, Gravy must have written it for her –

KATEs' PLACE
A mouNtayN of SPyces aNd my BRESTS like towers, make
hast my Belovd
If lockt or NO aNswre, doN't Push – come agiN tommorow

The door was slightly ajar: I called her name, no reply: I went in.

She lay tumbled on an unmade bed, empty gin bottle in the
crook of her arm, gin spilt on coverlet and floorboards. Her
mouth was wide open and she snored like a barrel organ ...
Was I taken aback? Had I thought I could trust her? Because
I'd passed the tests she'd thought fit to put onto me, did I suppose that she too might be tested and prevail? Ah no, I had
no right to assert what she *should* be, or even what she *used*
to be, only to know her, to cope with her, to love her, here,
now, this pathetic garret, this unhinged and haywire morning
... Cope? on my own I'd have been helpless to deal with her:
but it seemed I was not on my own, it seemed that if not myself
it was the shape of Paschal Furey who swept forward and hove

her up from the mattress, whispering into her ear, calling into her ear – "Scharhorn Scharhorn Scharhorn, sweetheart wake up, wake up y'stupid bitch, he's coming to London, oh God help us, Kitty, help! whatever d'you think we can *do?*" That could not have been Paschal, it must have been me. She staggered to her feet and I was most certainly alone with her, just me and my disgusting darling: I pulled the filthy shift off her, induced her to crouch in her big tin washbowl, poured water over her from the bucket behind the door, and found there was still heat in the ashes of her fire. Sticks, coal and a blast from the bellows, before long I had a kettle boiled for strong coffee, oh but there was no time to lose, I was cursing her continuously, and attempting to read her the news-cutting; when she laughed, I could have smacked her in the face.

"Didja say the 17th?" she crowed. "Jasus Mary, have yeh no notion o' the meaning of the day? D'yeh tell me you've never heard of the sanctified glory of Ireland? Christ, Jack, I've a week to get sober – leave me alone! – and then, boy, the Day of the Deed." She launched into rodomontade, here and there a little bit akin to good sense, the rest of it bleary maundering. But even at her most crapulous, she was scheming like Guy Fawkes, swift, bold, incomprehensible. She drank coffee and threw it up. She pulled herself into a skirt and befouled it when she had to piss. I helped her to find another one. She scrambled around, and swore – she had lost one of her shoes.

At last I had her settled and more or less cleansed. I could now *discuss* Scharhorn with her, rather than simply eavesdrop onto her bloodthirsty self-communion – my God, but this had wasted the whole morning.

I read the news-cutting to her again, to make sure she took it in: she had already taken it in. Through the tail-end of the fug of booze, the obsession of her life was shooting forward like a whaler's harpoon. Ways and means, preparations, they'd clicked into her brain in an instant. "St Patrick's Day in the morning? McGurrell could never say 'No', no nor any o'them New York Skirmishers – Jasus Mary, Jack, we have 'em grilled!"

"We don't know who keeps the dynamite."

"McGurrell keeps the dynamite. D'yeh think I'm after spreading me two legs up an' down this poxy river just to find out nothing at all? ... O Jack, don't yeh see it? McGurrell for the day that's in it'll be *lepping* to let yeh have it; just see if he don't – Jasus Mary he can't not!"

I was actually before her here – as soon as she'd said "St Patrick's," my low-church slow-church anglican mind turned a hysterical cat-in-the-pan: all at once I was alive to a streaming possibility. (Bright green and streaming scarlet. Oh terror and excitement, ha.) But even so – "We don't need a bomb, Kitty, to kill one single man in a crowd at the Mansion House. If we're close enough, pistol or knife ... if we can manage it at all ... if we can." Was I beginning to have second thoughts? "This Scharhorn, y'know, only did what Victoria wanted him to do."

She made a face, sipped her coffee and tried not to be sick again. "Jack," she said, cold and deadly (though her hand shook till the cup danced a jig in mid-air). "D'ye tell me Victoria told Scharhorn to kill my daddy? Ah the hell with Victoria. She's behind her castle walls. And besides, she's not a woman, she's a fucking empire, so she is: let the Brotherhood deal with empires, that's what it's for. But Scharhorn, he's personal, and *he'll* be at the top of Lombard Street. D'you forget he has a ship? Bomb for the ship, pistol for the man ... Knives? I don't think so, not with a knife, I'd a feller knifed in bed beside me once ... So *you* go to McGurrell, *you're* the sworn soldier, you tell him we have a use for his gear. To be sure Jack Harrington-Nee can think of a way to persuade him? Dear Jack, y'can o'course, doncha have the education? Go."

of KF's Bed: a Wraith
Knifed beside her? Who? Whose hand on the dark jealous hilt?
Who could not bear to see another beneath her quilt?
I could not, for one. For if I had –
Why, then the whole globe might topple and tilt,
Why, then my whole brain might burst in my head blood-red.

I found McGurrell in a rare taking. His breath came in explosions like a grampus; he snatched at me to pull me toward him: "Where the hell you been, boy? Didn't y'hear me calling you in? Begod I don't pay you to absent y'rself around the docks!" Which was exactly what I was paid for, and the men in the warehouse looked up from their work in astonishment. He became aware of the open mouths and dragged me by main force into the office.

"Now," says he, eructating, gasping, as he compelled himself to keep his voice down, "here's a terrible bloody thing. Them fellers from New York have giv me the word, look at this, look at it!" He flapped a telegraph flimsy in front of my eyes, too quick for me to read it. "'Tis encoded o'course, but what does it mean only the middle o'this month? We're to place and time the dynamite for the list of targets already afforded, that's the railways and the underground and begod the House of Commons! we're to choose our hour and date and let them know instanter, and six o'the bloody jobs is put down to this Circle! godsake boy, do you not real-ize it? 'tis the London bloody Docks Circle, that's me and it's you and maybe the mot and who the hell else? How'll we ever – no more than three of us – get a whole half-a-dozen infernal machines off of our hands into the proper settings undetected and all-at-a-go, willya tell me that?"

He wouldn't have let me say a word, but I broke in on top of him, nearly as frantic as himself. I forced him to hear about Scharhorn, and he heard about Scharhorn's ship, and he heard how St Patrick's Day cried aloud for the Deed. I changed tone, I was sly, most seductively treacherous – the subtlety of the Cambridge man to flatter his amour-propre – did he really think it appropriate to have the Yanks taking over the whole direction of his enterprise, when here at the toes of his boots was a chance never to be repeated, and a chance furthermore that two of us, three of us, could handle like a mug of hot soup?

He hushed me with a wide, wild gesture of despair. If New York got the notion that London Docks Circle invented and created its own operations outside of disciplinary control, and for no reason but to cover up discrepancies of recruitment, he

(McGurrell) would be shot – no metaphor! he meant it – "Shot," he reiterated, slumped behind his desk, "shot dead as a gutted mackerel, tipped into the tide like Coogan."

"Coogan?"

"They shot him dead, boy, dead as the mackerel, two loads o'buckshot in the bag of his belly and he didn't die quick. I was there and forced to see it, O God O gracious God." Even as he lamented his jeopardy, he watched me with artful attention from the corner of a piggy eye ...

He took a moment to breathe; he said, slowly, "On the other hand." His voice was slowly sanguine, although it wavered even yet, and the sweat ran down his face. "You tell me this royal admiral man gets his dinner from the Lord Mayor upon St Patrick's Day, glory to God! – begod with such a stroke, we'd have no need at all at all to deploy the rest o'the dynamite, at all events not before we have a way found to fill the deficits."

And then he bethought himself. "You understand, Jack, of course, if I do draw expenses for Brotherhood men who may be off at sea or on their backs in the hospital, 'tis only be way of an investment for 'em in their absence, no question of any class of a cheat – ah sure, y'do understand me?"

I told him of course I did.

He groped in his desk for a bottle of whisky, poured himself a stiff drink, and went so far as to pour one for me – unprecedented. "Why, Jack, if the admiral man can be put off the walk, and at the same time his flaunting bloody gunboat blown away in a shower o'rivets the breadth o'Tower Green – why, *there's* a defeat for the navy of Victoria that'll – that'll – why, Trafalgar Day'll find itself scoured outa the almanac. I can tell you, boy, be the same token, it'll take New York by storm."

I know now that McGurrell was not only a bungling Centre but an equally incompetent provocative-agent on behalf of yourselves at the Yard. And suddenly, that morning, it had leapt into his fat head how immediate and contradictory were the duties expected of him – on the one hand he must organize the deadly activities of a Circle that did not exist, on the other he must deliver as many as nine active members of that Circle into the arms of the law and fully incriminated. If he couldn't do the first, the second was made impossible. New York would be ready to shoot, the Home Office very possibly might bring him to the gallows out of spiteful frustration. Or at any rate, penal servitude. Or if not quite that, then certainly no more rhino. He was blocked at both ends and hopelessly grabbing for the scantiest fragment of hope.

So in breathless haste and scramble he began to shape my unlicked plan for me. Of course, what would he suppose but that the prestige of the London Docks Circle had been my first burning thought when I gaped at Tuesday's *Times*, Page 4? He knew nothing of the cruel tale of Paschal Furey and his implacable daughter; he knew nothing of Palinurus. How should he suspect the daft and murky truth: that Kitty and I didn't care a flea's fuck whether the Brotherhood got the credit or not? We did intend to leave some sort of – of a – a testament, somehow, we'd not decided how, as to what we'd done and why. In any case, I do believe that neither of us expected to live beyond the Deed. Which is why Kitty got drunk and why I'd given up any attempt at regular writing ...

Never mind that for now. McGurrell's plans. He asserted that his warehouse was bound to be given the Admiralty contract for *Scaramouche*, replenishing her stores as soon as she arrived in the river. If necessary, he assured me in a most intimate confidence, he'd even go so far as to tender below cost: this was no bloody occasion to put profit before national honour. Government, he said, had often availed of his services; his name stood good in the highest quarters; competition was afraid of him; he had his patrons, so he had, who'd see him right. Now, as part of those services, wouldn't a case of Old Cherokee Remedy be carried aboard amongst whatever the hell else? and make no doubt, boy, with all the ceremonial tantantara neither steward nor loblolly man would conceivably be checking it bottle by bottle, at least not till the beanfeast was over, and by then – why, by then -   But no further plans without the Stonecold Kate, a vinegar-jane and a crab-louse, but if we weren't to let her in on it, she'd surely tear out our windpipes. You'd go far enough before you'd outsmart that contrary little mot. Not to fetch her to the warehouse, though, too many ears on the floor; but the snug of a pub, the Marlinspike, sure didn't she doss herself in the alley alongside? He'd see me there ten o'clock tonight.

The Marlinspike, from its name, should have been a roaring house for sailormen and the trulls and the crimps and interminable rowdy song, but somehow it had deteriorated into a wretched thieves' kitchen where twos or threes of scabby-faced men bent over their gin in alcoves, whispering closely. McGurrell was at a table with grilled sausages, a hot grog and a dirty corner-boy in a scotch bonnet. They had a racing-paper spread out between them; they seemed to be exchanging tips. When he saw me arrive, he picked up his plate and glass, left the paper with Scotch Bonnet, and nodded to me to follow him. We approached a back room, kept empty for us by the barman. He called out to the latter, "Get her in."

The barman said, "She's in."

To McGurrell's annoyance, so she was – he hated to have anyone know more than he knew – she'd been waiting there for some time, white-faced and sick-looking, but demure as a prebendary's niece, refusing drink (thank God for that), refusing food, demanding we came straight to business.

She had been thinking and muttering and prowling the town all afternoon and prowling the floor of her garret all evening, she had certainly contrived the broadest of broad concepts of how the event should proceed. "You first of all set your timing device for midday the 17th. Himself and his crew'll be all out of the ship be half-eleven, for parade and inspection and march to the Mansion House and Sunday-best duds the lot of 'em. No-one left aboard but a harbour watch, bosun's mate, couple of boys, that's all, none o'the gold lace. Fair chance they'll save their lives, the dynamite's not that extensive, just so it blows us a hole in the hull – sure, that's the only requisite, right? My daddy died in a navy-ship, I don't see me way to be slaughtering him all over again in this one, how do *I* know who'll be in the engine-room?"

McGurrell snorted. He said slaughter of the British Empire, all its lackeys and mercenaries, was the one thing we were here for, never mind their fucking rank ... I wondered how many goes of grog had he already taken? There was an unsteadiness about his jowl, a kind of wobble, not reassuring.

Kitty was derisive. "Christ, yeh haven't thought about it, not at all, have yeh? Amn't I telling yeh, 'tis the gold lace to be slaughtered, and that's it! because that's alone what we could call a Result, an Execution, and the Glory of the Day! Jasus, McGurrell, I wonder are yeh game for it, for all of your wheezing and rant? Never mind the sodding ship, I tell yeh the Deed is for the marble halls of London, Jasus Mary the stately Mansion House, the Bank, the Royal Exchange, at the feet of the Lord Mayor, hurl this Scharhorn's blood an' brains into the *face* o'th'Lord Mayor – but how in shite's name do we get there?"

I said, "Through the back kitchens? Barely likely we'll be sent an invitation for the front hall."

I'd meant it as a sort of joke to ease things with McGurrell: he seemed ready to quarrel with Kitty – was he jealous of her? her ruthlessness, her vigour, the clear way she'd reconnoitred the enterprise? Of course she had shown she knew something more than *he* knew ... To my surprise he took me seriously, his unsteadiness abated.

"Barely likely, boy?" His smile was the crawl of an earwig. "Why so? The Lord Mayor's a char-*acte*r, as popular as all get-out and a democrat to the heels of his feet. To be sure if you prefer that a regular invite's the way to fix it – to be sure, we can see you provided."

He suddenly chose to emit a snatch of song: –

> "For Francey McG's y'r only man
> To find an' give whatever he can,
> Whatever he can, whatever he's got,
> And what's he got? He's got the lot."

Having given off his ditty, he seemed to feel better; he felt able indeed to exult over the pair of us, knowing something that we didn't know: "All I ask for is a day or two, an' a day or two is where we're at, thank God ... Gentleman citizen and lady wife, clothes, hats, julery and a deckle-edge card to declare your boney-fideys. You'll see."

*

In fact we had more than a day or two – at least a week to go before the 17th – much could be *fixed* before then. We might even in the end (God help us) succeed in our hoped-for, our hateful, our exhilarating devil-dance.

It was only a few hours since I'd thrust myself into Kitty's lodging; she said nervously that she guessed she could do herself no harm by bringing me up there again – after all, 'twas only next door? She seemed anxious to show me the room, like a little girl with her school-prize needlework; and indeed there'd been a great change since midday. She'd done a deal more than prowl – she'd tidied, swept, scrubbed and dashed the place with rose-water; empty bottles, dirty linen and so forth were thrust out of sight; a bunch of early primroses sat in a glass on the table. The birch-rod ("for to heat up a certain class o'cockster, don't ask") had been taken down from its hook and put away. However, her Parisian "art-photographs" stayed pinned to the wall, beside some chromo-lithographs of pretty little countryside scenes. There was also, not so comfortable, what she called her "holy picture," Judith and Holofernes: blood on the broadsword: naked corpse without a head: naked murderess adorned with jewels, sliding her gorgeous robe gracefully over her shoulders, while the slavey shoved the head into a bag.

No less gruesome, our chat concerning the Deed. It was clear we must tell McGurrell only enough for him to think he had his hand on the helm, while she and I in private rehearsed our every step as far as we could foresee it, every step, every word, every gesture. This was the room where we'd fix it, she pronounced: she'd manage without *cocksters* for the time being, she'd just enough money put by, and she didn't want to come to my basement, it "made her ashamed," she inexplicably told me.

So. Every evening, that's what we did. I wrote a new card for her door: –

KATEs' PLACE
I'am Not well, <u>keeP away</u>, **fever !** weN I'am BETTER I'll Put the
word out.

Fever indeed: those entire seven days reeked of it. From the moment Kitty and I walked out of the Marlinspike, it had come to me that London was no longer the same city I'd been hitherto aware of in the lamp-lit darkness; now there was a new outline, a new bulk, a livid new sheen upon streets, vehicles, porches, rooftops, towers – the very horses had the look of the painted steeds of a merry-go-round and all the men and women were Mr and Mrs Noah from a toy Ark, repeated over and over again; the only difference was the blood that seemed to fill their eye-sockets and trickle down their cheeks. Not red blood, nor purple, but a slimy sort of green, the glistening dark green of seaweed. I didn't see it in *Kitty's* eyes: hers were now so pale I could barely distinguish the blue-grey from the white, and the pupils were like tiny specks of soot.

(This sickening perspective was to come and go throughout the week, intermittently, unpredictably, for no more than a minute at a time. Not so much an hallucination but the *illusion* of an hallucination.)

I do have to write about this fucking. She'd straitly determined NOT, but that was in the days of dream-it-an'-guess, that was before we knew how we were harnessed irremediably together till the very end. So now she changed her mind, and every night we'd have been at it, except for our preoccupation with the -   It makes me cringe as I write, as I've already cringed. But I'll be candid. It turned out that what she craved for, I was suddenly impotent to give: it turned out that what she *thought* she craved for, she didn't really want. So now every night, after hours and yet more hours of outrageous preparation for the -   Collapse into her bed for immediate sleep, lifeless,

215

wasted, drained. In her dreams she cried out most lamentably, and she told me that I did, too. But whatever my dreams might have been, by morning they'd gone from me, obliterated. Nor throughout that week was I harried, day or night, by the host of my *familiars*. My head was most mercifully quiet. Palinurus alone continued just outside the range of my vision, but happily a great way off, I could no longer hear him *wallow*. I supposed I had at last attained their trust, now that I had absolutely decided to carry out the –

After dark on the 14th, McGurrell called us again to the Marlinspike: he gave me the 'deckle-edge' he'd talked of. Upon its ivory surface, in superlative copperplate, I read that His Worship the Lord Mayor had the pleasure to invite Jabez Fitzgerald Esquire MP, and Guest, to the Mansion House to witness the conferring of the Freedom of the City – *and so on and so forth*. Dress formal.

I was horrified. "But I'm not Jabez Fitzgerald! Godsake, man, it's ridiculous. And they'll see that I'm not, the very minute I walk in on them."

"Ah no they won't, not at all; nobody knows what the silly feller looks like, sure he was only elected last month and he's spending St Patrick's with his family an' constituents in Ballinasloe."

"But 'Dress formal'? How can I possibly – ?"

"Easy now, be easy, didn't I promise you? I did indeed." He handed up two bulky carpet-bags from under the table. "Here's yours, so. And here, Mrs FitzG, will be *yours*. An' take note, please, the both of youse, I want 'em back in spotless condition, as soon as the – as soon as the activity's accomplished ... Don't open them now: you take 'em away and try 'em on in your own good time. No reason to believe, with a smahan o'care, you can't make yourselves look like a back-o'-beyond Home Rule politico and his high-aspiring Galway wife. You'll not have to talk, you'll not have to do anything, except – well, except -   By which token, in the bottom o'them bags you'll find pocket-size revolvers and two lots o'ball-cartridge. You'll need a bit o'practice? this pub has a good cellarage, soundproof, I have it settled with the landlord. Practice-cartridge in the yaller wrappings. Don't use the other till the day, it's extra-special soft-nose, we don't want it wasted."

"Oh yes," he added. "Expenses: five sovs apiece, for cabs and the like, here y'are ... Begod I'd make it more if I could, but they keep a strict check on me finances, know what I mean? New York's nothing better than a nest o' begrudging Shylocks."

The pistol-practice. We neither of us proved good shots; but we swore, were we close enough to smell his breath, we'd have the nerve to aim and hit. I have to write that on St Patrick's Eve, when our last practice was over, the flare and the crack of the cartridges seemed to have breathed its own fire into the exhausted chill between us. There was straw heaped up in that cellar, we came together on it like a pair of weasels, just the once. I have to write, it was a coupling that owed less to the tenderness of love than to the terrific proximity of – But I also have to write that I already knew I was in love with Kitty Furey, profoundly, incurably, for ever and ever. Which does NOT make me cringe, and be damned to you. I can't say if she felt the same about me.

*

On St Patrick's Day at dawn, McGurrell's cart, with McGurrell himself at the reins in a clean collar and a bright tie-pin, and myself beside him (very much the underling), trotted onto Tower Wharf to unload the ship's requirements – wardroom-stores, medical stores, cases of tinned food, coils of yarn, paintbrushes – small items, all of them, but the sort of thing a careful captain will always top-up upon arrival in port – any port, home or foreign: the ship must live. It was a grey, damp, sunless morning; even in the drizzle *Scaramouche* showed herself a lovely little vessel. Routine tasks, washing the decks, polishing brasswork, had already begun; the men joked among themselves about the long night of shore-leave that would follow the day's ceremonial. My job to keep an eye on the working party who'd fetch our gear on board; as I loitered about for them at the foot of the gangway, I caught an unexpected glimpse of the rear-admiral. He appeared upon the quarterdeck beside the officer of the watch, looked around him importantly, and then vanished down a companion ladder. He was but half-dressed, in his shirt-sleeves as a matter of fact, and hatless. He wore pince-nez, and carried a bunch of papers which he shuffled into order as he glanced toward the wharf. I had the impression he was irritated by the untidy pile of stuff from our cart, but he made no comment. He had aged a good deal in eighteen years: fatter and balder than I remembered, and his fancy blond dundrearies were now a square-cut beard, streaked with silver.

It was hard to believe I was looking at a man who should be dead within six hours, whom I wanted to be dead, whom I intended to be dead.

While McGurrell and the ship's paymaster checked invoices, I followed the medical stores below decks, "to make sure there's no jolting: these bottles have been known to effervesce." I saw the crucial packing-case handed down through a hatch to a lazarette at the level of the waterline, exactly where we'd planned for it. Good.

I rode with McGurrell on the empty cart as far as the East India Dock Road, where I left him and sneaked home to change my clothes. We had not spoken about the Deed, not one word, our eyes had not met, we were as nervous as foxes in a barnyard full of dog-stink and snares ...

Ah, but I thought I could sense Palinurus, coming closely in toward me, like mist within the mist.

In my basement I stood stripped and washed my body top-to-toe, I shaved off my beard, I trimmed my rough red moustache to a neat line and darkened it with brown boot-polish, I slicked my rough-cut hair with dollops of macassar oil, I polished my spectacles. The morning suit was not a good fit, but never mind, there'd be crowds all around me to mask any gawkiness; and never mind, I'd not seen myself so nattily togged-out since I came down from university – no, not even then, because

I'd always worn dead black, and now there was a lilac cravat, cream silk waistcoat with sky-blue stripes, a pair of dove-grey trousers, collars and cuffs that'd blind a lurking pickpocket. Altogether too notable for the neighbourhood: I huddled it under muffler, cloth cap and raggedy cloak, and went limping on a cane toward the hospital in the Commercial Road like a down-at-heel outpatient.

I wandered into the casualty waiting-area, and looked around at the sub-fusc collection of habituals, as though vaguely expecting a friend. No-one took notice of me, so I went through into the men's lavatory and made use of a cubicle (maybe I'd not have another chance? was it the last crap of my life? I had to laugh.) I hung my cloak on the peg inside the cubicle door, and left it there. The soft cap went into my trousers pocket – I thought it might prove useful after the - after -   I'd been carrying a shiny topper beneath the cloak: I tucked it under my arm and strolled out by another door into a corridor I'd explored a few days earlier; it led to the side entrance where cabs and carriages drew up. Here I might be taken for some sort of medical man; the doorman indeed saluted me and called me "sir" – did I want a cab? I told him not just yet; and waited, very casual, twirling my cane, hoping he wouldn't see how I twitched and gnawed at my lip.

I need not have feared, for at last, here she was! exactly as arranged, also from inside the hospital, also in improbable new plumage. If I looked like a yellow-press reporter trying to sneak into a society wedding, my Kitty had the air of a delinquent servant-girl in her mistress's clothes, purple skirts dragging the ground, a bustle like a bunch of red cabbages; black bodice far too tight, it might have been the skin of a beetle; short blood-red jacket; snooty little blood-red hat that tottered on a pyramid of braided black hair full of combs. Purple parasol at her wrist. Black hat-feather, black gloves, a black handbag dangling with the parasol in front of her loins. Brooch at her neck, rings on three fingers, tortoiseshell buttons up the side of each boot. She offered me a po-faced bob of a curtsy, I gave her a bow, she took my arm with a sneering attempt at Belgravian hauteur.

I thought McGurrell had made monkeys of us, no doubt at an advantageous discount.

Kitty's snubnosed Yankee pistol was in the handbag, where else? with a message I had written at her dictation round the edge of a playing card, the Queen of Spades: –

> **REVENGE** for <u>**Paschal Furey**</u> RIP, on board the Carausius, an engine-wright
> my lovely daddy, drowned & murdered   + 1868 +<u>Kitty's here</u>

My own pistol lay inside the breast of my cutaway coat. I'd put my brother's photograph into the watch pocket of the waistcoat, my own message on the back of it, thus: –

> **In Memoriam Palinuri Harrington, Midshipman,**
> **HMS Carausius + 1868 +aged 14**
> AVENGED Ah, brother: grandfather: father: all paid at last and shall we meet?

"Now then," says I to the doorman, cool as a glass of champagne. "We are ready for that cab."

As the hansom clip-clopped toward the City, I began to be distressed by dazzle from the sun; we swung into Gracechurch Street and it was glaring at an angle straight into the front of the cab, pretty nigh burning my eyes out – I've already referred to the intermittent oddity of the appearance of things the last few days – this morning it was redoubled; I could not speak of it to Kitty; all I could do was endure it and trust it would not *foozle* me when the moment came to -   Our plan was to enter with the invited guests, to mingle separately with the mob at the buffet, to get as near as we could to the rear-admiral and to -   One from either side of him. We hoped to be able to keep the pistols beneath our napkins and plates, and to drop them privately to the carpet while everyone's attention was seized by the man's collapse. And then we'd shuffle out of it, or we hoped we'd shuffle out of it, or if need be we'd *hurtle* – we'd no choice but wait and see how our destiny was to be carved.

We had the cabby bring us into Eastcheap, near the Monument. We thought it would be prudent not to go direct to Mansion House but to saunter from a distance, our eye upon the dispositions of police. And there did seem to be a great number of police. Almost as though – We were down from the cab and I was fumbling for the fare, when Kitty touched me quickly on the wrist: "Pay him and walk straight into the archway," she hissed. I didn't know what she had seen, but her voice was tense; something wrong; I must be casual, cool, do what she said, no panic –

"Keep the change."

"Thanks, guv'nor, y're a toff ... 'morning t'yer."

"Cheerio."

Whip cracked, hansom away with a whinny from the horse. Pavement middling full of sunshine. London about its business. Kitty out-of-sight entirely until I saw a gloved hand and a parasol behind a pillar four yards away. I stepped sideways into the same shelter, we might have been two sweethearts taking time off to kiss, so we kissed and I peered past the edge of her veil. Over there at the top of Fish Street was the entry to the Underground: a squad of bluebottles, sweating in their heavy uniforms, moustachioed like Turks, came running up the steps from the station – oh, oh, as it were from the smoke-hole of Tophet, didn't I tell you already, "Tophet"? A number of them had arrived already and were being deployed around the area by some sort of plain-clothes trap, very busy in the midst of them, pointing with his walking-stick, gesturing them to their posts at every corner of the open space where all those streets meet at the north end of London Bridge. He was a long, lean, lip-curling hardcase, with an ulster down to his ankles, and a flat-top felt hat.

Kitty clutched me close, she was trying to speak calmly, she was shuddering with fear. "That man," she quavered, "there, with the stick; oh God, Jack, Scotland Yard, chief inspector is the least of it; why, look, he is *in charge*. Would that be why he begrimed himself to sit in a scotch bonnet with McGurrell in the Marlinspike?"

"Oh Kitty, so he did. Oh Kitty, I think we're dead." Staring at the man, my eyes hot and watery, I lost him for a moment in the dazzle; when I looked again he had crossed over into King William Street and was bustling some of his men in that direction.

Her face drained of all its colour, Kitty nonetheless *recaptured* herself; her words were the flick of a whip. "Round the little side streets, so. Before he can see us. One way for you, another for me, we'll meet at the buffet."

God, she was quick but we'd no time to spare; and I was sure she was quite right: we had but the one chance, to be in there before we were recognized, which was to say before Scotch Bonnet arrived at the Mansion House. He seemed to find his crushers slow to comprehend what he needed. He seemed to be reviling them ... I wonder, now, how confident were you all at the Yard, that McGurrell knew as much as he'd been paid for? He'd never have wished to admit that a pair of louche amateurs could run away with the heart of his outfit? Well, we had: and we meant to *stay* away: we were resolute and bloody hungry: we were sharks in a lagoon full of the tentacles of questing squid.

We hurried into Cannon Street station, merged with the railway crowd in and out of the booking office, separated, strolled away from the station and made our ways to the Mansion House, dodging through back entries and unfrequented courts: myself to the west behind Bow Lane across Cheapside to Gresham Street, while Kitty struck up the alleyways between Walbrook and St Swithin's Lane. McGurrell was bound to have notified our clothes to the Yard. But he hadn't known I would lose the beard (and now the spectacles, into my pocket; although that trick made its own problems); neither could he foresee that Kitty would come upon a queer little allsorts stall at the railway station, would affect to break her parasol and replace it with another one of very different appearance – white and gold instead of purple.

It took me ages (or it seemed ages) to get where I needed to go – every street-end and court's corner was shadowed by the traps – but absolutely they seemed not to see me – almost a miracle, invisibility like Simon Peter in flight from King Herod's gaol – at all events I dodged them.

But when at last I reached the Bank, half-blind with the sweat running into my eyes, how the devil was I going to find Kitty? For the sunshine no less than the Deed commanded her to open her parasol – as indeed with all the fine ladies that morning – nothing to be seen in front of the Mansion House but a flowerbed of these bright twirling folderols interspersed with tall hats – fringes and brims hid nearly every face – amid such an outdoor throng, police descriptions must be hopeless ... Rozzers nonetheless everywhere, nodding, conferring, glowering, their helmets like clusters of ninepins.

I had not expected how much of a to-do was to be made by the city fathers, a royal wedding might have been more modest. Did they deliberately honour a vigorous naval officer as a show of disdain for Gladstone's Egyptian dithering?

So. The chief part of the ceremony would take place in the street, ostentatiously spread with red carpet, as were the steps to the Mansion House portico. Red ropes in all directions. Flunkeys in knee-breeches. Lines of redcoat soldiers along the edge of every pavement to hold back the crowds – City of London Volunteer Battalion (somebody said), and already I could hear the rattle and heart-catching squeal of their drum-and-fife band on its way from Tower Wharf – any minute, the parade would be on top of us, and oh where was Kitty? If she'd missed me, she'd never get in among the nobs, there was only the one invitation and I had it ... And that's when it fell like a guillotine: they didn't need to *recognize* us! the invitation was a snare, McGurrell's most treacherous snare! no Fitzgeralds could make themselves known within a half-mile of Mansion House without the darbies on their wrists incontinent. I'd thought of it almost too late, would Kitty think of it? of course she would ... But where *was* she?

(You might say, by the by, that the proofs of McGurrell's double-dealing were not conclusive. Oh but they *were*, though. Had you seen those two in the Marlinspike, head-to-head with their whispering grins ... Don't waste my time.)

The last stragglers of the Lord Mayor's guests were shuffling up the steps at the west end of the Mansion House portico.

Could I see or couldn't I, inside the pillars, the helmets of a couple of rozzers next to a flunkey's powdered head? were they checking invitations? my eyes so hot and wet, such blinking and squinting. No good.

The plan was lost. And where was Kitty, where? She was lost, I was lost, finished.

Drums and fifes at that desolate moment came swaggering in from Cornhill to the tune of 'Heart of Oak', the music almost drowned by cheers. Behind the band, the crew of the *Scaramouche*, blue jackets, white bell-bottoms, wide straw hats and cutlasses, marching in fours. Behind the sailors, two four-horse open carriages, full of ladies with parasols, and nodding cocked hats. One of the hats was Scharhorn's, lifted from his genial head as he bowed right and left to the citizens. I noticed he was no longer wearing his pince-nez. I noticed it even though the whole scene slid in and out of focus, as though a telescope were unaccountably lengthened and shortened. The band played 'Rule Britannia' and counter-marched in front of where I stood, at the corner of the Bank. The sailors wheeled round the little square and came to a halt. They were drilled into two ranks for the carriages to be brought up between them, facing the entry to the Mansion House forecourt.

The ladies were handed out, followed by the *Scaramouche* officers, and finally by Scharhorn. They looked about them and beamed with pleasure. A stately little group, the Lord Mayor and his aldermen, had descended from the east end of the portico and came forward to greet them. I saw as it were in a dizzying flicker of light, a mace and a huge sword, scarlet robes and gold chains, a man in a fur cap. The Lord Mayor took off his cocked hat and said something inaudible to Scharhorn. Scharhorn, having replaced his own hat, doffed it again and said something to the Lord Mayor. There was a scroll of parchment, and a bunch of huge keys on a cushion. The drums and fifes had stamped to a halt; they began to play 'God Save the Queen' ...

Could I aim, fire, and hit, from where I was? Ah no! my useless eyes, and far too far away, far too many in between. Ah no, an army marksman I daresay might have done it, or one of those Texas pistoleros, but -   Was it possible I could wait till he'd been into the Mansion House and out again? But I'd have to wait for hours, unless I -   Where could I lurk and avoid suspicion? I peered about me in all directions: to my left, across Threadneedle Street, in front of the Royal Exchange, I saw a framework of scaffolding round the plinth of a great statue of some marauder on a horse, cleaning or repairs, no doubt: but its height now overflowed with jingo tumult, young hooligans waving bottles and flags. I saw first one peeler and then another, and then several, make an unsuccessful effort (from a distance) to order them down. Maybe, if I got myself in behind that plinth, I could -   From in behind that plinth came Kitty Furey at full speed.

She had hoicked up her skirts into the waistband of her frowsty pantaloons, and she ran like a rat, dodging soldiers and traps left and right.

Her hat had come unpinned and her hair flew out behind her. She had lost the parasol. She had kicked off her high-heeled boots and ran in her stockings, swinging her handbag from right wrist to left hand; she plunged her right hand into it and brought up the pistol. Ceremonial soldiers, ceremonial sailors, were baffled by their own discipline – could they break ranks and snatch her? at any rate they didn't – and the peelers had been so busy with the louts on the plinth that they'd missed her until too late. But *I* was not too late, *I* could get to Scharhorn even before *she* did, support her, reinforce her, prove to her that I was *there*, my God I was her own true love and my pistol was - I fumbled for it in my coat and took one great stride forward, my toecap tripped the edge of that damnable red carpet, I staggered and would have saved myself but for a cast-iron bloody bollard that caught me on the inside of my left thigh.

Intolerable pain, through the muscles of the groin, or the sinews of the hip-joint, or the strings of the testicles, or heaven knows where – and it paralysed me the way they say the electrical light will paralyse if you pry into its apertures. It was all I could do to pull myself straight and keep standing, one leg and a cane and the second leg a damned redundancy that folded up beneath me.

> *of Murder and no Murder: a Wraith*
> Finding out how to fuck
> I found instead I could kill
> But my foot told me no, and I fell.
> Was it only ill luck
> Or a conscience in ruin
> That so flailed at my loin and my groin?

As for Kitty – nothing at all, so it seemed, between her floundering, pounding heart and the atrocity of REVENGE – her disorder and haste, the beast-like roar of her exertion, tore apart the solemn stillness enforced by the national anthem – I saw her as close to Scharhorn's medal-plastered breast as a woodcutter to a tree-trunk – she pointed her pistol and –

Nothing. She pulled the trigger again, again: nothing. It was not possible: one chamber after another of a well-tested weapon missing fire and by *accident*?

Not possible? *Of course* possible, no accident neither. For who gave us the cartridges? and who else could have tampered with the "extra-special soft-nose"? (To prise bullets out of the casings, pour away powder, jam the bullets in again?) Of course McGurrell had tampered: would the Yard have permitted otherwise? And some interfering entity, Lord of Hosts, Prince of Peace, must have stolen our wits, or else why did we not suspect? Practice-cartridges had worked perfectly, why *should* we suspect? My own pistol just the same, *must* have been just the same, no point in even trying it.

Scharhorn and all those near him stood like window-dressers' dummies, staring blankly at this madwoman and her gun with nothing in it, all too swift, all too silly, all too *pointless* for immediate fear, until they saw -   No doubt you will think that what I say *I* saw was the result of my eyesight, already that morning confounding the process of thought. Think what you want: I shall tell. I saw the shape of Paschal Furey drift softly round from the side, to whisk the pistol out of her gloved hand, and (all in one movement) put into her hand something else – something that glittered, small, sharp, silvery-green – she hurled herself against Scharhorn, she drove it at his neck. It was a shard of broken bottle: it should have caught the jugular and he ought to have died of it, blood flooding everywhere. Instead, it clove the thick gold lace of the high collar of his full-dress uniform, slipped upwards and stuck. It tore his cheek, a two-inch gash, spurting and appallingly sudden, but no worse. He cried out and recoiled against the door of the carriage, she dropped the shard and *she* recoiled, both of them in a state of shock ... She'd said to me, *not with a knife.*

D'you insist, being policemen, that she'd had it all the time in her handbag? d'you insist you had reason (there and then) to believe she was very likely hiding further items in the handbag, her reserve armoury? a poisoned knitting needle, a phial of vitriol? And action had to be taken in accordance with that belief? So. Argue as you wish: I have told.

She recoiled; she looked around her; she stood weaponless, waiting; she nervously plucked at her skirts to restore her decency; from where I stood, I couldn't see her eyes.

Scotch Bonnet came loping toward her over the flagstones out of Mansion House Place: he held a short-barrelled repeating carbine under his right elbow. He fired it as he moved, one bullet after another, slamming the trigger-guard down-and-up to reload. By the time he got to her, she was spreadeagled on her back across the carpet, every limb of her in spasms with the force of her destruction – an old sailmaker showed me once a voodoo-doll from Madagascar; ah! that was her, a bunch of rags, purple and red, spikes of pitch-black horsehair, straw.

Around the bewildered Scharhorn the city fathers, the fighting-men, the subordinate citizens, the lackeys, ran together from all sides in a loud-lamenting vortex. The only one of them to go toward Kitty was her killer; he made sure she was dead, took a cape from a constable, covered her face. As he did so, his eyes travelled, looking everywhere for me or for somebody like me. (Oh yes, and one of his bullets must have hit one of the Lord Mayor's footmen, the poor fellow had fallen screaming among the hoofs and the dung of the carriage-horses, nobody took much notice, he'd have to wait his turn.)

Palinurus, on my shoulder, was purring into my ear a strange and soothing rhyme:

> _Last Wraith of All._
> Pious Aeneas, time to go;
> Queen Dido your love is dead.
> You must leave her, heart and head,
> The poet says so – go, go, go.

*

With that shameful gelded handgun untouched inside my coat, I replaced my spectacles, pulled my hat over my brow and hobbled away along Poultry amid a whole crush of people doing their best to get out of danger. Bluebottles in quantity were coming the other way. Yelping and barking; the clatter of their feet like coal off a tilted tumbrel. I saw a back entry and immediately went in; I held on to a window sill to fetch a series of belly-wrenching sobs, until at last with a deep breath I dredged up my reason from wherever it had sunk. I was among dustbins in a sordid recess, out-of-sight from the street. I changed my hat for the cloth cap, and dropped both hat and pistol into a bin. I took off the cutaway coat and dropped it into the bin, together with collar and cravat. I thrust my hands into the bin for ashes and general muck, I smeared myself all over, clothes and skin. At a superficial glance, I was a drink-sodden derelict, a type not looked at closely, not even by the crushers: so I hoped.

I was moving with difficulty, but as fast as I could, toward Cannon Street station once again – I didn't know what I'd do when I got there – just to keep myself enclosed in the thick of the multitude, as already that morning, how long ago? surely hours and hours ago? in fact, I'd say, scarce twenty minutes.

At the station the surge of the crowd was toward the Underground, so I followed, flung out my money for a destination as far away as I could think (Hammersmith, was it?) and stumbled down steps to a platform. Tophet. A train was just then arriving: the sulphurous reek, the roar like an avalanche, the agonized whistling, the cinders and soot from the chimney. I had no time to see the direction-board, whichever way it went would be *my* way, I dragged open the door of a compartment and threw myself inside with maybe a dozen others. An astonished passenger, already there and ignorant of the homicide above ground, told me it was the Circle Line, anti-clockwise: he himself was going to King's Cross and what on earth was the matter with everyone?

I let the others inform him. My brain all the morning had been working like a pile-driver; now it gave up altogether. The bloody mask of Kitty Furey (that man's vindictive bullets had smashed into her forehead and face) merged with the swollen features of my long-drowned *familiars*, all of them back again as horrible as ever they were, cramming the death-black tunnel as the train rocked and bellowed upon the curves.

I was actually carried right round the Underground system two-and-a-half times before I began to comprehend where I was. On the third circuit, at Mark Lane, nearest station to the Tower, a pair of bric-à-brac vendors climbed in. They were on their way to the Portobello Road, all agog because of the bomb that had gone off – or rather, had *not* gone off – in the bowels of the *Scaramouche*. "A smoke an' a sizzle, that was all; piss-poor dynamite, the feller was saying, or else – what'd he term it? – flawed linkage at the detonator? But they'd called out three fire-engines an' all the tommies o' the Tower garrison, how's that for a game of sojers?" They had heard only obliquely of what happened at the Mansion House: I let others in the carriage inform them.

What was I to do? Where to go? Where *could* I go? *How?* I had no money in the wide world beyond McGurrell's five sovereigns, less the cab fare from the Commercial Road and the fare for the Underground (and in neither case had I waited for change) – I couldn't go back to East India Dock Road, or to anywhere else where McGurrell might have posted the news. My family? No good. Any clergymen, ex-colleagues? I knew several, but they'd certainly turn me in. Old friends from school, or Cambridge? I never *had* any friends, at school or at -   No! wait, there was Wadsworth, he and I once read poetry together; Browning, was it not? in his rooms in Sidney Sussex College ... Hadn't I heard he was now a solicitor with a prosperous practice? and he lived, I was almost sure of it, in Westbourne Terrace. Old Billy Wadsworth, such a very sanguine lad and a liberal and almost a socialist, at least he would know what to do ... Praed Street was the nearest station. I would find Billy's house; if he wasn't at home, I would sit on his doorstep till he was. Get out at Praed Street.

* * * * * *

At this point, Jack Nee stopped writing. He sat staring for a few minutes and then swept all the finished pages off the table with one swing of his arm. The inkwell went too and made a splatter over walls and floor and the lap of the detective sitting in the corner. Nee said, "Get out at Praed Street." He said it quietly, over and over, staring motionless at the wall-tiles in a trance of stupefaction. There was nothing more they could do with him.

Apart from his interminable Statement, and apart from an earlier report by McGurrell, all they knew of him for certain was that on the afternoon of St Patrick's Day he had just reached the top of the stairs of Praed Street station, and was about to stagger through the booking office into the street, when the infernal machine exploded.

It was a dynamite bomb, wrapped up in an old sack, and hidden in a rubbish bin a few feet away from the ticket window. Detectives were sure it had nothing to do with McGurrell, whose activities (as overseen by Special Branch) were confined to the East End and the river. McGurrell had in fact warned his handler at the Yard that Irish-American Skirmishers might soon be expected in Britain: probably this bomb should be at-

tributed to them. In fact it soon proved to be the first of a series that terrified the public, though by no means as decisively as the Brotherhood must have hoped.

When the grotesquely mutilated Nee was eventually discharged from hospital, detectives had thought he might give clues as to how to catch the Skirmishers – if not, he would in any event present what might be called an authentic foot-soldier's-view of the Brotherhood – not at all the same thing as venal informations from the likes of McGurrell. So they'd allowed him full scope to write what he needed to write, whereby, to be sure, he admitted his crimes, but otherwise – chaotic hotchpotch! unbalanced and worthless fantasia. Indeed, if it were to be accepted as a true bill, it would make nonsense of the very raison-d'être of the fledgling Branch and its carefully nurtured picture of an implacably efficient transatlantic conspiracy; the press would only mock, and government curtail the huge new security budget.

In the end it was decided that Nee was unfit to plead, by reason of mental incapacity. His identity moreover was not at all clear.

The Harrington family denied all knowledge of him – although they agreed there was at one time a young man, Aeneas, deacon of the Established Church – they understood him to have abandoned his ministry to cavort abroad (the West Indies, they thought) with a sect, or sensual cult, half-pagan, half-popish, inimical to English religion. How could a true Harrington recognize the kinship of such an apostate?

William Wadsworth, solicitor, insisted he could remember no Harrington, at Cambridge or anywhere else, nor had he ever had dealings with anyone called Aeneas. Appalled to have been even mentioned in a dynamitard's deposition, he threatened the police with an action for criminal libel.

Grace Plaistow, cookshop proprietress, spun a reel of improbable yarns, tragic, romantic, obscene, regarding men called Nee or Harrington and the woman known as 'Irish' Kate: however, she was under indictment for running a disorderly house and she obviously sought to obstruct police enquiries.

Jack Nee was committed to Broadmoor: he had blown up nobody and shot nobody, but his alleged memories were so wild it was judged safer (in the public interest) to keep him out of harm's way for as long as was convenient. He seems to have died in confinement.

Part 3:

Yorkshire

LIZARD UPON TWO LEGS

The Yorkshireman Silas Oldroyd, "a good old-fashioned news-paperman" (as he liked to describe himself), was haunted for years by an indefatigable parasite, an inherited proprietorial critic-cum-admirer-cum-collaborator, who refused to leave him alone. The creative skill of such a fellow was to occupy a vacant space in a writer's imagination and contrive to make it his own – it didn't matter what sort of writer, or of what quality, the thing was to hold on tight until something some-how came of it, like a boil breaking out through the skin. Not that Silas's imagination had ever amounted to much: he was a literal-minded stick-in-the-mud, but he nonetheless came to fear that his uncovenanted praise-singer, upright indeed upon two legs and adopting the shape of a man, was in reality a spe-cies of extra-terrestial **lizard**, telepathically wished onto him by the bitter contrariness of his dead father, or his dead mother, or both, for no other reason than to wither his unconfident spirit. As he had always taken pride in his northern good sense, it disgusted him to entertain so irrational an obsession: he kept it secret from everyone, he hid it deep inside his breast like a murderer's guilt.

From the mid-1950s through the '60s and into the '80s, Silas followed his trade in the coal-and-steel districts of his native county. He styled himself 'Spike,' a desktop moniker redolent of a rugged or cynical sincerity. Each week he contributed his brisk little items to **The Barnsley Chronicle, The Sheffield Star** and **The Dearne & Don Intelligencer**, until the editorship of the **Intelligencer** fell vacant and he exerted himself so far as to apply for it. They gave it him without question; his unadven-turous competence was exactly what was required for a wary twelve-page tabloid full of small ads, football, cricket, bowl-ing, colliers' weddings, racing tips, and a sordid substratum of

*police news. Most of the latter dealt with violent assault in
alleyways behind public houses. He coped with the job pretty
well, although it was without doubt a depressing routine. As
he said often enough, his work was "nowt if not realistic ... a
man must live in the real world."*

*In his later years, having moved to Ireland to attempt the
unlikely lifestyle of a serious novelist, he would expand upon
this theme.*

"My dad, d'you see, never did live in the real world. Wouldn't
live in it, ever. Took one look and left it. Abandoned it, no nonsense. Or rather, you could say, the real world abandoned him,
ran away from him, pushed him out into the dark. He was a
genius, the arrogant old bastard, and my mum, d'you see, was
mad. Don't misunderstand me. When I say 'genius,' I don't
mean Shakespeare, I don't mean honoured all over the world,
Nobel Prize and all the rest of it. Bloody hell, no. He was a
schoolmaster, and a bilious one (don't I know it, I was in his
class), but nonetheless he wrote these books, 'story-books,' he
used to call 'em, worked hard to get 'em published by a hand-to-
mouth firm in Leeds; to begin with he'd to pay for 'em from his
own pocket, so I'm told, I was only a lad at the time. Aye, but I
do insist they were marvellous books in their way – regionally,
of course: language and allusions were indeed highly regional, nonetheless a bit too offbeat for the region, yet not offbeat
enough for the Soho modernists. That's to say, most of the
books: there was one exception, a story that -   No, but that
story's quite another story. No, if I was pushed to it, I'd say his
stuff was a mix between Thomas Hardy gone northern, Gerard
Manley Hopkins and Leland's *Itineraries.* He liked to describe
himself as a topographical poet or a poetic topographer, min-
gling fiction with folklore with irregular verses with local history with – well, with – not to put a tooth in it, he called it 'a
healthy eroticism,' his prig of a publisher called it 'smut,' and
finally broke relations with him after the last book was hauled
off to be burnt by the Huddersfield vice-squad – that one did
have an eventual big sale, because he reissued it as a *samizdat*
duplicated typescript and sold it by post or from the boot of his

motor-car and this time the cops didn't notice, or they turned a blind eye – we were well into the '60s by then, Lady Chatterley set free without a stain on her character or even on her knickers, the dear woman … Talking of women – "

At this point, if he was sitting at his usual fireside in the snug of a Galway tavern amidst a boozy middle-aged crew of Connacht literati (solicitors, newspaper stringers, auctioneers, insurance reps, the odd bank manager or teacher or doctor), he would leer through the tobacco smoke and extrude one of his pungent anecdotes, some recollection, perhaps, of old adultery or bigamy or incestuous buggery as originally reported in the **Dearne & Don Intelligencer** *in the days when "a certain posture" or "an intimate activity" were the nearest a reporter could get to "the sweaty naked hairy truth of our vile and human condition," – such were his growling adjectives as he slurped his whiskey and smacked his hands, all mottled with liver-spots, palms-down onto the table to mark his peroration. Most of the men present would have heard his tales before, but they were content to endure them again because then they could cap them with efforts of their own, and the bawdy bravura of competitive narrative would continue for hours. As a rule he failed to notice that the whiskey and good company had allowed him to digress from what he'd intended to say – sometimes, indeed, he did remember and then he'd force the conversation back with an angry twist of his shoulders and a deep catarrhal bark at the back of his adam's apple:*

"I *was* about to say that talking of women brings me inevitably to the memory of my dear mother. Miranda Silkston, political cartoonist for a whole range of way-out lefty journals. When I call her mad I do not of course mean she was certifiable into a looneybin: rather, like so many English girls of her generation, she had become disorganized, disorientated, by the abrupt reconstructions undergone by her sex; she'd have been born, as I calculate, the very August of '14 upon the outbreak of war; her earliest recollections of her own mother must have been of a strange khaki figure, girded and swathed in a long-skirted uniform, under a scout-hat cocked at one side – a female Jehu, as it were, terrorizing the roads of Britain at the wheel of a military truck. Oh aye, I've seen a photo. And after the war, with her newly-acquired vote and your Irish rebellion and the unemployment and the General Strike, this khaki-clad termagant became a surrogate Britannia, damning the proletariat for its unpatriotic recalcitrance, crying hurrah for the Black-and-Tans and getting herself appointed to the magisterial bench in Doncaster, where she sent trade-unionists to prison in a fervour of angry triumph. Eh, bloody hell, my grandma! – I tell you she terrified.

"So it's therefore no surprise that Miranda turned out a communist. But here comes the madness. She was not only a frantic hater of the likes of her own mum but she refused to be bossed around by Karl Marx, whose doctrine, she believed, was marred by an obscure and complicated flaw which she was always on the point of definitively exposing. As a result she could never accept the party line upon any question whatever until it was first examined and analysed in relation to this suppositional flaw; she lost her rag with them in '39 over the Hitler-Stalin pact, so they slung her out, so she joined a gang of Trotskyists and *they* slung her out, so she formed her own outfit – she called it the People's Progressive Revolutionary Tendency (PPRT) – someone in the mainstream Left derided it as the Pan-Pennine Roughage Tract and the nickname stayed with her. But she was a big strong Doncaster lass and stood no nonsense from nobody. Neither did my dad. He'd married her because she was what she was and she'd married him for ditto. She ran her little tendency from our cottage in Craven of Airedale and held its crosspatch meetings of three or four fanatics in the hall of the Skipton grammar school where dad taught English and History – until the school governors discovered what she was up to and – aye, right, they played merry hell with poor old dad and they slung her out, what else?

"I should say that at that school, while I suffered not only the regular schoolboy angst but also a very marked strategy of parental non-favouritism, I did manage to imbibe a damn fine old-English education. None of your Labour Party comprehensive-school rubbish, let me tell you, if you know here in Ireland what that means. You'd best just hope you never do know. I should say that not long after leaving that school I was suddenly persuaded I had to become a writer. Now, it absolutely wasn't my dad that convinced me, rather it was -   Oh it don't rightly matter who it was, but I made up my mind: journalism, novel-writing, poetry (would you believe?), and I've never looked back."

By the early 1990s he thought he might finally be rid of the lizard-thing; he still wouldn't talk about it; even to think of the whole sorry story (and how it ended) made him deeply ashamed. If he seemed to be edging too close, by way of excessive chat about his upbringing, for example, he'd shy away directly and shut up. And then, unexpectedly, he took up with a warm-hearted German who owned a New Age craft-shop in Galway city; alone with her in bed, amidst the mingled odours of sweet herbs and gratified sexuality, he simply yearned to tell his tale and no evasion. Such a wonderful confiding friend, this big blonde Ute with the round white arms, even more of a friend than a lover: she listened to him, every word.

"Fact is, love, I have to tell you, d'you know I've never talked like this to anyone, not truly having had the chance since -   Aye, in my mid-teens, my very first days on the *Chronicle*, there was this long-leggéd girl, Sal Pethybridge, editor's secretary, oh I'd talk to her allright, no end to it, and a sight more than talk – she was three or four years older than me, and she and I, we used to -   That's to say, she used to, I was too young to instigate owt of it – if she danced I crept, if she hollered I chuckled – aye but I was chuckling every delicious inch of my skin.   Like, she lived the 1960s when the 50s were still with us, that's hindsight. But as soon as she got a chance to get wed, why, she took it – and all of a sudden she was Mrs Len Hopwood with a bloody great diamond ring and a bloody great pram with a sweet little kid in it that was quite likely mine, d'you know, but I didn't dare ask. Hindsight again ...

"Never since then, my love, never since my lovely Sal, until now: and it's better than ever it was, now, today, tonight – for all my grey hairs and whatever's gone wrong with my right leg's circulation.

"Fact is, I have to tell you. It all began with Sal and it damn near made a muck of me, at least until ten years ago. The lizard. I have to tell you. It was a gorgeous day in May, and me and Sal had taken the bus ten miles and more to the top of the moors west of Penistone; there was no question yet of another man's wedding-ring; we lay among the heather in a bit of a ravine, bare as penny whistles, in and out of this little beck, brook, rill, cool rocky torrent hidden by the young bracken and a handful of wind-stunted trees, the sun flaring down at us fit to broil us like rashers – you might say we took a risk, there'd be hikers galore on the moors at the weekend, but it wasn't the weekend, it was Thursday and the *Chronicle* went to press on Wednesday, we had our weekend midweek and nobody to trouble us – so we thought.

"We'd brought a bottle of wine and ham-sandwiches in Sal's haversack and there we were, munching and drinking, and all of a sudden there he was, stood on a boulder over against us, propped elegantly upon his walking-stick, peering steadily right at us through very narrow eyelids like the Lord God in paradise garden on the watch for naughty apple-cores. Sal gave a squeak and ripped off her headscarf to cover herself, as well as she could with so frivolous a fragment. Me, I was shocked speechless. I'd the haversack on my lap and I damn well kept it there.

"He spoke. A dry, harsh, quiet croaking in an accent I couldn't quite place – it might have been Scots, it might have been Irish – a certain blur to his articulation, it might have been from drink. 'Bear with me,' said he. 'I'm not here to spy; mere chance I climbed the bank; what a fair, golden picture you make in this incomparable sunshine. But young man, I have seen you before; you are son of the poet Oldroyd, from up beyond Skipton. D'you live now in these parts?'"

"I stammered something about Barnsley, temporary place of work, lodgings away from home, my dad had thought it best, only temporary, perhaps, but -   He nodded understandingly, swayed a little on his feet, gave the impression of a man who was about to sit down for a prolonged and easy chat. But Sal wasn't having any. She swore at him, she ordered him off without waste of time. He tipped his hat, turned aside, walked a few paces, stood still with his back to us and piddled against a rock. Then he departed, silently, *fluidly*; but of course he had spoiled our day. Sal swore at me for being so feeble as to reply to his 'fucking sauce.' He was some sort of pervert, she proclaimed: and I ought to have known it. We got dressed and packed up; as we did so, a small cloud came over the sun and the afternoon felt suddenly chill.

"It's necessary I describe him, it occurs to me you might meet him, one o' these days: eh dear, it's not impossible. Some folk think he's dead, others aren't so certain. Anyroad, if he comes, you should know that it's him, get clear before it's too late. At that time – he might have been no more than twenty-nine, thirty – he was already lizard-like but had yet to develop his mature characteristics. His moustache, for example, was no more than a tight little line of blond bristles, all but invisible in certain lights. No sign of his subsequent baldness: every hair was in place, trimmed very short and carefully combed. His clothes were precise; but curiously *off*, for a day's bog-trotting – a well-fitting straw-coloured linen suit – it'd have looked well in a Singapore finance-house – paisley-pattern cravat, panama hat. His beak of a nose was prominent indeed for a man of such short stature, his cheekbones hard and ominous, his eyes so desperate pale you could say they were colourless, and he never seemed to blink – everybody blinks a little – not this one. Teeth: he had too many teeth. And a twist to his shoulders you couldn't put a name to: not exactly a deformity, more of a habitual posture indicating – what? just his damned curiosity as to who might be round the next corner, if you understand me?"

Ute shifted her position in the bed – she had a cramp in one arm, she had lain too long holding him while he rolled and tossed and gesticulated with the force of his narration. She

*suggested, as tactfully as she could, that if this tale was to go
on for any considerable time, he ought to bear in mind she had
a living to earn, a shop to look after, she needed to be up every
morning before six. Why would he not write it all out for her?
He was always complaining that he could not settle down to
serious literary work, here was his opportunity, no?*

*He grumbled and grouched for a while, but she sweetened
him with her hands and her tongue and her lips; at length he
agreed; he set himself to sleep in good comfort beside her, running over the essentials of the story in his mind, at first while
still awake, recollection at full power, and then in the moist
warmth of his dreams. Next day at sunrise, when Ute went
downstairs to her shop, he ignored the breakfast she'd left for
him and made haste to his rooms in the Bowling Green. Without reflection, he began to type. To begin, he summarized what
he'd already told her. Then he kept right on going, into what
might (if he was lucky and the strain of memory held) become
a regular Chapter Two. After the manner of his father, he seasoned the prose with slivers of verse – useful springboards, he
found, for his flights of imagination.*

*

So now instead of speak I write to spread my rage and pain
All over paper; read it and think and read it all over again
To chew up my life in midst of my food and drink
Till down it goes *out!* and shot down the drain.

It may well be that much of what follows doesn't altogether
hang together, that I ought to have asked a few questions, investigated phenomena, behaved (in short) like a man of sense.

I couldn't, I can't
I just didn't want.
Didn't even try
Don't know why.
No, I don't lie.

Lizard indeed, that fellow was, and no I don't lie, he slid and he crept and he sprang: no more than a week later he's suddenly at my elbow when I'm out on my cub-reporter's beat. I'm awkwardly trying to interview the witnesses of a traffic accident just outside the *Chronicle* offices. A milk float's been hit in the solar plexus by a youth on a motorbike; the milkman sitting in shock on the curb, moaning over and over, "Eh but they'll murder me back at t'Co-op, there's fifty gallon spilt if there's a pint ... eh but they'll murder me ... *murder.*" The leather-clad biker lies prostrate, unconscious; he's been flung right through the milk float and all its load; his legs and arms spread out like a starfish, his face in a great puddle of milk and broken bottle-glass, it's slowly turning pink with his blood. A policeman, also in leathers and fresh from his own motorbike, is noting bystanders' names and tetchily keeping them away from the injured rider: "There's an ambulance been called for," he reiterates. "It's proper procedure never to touch the victim 'cept to cover him with a blanket if conceivable and I don't see no blanket – does anyone have a blanket? Nobody? Allright then. Move along ... There's an ambulance been called for ... (*etcetera.*)"

A sudden waft of whisky into my nostrils. Lizard-man is grating, blurred voice amongst hiccups, into my ear, "Gup. Surely good practice to borrow an overcoat. Why, gup, why don't somebody lend him an overcoat?" I turn and look at him; not at all surprised to see him; even now I can't say why. The day is cold for early summer, east wind without sunshine, but he himself wears no overcoat, only a scarf around his neck; he's changed his linen suit for brown tweed, his panama is still in-situ. Whereas I'm in a duffel coat, snazzy, flashy, sharp, damned stylish for the time and place: wooden pegs instead of buttons. I take what I assume to be his hint and drape it over the biker. Sheepish enough about it, I'm sure: I feel I've been somehow caught out.

And then I saw Sal. She was flattening her nose on the inside of the upstairs window of the *Chronicle*, with L. Hopwood, editor, unnecessarily close beside her. Lizard-man tipped his hat to her, gave her a hiccup and a show of his teeth; she took a great deal of umbrage and abruptly withdrew herself. (Nor did she speak to *me* for the rest of that day; I told her it wasn't my fault, but what the hell? these things are like that.) Lizard-man slipped away, somehow lost to sight behind the constable's bulky shoulders.

August was the next time I saw him. It was Barnsley Feast Week, the public holiday, when crowds of raucous families went off by excursion train to Blackpool or Cleethorpes: *my* train, by contrast, was very dull and ordinary, it took me into Craven to visit the parents. Not because I wanted to: but I'd nowhere else to go and no spare money to go with and Sal was turning cold on me. The bus from Skipton station brought me to the bottom of the lane where I could see our old grey cottage and its bit of a barn perched on the hillside, with the rough green field below it that we called a front garden. It was about half-past one, nearly time for Saturday dinner. There were three deck-chairs in the garden, two of them empty. One of them bore the slender thighs of Lizard-man. I walked up that lane in a state of trepidation. I damn nearly turned right round and went back to the bus-stop. Except there'd be no bus till nigh on teatime and I needed some lunch.

As I opened the gate, Miranda came out of the house with a tray of glasses, brandy bottle, soda water and so forth: saw me and waved, beckoning me in. Lizard-man looked up: saw me and tipped his panama. Dad came out of the house: saw me and went back in again.

Miranda said, "Sit down, love. Your dad can bring his own chair. Supposing he wants to join us; I don't know; I didn't ask him. This is Mr Lee McStarna, Chicago."

"Los Angeles, ma'am, currently. I was reared in Chicago."

"All one and the same: McCarthy and his goons spread a wide shadow everywhere, don't try to deny it."

"Ah, no no, Miranda, bear with me! not so much to deny as to qualify. Senator McCarthy is an asshole much regarded in some quarters of LA, but Chicago don't go for him. They breed their own bigots. All told, though, he *is* the reason for my presence in the UK. And your good husband, ma'am, is the reason for my presence in Yorkshire."

I was puzzled. He knew me, he knew my father, at least as far back as May and the Sal Pethybridge business ("the poet Oldroyd," right? "from up beyond Skipton."?) So how come he was serving her such elementary information? She picked up very quickly on people and got things right about them at once. Was this the first time they'd met? So how come he was on first-name terms with her?

I fancied that this Lee McStarna had her as puzzled as I was; I have since come to realize that presenting an enigma was the keynote of his social strategy. But I didn't see it then, and I didn't dare speak in case he brought up Sal. Miranda wouldn't relish Sal one little bit: "cradle-snatcher," I guessed, would be her kindest comment. Arbitrary blue-black threads of Doncaster police-court prudishness interspersed the glittering weft of her radical personality – you never knew when loose ends might surface. And she was always incorrigibly jealous. Eh God, and the police might be more than a figure of speech: I'd been and gone and forgotten I was only fifteen when Sal for the first time
- And then my father re-emerged from indoors. He was laden with the old rocking-chair that belonged by the sitting-room hearth; he supported it on his shoulder with one hand; the other hand carried a jug of lemonade and an old china mug with a donkey painted on it – they'd given it me when I was three, what the devil kind of point was he trying to make? He was in shirtsleeves and striped braces with an ancient straw boater on his head; he looked like the man who hired out punts on the landing-stage at Ilkley: eh God how I wished I wasn't there.

I should explain about my father – he wasn't a bit like me – not at all tall and gaunt, I got that from Miranda – nay but he was built like a postbox on the street, short, squat and florid, with a slit of a mouth you could drop your letters in (supposing you were so minded), his dark eyes behind his glasses were peppercorns in sausage-meat. The lads at school called him Tightarse because of course he'd been christened Titus. (My granddad being a Methody preacher who showered the biblical names end-to-end of our extended family.) The lads of course knew nowt of his story-books. At all events, here he was, puffing with exertion as he signalled me out of my deckchair. "The rocking-chair for young master," he snarled. "Mr Silas, you must understand, is a hard-working hard-nosed newspaperman, which is why he's been in Barnsley the best part of a year with never a visit home nor so much as a picture postcard, so he needs to relax at his ease. We wouldn't even be aware he was still alive, if I hadn't now and then had a phone call from my old protégé Len Hopwood to tell us what he was at. What *are* you at, anyway?"

Eh God, what had he been told? More to the point, what had Sal been telling Len?

"And no, boy, you don't have a bloody b-&-s. You're well under age and anyway it's not yet dinnertime. Lemonade in your favourite mug: donkey for a donkey." A very old family joke; I'd never enjoyed it. He guffawed and cawed and brayed and delivered a rendition of how he imagined I went about my work. "'Mrs Gobthwaite, do excuse me, *Barnsley Chronicle* here, just to notify you that your good husband half-an-hour since was cut to pieces by a rotary excavator on his building site, and as a grieving widow have you any message for our readers?' Well, had she? did she? have *you*?"

I was distressed, and at the same time excited, by a rush into my brain of images of Sal, long legs and her slow sideways smile. Eh God as a result I entirely forgot (for the first time ever) all fear of my father. I cried out at him in a flurry of resentment: "No I haven't and I never would and if I did I'd not tell you. For the best part of a year you've been pronouncing to the world how you alone and your influence with the free and independent press got me a job in a first-rate newsroom: so don't you dare *despise* the job in front of – front of perfect strangers, not right and not fair."

Old Titus looked startled, and glanced at Miranda to see what she thought. Miranda glowered. Obviously neither of them knew what next to do with me. We sat for a long time in silence. Goes of b-&-s were poured and drunk. Lee McStarna all this while showed me his teeth as though he was in some way my mentor and was anxious to see how I'd deal with a family wrangle. When he heard "perfect strangers" he'd nodded as it were in approval.

He decided to fill in the silence. "Not quite strangers," he growled, hooding his eyes suggestively. "I came here to meet a poet." His teeth at my father. "And a polemicist." Ditto at Miranda. "You're both of you so well-known in the Dales, what could I do but pay my modest homage. But there's more," he went on, "is there not? You never told me your son was so fresh and debonair, so much of a morsel for lovely leaping wild, wild women, hey?"

I must have blushed as red as Miranda's politics, and then I was sick-white and sweating: if she noticed she misinterpreted. "Women?" She fired up at him. "He's far too young for women; I sent him to live in Barnsley with Tabitha; she swore to keep him clear of all this bourgeois shit." True enough: Sal and I had had the very devil of a labyrinthine intrigue to outsmart the venomous Tabitha (older cousin, much older) and to organize our trysts.

"Ah not at all," exclaims L. McStarna, "No suggestion in the world that he's actually on the job. No, but what he is, is a humming little honeybun potential, no end of cute, and when he comes to know himself, his poetry and his fiction will outdo the Californian Beats, you mark my word. The Beats not quite heard of in England yet? They will be, they will be, mark my word, and your son will be numbered amongst them. But bear with me – " He holds up a hand to check their righteous dismay; I become aware of the slur in his voice: b-&-s. "Bear with me – I did not say he would outdo his own father. If ever he does that, that – you can call me a man of neither good luck nor smart perception. Silas," he exhorts me. "Silas, Spike, whatever the name, expand beyond the newspaper. Oh yes, you can do it. True love, if ever you find it, find, will show you the road." He turns to my mother, "Miranda, I'm *on* the road, I've a train to catch for – for London, why not? My dutiful respects, ma'am, and to you, sir, likewise, likewise."

He gropes vaguely for a briefcase that lies at his feet, some-how discovers it, sways himself upright (but slightly twisted) out of his deckchair, walks to the gate with precarious steadi-ness ...

"How bloody many did the smarmy bugger drink? *I* didn't count 'em, *you* should have done." Old Titus as usual taking it out of his wife. "If he gets into Skipton without being hit in the back by the bus he's too early to catch, it'll be a bloody great wonder, damn his eyes, bah." Old Titus as usual has had more drinks than anyone else. He bellows as it were to a non-existent tribe of servants that it's after two o'clock and why isn't his din-ner on the table? He stumps up the slope into the house.

Later on, in the cool of the evening, Miranda and Titus be-tween them sit me down to make it clear that L. McStarna's diagnosis of my problems (insofar as I could have any prob-lems, at my age) is not to be taken seriously. They tell me all about him, at least they tell me what he's told them: it is by no means consistent. He is an American, or maybe an Irish-man emigrated to America; he's directed films in Hollywood, or maybe scripted them, or maybe run a theatre company where movie-stars indulged themselves by playing to live audiences; or maybe he hasn't actually *worked* in the industry, but comment-ed upon it as a journalist, or else as a short-story man, or else as a radio DJ; his radical politics getting him onto a McCarthyite blacklist with a spell in the slammer, or maybe he gave in and has "named names," to his own enormous shame, and is boy-cotted by colleagues – either way he's had to flee and his whole life is blighted; or maybe his exile has stripped him to the very soul and swept him into the first real sea of freedom he's ever experienced: he is currently surfing the time-honoured liberties of Great Britain while he survives as a freelance something-or-other in London, or maybe he lives on the dole. He has implied he is a speculative tout for a series of avant-garde publishers on both sides of the Atlantic. Can he do anything for my father? My father thinks not, and he'd rather he didn't try. He drinks, says my father; he tells lies, says my mother; and today was his first meeting with either of 'em. Or was it? I never found out.

They compete with each other to say what they need me to hear. They drink, they tell lies, they are by no means consistent.

*

After five years or so I saw him in Sheffield. I had not long been demobbed from my service as a conscript soldier, I was more or less an adult man with wide views as to adult society, I was living in that city in my own little packing-case of a flat undisturbed by Tabithas and such, I wrote a column for the local paper – 'Scraps and Scribbles from Spike.' This man L. McStarna was hooting stinking drunk on a kerbstone in gathering dusk, under the east window of the cathedral. His feet were in the wet of a blocked-up gutter, he was singing, after a fashion: –

"Oh Charlie, rusty Charlie,
Fills his belly with beans and barley."

He beat time on an upturned cake-tin with a big metal spoon. On either side of him were liquor-sodden derelicts, a purple-faced old man and a woman like a consumptive gorgon. Strange, L. McStarna's clothes were not altogether a heap of ruin, although worn-out, ill-buttoned and unclean, and he seemed to have been regularly pissing his pants – but good quality Dak pants and his stringy neck garnished with a polka-dot rag that had once been the modish cravat. And strange, strange, as soon as he saw me he hailed me by name. (Eh God, but I'd hoped to slide past him unrecognised – well, you would, wouldn't you?)

"Spike!" he shouted. "How's the fucking? How's your asshole of a poet father? How's your cunt of a commie mother? Have the cops got her yet or does Leo Trotsky's ghost stand erect between her and all harm? You and me must meet and talk, boy: because I need to hear it from you, how goes the masterpiece?"

His ghastly companions started to laugh and he turned on them in a surge of fury, pushing them over into the gutter and

throwing their caps and ragged shawls across the wind. Then
he took up his song where he'd left off: –

> "Hit him on the head, boy, shove him in the clink,
>   No more dope for him, no more drink."

The ghastly companions, having pursued their bits and pieces
and gathered them up, came crawling along back. I thought
they might have attacked him; I looked around for some help,
a constable maybe; of course nothing doing, this was Sheffield,
wasn't it? But it seemed they preferred to make peace; the old
woman fondled him, the old man passed him drink from a bottle in a brown paper bag. He was singing again: –

> "Leave him to lie there all on his tod:
> Christ, that'll teach him to call himself God."

I hurried away as fast as I could go.

And then he turned up at my flat – not immediately, there must
have been the lapse of about a month, but as I remember it, it
seems the very next night. Late night. Bloody well midnight.
He was as silent on the stairs as a lizard and he rapped my door
with such peremptory emphasis as to give a right stoppage to
the unprepared heart. I opened with some apprehension. He
came in, he twisted himself round the edge of the doorframe,
he narrowed his crafty pale eyes at me, he showed me the teeth
underneath what was now a strong dust-coloured 'tache, the
sort of bristles you'd see on a quartermaster-serjeant behind a
pile of dodgy dockets. His clothes were as I had noted them
in the street, rather dirtier if anything. The hat was a crushed
trilby, plastered with muck, tilted over one eye, dark green with
a ragged ribbon, jaunty, impertinent. He wore a fresh yellow
rose in the ribbon. He stood in my doorway, one arm akimbo;
the other one held out a bottle of some cheap, sweet, port-type
wine.

"This is to show you," he said, "that you can walk past me in disdain, if you wish: but I don't walk past you. I return your smug snub, you long string of unravelled knitting, with a gift from a full heart. Open it, drink it, and I'll drink some too. If you really mean to be a writer of zeal, power, precision, you'll need to say 'hello' – my God, much *more* than 'hello' – to the street people, because we are the backbone of this country. Mahatma Gandhi (may he rest in peace) would have called us his 'Harijans' – *the People of God*, as you'd know if your education had comprised the real world.

"Don't apologize," he interjected, after a long brooding silence: he saw I was about to speak. "It's a sign of weakness."

"That's what John Wayne says." – in default of apology he did seem to look for a comment and that was the best I could think of.

I tried to appear at ease, not at all effectually: he was reclining on my sofa and swigging from the bottle. I'd given him a glass; he'd set it carefully on the floor and had instantly forgotten it. Every time his hat fell off, he grabbed for it and put it on again. I daresay he didn't wish to exhibit his patch of bald skin, yellow and shiny, nor yet the grey hairs mixed in with the red. "In film upon film," I continued. "Does he write his own lines, d'you think?"

"'That'll be the day,'" he growled, in the actor's very voice. "Let me tell you, it's a question whether he can write his own name. No no, some asshole of a scriptwriter delivers him the lines and then he has 'em inserted over and over, film upon film. I guess I ought to know, didn't I write a good half of them myself, till he chose to sniff my politics and thereafter – *kaput*."

He sprawled there for hours and talked, endlessly, slowly, ponderously censorious, constantly contradicting himself, one slanderous tale after another about the great persons of Hollywood, each character (as he presented it) responsible in some way for his own current collapse onto the skid row of Sheffield – why Sheffield? he wouldn't, or couldn't say – only to mention, sideways, without emphasis, that a return to the States was impossible because the US Marines were after him for desertion. Had he fled from the Korean War? Another question which he failed to answer. I began to wonder if these apparently fuddled evasions were not some sort of spiritual challenge, the stock-in-trade, no less, of a Mahatma-esque guru. Eh up, did he see me as a likely disciple? He went on to ask about my own small soldiering: I'd escaped being sent to Korea, and it seemed to infuriate him. The British Army, he informed me, was a clapped-out ratbag of skrimshankers, pinkos and fags. General MacArthur, whatever they said of him, had been hewn out of solid platinum, a fact I'd no right to forget.

I hope I don't suggest he was nowt but a drink-sodden bore – fact was, I was fascinated, as he switched his reminiscences from one famous name to another, and not only in movieland – war, harlots, gangsters, the horrid world of the down-and-outs, the huge corruption of politics in the cities of the United States. Then all of a sudden he asked, did I ever go back to the cottage in Craven? Like a fool, I told him yes – my parents were off to Doncaster where Miranda's tyrannical mother was feeling her age and demanding company – she had a will locked-up in her desk, always capable of alteration, they could not ignore her. So the cottage would be vacant for at least a long weekend and I'd thought I might make use of it – "A man doesn't have to be in Sheffield to write for a Sheffield paper."

"No," says he, "he don't. Tell you what, I'll come too."

Like a fool, I said, "Why not?" – although I shuddered at the implications. The fact was, he did flatter me with all his knowing talk, and flattered me even more with his constant implication that I was only a footstep short of Hemingway or Norman Mailer, if I could but put my mind to it. I must bathe in the needful experience, he insisted: I hoped he didn't mean I ought to drink around the clock and sing with my feet in the gutter.

And then he fell asleep, only to wake me four hours later with a bellow for a proper breakfast – I had cornflakes in my cupboard and not much more, where the hell were my bacon and eggs? He was just like my dad, damn his eyes.

So we caught a train that very morning, then a bus, then we were there. It was raining. I found the key to the cottage where they'd left it under the mat, and we went in. The first thing I saw was a letter from Miranda, addressed to me, propped up on the mantelpiece of the parlour: –

Silas, if you're there,

You always say you want to come when we're away, for your peace and quiet. Why peace and quiet? An active young man needs noise the way an engine needs fuel, a revolutionist needs more than noise – downright confrontation – as well you know. But if you must make your sentimental terms with nature, as per that fink Wordsworth, who am I to stop you? You'll find cold chicken in the fridge. You're not to bring any of your press ruffians into the house, you know how Titus would hate them to fumble through his privacy, I'd hate it too.

Your mother, in haste X X X

– my mother just rang us for the third time this morning – and the car giving trouble blast it – I'd told Titus, why wasn't it in for repairs? Carburettor, no damn good. The man's a fool.

Right: so here I was and here was the chicken and here without doubt was a ruffian, though not quite a pressman – I'd best hope he'd behave himself. But of course he could not. The first thing he did was to search for my father's "privacy" – that's to say his notebooks and loose drafts, heaped any-old-how in bedroom and study. He went further: he ferreted out a locked chest full of ancient yellow typescript shoved behind a chamberpot underneath the marital bed, and he opened it with a – eh God, it was your actual picklock, on a bunch of keys from his pocket – he cried, "Ha! this is the business! Spike, we've struck oil!" He stretched himself like a cut-down Rokeby Venus on the top of the marital bed with his dreadful sticky wine, and the hitherto unknown works of the Genius Oldroyd spread around him across the counterpane.

"You serve the chicken," he ordered. "Make a mayonnaise and we'll have it with a bunch of lettuce."

He snarled in contempt at a great deal of what he read, mostly the latest stuff. And then he came across an unpublished tale dated 1938, the year I was born: the year of my parents' marriage, in point of fact (something of a shotgun job with furious magistrate grandmama shouldering the weapon of threat). He read bits of it out aloud to me in a dragging dry voice, a villain's voice from melodrama, while his fingers smeared the pages with salad: I had never come across, let alone heard of this particular piece: it was quite out of all expectation, being three times as revolutionary, fiery revolutionary, damnable *explosive* revolutionary, than any of Miranda's pamphlets – pacifist into the bargain and sexy to a degree that would have startled Dionysus.

"D. H. Lawrence, how are ye? This pro—progenitor of yours had balls, he being *young,* like a wolverine in rut, have I the word for him? and a pecker the dimension of a spadehandle, so he had. Jasus, what happened him?" He'd laid hands by now on my father's best whisky; in drink he was becoming more and more Irish with every gulp. He ran a bitter running commentary upon old Titus's life and works – he had previously read, so it seemed, the few printed volumes – now that he had before him what he took to be the full perspective, he was able, so it seemed, to trace a weary history of decline and selling-out.

He suddenly interrupted himself by vomiting across bed and papers: nasty beast, he rolled over in his own mess, tumbled to the floor, and slept.

I was in despair; I couldn't wake him; my best resort was clean up everything as near as I could get to his horrid margins; Jeyes Fluid in a bucket of water; I took the desecrated papers into the garden sunshine and pegged them out on a clothesline; they'd dry, fair enough; I was greatly afraid that the stains were indelible. He awoke in the late afternoon, pulled himself up by the bed-leg, shook his head mournfully and said, "Sorry about that." Then he wandered into the living room, sat down in Titus's armchair and began busily writing in one of Titus's notebooks. Then he tore out the page and passed it to me. Big sprawling letters, arrogant underlining, green ink from his fountain pen, who the devil did he think he was? He had written: –

22 years ago, this tale 'The Red Hot Dungfork' should have burnt out every brain in the land.

Too late for it now. Can Spike rekindle? Oh but he MUST.

Was it possible he could be right? The question snapped into me as though shot by a staple-gun. It hurt me, it angered me – or *he* did, which came to much the same thing – and I must admit it excited me, although *he* did not excite me, that has to be made clear, no he disgusted me, he had conned me, he had bullied me, he was running me into unthinkable family trouble and how the devil, how the hell, how the *fuck*, was I going to get rid of him?

There wasn't a bus till tomorrow morning. And if I rang for a taxi, would I be able to compel him into it? I was taller than he was and perhaps a good deal stronger – I doubted that he had indeed been a US Marine – more probably an orderly-office clerk in a home-service outfit – but even so – Right: I would make the call and then we'd see what we'd see.

"Hello? Garfield Cabs? Can you send a car please to Old-royd's, at High Riggs, quick as you can, miss? One passenger, Skipton station."

"Aye, right, love: we've a car on t'road up there already, he can bring back your passenger on his return, right? Ten minutes, no longer."

"Hey, no, wait – " Too late, she'd rung off. We were the only bloody house at High Riggs, was it a mistake? no! because it must be -   Eh God but their own car must have broken down *as per usual* and they'd cut short their visit or not even made the bloody visit and then they must have -   However I tried to shape it, every stage of my misfortune (*they'd* call it my iniquity) was about to be unravelled before their very eyes...

And so it was. However, I'm bound to say he went quietly. "Of course," he murmured. "Most inarope—pri—ap—appap-propriate behaviour, no choice but apologize, your leniency is noted and appr—preciat—appreciated. Sir." He said it first to me and then to them. Then he said to Miranda, "Madam, the Man Upstairs will surely bless you." He tried and failed to kiss her hand, and fell reeking into their taxi before they'd so much as got the luggage out.

I won't go into detail as to what happened next. Just let's leave it as the worst of all those *things* between me and them.

I never saw them again, or hardly ever.

Nor was I to see L. McStarna for years. I bode in peace and quiet in Sheffield and worked. It looked as though he'd left the district: I hoped he'd left my life. But not quite.

*

In 1968, I was thirty.

The year of the student riots, right? Even in Sheffield. It is a Wednesday in hot, hot June. I am at work on an article for *The Dearne & Don Intelligencer* about the 'manifestations' at the local art school – the kids having occupied the principal's office and 'liberated' his private bog – or summat o't'sort – any road, my job is to make it look a daft little hooligans' eruption, quite alien to good solid Yorkshire wage-workers, colliers, foundry-men, railwaymen and so forth. I've been down to the college to take a look at it and the girls all so strong-faced and determined and quite gorgeous in their bell-bottom jeans and summer tops that I've fallen in love with half of them and can't bring myself any too easily to write what's expected – and what, in point of fact, I believe to be true, I've no patience with home-made revo-lutionists. This is not to the purpose, except to make the point that I'm feeling brim-full of the penetration and sensitivity of a real writer – just that I've not been able to settle down and do the writing – any road, not yet.

A letter arrives by the evening post – oh aye, we still have an evening post, England is still England, tha knows. It's from old Titus, it's over the wall, aye he's always been queer but this is the queerest: –

Look here, boy,

I've got to talk to you. Meet me off the train Wednesday, due 6.36 pm from Leeds. I can't tell you why through the post. Hope you get this in time: emergency: phone or telegram out of the question in such an exigent. EMERGENCY. Look here, only you can prevent me committing this murder.

In horror, Titus O.

Wednesday already, I've no more than twenty minutes to get to the station, if indeed I want to get there. Bloody ridiculous, his stupid letter was two whole days on the way, he could easily have left out "murder" and sent the message down the wire. But here he comes tearing towards me along the platform as though he has indeed killed, turning his head just the once, as though in fear not alone of the police but the Furies of Aeschylus: his face blue as lead and his eyes rolling bloodshot. "Into the buffet," he gasps, as he fixes his fierce grip onto my forearm, "a drink before all else. And then you shall hear. Oh dear God."

"The buffet isn't up to much. There's a comfortable pub not ten minutes' walk away, wouldn't you prefer to – "

"No no, no time. Got to – got to – talk. Here – order me brandy. No soda. No."

He's dragged me inside and to a corner table where we're more or less private. I buy the drinks and sit down opposite him and he grabs once again at my arm, pulling at me so that my ear is within inches of his mouth, biting distance if he so wishes: I'm seriously alarmed. I've never known him so unbalanced.

For a man who's demanded to talk, he is slow enough to begin, mouth opening and shutting, huge rasping intakes of breath. Up to me to start first? the more direct the better. So, "Your letter said murder. Murder of who?"

"Of *whom*," he snaps, ever the schoolmaster. "Of your mother. Miranda. Who else?"

"Eh, God, but dad – " I am absolutely unable to measure him. I must be gaping like a codfish.

"Don't you eh-God me, boy: just tell me what to do!"

"Well, I will, I will, if I – No, *you've* got to tell *me*. Why. How. What happened. Some sort of reason."

"Eh reason. Eh there's reason. It walks on two legs and calls itself McStarna. *You* know him well enough, *you* fucking brought him." This is the first time I ever heard Titus use such language. My mother is foul-tongued enough, but he's never responded or given even a hint that her obscenities register with him. Moreover, what he says is untrue – the first time L. McStarna came to High Riggs, he was there before I was and I'd nowt at all to do with it.

So I wait, carefully silent, and at last it all comes out.

Not long after the day that the drunken creature piled into that taxi, leaving the cottage a sodden wreck and Titus's years of writing pillaged and scattered, it seemed my mother entered into a process of private contact with the hideous homunculus. He'd taken to phoning her in penitential terms. While she instinctively loathed religion, a religiously humiliated person (actually applying for absolution from *her*) was a novelty that drew her like catnip. He asked her not to tell Titus, protesting that it was all because of his adoration of Titus's writings that he put himself in this painful way at her feet and hadn't it best be kept secret? – he did not dare expose himself to the great creator, not yet, not just yet ... He would ring up from Sheffield, and then from London, and then from the north of Ireland, at unpredictable intervals, always apparently sober, and as eloquent as Tartuffe.

A year ago Titus chanced to be home with a bellyache instead of down the valley in his classroom; he answered the telephone in the middle of the morning; Miranda was plucking onions in the garden; L. McStarna's oleaginous syllables piled into her husband's earhole before he had a chance to stem them.

From then on, L. McStarna was never out of the way – if he wasn't on the phone to Titus quite as often as to Miranda, he was sending him unsolicited gifts of books by the sort of morally-positive authors whom Titus most despised, together with picture postcards of vaguely inspirational bits of modern art with comments on the contents of the books – 'page 54, dear master, a drastic account of the carnage of battle that should make even the most militant warmonger think twice, etcetera.' – this *dear master* tag was perhaps more intolerable than any other of the hideous man's insinuations. And moreover he made promises, specious, improbable. Titus didn't seem to want me to know exactly what; at all events, he skated over them.

The next stage, no more than six months ago, a personal sighting. Miranda had heard from a Trotsky-comrade of a newish breed of cowboy picture, the Spaghetti Western, "quite a different animal," she assured Titus, "worth consideration at the highest political level, believe it or believe it bloody not."

"She commandeered me to go with her to something called – *Good, Bad, Ugly,* was it? – that was playing in Leeds. Quantities of treacherous American bloodshed, I had to grant her that: but its hot photographic and musical ambience continually promised us venereal as well as homicidal depravities, and it failed to come up with the goods. Never mind that now. There was an actor in the film, a villain, on-screen at the very beginning, what was his name? Lee something?"

He describes him and I tell him, Lee Van Fleet. Well, it appears that as soon as this Lee made his appearance (shooting a man dead in the desert, quick sharp), Miranda gave a gasp of alarm? or was it erotic excitement? Titus paid little attention, until two-and-a-half hours later as they walked out into the Headrow, when it was *his* turn to gasp: no alarm, no sexual arousal, but "consternation, undeniably. On the far side of the street, this creature, d'you see? this fleeting simulacrum of the cinema villain we'd just been watching, and who'd jabbed, as it

were, his psychological bodkin into your mother." But it wasn't
Lee Van Fleet, it was someone much shorter, hideous Lee McStarna, saturnine and watchful, his moustache crisp and cultivated, his eyes like two fireflies, black broad-brimmed hat, anklelength trenchcoat – Titus saw him, he saw Titus, he gave a twist
to his torso and vanished. Yet there he had been, *patrolling*, in
the next nearest city to Titus's home – "and why did he present
himself so like, so fearfully like -   Be quiet, boy, I can tell
you why. He knew this actor in Hollywood and modelled himself upon him – maybe borrowed his first name, or maybe the
coincidence of names gave him the cue – and if he dresses like
the actor, will he not behave like him? A cold-hearted killer:
I put it to your mother. She ignored me. Dangerous, so very
dangerous."

Killer or not, within weeks he began coming to Skipton. From
Leeds? Titus cannot be sure: "but my sharp eye is sharper than
many might think," (a sudden flash of intimidatory classroom
manner) "for despite the transparent prevarications of the hideous bloody man, it would seem he did enjoy a certain habitation in a degraded area of Leeds." Or if not Leeds, Bradford.
But here he was, in Skipton, he hung around near the grammar
school, "he absolutely buttonholed me as I was getting into my
car to go home." Three times this happened and Titus brushed
him off.

The third time, Titus tells Miranda about it. Miranda curses
him for a curmudgeon: "He only wanted to pay us a visit. Next
time, you offer him a lift, damn you. He worships you. You
have few enough in the way of fans; it's monstrous you should
alienate them so." So Titus, in awe of his wife, does what she
says, and since then the bloody fucking hideous man is never
out of the house. No, these days he's neither drunk nor disorderly about the place (Miranda offers him sherry and such and
he seems not to accept it, although Titus suspects he carries a
hipflask and does his toping in private in the bathroom): he
just won't stop talking and won't leave when given the hint. It
seems he's taken a room at the Drovers' Arms, half-way over the

moor toward Wharfedale. He regularly walks the distance in all weathers, and after dark as well.

He's not yet been run over by a car on a wet night. Oh no, no such luck.

Titus blames Miranda.

She is courted by L. McStarna and at the same time abused, he travesties her politics in improvised song, as a jocular adult might mock a little girl who's pretending to be a fairy queen – for example:

> Ho-ho, Ho Chi Minh
> Too many whiskers on his chin,

or:

> Aldermaston in the distance
> March and march and show resistance:
> Marching assholes night and day
> The wind shall blow your bombs away,

or, by way of a surging rhetorical finale, *recitativo*:

> Bear with me! for I assure you,
> workers, peasants, soldiers, you shall
> at last be a just and happy society,
> even though I have to send
> every single one of you
> in my cattle-waggons to the labour camp!

– and believe it or believe it bloody not, she makes no remonstration; why, she suffers his gibes in masochistic ecstasy. Thus Titus blames her and indeed goes further, he angrily scorns what she's doing and then fears it and at last hates it – until the scorn, fear and hatred are transferred from the doing to the doer. "I say she is his *instrument*," he cries, "demonic possession, what else!" and he roars for another brandy. When I fetch it, he roars no longer, he lays his head in his hands and whimpers. "Better I shouldn't kill her," he tells me – or rather, tells himself and lets me overhear if I can, such a still small voice he's suddenly found, I've never heard the like from him, never – "I love her. All these years," etcetera. He is speaking exclusively into his brandy-glass … Then, abrupt, without warning, and loud enough to startle the barmaid across the room – "No: I'll kill *him*. He'll be there now. I've just time."

*

He must have noticed what I hadn't, the reiterated crackle on the station loudspeaker to announce the next departure, the seven-ten for Leeds and Carlisle: the announcement repeated as he ran from the buffet so fast I couldn't catch up until his foot was on a carriage step of the north-bound express and the guard blowing his whistle and a porter running down the plat-form slamming the doors. "No no, you mustn't, eh God what are you thinking of? You mustn't, you mustn't – no no-o-o!"

He cut me off with nowt but monosyllables, "Shut your gob, boy: if I must, then I have to, that's it!" – he was inside the car-riage, I was on the platform, door shut, train moving. If I'd been an instant quicker I could have been in the train with him, fetch him home, calm him down, keep him and – and the others from – Eh God *I* don't know what I could have kept 'em from. Hopeless.

> Tried in vain
> To get on that train
> I couldn't, I can't
> I just didn't want.

I was wondering, stood alone there on the railway concourse among the last of the evening commuters, would I do right if I went to the police? At all events I decided not.

> Couldn't and can't
> And just didn't want.

As for what happened, when he got to High Riggs. I can tell you what Miranda told me the next time I saw her, upon the day of the funeral.

It had been so very late, and dark, and wild with rain (as she explained, with all of her customary crudeness) – "a biblical fucking thunderstorm, and his taxi came sweeping up the road. As usual, he had the driver *parpity-parp-parp* on his horn like a teenage fucking halfwit trumpeter to alert me in the cottage as if I couldn't possibly have heard the car itself, or as if I was waiting there, *wanting* to know he'd arrived." He jumped out and up the garden and into the parlour soaking wet, caught his foot in the hearthrug, fell into the grate and all but set himself afire. She formed the opinion he was hooting stinking drunk (as indeed he was, it later became apparent that he'd stopped in Skipton until closing-time), whereas the beady-eyed L. Mc-Starna, sitting softly in Titus's rocking-chair, was as sober and judicious as a well-seasoned pedagogue.

Titus lifted up his bleeding head and glared at L. McStarna. His language was a disgrace, insofar as it was decipherable. L. McStarna said, "I think y'r man JC would have turned the other cheek here: Gandhi-ji likewise (may he rest in peace): passive resistance. I'm trying as hard as I can: but it really is no picnic to listen and stay cool. Why wouldn't I take a stroll in the garden?" He turned his eyes away from the pair of them and walked out of the front door with his neck humbly bent and his hands clasped on his chest.

Miranda claimed she was repelled by this "fake religiosity," this petty-bourgeois attempt to assert personal familiarity with Gandhi by adding "ji" to his name. She claimed without evidence that it was an affectionate Hindi suffix as used within an extended family and he'd no right to appropriate it. (I knew nowt about it: but I did know she had mixed with Indians in her art-college days, so I took her at her word.) And as for "JC," was he talking of the president of some transatlantic uplift-outfit, or what was he talking of? He'd sounded like a liberal parson trying to ingratiate himself with a gang of navvies. He had, she said, often irritated her, but this time it was beyond all bounds. She screeched into the night after him that never again, never again, she'd have nothing to do with him ever again.

With the lizard out of the house she felt able to attend to my father. She knelt down beside him and took him by the ears and shook him, "to pluck," she said, "some fucking sense out of his brainbox." He had stopped cursing. She looked into his eyes and shuddered, for only their whites were visible. He was making an unusual, unnatural gurgling sound in his throat and saliva seeped from his lips.

After two or three minutes of this, he fell silent and lay still, her arms around his shoulders, and it came to her that he was dead.

She hadn't known, till the doctor told her, that Titus had had an ailing heart for years and years and was supposedly taking pills for it: never mind the bloody pills, he'd swallowed so much booze on top of 'em that a shattering thrombosis was the only possible result. Even had she been aware of it, there was little she could have done. She kept quiet about L. McStarna (who had positively disappeared); privately she held him responsible, not herself, mark, never herself. I thought it was her fault quite as much as his: I refused to believe it was *my* fault. If I'd gone to the Sheffield police, would they have stirred up their Skipton colleagues in time to keep Titus alive? Assuredly not, I consoled myself. And yet, perhaps, perhaps ... Eh God such damfool nonsense, farcical speculation, how could anyone be sure of such a thing?

*

My father's will was an odd one. Or rather, it was supplemented by a very odd codicil. The main text was straightforward. He left his inconsiderable moneys and the cottage and the car, and all his books and manuscripts and so forth, to Miranda. (In her own will, written within days, the books and manuscripts came to me, the car and the cottage went to a breakaway faction of the Anti-Apartheid Movement, while the several thousand quid of her own personal savings were bequeathed to the 'Squatters' Coordinating Council' in Leeds, a barely legal collocation. Typical.) But Titus's handwritten codicil, and notably the codicil to the codicil, caused us to look strangely at one another – when I say "us," I mean not only me and my mother but all the unexpected relatives who had suddenly emerged from the jungles of oblivion like those devoted Jap soldiers turning up now and again on remote Pacific islands, enquiring had Hirohito won his war? The codicil was dated about a week before my father met me on Sheffield station. It had been composed without the help of his solicitor. For witnesses, he'd waylaid a couple of colleagues in the masters' common room during morning break: one of them taught French and the other Callisthenics: neither was a personal friend.

CODICIL. I decided to write this because it crosses my mind that my will may have to be read rather sooner than anyone expects. And I need to amend it, thus: one especial manuscript is to go to my son Silas, not to my wife, if you please. This is the one that he all but destroyed when in his cups – some nine years ago, was it not? A 100-page story dated 1938, I'd typed it out untitled, but somebody scribbled at the top of it, <u>The Red Hot Dungfork</u>. Not bad, eh? but in green ink? At any rate, you'll easily recognize it. I leave it to my son Silas by way of a piece of homework – he's always been remiss in that area, let's see if this will bring him up to the mark. My son Silas is not to publish any of his own work until he finds a publisher for this one of mine: unbreakable precondition: let the executors look to it. My son Silas allowed an obnoxious individual to sully the unfortunate MS and (I suspect) to insert an impertinent title – green ink, indeed, unspeakably vulgar – so my son Silas must recollect how that individual claims a certain expertise – so let that individual be consulted by my son Silas in regard to potential publishers. I doubt that the offices of the <u>D & D Intelligencer</u> provide much in the way of experience in the marketing of experimental literature of the highest class, which this story damned well is and L.

McS. knows it is. Let the executors seek and find L. McS., if he's not in the neighbourhood. Now that I'm dead, I don't care how close he comes, if he can be used for my posthumous benefit, or indeed for the benefit of my unthrifty son. But he is a hideous man and so for God's sake keep him far far away from me for as long as I'm still alive.

CODICIL to the Codicil. Oh yes, and folk who find an overplus of irritation in this bequest are too ignorant to comprehend the affection and respect between a father and his only son and vice-versa. Young rips have a need to be chastised; and let not my son Silas think I didn't know about pretty Mrs Hopwood (as she now is). That daughter of hers must be nearly thirteen. Silas should give her a respectable birthday present, now she's becoming a teenager. He can have the little china kitten for her that sits on my desk, it's the sort of thing a girl would like for her bedroom; I'm damn sure Miranda won't want it.

There was silence a full minute after all this was read out by the solicitor. "Non-compos-mentis," declared the first executor, my uncle Barnabas, of Messrs Oldroyd, Sugg & Co., Mill-wrights and Weighbridge Factors, Bolsover. He was the first person in the room to speak, he spoke with pragmatical finality. He was a right old-fashioned manufacturer with no nonsense about him, damned good for British trade.

"Oh no, sir, your brother was by no means non-compos," retorted the solicitor (second executor). "Any will made without legal advice has a look of derangement. But the bequests are quite rational. We should certainly hand over the manuscript and the – ah – kitten. We can safely ignore the preconditions as to what our friend Silas may or may not do in regard to publishing. Or in regard to the birthday of – of this ah-h'm child. The codicil does not have the legal status of a contract. It merely expresses desires, to which Silas may accede, should it seem convenient."

In a voice of distilled vinegar, Miranda enquired what was to be done about this mysterious "L. McS."? At least, she hoped he was mysterious: if he was who she thought he was, she didn't want the whole tribe getting in on the sodding search for him, whatever nasty racket Titus in his last days might have tried to set up.

The solicitor assured her that the gentleman in question need not be "sought beyond reason." If he came forward on his own account, well and good; but otherwise -   The solicitor clearly agreed with me and my mother that it was a bloody bad show for a dead man in his grave to sit up and muck folk about with preconditions, codicils and such. We were sitting around in the cottage parlour like a treeful of despondent rooks, having just returned en masse from the cemetery, so I got up from my chair without any more nonsense, and pocketed the kitten. I said I'd prowl for *The Red Hot Dungfork* after everyone had gone, meanwhile there were egg-and-cress sandwiches, cold meats, tomatoes, parkin – all on the kitchen dresser, and sherry or gin-and-tonics if tea didn't satisfy.

I took it that the codicil was a desperate attempt by my father to somehow mitigate his biliousness toward me, to *approach* me, even: did it not strike him that he had to be dead before I could be aware of it? And then again there was a sort of forgiveness implicit in the codicil, for my failure to advance any further in the literary world than 'Scraps and Scribbles,' or 'Foundryman had fifteen pints prior to assault on tram-driver, court told.' Forgiveness also for my acquaintance with L. McStarna. And, equally also, for long-leggéd Sal, whose girl would get the kitten, okay: an anonymous packet through the post.

Maybe one day I might gather the courage to look 'em up, but-   Of course I would do my best to have *The Red Hot Dungfork* published, though indeed I had not read it, barring the disconnected bits I'd heard read out by L. McStarna. I'd nothing but the latter's doubtful word that the rest of the hundred pages would prove of equal quality. Nor would I bring him in to help me edit, or whatever. End of *that* thought, dear dad.

A fog here I've never been able to penetrate; even the attempt is – is abhorrent. The Titus who wrote the codicil was not at all the same Titus as the hysteric a week later who tore down the Sheffield platform. What had happened in between? Miranda must surely have done something, said something, which he couldn't bring himself to tell me – something perfectly bloody dreadful – foul pictures form in the mind. Had he one day found her in nowt but her skin and her wrinkles, on all fours across a pouffe in front of the fireplace while L. McStarna, dog-like, scrambled up behind her to -   ? Or maybe did she crouch like a massage-parlour whore above L. McStarna's meagre thighs to *work* upon him with her tongue till he -   ? My Christ but that's more than enough. Oh but in due course I certainly would have asked her, I'd have *forced* her to respond, I'd have savaged her like Hamlet did Gertrude, I'd have -   In due course? oh no no, she fell ill, didn't she? how could I put such a question when the woman was dying?

For Titus's death destroyed her. Within six months she had followed him: at the age of fifty-five: a cancer of the ovaries: psychosomatic, we all said. She was not so much fickle as contrary; without doubt she loved her husband but deplored so much about him that she seemed to detest him. There were times when she saw him self-tortured in the throes of such precision and pedantry and pusillanimity that it was all she could do not to kick him in the gut. (In particular "pusillanimity" when he demurred at some new political stunt of hers: as it might be, slashing the tyres of Labour Party councillors in the town-hall carpark.)   Her contrary spirit must have attracted her – for a time – to the contrariness of L. McStarna, and then in an instant turned her against that measly interloper. Mind you, a most vehement, violent, terrible instant and she never recovered from it. About her, I'll say no more.

Every time I hear dirt from a woman's angry mouth, I think of Miranda and my heart turns over ...

I should add that L. McStarna manifested himself at neither funeral. Years later I discovered that when he left High Riggs for the last time he had travelled straight to America, where he was wed within a couple of months to a Dr Rebekah Vogelsang,

Lecturer in American Mythology at a college in Nevada. (The desertion rap from the US Marines was apparently not activated; had it ever existed?) And then, as I understand it, the marriage ran itself headlong into an inimical environment. L. McStarna amongst the faculty of a highly conservative campus was a scorpion in a wasps' nest – he was armoured against their stings, whereas *his* sting, promiscuously flourished, made their habitat intolerable. The end came (I am told) when Dr Rebekah induced him to go with her to a wife-swapping barbecue hosted by her head of department. It had been hinted that if she really wanted *tenure*, she had no choice but to take part. L. McStarna discovered that the lady he was paired with, trophy-wife of the Professor of – of Anti-Communist Studies, could it possibly have been? – he discovered she was regularly pinched black-and-blue by her ageing husband; it was his only form of sexual expression, it hurt her quite severely and she was sick of it. She showed L. McStarna the moonscape of livid bruises all around her most intimate parts. Alarmed at the sight, and outraged by the thought that at that very moment the professor was up to his tricks with Dr Rebekah, L. McStarna hurtled regardless through the house into the garden and back through the house, throwing open every door until he found them. (I'm told that he made himself a right ribald spectacle, priapic pint-sized satyr, observably *steaming*, eh the daft bugger.) He did serious damage to the area of the professor's groin with the neck of a broken bottle.

I heard nothing of all this for years; but when I did hear I was startled to realize that L. McStarna was not quite the phantom I had often thought him. He must actually have enjoyed an autonomous existence, not tied and never *was* tied to my father or to me or to my memories of Miranda and Sal. If I were to die, he would continue to live. To be sure his Dr Rebekah continues to live: only last week in the Galway public library, of all places, I found a book she had written. It dealt with fantastical legends spun out of the American Civil War, an interesting subject, wouldn't you think? No: dryasfuckingdust and immeasurably scholarly. In her preface she'd inserted a word of thanks to "Lee, my ex-husband, for his herculean labours at the proof-reading." I considered getting in touch with her, a letter, a non-specific greetings card, a fax? – but my heart failed me, it was too much of a muchness with long-leggéd Sal and her daughter ...

How come I never knew the name of that daughter?

*

So what next?

> A dreary orphan's life and all alone,
> No folk nor home to call my own.

I worked hard with nobody's help to get *The Red Hot Dungfork* published, a slim novella: only three reviews, one in *Peace News* middling good, two others decidedly bad (*Yorkshire Post* and *Times Lit. Supp.*): sales were poor. And not a word from L. McStarna, never mind that he'd somehow at some time given my father the impression that he and no-one else could convey the book into print for him. Did he even know that Titus was dead? Be sure that he did: he had antennae like a stealth-bomber ... I ate and I drank and I often drank too much, I conscientiously produced the newspaper, a factitious hollow nothing, banal and jejune. As for my own attempts at literary fiction –

> I wrote and wrote and yet I could not write:
> My mind brim-full of greatness, bright, alight,
> Ungraspable. I tried to swarm the greasy pole,
> I swore to God I had the skill
> But again again I slipped and fell.

There was nowt wrong with my vocabulary; but over above the time-wasting demands of newspaper drudgery, I just couldn't order the words hand-in-hand with the ideas.

When they made me editor, the *Intelligencer's* proprietors had me live over the shop – that's to say, a cosy enough flat upstairs from the offices and newsroom. It lay in the township of Wath-on-Dearne, a dark low-roofed straggle of grotty brickwork along the valley of the little black river, along the side of British Rail's marshalling yards, where they made up the coal trains for half of England. There were collieries on the edge of town: before long they were in a state of fury, the miners in the process of toppling Ted Heath's smarmy government, the *Intelligencer* trying to find an honest but prudent attitude and adopt it pretty smartly if we didn't want brickbats through our plate-glass and maybe flaring petrol into the mail-box – it was indeed *that* kind of industrial emergency, worse than ever I'd seen. I printed Open Letters to the government, not exactly supporting the miners' union – I couldn't quite bring myself to the pitch that I'd seem to duplicate my mother's atavistic levelling rants – but I did make it clear that the Fourth Estate in Dearnedale would not stand for Tory bureaucrats riding roughshod over human rights, and so forth.

My proprietors didn't like this. Right, well, one of them didn't: another bloody atavist, a squirearchal Boadicea, Mrs Geraldine Manningly-Hoax of Hoax Hall on the far side of Barnsley, the last of the old country houses in the south Yorkshire pit-district to contain its original family. Prior to nationalization, the Manningly-Hoaxes had owned the pits as well as the newspaper; in the 1970s they behaved as though they still did. Right, well, *she* did, at any rate, and we had a roaring stand-up row in the newsroom in front of my two reporters and the typist. I not only stood up, I stood firm. I asked her which would she prefer – a newspaper that sold all its print-run or one that used *her* words instead of its own and was read by hardly anyone? I asked her how many of her fellow-directors agreed with her, if any? She declined to answer; she turned on her heel and click-clacked out of the building to her deferentially chauffeured Bentley. I waited some days to be sacked. Nothing happened.

To tell truth, I was disappointed. I'd had enough of the *Intelligencer:* I'd have been glad to walk away on a flaming point of principle. And when our egregious prime minister put the country on a three-day week and all the lights went out in the middle of the darkest afternoons, it was a damned uncomfortable job to be stuck to.

To tell truth, my life was dead. I was utterly depressed by politics, not only the coal situation: there was torture and a concentration-camp and paras running amok in Northern Ireland; Whitehall conniving at a sadistic serjeant-major in impregnable charge of Uganda; asset-strippers let rip everywhere; ancient county-boundaries thrown to the winds as though a cack-handed toddler went berserk with his big sister's jigsaw; while a sort of ministerial Geraldine M-H. snatched the kids' milk and nobody stopped her. To vote Labour was not the solution, I had never voted Labour, Harold Wilson was a squit and a squirt. I could scarce compose an editorial without having to delete unacceptable expletives by the dozen. My personal relationships were a desert. There seemed no woman anywhere who'd agree to share my bed, scarcely even my beer in a pub or my jokes and a sandwich in the office. Such females as I'd attempted, all the way back to lecherous Sal Pethybridge (although indeed Sal was uniquely and absolutely *mine* for a full half-year), had invariably ended the business with yelps of "possessive," "bossy," "censorious," "who are you to take me for granted?" I desperately needed to be told with authority that at the age of thirty-five and upward (going on for forty, to tell truth) I was after all worth something. There's a folk-tale I vaguely remember from my childhood bedtime stories – Titus usually read them to me, very rarely Miranda – *The Man Born To Be King*. Right. The details maybe not so right, but I have a recollection that the messenger who brought the news of the hero's destiny was no good angel but a Rumpelstiltskin species of demon. Is it possible I hankered unwittingly for the long-lost Lee McStarna? Did I need the likes of *him* to inject me with energy? Had my confused and confusing father, with his confused and confusing codicil, seen something I could not see? Nonetheless, L. McStarna had brought me news – *intimations* at any rate, however snide and mischievous – of my own potential destiny, they stuck with me, they did, I was that bloody gullible, and oh I can't deny it, I was beastly afraid of him – which is to say, afraid that one day he'd reappear and all the questions I'd ignored would be crying out for answer.

General election. Labour won. And Labour couldn't cope. I used to say so, over and over again in my editorials, and in my traditional 'Scraps and Scribbles' stuff for other northern papers. Mrs Geraldine M-H. was good enough to tell me I was at last "giving satisfaction," while the Miners' Union PR, with whom I often had a drink, said "he wished on the whole I was writing summat more positive, but bloody hell he couldn't disagree." I should have been pleased with myself: 'Scraps and Scribbles' were no longer entirely local in their appeal, I was syndicated to weekly journals as far away as Carlisle or Leicester. Even sometimes London, for *The Daily Telegraph* took to reprinting anonymous excerpts from my columns for its own political advantage and under its own title, usually something like 'Daft Sparks at the Socialist Coalface,' no great increase in my reputation but the money was solid.

To tell truth, my life was dead.

*

The next time he showed himself would have been about the time that Cyclops Thatcher shut us all into her dark cavern to gobble us up. 1979? OK. There he was, at Doncaster races, on his two little legs in the grandstand, some seven seats to my left and two rows in front, shoulders twisted with excitement as he peered through his binoculars at the runners of the three-o'clock. When the race was over (I'd lost, but I gathered from the frenzy of his fists and forearms that for certain *he'd* won something), he was swinging himself jubilantly around and around as though in search of an expected face – why did I think he must be looking for *me*? I cowered down behind my race card and pretended I wasn't there. However, I kept my eye on him, one eye below the corner of the card, if only to make sure that it was him. He still wore a long belted trenchcoat but his hat for a change was now a cap with a shiny peak. It might have passed muster in a Moscow workers' soviet in 1917, and he wore it precisely centred above the nose-piece of his wraparound sunglasses. His whitey-grey moustache curled at the corners of his mouth. His teeth were displayed like forks in a cutlery canteen. He employed a neat bow-tie to tighten his stringy neck ... I realized with dismay that he was suddenly on the move, excusing himself along the row to reach the aisle. My seat was next to the aisle: if indeed he was making for me, I could effect my escape before he was clear of knees and feet. No, I did not move. And no, I can't explain why not. I was the rabbit in the car's headlights, sat there to be run over.

"You've the appearance of a rabbit in the headlights of a car," he cried, as he teetered up the aisle toward me. (Why sunglasses? it was a very dull day.) "Paralysed and palsied and probably cataleptic. I take it you've had no luck. 'Unthrifty,' as your father diagnosed in that momentous codicil." (Who the devil had told him that?) "I take it you did not lay your money on Fortunate Boy. *I* did. I rejoice. I shall buy you a brandy-and-soda." Without waiting for my acceptance, he glided on into the lobby at the back of the grandstand and so into the bar. He seemed smaller than my memory of him, though it must have been an illusion – only very old men will actually shrink and he could not have been much more than fifty. His gait was as it always was, precisely-placed strides with a slight wobble at the knees, asymmetrical stoop of the shoulders, probing movement of the neck, his indefinable lizard-look that led one to think that at any moment a thirty-inch tongue would shoot from between his teeth and catch hold of a butterfly. But he didn't need that. *I* was his butterfly.

In the bar he asked me, "What news of the masterpiece?" I gave him some sort of evasive rigmarole, which he was polite enough not to question. I asked what was *his* news. He spoke at length about America, not about himself in America exactly, but an episodic run of sexual scandal from the college campuses, military/industrial appointments to academic posts, and the ease with which legal sanctions could be evoked upon anyone in those circles who did not altogether toe the line. I gathered the local police would be in the pocket of the faculty, provided the faculty was sufficiently right-wing; I more or less gathered that he had languished in gaol as a result of such a compact, but when I pressed him for details he proved as evasive as myself. Then he suddenly murmured he had a train to catch for King's Lynn, "oh and by the way, congratulations!" and what a good thing, was it not? that we'd met one another again. He slipped away through the throng, leaving me nonplussed with a half-empty glass and our next drinks ordered but not paid for. (His drink, I may say, was a soda without the brandy: he didn't say how long he'd been on the waggon.)

When I got home that evening, I found a telegram waiting for me. From Paris, of all places. At first I thought it must be somebody's mard-arsed prank:

CHER MONSIEUR TO CONGRATULATE YOU AS NEXTOFKIN POSTHUMOUS THAT THE RED HOT DUNGFORK BY T. OLDROYD IS AWARDED LE PRIX EDGAR POE AMOUNT STERLING £5000 TELEPHONE PLEASE TO CONFIRM YOU CAN RECEIVE

– and a name and a phone number in Paris, which of course I rang first thing the next morning, expecting imbecile cackles of laughter from God knows what supposed friend on his daft holiday, but no, a most courteous French lady speaking very pretty English, who explained that the Prix Edgar Poe was the only French literary prize given for a work in the English language (untranslated); it had been endowed by Victor Hugo in gratitude for the British democracy that had afforded him refuge from Napoleon III; it was incredibly prestigious, although the money was "but small, hélas." Apparently a copy of *The Red Hot Dungfork* had recently arrived in Paris, a leading French poet had read it and had been overwhelmed, had passed it on to a leading French critic, who was likewise overwhelmed, and was the mistress (as I gathered) of one of the judges, and the judges themselves would be arriving to present me with the cheque and an illuminated scroll at the French embassy in London on such-and-such a date.

Do not ask me what L. McStarna knew, if indeed he knew anything. Do not ask me what he was doing in King's Lynn or why he was back in south Yorkshire within the fortnight. In Barnsley in a corner of the lounge bar of The Three Cranes, I sat with some of the lads from the old *Chronicle;* we were supping ale in quantities (I think it was Chas Buswell's birthday) and I was holding forth as usual, boasting on behalf of my dad, I daresay. I became aware of the glint of L. McStarna's dark glasses between the shoulders of some men in another part of the lounge, I could see him through an archway behind the barmaid. When he saw that I saw him he held two fingers against the peak of his cap, like a Boy Scout saluting, and disappeared.

Well, I went up to London to the embassy, and it was a great day, or would have been, if only Titus had been there or even Miranda. I felt it necessary to tell them so, more than once. Sorry to say, I'd got foxed on their champagne; I gave thanks for the prize with a disgusting maudlin speech, soaked in tears and family hypocrisy. Later on, I made an emotional play for the French lady who'd been on the telephone. (We were staying in the same hotel.) I don't believe I succeeded, but the booze shut down my memory; the best bits and the not-so-good became and remain a blur. I fancy I had hoped that despite her Parisian chic she might enjoy me as a specimen of Anglo-Saxon rough trade. I did meet her next morning in the coffee room; she was tactful, she was agreeable, we walked out into the foyer together ... L. McStarna slid up to me, alongside my elbow, with a grin and a grisly murmur, "Bear with me," he said. "I'm not here to spy. But doesn't this justify everything? Haven't I made good my promise to *the master?* And now are we not free for the new masterpiece, yours?" And then he was gone again, and then I didn't know whether he'd been there at all, and the French lady was looking at me with – with tact, and a certain *concern.*

*

After that he became a constant presence, sometimes stopping me in the street to talk, sometimes overhanging me in pubs and cafés, sometimes calling at the *Intelligencer's* office to offer me "a word to the wise," sometimes he'd just walk past me in silence. On one alarming occasion, as I drove down the motorway to Newcastle to report on a teachers' conference – it was thought they would be launching industrial action against the government, with ramifications for any of my readers who had kids in school – I became aware of his huge-nosed profile scarcely eight feet away from mine – he had come up on the fast lane and was now driving level with me, staring straight ahead either side of the nose – as he accelerated to get beyond me he turned his neck sufficiently to show the quick flicker of the lens of his sunglasses and the quick sideways flourish of his teeth.

Whenever he found time to hold a proper conversation, as opposed to a mere *appearance* like a saint in a mystic's vision, he narrated bits and pieces of the adventures of his life, never entirely connected together, but highly seasoned with his defamations of well-known persons – "assholes," they always were, and up to all manner of ignoble malefactions which had yet to be made known to the world. "Bear with me," he would urge me, "bear with me when I inform you that I *do* know what I'm talking about. You do not show respect by your sceptical smirks and tut-tuts: these are confidences that any serious literary man would treasure, and *I* show respect by passing them on to *you*. Don't you see, you can use 'em in *dhe buke*, you don't have to give the real names, you ought to be at work at your notes, dammit: you do have the shorthand, do you not?" I don't know whether he knew that the novel I had claimed to be writing was no more than a half-dozen fallacious stabs at a title-page and first chapter – I changed the name of it each time I decided to make a new start – plus a bundle of loose-leaf sheets scrawled patchwork-style with little thickets of notes in black ballpoint and divided here and there by asterisks. By and large a good deal of it must have been lifted from his anecdotes, but I'd already forgotten what most of the notes signified, and my handwriting's so bad I couldn't bring myself to pick 'em over letter-by-letter in the hope I might refresh my memory. L. Mc-Starna, however, had made up his mind that what he insisted on calling "dhe buke," in an absurd cod-Irish accent, was well underway. Indeed I sometimes thought that *he* thought he was the one who was writing it, he kept on inventing (and attributing to me) troops of potential characters of a degenerate and murderous sort, to be involved in strange conspiracies to violate virgins, desecrate churches or synagogues, start wars, draw honoured statesmen into the paths of sodomy, and so on.

I would dutifully make notes, in shorthand on the offchance he'd demand I read them back to him; I would occasionally put questions in a forlorn effort to locate his narrative *somewhere* – e.g. "Didn't you say this two-star general was already a practising pederast? So why should the boy need to tempt him to look at nude photos? Lee, it doesn't make sense."

"Don't be bloody silly," he'd say. "It's the way these scumbags work. I'd ha' thought that you as a journalist'd be alive to their little games? Full of shit, the lot of 'em. But drop it if it don't fit. Why don't we talk about Rebekah? Make some notes, make some fucking notes. She's a girl in a million, and you've got to get her through this tragedy." I hadn't at that stage been told the name of his ex-wife, I was working on the assumption that 'Rebekah,' pathetic heroine, was a creature of his muse – *my* muse, as he would have it – anyway, I didn't believe a word of her.

For more than a few years I endured his comings and goings, his patronizing of me under guise of idolizing my yet-to-be-manifest talent, his retro-patronizing of old Titus, his inclusion of me as it were into his own family as a sort of honorary relative for whom he would work wonders in the literary world. He would slander my mother abominably and then declare his undying devotion to her memory. He would disappear for a month or two, and suddenly return to be at me day after day for weeks, and then he'd disappear again.

At last, like the ugly growl of an explosion in the depths of a coalmine, came the slow, ominous notion that I could, here and now, change all of my circumstances at a stroke, and that moreover if I didn't, I'd be done for. I say, slow: the climax was anything but. Revelation, epiphany, unlooked-for, electric, upon a dismal wet Tuesday, in the steam of my bathroom at seven in the morning. I looked in the mirror, my everyday before-breakfast blinkings and grimaces, thinking no ill; what I beheld was worse than hideous, it was downright uncanny. For the first time I saw (and I might have seen it ages since, had I only had the eyes for it) just how like L. McStarna I had grown. Not absolutely a replica – I couldn't be that, I was at least six inches taller – but my cheeks were parchment hollow, as though to emphasize the forward thrust of the nose; eh God I was scarce beyond forty! my moustache already grey with exactly his orange-tawny streak from the nicotine at one corner, my crown as bald as his in precisely the same pattern, and as for my teeth! since when had they become such a cheval-de-frise of dark discoloured *prongs?* Moreover, my posture, the hunch of the shoulders, the upturned irritable chin, the haggard and scaly neck, was – Nay, I'd never ever been such a shape. Or had I? "Liberate, liberate!" – I was barking uncontrollably.

It so happened that that Tuesday was the very day I was called to an important interview with Arthur Scargill, charismatic boss of the Miners' Union – a Barnsley man whom I'd known on and off for most of my professional life – I'd every reason to believe he was about to reveal to me, exclusively if you please, the unpublished arabesques of his long-running tango with the National Coal Board. It was altogether a rewarding tribute to my integrity as a pressman. And in the upshot, I was not disappointed.

I was nonetheless considerably alarmed. What Scargill told me was neither more nor less than a declaration of Total War. Maggie Thatcher, he'd decided, had refused to allow coalfield recalcitrance to topple her like Edward Heath; instead, and by way of the Coal Board, she would annihilate the miners and indeed the mining industry, much as Good Old Geraldine might let loose her bull terrier against an intruder in Hoax Hall. He gave me chapter and verse for it; and assured me that the union

would fight her to the hobs of hell and even seek a general strike
on the model of '26, if it was forced to – "if we're forced, Spike,
if we're forced, and we'll not make the same mistakes a second
time; we can win and we shall." I didn't think they could but
of course I wouldn't say so, not to his face, I'm not that sort of
interviewer: I go with the flow and chew over my reservations
afterwards, in an article on the same page maybe, under one
of my pseudonyms. I've got bags of integrity, and no-one can
dare say different; but I can also be a dead crafty bugger when
I have to.

I came away from the interview with one very strong impression on my mind: there was going to be all manner of mayhem
very soon and enormous scope for solid journalism, involving
(and this was the worst of it) men whom I knew on both sides
of the quarrel: scabs, boycott, *riot.* I detested the very idea. I
wanted no part of it –

> Couldn't and can't
> And just didn't want.

All that I did want was a prize for a great novel.

> Eh God, so I did! and just like dad had
> Nor did I want it after I'd be dead.

Add to which: if I tried to run a newspaper in the thick of
Scargill's War, my brain'd shut down upon anything and everything else, I'd go mad with overwork and frustration. As it was,
the only sort of journalism I felt capable of just then was silly
little 'Scraps and Scribbles' which didn't overpower the imagination, and they damned well didn't fit with what was coming
from over the hill.

I told all this to L. McStarna.

Why on earth should I confide in him? God knows, but I
did. And he said, "I'll give you a watchword. KEEP CLEAR.
Get out of it, move – if you need to finish *dhe buke,* you'll nev-

er do it here, if indeed you've even begun it. Find somewhere else. Write up your interview, it's a swansong: tell nobody. Then go." Which should have been his exit-line: but he turned around in my office doorway to add, "Keeping Clear, very likely, could be the backbone of *dhe buke*, could link together all the subplots, d'you see? Wouldn't it make a good title? Think about it, anyway."

*

Would Ireland be a good place to live in and Keep Clear? The point was, if I did at long last complete a masterpiece, the Irish government would regard whatever I earned as the reward of *creative writing* and thereby not liable for income-tax. I saw myself swimmingly rich in a landscape of brown bog and green mountain, free for ever of the bureaucratic leeches, free (above all) to expand my imagination and let it go, let it go, with the flow. Of course, in the north-east corner they were breakfasting on blood and horror; oh indeed I'd Keep Clear of all that – a man at *The Sheffield Star* had had a camping-car holiday the length of the west coast from Donegal to Dingle – never any trouble, he said, once one got used to BRITS OUT graffiti on gable walls here and there, and at times on the surface of the road – fact was, he said, the rural people loved having the English in, provided the English were not only punctilious with the cash but slick and smooth in their praises for the warmth of the Irish character, its generosity, hospitality, tolerance, and so forth – I'd soon get the hang of it, he said. Nor would it do any harm, he said, were I to hang out a black flag when the next lot of IRA men died upon hunger strike

To tell truth, he wasn't wrong.

I went over with the car and travelled much the same route he had taken. I was captivated by the landscape and found the folk, on the whole, as pleasant as he'd described. I found the estate agents more than ready to listen to my requirements. I found a whitewashed hillside cottage some thirty-odd miles north-west of Galway, very much in the wilds, ideal for a wild-hearted writer. It was in a state of semi-ruin but the price was so low that what else could I do but take it? I suppose Eve took the apple in the same light-hearted way. Anyroad, I'm a Yorkshireman, I don't buy pigs in pokes, I made sure the agent put me in touch with a builder who'd estimate for repairs before I clapped hands on the bargain.

These days I'd not be so daft: but the break had to be made, and I'd made it, and d'you know, I still say it was worth it, however much of my money that blackguard of a builder shoved into his bloody trousers. Nor did he hurry himself, while I camped in a pair of rooms in a down-at-heel township called Leenane. Right: so we live and learn.

As soon as he had the roof on, I moved in, holus-bolus, and never mind the paintwork. I did have some work to keep me busy and bring in an exiguous cashflow. I'd made arrangements with a number of editors in England to keep sending them amusing pieces, social, domestic – observations germane to my new Irish experience – I thought 'Spike' would be too near my old Yorkshire concerns, so I found a fresh byline, 'Captain Macmorris.' (Pioneer stage-Irishman from *Henry V*, rather neat, right?) And I played every day, at least for an hour or so, with the manuscript of *Keeping Clear*. If I couldn't write it here, I told myself, I'd never bloody write it.

I was finally settled-in, with my feet on my own hearthstone, by the middle of '84. By the middle of '84, the Scargill-Thatcher war had broken out in all its fury. My replacement at *The Intelligencer* – Chas Buswell, late of *The Barnsley Chronicle* – dropped me a line to let me know that good old Geraldine and her friends were holding the paper to ransom: either it denounced the miners as the prime minister demanded ("the enemy within," right?), or the directors would be looking for an entirely new staff. Knowing good old Chas, I felt sure he'd cave in: and he did. Eh God, I was that happy to be Keeping Clear.

Even happier when it became apparent that L. McStarna would not crop up. Two years in Ireland and neither peep nor cheep from the hideous gnome. Wittingly or unwittingly, this time round I decidedly did not hanker for him. My addiction, if that's what it was, was damn well cured. He couldn't try to write to me (I'd successfully avoided letting him know my address); he never seemed to have any address anywhere, so I couldn't write to *him*. Moreover, I was still waiting for a telephone to be installed, always a slow business in Ireland. Nonetheless, I was darkly afraid that if it suited him to find me, he'd arrive.

The one who did crop up – disturbingly enough for Captain Macmorris and his mordant pen – was the President of the United States. Mr Reagan (so they told us) had been born of Tipperary people; with an eye to his approaching re-election, he'd pay a visit to his granddad's birthplace. White House publicity hacks would inspect village and villagers for photo-opportunities – unless it was all too sordid, when they'd have to think of something else. He would naturally be in receipt of a fulsome political welcome in Dublin, and would address the Irish legislators en masse. He would also be in receipt of an honorary doctorate-of-law from Galway University. This latter was sufficiently close to my front gate to make a detailed hour-by-hour account a professional necessity: especially as the hostile demonstrations were already being planned. I must get the inside story into the provincial English press in a style twice as vivid and better-informed than the standard reports from Reuters and AP; if I couldn't, then I -   Eh up, this could be the end for Captain Macmorris! and he'd not been in business much more than eighteen months; real Irish politics were altogether too heavy, way out of his brief, they were bound in some way to be wrapped up with gunmen, they were not what he'd been created to deal with, they were -   I envisaged not only riots but riotous policing; the Garda Síochána had a malodorous reputation when it came to crowd-dispersal.

Excruciating paradox: how as a journalist I felt impelled to be in the thick of these affairs! how as a self-protective novelist I longed to be nowhere near 'em! what *was* I to do? Forget Arthur Scargill – the carry-on in Galway would be my the genuine swansong – once I'd pulled it off, there was nowt between

me and the masterpiece. Oldroyd's *Keeping Clear,* best-seller of
1990, "a majestic flash-flood of erotic passion athwart the chill
dialectic of fermenting civil strife, every word a blazing cameo."
(I could write the reviews today, as I light-heartedly wrote 'em
yesterday, even though I'm not yet able to finish the book itself
– well, not altogether finish it, but I *have* made a sort of a start.)
And if I didn't pull it off? In the bottom of my heart I could
foresee myself so depressed, I'd never write another word in all
my life, I might just as well give over here and now ...

My difficulty was, I had not really made up my mind about
Reagan, nor was I sure what my readers might think of him.
In the cinema, I had always enjoyed him. In politics, wasn't
he something of a jovial idiot, of no great use in high office? I
really couldn't rate him as an unqualified fascist beast devouring the heart of Nicaragua. I knew nowt about Nicaragua and
cared less. Dagoes were Dagoes (I used to think), whichever
way you cooked 'em, always on the clatter with their tuppenny-
ha'penny revolutions and their samba and flamenco and som-
brero-covered bandits ... So hadn't I best find out just what
was wrong with good old Ronald to put the Irish in such a
kerfuffle? To start with, it seemed, the people and media were
far more troubled than the British about United States' miscon-
duct in Central America. The Sandinist revolution was seen
as more catholic than marxist; denunciations from the catholic church (at any rate from the Bishop of Galway, so close to
my front gate) had actually caused Reagan's vice-president, one
George Bush Snr., to be sent across the Atlantic in advance of
his boss to remonstrate with press and TV ... Moreover, there
was an outbreak of academic rage at the announcement of the
doctorate-of-law only weeks after the US Navy had sown mines
in Nicaraguan harbours. If the president knew what he'd done
(it was argued), he was an international criminal and unfit for
such an honour: if he didn't know, he was too ignorant for university recognition. At least half of the faculty refused to attend
the ceremony ...

A proposal that provoked more mockery than indigna-
tion was the vainglorious motorcade whereby Reagan would

traverse the city, stopping en route to address the populace; to address them furthermore from the very spot in Eyre Square where his predecessor J. F. Kennedy had made a glowingly successful speech way back in the days of innocence – 1963, or thereabouts.

So the visit was already in trouble. What would the protestors do: for that matter, who *were* they? What would the Garda Síochána do? Would its expressed liberal intentions be reflected in the conduct of individual Guards? If indeed there was to be violence, how on earth should I report it? As amusing and Irish, or impregnate with the savagery of terrorism and cold war?

Doubt, dilemma, *stress* ...

It'd be about a week before the presidential arrival: I'd come down to Galway on a showery Saturday morning, to shuffle among the tourists in Shop Street, to try to feel delight for the brief breaks of sunshine, to take a nervous dekko at the anti-Reagan crowd with their placards and little table and petition for people to sign. Organizing the signatures was a bright-eyed love-child in hippyish raiment, all flowing and flowery; her gentle smile crept between my legs to trouble my genitals, like the south-west wind in an apple tree. It made me want to cry to see such a sweet pre-raphaelite damsel mixed up with this dodgy demagoguery. But the smile was not for me. It was of course for the public in general: in particular, for L. McStarna.

He stood sideways to her table and grinned into her smile. But wait! was it not the fact that he was *refusing* her his signature? That he grinned like a dog and then presumed to say No? I was so mad at the sight of him, so smug, so flirtatious, so short-arsed and *huddled*, so spitefully godawful, in the face of that girl's quite poignant disappointment, that I was over the street in two strides and jabbing down my own name without so much as a glance at the text. He said, "You're mistaken; this is not the class of business you ought to be connected with; remember this isn't the UK; these things signify." Citizens were clustering behind me, to await their turn at the table: I thought, if we must have an argument, it had better be out of earshot. I moved up the street and he moved with me, walking too damned close to me, his hand on my forearm. He was wearing one of those green, waxy, thigh-length waterproofs that the gentry affect for gymkhanas, his hat was a tweed fisherman's item with the brim pulled down all round. He might have been the agent of the Earl of Whatsit, come to collect his lordship's ground-rents.

I said, "Who are you to tell me it isn't the UK? You're as much a stranger here as I am."

He said, "I was born in the town of Letterkenny, we had no running water and not even an outside jakes, we'd to empty our shit-pots into the gutter of the fucking street, the Ireland of de Valera, how are ya? so don't you tell me I'm a stranger." And at once one of his vexatious changes of tone, from turkeycock anger to a sly and comfortable intimacy: "I grant you that Reagan's a red-baiting asshole, but as president of the United States, where I myself have been privileged to apply, and so forth, for their citizenship – no no, *as president*, don't you suppose he deserves respect? Gandhi-ji, may he rest in peace, would have given him respect: he'd have said, 'include, never exclude.' JC would have asked us to render unto Caesar. A matter of peace, justice, fair play, d'you take my point?" A group of important suits was planted at the entry into Eglinton Street, obstructing the traffic, referring to clipboards, pointing upwards at cornices, reconnoitring sites for flags and such – the star-and-stripe motif, hopefully to be subsidized by the corporation for every shop on the processional route. L. McStarna slipped in between them; they irritably stepped aside; one of them gave him a nod of acknowledgment, cool and curt. L. McStarna took advantage. "Bear with me a moment, Councillor," he murmured deferentially. "Spike, you must meet my good friend Councillor Tobin. Spike Oldroyd is the son of a glorious prize-winning writer, a glorious writer himself; and just now, know what I mean? he *is* the British medja. We need to make sure he carries away with him all the proper notions about Galway, I'm after warning him to take no notice of the negativity down the street."

The councillor gave me a fat unreliable smile, his scanty hair was dyed jet black, brushed flat across his pate and held in place by what might have been varnish. "O'course, o'course, o'course," he exclaimed, "We would be second to none in Galway in our defence of the right to protest, but we'd also be aware of certain elements who'd abuse that right in order to maintain a subversive agenda in favour, unspoken, of terrorism north of the border. As an Englishman, and fair play t'ye, you would naturally wish to priory-*tize* all measures to eliminate such an agenda. Priory-*tize*."

His companions were nodding and smiling agreement.

"I'd say," continued the councillor, "that at this stage we'd achieved a decent consensus to th'effect that the protest may legitimately take place, facili-*tated* by the authorities, the early morning of the day of the presidential arrival, prior to the arrival, prior; after that, we clear the streets; so one-and-all we'd be all set to give him the hundred thousand welcomes as is traditional, traditional, and to the credit of the city."

The companions joined in with, "the hundred thousand welcomes, traditional, traditional," and immediately turned their backs to carry on with the survey. Something of a brush-off for L. McStarna, had he hoped to impress me with his prestigious local contacts; but it didn't defeat him; no more than a minor obstacle, he deftly made his way round it.

"Billy Tobin's a pompous asshole, profoundly corrupt," he confided, as we walked up into Eyre Square. "If this Reagan jamboree's anything like a success, he'll have thousands in his pocket from certain hoteliers and such – ah, sure, th'old brown envelope. But he's not a man to antagonize. So you'd best take care what you write. Y'see, let me expound you the problem: within this anti-Reagan protest-nonsense are any number of multiple strands: there's some more subversive than others. If the Sinn-Féin IRA strand is the one that's perceived to be strongest, then the only thing to do is Keep Clear. Or otherwise, otherwise, God knows the damage y'could do."

I had to say it. "Right: so your inclusiveness, by way of Gandhi and the Son of Man, does not include the inclusion of Sinn Féin?"

He didn't like that. He gnashed his teeth at me. "Sinn Féin's a heap o'shite. And in this country, that's it. They'd infiltrate everywhere, give 'em the chance. Go an'write y'r fucking *buke* an'get wise."

Throughout the week he kept away from me. He had disgusted me, damn his eyes, and so had his good friend Billy Tobin. So against my better judgment I made up my mind to immerse Captain Macmorris heart and soul into the protest. I began by catching all manner of vox-pop, from protestors and anti-protestors, notables, nondescripts, tourists, writing it up and sending it off. I scornfully wrote up the corporation's arrangements for the day and sent it off.

*

The day comes: at first light I am out with my notebook and tape-recorder. To "facilitate" the protest, the authorities have ordered it held in a carpark at the back of the cathedral, within two hundred yards of the processional route, but entirely out of sight of it. The route itself runs from the dog-racing track, ad-hoc arrival-point for Reagan's helicopter, through a zigzag of streets to the university campus. The pavements all the way are lined with gardaí, while sharpshooters (Irish? American? no-one is quite sure) lie hidden on appropriate rooftops. Eyre Square is especially protected: there are scores of gardaí in uniform and plain clothes, augmented by a swarm of hard grey faces, dark glasses, two-way radios (US Secret Service, snarling their orders left and right in Clint Eastwood undertones to the Garda Síochána, to the city councillors, to the university bigwigs, to the public at large.)

Despite the "facilitations," several knots of demonstrators defy authority and turn their backs on the cathedral. Contumaciously they seek to establish and conceal themselves amid the general throng of citizens who are beginning to fill the streets, expectant and curious. I see rolled-up 'Nicaragua Solidarity' banners awkwardly shoved under anoraks; I see the Secret Service take clandestine note of them; I see grey faces mutter grimly into the ears of the gardaí; I see gardaí fumble for truncheons and make ready for a sudden rush. I see Lee McStarna sauntering about to chat jovially to this garda and that; they are not quite so jovial in return; rather shy of him, I would have thought. At the top of Eyre Square, as near as dammit to the site of JFK's long-gone rhetoric, is a forlorn little coven of rain-washed folk on hunger strike, huddled upon folding chairs with blankets around their knees and placards propped beside them:

7-DAY FAST against US Imperialism
Reagan Go Home
Galway Is Disgraced by Your Visit

I have taken intermittent note of them during the week. Oddly, the Garda Síochána has made no attempt to move them. I ask an inspector why not. "Ah, well now," says he, on his cordial best behaviour with the press, "we're not in the business of destroying the freedom of speech." (Voice lowered to a confidential growl.) "Not but what some of our conscientious American brethren would have preferred a robust enforcement." (A furtive gesture with his thumb towards a nearby grey-face.) "I told 'em their objection was more a matter of aesthetics than hard-nosed security. For whatever reason, they didn't choose to press the point." He's being disingenuous: I've heard a different tidings.

There's a local newspaperman who does his drinking in the guards' favourite pub, he gets told things in confidence, he tells 'em to me because I'm a Brit and he likes to brag about his connections. Garda Special Branch Intelligence (so it seems) is shit-scared and under pressure. The burgeoning demonstrations have all of a sudden thrown the Dublin politicians, the Galway potwallopers, the university brahmins, into a state of preposterous panic: they are obsessed by the thought of a public-order catastrophe, all the more so when they reflect that Reagan's bodyguards are armed to the teeth and would happily slaughter anyone who might be deemed *inappropriate*. Desperate visions prevail, of "IRA/Trotskys" making riot against the slow-moving motorcade or in the middle of Reagan's speech, of an innocent citizen prone in a splatter of gore, and worse, worse! – a guilty citizen. To say nothing of the president himself shot dead … At the very least, they argue, the procession should be speeded up, the speech cancelled, even though that same speech is a major element of the man's electoral image. He's a popular boss, right? but he still needs the Irish-American vote; his White House fixers must be given a convincingly weighty pretext if they're to cut short the razzmatazz. My newspaperman friend whispers that the guards in their satiric humour have indeed found a pretext – none other than that harmless nuisance, the 7-Day Fast, bespectacled bleedinghearts who can't possibly be removed without the worst kind of publicity – after all, this is not Latin America – could friendly old Ronald be seen to deprive his friendly fellow-Irish of all those civil liberties that their kinfolk in Boston so deservedly enjoy? Moreover, the gobshites of the 7-Day Fast are denizens of the locality, the Guards know who they are. "By the same token," they reassure their stateside colleagues, "'tis the ones that we *don't* know, sure this same 7-Day Fast could be a cover for God knows who. D'y'see what I mean, now?"

The point is made, and taken. The sly implication of undetectable Outside Agitators turns the scale. The 7-Day Fast is left in the rain where it sits, the Secret Service reluctantly accepts the need to keep it there.

Because it's there they do not dare

Let their man set his shoe (not for me, not for you)

On an inch of John Kennedy's square.

No speech: and the motorcade must whirl across town at 75 miles an hour. (The official excuse is the unchancy weather.)

I have already taken a stroll to the cathedral to assess the "facilitated" demo – serious, respectable, largely middle-class, buckets of outraged oratory from priests, a protestant vicar, disaffected lecturers, the local unemployment industry, Sinn Féin (yes indeed), and the provincial left-wing fringe. Allegorical black balloons are let fly in a huge cluster beyond the rooftops, but the wind's in the wrong direction, Reagan can't possibly see them ... And now I'm back in the town centre, waiting in the rain for him to come. Damn his eyes, he's going to be late. But then these great personages are always bloody late – I remember Harold Wilson arriving in Barnsley two hours late and more, to open a – an art school, was it? or a new wing for the hospital? ... L. McStarna has been in Eyre Square, he's hurrying away, face red and swollen, teeth clenched, something has enraged him. He's aware of me as though by magic (I am striving to hide myself under my umbrella), he changes course to accost me, the only way to stop him accosting me is for me to accost *him* and perhaps to dumbfound him and then he'll go away. I say, "Your friend Gandhi'd be fair chuffed to see the hunger strike, right?"

He comes to a halt and glares. He's not just a lizard, he's a card-carrying gila-monster and I don't like him near me: has the sight of the 7-Day Fast scalded his eyes with a spurt of jeal-ousy, as it might be the excrement of skunk? "Gandhi-ji," he grates, and his impeachment of me brooks no escape, "Gandhi-ji the master pursued his onerous fasts for the spiritual edifica-tion of the people of India, his primary purpose; and only after that did a political agenda come into play. Which I took pains to point out to these self-righteous assholes. They told me to fuck off: they have *no* primary purpose, they are jack-in-a-box reactionaries who jump up when the subversives whistle and drop down when they hear 'em cry 'stop!' They are stupid fuck-ing henchmen, that's all. And *you* can fuck off, I've nothing to say to you, nothing."

I ask him, "What subversives?" He has me cornered against a shop doorway; saliva jerks from his mouth as he furiously evades the question. Instead, he swoops incontinent into a foaming diagnosis of atheistic prejudice as a syphilitic chancre infesting the body politic, of cynical spirituality clapped onto the sore like a second-hand bandage befouled with pus, of gun-men and ex-gunmen, of the crimes of de Valera and the bishops.

For a man with nothing to say, he's breathtakingly garrulous: and why not? is it not his last word before he casts me off for ever? He says he is a damned good catholic; he says he's no fucking time for the pope -   Whether he has or he hasn't, he's abruptly cut short: there's tremor through the crowd, murmur of anticipation, tentative beginnings of applause; the roaring Garda motor-cyclists, outriders of the presidential progress, are at the top of the square and about to erupt into Willamsgate Street. Suddenly Lee McStarna makes haste to make trouble; he's seen a placard he believes to belong to Sinn Féin; he's seen a bold youth at Moon's Corner thrusting it forward from amongst the spectators, behind him two or three others; here indeed is the immediate answer to my question, *here* are the subversives, oh yes! As though launched like a firecracker, he throws himself across the street, oh yes! he will deal with them, oh yes! Scuffle all over the gleaming wet tarmac right in front of the outriders; one of them skids and falls over; eh God what a speed the man was going, he's lucky to survive it, the people he falls amongst are also damned lucky to bloody well survive. The procession ploughs on regardless; the darkly-glazed, bulletproof windows of Reagan's car are shut tight and impenetrable – no smiling face, no condescending waving hand – and it's not even clear which of three identical vehicles actually *is* the crucial car.

("Bedad but the Galway people are prodigious disappointed." "JFK rode in an open-top, shaking hands with all and sundry." "Bedad JFK was the business, y'r man today's no better than a hypocritical old charlatan." "But at least he's still alive, man; JFK's open-top ended its run in Dallas, finished, dead, done." For days the entire fuckup will be loudly disputed up the town and down, a gleeful *didn't-I-tell-you?* so palpable you could paper the walls with it.)

The motorcade has gone by, the rain's finished, the sun's out, the crowd is dispersing, the injured motor-cyclist is being loaded into an ambulance which has somehow arrived from behind, and I see Lee McStarna manhandled toward a squad car by vindictive detectives. His sunglasses are broken and hanging loose, there is blood all over his face, his clothes are quite shockingly disarrayed – I am reminded of the day I came upon him in the Sheffield gutter, hooting stinking drunk and beating out his dreadful song. The Sinn Féin people (if that's who they were) do not seem to be under arrest. US Secret Service agents are either arguing with gardaí or vivaciously congratulating them, I'm not near enough to be sure. Nor am I near enough to respond to the anguished look and the hoarse, frantic cry that I receive from Lee McStarna just before they fling him around and force him head-down into their vehicle. I stand there stock still, I look on in silence as they beat him and abuse him and dispatch him without mercy upon his Via Dolorosa. I turn quietly away from the degrading sight. I Keep Clear. Did he not recommend me to do exactly that?

I am no Wandering Jew to travel the world in an endless expiation. And yet I must ask myself, has he got himself arrested of deliberate purpose to fill me with guilt? He knows I've not yet been able to write the book he wants me to write: is this how he's fixed it to punish my inadequacy? Eh God but I see no end to his malice.

Old Titus in the grammar school, as he spouted his Eng. Lit., would bark at us and revile us to incite us to read more widely, more gaily, more aggressively, than the curriculum prescribed. He dug out a series of poets who had never quite fitted into critical convention. One of them was John Skelton, over four hundred years dead: I felt an immediate kinship. Here's a small caustic sample of his verses; who knows what provoked him to write them? At all events, I never forgot them and now they are corroding my soul.

> Though ye suppose all jeopardies are past,
> And all is done ye looked for before,
> 'Ware yet, I rede you, of Fortune's double cast ...
> That when ye think all danger for to pass,
> 'Ware of the lizard lieth lurking in the grass.

I walked out of the centre of town to a side street near the Headford Road where I'd parked my car; I got into my car; I drove straight home to my mountainy cottage. I had a press ticket to the campus solemnities, but I couldn't be bothered using it. I did not foresee that anything very interesting was likely to happen there. (I was right: nothing did.) Once I found myself alone and private behind my well-bolted front door, I drank myself stupid and went to bed. For the next week I neither read any newspapers nor wrote for any newspapers. At the end of that time I had to earn some money: so Captain Macmorris crept to his typewriter to spin a facetious little web about hard-nosed American security and Irish insouciance, oh they'd print it in Lancashire but I knew it was a hotchpotch of cliché and I damn well didn't care.

It was quite some time before I found out (from my newspaperman friend and other sources) a few details of Lee McStarna's trouble. It has to be understood how the gardaí were so pleased with themselves at having outsmarted the US agents, that when roughhouse erupted in the very eye of the motorcade, hurling one of their fellows into hospital, the fury was beyond measure. They rushed from all directions to tear the tripes out of the culprits. But the culprits had adeptly dropped placards and scurried out of sight into the hinderparts of the crowd, and so into a labyrinth of alleyways and back yards. Lee McStarna on the other hand, bursting with self-importance, preferred to stand forward as the Keeper of the Peace, the Upholder of Police Authority; the police (he implied) had been ludicrously caught on the hop. Which did not endear him to them. Still less so, when a Secret Service man came hurrying out of breath to inform the Garda Síochána that "Hey, man, we know this motherfucker." (Deadpan professional diction self-destructing at every gasp.) "Like, we eyeballed him an hour ago and -   Hey, we've just this minute been able to check him out with -   On the FBI database as a fugitive felon. Indicted in Nevada on a bodily-assault rap, '71 through '72. Released on bail pending appeal, breaks bail and flees the country. The FBI notate him a violent psychopath. So what'll you do?"

What they did is what I saw.

And after that, who knows what happened? The arrest of Lee McStarna was never announced in the media, nor was he prosecuted in open court. Nor did anyone in Galway ever see him again. I heard of three possible explanations: –

1. Charges were dropped for fear of untoward embarrassment, whether in Galway, Dublin, or the White House; and he'd slipped out of Ireland in his usual saurian fashion.
2. He was placed in the hands of the Americans and illegally extradited, an occult midnight affair on a secret CIA flight from Shannon, again to avoid embarrassment.
3. He died in Garda custody during intense interrogation – the Special Branch 'Heavy Gang' being desperate to discover his part in any plot to assassinate Reagan, if there *had* been such a plot; or if there hadn't, to convince their chiefs that the US Secret Service had lost its marbles.

These hypotheses were well known to 'the dogs in the street' (i.e. every journalist, large or small), and were the subject of private gossip; in public, never a word. Eventually the man was forgotten and nobody any longer was concerned to question his fate. "Nobody" includes me: I made an effort, largely successful, to stop myself even thinking about him. It is a fact, and today I am able to admit the fact, that I had now and then been glad of his talk, *greedy* for his talk, I'd go so far; because I cannot deny that he was a bloody good talker. And at last, I do believe I can almost discern his mindset. He was a species of lapel badge, a horridly personal version of such cringeworthy messages as I ♥ NY. Once he found out how good a writer my father had been and how famous he might become, Lee McStarna set out upon pilgrimage to Yorkshire to pin himself to the old man's coat; in case he were not made welcome, he drove his parallel prick into mine. (I ♥ TITUS? I ♥ SPIKE? the gorge rises.) How he longed to write my novel! He was a hideous pest; yet I had thought him an essential pest, if ever I were to outshine my progenitor. *Keeping Clear*, I had thought, once it got into print, supposing it did get into print, would need a fervent dedication – 'to Mr L. McS., the only begetter,' and so forth ... Right: I was generous enough to contemplate such a gesture. The difficulty was that his begetting was no good and was doing me no good. The book itself was no good. Like a feeble-minded Frankenstein I had been attempting to miscegenate the style of old Titus with the subject-matter of Lee McStarna and the consequent crossbreed was dead on the laboratory table: had it lived it would have been a lumbering zombie , so I'd no call to shed tears. No: I had been glad of him, eh God I had *hankered* for him, and now I was so glad that he'd gone.

Right: I was free. And totally empty. Puddling and piddling around with odds and ends of silly journalism, growing old, wasting time, I was nohow, I was nowhere ... until, almost desperate, I came down from the mountain, rented a flat in Galway, and astonishingly fell in with my bountiful, gaudy Ute, my roly-poly German Goldilocks, revelation of towering delight, trumpet solo from *Messiah*. She says, "Write it or leave it alone." .

So he wrote. Ute read. She said, "O my beloved, you have cringed, you have wept, you have denied. But no need. Your story, as you tell it, defeats calumny: for you yourself have made record of so little good of your own self. And therefore no longer are you called to be ashamed of your shame. **Überdies***, you can laugh at it and I think that you do laugh.* **Überdies und überdies***, your cruel notion of this lizard-man Lee is not perhaps altogether truth? Invention, perhaps, of the malice of the son of your father? Would you swear before a judge? ... But then I think, how much is it better for you in your grey age that you write this furious fiction than piddle and puddle all your newspaper-***Dreck?** *your* **Zeitung-***dross?* **ja?**

– week by week your current garbage! **Ach Gott,** *you will soon be well able to live in the real world, my own world, my own bed, need I hint further? ... I say no more about it: you will think and then again you will write. We have between us this evening drunken more than enough. Soon it will be time we go to sleep."*

A Plot to Crack a Pisspot

On the north Yorkshire coast, toward the end of the twentieth century, there lived a fifty-year-old gentleman with a notable history of literary attainment. Out of nowhere in particular a very queer tale about him began to be whispered, darkly subterranean and quite devoid of proof: many of those who listened to it hoped gleefully that it might be true, it satisfied so many jealousies. It suggested that this man had been the target of a murder plot; and that the plotters were no mere criminals but some of the best-known names in British cinema.

('Murder' may be over-strong: it is possible that all they sought was his irreversible absence while they devoured his notability and thereby saved their own – did they really require him stone dead?)

His name was Henry Pellinore: his unfortunate nickname, which dogged him the length of his life, was Pisspot. Once heard, it was hard to forget, probably because he somehow contrived to *resemble* a pisspot in an allusive sort of way: he was pursy and sweaty, physically uncouth; as a boy he had exuded a fetid bodily odour; however often, however thoroughly, he washed, his schoolfellows would give him news of it. At the time of these events he no longer stank; or if he did, it was well covered by the reek of his pipe-tobacco; but even so there remained an indefinable personal attribute (superfluity of saliva? a sort of gurgle in the voice?) that caused a slight withdrawal from his immediate neighbourhood whenever he was in company. Only the *slightest* of slight withdrawals – his reputation as a writer meant that he had to be welcomed and talked to, his meals and carousals shared, by professional commentators and insincere toadies alike, as well as by a number of genuine admirers. He was a bachelor; but he had now and again found women who would allow him to make love to them, the intensity of his work had its own seductive power. Now and again he was said to be "Byronic," for indeed he'd been lame since child-hood (predatory teenagers having knocked him off his bicycle in a squalid little alley the wrong side of King's Cross), and he walked with a stick, which somehow served to dignify him. In short, he was only repulsive if you felt a need to be repelled. But the nickname nonetheless stuck.

He wrote parable plays in the epic manner of Berthold Bre-cht, stories as sparse yet as full of erotic implication as the tales of Karen Blixen, quiet haunted poems that seemed to share the muse-dictated visions of Robert Graves: but his work nonethe-les was taut and original, you did not think as you read it of the author's models – it was always "pure Pellinore" and delighted the critics. The book-buying public was less enthusiastic; with-out doubt he was an acquired taste.

His home, Dryghtskerry House, about halfway between Whitby and Redcar, was a tall, square, blank-faced barrack daubed with unseemly pebble-dash. It had been built in the reign of George III by a local squire who had none of the good taste of his era. Pellinore's grandparents had got hold of it cheap, for use as a private boarding school. The school was dis-solved soon after the first world war – a complicated disgrace of adultery, pederasty, political subversion, God knows what ... *Pellinore* probably knew, but he never let on. (It may be that he fictionalized the supposed misdemeanours into one or more of his works; but if so, he fragmented them and disguised them out of all recognition: he was a master of the coverup, both in literature and life.) At the beginning of the '70s he inherited the property from his mother; she'd indulged herself in Soho with a bohemian existence as model and mistress for a series of artists; she rarely came north and took little care of the place. It was more or less a ruin when he moved in; gipsies had squatted in it; the army had commandeered it during the war as a billet; young bikers from Teesside came by night to drink and drug. Pellinore mended the windows, patched up the roof and that was about all. He couldn't afford anything better, being encumbered by a long history of secret debts and disreputable expenses. He was aware that the local people called him a miser. He had little to do with the local people. They lived at a distance, in the village of Dryghtskerry Staithe down a dark, dank gap of the cliffs; Dryghtskerry House was on top of the cliffs and away to the north, keeping itself to itself.

Nevertheless, he was not quite a recluse. Yorkshire was his home but he was never at home there to anybody; whereas in London, and only in London, was he able to relax his fetter-locked northern caution and give himself up to communal flexibility. At least once a year he would take the train to town, see his agent, see his publisher, see any theatre directors who might have a prospect for him, and in general organize his work for the next few months. He had busily convivial connections with the 'better class' of journalist – which is to say the ones most likely to give him a puff on the arts pages of their broadsheets. Conviviality had its limits: he preferred not to go to parties and such where he might have to mix with fellow-writers; in any case, the kind of bragging proclamation he was inclined to present to the media made the fellow-writers unwilling to mix with *him*. Worse, he had labelled some of the most celebrated with infantile sobriquets, no doubt out of resentment of his own nasty nickname: thus Samuel Beckett became "Bandy Rickets," Philip Larkin (in a snatch of bawdy song) "a yard-an'-a-half o' Parkin hanging down below the knee," and William Trevor "Drizzly Weather." He told scabrous tales about authors' wives to his toadies from the press. As for his female colleagues, he avoided mockery: he simply dismissed their work with the abrupt rudeness of a job-centre clerk.

There were certain metropolitan areas of ancient acquaintance which his mother had frequented in her rackety fashion, and where (for her sake) he was still welcomed. As soon as he arrived in London, the smell and the roar of the city would draw him like a blind man's dog to pay a furtive call upon one or other of these 'households.' For instance, a penthouse flat on top of an office building in the purlieus of Langham Place, tucked in behind Broadcasting House: here he might find a delicious assortment of greasily pliable persons of any sex and all ages with whom, by advance notice, he could do almost everything he yearned to do (or he could loll and watch *them* do it). They were costly associates for a man-of-letters who had never been a best-seller, and he needed all sorts of passwords and coded phone-messages to get in; as a rule thirty-six hours in their hot transgressive chocolate-box was more than enough. He called these aberrations his "Dr Jekyll picnics," while the austere little Pisspot he'd left behind at Dryghtskerry House was of course "Mr Hyde," legendary identities back-to-front, upside-down, just to prove to himself he didn't take his quite serious depravities as seriously as all that. To be sure, all this secret shape-shifting failed to make him happy, but he couldn't do without it, and at least he was confident that nobody knew.

Dryghtskerry Staithe had at one time been almost prosperous – oar-and-sail cobles, and (in due course) petrol-engined drifters, went out in all weathers to seek the shoals of herring up and down a most deadly coast, precarious livelihood over many generations for the three or four extended families of the cove. And then the herring went away. By the time Henry Pellinore had his house in watertight order, there was only one sizeable fishing-craft left at the staithe, and its skipper earned his money carrying holidaymakers round the headland. Nearly every cottage in the village was a bed-and-breakfast kept by women; the men drove off in their cars to the the Whitby dole-office or the factories of Middlesbrough. But even as a summer resort Drightskerry Staithe was pretty much a calamity. There was no proper beach, only shingle and a great shelf of dangerous rocks (the original Dryghtskerry, from which the place derived its name); the sun did not shine on it, except briefly in the middle of the day; the coast at this point faced nearer north than east; the cliffs that hid the sun were black and overpowering. The county council, in a futile effort, built a short promenade with kiosks, but had to cut down on its 'amenity fund' before the job was finished. With a similar doomed optimism, the Captain Cook Free House (which had always faced away, being a sensible pub, from the cold sea and the storms) turned itself around and elongated its back yard into what it called a beer-garden to overlook the promenade. At the same time it changed its name to the Captain Cook Hotel, put a 'chef' in the kitchen and a new wing behind the kitchen with a 'cocktail lounge' and 'en-suite bedrooms.'

One day in the mid-1980s, Henry Pellinore came sneaking into the cocktail lounge to sample the wine and despise the chef's buffet-lunch. "What we need," he said to the landlord, "to make this place go, is a festival. Aldeburgh, Glyndebourne, why not Cannes?"

He meant it satirically, but the landlord was desperate, for already it was June and his hotel had no bookings to speak of. He was perhaps rather afraid of Pellinore (whom he thought of as one of those immoral intellectuals), and was certainly afraid that if he were to say too much the man would make a fool of him. So he shrugged and offered nothing beyond, "Nay. It's a thought." Nonetheless, there might be reason to mull over what had been said ... thereafter to mull it over together with a few friends ... and together with some county councillors ... thereafter with the local MP ... to persuade them all (together and separately) to make approaches to the regional arts council ... and thereafter to one Jedediah T. Fosdyke, a fatcat American, TV executive and ardent Anglophil of Yorkshire ancestry, who'd built himself a species of hacienda on the edge of the National Park in the neighbourhood of Pickering. Moreover both the MP and Mr Fosdyke had potent connections with media.

All of a sudden, the thing was done.

It was agreed that opera or orchestral music would be far too costly to set up, at least to begin with, there being nothing in the way of a theatre or concert hall. But for film, on the other hand - Dryghtskerry Staithe had a spacious old lifeboat house, which had not held a lifeboat since the Whitby crew motorized theirs and made themselves available for many more miles of coastline. There was room under the rafters for a raked auditorium to contain nearly two hundred people; the end wall was just wide enough for widescreen. No doubt there was a rough, rude look about the expedient, but it soon became a selling-point, a whiff (as it were) of salt, tar and fish; audiences could walk straight out of the side door below the promenade, down the slipway onto the beach toward the Dryghtskerry and the excitement of the rolling tide. Hugely picturesque: of course by no means Cannes, but small, select and very expensive (as Mr Fosdyke had taken pains to ensure): neither was it disdained by a succession of foreign filmstars of very nearly the highest class. In order to spread the benefits of the festival, business people made the forcible point that there was small enough difference on this coast between winter and summer, so why not attract visitors to an indoor entertainment twice a year instead of just the once? – "Hey," cried Mr Fosdyke, who approached all his media projects as though they were baseball games, "hotdog hotdiggetydog, WinterScreen and SummerScreen, I can see the ads already: wow!"

One might suppose Pellinore would have been invited to join the committee; after all, the whole thing had been his idea. But no: he was not wanted. There were a number of reasons. Firstly, the committee included a strong local element that did not like him. Secondly, even had his neighbours liked him, there would have been a dour north-country suspicion of his origins – he had taken over Dryghtskerry House quite out of the blue, nobody being aware of his existence. And then when folk *were* aware, they heard rumours that dismayed them (and dismayed the MP, who had his eye on the chapel-going vote). If Pellinore bore his mother's surname it must be because neither of them knew who his father was: altogether too many candidates. His mother, too, might not have been the daughter of *her* mother's husband – the school-keeping Pellinores (headmaster and matron) had separated before the girl was born and there were all sorts of whispers about one of their teachers who perhaps was the matron's lover, and who died under curious circumstances. A few old people remembered the affair but refused to discuss it; they primly preferred to "preserve the good name of the district." Thirdly, Henry Pellinore was by no means as well-known as he would be in fifteen years' time: his name was not yet a *name*. And fourthly, as between literature and cinema, a curious two-way brand of professional rivalry kept him apart from the festival's artistic directorate.

As soon as he understood that nobody wanted him, the little Pisspot wiped the sweat from his face and retreated without a word behind the blinds of his funereal house; he sat himself down in a fug of consolatory tobacco and got on with his writing. After a year or two an estate agent came to see him, to ask if he would consider selling the property for conversion into a four-star country-house-style hotel? the festival promised so well and the view from the gardens "would be only to die for, if the yews and rhododendrons could be maybe thinned out a little?" The fellow was lucky not to be thrown over the cliff.

It might seem that things should have changed, as year upon year Pellinore's fame augmented: he won the *Evening Standard* Best New Play Prize, he was short-listed for the Booker Prize, a three-page in-depth illustrated interview appeared in the *Sunday Times* supplement. Without doubt he was now a name. Film-festival visitors, year upon year, kept asking about him – and why should they not? didn't he live just above there? wasn't his ogreish crankiness part of the spirit of the place? was he never to be introduced to the ticket-holders? But the festival committee continued to shun him. When its personalities were asked for a reason, they seemed at a loss – except vaguely to aver that *he* had shunned *them*. Certainly he never spoke to them when he passed them in the street, but he did not altogether ignore their cultural offerings. Each season he would hobble down to the lifeboat house once or even twice to pay out his cash for his very expensive seat: the films he chose were invariably the quirky ones with the smallest audiences, a documentary about an abattoir in Bolivia, a German-language version of the life of James Clarence Mangan. He was not often recognized; in his nondescript grey pinstripe suit he might have been anybody; a lawyer's clerk, perhaps, or a TV licence inspector. A distinguished author? Surely not. He never hung around in the Festival Club at the Captain Cook to hobnob with the mondo-ciné. He never under any circumstances set foot in the Hardrada Hotel, the brand-new, seasonally-flourishing establishment they'd erected "in despite of him" when he refused to let them purchase his house. (It was three-star, not four-star, and a high-priced taxi-ride from Dryghtskerry Staithe, but several local girls worked as waitresses and the foreign filmstars were sometimes induced to stay there.) Meanwhile, year upon year, the festival extended itself; it would soon be too large for the lifeboat house; a regular state-of-the-art multiscreen was already being planned for the top of the hill, alongside the carpark, within sight of Dryghtskerry House ...

One WinterScreen season – was it 1998? – Henry Pellinore decided to treat himself to a new film by a new British name: he was intrigued by the almost insulting curtness of the blurb in the festival programme. It read as though the organizers were somehow ashamed of their choice.

> **CLAPTRAP** (*UK, 60 minutes*) documentary: dir., Gunnhilda Stroll.
>
> Stroll with handheld camera is tendentious fly-on-wall through all phases, fund-raising, pre-production, shooting, post-production, of iconic drama-doc *Raves (1995)*, Brit director Tip Landmann's in-your-face re-creation of Tory era's racism, youth riots and alienated underclass in an Essex sink-estate.
>
> **NB:** *Festival-goers of two seasons ago will remember our SummerScreen scoop of Landmann's* **Raves** *prior to TV screening, by special permission of Channel 4, plus personal appearances of leading actors Vinny Bostick and Tulip – now we can announce a repeat showing (Sunday 9.00 pm, see p.12) of this definitive socially-crucial drama as the final item of the festival, followed by question/answer session, preceded (8.00 pm) by master-class with director Tip Landmann.*

A study of the hour-by-hour work of an acclaimed director, presumably by mutual agreement, so what did they mean by tendentious? Pellinore had a wicked hope that trouble might be on the brew. Had somebody quarrelled with someone? He noted that *Claptrap* was being screened at the absurd hour of nine-thirty in the morning, when most of the festival crowd would still be in their beds. The discrimination was blatant, yet after all the film had been accepted. Tip Landmann of course was a member of the festival committee; but even so, why should his *Raves* be shown for a second time? Some species of quid-pro-quo? A notion here, thought Pellinore, for a murky short story, a lively possibility of sexual-artistic intrigue with a fictional equivalent of the mysterious Ms Stroll, no matter whether her film should prove to be good or bad.

In the upshot, remarkably good; and the lifeboat house, remarkably, three-quarters full. Beyond all denial, the film was 'tendentious.' Nearly everybody caught up in it might well sue this Stroll for libel – except that they wouldn't, because they'd only look ridiculous. Stroll's camera-view of Landmann's leading actors was already an incitement to ridicule: Tulip, black and beautiful, tabloid-hyped 'celebrity model,' appeared a petulant ignoramus; Vinny Bostick played an inarticulate skinhead off-screen as well as on. Tip Landmann himself came over as a cut-price Groucho Marx with a pony-tail, thoroughly untrustworthy; while the beneficent Fosdyke (*Raves'* principal money-man) revealed himself in conference with producer and director to be an unconfident hysteric, almost a racist – for heaven's sake, the exact opposite of his public persona. It was hard to understand how Ms Stroll had contrived to keep herself in place during many of the episodes – surely they all knew she was there? surely they could have sent her packing if they hadn't wanted her there? "Oh dear oh dear," thought the smug little Pisspot, as the film came to an end, "vanity of vanities, all is ... etcetera. Once she started shooting 'em, they couldn't keep away from her lens. But I would one of these days like to ask her about – "

Even as the wish crossed his mind, a diminutive woman came scurrying down the aisle. "Hang on," she gasped. "Hold it. I'm not supposed to be here, not *announced* to be here at all events, but the next screening isn't for another twenty minutes and the guy on the door said I could give you my tuppence-ha'penny-worth, that's to say if you'd care to hear it. Oh, yeah, I'm Gunny Stroll. It would have been better if I *had* been introduced."

She explained that she had heard that some people in the media ("art-holes of the arse-supplements," as she put it) had insinuated there was bad blood between her and the committee on account of defamatory misrepresentation of persons and events in her film. In the absence of any of the committee (she pointed out that Fosdyke or Landmann could have put in an appearance but clearly had decided otherwise), she unfolded a list of the supposed defamations and demolished them with throwaway scorn. "What you have seen," she said, "is true, because what you see is what we got – when I say 'we,' I mean of course *me*. I was there with a teeny-tiny camcorder, and most of the time I was down below the level of the furniture: in fact they forgot about me, and that's where the trouble lies." Pellinore thought it would have been easy to forget about her; she resembled a small rodent, a shrew perhaps, or a vole, red-blonde and bespectacled, with short-cropped tousled curls, well able (he thought) to hide herself in the corners of skirting-boards. She might have been thirty or a few years more. Freckled. She wore a black leather jerkin and an off-white polo-necked sweater. Her speech was swift and diffident – she stumbled over words and lapsed now and then into indistinct mumblings like an old-fashioned method-actor. A curious accent, Yorkshire with a hint of moaning wind on distant hills, maybe some brand of Scandinavian. "Questions?" she asked. "Anything at all – hate the movie if you want to – if you do, I'll hate *you*, but who cares?" A murmur of appreciative laughter from up and down the auditorium: this hunted, gingery creature must have something of a cult going.

Pisspot Pellinore, smart as paint, was ready with his question; but it came out with unusual awkwardness. "No but it's not so much what we think of the film, though: is it? No but it's -   They've *scanted* you in the programme details, given more space to *Raves* than to *Claptrap*, even though *Raves* has its own blurb on -   There we are, page twelve. It's far too early in the morning. Nobody introduced you. What I'm trying to say, is -   Let's live in the real world. They let you make your film because the idea of it kindled their gonads for 'em, then they wished they hadn't because it showed 'em up as a gang of chancers, but they couldn't for very shame keep it out of the festival, so what do they do? they conspire it won't be noticed, yet somehow it *has* been, so where d'you go from here?"

Ms Stroll gave him a sudden brilliant smile; it seemed utterly for the instant to transfigure her, body and soul – or could it be that Pellinore was falling in love at first sight? By all normal standards of sexual attraction, she was no pocket Venus – but neither did he resemble the strenuous Mars ...   "Yeah," she said, "conspiracy." She rolled the word around in her mouth as though sampling a jujube. "An American point of view, yeah? but I'd guess you're not an American? Neither am I, but I worked there two-three years, and every day there the same question, did Kennedy get shot from an upstairs window or the slope of the grassy knoll and in any event at whose order? LBJ's? But one question not so frequently asked: suppose LBJ did *not* give the order, whom did he know who knew it was to be given? y'see what I'm saying? anybody not?"

There was a buzz of general bemusement, people trying to indicate that they didn't quite see, yet anxious not to sound stupid. Pellinore, however, knew exactly what she was saying; intuition tingled inside him from toes to the lobes of his ears. (It occurred to him that Venus had accepted hand and bed from the uncouth Vulcan, although the poets did suggest that her marital ecstasy faded away in short order.) The next few questioners avoided contention and kept strictly to technical matters – what sort of camera did she use? how did she get over the interferences on the soundtrack? and so on and so forth – and the session seemed to come to an end ... But no: she returned to "conspiracy.".

"I guess some of you were bothered when I lapsed into ambiguity? let's forget ambiguity, let's not be prudent, because I've got a question for *you*: see how you answer it: I give you full permission to run me, if you can, into a corner. Here we go: 'I already laid out for you all the truths of *Claptrap*, one after another in line: so if I told you the truth and if you believe that the movie tells the truth, does that mean it's not malicious?' Anyone give me an answer?"

They were caught unawares; for a second time, the buzz of bemusement ... Once again she smiled at Pellinore. "I'll give an answer," he cried; he was up on his feet, he was no longer awkward; his rhetoric flowed, he began to gesticulate, even began to rant. "Truth is neither good nor bad. The truth of your film is how do they do things? they're competitive professionals in a collaborative artform, they scheme and manipulate, thrust all their wit into half-wits to get the half-wits to do what they need. They assumed you would know this; they assumed you would never tell; you're a fellow-professional. And *that's* where the trouble lies: you violated the mystery, you revealed the masonic rituals, you laid open the CIA's plans for the next third-world coup: in short, you're a traitor. Am I right?"

"No," she retorted, "all the way wrong. Not at all a collaborator, my movie's *my* movie, I even did most of the editing myself and that's more important, a sight more difficult, than shooting it. And don't call me professional. I'm a bloody little amateur, I never went to film-school, I'm beholden to none of these twerps and they ought to have known it. So ought you: it's in the programme." She was annoyed. She had thought this ugly fellow had understood her but he hadn't. She turned away from him, blinking, looking out for raised hands at the other side of the house.

A young man, student-type, out of the shadows and rather too aggressive for good manners: "If that what you said is the view that they had of you, like -   Right, so what made 'em let you in?"

Her response was none too friendly: "What d'you think? I was nice to them, him, the jolly Jed Fosdyke, *him*: years and years I've known the man and I worked for him once, never mind how, it wasn't in movies, but I wanted to make movies, he indulged me, he owed it me: I told him so." She stopped in a fluster; she suspected she'd said more than she should have, almost guiltily, she paused and then added, "With the result that *I* owe *him*, so I am in fact beholden, I told you a lie; one of these days, I daresay, I'll have to pay."

End of session. On their way out of the lifeboat house they were all handed voting-forms, to assess their view of the film; the last day of the festival there'd be prizes for various categories and the audience vote was sovereign. Pisspot Pellinore wiped the sweat off his face and limped slowly up the hill, to tuck himself into his house, to persuade his housekeeper to make lunch, to consider the next turn of his sour new novel about corrupt politicians, provisionally entitled *The Slutfund Compromise;* the January sea-fog crowded in under his armpits and bit him to the bone; he felt old and depressed and – not to put a tooth in it – snubbed.

What had she meant? – "It's in the programme." Had he missed something? He pulled the crumpled brochure out of his pocket and spread it on the kitchen table ... Ah! so that was it. A whole page of advertisements (which he hadn't bothered to read) also contained autobio-bits of the directors of some of the shorter films, the not-so worthy films, the festival's *second eleven.*

> **Gunnhilda Stroll** (*Claptrap*): born Huddersfield 1965; two years at Bradford Art College (mixed-media installations, performance-art events); went to USA 1985, McJobs in seven states, street theatre, guerrilla graffiti; billy-clubbed & injured when police-riot broke up anti-capital-punishment demo 1988; busted by Houston PD & deported. Came home knowing how to wield camera in tense situation. Has wielded it ever since.

"Okay," reflected Pellinore. "Tough cookie. No wonder they conspired. Bit of a shame, though. Keep out of her way."

Upon an impulse, on the last night of the festival, he went down to the lifeboat house to buy a ticket for *Raves*. He was vexed to be told they were sold out. Having slipped and slid all the way on what amounted to a toboggan-run of frozen slush, he decided not to go home again at once. He swallowed his bile and hauled himself up the short but perilous lane, part stairway, part cobblestone ramp, to the Captain Cook. A meagre old cove, in a Barbour jacket, green wellingtons and a gentleman's-relish tweed cap, stood blocking the way across the narrowest of the irregular steps. A rim or ruff of untrimmed silver hair stuck out on either side of his cap. His eyes seemed afire with resentment behind thick-lensed glasses. With his short torso, big nose, soup-strainer moustache, whitey-yellow goatee sticking up from an upturned chin, he had somehow the doomed appearance of a Confederate colonel about to be defeated by a battalion of freed slaves. He doffed cap very deliberately, giving a curt little bow. The frosty rays of a street-lamp caught a gleam from the bald dome of his skull. "Mr Pellinore?" he rasped, like a jackdaw with a sore throat. "Who else, but the acclaimed Mr Pellinore? An honour, indeed, as always ... Bear with me," he continued, confidentially familiar, grinning with all his teeth, jamming his cap down again in the middle of his halo of curls. "Only to say that being so close to your threshold in connection with the festival, I naturally desire to pay you my respects, as always. I am in fact consultant upon a new script for this asshole Landmann, he calls it *Aggressive Beggary* or some such pseudo-sociological garbage; I am fortunately able to work with his excellent lady-writer to augment, from my wealth of – ah, may I say, my experience? – augment her inadequate knowledge of the – ah, mendicant community, in the interests of fair play for my good friends the street people ... You're unwilling to remember me? Okay, let it be. Peace and love."

He had been standing, neck slightly off-centre, in a queer questing posture, from which he now dodged sideways past Pellinore and down toward the beach before Pellinore could frame a reply. For of course Pellinore remembered. The fellow's name was Lee McStarna; his origins were obscure but he'd certainly worked in Hollywood in various capacities and nowadays he hung around at film festivals and literary events, pontificating, offering advice. (Touting for work, in point of fact; sometimes he got it.) Over a period of years during the later 1980s he'd harassed Pellinore beyond endurance with an air of appalling proprietorship, haunting and stalking him as "my exemplary comrade, the one writer in England with a glorious greatness of compassion for the dispossessed" – which Pellinore of course believed to be true but did not need to hear from a range of eighteen inches any time that he hoped to be alone. In the end he'd told McStarna to go chase himself or be chased, a dismissal as brutal as he could make it, even invoking the police; and the bloody man had gone. So now he'd cropped up again. At least, at this moment, one small mercy: he was headed in the opposite direction ...

The Festival Club (*aka* the cocktail lounge of the Captain Cook) was cavernously empty save for the landlord and his barman, who were hanging up decorations. Pellinore scowled. "Good God, what's it for? We've already had Christmas."

"Last night of the WinterScreen, Mr Pellinore, farewell reception, soon as this master-class business is over and the final picture-show and that. Nay: they'll all be up here, we've to make it an attraction, we've had a caterer in from Scarborough and all. I took it you'd have been invited?"

"Oh I was, now you mention it." (Indeed perhaps he had been; his letterbox was regularly cluttered with promotional bumf, which he regularly binned without opening.) "I hope that your caterer goes in for smoked salmon. I'm very fond of smoked salmon, on brown bread. I'll have a hot port with lemon."

He sat down and nursed his drink, stuck his pipe between his teeth, watched a waitress at her work. Her busy little bum was like a dimpled tangerine; she bent down and straightened up and bent again to spread the tables with bottles and glasses and platters of kickshaws ... He could not make up his mind whether he should leave before the crowd came in from the life-boat house or whether he might wait and then force himself jovially upon one or two of them and compel them to be jovial with him. He could sneer at their films and watch them try to laugh at the sneers: he was well-practised at that aspect of the conversational art. He realized with great annoyance that he had actually wanted to see this bloody *Raves* – not for its own sake, but because of Gunny Stroll and her *Claptrap*. Why on earth hadn't he booked his ticket when it was still possible? Because he had NOT wanted to see *Raves,* that was why: it was only too clear from *Claptrap* what sort of clichéd rubbish it'd be. Okay, so he contradicted himself: like Walt Whitman, he was large, he contained multitudes. O God he was NOT any longer the sole customer in the lounge, he was snarling aloud to himself and waving his glass about, this newcomer must think him a dangerous lunatic – and O good God who *was* she? Gunny Stroll, was it possible? he'd thought she was long gone – but surely that was her, scuttling into the darkest corner, in a hooded anorak sprinkled with half-melted snow, her telltale hair quite hidden and her spectacles for the moment off? This was worse than embarrassing, it was a psychological earthquake, no he couldn't face her, he'd have to go home, now, at once, this very minute, in what seemed to be a blizzard, and O God he'd caught his foot on a table-leg and spilt what was left of his port.

She was peering at him doubtfully, then she stood up, pulled out her glasses, put them on, peered at him again, recognized him and (to his alarm) intercepted him on his way to the door. "Hang on," she gasped. "Hold it. Your questions and so on at the screening the other day, some were good sense, some of 'em way off the mark, till I wasn't sure were you genuine or were you a plant from the gang. Y'see, I didn't know till after who you were; it made me kind of rude. Why are you here? they told me you never came here, shunned the glitterati, yeah? and good for you if you did. So why? Are you waiting for the highly professional Tip and old Jed the Carson City usurer, with all the rest of the twerps, to come surging up from this so-called master-class and then you'll insult them?"

"Do – do – d'you suppose I'm that reb-rebarbative?" O God and she was smiling. His words were on the slide into the sort of nervous stammer he thought he'd left behind when he'd done with primary school. He was aware that he too was smiling – no, bloody well grinning, uncontrollable inanity – but no, he couldn't help it.

"I guess not," she gabbled, as nervous as himself, "but *I* am. I arrived tonight all set to ambush the master-class when it came for its drinks and not to let 'em go till they'd sent for Security and made monkeys of themselves chucking me out and maybe breaking my neck on the ice. And don't think this place don't have any Security. Everywhere Jed goes, *it* goes. Tell you what, though: my idea was not a good one. I'd have to get drunk to carry it through and if I get drunk I can't talk straight. On the other hand, now I know who you are and now that we've met, there's some straight talking in my mind from me to you and vice-versa. That's to say, a sort of project, an -   Ah-   Like, an attempt at -   Oh fuckit, you'll be interested for sure; but where can we go to discuss? Certainly not here. Maybe the other pub, what's it called, the Mainmast? A bit of a hole, but the festival crowd don't use it."

"No, not the Mainmast, I'm barred from the Mainmast, I'd a row in the bar there with a man that spread rumours about me. But what d'you mean, project? Are you serious?"

"Do I look like a joker?"

"No you don't. It's late and it's cold, maybe we should meet tomorrow. Where are you staying?"

"Over in Whitby, a motel-style joint in a back suburb, like a row of concrete-block mortuary chapels, did the festival pay my expenses? it did not ... Oh look at that fucking snow, will you look at it; I do *not* fancy my chances on the road, not at all, but I *was* wondering – "

"I was wondering – " They spoke both together, and the same three words; they broke off together and laughed. Pellinore stopped laughing and was suddenly decisive. "It's a long wild walk up the hill but it's safer than driving to Whitby; what d'you say to my house? Central heating's unreliable but I've the makings of a good log fire."

"Then we'd better get out of here before all the twerps are on top of us. Hold on, let me swallow my brandy."

She had tucked her trousers into Wellington boots; he hadn't and his shoes very quickly filled with snow. She needed to lay hold of him and physically haul him over some of the steepest passages of the road; but in the end they reached his door. He told her he felt like Scott of the Antarctic, if history had been different and Scott had been rescued by Amundsen's wife. Hectic and humiliating; but the housekeeper had left a mutton casserole to keep hot in the oven and had banked up the ashes of the fire before grumbling off home through the snow (she was the great-niece of the old school handyman; she lived across the yard in what had once been his cottage).

The house was all but unfurnished. There was an abundance of rooms, great dormitories, queer-shaped boot-cupboards, a range of dreary classrooms (some of them still bearing blackboards and maps of the Holy Land), but the only ones habitable were a bedroom and bathroom upstairs, the living-kitchen with a scullery downstairs, and Pellinore's study in a sort of conservatory at the end of a long passage with a view across the bay. He gabbled a confused explanation, excuse, apology, to Gunnhilda, piled timber onto the fire, and crouched down in front of it to work the bellows ...

Even before he had the food out of the oven, she too was talking and talking at such speed that his faltering words came to a dead end: he tried hard to keep track of what she had to tell him.

Or rather, to put to him. She wanted to make a film of his life and his work, she had not intended to declare it so soon, not for another year, maybe, but -   She blurted it out, half-shy and half-violent, that he was known so very well to be a recluse, so she'd never expected to meet him at the festival, but the way in which she did meet him made it absurd she shouldn't declare herself, so here she was, *declaring*.

He was instantly suspicious. He glared at her across the casserole, ladle poised to serve the stew: his glasses were all steamed up, his mouth was twisted, he looked perfectly baleful. "My life," he muttered. "My work." And then, with a snap of his jaws, "How much of my work do you bloody well know?"

"Enough," she said. "Can we have the grub, I'm starving? Thank you." (he relaxed, filled her a plate, passed it to her) "I read your *Kings and Captives* while I was an art student, it excited me and infuriated me for weeks. Then I saw your *Traffic Lights* when the 7/84 Company brought it on tour, and a boyfriend of sorts gave me the first of your poetry books which I kept by my pillow until he took himself off. Since I came home from the States I've caught up with most of what you've written – you'll be able to point me to anything I've missed. I haven't liked all of it, which might well be an issue to be gone into in the movie? like, why should one book of yours tell a powerful story and another one just rubbish? We could work it all out together."

Pellinore was seriously intrigued. He'd had such a proposition once or twice before and had always refused, untrusting and suspicious; but here was this extraordinary 'pocket Venus' (he *had* thought she was no such thing, nonetheless the idea struck deep into his fancy), so wildly different from the smooth operators who'd previously approached him ('twerps' in fact; *her* word and it too struck deep); constructing a film with her would assuredly 'kindle his gonads' to some decisive purpose; already just to imagine it amazed him and thrilled. Of course he could make a putty-nosed clown of himself for ever-and-a-day if he agreed too bloody smartly; but even so, why be afraid of - He was after all a Yorkshireman, there was at this stage the one thing he ought to seek to know: "How d'you intend to get funded? Arising out of which, how did your *Claptrap* get funded? Nobody at the screening thought fit to enquire."

She seemed to be about to prevaricate. "Good question, let's see how to answer it, for *Claptrap*, it was by way of a private

subsidy, that's to say, I -   Oh why can't I be frank for fuck's
sake? – I was funded by Fosdyke. Yeah. He paid for both movies, he hadn't expected them to – to – *collide*, and when they
did he had a problem, which he solved by the cold shoulder for
– for the weakest one, the smallest one, mine. But I think he'll
find out, it was *not* the most vulnerable. No." She was grim,
she was implacable; a harsh moment of silence while she held a
chunk of bread suspended in mid-air, and then she was smiling
and chewing the crust as though all of her troubles were forgotten. "As for *our* project," she continued lightly, "Fosdyke don't
know it, but I've money in the bank, legacy from my snuffy old
dad, he died only a year ago, he hated what I did with myself,
I was supposed to be an estate agent like him and he never got
over that I wasn't, he did sheer fuckall to spring me out of gaol,
but mortal sickness turned him round, and I'm secretly almost
rich. Isn't it wonderful?" Again, such a gay smile, and all melancholy blown away, so why wasn't Pellinore convinced she was
telling him the truth? – or at any rate, all of the truth? At any
rate, it did seem she could afford to make a film.

"It'll still be amateur hand-held camera, just you and me, be
confident I'm not going to descend on you with a whole crew.
The greater part of the business won't affect you, post-production, editing, laying in music, voiceovers, titles, I hope *not* with
waged help or not too fucking much of it, maybe Ricky if he's
willing, I'll keep it far from you unless you really want to look
and learn. Perhaps you do? Do you?"

Looking-and-learning, as it were at her very elbow, seemed
at this stage too intimate to contemplate. So he waved away
her question and asked her another of his own. "You'll edit it
yourself? Now that's a heavy skill, you don't need to tell me.
You never went to film-school, you make a mockery of 'master-
classes,' so who taught you?"

The gay smile had faded; she looked at him sideways. "Oh,"
she said quickly, "I did get some guidance, it was neither here
nor there, one of Fosdyke's people, when I was -   It was part
of a sort of deal; like I told you, he owed me." A sudden, almost

spiteful note of challenge in her voice: "Why do they call you Pisspot?"

This was not comfortable; he wiped his face and stammered. "Why? – oh no, no. I – I'd really pre-prefer not to – "

"Okay," she said, with a shrug, waving it away, waving *him* away almost. "You don't have to answer me now. It'll crop up in the movie, it'll be that sort of movie; that is, if you agree to it. I'm telling you now 'cos I don't mean to lay snares."

They continued eating for some time, without much conversation. Pellinore switched on the television, a maladjusted old cabin-truck of an apparatus; the reception was poor, the programmes banal; Gunnhilda said she really didn't want to watch total rubbish; he switched off. There was a small contention as to who would do the washing-up, which she decisively cut short by going and doing it. Then followed some fumbling nonsense about beds – he was shakily earnest not to seem to be attempting to seduce her, she was no less determined to show herself careless of all such guff – in the end his double bed upstairs was to be hers, while for himself he ferreted out a sleeping bag to go on the couch beside what would be left of the fire ... that's to say, once they'd finished their last drink. They agreed to defer any decision about the film until morning. He opened a bottle of brandy. He found her some cigarettes and lit his pipe. As they smoked and sipped she was watching him narrowly. He felt she *descried* him as an object of her work, neither a friend nor a colleague nor even an ad-hoc host. This was not comfortable. He was tired and preoccupied, uncertain, apprehensive. What had he got himself into?

She soon went up to bed; he sat by the fire, sucked at his pipe, brooded. If *she'd* thought fit to question him as to where he got his nickname, how come *he* couldn't summon up the wit or guts to ask about her "deal" with Jed Fosdyke? She had not given the impression that it was anything to be proud of. She'd said that she'd "worked for him." Was there an implication that the work had been – not to put a tooth in it – in some sense ignoble? Why, she could even have been his wife: any shape or size of a footloose woman was liable to find herself married (at least for a brief period) to one of these outrageous tycoons, and Gunnhilda was the sort who might well call it "work."

In the morning they came together for breakfast. He boiled some eggs and made toast. The snow had largely disappeared; the north wind had swung westerly, and the TV was announcing that the coast road to Whitby was already clear of ice. Gunnhilda had left her car at the top of the village; he walked down with her through drizzling rain to see her safely away. Nothing was said about the film until they were actually in the carpark and about to say good-bye. She looked at him sharply. "Yes?" she demanded, "or no?" Her fists were on her hips, her chin was thrust out, she looked ready to punch him on the jaw. "Yes," he said. She threw her arms around him and kissed him, she jumped into the car and drove off, he stood stock still in the wet and wiped and wiped his streaming face.

An hour later, he's in his study to sort through his notes for the day's work on *The Slutfund Compromise,* his telephone rings and it's Gunny – "Hi! hey! it's Gunny! my God what a fucking turnup, I'm no sooner over the doorstep of the motel than I get a fucking phonecall to call the festival office and hey! I've fucking WON – first prize for documentary – and they're giving it to *Claptrap*! If I'd been there last night instead of in your - your clifftop penitentiary swallowing hotpot – why, they'd have handed me the cheque and the diploma and oh fuck! I'd have watched their fucking faces as they did so! Hoo!" She's chortling and squawking like a foulmouthed schoolgirl with an unexpectedly brilliant result for her final exams, "Come to Whitby," she yodels. "Come come come, *come*! Oho sweet little Pisspot Harry, you-n'-me we have to celebrate – let's have lunch."

She sounds drunk but she can't be drunk, not yet, it's no more than ten o'clock, and he doesn't like either Pisspot or Harry – familiarity might be tolerable *after* she's made the film about him, if she ever does make the bloody film, but on the other hand –"Most wonderful," says he, "majestic and precellent, you are a marvellous practitioner. I'd say lunch would be most apposite, I'll meet you at the motel and we can eat at the Harbour Bar, if you're partial to seafood." He deliberately speaks in measured pedantic phrases, so as to muffle his own excitement from himself as much as from her. This woman is more than *something*: he must not, oh must NOT, take hurt or offence at her raillery. It might even be strategic to give raillery more scope - That is, if he really wants her to - He is unable to settle to work, he goes for a soaking walk along the clifftop, returns home to wallow in a very hot bath where he sponges and scrubs and soaps himself with a manic-obsessive thoroughness, and then puts on fresh clothes from the skin out. All the way as he drives to Whitby his windscreen-wipers ply their repetitive silly trade like the hands of an incorrigible wanker (so he imagines: but how on earth does his imagination fetch up such a concept, now, today, why? He must nevertheless make a note, it might be very useful, he could transfer it into *Slutfund*.)

This was ten o'clock on Monday morning.

At ten o'clock on Tuesday he strides out of her room, or cabin, or shanty or whatever it is, at that morgue of a motel; limp or no limp, he *struts*; all night he has floated like a garland of Hindu marigolds in no mere waterhole of sex, but a vast Ganges of true affection; he is unable to contain his triumphant exultation, he flourishes his walking stick as though it were a drum-major's staff, he chants half-remembered passages from *Don Giovanni*, fragments of Leporello's list of his master's conquests – "and here in Spain there's a thousand and three!" – well, more or less ... He has left her in her naked bed, not to drive home to Huddersfield until twelve, so she has said; she is curled-up in the duvet, hidden, warm, asleep – he hopes a deep, deep sleep of contentment and venereal peace.

Two months later, in the wild days of April, he went up to London for one of his regular visits. He had an unproduced play still lingering on his agent's shelf, maybe some trendy director at the National could be persuaded to - But first, to Langham Place! for now that the moribund Yorkshire Hyde had disconcertingly come to life and his veins so thick with good blood, unworthy London Jekyll must somehow be *dissolved*. Beyond contradiction, those days were finished and done. But dissolved how? Surely by means of one last unbridled abandonment, if only to find what he would lose (what would his *work* lose) if he truly said goodbye to -   Entirely against intention, if not against will, he stayed in that damned penthouse three times longer than ever before. Afterwards, imperceptibly afterwards, it *must* have been afterwards, as he sniggered and growled along Wardour Street in the middle of the afternoon, not yet fully freed from five days' lewd succession of mesmeric images in two dimensions, or was it three? or had it been in tactile verity the pitiless carnal deed, and how many times? – or simply the shards of an hallucinatory dream? – his appraisal of the occurrences still swirled in a cloud of narcotic unknowing, and he'd had to shell out for them more extravagantly than he thought possible. "Inflation, dear darling Harry," so one of them had tried to console him, "do try to have some sense of the pressures of the world, the *real* world, you ugly duckling; why don't you live in it?"

"Real World" – that's what they'd said, he remembered it, yes he did, and the remembrance stopped him short between kerbstone and lamppost, his imbecile serenity riven asunder by an enormous bloody question that had not until now occurred to him: how much of Dr Jekyll should he confess to Gunny Stroll? He wanted her film to be honest, O God he had such need for a paradigm of truth ... He caught onto a bollard to restore his balance against a squall of rain and howling wind, he fumbled for his pipe, O God his tobacco pouch was empty; he must strive to find his way to his favourite shop in the – the Charing Cross Road, was it? and replenish. Only then the Real World! only then could he search for his agent, or scour the town for his publisher about the jacket-design for *Slutfund:* interruption to his planned routine and it vexed him like a pebble in his shoe.

It vexed him even more to see the louche Tip Landmann come loping out of Old Compton Street: a corkscrew of aggravation that mutated into compressed derision, a horrible silent shriek, when Landmann deliberately crossed over the road to greet him.

The director, as usual, strove for the outlandish visual – a kaleidoscopic mixter-maxter that caused Pellinore to blink and wink – black-green-and-yellow striped poncho, white leather sombrero, long greyish pony-tail in a chunky clasp of Whitby jet and red coral, white cowboy-boots painted with bleeding red hearts, mirrorglass spectacles like a Texan traffic-cop. He positively *confronted* Pellinore, a cobra rearing up from its coil; he held out an impudent hand. Pellinore tittered with rage, but felt he had to shake it: he strove hard to aim his own hand with some degree of accuracy ... A warning voice inside his head was insisting, "No no no, *don't* let him see you've been *at it,* he'll only make use of it to – to – how the hell should *I* know for what he'd make use? Play along, along, yes."

Landmann averred, in the friendliest possible fashion, that he was shattered he and Pellinore had not met up at the WinterScreen, but he knew Pellinore liked to keep his own space and he wouldn't for the world invade it, bullshit and congratulations upon Pellinore's latest book. He turned and took Pellinore's arm, to lead him unresisting round the corner into Old Compton Street and an inviting pâtisserie. "Croissons? café-au-lait? thank Christ they're not calling it 'latte.' Don't you agree, wasn't it brilliant when little Gunny won that prize? Not that she'd ever have got it if she hadn't had Ricky Rospovitch to look after her editing, now that's a boy with talent, but the festival was offering no prize for editors, maybe next year we could – "

"She edited it herself. Did she not?" Pellinore's mind was suddenly quite blind to the dross and dregs of the ignominious Jekyll, to the cocaine in a laundry-basket, soixante-neuf in the dressing-up closet, treacle, two-way mirrors, WC with a busted ballcock – all the detritus of Langham Place was instantly swept from his head. For now he had to work so bloody hard and dangerously to keep his stutter under control, to choose his words with elaborate care – there was something going on here, he *must* be aware of it, entirely aware. Men like Landmann were never so speciously friendly without occult purpose. "Did she not?" he said again.

"Did she?" Enigmatic. "I'm told that she may have said so after the screening of *Claptrap*. I'm told she may have said that she'd worked for Jed Fosdyke and Jed Fosdyke was now in her debt. Did she?"

"Did she? I don't remember."

"You ought to remember. You had the devil of a long lunch with her in Whitby, and all o'that. Plenty of time for her to tell you how she -   None of my business to ask you what she told you."

Pellinore's *cloud* had vanished. He could see Landmann now with a cold and dreadful clarity. Kaleidoscope? nonsense. This man was no longer an impressionist painter's flowerbed, but a sharp, precise operator, indeed a damnable spymaster who was talking very much to the point. Aha, though, but *what* point?

"Jed Fosdyke, as you know, is a most bountiful man. Without him I could never have made one single movie. Moreover he knows good movies from bad. And moreover he's most stalwart against cruelty and injustice." (Landmann's tone was strangely forensic; Pellinore felt that a disconcerting "but" must surely be in the offing.) "Maybe ten years ago, he paid a visit to his aged great-aunt in Saratoga, an old battleaxe of a Yorkshire-woman, yes? who took in monthly piles of radical journals. In one of them he read how a bold young chick from Yorkshire had been arrested in Texas under very vicious circumstances – the Bush'n'oil political machine was all geared-up to make a blood-fucking-pudding of her – she being a foreigner, outspoken and caustic, you know how it goes. Christ, but it looked like she was facing without good friends a truly Texan length of gaol-time. So Jed flew straight to Houston and he bribed, cajoled and blackmailed until he got her out of prison and fetched her away with him to his house in the Bahamas – he'd to undertake to remove her forthwith from the USA. So what was she to do? She didn't have the money to fly back to England. She was in effect Jed's guest till he fixed her next move for her. And himself the most generous host. But." (Ah: there it came.) "But also, *employer.* D'you see, I have to tell you: if I speak of his – his weaknesses, it is only because they are the means to an understanding of our excellent little Gunny, such an understanding as I fancy you will need." (Pellinore was wiping the sweat from his face. This conversation was all wrong, this damnable man was all wrong.) "I have to tell you that Jed Fosdyke came into movies and TV only because since his earliest years he's been an unconscionable voyeur. And he pays the highest prices. In particular he loves to inspect certain female – ah – commotions; like, a turmoil of small women with small tits and round arses, angry little sapphic athletes, he can't get enough of it. Gunny was first-class at that trick, he showed her to me himself, through his scandalous two-way mirror. So that was her work for him, she owed him and she had to pay, d'you see? Oh dear, I see you do see." (Pellinore was shaking all over, partly at what he was hearing, partly at what he must once more, and unwillingly, recollect from the *cloud of unknowing*.) "Now whatever you may think, old Jed is no Tiberius. When he saw that little Gunny had had, you might say, enough, he asked her what other work she thought she could do, and she told him, 'make movies.' So he passed her on to me and I took her to Mexico as my pupil/assistant, I was shooting *The Pistolero,* I have to tell you she proved herself in the job one hundred percent – oh, and a word to the wise, okay? I never again saw her bare-buttock naked, not in the whole of that time, I dunno if anyone else did – like, you might care to think about my second assistant, name of Carlotta, black-eyed gap-toothed chick from Vera Cruz, I'd say *she* was a possible to have got to know Gunny rather better than -   No, I'd better say no more, or -   Oh fuckit, here's a fiver for the grub," – a harsh, abrupt conclusion that left Pellinore struck rigid and wide-eyed in his chair; he watched Landmann swoop out through the tables into the street; he could summon not a word of response.

Of course Pellinore did not know that from now on the murder plot was an incipient entity: but then Landmann didn't know it either. Nonetheless, with a light-hearted order of croissons and café-au-lait, a process of crime had unconsciously been set in motion; within months it would be irrevocable.

There can be no doubt that Tip Landmann, long-legged, bent-kneed, moving ever at sharp angles like a knight on the chessboard, had seized the chance occasion deliberately to pollute Pellinore's mind against Gunnhilda – against *working* with Gunnhilda (that's to say), for it was more than a matter of trivial personal jealousy, it was a highly professional ploy. During the months since WinterScreen, it had come to his ears that young Stroll was considering a Pellinore film ("Pisspot picture," he snorted to himself.) If it was true that she'd been fucking that celebrated author, that owlish and unlovely boggart, she'd gone far beyond the call of duty: any film that emerged from their congress might well be a 'conviction-driven' project of authentic cinematic weight; in short, a discernible threat.

Landmann's view of Stroll was uncomfortably complex. To begin with, he had thought to claim her gratitude for getting her out of Fosdyke's seraglio. In Mexico, as his apprentice, she seemed as humbly grateful as he could have wished. Maybe he praised her work too highly and gave her an excessive conceit of herself; at all events, she shied away from him when he made her a quite natural pass, and her manner of refusal was both clumsy and hurtful – inadvertently hurtful just *because* it was clumsy, but Landmann chose to interpret it the other way round, that her gruffness was deliberate, she knew it would give pain. He pretended he didn't mind, he pretended to brush it off, but from then on he watched her with his patronizing affection now darkly blended into obsessive suspicion. For he had sat and he had smirked and he'd enjoyed her humiliation, "barebuttock naked" indeed – as a clergyman's son from Bletchley he was well enough brought up to remember the occasion with guilt. (He remembered it every day.) She did not know he had seen her, until suddenly in a jealous rage he let slip about the two-way mirror. They'd finished shooting his *Pistolero* film, there was no reason for her to stay anywhere near him save for friendliness: friendliness now was out of the question. Within the hour, she'd demanded all the money due to her from the film company, and was on her way to the airport. She chose not to say good-bye to him. That hurt him more than anything. Affection and suspicion were thereafter compounded with hatred. And hatred meant surveillance, whenever he could contrive it. He had nothing to do with her for at least five years. He worked overseas for most of that time, but he continued to keep a rather fatuous watch upon her by means of the internet, and (at least once) by a private detective. He chewed his mobile lower lip and never ceased to *remember*. Meanwhile, Gunnhilda's skill improved with experience; she made vivid and satirical short documentaries; she fought like a terrier for the funds with which to make them; they were occasionally screened at clubs and small festivals; some of them cropped up at unlikely hours on Channel 4. She met Ricky Rospovitch, a devoted young geek of an editor, whose genuine friendship was gentle and undemanding: he taught her a good deal of his trade. Between them they achieved a build-up of underground acclaim, the "Stroll-club," as Landmann called it: he wondered what to do about it.

Until at last he had a film to make in England. This was *Raves,* which he believed to be his most important project ever. Jed Fosdyke, who shared his belief – "wow, boy, your fucking flagship!" – suggested a spin-off, a film of the filming, to "nail it down, boy! fix it! for posterity for good and all, into the archives, wham."

Tentatively, Landmann wondered if little Stroll might be asked to direct the spin-off. Even so, even yet, he still felt he had to patronize; but his deeper motivations were obscure, even to himself ... He implied he felt an urge to rehabilitate himself with her. Fosdyke took this at face value, he hated cross-purposes among his dependants. But he too was inclined to be tentative: "You reckon she's good enough for it? it has to be good."

"Oh she's good, Jed; she's damned good; all her work since *Pistolero* has justified your trust in her."

"Yeah? I guess that's good. I don't regret letting her go from the- ah - from the other - Face-wise she's a dog, though

she was slick, quick and hot enough to -   Dead-white skin
and freckles, I dunno. I guess Irish-red pussy-fur *is* an acquired
taste. D'you suppose she might be Irish? I had my people ask
her once, she kinda laughed."

"When she laughs, it's *not* so good, ominous rather – don't I
fucking know it? But no, she's not Irish. Yorkshire father, Ice-
landic mother. They say there's a lengthy string of Irish DNA
in Iceland, d'you ever hear that?"

"I guess not. I guess there's no harm though, in backing her
for the project. Would you say, certain guidelines?"

"No more than to make sure she keeps an appropriate low
profile; I imagine she's well able for it."

"I guess it could fucking backfire. You say 'ominous'? *I'd*
say she's bold enough for a bagful of cluster-bombs, the Houston DA told me she flew at the eyes of his cops like a rattle-
snake. Hell, Tip, I need reassurance here, *reassurance*, fuckit.
I can't accept it should all go to shit. Lemme think about it,
four-five days?"

Landmann knew Fosdyke well enough to disregard the man's
habitual neuroses: Gunnhilda from that moment was effectively on the books.

It is hard to know what sort of film Landmann expected
from her. Of course a vivid endorsement of his own talent by
his own ex-pupil would augment his prestige, but was he quite
sure that rancour and frustrated desire did not tempt him to
hope for her failure? Whereas Fosdyke wanted little more than
a series of exciting previews to give useful publicity to *Raves*.
He didn't get them. One look at the finished *Claptrap* and it
was clear it could turn Landmann's drama into a laughing-
stock. It was also clear that *Claptrap*, taken strictly on its own,
was something of a masterpiece. Certainly the two films must
not be shown in the same bill. Distribution of *Claptrap* was
deliberately held up; it was only released after *Raves* had received all the good reviews it was likely to get, and after Gunnhilda's instantaneous legal proceedings had been settled out
of court. As part of the settlement, Fosdyke and Landmann
undertook to include *Claptrap* in the WinterScreen programme.

The award of the prize was beyond their control: it infuriated Landmann that he had so misjudged her reputation, Fosdyke laughed drearily and made jokes about her private parts, but both of them were severely jolted. So were a good few of their professional associates. The gathering power of the Stroll-club was now a serious problem.

Gunnhilda, as it were a one-woman multitude of honey-mad bees, positively *swarmed* upon Pellinore, holding him in thrall from May to August. She went backwards and forwards between Dryghtskerry House and Huddersfield; whenever she was with him she talked to him endlessly in order to induce him to talk – his reticence drove her "wildwood fucking mad," she shouted – and immediately a gush of tears and insensate apology – when he did talk she recorded it on audio-tape. She took the tapes home to Huddersfield and laboriously transcribed them. She said she would need "to pull him verbally inside-out before she could make a script of him." A slow process, she said, she took it step by step. He secretly had words with the bizarre private phenomena he thought of as "The Three Weird Dreamers" (neither angels nor furies, these creatures of his imagination had long ago arisen from the Bible classes of his second-rate private school, stewed up in his mind with pre-Hellenic myth and his mother's acrid anecdotes); he gave them fervent thanks that he'd finished with his visit to London before Gunny arrived with her tapes. He kept his mouth padlocked on the subject of London, whether orgiastic antics or Landmann's nasty tale-bearing. The latter had distressed him – irrationally indeed, for why should her misadventures of the previous decade be a burden to her lover today? Or indeed to herself in his company? For if she didn't know that he knew about them now, would it not be all the same as if he had never known? And if he could make himself believe that Landmann was not only a shit in a sombrero but also a mischief-making liar, then in practical terms he (Pellinore) knew nothing, and the man who knows nothing has nothing to tell. However, he was still distressed; as a result, his occasional love-play became angry and spiteful.

She didn't seem to mind; she assumed he was under the strain of her interrogation; strain was inseparable from the job; in any case she herself had very little libido to spare, it all went into the script and the storyboard and eventually the camera and if he didn't like it he must lump it. The work was going well and that was all that mattered – she gave a crow of raucous triumph – she had, she exclaimed, his person, his history, and "the enigma of his poet's daemon," very nearly stripped down to the skeleton.

"Very nearly?" he said to himself. "Let's hope that we can leave it there."

But she went on to ask him, for the first time since that WinterScreen supper, "Will you tell me why they call you Pisspot?"

"Not yet."

"When I come back from London?"

"You're off to London and you never said? What the hell's it all about?"

They had been walking hand-in-hand along the cliff through his derelict garden, it was all very sweet and agreeable and she could think of no reason he should be so startled: it would only be good sense for her to talk to his agent, his publisher, or theatre-people he'd worked with. But then she said, "Soho. I ought to roam around Soho, fetch up any memories you may have of your childhood there? If I hit anything interesting, I'll bring you into it for filming, but at present it's no more than a reconnaissance and I need you to give me some names and addresses ... Oh God, Harry, what's wrong? I can't bear it when I see your poor face all mottled with red and the spittle at your lips – oh for God's sake, won't you tell me?"

The sudden anguish in her voice wrenched away his imaginary padlock. In a rush of humiliation and shame he told her all about Dr Jekyll; he told about his mother, the dreadful old carcases who'd known her, the lamprey-like young creatures they'd been grooming for years expressly for the likes of him; and then, without daring to look her in the face, he told about his meeting with Landmann – "Now that you know what I'm up to when I'm – when I'm otherwhere, wouldn't you say you *recognize* it, wouldn't you say we're two of a pair?"

"Why should you believe that Landmann told you the truth?"

"Did he or didn't he?"

"Oh he did, I don't deny it. But I ask, why the fuck did you *believe* it?"

There was a long, fearful silence between them. At last, in a tremulous voice, he ventured a question: "Is that *it* then? There'll be no more filming, no more – what? – no more hotpot, no more laughs and jokes for us, no more *bed?* Okay," he said, "I can hardly complain, I've finished it for you, haven't I? – for you and for me."

Her face was a blank mask of nothing. Her mouth a narrow trench, just sufficiently open to display the clenched teeth inside it. Her eyes were as dull as old pewter and fixed upon the waves that rolled in upon the Drygyhtskerry a hundred feet below. "If that's what you think," she murmured, "let that be your choice. Except for the filming: you don't prevent me filming by backing yourself out, on account of your abject mistrust. If necessary I'll make a movie about a dead clever writer who's as abject as a turd in a baccy-box. Oh yes and without his consent. But be assured I'll make it: by its very entanglement of drivelling contradictions, I am forced to make it, *forced.* And no remedy." She walked past him and over to the edge of the cliff. Her voice seemed to break, she turned quickly towards him, not exactly smiling but he saw her mouth curled crooked at one corner; good God she was laughing at him. "Of course," she faltered, "if – if you could agree, I'd be glad of your help." He stepped forward to hold her. She avoided him and ran into the house.

So she went off to London to dig up God knows what. True, they were partially reconciled, but the emotions of both remained turbulent to the point of centrifugal disintegration. No postcards between them, no e-mails, no phone-calls. He tried day by day to wrestle with *The Slutfund Compromise,* but got nowhere – he gave it up and turned to verse, reams of it, autoerotic, full of beastly self-pity – he saved it in his usual way, in case he might deliver some of the warmer passages to Gunnhilda, "one of these days" – then he had a change of heart, thrust the printouts into the fire and deleted the poems from his computer. Maybe it was time he definitively deleted *her?* she could never make a film in the face of his refusal? or could she? He took to bringing daily bottles of brandy up from the Captain Cook and gulping them in his kitchen, he didn't wash, he forgot to shave, his housekeeper gave notice and got another job (at a smaller wage) in the Hardrada Hotel. All his old bad smells were accumulating around him. "Oh God," he groaned, "what a mess. Two-way mistrust is a two-way fucking mirror." He addressed his despair to the Weird Dreamers: he knew they sat out there in the dark: he was sure he heard them laugh ... And then came SummerScreen. The plot was beginning to ferment.

An informal meeting, on the beer-garden terrace of the Captain Cook, a week before the festival; the sun for a wonder ablaze through the gap in the cliffs. Jed Fosdyke is there, sprawled in a deckchair, in his white baseball cap and yellow chinos. His thick grey beard trimmed close to his jowls. On either side of him, at two tables, sit Tip Landmann and the creative talent, known collectively and absurdly as 'Team Landmann.' They're called together in Yorkshire for hasty post-production work on *An Aggressive Beggar*, as usual a 'condition of Britain' exposé, produced as well as financed by Fosdyke, bits of it scheduled for this year's SummerScreen as Work-in-Progress. Jed has rigged up a studio-cum-conference-room five miles inland at the Hardrada, but allows them the odd few hours' self-indulgence by the seaside, not as a rule an occasion for serious business; today is an exception. Their première of another searing work is to open the festival: a sarcastic portrayal of Ramsay McDonald and how he trashed the Labour Party nearly seventy years ago. Nothing to do, according to Tip, with Tony Blair's *New* Labour – "But if they think the cap fits, let 'em wear it. Ha." They are all very pleased with this film and congratulate themselves on being the first out of the Cool Britannia syndrome to really bite the hand that feeds them, or that wants to

think it feeds them: they look forward to making a stir. Sitting
alongside them is Cornelius Hagan, a director from the Irish
border country, whose documentary, *Doomswatch,* another
festival highlight, will vivisect the British 'Civil Defence Fraud'
and celebrate the protestors of Clydeside Faslane in their struggle against the Trident nukes. Hagan is a freshman in this particular gang; but he has hopes that Fosdyke might produce his
new feature film – Jed already has the script and has told him it
"looks good, it looks great, it looks – wow!" – which might or
might not signify, but at all events Hagan is keeping well in with
all of them. Also present, though not absolutely of the party,
is unfathomable Lee McStarna; he lies back in a deckchair a
little out of the general sightline and sips at his mineral water;
from below the brim of his seasonal panama he has apparently
picked out a ship on the glittering horizon and is puzzled as to
its destination and cargo.

A new subject for discussion. Tip's trusted researcher, a film-
school graduate, Brick-Lane Bangladeshi, in suntop, designer
jeans and jewellery, may seem half-asleep but she makes a most
competent report: "She's not any longer in Dryghtskerry Staithe,
that's for sure; but the landlord of this joint says she's been in
and out of that filthy house up the hill – like, for months, Tip,
all summer, dead intimate. She was asking questions round
the village but the locals gave her nothing; like, she wanted to
hear all they'd ever known about the Pellinore extended family.
Sounds like she was well into her research, yeah?"

"Yeah," replies Landmann, with a careless yawn as if nothing very much is important. "Was she *living* in the house?"

"You mean, like living *with*? I wouldn't say M'sieur le Pa-
tron was precise, but he winked and jerked his elbow and he
-     What does it mean, Tip, when a Yorkshireman brays out
'Nay' like a donkey refusing to move?"

"It means our little Stroll is most certainly preparing a massive cinematic hallelujah to Yorkshire's fucking finest: I think
she should be stopped."

"I'd be glad to hear you tell me why." Jed Fosdyke drawls his
question, but his eyes are very tight and fixed upon Landmann.

There is an apprehensive stillness throughout the whole group. Nothing is quite as it seems and they all know it.

"Okay." Landmann shifts himself from his indolent posture and leans forward over the table; he chews his lip for several seconds before he continues. "It's easy to sneer at this clown of a Pisspot, those of you who don't know too much about what he writes or what people think of it; the fact remains he is well on his way to becoming a National Treasure. I've been picking up talk where it matters. He is due, overdue, to be celebrated big-time. If it don't happen now, it'll happen next year. A milepost of a TV tribute, a feature-length movie, all sorts of reverential shit analysing his body of work and chatting-up his pals, and after that no doubt the backlash, to debunk his pretensions, explore the sordidity of his house, get soundbites from his enemies, discover inappropriate sex. If the two were combined, you'd have something unique – tribute and demolition all in the one movie. *If* they were combined – and who should combine 'em but Team Landmann?" Appreciative murmurs all round. He quenches them with a glare. He has horrid authority when he cares to display it. "Okay: but we can't. A marmalade kitten has got to him first, scratching and tearing its way into his trousers. I tried to forestall her when I ran into him in London, it don't seem to have worked, he still has her there and she's poison. Okay, she's as sharp as a cobbler's fucking prick; she's blatantly unprofessional and she fucking grassed us up, made unmitigated arseholes of us with that rubbish of a *Claptrap*. If she can do Pisspot, she'll win another prize with it and it won't just be at Dryghtskerry Staithe. And where will it leave the fucking staithe, think about that? Won't it show the world there was this marvellous man, living just above our heads, and our self-promoting film festival never asked him, never once, even to sit on the committee, let alone saunter down on his poor old fucking walking-stick to spend an evening as guest of honour? Think on, as they say in these parts: my friends, we are in the shit : our only way out must be at her expense, she is therefore *expendable*."

"Hey, Tip, the hell with it. Paranoia, paranoia, if we were as bad as you're trying to make us believe we are, who's to say we couldn't fix the brakes of her car? there's some evil steep roads in the region, d'you read me?" Jed Fosdyke might be trying to defuse things by over-the-top satire, but it doesn't quite work. One or two embarrassed laughs and the silence once again is complete.

Lee McStarna puts an end to it with a voice from the back of his throat, and still with his gaze (as it seems) on the sea: "If you people had any conception of spiritual renewal, you would never express yourselves in terms of parody. As a literary form it is basically dishonest. You need to learn to stay safe while tuning-in to the invisible world: to be sure, in some sort we can all sense psychic vibrations, but how are we to know that we sense them correctly? And if we don't – disaster." At this point, the features of the Irishman Hagan are crossed with a spasm of apprehension: it is as though there is suddenly some telepathic intrusion into his consciousness. McStarna pronounces, without so much as a turn of the head in his direction: "My good friend, Corney Hagan here, has the appearance of a man who sees what I mean. Your argument, Fosdyke, is sound as far as it goes, but inaccurately focussed: let me tell you I'm not going to tell you what you should do to make it accurate. Bad karma, bloody damned bad." He uncoils from his deckchair, shows the full range of his teeth (smile or snarl, who can say?), lifts his panama to the ladies; he walks delicately, as though his feet hurt, from the terrace into the cocktail lounge. Nobody has taken much notice of him; he's only said the sort of thing he ordinarily does say, karma, and so forth. Maybe Fosdyke has taken him seriously; if so, he doesn't let on.

Hagan decides to adopt a rumbling characterization as the hardman from County Fermanagh. "I thought I'd meet no more of this class of lillibullero, now that your man Bill Clinton's the height o' the tide with his *peace process*, is that not the buzzword, yeah? in England, not the buzzword? I've heard enough death threats to know when they're valid. To kill *her* will do nothing. For it's nothing but ridiculous. Look for your proper target."

Another long silence.

Says Landmann, slowly, carefully, as delicate as Lee McStarna's feet – "Whatever sort of movie Stroll is compiling, it clearly – from her closeness to him – is to be based upon the Pisspot's words and deeds over the next few months. If she *were* to have an accident, say descending a steep hill, she couldn't compile it, could she? But could anybody else? The grubby little drunk up there on the clifftop would have lost his unexpected true-love – irreplaceable, no? for who'd want to take her place in such a muckheap of a bed? – would he not be collapsed with the shock of the deprivation? – as dead as herself, in point of fact. He'd stutter himself into silence and would tolerate no more cameras, the project would be finished and gone. But suppose, in the midst of her filming, he himself is finished and gone – like, for long enough, maybe, to call halt to her work; how's she going to handle it?"

Loretta, his script-writer, a leathery cruel-eyed woman of fifty, gives a scream like a seagull. "Hoo!" she cries. "*She'd* not be collapsed with any manner of shock or grief, oho not that one, no! if she carries a cunt at all between those bandy short thighs of hers, you'd find it stuffed with stinging nettles. No, she'd never endure any manner of *halt*. It'd be off with the old and on with the new in five minutes, scouring the continents for a fresh project – which she'll get, on the strength of her *Claptrap*, oh she will get it! – and all her Pisspot preliminaries up for grabs! *Our* grabs, why not? Hey, Jedediah, would you stake us for a bid?"

"I'd do better than that." Fosdyke is judicious, his utterance for a change devoid of middle-American rodomontade. "I'd bring her in herself, with her research and her material, on the strictest terms and conditions, to be a non-executive partner with enough in her bank account to keep her polite and to finance whatever fresh project we could shunt her away on. I take it, Tip, we can construct a Pellinore movie without Mr Pellinore, and it wouldn't be *her* movie, okay? and all the circumstance would be so tragic, we'd be busting with kudos before we'd even begun ... Yeah ... That's to say, unless – "

Nervously about to go back on everything he's just propounded, he exerts an agonized self-control, shuts his mouth hard, jumps to his feet and canters off in a sort of panic. This concludes the meeting. No-one for the moment has anything to say. Tip Landmann stands up; he glowers at them, chewing his lip, turning his glance very deliberately from one to the other, a glance that *forbids* them to have anything to say and they obey it – even Cornelius Hagan, who is not exactly bound to either Landmann or the team.

Says Landmann, "Okay, people, sufficient drinks and sunshine, we do have some work to do." They all leave, like schoolchildren called in from the playground. Hagan turns back when Tip softly touches his arm. They talk together quietly for a short time and then separate. Tip swings his long legs quickly up the hill to the carpark, catching up with the others as they board the company's people-carrier. Hagan chooses the opposite direction, down the slipway to the jagged beach, where he stumbles among seaweed, cursing, complaining, getting his feet wet and planning wickedness.

With Stroll still in London, and himself in a primary state of breakdown, Pellinore ignored the opening of SummerScreen, not even troubling acquire a programme. But he did need his brandy and he needed to go to the Captain Cook to buy it – he could have driven into Whitby and bought other things as well, but the trip seemed unduly onerous, and his tobacco and tinned beans were also available in the little shop down at the staithe – he knew he was likely to run into festival people and he knew he looked dreadful, unkempt, dirty, buttons missing from his suit, even flybuttons for God's sake, but that was *their* problem; for was he not a writer and the hell of an important writer (who just happened temporarily to be undergoing a dose of writer's block)? He had a right to whatever appearance he thought fit, they could all go chase themselves. As he shambled down the hill, he thought he saw that adhesive nuisance Lee McStarna coming out of the post office. The very sight of the bloody man thrust criminal carnage into the forefront of his thoughts, an anger as totally out of proportion as the rage of a jealous child, it crammed his loose-hinged mind into a vortex of horror and gore ... He plunged through the door of the Captain Cook's off-licence. The girl who came to serve him stared at him oddly – "Oh, Mr Pellinore, I wor to ask you this afternoon if you'd thought to come in, would you maybe pop upstairs to the lounge, it's like an invite from Mr Fosdyke and that, says he'd treat you to a drink?"

"Good God, whatever for?"

"Nay, I don't know, Mr Pellinore; I only give the word as it wor given."

She wrinkled her nostrils and shaped her mouth into a pout of disgust at the reek of him, opening the door behind her counter that led to the service stairs: he crept through and went up with his bottles in a plastic bag: the Festival Club (aka the cocktail lounge) was full of disconnected cinéastes, fluttering about with drinks and sandwiches like very noisy starlings: he would have turned tail to go down again, but Tip Landmann prevented him and clutched him almost amorously by the upper arm: "Come along, Harry, come." *Harry?* Never in his life had even the most suppliant moviemonger presumed to call him Harry. Except, of course, just one ... "No, come, we're all good friends here. Harry, my friend, we have a proposition. What'll you drink?" The answer was distressingly obvious: they fetched him brandy. He found himself sitting in a tight little group of Team Landmann plus Fosdyke; he knew them all by sight, save for a bulky ruffian with muttonchop whiskers and Aran sweater, introduced as "the bold Corney," and apparently the focus of the meeting – somehow they had managed to cut themselves off from everyone else in the lounge; even before conversation began, they had silently defined themselves as a *cabal*. This was the plot; these were the plotters; they had him where they wanted him, half-soaked in liquor already but as much more to be poured into him as they could pay for. On the other hand, they didn't want him stupid. Nor *was* he stupid: although he sagged in an unsightly posture and allowed little driblets to run out of his mouth, his right eye behind a smeared spectacle-lens was formidably bright and clear. (As for the left eye, he kept it shut: let them worry until sunset as to why he should wink, he wasn't going to tell them. No sign of McStarna. For which the Dreamers deserved thanks. "Deserve thanks," he mumbled. "Deserve.")

They all look towards Corney Hagan, who clears his throat and takes his cue. "I have," says he, "a script, a picture I'll direct myself; ninety-minute feature on the winding-down of armed struggle in the north of Ireland, how a number of guys from either side of the divide have been gung-ho gunfighters heart-an'-soul since their teenage: where do they go from here? does it wreck their lives or fulfil them? Now," says he, "I'll shoot most of it in Ireland, avoid professional actors, get stuck in to the *real people*, like De Sica did, Rossellini, know what I mean? There's some of it to be shot in Yorkshire, as it might be near here. I'll tell you what I need," says he, with increasing intensity, "I need a middle-aged to elderly Brit, who's been a serjeant in the army, has seen things and done things in Ireland that – oh Christ, they wreck his life. Years of fucking bloodshed, it's all gone for nothing. He's a used-up fucking murderer and nobody wants him. Suicide at the edge of the sea, as it might be the Dryghtskerry rocks. Desperation! Intolerable!" He is shouting, waving his arms, he becomes aware of it and quietens down. "No no," he says, "he don't die, but the experience exalts him – know what I mean? – into a new fucking region of consciousness. I thought *you'd* be the man to play him. Aye, Mr Pellinore, *you*."

Pisspot shuts the right eye as well as the left, he sits without a word for a whole minute in his self-made darkness. Then, still in the darkness, unforthcoming, resentful, insulted almost, he mutters: "God, I can't cope with this and there's no practicality, I'm not an actor, actors have a trade union, how'll you deal with that?"

"Can be fixed," reassures Hagan, to a general murmur all round of "fixed, can be fixed, *we* worry about it okay, no need for you to, fixed."

Pisspot again: "Not an actor. Never have been. Don't know that I want to be."

Landmann, very sarcastic: "Do us the courtesy of telling the truth, if the brandy will permit it. D'you think we don't know? Corney and I heard your lecture, two years ago, on the stage-and-screen portrayal, was it? of characters out of novels – ho, highly intellectual, but you saw fit to *imitate* for sixty minutes on end, the lot of 'em from Olivier to W.C.Fields to Henry Irving to Orson Welles and let's face it! you were bloody electric. You shot out of your skin like a rabbit from its hutch, and you'd hobbled onto that platform as a dirty old sponge, all slobber and sweat. Do yourself a favour, of course you're a fucking actor, don't come the mock modest with *us*."

"Corney says he needs you, what's wrong you should give it a try?" Jed Fosdyke is stern but fatherly. The general chorus echoes him, a vague reverberation expressive of disappointment that Pisspot won't jump to do his duty, just as in the old days, schooldays, horrible bullying back-of-the-bikeshed miserydays.

"Imitate," says Corney. "That's the word, man. Sure, your imagination will find you this old serjeant, you hear him in your head and you imitate him, so you do. It's a treat for you, you'll love it and that's all that's to be done."

Pisspot Pellinore wipes his streaming face with the end of his tie. His right eye is open again, he swallows from his glass. He is rambling to himself like an office calendar, listing days, weeks, months – and then, an irate and bleary outburst – "D'you suppose I've no work of my own to be getting on with? How much the fuck of my time will you force me to fucking give up?"

Hagan explains, very soft, very friendly, that to start with, nothing's needed beyond three or four days' location work – in Dryghtskerry Cove, nowhere else, right down on the Pellinore doorstep – the 'pilot project,' explains Hagan (with a splutter of technical jargon) whereby the movie will seek to obtain its funds. If all should go well, the experience happy on both sides, the money arriving on schedule, then a longer-term contract will of course be negotiated. A script will be in the post this evening, with the relevant pages marked. "No sweat."

Scarcely the appropriate phrase to employ at this juncture: Pisspot Pellinore's drenched in sweat; and worse, his dodgy bladder starts to leak into his trousers – he scrambles out of his chair and out doubled-up to the gents – he is angry and ashamed and conspicuous. He drops one of his brandy bottles on the stair. He does not return to the lounge. He rolls through the bar onto the street. The landlord takes indignant note of him and tells the barman, "Here, if that nasty bugger comes back, you're not to serve him. I won't have him on the premises till he knows how to behave, lightship of literature or not. He's a disgrace to this festival."

The next morning, with an unmerciful hangover, Pellinore took in from the postman a packet with the local postmark. This surprised him – if indeed it was Hagan's script, yesterday's unpleasant nonsense could scarcely have been cooked-up on the spot just to make a monkey out of him – no, it must have been *meant* – unbelievable. He dragged a crisp new script out of the wrapper: attached to it a sheet of headed paper.

Glasgerion Productions (film, TV)
Belfast / Edinburgh / Galway.
C. Hagan, Executive Director

The message was written by hand: –

as from Hardrada Hotel, # 237.

I promised it, here it is: 'If Death Should Be Dead?' Check pp. 93/94/95 for your character, <u>Jabez Robinson</u>. Really looking forward to having you on board. It's an honour, sincerely. Give me a bell (ASAP) to let me know what you think.

All the best – C.H.

If Death Should Be Dead? – a gaudy enough title, a bit too E. A. Poe perhaps? But it did suggest to Pellinore that the story might extend beyond utilitarian realism. It would even have encouraged him to read on if he'd not felt so abominably poorly. He dropped the script on the kitchen floor to be dealt with later;

he'd be more in control at the end of the afternoon; he was by now used to the toxic aftermath of his binges and had learned the best way to mitigate it; but oh how he wished for Gunny to come back and take him in hand. All his dismal loneliness over the past quarter-century (which he had brusquely denied and then illogically endorsed as the necessary environment for first-class work) had come piling up onto him, as it were, in one month and it crushed him. He subsided across his sofa, supine, open-mouthed and dead to the world. At half-past five he aroused himself and drank brandy: then he boiled an egg and ate it with last Friday's stale bread: then he drank a mug of coffee and was violently sick. After which he felt well enough to switch on the television for the six o'clock news, where Tony Blair in swankpot-mode annoyed him so much that he grovelled on the flagstones for Hagan's script in default of anything better – he was certainly not ready to return to the *Slutfund* job, at any rate not until -   Never mind about 'not until.' Had he really thought Hagan's title encouraging? If he had, it must have been days ago. How long had he been bloody well blacked-out? But on the other hand (he flicked through the pages) he remembered the Irishman as polite and good-natured. He'd seemed not to be part of the Landmann gang, so it was doubtless only decent to give his proposition a chance.

It took him nearly twenty-four hours to decide what to say to Hagan. He rang the Hardrada and asked for room 237: a bad time to call: all these SummerScreen chancers would be either in the lifeboat house or ornamenting one of the bars: astonishingly the phone was answered – no, it was not Hagan, it was (good God) that fearsome Loretta woman, yelping into the handset like a she-wolf on a mountain. "Ah you can't talk to him, he's in the shower and well he needs it, tell it to me and I'll tell him, you like the script? of course you do, it's a crackler, I'm just looking it over for further amendments, the Jabez character's massive, you'll do it? of course you – "

Amendments? Further? Had *she* had a hand in the writing? Not auspicious, if she had. And in any case – "No." Which pulled her up all standing. She'd been clattering on as peremptorily as Gunny. Were all of these film-people unable to punctuate? "No. I'll tell you why. I – I – ah – listen, will you, *please.* That Jabez isn't me by a long shot, I'm not at all an army type, let alone an NCO type, I don't have the experience or the skill to -   I'd only make a horse's arse of myself, I know it, so don't, please – *don't* try to persuade otherwise. Sorry. I should tell it to Mr Hagan himself."

She gave a crow of what might have been meant for sympathetic laughter but sounded more like savage mockery. "Oh ho by all means tell him, but you're going to change your mind, y'know, you couldn't possibly let this go unless you'd really truly got work on the stocks we wouldn't dare interrupt? (Hagan, my son, are you there? – I have him on the blower, he says No.) So here he is this minute: Hagan to talk to Pellinore as naked as when he was born, dripping water all over the carpet: so, Pellinore! you tell him and see what he says." .

He told; and then he added: "Mind you, I do – do think it's a fine script, even when -   I do think your Jabez Robinson is surely too old for me, if -   As I take it, his atrocities in Ireland are all over by '73 and then he's discharged unfit, that's twenty-five years ago, he could easily be hitting seventy, okay? Look, I don't – I don't want to leave you out on a limb with this. D'you know a man called Lee McStarna? He's here at the festival, I'd say he fitted Robinson like Cinderella into the slipper, look him out and see what you think? So if – if you like him, I haven't let you down, okay?" No, but he'd let *himself* down by this incorrigible stuttering, he ought for very pride to have couched his refusal in dignified periods. He could do the late great Churchill as well as any actor with a backbone and two hands, but he couldn't do great Pellinore to save his very soul. Oh how he wished for Gunny to come back, where *was* she, oh where?

Nor was his misery finished. Hagan was still at it, persuading and persuading, smooth treacly voice, the harsh Ulster burr so sweetly softened down to wheedle and woo. "No not at all, I do know Mr McStarna, but he's not – not at all – no. And his voice isn't right, more Americano-Scots, I'd say, than demo-

graphic Brit. By which token, Mr Pellinore, I most genuinely
assure you that yourself and none other can – "

With a barefaced lie about the gasman being at the door to
read the meter, Pellinore swore to call Hagan back in – in –
twenty minutes, and rang off. Once again, he was up against
impediment in his speech, but twenty minutes should be sufficient; he was only playing for time, of course, because he truly
did not know what he ought to do. He'd recommended the
obnoxious McStarna for no real reason except a sudden gust
of remorse for gratuitous incivility, both yesterday and in the
past; but he knew he'd be just as rude again if the occasion came
up. Had Hagan received the recommendation with the slightest appearance of intelligent approval, Pellinore would have felt
absolved of further action: but he hadn't. And then there was,
was there not? in the interstices of Pellinore's psyche, a strong
secret lust for the stage, which for long he'd pretended wasn't
there – ever since, in point of fact, a little amateur theatre club
in Notting Hill Gate had turned him down at an audition in –
why, it must have been 1967 – surely not so long ago as that?
(oh but it was.) ... Twenty-five minutes by the kitchen clock,
twenty-eight by his watch, he telephoned the Hardrada once
again. This time it was Hagan on the line, not best pleased at
being cut off for a gasman. "Well? Did you hear what I was
arguing, Mr Pellinore, did you take but one word of it in, because – "

"Oh I did I did I did, and I'll do it. Jabez bloody old Robinson, whenever you're ready, and that's it."

After all, it was only three pages of the script – the suicide
attempt, in point of fact, with very little dialogue – he did not
suppose he would actually have to flounder in the sea until
dragged to safety by the ex-IRA man who had floated up like
a ghost out of the serjeant's past – maybe indeed a ghost, the
script was grimly ambiguous. He vaguely thought of "stunt-
men," and washed himself, and shaved – the whole notion of
Hagan's movie was bringing him alive again. He limped his
way down to the village, smiling and sober, bought a ticket for
a film about con-artists in Nigeria, greeted various festival per-

sons (who were not sure whether they wanted to know him or not), and spent a respectable, critical, enjoyable couple of hours in the lifeboat house. He avoided the Festival Club, lest they chose to refuse him service.

He was astonished to be called to the cameras only a week after the end of the festival: six in the morning, Dryghtskerry Cove. He had heard nothing from Gunny, which was a pity; she might have wanted to film him being filmed. He found Hagan and his unit already in occupation of the cove; they would work there all morning, until holiday-makers arrived in such numbers as to cause an interference. He was the more astonished when he realized the unit was made up almost entirely of Team Landmann people. Landmann himself was not there, but Pellinore saw Jed Fosdyke perched on a rock, keeping a eye on things from a discreet distance. Loretta seemed to be very busy close under Hagan's armpit, holding pages of script fastened to a clipboard; she was making notes on them with a biro as he spoke; a small cheroot smouldered dangerously between her lips. Landmann's cinematographer was behind the tripod on a stretch of sloping shingle; that elegant brown research girl with the flying black hair and all the bracelets was kept running hither and fro upon obviously vital errands; Jed Fosdyke's personal assistant was sitting up there beside him, whispering into his ear. Certainly this would have been no place for Gunny. There were others hanging around whom Pellinore did not know: one of them was a bald round-shouldered Irishman with a face like a barbecued cutlet; he introduced himself as "Teigue O'Hoey, Mr Pellinore, Hartlepool Irish, for what it's worth – I'm to play the bould Gilfillan, your rescuer, so they tell me – your Nemesis, by the same token. Sure I've never done this before, he's after picking me out from the Seán South Republican Club in Darlington, I have at least the appropriate take on the politics. What about you?"

A hundred yards away, at the top of the slipway, a man in a panama hat was leaning against an upturned boat, neck twisted, head averted: it looked like Lee McStarna. Pellinore had no time to wonder about this, for he was just then assailed by the strong hands of a young woman, who'd begun to change his clothes for him; uncomfortable and awkward, in the direct path of a vigorous sea-breeze. She replaced his pinstriped trousers with thick corduroy, his suit-jacket with an army-type dark green pullover, and his mackintosh with a denim jerkin. She crammed a brown pork-pie hat onto his head; a size too small, he thought; she told him it looked right for the character. Meanwhile he did his best to reply to the Nemesis man with a cheery witticism about the ineptitude of Stormont, but he was distracted by the circumstances, irritated, unable to frame words – his attempt at political banter sounded more like a concealed insult. The Nemesis man looked blankly at him and moved off, bewildered rather than offended. But this couldn't go on. What the hell were they all waiting for?

At last Hagan came over to him, bluff and commanding. He said, "You look grand. Keep the hat on the centre of the head; if it's about to topple off, stop whatever you're doing and straighten it. All your life you've been a stickler for your formal appearance, even now in the last stages of – you've read the script, yeah? – the last stages of moral collapse. For this first shot, what I'd like you to do, is to start at the top of the slipway, over *there* – Hasina!" (he was suddenly roaring like a bull for the research assistant) "Hasina, d'you hear me? would you please ask Mr MacStartrek to remove himself pronto?" (a pause while the girl sped towards the disconcerted Lee, waving him away; he might have been an intrusive bluebottle) "Okay, Mr Pellinore, from the top of the slipway, you'll hear me cry 'Camera!' and then I cry 'Action!' and then you come down as fast as you can, running and hobbling across the strand, know what I mean? crippling yourself into closeup down this way, down *here,* oh yes and brandish your stick in the air, you're all but demented entirely, and – Okay, we need you to lose the spectacles, stash 'em in th'auld pocket and –Okay, don't forget to keep up the military bearing, even when – "

"Brandish in the air? Out of the question. If you really need me to *run,* half-blind without my glasses on this graveyard of

a beach, then the stick is my third leg, I'm bloody hell not safe
without it. And neither, I daresay, would be poor old Jabez
Robinson, demented or not."

"Ah. See what you mean. We are of course insured against
-     Do what you can. The essential is two things: you come
down like the clappers, you're as mad as a cut cat. Okay? Away
you go, so. The best you can."

Six times they had him totter at high speed down the shingle, each time it seemed more difficult and indeed much more
painful, each time he was exhorted to do it "more soldierly,
stiffen the back!" or "faster, faster, quick-quick chop-chop!" or
"madder, man, much madder!" Also, they'd given him incoher-
ent phrases to be called out as he tottered. When he (or rather,
they) had got it more or less right, they took interminable close-
ups of his staggering body and his face in the throes of extreme
remorse. They then allowed him out of shot to sit on a rock
and watch Hagan bully someone else for a change – in this case,
Teigue O'Hoey, who at this stage had nothing to do except *slink*
in an inconspicuous fashion along the beach under the cliffs, but
who seemed unable to comprehend his instructions. Pellinore,
determined to enjoy himself, had uttered not a word of protest;
O'Hoey lost his temper and swore. But in the end all was resolved; the young woman in charge of costumes brought coffee
from a big thermos she'd laid ready on the breakwater; the two
exhausted actors relaxed. Hagan and his team set up shots of
three or four locals manoeuvring a boat down the slipway, to
be launched when the tide was well in, for which force of nature
they all had to wait throughout the greater part of the morning.
Sandwiches were produced as a backup to the coffee.

While they were waiting, a second camera crew appeared
and took its place on the far side of the slipway. The costume
girl snorted: "Yorkshire Television, two hours late. Hope
they'll have brought their own coffee, they're not having any
from me."

"Television?" Pellinore was startled. Nothing had been said
about television.

"Their local cultural programme. They'll no doubt want an interview. Local culture, local author, booster for the tourist trade – booster for the new multiplex, if and when. Corney says they're not to bother you till after he's finished the shoot. You don't mind if they film you while you're filmed?" No he did not mind (but he should have been told and it should have been Gunny); he just hoped they wouldn't record him if he *did* make a horse's arse of himself for the couch-potatoes of Cleveland. He should in any event have been told ...

At last the boat was afloat; its indigenous crew rowed it out on the choppy water and back again three times, until the re-flections of sunlight off the wave-peaks caught the camera at the proper angle, or whatever; small clouds persisted in hiding the sun; every time they did so, Hagan threw curses at God. The sea had already rolled in over the wider levels of the beach; only the serrated rocks of the Dryghtskerry stood out through the breaking surf. Layered with seaweed, they were sparkling green, black and silver under constant crashes of spray; they were slimy dark teeth in a growling, belching mouth. Hagan looked at his watch, looked at the sea, looked with a peculiar intensity at Pellinore. His jocularity tended to the macabre: "Okay, Mr Pellinore. The tide's where we want it, the rocks are where I want 'em, I want *you* on the rocks – *if* you'd be so good, sir. 'Tis just about time for your suicide, so it is."

He now begins to issue his tortuous instructions for the attempt at self-slaughter, a precise plotting of Jabez Robinson's every move and utterance; he speaks close to Pellinore's ear in an omi-nous, slow voice, pregnant with emphasis. Even before he's fin-ished, Pellinore makes an objection: "Wait now, wait a minute, please: this is not according to the script. It says clearly that this terrorist man, what d'you call him, Gilfillan? – says clearly he grabs hold of me *before* I get into the tide, but now you tell me different? I'm to jump over all of those boulders, all on my own with my leg, and the Gilfillan character fifty yards away? And what about the stuntman?"

"What stuntman?"

"You assured me over the telephone that any dangerous bits would be done by the stuntman."

"Aye, in the final film. But this is a pilot, we shoot on a shoe-string, have you e'er a notion how much a stuntman costs? We have to do without him, I thought I'd made that clear."

"No."

"It is, I must tell you, a fact that Loretta and I have, if you like, *clarified* this part of the script since you had it. I ought probably to have let you know ... Wait a minute. I have a thought. Wait! and we'll see how it goes."

There is no doubt that Hagan is nearly as discomposed as Pellinore; he goes over to the cinematographer and confers. Loretta joins them. Hasina is sent up to talk to Fosdyke. As she runs, Pellinore's eyes are transfixed by her gait, his concupiscence inappropriate at this particular moment, but she does wear very tight jeans; replacing his bi-focals to give himself a sharper view of her adroit physique, he becomes aware, above and beyond her, of a singular grouping across the top of the slipway. Jedediah Fosdyke stands motionless, intent, between Landmann and – unaccountably – McStarna. There is something hierarchal about their pose, each one with feet slightly apart and arms crossed in front of the breast; they resemble three uncanny statues set to guard an ancient temple; were they women, Pellinore might well take them for his Dreamers ... The girl comes panting up to them, they break ranks (as it were) to hear her message; in so doing they also break the momentary spell they have cast upon Pellinore. Very odd.

He turns away, with a sudden stab of violent headache. He looks at the Dryghtskerry. He remembers – as he has often remembered, but this time it is so lurid as almost to blind him – how his mother would tell him how the man she believed to have been her father had been chased by police upon that clifftop just up *there,* how he'd flung himself in his handcuffs into the height of the midwinter flood-tide to drown rather than face a "traitor's gallows," how he'd fought and he'd killed for Michael Collins's IRA and the freedom of Ireland. Why, some of his bones are very possibly even now (after nearly eighty years) slithering like spillikins among the weed in the cracks in the rocks. It's horrible to think about; Pellinore's head hurts most horribly.

The sequence is to be shot with a hand-held camera; director and cinematographer have been galumphing from rock to rock like a pair of seals, exploring the options. And now Hagan, vehemently agitated, leaps toward Pellinore: "Look, man, we've to do it *this minute,* any more delay and the tide's all wrong, would ya look at that unmerciful stirabout among the crosscurrents already. We can't keep the boatmen out there any longer, and fuckit, man, you're gonna make me lose the fucking sun! So I'll tell you what we do. We'll not record sound, none o' that dialogue we've given you, it can all go down later, no crying or calling, will *that* make it easier? – and I'll talk you through the whole action, like D. W. Griffith with th'auld megaphone shouting the battle of Gettysburg – you listen to every word and you do what it says! One step at a time, man, one step and we're there ... Okay, you're up for it. Glasses off, stick in your fist, take a run like a bloody hero and the camera'll pick you up – GO!"

A nightmare revisitation of school afternoons on the rugger field, a terrifying illusion of boots, buttocks, scrum-caps, flying fists and mud, with a ball in the midst of the scrimmage, the games-master yelling at him to "get down and into it! and never mind your stupid leg," catching him by the scruff of the neck, viciously compelling him where he did not want to go, where he *dreaded* to go, good God! and here's this thug Hagan at the same uncouth tricks ... But at school he was no more than a swot of a 'scholarship boy,' unable to prove to his fellows that he was not therefore a wet or a weed or a miserable Pisspot. Upon this strand he's the Dryghtskerry chieftain, proprietor of his own house, the rightful *inheritor* of the sepulchre beneath his feet – most certainly he has no need to prove anything to anyone. Except to himself. He has given his word to conscientiously mutate into this deranged old mucho-macho Robinson: if Henry Pellinore gives his word, Henry Pellinore keeps his word (not always true, but good God there's no time to analyse anomalies). How can he let slip his one chance to exhibit himself leaping and howling in the dark howling breakers of the ocean? why, dammit it's sheer Burt Lancaster – whose grinning athletics he had so fervently admired even when funking the rugger scrum. Good God, at his age he's a better man than Hagan, though old enough to be the bugger's father. Once again, the bellowing, "GO!" – and Pellinore goes.

Someone has put a loud-hailer into Hagan's grasp, minor technological advance upon Griffith, he doesn't have to shout; but he does, and immediately a tremendous tumbling cataract of command is vomited out of it, totally disproportionate to the width of the location – "Camera! action! catch the fucking action! Mr Pellinore, your left foot on the sharp rock, over *there!* Right foot past it onto the ridge on your right, on your *right,* man, don't you hear me? Straighten your hat, centre head, wave the stick and stab it downwards – jump for the next big rock, I said *jump!* – no, you can't make it, you miss it, down down down, that's how we need it, you're on all fours in the water – now up with you, *up!* up, man and *forward!*" And then, in baffled anger at his actor's unhandiness – "CUT! No, Mr Pellinore, *no* – you're listening for the word of command, I can *see* you're bloody listening – you've to understand it intuitively and do it even as I say it – come back above tide-line and we'll try it once again." Once again. And once again. It gets worse: the instructions come quicker and quicker, contradictory, hysterical, as Pellinore's bad leg seems about to buckle under him. Surges of pain from ankle to knee: the like of which, not since his schooldays -   Why the hell is he sinking so fast into his schooldays? Oh how he wishes for Gunny to come back, where *is* she, has she forgotten him? where oh where?

(It was, though he didn't know it, at this exact moment Gunnhilda Stroll turned the corner of the lifeboat house. She had just arrived from London after a tiring night-time drive, to find a scruffy pencilled note wedged into Pellinore's doorknocker –

GUNNY, if this is YOU? I'm not in, try the beach.

Cameras rolling to GLORY.

WHO'D BELIEVE IT? I'm a STAR. HP.

She obediently tried the beach; nobody saw her; she saw *them* with indignant apprehension.)

"Once again, you bloody auld Pisspot eedjit, if I say 'left,' I mean fucking *left*, left foot, left hand, left bollock, you miserable bollox, left left left – !" Hagan has gone beyond all bounds of permissible drillyard, but Pellinore refuses to resent it, he'll take any slight, any insult, any injury indeed, if only he can finish the man's damnable pilot according to script, according to direction, according to his personal *pride* – and if possible finish it in better trim than Hagan. Hagan's face is white as a fish-belly sprinkled with blotches of red, Hagan's mouth is discharging streams of black coffee mixed with phlegm, Hagan's woolly cap with its ludicrous bobble has fallen into the sea; a breaking wave has caught him, he's sodden to his great thick armpits. Pellinore long since has attained the same condition, but he grimly has *endured* it, already he is used to it, not possible it can get worse: whereas Hagan is falling to pieces. Pellinore glares up at him, from his knees in a foaming eddy where the tide rushes into a rock-pool; Pellinore cannot stand; Pellinore is three parts drowned; with all the defiance of a captured ninth-century berserk thrown into a snake-pit, he cackles outright with laughter at the baffled contortions of Hagan's ugly mug.

Hagan, twice as wide as the little Pisspot and a good eight inches taller, drops his loud-hailer regardless and grips the despised creature by the throat. He whirls him around through whirlpool water like a strangely bewhiskered washerwoman mistreating a bundle of smalls. It could end in most terrible consequence, but it doesn't. For there is trampling and shouting down the shingle, horrified men and women racing to intercept fatality – and the first of them all is Gunnhilda.

She leaps at Hagan's back and *clambers* – she is a marmoset riding a rhino – she has her hands round his neck and throttles him with her small sharp fingers even as he is throttling Pellinore – but this is no good, the neck of this hulking bravo is an impervious cable – she shifts her fingers upward and goes for his eyes. He screams; he lets go; Henry Pellinore falls backward under an incoming wave. Everyone presses forward, everyone lays hands on him to pull him to safety, everyone so eager to rescue that no-one can stop the whole pack of them rolling over and over in the convulsive undertow, scratched, scrabbled, lacerated by the ridges of the Dryghtskerry. Landmann is foremost and Fosdyke just behind him. Everyone is there but no-one is of any real use save Teigue O'Hoey, scaffolder by trade; he deftly watches his moment, husbands his wiry strength, and levers the strugglers one-by-one from the entanglement and up onto the shingle. It seems at first glance that the only ones to keep out of it are the TV crew; they are there to record cultural happening; none of their business to take part in it. No, that's not true: there is another who takes no part: hoar-headed, beady-eyed Lee McStarna; he observes what he needs to observe and then trundles inconspicuously up the slipway, in behind the lifeboat house, into the shadow of the twisting lane that will bring him to the top of the village.

The marmoset Gunnhilda, first into the fray, was apparently the first to recover from it, despite a shining red gash across her forehead. She staggered from the grasp of those who might have been trying to support her; at once she began to denounce everything and everyone – oh without doubt she had seen what they were up to! a deliberate attack, "a murder!" she was hollering, the premeditated murder of a better man than any of them! an older man, a shorter, though no less fucking fat than the slob who'd assailed him! Her words were not coherent, she was spewing salt water, but Landmann and Fosdyke saw at once what she was trying to say; they tugged her briskly between them out of range of the TV; the latter was just then concentrating upon Pellinore, victim/celebrity, shouting silly questions at him even before he was out of the water. A man from Fosdyke's 'security,' which had *not* been mixed up in the melée, had run for the unit's first-aid kit; in this valise was a certain syringe; Landmann knew all about it, knew all about its contents; concealing his action behind Fosdyke's flapping anorak, he grabbed the syringe and stuck it straight into Gunny's left haunch. She passed out. "Out cold!" screeched Fosdyke. "Gonna die on our hands, Jesus Christ. 999, call a blood-wagon, quick as a darky's dick – DO IT!"

'Security,' on his mobile, obliged. "Ambulance as soon as they can, Mr Fosdyke, but it has to come from Redcar, and it's over-steep here for 'em to drive it down to t'staithe – can we carry her betwixt us as far as Captain Cook, or are we forced to wait for an NHS stretcher?"

"There's a stretcher in the lifeboat house," said Landmann. "We'll use that. Go with your mate and bring it." Quietly, aside to Fosdyke: "No problem, she'll not wake for another two hours – chances are she'll not remember what she said – that's the way the drug takes 'em, general rule. We'd best have a word with that blundering bull Hagan – I'd no notion he'd make such a fuckup."

"First things first, hell! get rid of the TV, rid of it, knock 'em down if they won't go, can't they see it's an emergency? – Christ, man, where's Blunt? Rigby? where?"

"Gone for the stretcher, Jed, didn't you see? Keep it calm, keep it quiet. Jed, we do *not* need strongarm; no, Jed, this isn't Nevada. I'll have a choice word, I'll *tell 'em the tale,* that's all." He spoke earnestly to the TV reporter, who reluctantly ordered her crew to pack up and make themselves scarce: it hadn't been the sort of event she'd expected and she wasn't at all sure how much of it was any use to the programme; unmanageable rough-house was not what she'd been sent to record.

Now that he saw the back of the media reptiles (whom he'd personally invited to the shoot), Jed was able to rein-in his panic and re-assume the authority of dollars. He turned his frozen glare upon Hagan. Hagan was not fit to offer any articulate reply, as the chagrined moneyman reviled him like an old-time plantation-owner excoriating his overseer for the costly mortality amongst the workforce in the cotton-field. What in hell (for example) did Hagan think he meant when he bullyragged a monumental Booker-Prize shortlister in front of the whole fucking crew, in front of the fucking TV? sonofabitch, did he think he was at work in a Roman circus? The whole point, the whole fucking point, man, was to have – to have – hey, hell, *Tip! for fucksake*, willya tell this fucking meathead what the fuck was the fucking point! Christ, I don't *know* any longer. Just tell him. And tell him he's fired."

Landmann took Hagan aside and spoke to him gently. The Irishman seemed to be in shock, he shook his great head from side to side, rolling his eyes, dripping seawater from his un-trimmed hair and extensive mustachios, trying to talk but not succeeding. Said Landmann, "He can't in fact fire you, he's not your employer, but face it, Corney, you're in trouble. Like, I don't see his money coming into Glasgerion to pay for *If Death Should Be Dead?* And when Fosdyke won't pay for it, who will? I'm telling you, he's that angry, he'll spread the word through the industry: you'll find yourself bloody well black-listed. As it is, I'm under orders to fetch my people out of this pilot of yours: *I* can't ignore his orders, whatever *you* might have thought you'd get away with."

Hagan found his voice. The small voice of a small boy caught pulling his sister's hair. "Not right. It's not fair. Sure, I know I kinda lost it, like, but they said – *you* fucking said, you slews-thering gouger – all I was to do was to get him into the rocks and – and *break* him, that's what was said, and don't you tell me Jed Fosdyke wasn't behind it. Christ, man, 'twas a *done deal*: if I put him off the walk, I'd have backing for the movie, so I would; you know it, Fosdyke knows it. Christ, you have me fitted-up like a drunk in a hoor's bedsit."

"You had *me* fitted-up, I told Jed you were a hardman, but with brains; and he believed me. Who told you 'break,' hey? who said 'put him off the walk'? The only word was 'acci-dent,' and how *could* it be an accident when your two fucking fists were tight on his adam's-apple and everyone a witness, not least that squawking tart from the Yorkshire TV? What do *you* think she's going to tell 'em when she gets back to studio? You'll be lucky if you don't have a visit from the cops."

"Cops? There's things *I* could tell the cops, if any of 'em come to – "

"Never fret yourself. They won't. Jed Fosdyke'll fix it with 'em, it's the kind of thing he's good at. Look, it's over, it's done with, forget about your pilot. Go back to Belfast, carry on with your TV commercials, and – and be patient and wait. Say, six, seven weeks. By then good old Jed'll have had his second thoughts – I'll make it very clear to him you're due some compensation for – well, for putting yourself on the line for him like a regular dumbcluck and – and I suppose for going quietly when you were asked. Deal?"

And how was it, all this while, with poor little Pisspot Pellinore? In the frantic hullabaloo, the recriminatory shenanigans, he was more or less forgotten, save by Teigue his fellow-actor and the young woman who'd dispensed the coffee. These heroic souls were still waist-deep in water, pulling and hauling to extract him from the peril of the rocks, the slippery unseen abysses, the eddies that surged amongst them at this stage of the flowing tide. What had been a strong sea-breeze was now a gathering gale, the breakers on the Dryghtskerry were nearly the height of a man. When Pellinore at last was dragged out from under to lie prone on a bank of shingle, he gurgled and roared for lack of breath, and his face and his hands were a pulp of pumping blood where the rock-limpets had torn him. (His walking-stick and spectacle-case travelled in and out at every wave, beyond anyone's reach and promising to end up in Denmark.) Teigue would have given a heave to lift him to his feet, but he rolled over and shrieked with pain. The hip joint of his gammy leg had cracked, split, shot from its socket – at all events, refused duty – he could neither stand nor go. "Burt Lancaster my arse," he cried, inexplicably. "I wanted, but I couldn't and good God they wouldn't let me." He lay there and sobbed, his weeping, bleeding face half-buried in the wet stones. He had never been so unmanned since the inner-city hooligans thrust a stick into the spokes of his bike, all those years ago in London (forty years, more than forty? had he forgotten how to count?), and they did it, so they said, because he pedalled down the line of their foul back yards as cockahoop as any rent-collector. The bike had been given him, only that very same day, his ninth birthday, good God, by his wanton, inconsistent, beautiful mother – good God, how he had loved her, how he'd watched her with her flash companions in the floodtide of her turpitude, how ungrateful he had been for the warmth of her stubby white hands and the husky caress of her voice.

He lapsed into semi-consciousness. Loretta the script-woman came and stood over him. "Why, he's worse off than she is. We're going to need that NHS stretcher. Hey, Tip: they'll be sharing the ambulance. Sweet."

Tip, in a hoarse whisper, down upon one knee to put a finger on the pulse in Pellinore's neck: "If he's not properly out, he'll see her and he'll talk to her, they'll compare notes, we can't have that. What the hell fetched her back here this morning? All the grapevine had her safe in the Smoke for at least another month, scouring Soho and Fitzrovia for Pisspot's old wanking-tissues ... Sod it, Loretta, I had but the one jab in the valise – we'd meant it for him, not for her – fucking irony, wouldn't you say?" As he spoke he was rummaging deep down among the first-aid stuff; he found some capsules (he didn't say what), he loped across to the breakwater, shoved what looked like a whole handful into the half-empty two-litre coffee thermos, shook it up to dissolve them, told Loretta to hold open Pellinore's mouth, trickled it into him regardless. Much of it ran out again onto the strand, but – "but he's swallowed enough to bring down a carthorse. We just have to make sure the hospital don't think they're to be treated side by side. Take my car – here's the keys – get to Casualty before the wagon. Jed'll go with you, he's not fit to drive himself, but we need him there to lean on those dodgy doctors. I have to stay here, clear everything fucking up, I'll ride to the Hardrada with all the others in the people-carrier. And I'll follow to the hospital. Oh what a washout, what a putrefying syphilitic washout." He stood up and surveyed the beach, now little more than a narrow ledge of tumbled stones close under the cliffs; the tumultuous breakers ever nearer and nearer. In half an hour the tide would leave no beach at all. It was high time for everyone to go. So far, save for the humiliated Hagan and the amateur stretcher-bearers with Gunnhilda, nobody was going – these film-makers no longer bore any semblance to a unit, just a scatter of bewilderment at sixes and sevens doing this and doing that when somebody told them to, but –Landmann cupped his hands round his mouth and bellowed (the loud-hailer being lost beyond recovery): "Will you listen, will you listen up, Hasina, Conrad, Julia, Mr O'Hoey, *everyone!* No more work for Glasgerion today, maybe not tomorrow, maybe never! as of now the pilot-shoot is totally *on hold!* Everyone please help to carry the gear to the carpark. Okay, okay ... Mr Fosdyke, has Loretta told you what I think we ought to do? Be so good, sir, as to go with her – that's the way, sir, she'll take your arm, I'll see to Mr Pellinore as soon as the stretcher arrives. He's *my* responsibility, absolutely, sir, mine."

Jed Fosdyke, picking his way toward the staithe, leaning hard on Loretta, seemed all of a sudden as old as his age; not exactly senile, but far too worn out to make up his mind to anything. Once he was at the hospital, with men and women in white coats deferring to his status, he would surely reassert himself – Landmann had often enough observed his resilience – although today was a step beyond any previous exigent – today, before sunset, might well involve police. Landmann did not know how deeply Jed would know the quirks and quiddities of the North Yorkshire force. No: this was *not* Nevada. Accusations of murder would cost a sight more trouble to fix than any old festival traffic-problems ... Two ambulance men in yellow waistcoats were stumbling down the slipway; they carried a stretcher and looked about for their patient. The costume girl, going up with her arms full of garments, managed to wave one hand to indicate the prostrate Pellinore, around whom the waters were already beginning to curl. Landmann had his back turned; he was staring out to sea; he was contemplating immeasurable disgrace.

In the evening, in a visitors' waiting-room of the Teesside regional hospital, there's a curious little colloquy – Landmann and Loretta crouched over a table with polystyrene cups of coffee from the slot machine, amid families sitting in clumps at various distances, each family seemingly preoccupied with very noisy children, to say nothing of the sombre misadventures that have brought them here (traffic accident, heart-attack, stroke, and so forth): thus no great note is taken of what amounts to a spinoff of the original conspiracy. An ineffective spinoff, moreover: neither party to it knows what will happen next or what to do if it does happen. Now and then a nurse or doctor comes in through a pair of malachite-green swing doors and takes away one of the anxious families to give them news of friend or relative – there seems a good deal of weeping and sobbing and comforting going on, and children getting slapped: no doubt death in several aspects on the far side of those ominous doors.

Landmann says: "They wanted to know what we'd given her. Seemed to imply – suspect – an illegal substance, whatever. I said it was a sedative. Jed said it was a sedative. Hell, he was the one that loaded the syringe. And where *is* he, anyway?"

Loretta says: "They pumped out Pisspot's stomach. Said another hour and he'd be pushing up daisies, all those pills you shoved into him. Not illegal in his case, just panic-struck and fucking stupid. His hip's broken. They think he's concussed. *I* didn't see him hit his head. Did anyone see him hit his head? Did *you* hit his head? Did that cretin Corny give him a bash with the bullhorn? At any rate there's a -   O Tip, there's a hole in the man's skull wide enough for the nose of a bottle of ketchup and his blood and his brains are -   Hullo, though, Jedediah? and where the fuck's he come from?" – for Fosdyke has entered the room through the green swing doors, which means he's had irregular access to areas of Intensive Care, which means –

"Okay, people," declares Jed, sitting to table cool and calm as a glass of milk, not at all the same Jed who needed all Loretta's succour to fetch him off the beach less than seven-and-a-quarter hours ago. "I've been hunting up some guys who call themselves Mister, not Doctor, which is big in this health system, yeah? and here's how it stands. Little Stroll has nothing wrong with her bar the after-effects of the jab, they'll let her out tomorrow morning. They will *not* let her talk to her Pellinore, they didn't need me to say so, though say so I did; nobody can talk to him for a matter of days; if there's brain damage, not even then. Not even the cops."

"Christ, have they been called?" – Tip.

"*Why* have they been called? O Christ." – Loretta.

"Ms Stroll did some chattering the minute she came out of the fog; I was there at the bedside, but so was the nurse; hell, the nurse heard it before I was able to – was able to *fix* it. Just the one word."

"Murder."

"Murder, Tip, you hit it, yeah. I interjected that friend Cornelius's script talked murder from first page to last, it must have stuck in the mind of Ms Stroll. The nurse wasn't convinced, said she was bound to report it, I had to pretend I didn't give a damn, so I left her to listen to whatever else Ms Stroll might say – and now, I guess, she'll be talking to detectives. So shall we. And, people, we do *not* try to bamboozle them. We are helpful and courteous and as *un*helpful in the upshot as any three responsible citizens conceivably can be … Let's forget about detectives. Let's think beyond detectives and consider our options in the likely eventualities."

Jed is now chairman-of-the-board; his mobile fingers spread out on the table as though at the keys of a piano; each process of his thought illustrated as it were by a new turn of the silent music that he plays all the time he talks.

"Shall we say Mr Pellinore recovers? Inevitably Ms Stroll will tell him what she saw, what she *thinks* she saw, what she deduces. But who can he sue? Glasgerion Productions? Hell no, they'll have no assets, indeed they never had and I can make damn sure they never do. Me? You? No no. We lent certain resources for a young colleague to make a pilot, we trusted he knew his business, we ourselves are as badly let down as Mr Pellinore. So that's where it stays. And no doubt she'll carry on with her movie; she'll refuse to let us buy her out, given the turn in the circumstances since the notion first came to me. Our view of that movie is the same as it always was: after the insults of *Claptrap*, it is not an acceptable project. So how do we stop her?"

His fingers for the instant hover motionless in the air; as it were for the end of the First Movement.

"Shall we say Mr Pellinore *don't* recover? No perceptible difference. Ms Stroll will surely come allover Irish ginger in defence of his life and work, she'll carry on with her movie as a passionate commemoration of the sneering bastard. *I* don't forget what he said to me at the Captain Cook that time, press conference for the first SummerScreen. *I* don't forget the way he asked me why he wasn't on the committee. Okay. So if we can't buy her out, how do we stop her?"

"You seem very confident." Landmann is not confident. "The last time I talked to you, you hardly – "

"I hardly. Yeah, sure I hardly, wow. I was a rich sonofabitch under stress; I often am but I get over it. Which is why I'm goddam rich and you're not."

This is a joke, and Landmann very properly laughs; none the less, he persists. "You thinking of – of *fixing* her? How? A straight quid-pro-quo? Might prove difficult. She's got more on you than you've got on her."

"Has she, Tip? Like what, for an instance?"

Landmann doesn't answer; he stoops over his almost-empty cup, twirling the spoon around to dissolve the last grains of sugar; he might be a forensic pathologist peering into a cadaver. Fosdyke stares at Landmann as though he's no idea in the world what this jerk can have been talking about. Then he says, very slowly, "Okay. She might consider using it, but in the end she won't, Tip, because – think about it – because it was her as much as me, her as much as *you*'n'me, and I guess she'll never again in all her life want to feel that *small*. Which she sure will, if she tries to revive it. So she'll stay in denial about – about whatever the hell might have happened there, one time, the Bahamas. You and I, ditto: understood?"

"Understood."

"Loretta, my honeybun, you don't understand – so is *that* understood?"

"Understood." – Loretta was never in the Bahamas, but she needs no chapter and verse as to Jedediah's playtimes.

"Okay." Fosdyke back again on an even keel, fingers making music, mouth smiling dangerously in the heart of his whitey-grey bristles. "Now, Tip, you told me she's been in London to research Mr Pellinore; the way you told it made me think she was more probably digging dirt?"

"Wanking-tissues." – Loretta.

"If you say so, my sweetlips. Tip, I'd be glad for you to elaborate?"

"Why, I'd guess that she gradually discovered how her cherished Henry Pellinore – whether celebrity man-of-letters or personal bed-friend, *all* of him – was acting too impenetrable for any serious in-depth movie. He won't tell her who he is, so she has to go seek. His life in London as a child, his visits there as an adult. If she's found out what I suspect she has found, she'll want to bury it pretty damn quick. He has his own strange tastes, this self-sufficient genius, he takes pleasure in – "

"I'm sure he does, we all of us do, we all know we don't need it advertised ... I hear what you have to say, I put forward a scenario: Ms Stroll is informed that if she proceeds with her movie, everything she wants to bury will be leaked onto the internet, anonymous, unattributable, gradual. She will read about a 'lovers' tiff' gone vicious, and how her consequentially vicious little movie will smear and debunk said lover for the sake of the fast buck, the sweaty sensation. The word 'paedophile' will surface – it won't need any proof – once heard, the man's biography is contaminated before it's told. Loretta, my lambchop, you called her a nettle-cunt; hell, girl, she's crazy in love with the guy! – hey, Tip, don't you get it? she'd rather die than debunk him, but any other sort of movie – like, hailing his greatness – would be trashed in every scandal-sheet as a pack of lover's lies. So she can't make the movie at all. *She* can't, *we* can. All that we need, my dirty young friends, is to find a director. Agreed?" Fingers running into a final cadenza, "Slam Dunk!" cries Jedediah T. Fosdyke, and the weary, worried loved-ones of

desperately afflicted patients look up in disgust at the yawp of
this hand-smacking Yank. "Slam Dunk!"

And Slam Dunk it more or less was. Pellinore lay in hospital
for months, and eventually emerged from his coma. Gunnhilda
came every day to visit him; when they discharged him, she
brought him home to Dryghtskerry House and looked after him
day by day, taking him out in a wheelchair, helping him walk
upon crutches, helping him walk with a stick but no crutches.
Until she was sure he was quite well, she thought it better to
say nothing about her film, or about what had happened on the
strand. Strangely enough, he didn't enquire. Nor was this the
only thing about him that was strange. He was able to speak
clearly, but he seemed to prefer not: he would growl his requirements in a voice so low and so vague she could barely hear it, let
alone comprehend. He never made love. He said, "I mustn't,
there's the three of 'em sitting out there on the end of the reef,
they open their great white eyes at me one after the other, they
say 'No.'" He avoided any return to his writing. She asked him
why; he grunted, "What writing?"

Depressed, but not yet hopeless, she waited for several
weeks.

Then she showed him his half-finished typescript of *The
Slutfund Compromise*. He looked at it as though it were an
unjustified telephone bill, he riffled the pages contemptuously.
"What *is* all this shit?" he asked. "Did you write it? Why
should I read it? D'you think I don't have better things to play
with? Get your knickers off." He threw himself at her like a
dog worrying a rabbit, attempted to strip her and bend her over
the kitchen table and -   Or he would have done, had he been
able for it. But he wasn't. Confusedly aware that something
somewhere had gone rotten, he seemed to want to hit her, but
his fist struck the empty air; then he fell into a corner where he
cried his heart out. So did she, in the opposite corner ... She
took him back to hospital, despite all his whingeing and his
helplessly passive resistance (she could organize him by degrees
much as you'd house-train a dog, even a rabbit-mauling dog).

In the hospital they studied him, gave him a whole new compendium of tests and put some questions. They put many more
questions to Gunnhilda. They told her, in sum, that this was
as good as it would get. There had after all been a measure of
permanent brain damage: he could follow a normal existence –
as, for example, a gardener's assistant – but an *abnormal* vocation, to be playwright or novelist, was out of the question. She
said, "I can't do this. I've only known him for a year. If I leave
him, can he fend for himself?" They were shocked by what they
conceived to be her callousness; but how could she be forced to
spend the rest of his life as his carer? She said, "I'm not a carer:
I make films: it's the only trade I know, except for – "
"Yes? Except for what?"
"None of your business."
"The best thing to do would be to talk to Social Services."
So she talked to Social Services. She put them in touch with
Pellinore's agent and his solicitor. Then she went away, entirely
away, she could not bear to be near him.
All this time Jedediah T. Fosdyke was pestering her with letters and e-mails and phone-calls, which she ignored. On the
day she finally decided to take herself off, she received one last
e-mail. After which, nothing. He wrote: –

Hi! This is our terminal offer for whatever material, disc, tape,
film or paper, you may have on Henry P. If you don't let us
purchase, you won't be able to use it or pass it on to anyone
else, it'll go totally to waste because the Fosdyke/Landmann/
Screenwork Creative Association as of now holds sole rights to
the life of HP, as contracted and paid for through his agent. And
hell, Gingerpuss, let me tell you: we do not hold those rights
in order to suppress them. We mean to make the movie. Let
me tell you the director we've chosen. Wow, he's the man
McStarna, Hollywood veteran, his CV starts years before his
location work on Huston's *Moby Dick*, one hell of a long long
trail in motion-picture history. The guy deserves a comeback.
Hey, we were fellow-residents of the great state of Nevada one
time: I got him out of the Reno slammer after a playful indiscre-

tion against the corruptions of US patriotism, same as I did for you in the even greater state of Texas. He's something of an expert on HP, but he could use your expertise too; I'd pay you well for it! you'n'him could swop your jail stories, you could show him the bite marks on your round little, freckled little ass. Let me hear from you soon, or for fucksake let me NEVER hear.
– no kidding, your aged father-figure, JTF.

A year or so later, Pellinore's agent wrote Gunnhilda an un-expected letter. He explained how he'd been passing through North Yorkshire, and something had prompted him to look in on his old client in an expensive residential nursing home near Scarborough. The fees for this place were being paid by an anonymous benefactor. ("Fosdyke, of course: disgraceful hy-pocrisy.") He found Mr Pellinore utterly immersed in what was now the chief business of his life – he was covering an entire wall of his room with squares of newsprint and coloured paper, a sort of chequer-work collage to chart the sprawling ground-plan of a labyrinthine apartment. On several score plain postcards, he'd used his ballpoint to scribble indications of men and women in curious postures and clusters. For their exiguous clothing, he'd gummed loosely into place bits of feather from a neighbour-ing henhouse; they fluttered when he puffed at them, revealing every indecent detail that might be imagined by a prematurely ageing debauchee. He said he would attach these cards to rel-evant rooms on his chart, to *humanise* the space by examples of human activity. ("I was surprised the nursing home allowed it. Fosdyke's persuasion, no doubt.") He had already pasted up a reproduction of a painting by a follower of Lucas Cranach, 'The Three Graces,' nude and disconcerting – two had their backs turned, looking coldly over their shoulders, the one in the mid-dle, full-frontal, wore a hateful, terrifying smile. Fresh dabs of white Tippex blotted out their eyes. There was a label.

3 WEIRD DREAMERS?
They look after Dr Jekyll:
Ssh! & they know to be silent.

– inscribed by Pellinore with meticulous calligraphy. The agent wrote that he never saw a chap so happy and serene. However,

> – that film they slicked you out of is at last underway: a crew from Fosdyke/Landmann was packing up its gear at the nursing home when I called. They seemed to have been concentrating on poor Harry's peculiar artwork, an emphasis I didn't much care for. Contractually speaking, there is nothing we can do about it, nor about their choice of director, an Erich von Stroheim manqué who gnashed his septuagenarian teeth and barked at all and sundry. One of the nurses whispered to me that he put her in mind of the Grim Reaper.

Yorkshire Pudding

Chaucer knew all about the region, even though he may never have been there.

> *Lordinges, ther is in Yorkshire, as I gesse,*
> *A mersshy contree calléd Holdernesse,*

– and he seems to have understood the isolation of the inhabitants, reserved and watchful, minding their own sardonic business, standing no nonsense, building great churches, yet not giving a farmer's fart for the clergy. Westward from the reclaimed fen, beside the lower slope of the Wolds, sits the market town of Kirk Deerwood: a throng of red-tiled roofs round the bright white limestone towers of a tall thirteenth-century minster. The town is girdled by white limestone, the broken fragments of defensive walls, nearly as old as the minster. Despite misadventures of rebellion and civil war, the citizens contrived always to secrete their tight-lipped pride in the virility of this ancient architecture and the decorum of its history – a history passed on from one generation to the next in the shape of a species of folk-tale, evocative, picturesque: –

Thirteen hundred years ago, in the days of the Old English and their Seven Kings, a dispossessed bishop came splashing through the sodden woodland with a half-dozen grumbling monks, to mark out a site in the very glade where he was born, to erect a minster with his own hands, and to live in it till he died. Retired from power and worldly churchmanship, he pointedly devoted himself to conversations with God; he offered prayers for the souls of the barbarous local people (many of them his kinfolk, not all of them Christian), even as he sent up an unending recrimination against the carnal simoniac who had chiselled

*him out of his see. His minster was no more than a narrow
dark shed of a chapel with scanty outbuildings, whitewashed
timber and thatch, altogether expressive of its founder's humility. The humility, although reluctant, appears to have been
effective. In his old age he discovered he could now and then
work a small miracle. He cured chronic outbreaks of swamp-
fever, he cleansed a swineherd's daughter of her uncontrollable
sexual frenzies, his prayers put out a fire that would have destroyed her father's pig-sties. "Hallelujah," he is said to have
said when he knew he was on his deathbed (and many thought
him mad for saying it), "God's Grace and the People of God
will turn this mildewed cabin into a temple more splendid than
Solomon's, more glorious: yes, I prophecy." And so, it came to
pass – the adjacent acres of tree-entangled swamp were drained
by the system of ditches and sluices that he and his favourite
pupil had devised between them as he lay sick – was it not a
posthumous miracle that that pupil was infused with sufficient
of the bishop's spirit to persuade reluctant peasants to dig and
dig until the land was dry? The fever ceased its ravages; the
region began to live. And so today Kirk Deerwood Minster,
unparalleled vision of pinnacled sublimity, fetches-in camcord-
ing tourists upon the plangent cry of "Heritage." Wasps to a
saucer of jam.*

*

This story, however, is to deal with a time when the package-
tour scarcely existed and English tourism generally was as yet
in a small way, indeed primitive, offering little beyond excursion trains, chartered charabancs, and a few youth hostels; at
least throughout the countryside inland of the Yorkshire coast.
Mr Frank Fouracre, mayor of Kirk Deerwood for the year of
1932, was not at all sure he wanted more of it. On the other
hand, he did recognize that the quality of the place attracted
discriminating visitors and that this should be kept up. He was
a solicitor, respectable and respected, leading figure of the local
Conservative Party, treasurer of the cricket club, and church-

warden at the minster, where his elder brother, the physician Dr Charles Fouracre, trained the choir and played the organ. Charles wore a bristling grey beard; Frank (by contrast) had something of the look of the pictures of Mr Pickwick, bald, bespectacled, kindly and plump – one might even say *baby-faced*. A lifelong bachelor, he had lived for years with his brother and his brother's family in their big Georgian house. A posy of unmarried nieces looked after him very comfortably, and his sister-in-law Martha (though at times a little distant) raised no great objection to his epicurean dependence. His private life outside the house, outside the office, was beyond reproach, largely because nothing was known about it. He exuded a formidable discretion on such matters, other people's matters as well as his own – which was only to be expected, given the scope of his law-practice amongst the very best of the town, mercantile associations no less than private persons. He was trusted, he was deemed to be trustworthy, and nobody questioned it.

He was nearly seventy years old. Apart from his professional pettifogging, the good-humoured pedantries of his ecclesiastical concerns, and an odd affair of municipal sewage just before the Great War, he had probably never done anything of any real use to anyone in the whole of his life – until, without warning, the Holderness Bus Company belched out a reeking gutful of petroleum-flavoured arrogance. Pushed hard into what he called a corner, he felt he had no alternative: they had forced him to *take action*.

The last time he had been pushed into *what he called a corner*, "a damned squalid sickening corner," as he put it to his brother, "where hooligans relieve themselves after drink," had been roughly fifty years earlier, somewhere between 1881 and 1884 (local records seem to have been lost), and it was not at the hands of some overweening company but, more dangerously, the police. In those days he was *not* respectable, although well able to hide the fact; he was an articled clerk in his uncle's law firm, a pudgy and dissolute young rip, "Yorkshire Pudding" or "YP" to his friends. He consorted in secret with other dis-

solute rips, including certain subaltern officers of the 15th Foot
from the barracks at the far end of town. In order to cultivate
such very flash companions, YP needed cash, cash in hand, cash
on the nail, cash for all exigencies. He needed, in short, to
buy his way up, to a level of society which otherwise would
have been impossible to attain. The Army did not think the
Law to be quite so low as Trade, but provincial solicitors' law
was not at all the same thing as inns-of-court barristers' law.
Add to which, these young officers were all public-school men,
while YP's education had been confined to the Kirk Deerwood
grammar-school, and he'd left it at the age of fifteen ... They
tactfully let him know that their pay was less than meagre, yet
if they might rely upon good deep generous pockets, they could
show this jolly pudding of an apprentice-attorney all manner
of forbidden delights – could show him and *share* with him –
did he dare? Of course he dared. He worked overtime and
alone, week after week, embezzling by gaslight from a number
of trust-funds, not too much at a time, dipping an artful finger
here and a crafty finger there, covering up the defalcations with
a surprising access of skill: after which, in broad daylight, he
must deploy even greater skill for his lies to the bank manager
and the conversion of fallacious paper into veritable silver and
gold.

(*Congenital* skill? Possibly. No-one could ever be sure what
any of the Fouracres might be up to; they had always kept everything so exceedingly close. There was a tale they were rightful
but unacknowledged heirs of the ancient kings of Northumbria:
thus, by genealogical complexity, might they not lay claim to
the throne of Victoria herself? If so, they never said: the whole
town had heard about it: no-one could be *sure*.)

Upon the sultry afternoon of a Sunday in high July, YP and
a pair of his military friends went off in a hired dogcart with
the filched spondulicks, very sparkish, to discover what might
be found at 'Ma Kettlewell's.' This furtive but costly establishment lay three miles out of town where the ship-canal came
curling through the fields, and where prosperous local coves
such as corn-factors or keelboat owners could nourish their

vices well away from church and family: Mrs Kettlewell was discreet. Her house (legally speaking, her *disorderly* house) was surprisingly quiet and rural – it looked like a modest farmstead, it was in fact the remains of a mediaeval nunnery – a scattering of single-storey brick buildings, low-arched doorways, humpy patched roofs at all angles, and sash windows improvised within dilapidated gothic mouldings. There was a long walled garden full of apple trees, rose bushes, blackcurrants, gooseberries, unpruned and stifling among grass grown up to the thigh; as well as brambles and nettles, and here and there an awkward item of modern garden furniture in cast iron, the odd round table, a few leather-upholstered divans (piled with cushions when it didn't rain). On a pedestal near a corner of the yellow-brick wall stood a small leaden statue-group of a fat-buttocked nymph teasing a satyr, both of them on heat; it had been picked up cheap at a private auction in York and had since been improved by some merry customer with dabs of red paint at significant anatomical points.

In the midst of this green paradise, until nigh upon sunset, the would-be rakehells skylarked in their pelts with bottles of bubbly and a girl apiece, three bragging Adams, three wary little Eves. They began to be a little tired, feel their zest beginning to droop, perhaps; but YP's art and craft came to the fore once again to re-ignite. He'd conceived a new game, a delicate game, a cruel game indeed (for he was, it must be said, a nasty enough young fellow), to be played there and then amongst the foliage – supposing Mrs K made no objection. "Nay," she said carefully, turning a ring on her finger. "Nay, I've nowt against it. It's not going to hurt 'em. Not much. But of course I must charge you according. I take it you can pay … Let's see who you've got. There's Lily and her titchy sister. And Dolly, that's the mulatto. I dare say it'll brisk 'em all up. I dare say they're in need of it, being new to the business and bone-idle, *as* no doubt you've found." It so happened they were so new that Dolly and Lily might have been barely fifteen, the "titchy sister" maybe two years younger: but that only made it more fun.

YP explained the rules, with a sweet purse-lipped smile between the dimples of his rosy cheeks. It would be, he said, a sort of race: each gentleman to choose a girl and equip her for the contest by getting her back into her long petticoats, hauling them up from the waist and tying them in a bunch above her head (shoes on her feet, nothing else from the midriff down); her arms within the petticoats would of course be held immobile, and moreover she'd be running blind. The trick would be to start all three of 'em together from the statue corner and lay bets upon which would get first into the house – an obstacle-strewn distance of pretty nigh a hundred yards. The gentlemen would wield supple switches cut from the blackcurrants to steer the girls in the right direction, and in general "tickle their rumps." YP said he had seen it done in a hand-coloured print of 1798 (he'd been prowling the back room of a local curiosity shop among items marked *not-for-display*) – it showed how the soldiers dealt with rebellious Irish trollops who'd presumed to 'wear the green' – they drove 'em with canes along the main street of Newry, bare-arsed and muffled just so, as a lenient alternative to the gallows. The subalterns thought this to be excellent sport; they set to work, in great spirits.

YP's girl (the 'mulatto'), pleading to be *un*-muffled, weeping and squeaking, swearing dreadfully at every stroke of his switch, had lurched into the gooseberry thorns for the third successive time, when a shocking interruption put an end to the race – and an end, more or less, to everything YP held to be gaudy and good in his life. The county constabulary were raiding Ma Kettlewell's in force. Alas, the back door to the garden was padlocked; the walls were too high to climb; the revellers were trapped, in their breechless indignity. And no! there was no question of anyone begging-off by reason of soldierly status or the prestige of an uncle's law-practice. They all spent a night in the cells, boys, girls and an angry proprietress – she thought she'd enjoyed immunity, but the inspector who took her money had ceased to be an inspector. "Ill health" had provoked his premature retirement.

In the upshot there was no prosecution. Magistrates decided – after a quiet word from the colonel of the 15th – that the police might have been too zealous, and the good name of the regiment ought surely to be preserved. (The colonel pointed out that the 15th had its own sanctions for young fools who'd consort with inappropriate civilians to bring the Queen's Commission into disrepute: he intimated confidentially that those subalterns would soon wish they had never been born.) As for Frank Fouracre – well, if his uncle and father thought the matter best kept quiet, there was no point in antagonizing them by undue severity. The father in particular was highly influential. As Canon Charles Alcuin Fouracre DD, he was vicar of Kirk Deerwood Minster and rural dean into the bargain; more importantly, he had inherited an old coaching inn in the market-place (The Jolly Postboys), together with an interest in the East Yorkshire Stage-Coach Company, now defunct; he had since become a director of its successful competitor, the North Eastern Railway, and was negotiating the purchase of the profitable Station Hotel. He also, as it chanced, was a magistrate. Nor were the women indicted. Some undisclosed pressure persuaded Mrs K to transfer her enterprise to Liverpool, or was it Newcastle? – it seems her wealthier patrons advised her to remain, as it were, out of sight for a season, and then to slip away, as it were, by night; it seems they may have *subsidized* her discretion.

What the magistrates did not know, and what the senior Fouracres very shortly discovered after pungent and poignant investigation, was the shame of the plundered trust-funds. Sabbath-day lechery was disgraceful enough: but now, combined with theft – nay, *facilitated* by theft! – it must never be made public; it ought by rights to be a police-matter; it could not *possibly* be a police-matter; but whether by good luck or indeed by artful management, Frank's crime had been committed within the purlieus of Frank's family, and Frank's family could keep it close. Yet plainly his continued presence in a venerable parsonage, in a law office, in the courthouse, and at large upon town, chattering to the dregs of the borough like a monkey on a busker's barrel-organ, was most perilous and not to be tolerated. Why, the *ladies* of the family might hear what he'd been up to, let alone his uncle's clients and his father's congregation, and thereafter (once again!) the police, who'd assuredly be keen to ask questions. No, he must go abroad, purge his crime upon foreign soil, *make good* like a true Englishman – so where was a convenient place? His uncle could think of one. He'd done some business in Hull with an importer of colonial produce who had, he understood, a most suitable East Indian connection, a pepper plantation up-country from Malacca. Why should not Frank be sent there? to keep himself out of mischief and to dally (if he must) with cheap native drabs who'd fetch home no scandal to Kirk Deerwood? He might even learn the spice trade.

It was generally assumed that Frank went overseas from a spirit of gay adventure, and who was *he* to contradict? At all events, he went. It was full five years before he came back. And he came back an apparently serious person of grave sensibility and industrious habit. His uncle was on the point of retirement; accepting the good report given by the pepper people of Frank's conduct in the tropics, he agreed with Canon Fouracre that the returned prodigal should resume his law studies from the point where he'd left off, and – if all went well over a period of years – take his proper place as junior partner in the firm. The resumption was easy to effect, for Frank had been largely employed in the legal work of the plantation. In point of fact, though he did not say so, much of that work had been the justification of piracy, blackmail, and barratry – all for "the protection of trade." Civil order in the colony was nothing if not *volatile*, despite the worthy example of good English cricket played week after week by the English in exile. Frank had been no great shakes as a batsman, but he'd excelled as an impassable wicket-keeper; after a couple of seasons (and aided by the ravages of a cholera outbreak) he was undisputed team-captain and a sedulous corrupter of umpires.

His immediate superior in the pepper company was a gimlet-eyed Chinaman, Mr Wang, who pursued all sorts of interests beyond pepper. He had been carefully watching the procedures of the cricket-club, he'd quickly detected Frank's lack of scruple, he set about to instil in him such necessary discipline as might advantage the pair of them in many a dubious scheme. Frank was thus rewarded by a great deal more money than uncle or father could possibly have guessed, together with the loan of sundry concubines. Money was transferred to English banks under a variety of names; concubines were left behind in Malacca.

Canon Fouracre (already a widower) was fatally run over by a galloping horse-bus not twelve months after his son came home. He died frowning terribly at Frank – he had never entirely accepted the young man's rehabilitation – unable to put words to his suspicion, he'd frowned and kept silence right up until the end. From his will Frank obtained nothing but a half-share (with Charles) in The Jolly Postboys, which had fallen on evil days and now was little better than a seedy class of dram-shop. Charles gained the railway shares and the Station Hotel – he was unwilling to cope with the latter, so he sold it to Jethro Hurn, 'butcher and purveyor to the gentry,' the chief Tory in the town, a grim old champion stud-bull of the classic Holderness breed.

There was general disappointment that Frank had so little to tell about the events of his term of exile: people concluded he had had to work very hard in a hostile climate and that this may have clouded his spirits. He was offish with old friends, no longer laughing when they called him "YP." They tended after a while to avoid his company. As well they might: although he still kept up his cricket, he nowadays refrained from public houses, billiard halls, race-meetings and such-like. Instead, he chose to busy himself with *church*, pottering at all hours in and out of the minster, astonishing his brother Charles with a newly-declared interest in the anglican tradition of worship.

All this seemed to fit him to assume control, little by little, of the uncle's worthy practice. The old man's health was failing; no doubt he did not notice how his nephew had begun to steer the business down paths hitherto unthought-of in Kirk

Deerwood. Thanks to Mr Wang's tuition, the metamorphosis was accomplished most artfully: it involved a whole new brand of clients alongside the old ones, and novel transactions among seaports, Hull, Goole and further afield – never to the extent of litigation in open court, but rather the quiet (and malodorous) shuffling of financial arrangements in patterns that were hard to trace, were indeed kept so very quiet that nobody *attempted* to trace.

In due course the uncle died, of a weak heart further weakened by too many glasses of madeira. It was scarcely a dozen years since the Kettlewell debacle, and Frank was now head of the firm. He was just past thirty. Charles's elder daughters were growing into their teens; they regarded their father's brother with genuine affection, because to them alone in the whole of Kirk Deerwood would he narrate his oriental adventures – Chinese corsairs, opium smugglers, Dyak blowpipe-assassins, snakes, crocodiles, dancing-women in golden temples, tigers – some of it was even true, all of it was wildly romantic, and his curios were nailed upon the smoking-room wall to prove it – swords, kris-knives, opium pipes, shimmering lengths of patterned silk. At one time he was heard to say he should look about him for a house of his own – with one voice the girls cried out against such a loss, their parents succumbed to the plea, Uncle Frank continued snugly in the family home like a portly benevolent cuckoo-child, smiling his sweet little smile, telling nobody where he went at weekends.

That's to say, he *did* tell, but the information was so inconsistent as to be useless. He would speak of something called SAGA, denoting (so he said) *The Society for the Appreciation of Gothic Architecture,* or maybe *The Sculptural and Architectural Gentlemen's Association,* or maybe (when pestered by nieces) *"Silence, you Annoying Girls, Ask-no-more-questions!"* And then again, he would say that "saga" was Norse for "story," and a *story* is what it meant. He hinted to them, once, that it was "a trans-Pennine fraternity," by which he seemed to mean it held its meetings in Manchester, but he didn't exactly say so … As a rule he returned from these trips preening himself like a genteel little pigeon; a vaguely exotic aroma would pervade his clothes. But there is no doubt he did know a lot about medi-aeval buildings, and if he wanted to be mysterious in regard to his fellow-enthusiasts there seemed no reason to challenge him. Besides, as Charles put it, "When Frank makes up his mind to be *private*, we are better off not knowing."

In 1905 he made his first serious foray into local politics (in the Tory interest) and emerged from the election as Councillor Fouracre. In due course he became Alderman Fouracre. His attendance at the town hall was regular, his work on commit-tees and so forth plodding and correct. He was never contro-versial – except upon one occasion. This was during the first of his three terms of office as mayor, in 1912. The borough engineer made a presentation to the council of a new scheme for a sewage-disposal plant, explaining its technical excellence, its benefits to health, its economical cost. Drawings and pro-spectus were passed around the room, councillors grunted over them with increasing approval until old Jethro Hurn got them into his hands. He growled wordlessly through his great floor-brush of a moustache for what seemed like twenty minutes, and then he articulated, "Right. I'd ask Mister Engineer, do they have yan o' these a' Driffield?"

"No sir, I think not."

"Do they have yan a' Pocklington?"

"Not yet, but they're talking about it."

(Driffield and Pocklington being the two nearest townships.) The engineer thought he could see where this was going. He earnestly added, "They do have one at Scarborough; and Brid-lington, I know, has already requested an estimate."

"Right. Then I vote a' Kirk Deerwood we waste our good brass on nowt o't'sort. Nowt." This seemed to be final, a straight signal to the other Tories (for Tories as usual were by far the majority faction): the project was to get the thumbs-down.

But His Worship the Mayor Fouracre thought different. He had long been irritated by Hurn's excessive wealth combined

with his bloody-mindedness on all sorts of minor issues: he
was sure that the sewage work was by no means minor, was
vital to the population, and must not be put at risk by a mean-
minded small-town chauvinism. The result was an outburst
entirely out-of-place from the chair. Yet his manner as he delivered it was as diffident and understated as always. "I do
not suppose," he murmured, "that a more stupid, ignorant and
brutal response to an excellent presentation by a talented public
servant has ever been made in this council chamber. I must ask
for a vote in favour of the project. I must ask Alderman Hurn to
apologize." There was a horrified silence. Mortally offended,
old Jethro blundered out of the town hall, back to his butcher's
shop, back to his miserly set of rooms above the shop, back to
his wife whom he straightaway punched on the jaw. He did not
apologize; he did not resign; from then on, he ceased absolutely
to dictate the Conservatives' policy.

Frank Fouracre replaced him as local chairman of the party.

And the sewage plant was built, in full accord with the original plans.

A couple of years later, at the height of the hysteria surrounding the outbreak of war, a strange woman came up and down
the town, asking queer sideways questions about someone she
called "Yorkshire Pudding." She was short, sour, small-boned
and aquiline, black-eyed, black-haired, of a smouldering yel-
low-tawny countenance like oatcakes just out of the oven. Her
clothes were neat and unnoticeable. She wore a heavy brown
hat like a soup tureen. She might have been any age between
thirty-five and fifty-five. No-one she spoke to – in shops, at
market stalls, in the tea-rooms where she drank a glass of lemonade – had heard of any Yorkshire Pudding; many of them
laughed at her, because the name was ridiculous; because it was
the only name she had of him, whoever he was; because she
was a "darkie" and unusual. She began to trudge back to the
railway station, dusty, depressed, tired-out, when a scruff of a
butcher's boy came clanging on his bicycle over the curb of the
pavement, startling her, blocking her way forward. He blurted

out that as his chum up the market had told him who she was asking after, *he* was here to tell her that he *knew* who she was asking after, on account his mangy old boss forever cursed the bloody day that Yorkshire-bloody-Pudding had crossed him and ruined him. He asked the woman for money. She gave him half-a-crown, and he whispered a name.

It was already dusk, the last train for Hull would be leaving in ten minutes: she made haste to catch it. Her shadowy, weary features were aglow with something like triumph.

The following week, upon the Saturday, she created an *event*. She turned up at the Fouracre house, just outside the old town wall. It was the maid's half-day; the door was answered by Frank's eldest niece, Miss Veronica Fouracre, a tall, cool librarian in her early thirties. The visitor was disconcerted. She gasped abruptly, "Are you his wife?"

"What? Wife? Whose wife? Certainly not. What exactly is it you want?"

"Fouracre. This here *is* the house, I reckon? Yeah?" The accent was peculiar: possibly American, if anyone in Kirk Deerwood had been able to recognize an American voice.

"Yes. This is the house. But which Mr Fouracre? There are two, do you see. Dr Charles or Mr Frank?"

"Is he fat? Is he blonde? Does he *smile,* like a scuttling woodlouse? If he does and his name is Frank, hell if his name is Yorkshire Pudding, let him know that Dolores is chipping away on his doorstep; yeah, he needs to talk."

Veronica was so outraged and alarmed by the tone, by the language, by the formidable white teeth of this woman, that she positively could not answer her – all she could think of was to slam the front door in her face. But that wouldn't do. She heard no retreating footsteps: the creature was still on the steps and might, for all she knew, be proposing to stay there. She opened again and said, chillingly, "No. Mr Fouracre is away for the weekend." (Not, for a change, SAGA, but an army recruitment committee, most urgent.) "If you'd leave a message I will find you pencil and paper."

"No, you don't bother. I wrote it already. Hell, it wrote itself." She handed Veronica an envelope, addressed simply to "YP", in green ink. Without a pause she swung round and walked off, short quick businesslike steps, haunches angrily jerking, into Market Street through the arch of the ancient town gate; she was immediately lost to sight. It was all so very quick that Veronica wondered had she dreamed it? No, she hadn't; she held the letter ...

She had been strictly brought up to understand you never, ever, opened other people's letters, it was an absolute rule. And yet ...

Almost anything could be in the letter. *"Yorkshire Pudding?"* What on earth?

She was alone in the house. She went into the kitchen and steamed the envelope open. The handwriting (green ink on lined blue paper) was an uncouth sprawling scrawl, but legible.

Mr YP, heres to say hiya, I'm Dolly, remember? – still alive and remembring. Was in America, not any more. No good in America and theyr'e lynching agen, even in the north, Ku Klux, gotta get out of it fast. Or my boy in bad trouble. They said you was in India? OK are you home again? And are YOU remembring? Ma Ks' garden the old bitch and the switching you was giving me, leastways till the cops come? Hell, you no dam right to mark my little ass that way, it was 2 week before the stripes was gone. More than 2 week tho before the baby – 9 month as per usual – he had to be yours, we was all-fired careless that hot Sunday, yeah? He was a boy, hes big enough but not so strong, I call him Switch for a nickname, cos I have to remember. He was chrissened tho proper I guess – naming him Saul after what the preacher in Baltimore said was a bad saint that repented, thats me for dam sure. He's past 30 now and he's had hard times. Ive had hard times. Ive seen your house, heard about you in the town, your times has been good, no good the God that made em so.

<u>Them   thorns   you   druv   into   my   poor   thighs</u>
<u>Should   tear   your   tongue   and   blind   your   eyes.</u>
Send cash (not a check, I know two of that) to DOLORES
CALHOUN, c/o Jaspers, back-lane to the Land of Green
Ginger, Hull. Its a sort of sailors boarding house, no place
for a decent woman but where else can I afford?

Distressing, but no great surprise, not after the behaviour of its
author. Some of it needed further elucidation; but the gist was
unambiguous – Uncle Frank in his reprobate youth had done
what he ought not to have done. Perhaps his accuser told a lie
about the child. Lie or truth, she was a predator, and a har-
lot and a humbug. Veronica had no sympathy with unchaste
women, even when they were very young; she *expected* them (as
they grew older) to grow grasping and vindictive – all-of-a-piece
and made no better by the alien colour of this one. She avoided
any such judgement upon Uncle Frank, she was fond of him,
after all; it was well known that young men were bred-in-the-
bone feeble when in thrall to temptation. However, the hints of
cruelty, switching or whipping or whatever it meant, and thorns
moreover (unspeakable), were quite as loathsome as the – yes,
as the *scuttle of a woodlouse*. Veronica refused to contemplate
them ... On the other hand, she was most interested to know
what her uncle would do. She'd had small opportunity in her
quiet life to observe libidinous sinners confronted by the fruits
of their sin. It would be an experience.

So when on Sunday night he sauntered in from his patriotic
duties, she gave him the re-sealed envelope without comment,
and sat down with her sewing – just the one cool eye upon him,
maybe a little bit amused.

If she'd hoped she would see a vehement reaction, she was
surely disappointed. His face went very dark as he read, and he
tore the paper across and across into sixteen small pieces: but
deliberately, slowly, reflectively. She detected no quaver in his
voice. "Did *you* take this letter in, Nicky?"

"I did."

"Did you see the person who brought it? Will you know her again?"

"I did. And I will."

"If ever she comes back, send the girl for the police."

"The girl might not be in, not if it's another Saturday – I was alone in the house – "

"Then run for the police yourself. I think she's a small woman, yes? You're a big strong one, with long legs, she wouldn't stop you." They laughed; and that was the end of it between them. He was not going to tell her the story of Dolores; she was not going to tell him she already knew it. But his response had convinced her that the story was most probably true.

Not long afterwards, there was an *event* in the courthouse. Few people saw it, and it did not become generally known. The Fouracre family only heard about it by roundabout rumour which at length reached a verger at the minster, who passed it on to Charles. It seemed a small "native woman" in a big hat had started screaming in the public gallery when Frank was examining a witness. Her words were indecipherable, except for filthy curses and something about pudding. The constable on duty grabbed her and would have hauled her to the cells, except that Frank said he knew her, she was subject to derangement, she had nothing to do with the case on hand – best just to make sure she took a train out of town. This was done: she went weeping. Nobody thought much about it: the war news, the great retreat from Mons, fully occupied the public attention. (Who could have expected so frightening a failure in the very first battle?) Even so, Charles made occasion for a word with his brother.

"'Native woman,' Frankie? Suggestive phrase. Had she come from Malacca?"

"No, Chas, she hadn't. *West* Indies, I'd say, originally. Half-breed, light-coloured, I suppose they'd call it creole. She was in my office earler in the day. Complicated story. I gather she'd just discovered her son had joined the army. He was drunk and he was boasting that if he didn't get killed by the Germans, he'd come home with a gun and he'd know how to use it. He thought the world owed him a living, he despaired of ever getting it if he left it to *her*. By the same token, the army gives out a regular wage. Of course he wasn't going to be killed, rather too old for front-line service, and then of course, his colour - They put him into the pioneers, I tried to explain this, she ran straight off the rails, and there you are."

"I see. She knew your old nickname. Frankie, you *will* let me know if there's anything - I mean, anything not quite - Trouble with you is you never let *anyone* know. Important though, we keep it from Martha. I'd not want her to forbid you the house."

It did appear that Dolores Calhoun stayed well away from Kirk Deerwood from then on. If she wrote further letters to Frank Fouracre, nobody saw them beyond himself. And if, toward the end of the war, he sometimes wondered about a man called Saul or Switch who might have been carrying a gun, he made no show of apprehension and there were no more uncomfortable *events*.

And then came all the trouble with the Holderness Bus Company. For years it had been no more than a small local service, first with horse-buses, then with motors, from the railway at Hull to various villages of the Spurn Head region, and along the coast as far as Hornsea. At the beginning of the 1930s, while the great depression shattered both savings and incomes in random carnage, a few intrepid hyenas took their chance among the carrion – one of them was Bram Bramthorpe, the new chairman of Holderness Bus. He was a hard young thruster from Leeds with no time for weaklings; he let it be known he'd make damn sure that *his* company was no weakling, whereas he knew many others in the region most certainly were, and by God he'd give the clothes off his back (if need be) to buy the buggers up. Within a year he had absorbed three failing transport concerns, he had moved his headquarters from Hull to his own city of Leeds, bought scores of new vehicles, extended his routes throughout the whole of eastern Yorkshire. He fought all the other companies, he fought the railway, he cheapened his fares until only the rarest plungers would take odds upon his survival. Nonetheless, he survived; and he grew.

He sent a letter on his company's notepaper to the Kirk Deerwood corporation. For a regular business request it was weirdly uncouth, an aggressive ultimatum.

As the town clerk read it out, everyone in the council chamber looked at everyone else, dumbfounded. At last the oldest alderman (Liberal party) was able to stammer, "Why, such, I do conceive, must, why I suppose it *must*, be part and parcel of the – eh – the new style, Yankee style, 'brash' is what they call it? – we *have* seen it coming, fellow-councillors, ever since the war. Iniquitous. But have we a choice? I – I take it we must concede?" The letter said: –

Let's live in the real world. The north-western gate of your town (alias King Henry's Bar, alias Harry's Bar) has for years been an obstruction to traffic. We daresay it was an obstruction in 1414, if that was when it was built, but in those days they had sieges, it was meant to obstruct. These are not those days: be so good as to take note that Holderness Bus Co. has placed orders for double-deckers to be introduced on all major routes, as from the conclusion of winter schedules 1932 – 33.

We have surveyed your town plan, we'd say a set of worm-casts rather than a rational arrangement of streets: no thoroughfare fit for buses out of and into the town on the York/Scarboro' orientation except by way of Market Street, all the rest are alleys and ginnels impossible for more than bicycles. When the buses are double-deckers they'll find Market Street blocked by Harry's archway – we'd like you to pull it down, we await accordingly your suggested time-table of demolition operations.

We daresay sentiment for an old structure will hamper your speedy decision.

Very well: if the archway stays put, Holderness Bus Co. will have no alternative but to cancel all routes through Kirk Deerwood that we've scheduled for double-deckers, which means there'll be not one bus to or from another town available in your town, village-service only is all you'll get. Kirk Deerwood people will be stuck with the rail, and you know what train-fares are. Sentiment and competitive transport are incompatible. The prosperity of E. Yorks., at this time of slump, depends upon competitive transport, deny it if you have the guts to confront your voters with the lie in your mouths.

Yours etc., B.Bramthorpe (chrmn.)

PS: *enclosed please find our engineer's drawing of a cross-section of a double-decker superimposed on elevation of yr. pointed arch. You'll note how bus top corners must crash either side against masonry. Verb. Sap.*

All the councillors present agreed with the aged Liberal. Some of them expressed themselves more brusquely than others, affirming, in effect, that they *did* have to live in the real world, they should take it as it came, they should speak as they found (*etcetera*). Moreover, those big double-deckers were marvellous machines and they should think of how admiringly the voters would think of their elected representatives when they'd see the splendid vehicles come roaring through the streets. "Talking film-pictures aren't in it!" cried one enthusiast (also Liberal). "Them buses'll be here months afore Stan Molescroft at the Alhambra gets us his sound-apparatus, much though he boasts it: mark my words. It'll be a wonder if we *ever* see a loud-speaker in that picture-house, I tell you he's nowt but piss-an'-wind."

The mayor (Alderman Fouracre) ruled the remarks out-of-order; the Alhambra Cinema was not on the day's agenda and its manager Mr Molescroft should be notified if councillors wished to discuss him: his business was his own business, he had the right to make his own decisions. But on this matter of Holderness Bus – did anyone think that the company's proposal ought *not* to be to be accepted?

No-one did, and several voices demanded a vote. Frank preferred to temporize; he would first like to hear a suggestion that Mrs Throw (Independent) was struggling to enunciate; perhaps it might modify the shock of the proposal? To be sure, she wailed, the ancient arch was doomed, inevitable, dreadful! But might not the statue *over* the arch, of heroic King Harry the Fifth (who'd had the gateway built to keep out the Scots while he and his brave bowmen marched to Agincourt), be lifted from its niche *before* the demolition, and re-erected in – perhaps – the portico of the town hall? The carving was indubitably early fifteenth-century, to preserve it would prove that councillors had not abandoned *all* cultural ideals. She quoted Shakespeare.

Very badly weathered, exclaimed one of the Tories, that statue! – so let's have some serious thought here, let's do more than just preserve it! – re-paint it! re-gild it, crown, orb and sceptre, *the lot!* – Why (cried several others), Mrs Throw's notion, progressive and beautiful, full of education, should be carried nem-con! – whereat they all felt much less guilty. Maybe it was all for the best that they'd yield to the masterful Bramthorpe, if it brought about new adornment to this town hall they were so proud of – they might re-paint and re-gild the columns of the portico while they were at it, why not? Altogether warm and cosy. A buzz from the five or six people in the public gallery suggested that they too were feeling it was all for the best.

Until Frank, his eyes on his order paper, his diction (as always) muted and precise, gave utterance to his own opinion. Thus: "The letter is signed 'Bramthorpe,' I don't know him, I know *of* him, that's all. You can talk about Yankees, but it does seem to me that it might more likely have been written by this man Mussolini whom we read of day-to-day in *The Yorkshire Post*, it's been written by a bully, that's all. I don't submit to bullies, none of you should submit to bullies. We do *not* have to have King Henry's Bar demolished; no, that would *not* be living in the real world, it would be living in a world of nightmare where nothing that seems good is allowed to be good and all that is tawdry, trashy, catchpenny, *bad*, is to be hailed from the rooftops."

Even in his peroration he did not raise his voice; but he filled it with such slow passion as none of them had ever heard from him. They stared at him, amazed: he was the one speaker in that room to utter what they'd (all of 'em) been longing to say, but had simply not felt able – intimidated less by Bramthorpe's vulgar threats as by his calculated trickery, under their skins, into their minds, persuading them so swiftly that the hoarse asseverations of a bus company on the make must indubitably transmit the very Spirit of the Age.

Frank continued: "It does seem to me that he thinks that our town is an extremely boring town. Our history is a boring history, and is he wrong? – why, this very gate, the very walls it gives access to, never did stand a siege, and heroic Harry never paid a penny for the town's fortifications – *we* paid, at any rate our ancestors, boring little citizens, paid – out of their own pockets, and don't forget it – the royal statue, as you've said, is *weathered*, never been smashed by gunfire, dragged down by ravaging hordes, any o' that, oh no. Weathered. Likewise the walls have crumbled out of weary old age, that's all: neither royalist nor rebel, not Tom Cromwell, nor Oliver, gave orders to destroy them. Right, if we're boring, then we're boring, that's *us*, and I'd say it's no damn business of a company chairman to demand that we pull up our socks. His intention, he'd have us believe, is one of service, to bring folk from this place to that, quickly and cheaply and in comfort. But it's not. What it really is, aldermen, councillors, is to bring *himself*, Bram Bramthorpe, to a dozen sizes bigger than he is, bigger than he ever was, bigger than he damned well ought to be; and the only way he sees to do it is to make all the rest of us smaller. My God, it's going on all over the world."

He brooded in silence for at least an entire minute and nobody interrupted.

He spoke again. "It does seem to me that very boring people can, by taking careful thought, put a puncture here or there into these swaggering swollen frog-bellies; no, we won't blow them up, we'll just let 'em down – *ss-sss!* and a fart and a fizzle. It can be done."

Ah but how? – several voices all at once, with more or less the same question.

"It does seem to me there's but one point to consider. We do need these big buses. If they're too big for the archway, then something's got to shift. But who should decide what the *something* should be? Now, our arch has been standing for five hundred years, handsome stonework, elegant mouldings, irreplaceable. Whereas (as I take it) these buses may well be on order; but nobody's said they've been built. How difficult is it to change the shape of an unbuilt bus? Good Lord, I can do it here and now with this little pencil."

He sketched some lines on Bramthorpe's drawing, amending the cross-section of the bus so that it was no longer a squared rectangle as wide at the top as at bottom. Instead, there was an elliptical profile, the sides tapering in above the upper-deck seats and the roof losing its flatness to rhyme with the curve of the Gothic archway – fitting into it as neatly as a foot within a shoe.

Cries of delighted wonderment at the sweet simplicity of the mayor's notion, followed (after a pause) by the voice of predictable doubt: "We'll have a job to convince Holderness. It'll *cost* 'em, y'know, to change their specification, even it's practicable in terms of engineering. Who's going to persuade 'em, then?"

"I'll do it." The mayor was mysterious. "Don't ask me how. Don't even imagine you can *speculate* how. Oh by God I think I'm old enough to re-discover certain ways." As he spoke, he looked far older than his three score and ten: councillors wondered if he was beginning to fail. And he trembled a little, as though suddenly afraid ... But he was the man with the notion: what could they do but let him alone to nurture it?

(The public gallery was twittering, confused, not at all sure what decision had been come to, if any. The mayor's last few sentences were inaudible beyond the councillors' table, and the minutes were to give no indication of any sort of vote.)

Nothing appeared to happen for a whole half-year. And then Bram sent a second letter, much shorter than his first: –

OK. You win. That mayor of yours is a paunch-load of dog's dung strapped up with a gold watch-chain, if he was a few centuries younger I'd have had him waylaid in the street and trampled into bullybeef hash: I don't joke. But he's not and I can't and you win. So you'll see my double-deckers in the shape of bloody cucumbers, dodging through that old archway as smooth as rancid butter and I hope it'll make you glad.

Yrs etc., B.Bramthorpe (chrmn.)

Grossly defamatory: councillors were outraged, but Frank explained privately that it would be not at all prudent to take note of the libel. With a *what-did-I-tell-you* cackle of unusual laughter and a flourish of the wrists, he exclaimed, "Oh good God, should I mind that the rascal calls me dog's dung? Is it not, after all, his writ of surrender, a crying of 'Kamerad,' like a Hun on the battlefield?" And as Frank was a solicitor, he must know all about it, to sue or not to sue was his everyday meat and drink: they took his advice and rejoiced.

At the same time, they were puzzled, fruitlessly asking what conceivable inducements could have brought Bramthorpe so suddenly to heel; it seemed quite out of character for him to reverse his course of action without some very powerful pressure ... They knew of course that Frank had secured a council subvention for a private enquiry agent, presumably to find what could be found about the Holderness chairman. The results of this initiative stayed locked in the mayoral safe. Not that anyone had ever heard of anything particularly heinous in Bram's past – beyond the usual rough-house of profitable commerce, which surely he would *vaunt,* he'd not be ashamed of it, surely? Indeed it was whispered that the agent could uncover nothing that was not already public knowledge, in bits and pieces through the press and general gossip ... There was a slight hope (unrealized) for irrelevant but juicy items about the reclusive

Mrs Bramthorpe. According to the off-record gossip of local journalists, she was known to despise what she called her husband's "bounce" and his "twopenny-ha'penny bus-rides" – her indifference would drive him out of the house for days on end, to follow the county cricket at every match he could get to, important or otherwise. He placed private wagers on all aspects of the scoring, and he usually won. He was something of an expert at the tricks and turns of the game.

But then, so was Frank. And from this point the story grows more and more conjectural.

Frank knew Bram by sight, for he had often seen his picture in the business pages of *The Yorkshire Post* – mastiff-jawed and florid, in horsy tweeds with Brylcreemed hair brushed straight back from the forehead, recognizable anywhere. On the other hand, Frank himself was not at all conspicuous outside of Kirk Deerwood; he thought it most improbable that Bram would know what he looked like; in his light summer suit and panama hat he made an unexceptional figure on the verandah of a cricket pavilion, a pernickety elderly gent peering at the wicket through binoculars, at intervals giving out his low-voiced interjections, "Well played, sir, run again, run again," and the like. It was not hard for him to find Bram talking to him: Bram would talk to anyone at cricket, you just had to be near him and nod respectfully.

And then Frank (as we may guess) talked to Bram – about cricket in Yorkshire, cricket at Lord's, cricket in Australia, cricket in the Empire at large, specifically cricket in Malacca. From cricket he allowed the conversation to shift towards women in Malacca. Detecting in Bram a certain area of interest, he chirruped about young women in Malacca, very young (some of them), *unusually* young. Frank, when he chose to, could murmur in a man's ear like a winking and blinking Mephistophilis, a plump Mephistophilis, a bald old temptation as insidious as palm-oil.

The two of them met casually at more than one match; they had lunch together, more than once. They talked in whispers, as though ashamed of their own words. Frank deduced, lawyer-like, that Bram was quite unworldly for a successful young entrepreneur, especially when it came to knowing where to go for what he hadn't hitherto known that he wanted to experience. Frank was slowly induced to agree to assist him. The assistance may have gone further than a sweet reluctant smile and vicarious advice. It began with an address perhaps, a telephone number, a hint of "mention my name and there's nothing they won't do for you." (The name would not have been Frank's, any more than in the old days Mr Wang's name would invariably have been 'Wang.') But then Bram unexpectedly grew nervous, and Frank must take him in hand, Frank must be *beside* him, Frank with his own body must steel himself to *replicate* certain cruel and stealthy doings which should long ago have been left behind – if not at Ma Kettlewell's, at least in the East Indies.

Even as an expurgated version of Bram's second letter was being read out to councillors in public session (the reprehensible original had been privately passed around before the meeting), the mayor's bailiff tiptoed in to lay a slip of paper on the table in front of Frank. He scanned it with a snort of irritation. "Apologies, ladies, gentlemen: I require to make a telephone call." He pushed back his chair and bustled from the chamber. He was applauded as he went, by both council and public gallery. Not that they knew where he went or why: in fact he trotted very fast across the market place to his law office, saw his clerk was working late, sent him into the basement to replace certain files in storage, and immediately picked up the phone. There was something disturbing about his haste and his deportment – a faraway wildness of the eye, a streak of spittle at the corner of the mouth, an unusual kind of hiss in the breathing – it troubled the old clerk, who could remember no such symptoms all the years he had worked for this man. So he listened at the keyhole.

To start with, he could hear nothing; until all of a sudden Frank's voice came leaping out, astonishingly falsetto, astonishingly coarse, with the sort of hideous jargon any criminal-lawyer might be expected to know but not use: "You've no business ringing me, certainly *not* at town hall; I don't *need* to reassure you! I have said and I have said, you have sent us the letter and those pictures are *smoke*, there'll be none for the bogies, none for the Sunday mucksheets, none for your wife! Nor will the cunts grass you up, you greasy-tooled kid-clapper; young ones or old, I've had 'em cosseted like Javanese sultanas ... For a roaring business bravo, you have indeed revealed yourself between bedstead and bog! good God, what a gutless article. Did I promise you, or didn't I: quid-pro-quo? I tell you once again – if I wasn't a man to keep bargains I'd not be where I am ... So there *you* are, and be glad of it; finish."

Later on, and long past the regular end of business, the clerk had letters that needed to be signed. He found Frank at the fireplace, stooping, stirring ash with the poker; the chimney smoked vilely; there was an acrid stench. "Photographs, Herbert, negatives and prints, time-expired, and they cluttered my safe. Cluttered my life. We should all of us be rid of such nonsense, why not?"

The following night, at the town hall, at a quarter-past seven o'clock, the mayor in full regalia of scarlet and gold, with the mace carried at his elbow, and all the aldermen in their gowns, and the councillors, and the town clerk in white wig, came crowding onto the balcony, to be cheered by half the populace (for whom Frank and Dr Charles had announced free beer till midnight at the bar of The Jolly Postboys): a glorious celebration of Frank's most noteworthy, *only* noteworthy, public achievement since the row over the sewage plant ... And then, the very next morning, the luminous aftermath of his triumph, he collapsed in the courthouse with a stroke. They carried him home and he died a few hours afterwards. It might even be said to have been a *heroic* stroke; for it smote him at the height of one of his most sardonic forensic excursions, the defence of a farmer who'd castrated a neighbour's prize boar.

In his bed, as his ruined body struggled helplessly to stay alive, he was able to vent a few broken words, very hard to interpret. From the left side of his jaw to the lid of his left eye, his features were working in livid and furious grimaces like the gargoyles of his beloved minster. "SAGA," he kept on and on, desperation flooding his eyeballs. "You have to find SAGA ... have to find her, and her, in my desk ... here, you fool, not office ... key ... shoebox, ridiculous ... she was always ... and *she* was ... too." And then he cried he was blind, and the thorns were in his tongue; and then came a second stroke, more fearsome than the first, and he died.

At the bottom of his wardrobe they found a shoebox with slippers in it, newly bought and as yet unworn, still wrapped in the manufacturer's tissue-paper. In the folds of the tissue-paper they found a key. It opened the smallest drawer in the big roll-top desk in the smoking-room at the back of the house. This was the only portion of the desk to be kept locked; everyone else of the household used all the other drawers quite carelessly for their own concerns. In the drawer was a long envelope. In the envelope was Frank's will. Extraordinary: it had always been assumed that his will was lodged in his office, under the care of old Herbert. But this new document contained a codicil no more than a month old, witnessed by a Gerald Hobson and a Kathleen Ann Figgis. The Fouracres' housemaid was Mary Figgis. Gerald Hobson (so it emerged) was her boyfriend, and Kathleen Ann her mother: rather too sub-rosa, perhaps; even a little suspicious; but did it matter? For the witnesses were far less important than the codicil, whereby a thousand pounds were bequeathed to two women whom no-one in the family had ever heard of – Miss Audrey Trooper and Mrs Jill Rust, described as sisters, c/o poste restante, Manchester.

– additional reward for a recent service of very great price which can never be described, afforded me (dare I say it?) for the sake of old friendship, old delights, even for the sake of love: let it be known to the curious that these ladies are SAGA, always have been. Sisters Are Good At – ? at whatever they're good at. For long there was a space in their hearts and their house for serenity, my heart too. But then I had to seek for the darkness of their invention; they are nothing if not versatile, don't ask. I did promise them material recompense and here it is, once the executors disentangle my financial dispositions. It may take some time. I hope not.

What sort of *old delights,* and more to the point, exactly what sort of *darkness,* was never entirely revealed. Nor did the sisters get their thousand. Before the will could be proved, they were fetched into custody on extremely sordid charges: periodic prostitution of under-age girls, and the covert photography of their labours. A number of salacious snapshots were seized and retained by the Manchester police, who kept their own counsel as to whether there were any more of them anywhere else, or whether anyone in them could be recognized. It seemed likely that those portrayed were so rich or so notable that discretion (once again) had prevailed over zeal. Meanwhile the executors successfully challenged the codicil: the court ruled that in default of a more credible explanation, the bequest must be regarded as an *immoral earning.* The sisters went to prison for surprisingly short sentences. A sly and unwholesome pair: Miss Audrey, tall, blonde and bony, in vivid contrast to the grey-haired Mrs Jill with her plump, squat torso, wide mobile mouth and protuberant green eyes. They were murkily erotogenic in their late middle age, they had surely a great deal of pull.

So were they the means by which Frank put the pressure on Bramthorpe? Perhaps, but it's little more than a matter of lewd guesswork: no relevant transactions came to light and there was nothing recorded in his cheque-book returns. What did emerge from his various financial documents was an odd little cache of bank-draft counterfoils made out in US dollars (small enough sums) to Dolores Calhoun at a series of addresses among the islands of the Caribbean. These went back many years, were clipped together beside the will in the small drawer of the smoking-room desk; there was a short memorandum thrust in with them: –

This is what I've given her every quarter since 1914 (August), when she made herself known to me. If she says it's not enough, ask her how she has managed to live on it for so long? If she talks about Switch or Saul, she must be told that I deny him entirely – he probably exists but he is certainly not mine. God in Heaven, he's far too big, and blacker than his mother. I saw him at Hull station when they put the pioneer company on the troop-train to Dover direct. As I'd told her, he wasn't going to be killed. I'd desire the executors to continue the payments: a debt of honour, if any such thing bears any plausibility when set against the pattern of my life. But I did save the arch. That would have been honourable, had I not had to achieve it by means of great knavery. The befoulments of my youth have crept in to the aid of my age and B.Bramthorpe reaps the consequence   The devil with him, he deserves it. YP. (unwitnessed and dated the day before he died.)

And that's about all of the story of Yorkshire Pudding, as much as is known or can be guessed – save for one last inconclusive *event*. It happened at the end of the memorial service held for Frank in Kirk Deerwood Minster three months after his death. A tall, brown-skinned, grey-haired man was standing among the pews near the south door of the church while the congregation made their way out; he wore a Ronald Colman moustache, dark glasses, and flashy clothes that suggested he was some sort of tout – incongruous in such a setting and vaguely alarming. Charles Fouracre was in the organ loft, playing a lively *Trumpet Voluntary* to signal the end of the service; his wife Martha waited for him in a pew below the pulpit, fending off the vicar's consolatory chitchat. Their daughters, Veronica, Abigail, Dorcas and Sheba, were intercepted by the man, who obviously knew who they were. He told them who *he* was: he said (with a knowing sparkle of very white teeth), "I am your cousin."

Veronica was the first to grasp what was going on; she remembered Dolores; her jaw tightened, her eyes narrowed. "Mr Calhoun," she replied, "if that is your name, we *are* in a church, and we're not going to make a scene, are we? This is neither the time nor the place, and *I* don't believe you're our cousin – can you prove that you are? No you can't." No he couldn't. All he had to go on was the word of his mother. Ah, but had his mother always told him the truth? By no means.

Nevertheless, he kept smiling; with a flick of his hand toward the organ loft, he made one more attempt: "Is it possible that Dr Charles could – "

He saw these four tall Englishwomen staring at him in a row, frosty, unforthcoming, and as sharp as kitchen knives: his heart died inside him. Or it may be supposed that it died, because he slid obliquely across the aisle and out of the minster before them; when they too stepped into the churchyard, he was already loping away down Swamp Fever Lane, and so into Old Puddlegate without the briefest backward glance. He'd put on his hat – a Yankee gangster's pearl-grey fedora – at a cocky, cheeky angle with a twist to the brim; and no, perhaps his heart had *not* died, not quite yet. He had the self-reliant gait of a man who had had a go, had failed, and now was off to see if there was someone else, somewhere, against whom he could have another go. Impossible to deny that he *existed*.

YORKSHIRE SPORT

"I don't admire this style of play; I'd call it tedious, uninspired,
not at all entertaining."

"Entertaining? This is football, it's not meant to be entertaining."

[Tetchy exchange reported between two soccer pundits on Irish TV during
the World Cup 2006.]

Impossible to imagine a political personage of the twenty-first
century who'd dare assert his civic probity by abolishing football. Yet there was such a hero, during the late 1820s, in the ancient Yorkshire borough of Kirk Deerwood. He was Dr Alcuin
Fouracre; he was mayor of Kirk Deerwood; indeed he wore the
chain no less than nine times, and his attack upon the popular
sport (during his last term of office) was such a reversal of principle and expectation that the Tories reviled him as a traitor to
the common good, the Whigs made a mock of him as an unconscionable meddler, and the rowdies of the town threw stones to
break his windows.

In the days of Dr Fouracre's public service, little happened in
Kirk Deerwood not directly related to the tillage and pasture of
the wide surrounding countryside, and its supposedly prosperous John Bull farmers: tenant-farmers, most of them. Their
landlords were a tribe of autocratic squires and noblemen,
hugely wealthy from what had once seemed the unbroken gold-
en times of all those wealthy farms. Nevertheless, county by
county, rural England was inexorably collapsing into distress,
landlord and tenant united in dread that the French Revolution
was about to be reconvened under the disguise of Political Reform – such an evil phenomenon must never (so they swore) be
allowed to corrupt the Integrity of the British Constitution. No
better means to prevent it than their own John Bull corruption,

more effective than coercion, although coercion had its place. There were gallows, there were gaols, there were convict-ships to Botany Bay – but there was also, in Kirk Deerwood, the coffee room of The Jolly Postboys, where (on behalf of the Tory interest) Dr Fouracre disbursed funds to the voters. And that's why he held office so often.

He had always been a man to be relied upon, he was a man with a damned hard head, burly and pragmatical with a harsh voice deep in his throat; he was a man you'd not walk around in a day and a half. He was the best physician in town and he owned The Jolly Postboys and the stage-coaches that used it. It was an old English inn of the highest reputation; his teams of horses were renowned from Hull to Newcastle. He stood no nonsense from the Whigs, and (as a magistrate) was merciless toward any species of Radical. In fact, in Kirk Deerwood, Radicals were as uncommon as crocodiles – or almost so. Of course, there was the man Swayne, who was also an Atheist. Folk said he was a cobbler. Such fellows always *were* cobblers, according to the accepted patriotic mythology. In the case of Simon Swayne, the myth was an obvious slander: he certainly mended shoes, and he *made* them, what's more; but he also made harness and saddles and top-boots and travelling-bags and round leather hats as worn by horsemen; Dr Fouracre's coaching business would have foundered without his skill.

As mayor, Dr Fouracre had the privilege of "chucking off" at the annual Football Game. He did this from horseback, in his gold chain and scarlet gown, head and shoulders above the cheering crowd – a very rough crowd, it must be said – and the more times he came to do it, the greater the cheers. "Good Owd Alky," they called him, and made affectionate fun of his red face and bristling side-whiskers (which were seen at each successive game to be greyer and thicker and ever more stiffly pomaded).

The Kirk Deerwood Football, as it was played in those days, was an archaic survival. It took place on Shrove Tuesday, between two traditional teams or *factions* – OutTown who lived outside what was left of the mediaeval walls, and InTown, the dwellers within. No rules to the game save a prohibition, occasionally observed, against eye-gouging and tearing the testicles. The teams were not selected: any boy, youth, man, or strong young woman, was eligible to join in (if brave enough). A thousand players, maybe two thousand, would assemble at dawn two miles out of town at the top of Deerwood Common. The "chucker-off" would hurl the inflated skin of a sucking-pig, wrapped in a strong leather case, into the heart of the crowd, and the players would fight for it all the way down the hill as far as King Harry's Bar, the main gateway into town through the old wall: this gate was the goal. If the OutTowners kicked the ball under the arch of the Bar, they had won. If the InTowners kept it out until the strident noontide clang of the tower clock upon Kirk Deerwood Minster, *they* had won. The prize was a garland of evergreen, to be hung on the inside or the outside of the Bar, depending upon who were the victors; the victors claimed free beer in every tavern. Win or lose, all the players would drink and brawl through the streets until well into Ash Wednesday, thereby troubling the spirit of churchgoers, and arousing denunciations from the clergy. The divines of the established church objected chiefly to the overspread of revelry into an inappropriate season; they had never reproached the Football as such: Carnival had always preceded Lent and they weren't so imprudent as to interfere. On the other hand, the methodists were. Taking exception on principle, they regarded any Shrovetide enjoyment as a virulent popish remnant, and annually combined with certain shopkeepers to petition against the game to the mayor and corporation: an annually fruitless exercise. For the Kirk Deerwood Football had continued for centuries, had become (as many averred) a ritual as sacred as Lent itself. Sir Jocelyn Wetwang went further. This domineering baronet was a retired colonel of cavalry, a master of foxhounds, the squire of a bleak village on the crest of the Wolds, and the hardest by far of the local Tory magnates: he was heard to pronounce that "the hunt and the football are Pillars of the Constitution, one for the gentry and one for the plebs (but neither exclusively) and the two of them arch together to hold firm at the top like your minster-chancel vault: part, sir, and parcel of the honour of the realm."

Upon a biting winter's morning, when the cobbles of the market place shone black and silver under the hard frost and a grey freezing mist lay low over the rooftops, oppressing the chimney smoke and filling the narrow streets with a reek of burning soot, Simon Swayne tramped into the taproom of The Jolly Postboys and flung down a tangle of reconditioned harness onto a table. "Maister in?" he growled. "Let un know I've fettled his straps for un, girths, traces, breechings: let un know."

The potboy made a diffident and uncouth attempt at an excuse. His grunts seemed to indicate that Dr Fouracre was in the surgery at the back of the house with a very particular patient and was not to be interrupted. It was brave of the young fellow to come out with such a rebuff: a vexed Simon Swayne could be a dangerous customer, even from the far side of a bar-counter. Despite crooked knees and bowed shoulders, the shoemaker was well known as a stormy fighter; he'd never stop till he'd broken a bone. However, on this occasion, his humour was intrigued by "a very particular patient." So he gave a cunning twist to his asymmetrical gash of a mouth, spun a coin between his fingers, and sent it with a sharp flick toward the potboy (who caught it adeptly) – "'Particular?' Aye aye? There's ateing and supping in yon yah word. When a mayor sets to boast hissen to be *particular*, tha knows, ent it best for right-eyed folk to mek un *general*? Why else do they tog un up i'scarlet?" With which impenetrable pronouncement, he waddled out of the bar into a labyrinth of passages, up and down steps, around several low-arched corners, and at last through a baize-covered door into Dr Fouracre's empty waiting-room. Across the room, on a glazed partition with a linen blind pulled down behind it, the word *SURGERY* was painted in fat blue capitals, one letter to each pane. A crescendo of foul language surged from within, and then an anguished roar, and then another. Simon twisted his lips even further, sucking them between the gaps of his yellow teeth. As it were upon a sudden thought, he blundered straight into the surgery, a man (as it were) who carried help to a fellow-creature in mortal peril – "Whey-ey," he shouted, "I'm here, I'm fit and ready, who's hurt? *I'll* mend un, *I'll* shape un, *I'll* save his blood-an'-bones!"

What he saw was no more than he'd expected to see – the style of the curses was well enough known to him – although cries of pain from such a quarter were indeed a novelty, a pleasant novelty, to be sure, at which he grinned like a rural mooncalf in front of Punch-and-Judy. He had one swift glimpse of terrible doings with lancet, flannel, and boiling water, amid the thick dark hairs of a shrunken and elderly buttock – there was an eruption of great boils there, as it might be gas bubbles in a peat-bog – fit to make anybody sick at the sight of them – one swift glimpse before the doctor turned furiously upon him.

"No, Simon, *no!* Take yourself off out of it – OUT!" The man Swayne affected subservience, ducked his head in apology, and backed out; in the waiting-room he let loose a small but malignant cockcrow, and stayed huddled upon the bench there in a posture of demonic watchfulness – he meant to hear and to pay attention to whatever there was to be heard.

For the sufferer bent over the doctor's couch was without doubt "very particular" – none other than Sir Jocelyn Wetwang, Bart. The man Swayne had longed for years to take such a contemptuous grandee at a disadvantage, and today was his chance. "Eh dear," he was telling himself, a gleeful parody of sad compassion, "what a calamity! eh poor Sir Jocelyn, who'd ever ha' thowt it? blood-poison for a penny, rank gangrene for tuppence-ha'penny, eh dearie dearie dear," – and so forth, while in the surgery the baronet gobbled helplessly for words at the outrage to his privacy, and Dr Fouracre tried hard not to laugh. Sir Jocelyn was short, bald and wiry, between sixty and seventy, something of the type of a superannuated jockey, never seen without top-boots, even at this awkward juncture with his breeches dropped to the floor and his shirt-tails rolled up above his midriff.

"I cannot understand, can *not* understand, dammit, how you greet such an insolent scoundrel by his given name – I spare to say *christian* name – as though he were your pot-companion? God's sake, Fouracre, have you no sense of yourself?" (And here the man Swayne heard a grievous great groan as the doctor returned to his work.)

"Of course he's not my pot-companion. I do now and again employ him, hey? A smoothness between us does no harm? Of course *you're* never smooth with anyone." Dr Fouracre was all the more moderate for the presence of an extremist: in other company he'd call Swayne a scoundrel with the greatest of ease.

"What the devil does he want here anyway?"

"He's supplying me with harness, I suppose that's his pretext, hey? He knows very well I'd ha' seen him in the taproom, as always. He came on in here to make mischief. It's his character. Does it matter?"

"I'd say it very much matters. The political aroma of this precious town of yours gets worse and worse. *You* don't sniff it, damn it, 'cos you live in the midst of it: *my* nostrils are choked with it like a fart flying loose from an uncorked gut, 'cos I bloody well live outside. There's God's good fresh air up there on the Wolds, so a stench along the wind toward us is rather more than notable. I'm warning you, Fouracre, come Shrove, come the football, there'll be trouble, and *that man's* at the back of it. Be assured."

"He's three-fourths of a cripple. When did *he* ever play at the football? What's it to do with him, hey? What's *Shrove* to do with him, for the matter o'that? To my knowledge, he never showed respect to the Temptation in the Wilderness."

"All the more reason. He crouches in his den with his wax and his needles and he stitches his incontinent webs. I'm telling you, Fouracre: you'd best get a word to the soldiers. Come Shrovetide, you'll have a need for 'em, don't pretend I didn't warn."

Now the man Swayne may never have been an actual player, but he held an interest in the game which Dr Fouracre had for the moment forgotten; he was the craftsman who'd made the ball and every year when the struggle was over it was brought back to his shop to be examined and repaired and kept safely until next year. So, upon hearing the turn the talk in the surgery had taken, he sank to his knees and crept nearer and nearer to the door until his ear was positively against the keyhole. After mention of soldiers, there seemed nothing much more for him to listen to, just a long growling murmur of continued pain from the baronet, varied by sharp yelps, while the doctor hummed a tune as an accompaniment to his treatment. And then –

"Soldiers, did you say, hey? Nonsense. Absurdity ... Take care now: this may cause some discomfort."

"Of course it will, you do it a-purpose! *ah-ah!* ... A cobbler, do they say he is? *I* won't use him, I go to York for me bloody boots. His ruffianism is unbounded, I sent me coachman on an errand to the back-end of town so he's not here to horsewhip him for me – Christ's sake, with an arse on fire, how can I do it meself? Humiliating, there's the word: Christ! ... Ah, so you're finished, at last? I suppose I may pull up me britches? Send a boy on a horse with the bill and I'll send you a cheque: I do *not* carry cash into this town, whole damn place is a quicksand o'thieves ... Martial law, sir! and by Christ, we shall back you to the hilt. Where the devil is that coachman?"

High time for the man Swayne to make himself scarce. All of a sudden, he'd had a thought that seemed thoroughly to disconcert him. Twitching like a man at the commencement of a fit, he muttered and he sucked his teeth and he scurried down the passageways as fast as a big black beetle. No sooner was he clear of the house by the back door than the baronet's coachman came in at a run at the front, made all haste into the surgery and seized hold of his master's right arm. Dr Fouracre supported the left; between them they manhandled Sir Jocelyn, conveying him across the yard into his well-cushioned chariot. Thus he was driven home between the barren winter hedgerows; with continuous ejaculation of agonized oaths, he was remembering the French bullet they'd carved out of him at Waterloo; he was trying to remember had the military surgeon given him greater or less torture than his old friend Alky Fouracre? Humiliating: there was the word.

As for his predictions about soldiers, trouble, and incontinent webs, Dr Fouracre let them go almost as soon as uttered.
Such warnings from the irascible baronet were a regular entertainment, rarely to be taken too seriously.

Rather more than a month had passed, and the doctor as usual
was carving for his customers at the communal supper-table
in the Postboys parlour. (He kept up the old style: no flap-
doodle about separate seating or varieties of menu. He had
always enjoyed playing host in his own inn, whereas his father,
an eccentric scholar and schoolmaster, had lived elsewhere
and employed a salaried deputy.) Into the room dodged a very
dirty boy, peering through the candlelight for the doctor. This
rapscallion in smelly velveteens was well-known as "Caleb the
Cod," an oddjob from the dirtiest streets, an orphan and probably a pickpocket. He was carrying a dirty letter. He took a
penny for it from the doctor's hand; he snatched a leg of chicken
from a commercial traveller's platter; he was out of the parlour
as rapid as a rat. Dr Fouracre opened the letter.
   The handwriting was erratic and the spelling largely speculative; nonetheless it was literate, of a self-taught rhetorical lit-
eracy – the doctor had seen its like before – no, there was no
signature, but surely it had come from Simon Swayne.

<u>MR MAIYOUR & DOCTOR</u>,

It so chances I had overheeard certain words that Sir
J.W.(Bart) saw fitt to put into your ear on the occkasion
of the bubuckles on his crupper. <u>Marcial Law</u>, if you
reckollect.

God is my witness (even tho as thou knows I bow to no
church-deeity) but I am struck <u>all of an heepe</u> to be
forced to fill your eear with the perril I have since uncovered – YOUR eear, can you creddit it? and you as much
of a ~~blue bastard~~ tory as he is – do yo'not think summat
strange is gone wrong with me?

No dout you thouhgt these heere soldiers was to be fetch't to stop the People arising up, out of the bravery of the Football, for Justyce and Reform? As at Peterloo, 10 year since? A RADICAL Ryot, that's what you thouht? Eh nay, but the ryot Sir J.W.(Bart) has been so busy as to invent, will never be Radical but damnable Ultra-Aristo: yet astonnishyng, they will rannsack shops & houses appartayning to prosperous ~~lousebags~~ ~~citizens~~ratepayers! Poor men of Kirk Deerwood who might once ha'fouht for Liberty, now are bribed, bouht and sold, to be <u>HIS ryoters, never ours</u>, and damnable well payd – and yet he calls on YOU to call Soldiers to sabre them down. Loyal Men (so it will seem) to theyr Church and theyr King to lie in every Street in theyr Red Bludd.

His friends that have ordered it want to see this town a bye word for rappine and pillage and Militairy Mistake. They want to see Goverment – aye, Mr Maiyour & Doctor – your <u>Westminister Tory Goverment</u>, knocked therebye <u>all of an heepe</u> and thereafter overthrowin by the GREATEST of their friends in London.

NOT to bring peace and prosperrity, but solely to put STOP to ParlyamentReform.

And then to throw <u>out</u> your owld ~~bugger of a~~ King George IIII, and then to throw <u>out</u> his daft Brother William of Clarence – that daft, so they putt it, as to be very nigh a Liberal – and then to call <u>in</u> the other Brother, aye HIM, the one we fair shuddder at – Ernest Duke of Cumberland, arch-Reaksionarry of the Land & England's Nemysis – <u>cooup-detat</u>, I tell thee, CUMBERLAND FOR KING! With payne and chaynes and slavery for all of us right-eyed Britons, and our brave Kirk Deerwood Football to be the verry Pre Text.

Mr Maiyour & Doctor, I am suffused and oppresssed with
Black Remorse that I thus appeer to turn agen and inform
upon my erstwhiyle friends, the poor men of our town,
nay, of our own brave Football.   (So vileley corruppted
they are, that now they are nowt but my FOES and FOES
to Liberty!)   But terrours attend me, conscyience criyes
out at me, I shannot let conspirassy take place!

Mr Maiyour & Doctor, if thou'rt one of Sir J.W.(Bart)'s
Cabbal, there's nowt to be done: but if not and if thou'rt
ignorant of the maleofactyions that are afoot – then I
tell thee that thou'rt Maiyour here, aye thou'd best look
to it.

I am torn.

I NEVER SENT THIS LETTER. SUMMBODY LIKE ME,
THAT'S ALL.

Dr Fouracre took one look at this perfectly shocking document,
screwed it up and shoved it into his pocket, ate his supper with
apparent good cheer and took wine with the company. At last
he contrived to slip quietly upstairs to the drawing-room at the
back of the house. He was seriously dismayed and unable to
decide what to do.

He was a widower, his children fully grown and out upon the
world; his only companion was his mother, Mrs Selina Fouracre,
an aged lady of acute intelligence and enlightened religion, as
radical in her own way as Simon Swayne. Mary Wollstonecraft
(vindicator of the Rights of Women) had been her adored correspondent and the poet Shelley had once stayed under her roof.
Her late husband also had been thoroughly imbued with the
ideals of the Enlightenment; he died (in effect) of a broken heart
that the kings of Europe should have gone to such interminable
war against Liberty, Fraternity and Equality. Selina had always
given sincere praise to her son's work as a physician; as for his
Toryism and associated corruptions, she pressed her elegant lit-

tle lips together and preferred to say nothing. He knew what
she thought of him: *he* thought of *her* as a generous warm spirit
who'd flown a ridiculous flag in the wrong bloody ship for too
many years to be expected to strike her colours now.

On church matters, domestic matters, or matters (non-clin-
ical) concerning his patients, he always asked her advice. This
evening he astonished her by begging a *political* opinion: he
laid the letter upon her tea-table: she read it very carefully: he
confessed his dismay. He seemed to her suddenly the confiding
little child he once was, hurt and bewildered by the treachery of
a playground friend.

"Mama, I cannot think straight: why the deuce should he
send all this – this addled and gothical eggnog to *me?* Conspiracy, hey? It's absurdity. Is it not, Mama? no?"

"No, alas no, I think not ... But if you should persist in calling it eggnog, I shall call *you*, my dear, a silly-billy candidate for
the dunce-cap." (Thus she had used to cajole the smallest pupils
in her husband's school.) "Do you not see, your Mr Swayne is
a man in a despair? He has tried to persuade his hot-headed
associates that they are cruelly deceived – he has failed – so he
comes to you. Oh my dear Alcuin, you, an inimical Tory, are
the Radical's last resort. He imposes upon you a duty, don't you
think?" There was a hint of inner laughter behind her words.

Irritated and confused, the doctor began to bluster. "Aye
aye, Mama, but how? What? Where? I am at my wit's end.
I say *where* does he find the blackguardly ordure thus to be-
smirch His Grace of Cumberland?"

"Have you never, yourself, heard this *Patriot Duke* be-
smirched? If I am not mistaken, you do have some knowledge
of him, and of his sulphurous reputation? an incestuous rapist,
a predatory sodomite, conceivably a murderer? I'd suppose him
quite capable of usurping his brother's throne."

Dr Fouracre sat and cringed in a deadly disquiet. He was
well aware that Cumberland, whatever his private turpitude,
remained an inspiration, an incandescent John Baptist, for the
most retrograde breed of Tory; the doctor had never (in so many
words) dissociated himself from their rantings. "Hey, Mama,

no! You forget that this duke offered to help with the College of Heralds when cousin Frank would establish the antiquity of our family, direct descent from King Aella of the ancient Angles or some such extravagance – Joss Wetwang had written to his grace on our behalf. He sent a most courteous reply. Not that it came to anything, but clearly the man's a gentleman."

"A royal prince, at all events ... So we know that Sir Jocelyn is one of his correspondents. And we also know that both of them are leading men in the British division of the Loyal Orange Order. It purports to be a religious society: *I* know (and the Irish know) it is a muckhole of incontinent bigotry. These men, my dear, have loathed and despised your Tory government ever since it had the strange good sense to emancipate the catholics: they are certain that this same government will eventually give way upon electoral reform. I'd hazard that Mr Swayne may well be correct and that some such conspiracy does indeed exist – coup-d'état? bloodshed? QED, as I would tell the children at their elementary euclid. You would be wise, my dear son, to conclude that he *is* correct."

"Correct? Simon Swayne? Good lord, it is more than possible I am the victim of a hoax. Would it not suit him, hey? top and tail, to make a monkey of a Tory mayor? And he and that tomfool Wetwang are two mad dogs in one sack, only last month he burst into my surgery when I was treating Wetwang for – "

"Maybe he pursues a most personal vendetta. He would not be the first. But trust me, it is very clear he is profoundly beset, nay he is *haunted*, by this knowledge he has acquired. Good gracious, it has compelled him to become that hated thing, a government spy, an informer to the law! To the law, as invested in *you*. I cannot believe he is the man to devise so drastic an exigent, for no honest reason but *hoax*. O my dear, I beg you think of it: you are a Tory and I've always said, a silly-billy indeed; but you do stand, always have stood, for the Liberties of the Constitution. Do you dare see them eradicated in an inferno of mercenary violence?"

"O Mama, I have been so stupid, let so many improprieties. slip past my regard when I could have cried, 'enough!' In my heart I always knew that that vicious little Wetwang was a companion to be shunned, and yet for years I have frequented him, smiled at his vices, embraced his cruel opinions as inseparable from his jocularity, and inhaled far too much of his corruption: I was flattered, I suppose, by the apparent goodwill of a baronet. Of course you recollect how he helped me cover over the rash enormities of my youth, upon at least one occasion he protected me from the law. He called me Good Old Alky, and the world called me Good Old Alky. And now by his patronage I am mayor for the ninth time and this town under my governance is very likely about to – O God, it's about to *dissolve* ... Mama, Mama, what can be done? O Mama, what can I do?"

"Mr Swayne has surely *told* you? The football is the pretext. Every man in the plot will have all eyes upon Shrove Tuesday. If there is no football, they'll find it hard to stir up a riot. No riot, and so therefore no excuse to call in the troops. No troops, no subsequent bloodshed, no threat to the government. Surely your first step must be to forbid the football?"

"But that in itself would cause a riot. The football for centuries has been – "

"It has been a perfect nuisance and we can well do without it. At best it is a relic of barbarism, and Christians should be ashamed to support it."

"But I don't *want* to forbid it, Mama!" (Dr Fouracre was now so plaintive it would have been pathetic to hear him, but a man of any age left alone with his mother is never entirely an adult.) "I have always maintained it is essential to the spirit of the nation – for Christ's sake, the people have a *right* to their ancient sports – "

"Alcuin, forbid the football. Use your wit and find a way without riot ... And refrain, please, from eructations of your casual and degrading blasphemy." She rose from her chair and made a severe formality out of straightening her shawl. "As for the spirit of the nation, by which I suspect you mean the spirit of Toryism – did we not all think that our revered friend Mr

Wilberforce, down the road there in Hull, had shamefully betrayed us when he repudiated his liberal ideals, turned Tory and
went in with Pitt? yet even in the shadow of Pitt he contrived
to put an end to the slave trade – for him, surely, *that* was the
spirit of Toryism. It is late: I go to bed. Be so good as to ring
for my maid."

Nothing contributed more poignantly to the doctor's dismay
than the realization that this riot was not to be paid for in an
alcove of his coffee room at The Jolly Postboys, but altogether
outside that time-honoured arrangement. For years he had
been trusted to dispense the electoral bribes, and now the hysterical Wetwang (if indeed it *was* Wetwang) had arbitrarily determined to subsidize an entire mob through some other agent
in another place. Hey, hey, but here was paradox! it could well
be called an outrage, a damnable insult, that a Wetwang should
conduct a treasonous coup and deliberately exclude a Fouracre.
Did they think him too feeble to take part? ... Or no, was it not
more probable that their sense of his integrity had utterly overpowered them? Could it be that they were afraid of him?
  Hey, but he'd give them good reason for their fear.
  Blue bastards? hey, hey? – indeed and indeed.

Easter was seven weeks away. He had plenty of time to think
out a plan. And plenty of time for his plan to become known
and therefore useless. Impossible to announce in advance that
the football would not take place. Just as Swayne's unheralded
letter had pretty nigh shocked him into a paralytic seizure, so
Wetwang and his rabble must equally be caught footless, upon
the very day, at the last hour, the last minute, without chance
of a counterblow. And government must then be told what
had been done and why. The Duke of Wellington, as prime
minister, was the proper man to deal with Cumberland – if
Cumberland had to be dealt with – yet where was the proof to
incriminate Cumberland? There might never be any proof. Yet,
if Cumberland did indeed conspire, not only Kirk Deerwood

but the whole kingdom could be -   Let him dwell upon *that,*
and he'd run mad.

He must think out a plan and a practicable plan. Could
he risk having a word with the man Swayne? Their meeting
might be observed and reported. Swayne might deny everything. Yet he had to talk to Swayne. He sent for him; said he
needed to be measured for a new pair of riding-boots. He had
the measuring done in the sunshine of the innyard, combining
it with chat upon the upkeep of stable equipment. All very non-
chalant, while the ostlers and grooms at their work about the
place heard nothing but appropriate business. The matters that
mattered were inserted (one might say) out of earshot, from the
side of the mouth.

Something like this –

"The last pair you made for me galled at the top of the foot ...
See here, about that letter which you said you didn't write."

"*Ah* ... Leather wor soft eneaf, t'wor likely a swelled ankle;
they allus swell, tha knows, wi't'passage o' years; tha'rt none so
young as tha wert."

"*Spite of your legs, I know you for a damn good horseman*
... Let's leave the boots as settled and overhaul these stirrup-
leathers ... *If a man were to chuck into your arms a bloody
great blown-up pigskin* ... All but worn through at the loop, I'd
say it's finished ... *Could you keep yourself in the saddle while
you'd gallop round the fringes of a crowd o'damned rogues,
could you do it?*"

"*Ah.*"

"And the bridles need new buckles."

"Ah ... It'll cost thee."

"*What'll cost? Buckles, or – ?*"

"*All of it.*"

"Ah."

In this way some sort of unspoken (or barely spoken) agreement was reached. For two men so much at odds upon a general apprehension of life, it was remarkable how easily they understood one another.

The doctor made one further arrangement during the days leading up toward Lent: he rode over to Hull and invited an old acquaintance to dine with him privately at the principal inn. This gentleman was the major in command of a squadron of dragoons, posted to the seaport some years previously to repress a wage-agitation among the dockyard men, and kept there ever since on the off-chance. Ticklish ground, delicate table-talk: conspirators might already have tampered with elements of the army, the major might prove to be enraged over the catholic question, might even be an Orangeman. But in the upshot all went well. The old fellow (who had served in Spain) would not hear a word against the Duke of Wellington: if Wellington thought proper to coddle the papists, there must be some good strategy that would at length be revealed. It was nobody's business to query the battle-plan.

Dr Fouracre spoke of his need as chief magistrate for an armed and disciplined horse-troop to arrive without notice and be prepared to prevent riot. He did not specify *whose* riot. But he did point out his fear of a repetition of "that Manchester nonsense" – he meant the Peterloo Massacre. He did not say that at the time he had approved the Peterloo Massacre. But *that* time was not *this* time, and he urgently sought assurance that the soldiers were reliable.

"As I take it, Mr Mayor, you are asking me for military skill. If I can't give you that, by God, I might as well give over."

Late at night on the Monday before Shrove, the doctor (as chief magistrate) sent for two of his fellow-magistrates. He believed he could trust them – if he didn't overdo it and scare them off – one was the octogenarian vicar of Kirk Deerwood Minster, laughably mild in his opinions, and the other an impregnable Whig. They were to come to him immediately, by way of the stable door of The Jolly Postboys, and to let nobody know they were coming. In his coach-house, by lantern-light, the doctor demanded their endorsement of whatever action he might see fit to undertake in the morning. He gave them no time to ask questions. He took his Bible oath in front of them that the safety of citizens' lives was at issue; he offered them a paper for their signatures. Overwhelmed by the solemnity of his demeanour, they signed and went home trembling.

The events of that Shrovetide were to become subject all over the county to grotesque exaggeration, coarse satire and public contempt, so they had best be described here as drily as possible: let readers make their own assessment from a precise recital of fact.

It was a beautiful bright morning, dew on the grass, birds in the gorse bushes, and a vast refractory multitude swarming up the York Road towards the top of Deerwood Common – In-Town in white shirts over whatever else they wore, and OutTown with broad rainbow-striped sashes wrapped round their torsos – many of them had obviously been at the drink throughout the night – cooks and hucksters were already tossing pancakes and making a great sale of liquor from their booths among the bushes – subsidiary brawls were vehemently in progress, even before the pigskin made its appearance. As he rode up into the midst of it, Dr Fouracre concluded he had never felt such an ugly spirit so early upon the football day; it certainly did look to him as though the man Swayne had known at least something of the truth. Swayne himself was there, as promised, perched upon a tall horse from The Jolly Postboys, direfully vigilant beyond the quickset hedge at top of the hill that marked the boundary of the common land. Neither Sir Jocelyn nor any of his irreconcilable cronies was anywhere to be seen. So far so good.

Behind the doctor came the municipal chaise; it contained a pallid little attorney who was always discomposed by crowds; he was the town clerk and he carried the mayoral regalia. Beside him sat the town constable, silent and dour, a man with the strength of an oaktree but no more intelligent than an *owl* in an oaktree; the pigskin lay across his knees like a great baby in its nurse's lap. Dr Fouracre had told them both, just before they set out from town, what it was he expected from them: he had reassured them by reference to the dragoons, but they could not see any dragoons. They *could* see a half-dozen deputy constables, but such officers were useless in the face of real trouble, and everyone knew it. For the moment, the mayor's courage compelled the courage of his two officials; but how long would that last?

The mayor dismounted. The two officials climbed out of their conveyance. The clerk helped the mayor into the scarlet robe, the gold chain and the cocked hat. The constable started pacing out a circle around the mayor, as though to create an invisible sanctuary which the crowd might not enter. Nor did they enter it. Dr Fouracre, accoutred, sprang back upon his horse, the constable handed him the pigskin and took up a position between the horse and the boundary hedge, the clerk (livid with terror) scrambled up beside the coachman to stand on the box of the chaise and unroll a sheet of parchment.

At the top of his voice, with all the confidence of eight-and-a-half terms of office, Dr Fouracre bawled out: "You suppose that your Mayor has come amongst you to chuck-off. Here is how he does it!" He lifted up the pigskin in the wide grasp of his right hand and flung it as hard as he could – not into the crowd (already beginning to move into the first vortex of the game, upon the east, or town, side of him, before tearing away downhill on their violent course) but to the west, toward the hedge, toward the constable. The latter, with a crouch, leap and turn, caught the ball against his stomach and folded his huge arms around it. He carried on through the *turn*, away from the mayor altogether; he was running full tilt at the hedge. He now held the pigskin above his head in both hands, about to throw it over the hedge; he was perhaps five seconds too late.

As the constable ran, Dr Fouracre had continued to roar. "The football is finished! There is to be no football! The Authorities of this Borough have today put an end to it!" The crowd, taken aback, were yet not so astounded as to be unable to see how Good Owd Alky had somehow done dirt on them: they instantly changed direction and raced to reclaim their pigskin. (No-one seemed to notice the clerk, who gripped the coachman's shoulder to keep his balance, while inaudibly reciting a polysyllabic rigmarole – the law of the land insisted that on such an occasion the Riot Act must be read, it had nothing to say about its being *heard*.)

Distances had been ill-calculated. It was not possible for the constable absolutely to reach the hedge before his pursuers. The first one to grab him was a brawny great girl, a bargemaster's daughter from the river-wharves; apart from her hobnailed boots, she had not a stitch on her but a rag of a short petticoat and a glaring OutTowners' sash; her wild yellow hair had fallen loose from its ribbon all over the place; she grabbed the constable round the hips and would have brought him to the ground if he had not fallen forward across the hedge. Others piled in to help her. Their victim held to the pigskin, his arms outstretched beyond the hedge; he was unable to throw it, the assailants were so tight upon him. They screamed at him, "Our pigskin!" – "Our fucking ball!" – "Drop th'fucker!" – "Drop it, tha daft fucker!" – "Fuckit, man, why wean't tha let drop when tha's told?" – the more they were screaming, the more grimly he clung. They dragged him backwards and sideways to get at the pigskin. The thorns of the quickset wrought terrible hurt upon his face, it was a wonder he was not blinded, his jacket was torn from his back and his shirt into strips, he bled zigzag scarlet stripes belly-and-side as they dragged him – he gave one single cry, and let the ball fall out of his grasp.

But the crowd did not have it. It fell the far side of the hedge and was immediately scooped up by a dirty, darting imp, posted there in the thicket as slyly as Abraham's ram – it was Caleb the Cod and he ran with uncatchable barefoot speed to Simon Swayne on the tall horse; he flung the pigskin forward as he ran, while the baffled pursuers still tangled among the thorns. The man Swayne caught the pigskin, standing in his stirrups and all but pitching himself out of the saddle. He gave a whoop to the horse and a jolt of the spurs and was off at full gallop down the green slope of the common, outflanking the crowd by a wide sweep to the north. They had no hope of catching him. The Kirk Deerwood Football was over and done. But not quite the Kirk Deerwood Riot. It is probable it would have started then and there with a lethal attack upon the mayor and the town clerk – the constable was already forgotten as he rolled about, groaning, in the bottom of the hedge – had not certain men on horseback (supposedly the stewards who should see fair play in the game) suddenly started to behave like a pack of unmanageable sheepdogs. Not so much stewards as provocative-agents, they kept up a chorus of frantic cries, "Into t'town, into t'fucking streets, what d'you reckon y'r fucking paid for? get *on* wi'it. MOVE!" – and moreover they were obeyed, the angry mob surged away down the York Road toward the Bar, intent upon God only knew what extremity of plunder and havoc.

But the exercise was more strenuous than perhaps the 'stewards' had bargained for. Long before the potential riot arrived at the ancient archway, it had lost its dangerous density; it was no better than a weary, boozed-up straggle with no pigskin to be wrangled over to provide a sense of purpose. And the gates were barred against it – the ancient iron-bound gates erected in the fifteenth century to keep out the marauding Scots, a barrier as strong today as ever it was then. InTown and OutTown milled around on the dusty road, sulky and indecisive, once again getting up their own little brawls, while the 'stewards' drew together in a knot and conferred. And then an intervention: the two magistrates primed by the mayor had silently arrived, aloft upon the battlements over the arch, in their ominous black frock-coats and tall black beaver hats. They glowered upon the populace.

"Good people," proclaimed one of them (the clergyman from the minster).

"Good people," proclaimed the other (the impregnable Whig).

They spoke in alternate sentences, Tweedledum, Tweedledee. They were both desperately nervous; the mayor should have been with them and he wasn't; and as they were not sure what had happened up there on the common (except that there seemed to have been no football), they were likewise not sure that they were doing the wisest thing. However, having begun what the mayor had set afoot, they must carry it through with all possible éclat.

"You have heard the Riot Act."

"It means what it says."

"You must immediately disperse. If you wish to enter the town – "

"You may not do so through this Bar. This Bar all day today is a Prohibited.Thoroughfare. As is the East Bar at the entry to the town from the coast."

"And *when* you enter the town by such means of access as you find, you will also find all beershops, dramshops, public houses, wine-vaults, inns, taverns, and all kinds of hostelry, closed until nightfall."

"Steps have been taken to prevent you from forcing them open. Any such attempt will be met by the utmost rigours of the law."

"Good gracious, good people, you are honest sturdy York-shiremen, you overcame the base Napoleon, overcome your own base instincts, behave yourselves like Christians and do honour to your town and county. Through the liberality of your Mayor, a free feast of constant pancakes, hot sausages, mashed potatoes, cold ham and cold beef, will be ready in one half-an-hour upon tables in the market place, together with free beer for every one of you, OutTown or InTown, *in regulated quantities* – and that's all that you will get."

"It's a great deal more than nothing. Behave yourselves and deserve it."

There was a bewildered pause. The magistrates stood and glowered. The populace murmured and muttered and milled around on the dusty road. Then it seemed that the 'stewards' had come to a decision. They turned and walked their horses quietly amongst the people, persuading them to disperse in small clusters by way of laneways and market-gardens into different quarters of town, and to make the best of the sausage-and-mash – once again, they were obeyed, for what else could anyone do? Had they not been told, first football, and then riot? But now there was no football, so how could there be riot? Add to which, the would-be rioters were thoroughly out of breath ... The 'stewards', in the meantime, took their separate departures, unobtrusively in ones and twos, away from the town and into the countryside. They were none of them Kirk Deerwood men.

When the crowd reached the market place, and found trestle-tables laid out there with the beer-kegs and piles of food, and the staff of half the taverns lined up ready to serve them, the general bafflement was only increased – behind every table (to Assist the Civil Power) stood an armed horse-soldier in blue-and-silver uniform with a white-crested helmet, while as a guard for the shops and inns on every side of the square a score of such troopers sat their horses like equestrian statues, each man with one hand on the hilt of his sabre.

It did look at this stage as though Dr Fouracre's counter-coup was already a success. But all had not gone entirely according to plan. He had intended to gallop down the common, well in advance of the mob, and to be with his fellow-magistrates before the Bar could be closed. But the dreadful state of the constable had held him back. He first must ensure the poor man was carried in the chaise to a friendly farmhouse out of reach of further assaults. This took some time. Then he had to ride round the town through fields and copses until he found a way into the streets that was not already thick with hostile citizens. As it was, he was stoned at the entry to Swamp Fever Lane, and he reached the Sessions House just in time to see its windows smashed by a gang of lightfoot hobbledehoys. Inside, there was better news. Sir Jocelyn had just arrived with a choleric deputation to complain about Prohibited Thoroughfares. They were intercepted in the foyer by the major of dragoons and two corporals, who detained them "for their own protection." Dr Fouracre ordered them locked them up in the justices' library, explaining that it was only for an hour or two, that it was a pity their young friends had broken the windows and let in the east wind, but never mind – there were strong iron bars to keep the mob from lynching them (unless they preferred the cells in the basement); anyway it was all for their own protection, hey?

It is uncomfortably true that an amount of riot did take place. But no-one was killed and no property set on fire. The tables in the market place were overturned in a greedy scrimmage, with the cook from The Jolly Postboys thrust most indecently into her tub of mashed potato, head-down and legs-up, and all but stifled. The Jolly Postboys itself was attacked several times in the afternoon and at intervals during the night. Broken glass everywhere and obscene smears of filth. Throughout the night the soldiery patrolled with drawn sabres, keeping ruffians on the run from street to street. Coordination of disorder was thus effectively inhibited. There was no pretext for anyone to demand a complete Martial Law.

Swayne's shop in Minster Northgate was wrecked; Swayne himself had not come home; he had ridden clear away with the pigskin and indeed never did come home. In the end it became known that he had taken off for an indefinite stay with his married sister in Lincolnshire, or was it Rutland? – serious threats were out against his life – Dr Fouracre had thought best to dispatch to him in secret a large sum of money – compensation? or reward? It was in fact a hidden addition to a whole stream of outgoing payment, acknowledged and public, to the constable, of course, and of course to the cook, as well as to others who'd suffered slighter (but still deleterious) personal injury. And as for all the lawsuits for the damage to various buildings ... Nonetheless, Dr Fouracre told himself that by and large he had *saved the town*.

He certainly did not expect the tumult of disgusted censure that gradually enveloped him once citizens began to think about what had or had not happened. Can it be believed that *he* came to believe that he almost had good cause to agree with them? for had he not crushed the Time-Honoured Liberties of Englishmen? laid open the town to even worse trouble than the football? allowed a good man to be all but torn in pieces, and a good woman's modesty to be violated in the market place? In short, had he not made a damnable fool of himself, without a

morsel of evidence for this unspecified, obscure conspiracy that
he kept on and on about? For a time he sweated and writhed in
a torment of forlorn self-reproach, unable to convince the world,
unable to convince himself, that he'd acted correctly; yet neither
could he admit he'd been gravely misled. In his nightly prayers
he even railed upon God for bringing him into such proximity
with the man Swayne – who was irremediably gone, gone, gone
and could never be called to testify to the truth of his tale.

The remaining months of the doctor's ninth mayoral term would
have dwindled away in accumulated ignominy, had it not been
for the death of King George and the proclamation of the Duke
of Clarence as King William IV. No sign of any coup on behalf
of the wicked Cumberland, but who (besides Alcuin Fouracre)
would suppose that there might be? However there was a fresh
dilemma, relating once again to the Time-Honoured Liberties.
It had been customary, since who could say when? for a bull to
be 'given' to celebrate the proclamation of a new monarch – the
unlucky creature was paid for by the mayor or drawn from the
mayor's own stock (if the mayor, like Dr Fouracre, kept cattle
on Deerwood Common) and yielded with all formality to the
citizens for their sport: which is to say, to be baited in the market place by savage dogs, and inevitably killed – the dogs were
tossed and maimed – very often they were also killed – there'd
be a sluicing of foul blood down the channels of the cobble-
stones and drunken delight amongst at least some of the citizens
– while ever more and more of them, humble, gentle or clerical,
were nowadays finding such sport quite abhorrent ... Yet only
ten years earlier, when King George had been proclaimed, Dr
Fouracre (in his fourth term) had Given his Bull with scarcely
a qualm.

And now, once again, the custom had come round.

Sir Jocelyn Wetwang, cured of his boils but in a condition of
implacable feud toward the man who had cured him, intercepted the mayor in the middle of Monksgate, between the apoth-
ecary's shop and the gunsmith. "Hello there, you Fouracre,
damn your eyes! I'm talking to *you*. D'you mean to Give a Bull,

you snivelling Creeping Jesus, or do we extract it by force from your worm-eaten herd?"

This time Dr Fouracre had no doubts. He had rendered himself already so wretchedly unpopular, that a second pragmatic stride into the morass of liberal decency could hardly make things worse. If the Tory managers preferred somebody else, and somebody else's inn, for their regular election business – as already seemed to be the case – the eventual effect upon his profits would be calamitous. On the other hand, he could say good-bye to a violent and detrimental class of customer and his mother would be able to sleep at nights. Moreover, upon reflection, he really had no wish to be mayor for the tenth time ... He squared up to Wetwang, holding his walking-stick like a quarterstaff, prepared for anything and no nonsense (he could see the baronet's coachman and a bulky companion loitering a little way down the street; they carried cudgels).

"Sir, I shall Give no Bull. I have made my last concession, hey? to bloody-minded brutishness – you can take that and put it where it bloody well blocks you up. Furthermore, if anyone attempts to purloin any beast of mine or of anyone's, I shall prosecute, and no leniency. Take care you're not sent off to New South Wales ... Oh aye, and if you choose to set your rascals onto me – *I* see them there, they can hear me, yes they *can!* – be assured that they will travel in the same ship as you."

Extraordinary: for the first time he was truly *glad* he had stopped the football – not because he might have averted a treasonable plot, but because he now saw that the football in itself was brutish, that in fact he had always known it, and ought to have stopped it years ago. Similarly with the bull-baiting. He'd instinctively refused the bull for no better reason than that the demand came from Wetwang: but now it was apparent that bull-baiting was a nasty game and – well, that was it, it was apparent.

Dr Fouracre's refusal – in the open street, at the busiest time of day, forthright and overt – instead of making him more enemies, in fact went some way to restore his reputation. Many of the quieter sort (who had tended to despise him as something of an old-fashioned boor) now began to say that his football decision was no mere folly, and that the mayor was at bottom a humane and principled gentleman, cut from the same good cloth as his estimable parents. Sadly, they would add, a bad run of associates in his youth had led him astray, and (of course) the promiscuity of the inn-keeping business naturally inclined a man toward doubtful political fellowships. These views were held by liberals and also by some moderate conservatives. The latter may not have been aware of it, but the spirit of the age had been changing for some time and they too had changed – *unbridled* corruption was no longer acceptable, even among those who would have nothing to do with Reform.

Not that Alcuin Fouracre had anything to do with Reform, and he still abominated Radicals. A pity, though, that Simon Swayne had fled so precipitately – Alcuin was truly sorry he'd had never taken the chance to sit down with him and enjoy a cordial political talk, even though they had known one another for years, almost to the point of a genuine friendship – it might have been possible, for example, to find out how an uncultivated artisan had infested himself with such outlandish levelling notions, all very well for Alcuin's father and mother among their philosophical bookshelves, but as near-as-dammit criminal at a shoemaker's bench? – and why was the artisan so relentlessly acrimonious? – and why on earth should he pursue so nonsensical an object as Universal Suffrage? – and what *was* all that, anyway, about Cumberland and pains and chains? If Swayne really knew things that nobody else knew, did he not have a duty to tell?

Less-moderate conservatives continued to regard their mayor as at best an irresponsible clown, and there was sheer naked hatred for him in the slum-tenements down by the river. To avenge the loss of the bull-baiting, his windows were broken and his walls daubed for the second time that year. But scores of unexpected people came running to help him make good the destruction. And old Mrs Fouracre descended from her drawing-room and served them with free beer. The Kirk Deerwood Football was never played again.

YORKSHIRE TYKE

"Quis custodiet ipsos custodes?"　　*(Who shall guard the guards themselves?)*

[Juvenal, *Satire VI*]

There was a family in Yorkshire that lived by its wits and assumed the name of Fouracre. They claimed a blood relationship with other Fouracres in the same county, well-known citizens of the ancient borough of Kirk Deerwoood, who indignantly denied the connection. Three generations, grandfather, son and grandson, each in turn pursued the claim; they met with no success; they grew ever more vicious and abusive about it. This is the story of the third generation: how the grandson's baffled urge to belong to a noteworthy lineage mutated him by degrees into a species of human quicksand, to engulf not only himself but also the only woman in the whole of his life who might be thought to have truly loved him, or very nearly truly loved him: she never said, but he knew it well enough.

The grandfather was an enterprising vagabond of mixed race (African, Asian, Carib? who could tell?); he had emerged into public view from somewhere in the United States (or was it the Antilles?) in the early 1930s. He called himself Calhoun Fouracre, and put it about that he was the unacknowledged son of the late Francis Fouracre, solicitor, mayor of Kirk Deerwood, lifelong bachelor and ecclesiastical expert. When war broke out in '39 this Calhoun was nearly sixty but as keen as a collier's whippet; he secured a job with the army at Strensall Camp near York, civilian consultant for the upkeep and repair of motor vehicles. He was a skilful mechanic. He was also to prove himself no less skilful at the black market, a slick trade in spare parts and illicit petrol. In '42 he followed the column to Egypt, where he diverted consignments of Free-French military tyres to the garages of Port Said and found himself thrust into an insanitary local gaol. He died in the gaol – but not before he heard that a son had been born to him in York. In his last letter to the child's mother (an apparently unmarried cook in her thirties, who fried eggs for a soldiers' canteen) he wrote,

I sure am an old old hore-headed fellonious jiggety-joo but O my sweet honnybun, hotpoussy you may be but you aint no teenage jailbate niether, didnt we _do_ it? hey we _did_ it, Praise-to-the-Lord we did _all_ of it and I guess I'm truly proud. Call him Alcuin Frank Calhoun Fouracre, make sure you let him know where he comes from.

(Alcuin being the name of a supposed son of old King Aella, the supposed Anglo-Saxon ancestor of the Kirk Deerwood Fouracres, that very ancient family in their very ancient town.)

The boy grew up in a council-estate prefab on the outskirts of Leeds. His mother wore furs and jewels in all weathers, blonded her hair till she shone like the midday sun, and endeavoured to gather largesse from a series of unreliable "uncles". Alcuin Frank Calhoun learned a lot from two or three of them, but he stuck a breadknife into the fourth and was sent to Borstal. In Borstal he learned a few things more. By the time he too became a father, he'd already been a thieving teddy-boy and had developed into a struggling conman, not always successful. He liked best to have a go at the _badger game_, where he worked in partnership with a delicious slinky tart. She was part-Asian: like himself, an unexpected product of the war, her mother an RAF nurse posted to Calcutta, her father a Bengali medical student. Alcuin Frank Calhoun and herself would pretend to be husband and wife in order to blackmail incautious chappies who'd thought the tart was all their own for all night long in a low hotel. It seems that Alcuin Frank Calhoun was himself tricked by the tart into believing he'd made her pregnant. After eighteen months of quarrelsome domesticity, she left the child on his hands and skedaddled off to London with most of his spare cash, to look for a livelier young man.

(The fact was, he took after his mother; he thought he was smart but instead he was heavy and gullible; he took as gospel every word his mother had told him about that very ancient family; he never saw what his tart was up to until it was far too late.)

Out of filial piety he called his son Alcuin – a name fit to be jeered at in the circles where he commonly moved, circles where he himself was known only as Frankie-boy. He added another name, Ringo, this being 1963. Much to his relief, the baby was taken 'into care', to be fostered for fifteen years by one mercenary family after another. For all of that time Frankie-boy pursued his cack-handed career, disappearing into prison more than once, until he set himself at last to seek his son.

He indignantly reclaimed him in an outburst of fatherly emotion. To tell truth he badly needed an able assistant for his current work-in-progress, a complexity of scams revolving around variations of *mock auction*, or *dutch auction*, or *blind auction*, where the public might be induced to pay and pay again for mere rubbish, or for nothing at all. He was insufficiently specious to carry off this sort of spoof with any degree of ease: but Alcuin Ringo soon proved himself to be quick, clever, plausible, as well as lithe and violent, well able to protect his father if anything went wrong with the customers or the law. The father appreciated him, and became greatly affectionate toward him; the son in his turn offered some small affection, combined with a spice of resentment; the two of them carried on a most prosperous partnership in all manner of rackets and fiddles until the 1980s. By this time they were calling themselves:

4ACRES : 4SQUARE

Import / Export / Wholesale / Retail
Cash–n–Carry

Financial Services a Specialty

Not to put a tooth in it, they were a pair of greedy loan-sharks. They set up an office in Barnsley, where Frankie-boy had been told the council was corrupt and the cops incompetent. The 1984 miners' strike did wonders for the business, with families in sudden terror of hard times in every pit-village between Wakefield and Doncaster and south as far as Rotherham. The miners' union took pains to warn its members against these dubious '4ACRES,' but father and son became aware of hostile surveillance and were careful to keep on the safe side of the law. Not that it mattered much, for the police were glad enough to see strikers fleeced and robbed; government had put the word out; it was a question, was it not, of the Enemy Within? whereas Frankie-boy and Ringo could be deemed essential venture-capitalists to save the soul of Great Britain ... Until (that is to say) a year or two later, when they revisited the notion of blackmail and brought the house down all around them.

It had seemed entirely reasonable. Ringo one morning was reading *The Yorkshire Post* to look for business opportunities that wouldn't be in *The Sun*, when his eye was caught by a death-notice: 'Miss Sheba Fouracre ... last of her name in Kirk Deerwood ... in her 101st year.' He showed it to his father, who cackled and chuckled and slapped his thick palms together. Miss Sheba, he declared, was "one o'them dry-cunt nieces of your granddad's fucking dad. He said they give him a right turnabout when he told 'em who he was, one time i't'fucking church; and now they're *all* fucked, must ha' been sat on fucking thousands, tens o'thousands, hundreds, sitha. So who gets it? *We* don't. Unless we go for that will, boy, as rightful fucking heirs, fucking challenge it downhill and up."

Unfortunately neither of them conceived the word "challenge" to mean a process of verification and lawyers' depositions. Frankie-boy had tried lawyers, once, upon the issue, and had been unpleasantly rebuffed. This time, he meant to make certain – if the Kirk Deerwood legatees refused to recognize his claim, he would settle to be paid to withdraw it. He foresaw at least a five-figure sum out of a six-figure total inheritance. He was sure that the peace and quiet of such sanctimonious muckamucks would be worth all of that to them and maybe more. He sent for the dodgy solicitor whom he used to safeguard his transactions, told him to find where the money had been left and how much there was of it: himself and the lad Ringo'd do the rest. The solicitor discovered a network of distant Fouracres (second cousins and suchlike) in Canada, Australia and Hong Kong, and one elderly man in London. Miss Sheba's estate had been divided amongst them – it was large enough, certainly, though by no means six figures – and the London beneficiary had most of it. So they dressed themselves up like wedding guests (sharp blue pinstripe, gorgeous waistcoats, floral buttonholes) and zoomed off up the motorway in their company-registered Porsche to intimidate the beneficiary.

They'd been told his name was Lambert and that he was a professor of Latin literature. Their entire understanding of professors had been picked up from movies. They assumed he must be short-sighted, absent-minded, soft as butter. He could hardly be the other sort – the wild-eyed Frankenstein sort – he had no laboratory, he did nowt but read books and write. How were they to know that in fact Joseph Lambert was the most contentious, cantankerous, controversial authority in his field, who'd spent his entire post-graduate life excoriating the flawed scholarship of anyone who dared publish one single timid paragraph upon Martial or Catullus? They came upon him at breakfast time, in his grim, gaunt Victorian mansion up a cul-de-sac off Highgate Hill; he was snarling and grinding his teeth over a new life of Horace that had been sent him for review. He gave them two minutes to explain what they were there for; his fury was at once transferred from inept biographer to floundering extortionists; Ringo lost his temper and pulled a cosh from his pocket; the professor, undaunted, ordered them out of the house, bellowing for his gardener to let loose the dog. Ringo struck out with the cosh, missing the professor's skull but breaking first his nose and then his collar-bone. Confusion and panic. The dog was a collie-type crossbreed, as choleric as its master and nearly as dangerous. It tore at Frankie-boy's calf as he fled down the path to the gate (he was terrified of dogs), but Ringo had presence of mind. He seized a spade that the gardener had left in a flowerbed. He swung such a blow at the conscientious animal as almost to chop off its head: it flung itself over and over, foaming and plunging and squealing. The professor, in an ecstasy of anger and pain, staggered to the telephone to dial 999. Father and son ran a-scramble full tilt to their car. Frankie-boy leaked blood at every step and roared like a sick walrus. Catastrophe unrelieved, the more so that they'd given the man their business card: he knew who they were, could find where they lived: neither he nor the gardener had had time to read their number-plate, so they'd get back to Barnsley unhindered – but after that? Catastrophe.

"Fucking leg," groaned Frankie-boy, as they spun off the motorway at the Dearne Valley sliproad. "First stop's Barnsley fucking hospital. Fucking tyke had fucking rabies, don't you argue. Get me there. Now."

Son deposited father at Casualty, drove home safe and sound, found no sign of police (at any rate, not yet), collected his passport and some clothes, travelled in a taxi across town to the bank. He withdrew all the money that could be moved without prior notice, then another taxi ten miles to Sheffield where he knew there was a branch of an Irish bank; he opened an account to enable him to draw funds in the Republic; then on foot to a travel agency and booked himself a ticket via coach and the ferry to Dublin. Something in his brain kept up a wretched rigmarole: "Custodial sentence, money demanded with menaces, father with previous, son with the cosh, oh the cosh oh the cosh, why the fuck did I go for the cosh? beloved dog viciously assaulted, and the pot, bloody blue pot, Jesus Christ why'd he put it where he put it? custodial, custodial." (Indeed they'd only got out of the professor's house by way of a priceless Chinese vase which was left in shattered fragments on the parquet.)

Ringo did not want to abandon the Porsche, but he felt it was too conspicuous; nor did he want to abandon his father, but he felt it would be easier for Frankie-boy without him. That cosh had destroyed their partnership, at least until the police had had time to lose interest.

From Liverpool, just before the boat sailed, he telephoned home. He was answered by a strange and cagey voice, it had to be the cops: was his father already nicked? At all events the business records would be thoroughly turned over – '4ACRES' was effectively demolished. Whatever he did in Ireland would need to be brand new. Change of name, to start with: a pity about the passport, he'd have to get it doctored, which wouldn't come cheap ... Calhoun was an Irish sort of name, he could use it for a surname. Alcuin was no good, likewise Ringo, both of them too conspicuous. He remembered what Frankie-boy had told him about the old granddad, that nickname, what was it? Switch? "Switch Calhoun" had a good gangster sound to it, it'd help him find a job where ability to intimidate was requisite, he didn't need to be illegal, what would be wrong with having a go as a nightclub bouncer?

*

For the next few years he groped his way precariously, keeping his head down. Frankie-boy (so he heard) had indeed been given "custodial." It was best not even to *try* to get in touch. He played one or two of the old con-games; but felt safer when he went for waged work, if it didn't need documentation – he was a bouncer in Dublin, then an enforcer in Waterford for a loan-shark (who sacked him because he knew too much about the trade); toward the end of the century he was hanging on in Cork, doing security at a dockside warehouse where they imported expensive cars, cannibalized stolen ones, and now and then received mysterious packages hidden in coachwork. He must have given satisfaction, for he held that job rather longer than usual, a year or more indeed – until one night in a pub he was accosted by a murky little man, whispering, buying him a drink unasked-for, whispering again, giving him to understand that something was about to *go down* in the warehouse on behalf of *certain elements* (some strand of the IRA, understood), and Switch should not be there when it happened; his Brit accent had been talked about, in this place and that; the Garda Síochána had been asking a few questions – *"know what I mean?"*

Switch knew. Before midnight he was out of Cork in his groggy old car, driving north towards Limerick. Limerick, so he'd heard, was already sewn up between its own ruthless gangs, no scope for blow-ins: better to continue to Galway. In Galway, it was now high summer, there'd be the arts festival, the horse-races, the oyster festival, all of them associated with an abundance of music sessions – crowds upon crowds of jolly visitors to work upon. Sufficient, as they say, to *give him a start* in the place.

He was at ease with these visitors, American, French, Italian, entering into their nervous good humour, recommending appropriate pubs or musicians or touristy tat-shops. He would sometimes employ that difficult conman's art which needs brazen effrontery combined with the skill to slide quickly out of danger – he would lead people to think that he knew people whom *they* knew in or from their own country, thereby to induce them to trust him with at least a small portion of their cash – for the purchase of tickets for a match or a rock-concert, from an eccentric middleman who "wouldn't sell to anyone he'd never met" – for an anonymous deposit on a holiday cottage, with a landlord who ran his business "a tad short of the planning acts" but was accordingly much cheaper – for an intro to "Celtic-style" varieties of carnal knowledge, in a city where such diversions were not widely advertised – to say nothing of the question of access to drugs.

With one thing, he was *not* at ease. That was this improbable and yet most hurtful, hateful link with the very ancient Fouracres. His real name was not Switch but Alcuin, he was always aware of it, his whole soul clamoured to *be* it; so bloody degrading to have to miscall himself for so many years in this ratbag of a country where nobody could be sure how many private armies lay hid in the bloody sewerage, and how far they were preserved by the cops. The message in Cork had given him the shakes, not to put a tooth in it: he ought to be (and why wasn't he?) where that deadly professor was, in a glowering great house crammed with prestige from cellar to attic, and a gardener, and a biting tyke.

Christsake, his dad had told him why the old granddad was called Switch, as well as how the granddad had been stuffed into great-grandma's belly; why, she was bloody well whipped like a pony, bare-arse naked in an orchard, by the paedophile Fouracre that fucked her – Christsake it was a family of psychos and kinks – *and he had a right to belong to it.*

Every day, every night, his troubled mind went prowling among these most troubling concerns; but he kept them inside himself, he had a living to earn.

One day during Galway Race Week, Switch Calhoun lounged in the lounge of the Great Southern Hotel, looking about him for a glimpse of the *main chance.* He'd supplied himself with a pre-lunch gin-and-tonic and was dressed like a man who might be the owner of a yacht (striped T-shirt and light linen suit) – the wedding-guest persona had long been discarded as altogether too crude. He became aware of a bit of a hubbub in a tucked-away corner – men and women clustering round a woman all on her own who seemed subject to a crossfire of questions – there were also flash cameras and – yes, wasn't that a TV unit with one of those furry microphones on a pole? Clearly a species of press conference, but oddly uncoordinated, as though the par-ticipants had not expected to be there. Switch couldn't see the woman's face, but the voice sounded strained, distressed even. He sniffed his *main chance:* he approached from the side, with care, avoiding notice, all ears. A quiet step to the right gave him a clear view of her profile, and surely he had seen her before? – on a TV chat-show, it must have been, two months ago at least – she was – oh soddit, why couldn't he remember her name? – she had anyway been highly praised for – for? – aha, and *he had it!* – yes! for her great work among female victims of cleri-cal sex-abuse – and she'd told how she herself as a girl had been abused by a priest on the very altar. And look at her! so cool and elegant, *suave* might be the word, if she didn't sit smoking like a turf-fire on a wet day, and if this scandal-slurping mob would allow her the time to think straight and give a straight answer.

Whereas, one and all, they were doing their best to confuse her and catch her out.

He listened and heard and digested. It seemed that her most recent exposure of a lecherous cleric had ostensibly been refuted, time, place and character of the man – moreover his supposed prey had turned out to be a drug addict, a gaol-bird, a compensation-greedy perjurer – and lesbian into the bargain, was it? Some tabloid must have run the story in all its tendentious detail – Switch hadn't bothered to read yesterday's papers beyond the racing pages, but apparently everyone else had – the whole of Ireland was claimed to be in shock and moral outrage at the pretensions of this lauded celebrity, her brass neck, her hypocrisy, making a mock of all the accolades she'd been awarded – not only had she regurgitated a tissue of most libellous lies, but when one of her assistants found discrepancies in the evidence, she was said to have used language against her that no decent person could endure or repeat.

In short, she'd been popular too long: it was time for the necessary backlash, the cutting-down to size, the ritual of national begrudgery. After more than a decade in Ireland, Switch needed no media-analyst to tell him what was happening. He heard her try in vain to stem the insistent questions, her voice ever more shrill with each successive protestation; in a minute, thought Switch, she would indeed be using language that no decent person, *etc.*

She'd been caught off her guard as she walked across the lobby. The press in fact was there to meet a cabinet minister down for the races, who was expected to pronounce upon the week's corruption revelations. He was still at his lunch, so the journalists must wait and make do with what they found; they had all but destroyed her and were about to wipe the floor with her, when a PR-person came tripping through the archway to let them know that the real press conference was all set up and ready for them in a private room with drinks – so off they went in competitive scrimmage, a pack of hyenas without a qualm and a half-eaten carcase left behind them.

Walking delicately, Switch came over to her; she huddled, pale and drained, in a miasma of smoke, and so tense she seemed to quiver. From her wide leather armchair she looked up at him as edgy as a rip-saw and wished he wasn't there; but he smiled with all his charm and said, "What you need is a minder. Okay if I sit here?" (Another armchair, nearby.) "I heard some of that," he said. "Nasty ... Don't worry about *me*, love. I'm not the press. Just a chap from over i'Yorkshire, down for t'races, same as you."

She did not return his smile. She said, "I'm not fucking worried. Just ferocious, that's all. And I'm not down for the races. I live here."

No more words for several minutes. They sat warily, appraising one another.

He saw: –   this bird, or doll, or chick, slightly-built, athletic; her shape might pretend she was no more than twenty, but the strength of her cheekbones and the lines between nostrils and corners of the mouth told a sharper story – she'd be thirty, thirty-five, no less; she was at work on her cigarette with quick, spasmodic puffs.   Brown hair, cut short, with a fringe and bronze highlights, very spruce.   Her breasts (Switch took note of breasts) were small and taut under a casual white shirt worn outside her black trousers; long legs in those trousers seemed as neat as a basketball player's.   Perhaps she did play basketball. Switch felt he would like very much to peel the trousers off for her, but hold it! it was early days, she might or might not be the *main chance* – he must move slowly.   He'd thought at the beginning she was on the verge of a good weep, until she said "fucking" with such harshness, and showed her teeth round the butt of her fag.   She was anxious to make a point there; he wasn't sure what point.

He suddenly remembered her name – why, of *course!* she was Cecilia Coppinger.

She saw: –   a short, slender, shy-looking man, about the same age as herself, sallow complexion and very black hair, wavy and left a little long; dark eyes and a dark chin (even though closely shaved) – he might have been a Spaniard, or at any rate a Connemara man, which sorted oddly with his flat Yorkshire speech. His face was thin and pointed; he evaded her eyes except when he was looking straight at them; when he did look straight at them his gaze betrayed no shyness, it was snake-like, cold and intense. But his voice was by no means cold – there was a chuckling kindness about it, and at all times a mischievous lift of one end of his mouth, not quite a smile, but the *spirit* of a smile. It made her feel she might trust him; maybe the chill of his gaze could mean steadfastness rather than cunning? But then, for twenty years she had trusted no male creature of any age or disposition – cunning, kind or mischievous. She had given up even *wanting* to. It was scary that with this one she should suddenly feel that she –

She must talk to him and unravel him, she needed to know who he was. She wished he wasn't there, yet she felt all of a sudden that she needed *him* to know who *she* was.

"If you heard it," she growled, "it's as well you should be told that none of it was true, barring the bit about language. That woman who worked for me had shown herself an eedjit and I don't suffer eedjits gladly."

"Of course it wan't true," he assured her, calm and reliable, the capable Northern Englishman. "I knew that afore they began. It's been obvious all the time you've been given a right fit-up. They want to shut your trap for you: you know what you shouldn't know: you've said what you shouldn't say. Dead obvious, really. You oughtn't to have fallen for it, if you'd had half your wits i'place. But how could you know, like, being as where you were?"

"Minder?" She lit another cigarette, as though to conceal her interest. "When you say minder, would that be bodyguard? or policy consultant? I don't want a policy consultant, I'm a one-woman show, dealing with women one-to-one; if they think I'm an institution, they take fright. I *had* a consultant, she was a messer not a minder, I swore at her, fired her out, look what she's after doing to me. You heard."

"Right, but take it easy. If not her it'd be others. No accident, tha knows; it was all planned." (He was precise with his bits of Yorkshire, dropping the odd phrase, sparsely, here and there, to remind her of his essential integrity.) "Mother Church, as they say, working up for the counter-attack."

"D'you know?" she cried aloud. "I'm only here to meet a friend, a *good* friend is how I thought of her: so where's she gone, why? She wouldn't be seen with me, is why." Her mouth (with the fag still in it) had the appearance of a three-cornered tear in an old tarpaulin, such bitterness in her words.

So: *stage one* was now in train. He'd planted his hints that he understood all the background to her trouble, more than *she* understood, very likely. She didn't seem to doubt his knowledge. He dared to move in a little bit further. *Stage two*: show her that he knew where she should go. "You'll never be able to prove that that priest was the sleezebag you said he was. You'd only the one witness, and they've taken her good and proper to Grimsby – "

"Grimsby?"

"Like, i'Yorkshire we say Grimsby's the place to get yersen slubbered in a barrel o'rotten fish. So for a while yet, there'll be nowt heard of *you* that en't wrapped up with *her* and the stink she gives off, drug-addict an' all o'that, I tell you it's lethal. Oh and o'course with that policy consultant too. You'll need a right flashy comeback to wash out the public memory – have y'another case on the go? like, another priest or a savage nun? like, one that you *can* prove? ... Yeah?"

Transfixed as she was by his relentless reptilian glare, she felt nonetheless there was warmth in his words: candid, she thought, humorous. She actually smiled, and responded with an equal warmth. "Ah don't be talking, I'm inundated, that's a fact – but who's going to listen to me now?"

"So long as the media's out to knock you, nobody'll listen: but you have to be ready for when they tire of it, right? Which is why you need a minder, or else they'll *never* tire of it till they get

you to give in – to admit you're a phoney – to crawl and display
your shame – 'CC's Shame' – they'll have it in their headlines
and they'll doorstep you for more. 'CC's Sex Romp Shame' – if
that's what they can find, it'll *do* you for ever. And not only
you. D'you have a husband, fiancé, boyfriend, girlfriend?"

As he asked her this, he leaned forward and laid his hand
on her hand. She did not exactly *jerk* in the hollow of the big
chair, but the psychological effect was as though she had sprung
from him like a starling from a gunshot. "Wrong question,"
she snapped. "Wrong move. I'd enough of all that when I was
twelve. So watch yourself, me bucko, or we're finished here and
now."

Startled, he pulled back from her. She stared at him until she
was certain he had properly understood her. Then straight into
business-talk, decisive and abrupt. "So you want to be the man
to keep 'em off my doorstep, yes? It's not only journalists, I may
be in trouble from regular thugs; if all you say is true, there's
more than flapping clerics behind what's in the wind, I've no
notion how deep it goes, but this is Ireland and I *know*. It could
reach to some very hard men, so I'm scared ... The point is,
you're no great size. How good would you be in a ruck?"

He had to consider this. Suppose she asked for references?
No way could he get references from the sort of jobs he'd been
doing. He played mock-modest. "H'm ... How good? Fair
question. Well, as to that ... "

As sudden and as rude as a belch at a burial, there cropped
up in front of her a pimply-faced man, beer-bellied, sweating,
in shades and a 'US MARINES' T-shirt – one of the press mob
who'd been at her before – he'd abandoned the minister, having
sucked in all he could use of the fellow's piss-and-wind – he saw
her still sitting where she had been – he saw her stare at apparently nothing. (He failed to see Switch, sunk in his armchair,
mock-modest.) Maybe there was more to be got from this bitch,
he must have been thinking, "or if not, I've wasted the day."
He took one quick stride and crouched down beside her, shoving his weasel features close under her nose. And he brayed at
her the very same question that Switch had so vexed her with.

"Boyfriend, you never tell us? Who is he? Or is it a dike? Our readers have a right to know, you know: you put yourself in the public eye, you take the shit as well as the sweeties: don't you fuck with me."

Switch uncoiled himself from his chair and all in one movement he had the man's arm with its tape-recorder twisted round behind the man's back and the man's neck bent horribly sideways with Switch's fist pressing tight at the Adam's apple. "Get out of here," a quiet instruction. "Out, or you're dislocated." He let go his hold. The man staggered a few paces across the deep-pile carpet; attempted to utter; all he could do was croak. He looked all around for help, but nobody in the lounge seemed to have seen what had happened, except for a waiter who stood there goggling and then shrugged and turned away. The reporter turned away likewise, shook himself, left: no doubt he'd write it up ("CC's KungFu Shock-Jock!"), but for now he was defeated.

Switch smiled sidelong, almost ruefully: Cecilia bared teeth in outrageous delight. They closed the bargain there and then. She named a wage, he accepted; she gave him notice he only held the job upon probation; after a few days she'd confirm it if she was still sure she needed him, and in any case she *wouldn't* need him once the nuisance was over, he accepted that too; he apologized for his tactlessness, and this time *she* accepted.

They went out of the hotel together. She paid for a taxi to bring them both to the racecourse, where she bought him a late lunch in the long bar under the grandstand, shepherd's pie and Guinness, to seal their arrangement. He was brooding about the tactlessness. Somehow, as he shovelled his gravy and carrots, it led him to acquaint her with all sorts of stuff he wouldn't as a rule deploy quite so soon. But this one was an unusual type: it would probably be helpful to have her fully apprised.

She was horrified at what she heard. She stubbed out a cigarette twenty seconds after lighting it. "My God! d'you tell me – your great-grandmother, she was not only black, but – *how* old? Fourteen?"

"Nearer twelve, so I've heard. That's how it was in them days. They'd to take it as it came. Brutal."

"God, but it makes me just ferocious to hear you ... Sure, you have great philosophy. But your granddad, did *he?* After all she was the one that reared him, they must have talked of it together – wouldn't he feel he should do something about it? Like confronting his – his father? *She* did, you tell me; why not him?"

"Confronting a lawyer? *She* got nowt out of it, *he* wouldn't, neither. He hadn't the skill, hadn't the proof, hadn't the funds, he knew that. And he was no more than a mechanic; and after him, my dad was no more than a Borstal boy, still *is*, the daft article – there was never the funds, you see. So we never did nowt, none of us. Now if *I* had the funds, I reckon I could and I would - Forget it, it's dead. What's alive is your campaign. I'd say you should go to ground, see nobody, talk to nobody ('cept these women you talk to, one-on-one, right?) till you've built yourself, like, this dossier that nobody's going to rubbish. How long'll it take?"

She took a moment to answer, flicking the flame of her cigarette-lighter up and down – her thoughts seemed to be elsewhere – the tale of his family had seriously upset her. "Oh," she said, stammering a little, "how – how long? No, a deal of the work's been done; maybe a month, no more than that ... Switch," she said, "wait! no, that's not your name, can't be. If that's how you want to be known, sure that's your own business, but I'd like to have your true name – by the same token, mine's a bit of an alias too. I wasn't at all Cecilia Coppinger, not when it happened, no. I was Bridget, so I was, and the other's the name of an aunt that took me in when me mam and me da, they - Jasus, they made out that I'd told a filthy lie out of malice toward the holy priest, they couldn't handle it, threw me away. Only for my aunt Cecilia, they'd have had me in the Magdalene Laundry or some such, know what I mean?" Her cultivated accent was dropping off under stress of emotion, and she reverted to gurrier's Dublin. "Know what I fucking mean? Mindya, I'm not telling ya the true surname, so I won't: Jasus, I never tell it, they're both of 'em dead and the name's dead, like it oughta be. But your name, you've a right to it."

So he had. So he told it her, Alcuin Fouracre; and yes, he did think, with sufficiency of funds, he could establish its lineage foursquare. "DNA," he argued. "Oh it costs, I'd need specialists: but there's nowt they can't do with a splash of DNA, I've seen it on the telly."

Well, he'd reached *Stage Three*. It was true that her smile was more sceptical than enthusiastic: but the sympathy was there and the notion of funds was definitely in play. He'd hooked her as firmly as she was ever going to be hooked. Wait and see then – till *Stage Four*. Which might be tomorrow, it might be next year.

An unresolved question: he'd no idea how much money she had. He gathered, as he'd gathered everything, from throwaway remarks (both today and on that TV show) that she was well cushioned at the bank. One of the reporters had made a crack about her "backers." Did they subsidize her to any degree, or just help her cover expenses? And she herself, didn't she administer some sort of charity, for research and maybe help toward the wrecked lives of clergy-victims? He wasn't sure about any of this.

In the meantime, should she want to know more about him than the urge to reclaim his name, he made a little mystery. He feared she might recoil from the uninviting truth. He said it wasn't quite the case that he was only in town for the races – he had in fact been in Galway for some time, he said he tried to "flog things, this and that, import-export," he skirted round a few vague images of cocaine-running from Colombia and gun-running from Libya, he gave a general impression of a canny entrepreneur who had been almost ready to set up a powerful series of property deals with powerful financial figures.

He finally admitted he was down on his luck, and Cecilia had saved his life.

This was a good line to adopt. She relished the notion that she'd been beholden in an awkward corner to a mischievous little rascal and was immediately able to repay him. By the end of the afternoon, she was telling him with glee that he'd brought her great luck with the horses. She placed her bets lavishly, winning more than she lost. By contrast, his own wagers were small and unsuccessful. He'd never been a racing man, exactly. Whenever he'd gone to the meetings it was to keep a sharp eye upon people rather than horses. He declared that if the bookies ever gave odds on punters' behaviour, he would assuredly win and win. This pleased her: it seemed to confirm his capability for the job. She told him he could forget about "probation", he was hers unconditionally. This was rash and she knew it, she knew it and she didn't care.

After the last race, he escorted her home, made sure there was no-one to hassle her, gave her a chaste handshake and went off to his "apartment." She lived in the upper half of a dignified stone terrace-house in Mary Street in the old city, while he had to put up with an exiguous tin-roofed shed at the bottom of a suburban garden – it was turned into a bedsit with cold-water sink and shower, and rented out as a *chalet*. Not so much residence as rat-hole, but it suited him well enough.

(Despite the warmth between them, he was altogether too cunning to let Cecilia know his address. He gave her his mobile-phone number, said she'd need no more than that. She did not press him: she believed he had a right to his secrets: no business of hers to uncover them.)

*

For three months, then, Switch *minded* Cecilia, and was good at it; she said so, but he knew it already. The drawback, it was dead boring. During the day, he would sit in a tiny room opening out of the stunted corridor that led to her office. He would read papers and magazines, listen to his Walkman, blink through lace curtains at the girls in the school playground behind the street, twiddle his thumbs and eavesdrop. Cecilia did not seem to mind if he sometimes smoked joints in there (she may not have been able to detect them through the reek of her Gauloises). But he had to be careful about his reading matter;

anything remotely pornographic and she'd send him packing; she made that very clear. She also impressed upon him that he must not be seen: the smallest suspicion of a man on the premises and her wounded clients would be scared clean away. For God's sake! some of these clients sat and talked for four hours at a stretch, sobbing and roaring as like as not, while his only way to her bathroom was plumb through the office: how could a man's bladder be expected to hold out? He put it to her, very gingerly; for the first time in their acquaintance she actually laughed; she found him a plastic bucket with a cover. God's sake but it was humiliating.

He certainly was useful to her. His little room had a back door onto a stair that led to a ground-floor passage and a secondary street-door. If she was bothered by anyone at the front door, or within it, she would blow on a loud dog-whistle that Switch insisted she wore at her neck; he would spring down his stair into the passage, and out onto the pavement to take the intruder from behind, a pantomime demon with a mouthful of hair-raising threats. Each time he tried it, it worked; the undesirables fled; happily, Switch did not have to *implement* the threats (which might have involved him in some difficulty with the law).

Every evening, she sent him straight home. He tried once or twice to offer her a drink in a suitable bar, or even dinner, but she always rebuffed him – nicely, to be sure, but a definite rebuff. He was no further forward with her, on a personal level, than he had been when they left for the races. But he knew from his eavesdropping that her *work* was further forward: the dossier upon certain clergymen was getting steadily thicker and thicker: she kept it in the office-safe where he fancied it must tick and fizz like an explosive device in an old-fashioned schoolboy comic, a shapeless parcel of iniquity with BOMB written all over it, for "Father O'B" and "Father MacD" – no names no packdrill, not just yet. He congratulated himself that this was down to him, his advice at their first meeting; otherwise she'd never have grown so potentially impervious to the tabloid darts.

Apart from the press, there were one or two *amateur* stalkers, half-cock corsairs who thought that repeated catcalls and revving up their motors as she walked along Wood Quay might provoke a reaction. Also, some women thought fit to revile her. They longed to have her in tears. Switch excelled himself, hurling himself at all of them, male or female, flapping his arms with the scream of an enraged seagull, or else he would glide up beside them to spit into their ears with astonishing obscenity. The fury of his onslaught would infallibly drive them off.

And then he would swagger, which was pardonable. He was due a bit of gratitude, right? – take it easy, it'd come.

She sometimes got abusive letters. She could not bring herself to read them; she immediately handed them to Switch for his opinion. He would relieve her by telling her that such letters were only in the post because the writers were too cowardly to confront her in person; usually he believed this. But then came a truly creepy one, a big buff padded envelope with a typed address-label; in it there was nothing but a three-inch square of cardboard cut from a cornflakes packet, and written on in purple ballpoint.

Cecilia was misled by its oddity of appearance; she had read it before she grasped its fearful purport. When she did understand, she flung it away from her in a slew of consternation, blowing on her whistle like a demented referee. Switch plunged from his closet, down the stair, out of the house, into the house and up again, to find nobody there but his employer on her top landing: "Switch!" she screamed, "Switch! What the fuck d'you think you're doing? I want you *here*, you stupid arsehole, here, here, here – look at that!" (This was the first time since she hired him that she'd sworn at him; important, he saw that, no time to mess about; he grovelled for the cardboard on the carpet.) "O Jasus, Switch, don't you see it? sure he's after disguising his hand, but he knows I know his turn of phrase, he means every word that he says."

The message was short, a queer mix of religiosity with prurience with a promise of most ugly violence. The writing was minute, print-lettering, sedulously executed, as unusual as it was sinister, for as a rule Cecilia's hate-mail inclined to the garrulous and scrawly. Switch narrowed his eyes, lifted the cardboard to catch light from the office window, and read –

by which Aperture shall the Holy Spirit (seeking vengeance for His Calumniated Saints) make His entry into you? by upper Mouth, or lower Mouth, or in between the cheeks of your impudent Situpon? by one of them or Allthree? be certain He will come and BEFORE YOUR DAY SHALL DAWN. 22 November, do we laugh? shall He penetrate with Godflesh or with grounden Steel or with Brass redhot? NO, you know not, until. NO, you must linger and possess your immortal Soul in Our Lord's good patience, as one of those 'Virgins' whose Lamps held less Oil than their privities. ah linger, you damned False Witness, in your fear.

"Christsake," he cried, taken aback and unaccountably angry with her, "what's all this about 'your day'?"

"I'll tell you in a minute, I have to catch the breath, O Jasus who'd'a thought it? Light me a fag, Switch; quick, they're on the desk there." She collapsed into a corner of the office, all cigarette smoke and shaking limbs. "'Tis her feast day, St Cecilia," she faltered, "Wasn't I planning for that day to hold my press conference, to launch, like, the dossier? – a good omen maybe, the coincidence of the name? – my solicitors have it in charge – give the names and all the details to the Guards and church hierarchy and as much to the media as is legal – he must have found out, somehow, anyhow, who can say? – he means to prevent it, he means to get hold of me before, he means to - O Jasus, to *make his entry?*"

Switch was as rancorous as a bad child locked in a broom-cupboard. "Press conference? Twenty-second? Christsake, barely more nor three weeks. You told me not a word about it. An'what about these solicitors, already they've the doings all ready to publish? Nay, not a word and why the fuck not?"

"'Twas none o' your business," she snarled. "You're here to keep me safe while I get after *my* business, I thought that was understood."

"And you *know* him, d'you say? Christsake, you could ha' let *me* know he's been at you before? If I'd had a bit o'warning, I could have worked a few things out. As it is – not so much as a month. I reckon you're dead right, this guy's no joker. At best he's a dangerous stalker. And at worst -   So who is he?"

"O Switch, I'm sorry, 'tis true I do know him; 'tis not true he was ever *at* me. Not in this way, anyway, no: but he did write to me once to tell me he'd come to see me and then he came, round Easter it'd be, a great stamping priest he was, spewing spit outa his great thick lips, raving urgent that that goat MacD (no I *don't* give you the full name, not yet!), urgent that MacD was innocent, falsely accused, blow the trumpets, thunder the drums, I must hear the truth directly and call off me dogs. I told him no: of course I told him no: I had already a power of evidence and was gathering more: so he threw me a load of guff about virgins and oil and false witness, and he lumped himself down the stairs and away towards Shop Street like a man in a bad dream. Jasus I was sorry for him, but what could I do? He'd been MacD's curate in a parish in Roscommon, he revered him, so he said, he could not bear that I should sit here, like a pig (he said) in shit, and tear a man's life to pieces. Okay, so now we can see what a priest'll come up with when he knows he *cannot bear.* And moreover he's six-foot tall and built like a belfry, you'd never be able to scrap with him and win. O Switch, how'll we deal with it, how? Jasus I'm shit-scared."

"You know his name?"

"O'Toole. Father Marcellus O'Toole. They've made him a parish priest now, a village beyond Castlebar – I have his address in the files somewhere – gimme a hand up, I ought to get it for you, Jasus I can't stand, ought to get it for you, for what good it'll do: he's a maniac, you'll never be able for him. Jasus, I'm shit-scared, he means to kill me once he's *had* me, and there's no use my going to the Guards without I can prove that it's him: you do see it, dontcha?"

"I do, and I see lots more." Why, it was as transparent as clingfilm. "I reckon this O'Toole knew all about MacD's doings, very like from the very start, lasses wi'their knickers down and that, in what they call the sacristy; watched him through the keyhole, like as not. And I reckon he's been at it on his own account, since; though you've not heard complaints, not yet. Which is why he's so desperate for MacD to be let off the hook, or MacD could drop him into it. They likely ended up as a couple, tha knows, trainer and trainee. And even supposing you cancel your press conference, he's still going to come for you, he needs to grab the dossier, he can't afford to leave you loose. Only one thing to do: I've got to get going."

She leapt up in alarm. "You mean that you'll leave me? Oh no, Switch, no, not now! Jasus, man: not now!"

"I don't mean owt o't'sort. I mean, get going and sort the bugger: I told you, I've been a bouncer; you don't have to be big. *Mobile* is the word, that's all it needs. In the meantime, think on: ent it likely all that tabloid crap had *him* at the back of it, O'Toole? We talked about plots but we didn't know the plotters; not then we didn't, any road ... Right, so I'll get going."

He felt impelled to display himself as ferociously determined. For this was a new situation: the first time she had been put into physical peril. It was possible the Highgate fuckup might be about to come in handy: that ill-omened cosh was still somewhere or other among his gear.

Cecilia found the name of the village beyond Castlebar: Kilcorca. "You're not going to go there? I don't want you making more trouble than we're already in, and he's bound to have the Guards on his side."

"Don't worry. Haven't I told you? – I don't go *making* trouble, I *solve* it, you pay me, that's it."

He swaggered, hastened home to the chalet, spent half an hour finding the cosh, swaggered with it to his car and drove north. Recollecting that tonight was Hallowe'en, he stopped at a shopping centre on his way out of town and bought himself some items appropriate to the season. He was not sure why, but they might come in useful for -   He was not altogether so determined as he'd let on; if things didn't pan out he might have to -   In fact he'd no idea *what* he might have to do. Except, somehow, keep Cecilia safe; and, somehow, in so doing, gain her gratitude to such a height that -   It was a bad gulping worry and it gave him diarrhoea. On his third stop to relieve himself, at a mini-market with toilet and petrol pump on a back road a few miles short of Crossmolina, he went to the counter for some chewing gum. He chatted a while with the woman who served him – a motherly gossip, she knew Kilcorca well and delivered a whole rake of quite scandalous information, particularly in regard to the character of Father O'Toole. It seemed that the man was already a byword.

*

Switch entered Kilcorca in gathering rain. It was just before nightfall, and he was pleased with what he saw, remote, dark and silent. For it is not so much a village as a crossroads in the bog, scantily equipped with a church and a house for the priest, a national school, a pub, a post office (soon to be closed down), a Garda station (already closed down), and no more than a half-dozen houses; the rest of the parish extending through desolate countryside, townlands, lonely cottages, for rather more than thirty square miles. He noted, as he motored slowly through, that what he took for the priest's house lay a good hundred yards from the church and was surrounded by a thicket of most dismal rhododendrons.

He drove around the district, killing time, until it was thoroughly dark. He turned off the road down a bit of a bohereen that led into a wood; inconceivable that anyone would have business there before morning. He left the car and walked in the rain for two long miles of misery all the way to the village; there was more traffic than was comfortable, but he'd pulled his black baseball cap down over his face (and why not? the weather was brutal); he reckoned that nobody would know him again. As he neared the first cottage, all lit up for Hallowe'en, he put on the mask he'd been carrying in his pocket: a grotesquely distorted skull, and anyone might be wearing it on their way to anyone's party. It made him feel somewhat secure.

There were lights on in the church; one window of the priest's house was lit up. Switch supposed that the priest was in the church and a housekeeper in the house: he had better not go to the house. He would hide in the rhododendrons, he hoped for no longer than a half-hour or so, and the bushes would give him some shelter. (In fact he had to squat there for a full three hours and got wetter and colder every minute.) People went into the church, and eventually came out again, hurrying under umbrellas to their cars, but no priest. Down the road, behind the pub, a chained-up dog howled interminably. Switch's bowels even yet were giving him no respite: he felt and smelt like a decomposing corpse, he was sure that he'd *be* a corpse before morning. Christsake, where *was* the dirty bugger? and what *could* he be doing, inside there?

It seemed maybe obvious what the dirty bugger might be doing, when a skinny little girlish figure in headscarf and plastic rainproof dodged out of the church and scurried away in the opposite direction ... And then at last, *himself*: the dirty bugger all on his own, open umbrella held up in the right hand, flashlight in the left. A flamboyantly traditionalist cleric, he was wearing soutane and biretta, he trampled the gravel of the path with magisterial energy, a rampaging rhinoceros, hard at work nonetheless to prove to himself he had nothing to be frightened of. Ah, but he had, though: for the beam of his torch caught a slight, sidelong shape that flitted amongst the shrubbery, a quick gleam of a ghastly face, luminescent, white as leprosy, and then it was gone. He stopped short in his tracks, dropping the torch with a soft little moan like a baby about to cry: "Mea culpa, led into it, *led*, against my will, by my eyes by my ears by my wicked companion, peccavi, unwittingly *led*!" – reiteration barely audible, as though already it had been uttered a hundred times over. He was wafting his open umbrella at arm's length in front of him, a pathetic attempt at a shield. Switch waited a few seconds and then suddenly ran at him, knees bent through the pouring dark, to lunge beneath the spokes of the umbrella, to drive his own torch like a piston into O'Toole's groin. Then the cosh into the man's face as he fell down heavily backwards, and again across his big bald head, and here and there all over him without mercy. And then a few small additional adjustments. Thus the job was finished and done, and the doer in rapid flight.

The rain had left off. Switch hardly noticed it: his turbulent thoughts were so darkly entangled with what he had been at, that an ear-piercing uprush of fireworks, a burst and a flare without warning from a bungalow garden, all but caused him to crash his car. He shook at the wheel like a tattered, disgraced battleflag in the rout of an army; he whirled into Castlebar far too fast for law or safety; he was fortunate to meet no traffic-cops. He bethought himself, he repressed himself, he reduced his frantic speed, he headed out toward Galway with some degree of common sense, his passage nonetheless signalled by bonfires (unregulated) and fireworks (illegal) in every townland all the way home: they might have been a mad celebration of his success.

He reckoned it'd be a while before the priest regained his wits. Maybe lie there on his churned-up gravel till the house-keeper came to look for him. Ah, and when she did, she'd have summat to see ... Success.

*

MURDER IN THE CHURCHYARD?
Bizarre Death of Controversial Priest
Gardaí seek Halloween 'Cult Pervert'

A clumsy piece of journalism, it sprawled across the lower half of the front page of *The Irish Independent*; it dropped hints instead of explaining itself; or perhaps the Garda Síochána had failed to explain; nonetheless, it was alarming and Cecilia was furiously alarmed. She'd heard nothing from Switch for forty-eight hours save for one abrupt message on her voice-mail to tell her, "Right, love, it's sorted." She'd resented his Yorkshireman's "love", and resented even more that when she tried to ring him back, he didn't answer. And now, after two sleepless nights, did he dare to come haggard and staggering up her stair like the survivor of a lost patrol?

All he could see through her curlicues of smoke was the teeth and the glare of a gorgon. Nor did she speak; she just thrust the *Independent* right up against his face as it might have been a warrant of arrest. Indecipherable silence for at least half a minute: and then she did speak, she accused him directly, she allowed him no scope for explanation or excuse: "This is you," she grated. "You. The soul of discretion. Didja not even *try* to talk to him, you blundering fucker? Beaten to death, it says, beaten. Oh but last night on the telly it didn't give his name, didn't say he'd been killed; maybe a heart-attack, I thought, I fucking *hoped*, so I did; and better wait till you came in – but this morning I see this, and I'm reading it, fucking *reading* it, and. And. And. What the fuck do they mean, 'pervert'? It says, 'sources claim the body was found surrounded by occult paraphernalia.' And it lists the paraphernalia: nothing at all only scraps of plastic rubbish from the supermarket. What the fuck did you *do* there, did you do?"

Switch was still bewildered and shaken from his own rapid dekko at the paper on the way up to Mary Street. (He hadn't seen the TV news; he'd preferred to watch Charles Bronson slaughtering the ghetto.) What did he *do* there, did she ask him? Christsake, he could scarcely remember; pouring rain, fireworks, and the dirty bugger *dead*? Murder? A bizarre cult? He stared at the newsprint as it tossed and swirled about beneath his eyes. "Hey," he gasped, "what's this?" How had he missed it the first time? "Hey. What sort of a report, for Christsake? All over the shop, it's not right, they've kept the top issue dead quiet, and why?"

"All right then, why?" At least, she was willing to listen.

He was excited, suddenly comprehending: "Because the Guards maybe think it could give 'em a clue, and it won't. It was meant to be *my* clue to bloody O'Toole, that's what – How was *I* to have known the dirty bugger would croak? I'd only knocked him sufficient to -   Aye, right, to knock him over. And everything I left there was for *him* to discover when he woke, that way he'd know where it came from but he'd never tell the cops, *couldn't* tell the cops, not without he'd incriminate himself. O Cecilia, don't you see? No you don't. Okay, right, here's how it was."

He told how he'd stuck a red devil-trident into the priest's biretta and spiked it to the ground; how he'd hung a phosphorescent little skeleton to dangle from the priest's spectacles, which in turn he had hung from the staff of the trident; how he'd spread the skull-mask across the priest's face. And then the *top issue* that the paper refused to print: he told how he'd stuck a square of cardboard under the spiked-down biretta, a message in waterproof purple marker, a message that only the priest would understand, but he'd understand it so damned well it'd close his mouth forever –

THE <u>VENGANCE</u> OF THE RAVAGGED VIRGINS
31 October
<u>To Hell with the Oil, to hell with the False Witness. Question is: DO WE LAUGH?</u>

He was pleading with Cecilia, he crouched at her feet like a mediaeval suppliant to the image of a compassionate saint: "Cecilia, Cecilia, I did *not* leave him dead. Aye, aye, you had it right, lass: heart-attack, why not? Eh nay, but that's not murder."

"I ask you again, did you not even try to talk to him?"

"O'course I tried to talk to him. That's to say, not *talk* to him, not as such. That's to say, I *waylaid* him, just so I could have a word, but -   Ah no, but you weren't there, you weren't there to hear his great feet crush-crush on his churned-up gravel, you weren't there to knock his cap off and then to see his great red bald head and yellow hair all around it like the crotch of what they called a foster-father when you were -   If you had been, you'd ha'known that such a great huge stinking stalking fumble-cleft could *never* be talked to. You needed him gone, so he's gone, what more can you want of me?"

She looked at him as hard as a carved granite gravestone; her words were flat and quiet. "What more can I want? O Switch, O Alcuin, Calhoun or Fouracre, whoever you are: from now on the answer just has to be, nothing. I'll write you a cheque, here, now, I have the chequebook in my handbag, handbag, where *is* it? where? for any wage or expenses I might owe you and a bonus, good bonus, substantial, you deserve it but you can't stay. Oh and I swear to you, not a word out of my mouth to *anyone*. What I know about this or do *not* know. And I swear it. You have to trust me." She wrote the cheque and gave it to him. When he attempted to speak, she laid her fingers on his mouth. (This was in fact the first time she'd ever touched him; it did not strike him as important; not at that moment, not just then.) "Go," she murmured. "Now," she cried. "O Switch, I implore you, please go."

To tell truth, he was not surprised. He'd come to her expecting the sack, and now he had it. Her gratitude? Aye, aye, to tell truth, his time as a minder had not been altogether lost, no-one could say the sum on the cheque was stingy: but nay, it was nowt to what he'd hoped to accumulate. Nay, there would be no *Stage Four*. Christsake, how *could* there be, when that dirty bugger O'Toole had thought fit to fall down dead?

Quietly, meditatively, Switch directed his feet to the other side of town, to lurk in his chalet and consider his options. He took up his mobile phone and began to ring round some friends and acquaintances (such as they were); he put the word out for another job.

Cecilia continued her own job, self-inflicted, unwaged, day after day, without him. He had minded her for long enough, she told herself; he had effectively served his purpose; largely thanks to him, the scandal had blown over (if indeed one could call it a scandal); she was no longer harassed; her public revelations on her own cherished saint's day, of the reverend ratbags MacD and O'B, were taken seriously by bishops and by Garda

Síochána, and accepted throughout the media as authentic; she was invited onto another TV chat-show where they let her say her piece without interruption or excess of snide questions.

Once again she had achieved respect.

She would not allow herself to think about Kilcorca. She tried not to allow herself to think about Switch. She had touched him on the mouth and it seemed as though her fingers remembered the feel of him, every day, all day, and quite against her will. This was a man who had maybe done murder for her sake, *hers*, no other motive, and all she could think of by way of reward was to get rid of him, chop-chop? Extraordinary that she harboured no guilt for this maybe-murder, only apprehension lest (however improbably) the truth might come out, and immerse her in what had to be an even greater scandal than the last one. Nonetheless it *was* improbable; at this stage it did not disturb her dreams. Oh but what did disturb them was the memory of her fingers for the warmth of his mouth. ("Jasus, that's enough, girl. Before your thirteenth birthday you'd had all you could cope with. Never no more, no more.")

Switch found another job. And then another, and another. He did security for a supermarket, he checked tickets in a car-park, he bounced for a nightclub with bits of bribery from the small-fry drug-dealers, he did wearisome small con-jobs for very little reward (his mind wasn't on the business, there were nerve-racking mishaps), he clamped cars in the street with bits of bribery from their drivers. Now that summer had come to an end, his ploys among the tourists were coming to an end as well. Altogether, he was sliding downhill. The faster he slid, the more his dreams were filled with the pride of the ancient Fouracres and the badness of their modern-day heirs.

He'd shown he could kill a huge-horned rhinoceros of an Irish priest, so what could he not do to a downright yelping dog in Highgate who called himself Professor? To be sure, not to *kill* him, but to strip him ballock-naked of all his wrongful gain. Even though he himself was (presumably) still wanted by the cops in London, even though the cops in Ireland would (most certainly) want him if only they knew who he was. If he did go to London to secure his inalienable rights, Christsake he'd need *cash*, first to hide himself, then to establish himself, these tricks didn't come cheap.

Over Christmas and into the New Year, he meditated morosely throughout the long dark nights and tried to relieve his mind with the seduction of women. He was good at it and they enjoyed it, once or twice they gave him money, and on the whole they didn't mind when he dumped them – he was good at that, too, deluding them into believing that they had dumped *him*, a technique that made everyone happy. Or would have done, had he not, little by little, become thoroughly obsessed with recollections of Cecilia, the stench of her Gauloises, her fingers against his lips, the gratitude she should have owed him, the funds that should have come with the gratitude, yet again the prodigious lawsuit that the funds should be paying for. He realized one night what a plague-sore was suppurating in the deep of his mind, when he suddenly terrified a Mrs O'Connor by calling her "Coppinger, you ironclad dike!" – even as he realized he was not going to achieve orgasm. No, it was worse than that: he clutched her by the throat and roared out that no more priest and no reward was one fucking *no* too many, that the sons of old King Aella were not to be farted at, and what would she do about it, hey? What she did do, was to run sobbing, with her clothes tossed on to her anyhow, bra and panties left behind, from his chalet to her car and so home: happily, Mr O'Connor was at a conference in Dublin, which prevented immediate disaster.

That amorous fiasco was the weekend before Easter. For the next five days Switch stayed banged-up in the chalet, abandoning his regular work with the car-clamp company, drinking hard liquor (perhaps), drugging himself (maybe) – as no-one came to see him, no-one knew exactly what he was up to – it is possible that all he did was stew under a heap of bedclothes, asleep eighteen hours out of the twenty-four, awakening now and then to peer blear-eyed at his black-and-white portable television, his feet on the floor only when he needed a small snack, pot-noodles or the like, and very probably a cup of tea. On Good Friday he forced himself to get dressed – which is to say, he put on a pair of trousers over his boxers, and a sweater over his T-shirt – and sat to table with a notepad and ballpoint. (He had pawned his laptop and sold his car to pay the rent and keep the TV; his life all of a sudden was most desperately hand-to-mouth.)

He was not a facile writer, he had trouble with grammar and spelling, but he knew what he wanted to record: he would set down every detail that his father had passed on to him of the Fouracre family claim, every anecdote, every name, every place, that had ever come up. He did his best to ignore the obvious weak link: as the grandfather had died before he knew his son, all the information had to derive from Switch's grandmother, that giddy short-order cook to the Strensall garrison who'd seemingly chattered like a well-paid supergrass and may not have been any more trustworthy ...

He concluded his account with a species of lamentation for the tragic inevitability of cause and effect –

If it wan't for them Fouracres: I'd never have koshed old Lambert
If it wan't for old Lambert: I'd never have come to lousy Ireland
If it wan't for lousy Ireland: I'd never have met Coppinger
And she'd never have got safe away from TV, press,
the starlking storking starkling priest
If it wan't for the starkling priest: I'd never have been shafted by Coppinger
She owes me for that
So why shouldn't she help me
prove myself a right Fouracre
as reconnized recongized in law:
& SO ShE'D Get The chance to get clear of all her detbs debts?
Will she see the chance & take it?
　　　　　Will she fuck

455

It'd be no more than proper if *he* should become her stalker, and damwell serve her right, at least until she -   Don't be daft: he had to laugh. Then he stopped laughing. Not so daft. She'd no right to shaft him without she'd even let his hand onto her tits, to say nowt of lower down between her -   Who *was* she, this Coppinger, to be so cutglass and lemonjuice superior? while a randy little guilt-ridden squealing and squawking estate-agent's wife the likes of Méabh O'Connor would -   How come he'd had *yes* from the one, at first asking; and *no* every time, all the time, unyielding, from the other? Christsake, it wasn't right ... Who better to stalk than a man who'd been paid to keep stalkers away? So why wouldn't he prove to her what like of a mouthful of teeth a first-class Yorkshire tyke could show? Have a go at her ankles the way old Lamberts' tyke had gone at his dad that time, snarling and *tearing*. Why wouldn't he draw blood? and if she thought he was rabid, so much the better.

He'd start today, Day of the Passion, Day of the Whip, Day of the Nails, Day of the Thorns in the Head – he understood where he was at, oh yes: he'd been fed with odd morsels in the way of religion from the first of his foster-mothers, how else had he fuelled his rage at Kilcorca? He understood well enough that God meant Pain and that today was the Pain of God. It was fitting, it was right, he went out to a phone booth. (He'd been told that calls from a mobile could always be traced: *she'd* guess who he was, of course, but he didn't need the cops to know it for a fact.)

Throughout the next fifty-four hours, he rang her up from one payphone or another all over the town, sometimes with long gaps between his calls, sometimes in a rapid succession – always the heavy breathing and no speech (except maybe a deep-throated chuckle or a miserable whine, or both). To begin with, Cecilia was asking, "Who's that?" Then it was, "Get off the line." And then, "Off the fucking line, OFF! or I'll have you to the Guards." Early on Easter Sunday, an hour before sunrise, the very hour that Mary Magdalene had words with a gardener only to discover he wasn't, Cecilia took hold of herself and told him, "I know you. Don't think I do not. You are Alcuin, you bastard, and it isn't going to work."

He said, "Oh yes it is. You know my right name, so you know what it's all about." He rang off.

After that, he left the phone alone. He'd gained a point, a great point. (He'd never have believed he could taunt her so quickly into calling him *Alcuin:* oh yes, she'd caught his purpose: now to consolidate, to diversify. Right.) He took to haunting Mary Street whenever he thought she might come out of the front door. If she didn't come out, she could look from behind her curtains and see an elbow or a shoulder of him, hovering like a mote in her eye just around the nearby corner. Being familiar with her daily routine, where she shopped, when she shopped, he could slip across the aisles of a supermarket, now full-face and staring, now on the move (crabwise) and not quite in sight, and then gone! just when she thought she could grasp him.

Certainly she was frightened, almost as frightened as at O'Toole's letter. Add to which, the news-media could not leave well alone; they kept recapitulating Kilcorca and wondering why the Garda investigation made no progress, which caused her to wonder, was Switch threatening her with total exposure, unless she -   Surely he was not simply scheming to *fuck* her? because, if so, she -   No, it must be for money, extortion for the family name, she ought never to have encouraged his -   And it went on for months. There were days when she never saw him, she would hope and pray that he was gone; but before the week's end, there he was, again and again, week after week, staring suddenly at her full-face and shockingly close, and flickering away from her like an instant of delirium. And then, for two whole months, nothing.

Had she known where he lived, she would have hurtled to confront him and to beset him in his own front passage – or would she? Why didn't she try to find out where he lived? Why was she so nervous of such an encounter? Was it fear, or a pricking of shame that somehow she had *failed* him?

No doubt she should have gone to the Guards. They are notoriously lazy (save when trundled to their duty by wealthy businessmen or cabinet ministers) but they have been known to prosecute stalkers if the victim can make enough fuss. So why did she not make the fuss? Because, if she did, how could she keep Kilcorca out of it? And she'd promised, had she not? given her word to the man Alcuin? – no no he was *Switch* and should *stay* Switch, that's all that he was to her. She had never, upon principle, broken her word once given; no, not even to a blow-in of an ugly creepy-crawly which is all that he was to her, an insignificant centipede, emotional and immature; she should never have admitted him beneath her roof; and now he was writhing himself all the way into her ear, all the way behind her eyeballs, the Blessed Virgin only knew where else ...

Whatever had possessed her to give even half a minute to his dream of a lost family? And yet she had listened. She had thought, as he rattled on, that it was the one thing that made him different, indeed it had determined her to confirm his employment. It seemed somehow so unEnglish, as in her ignorance she had always conceived the English, so up in the air like a swallow, so down in the waves like a porpoise, so out-of-this-world *poetic*, that she could not resist it. She'd loved all this fatuity of Fouracres, at the same time she'd despised it, oh she'd despised *herself*, it was shaming to remember how she'd smiled. ("CC's Shame" indeed, and much more than a pricking: a dirty downright swipe with a slash-hook.)

Nor could she pay for it: why, the thought was preposterous.

She'd rather give money to every bookie in Ireland than see it all vanish into the black hole of fees and court-costs for a crazy lawsuit that could never be won. She supposed she might have said so, but she'd feared to humiliate him. Moreover, did he not realize how very little money she had? – apart, that's to say, from the funds of her national appeal? the funds she had devoted to the women who called for her help? – she was constantly in the red – the rental of her two floors of a rotten old house was devouring her – woodworm in her rafters devouring her, O Jasus – why else did he think that she gambled so wildly?

Impossible to go to the Guards: all she could do was to leave him alone. In any case, for the past two months, it did seem that *he* was leaving *her* alone.

*

No he wasn't. It was the week once again of the Galway Races. "For my next trick, ladies and gentlemen, yobbos and tarts," Switch declaimed to his cracked little shaving mirror, "for my next trick, I swagger down Shop Street and I spend my last few fucking euros upon a morning in the cyber café. Christsake, I'm as daft as a brush." He completed the trimming of his pencil-line moustache. (He had recently grown it to remind himself of a snapshot he'd once seen of his grandfather: all his energy was coming back to him: daft as a brush, aye aye.) He sauntered out to swagger down Shop Street.

At the cyber café he registered himself an e-mail address – feralcleric@hotmail.com – he'd made it up, there and then, a fine flourish of satirical invention; he filled in the form with all the fictional detail required; he set about composing a circular letter. It was not altogether too difficult: the software contained a spellcheck which he could to use to good effect: the words seemed to flow like molten gold.

Madam CC, celebrity sex-victim and whistleblower, you all know her, is down on her luck. She needs urgently to fill her stocking with brass, boodle, lolly, & loot, or else she's dead and dried. So what can she sell? Her furniture's rubbish. Her car's fit for the scrapyard. Nought left for the market but herself. Let her friends gather round. For gents she'll charge €100, for kids under 17 and birds (lesbian) the cost is no more than €50, dead generous. Exactly how she'll earn it depends on on-site negotiation. No clergy need apply.

He added Cecilia's telephone number and signed himself "Jos. Lambert, Professor." He had a long list of e-mail addresses, her clients and general contacts, which she'd given him on one of their good days, on the off-chance she might need him to use it. The letter went to all of these, all-at-a-go and at no extra cost, what a remarkable thing was the internet! – if he'd had to send a mail-out by means of the post office he'd have been at it all day for Christsake, the price of stamps and stationery would have sunk him.

Most of those who received the disgraceful message were decent people who saw it for what it was and ignored it. Others, however, were Cecilia's enemies, or rivals, or friends who believed themselves exceptionally sincere. And some of them passed it on – as Switch had been sure that they would. Within a week the thing was public knowledge, via the tabloids again, via certain radio phone-in programmes, via the sort of triumphant gossip defined in Ireland as *the dogs in the street.* "No smoke without fire," was the regular comment, sarcastic or naïve, until no-one could tell who gave it any credit and who did not.

There is no need to go into the effect that it had on her. Had she known his address she would have gone round there directly and killed him. She did worse: she broke her word. She grassed him up. She bared her teeth, clenched her fists, wiped the hot brine out of her red staring eyes. She surged into the Garda Síochána, mad for revenge, a Mórrigu or a Brunhild from some bloodstained bardic saga. "Don't you snigger at me," she hissed into the face of the superintendent. "I'm very well aware you've read the e-mail, don't deny it, don't fucking deny it. You find the man who wrote it, you'll find the man who killed O'Toole ... Kilcorca? Halloween? don't tell me you've forgotten, you idle piece of shite – and if you think you need me to be arrested alongside o'him as accessory after the fact, before the fact, aider-and-abettor, co-conspirator, whatever, then I'm happy to oblige. O my dear Lord Jesus, only for that, I'll never be happy in all this filthy world, not ever again ... Would you believe me, I touched his lips?"

They took her at her word and held her for questioning. Then they went after Switch Calhoun. He was not hard to find: an employee of the car-clamping company showed them where he lived. They found him in bed at midday with two girls, first-year university students, all three of them drunk and drugged. He laughed all the way to the cells; in his cell he started dancing and kept it up till they fetched him to the interview room. He said, "Aye aye I sorted O'Toole, dirty great bugger, why'd you think I wouldn't have?" He subsided onto the floortiles and rolled himself into a heap, a urine-soaked bundle of contorted insignificance. In the light of Cecilia's statement, they took it all as a confession: it would save them a lot of work: they charged him with manslaughter.

Cecilia was charged as accessory, she pled guilty, she used no lawyers and all she had to say for her defence was that the court knew who she was, what had been done to her, what she had done. Under pressure from friends, she did offer in mitigation O'Toole's letter of threat and a printout of Switch's e-mail, thereby to indicate how her minder was a chip off the same block as her stalker, and how grievously she had been served by both of them. The judge studied them with sorrow; he had no choice (he said) only to issue a gaol-sentence, but he was happy (he said) to suspend it: she was free to go. She went without a word, leaving her friends nonplussed; she went home and sat and thought. She thought about an overdose of one of her many prescribed medicines. But then she also thought how she'd lie dead in her bedroom and someone would have to find her: O sweet Jesus, *who?* In an agony of repulsion, she sat to her laptop and began a day's work, her first attempt at it for months.

The media treatment of her trial was sympathetic. Consensus had changed since the previous scandal: she was no longer to be seen as a strident charlatan, making trouble for the sake of self-publicity; rather had she become a devoted idealist temporarily thwarted by incorrigible credulity, her unfortunate *tragic flaw.* She had freely admitted error and openly repented, now she should atone for it by continuing her labours (perhaps at a lower profile, with improved accountability), and so deserve support and financial contribution. Indeed, there was a vague suggestion that women such as her were an asset to Ireland, a National Treasure, one might say – strong but also humble, and as reassuringly foolish as anyone else when caught up for good or ill with persons of the opposite sex.

Switch Calhoun in the meantime was failing altogether to answer his helm: he had refused to fight the case, or properly to instruct his solicitor. When ordered to plead, he muttered something like, "Aye aye, sorted him, reckon I must have, couldn't tell for certain but was there a dog there?" He called himself Fouracre and addressed the court at random, going on about Father O'Toole's yellow hair and great bald head and somebody else's *pubic* hair; he said nothing in regard to Cecilia except that she was in terror, she had touched his lips "here, here, with two fingers," he was bound to protect her. Upon Hallowe'en, he cried, "all sorts of daft old ghosts was walking and talking, and that: ancestors and who the hell else?" "That's how it was," he snuffled. He mumbled against the back of his hand that after all he'd had no choice, "eh fuckit there was a dog and it howled and it howled." ... A psychiatric report said he was as sane as anyone else, but obsessed by ancient families and how children out of wedlock could keep them alive – this was not so much a mental disorder as a feature of his English upbringing, whereas the Irish of his class in these days of the Celtic Tiger were untroubled by such illusions. The judge told him he was a most violent man whose thuggery could not be excused by picturesque extravaganza. He must go to prison for ten years. In fact he was in Mountjoy Gaol for less than ten days. After that, they whisked him off to the Central Mental Hospital.

(He'd been insisting upon respect from the "ratty Paddy Irish," prison staff as well as inmates, he being Alcuin Fouracre and descended from -   For hours on end he would relate his lineage. He related it day-in day-out. When he took to biting people and barking like a crossbred collie, the authorities began to fear that his infuriated fellow-convicts would stab him in the shower.)

Since then, up to the time of writing, he has alternated between hospital and gaol: each time they put him back in Mountjoy, he is quiet and good-humoured for sometimes as long as a
couple of months, and then he breaks out again and the hospital
must take over. As he told a psychiatrist, "Nay, it's just like I've
got one foot in Ireland and t'other i'Yorkshire: ah, but which
one's where? Which the chokey, which the loonybin? Answer
me that."

Yorkshire Quarters

As recorded by Charles Aella Fouracre, Esq., Master of Arts (Cantab), founder and principal of Newton House School, a lyceum of liberal studies for the sons of his fellow-townspeople, Kirk Deerwood, Yorkshire, anno domini 1802.

To be read after his death by his beloved wife Selina and his beloved son Alcuin – and beyond them the world in general – supposing they can bring themselves, eventually, to publish.

Inasmuch as our once hopeful nation has walked so far astray that I fear it shall never recover the path, I have set myself the ordeal of compiling with unsteady hand this – this, what shall I call it? – this unhappy memorial. *My bodily health is failing, I cannot live much longer. Last Wednesday, I think it was, I passed the weary hours of my sickbed with Mr Dryden's translation of Plutarch's Lives. It struck me that the Grecian biographer, a cool enough narrator of many a strange and macabre proceeding, seemed distressed, nay repelled, by an incident in the life of L. Licinius Crassus (or rather, in his* after-*life): –*

When the head of Crassus was brought to the door of the Parthian king, the tables of the royal feast were just taken away, and one Jason, a tragic actor, was singing the scene in The Bacchae of Euripides concerning Agave and the head of Pentheus. The messenger from the battlefield, having made obeisance to the king, threw down the head of Crassus into the midst of the company. The Parthians receiving it with joy and acclamations, Jason took up the head and continued to sing the lyric passages –

We've hunted down a mighty chase today
And from the mountain bring the noble prey ....

464

The episode was undoubtedly macabre: but I did not find it strange. I have my own knowledge. I know more than anyone of the troubling events of some four years ago (rarely spoken of in the town, whether for shame, fear or guilt I cannot affirm). I know more than anyone of my feebleness of spirit that helped provoke those same events. All of which, to assuage my conscience, I am now concerned to record. Not quite an heroic philosophical example, not quite the serenity of the great Sir Isaac, whose name I bestowed so recklessly upon our Newton House for the edification of parents and boys: I fear I did not edify myself. But may I hope that after my death there may be found in these words some cause for contemplation, together with a clarified view of justice and injustice and how both qualities can owe their nurture to political exigency, likewise how political exigency can tear true love asunder and freeze the warmest house.

My dear son, my dear wife (silent wife and chill, indeed you have diligently cared for me since the violence of my recent heart-stoppages; but from duty, from natural kindness, rather than affection, is it not so?) – how long before we clearly see just who we are? how long, how long, before we are wise enough and brave enough to ask is there a cure for what we see? never mind whether we'd know how to apply it?

*

It is usually stated that the last time the British public was privileged to witness the horrid elaboration of hanging, drawing and quartering, as penalty for high treason, was in the middle of the last century. The condemned man was a Jacobite rebel and therefore obnoxious; the crowd was fiercely loyal to the protestant monarchy and therefore revengeful; even so, the process aroused more loathing than enthusiasm and is supposed never to have been repeated. In fact (as we in Yorkshire must infallibly recollect) it has been, once. But the proceedings took place far from the capital, and were so generally mismanaged that accounts of them seem never to have been honestly rendered, neither to government nor populace. It is as though those men responsible strove hard to ensure that their bestial imbecilities were well hidden and stayed hidden. Nor did it happen a half-century ago. Yet the hugger-mugger is complete.

Let me outline in brief the distractions of the realm in 1798. The late war against revolutionary France had dragged on since '93 without hope of success. Insurrection in Ireland had shown how easy it would be to invade and conquer Britain from both sides, east and west at a single blow, for did not French troops actually set foot upon the coast of Connacht, fighting their way into the very midst of the island? while Ulster and Wexford blazed with rebellion, and Dublin all but fell to egalitarian conspiracy.

Thus a Briton, in that year, who was proved to have had dealings with the rebels, the so-called 'United Irishmen', could entertain no hope of leniency. None. His name was Tom Tutton, a medical man in a modest way in our town of Kirk Deerwood.

His establishment was respectable: a surgery-dispensary in Minster Northgate, next door to the shop of a bootmaker-and-saddler, with a single gentleman's lodging on the first floor, above both shop and surgery. (His landlord, the bootmaker, a young man called Simon Swayne, dwelt at the back of the house with his wife, Mrs Janet Swayne. She was mortally ill, and they had no children.) Tom's patients were respectable: the better class of tradesman, the odd clergyman, old ladies and so forth. Among them, myself and family and the pupils of Newton House. Without doubt he was an ingenious physician; we trusted him entirely upon any occasion of sickness or accident. Why else would I have put my son Alcuin into his hands to be instructed in the mysteries of medicine? No fault of mine that a coolness grew between them. But I'll come to that later.

At the time of which I write, Dr Tutton would have passed his fortieth year. A saturnine dark fellow, lantern-jawed with flaring nostrils, he cropped his hair like a Parisian sans-culotte. His disposition was so rebarbative that the friendliest civilities between him and the world were difficult and were often balked. Not that he was quarrelsome: contemptuous rather, bitterly ironical, *reserved* would be the most courteous word. He seemed to discount all those who did not attain to his intellectual level, and in Kirk Deerwood that meant nearly everyone – with the curious exception of Simon Swayne, a very rude specimen of Yorkshire intractability, whose crippled gait Dr Tutton had striven to cure, at the same time attempting to ameliorate the chronic affliction of Mrs Swayne, in either case in vain. This double failure (combined with his earnest persistence) perhaps bred a mutual affection; at all events, the two men were a strangely devoted pair, drinking together, so it was said, until all hours of the night in the parlour of the doctor's apartment. It is possible they drank now and again with certain others, of a rough and contentious complexion, it is possible they discussed sedition. Songs were sometimes heard, most contrary to the ecclesiastical character of the neighbourhood – *Ça Ira* and the *Marseillaise* were said to have been recognized. None of us knew much about these matters until the day the blow fell, and when it fell Simon Swayne was out of the way in Lincolnshire – some dispute with his sister's husband over her marriage settlement, I know not what, but I think it saved his life.

Now it is a fact that eight or nine years previously, in those early days of revolution in France, I too haunted Tom Tutton's parlour; with many of like mind from all about our part of the county – schoolmasters such as myself, ministers of religion, simple artisans (I mention Swayne the bootmaker, having already mentioned him; other names are not relevant; to recollect them at the present time would embarrass beyond all reason, and may well put persons in jeopardy, even though a pretence of peace has lately been signed with the French). My boy Alcuin was usually present – as the doctor's amanuensis – he was almost sixteen and keen to hear new things. My dear Selina was also with us; she greatly admired Tom Tutton. There were times when her admiration was somewhat greater than I could wish. Certainly, she rivalled him in the leadership of debate ... Let me say at once that sedition is what we talked. Or at all events, what Mr Pitt and his cabinet would have called sedition.

We were happy to put up with Tom's caustic manners, because he (more than all of us) vehemently overrode the dismals of our bourgeois existence on the verge of the Holderness fen; nay, he exalted, with all the fire in his nature, the huge vigour of this joyful French somersault, *the world turned upside down*, indeed he led us all to sing the song that goes by that name, even those of us who had no music but roared like hungry seals. We cried out the great question, why could not the Palace of Westminster, and the lackey parliaments that infest it, receive the same treatment as the Paris Bastille? We looked to Mr Fox, maybe, and some of us to Mr Sheridan and even to Mr Paine, to lead the nation forward – and alas, that was it. Forward? We could see no further ... When the revolutionists went on to slay their king and queen, when they chopped down with falchions and cleavers the helpless men, women and children in their gaols, when they chopped down *each other* with the engine of Dr Guillotine, ah well, we were distressed. And how dreadfully was our distress augmented by the war that ensued! 1793, most desperate year: I said to Tom Tutton, and I was not alone to say it, "This revolution devours its own entrails. I do not know whether I can continue to make one of a club that would replicate it here."

He sneered, as of course he would. "So instead, our compassionate pedagogue will be one of a much larger club that will destroy it by force of arms? Shall you volunteer your pupils en bloc as the nucleus of a regiment? Send 'em oversea for the glorious Duke of York to march 'em up and down the declivities of the Netherlands?"

The next Sunday he accosted me on the steps of the Minster as I came from Morning Prayer with Selina – I think he never attended service – he was grim, but strangely hesitant (most unusual for him): in the end he blurted it out. "I mean to say, Fouracre, that that hobbledehoy lad of yours had best learn his trade elsewhere. His friends are not suitable." What was I to say to him? I did not know what he meant. The boys of our school, under their usher, were filing out of the porch behind

me; to bandy such words in their hearing was not to be thought
of, and yet -   It seems that Selina did know what he meant.
"I will tell you after dinner," she whispered into my ear. "In
the meantime, Dr Tutton, be so good as to say no more ... I
thank you." Tom did something abrupt with his hat, shrugged
and stepped briskly away. The boys were murmuring: I told
the usher to impose discipline: we all walked back to Newton
House in silence. It was our custom of a Sunday for ourselves
and Alcuin to dine in company with the senior boys. I was displeased to find Alcuin absent, neither had he been in church. I
confess that this disturbed me, so much so that I was unable to
cope with the improving conversation I always tried to initiate
at table. Selina made up for it with a light flow of talk upon the
dietary habits of the Hindoo brahman compared to the Mussul-
man dervish, or some such, and thereby diverted the boys – she
is skilled at these tricks. I am not.

After dinner, in our private parlour, she left all pretence at
lightness and came straight out with it. "It grieves me to tell
you, Charles, that Alcuin for some time has consorted with that
young Major Wetwang; this very week's-end they have driven
together to the country, out Pocklington way, to the Major's
deplorable father, for the hunting, the shooting, the roistering, I
know not what. It is not a proper house for our son to frequent,
and I told him so when I heard of it, only yesterday I heard of it:
he laughed at me, he kissed me, he told me not to trouble. But
I do trouble."

"Of course you do, good heavens. Major Jocelyn Wetwang
is a callow, galloping obscurant who defends negro slavery.
He demands the prohibition of a free press and the suspension
of habeas corpus. He is also a drunkard and a whoremaster.
He learns it all from his father, the bedridden baronet, ill-conditioned old cockatrice, who murdered a poacher in the days
when he could walk and moreover got away with it. Father and
son together, the pair of them are infamous." So I reviled Sir
Reginald Wetwang, only because his son took pattern by him,
whereas when *my* son ignored my example I blamed *him* and
not myself, inconsistent, contradictory. So I turned upon poor

Selina: such are the petty treacheries of even the most loving marriage. "And you knew it," I snapped at her. "And Tutton knew it, good heavens. When was *I* to have been told?"

"Oh Charles, our son is already eighteen, he is old enough to be a king's officer himself, if the king thought fit to have him, alas. Certainly old enough to make his own friends and discover their qualities, good or bad, for himself – how can you or I expect to *instruct* him? I was afraid that that was what you would attempt, so I chose to let things lie, to *keep all these sayings in my heart* (as it were) until I saw whether Alcuin would accept my advice. No: he has kissed me and laughed and gone off with the Major. And now he gets his congé from Tutton."

"For which I cannot condemn Tutton. But where shall the boy go next?"

Where he went next all but killed me. He used Jocelyn Wetwang's influence, and that of the baronet, to apply for a surgeon's post in Wetwang's regiment. At all events, assistant surgeon. "Loblolly boy" was the pejorative that came to mind. And no sooner had the notion struck root than Wetwang was recalled to the colours, indeed to that very Duke of York in the Low Countries. Our idiot Alcuin went too. "Aye well," he had blustered to me and to his mother, as the tailor scurried around him, sticking pins into his new uniform. "Clap and the fever in camp, sabre-slash and bullet-hole in the field, hey? Could old Tutton provide a fellow with anything so rich in the way of useful practice? even supposing his revolution came off? But, sir, to be serious: you've made it clear you hate what the Frogs are up to. So why reproach me that I take you at your word and offer my skills to our soldiers in the fight for liberty?"

I could have argued with him for hours that it was naught but a *horror* of liberty that caused government to join the kings of Europe in their war, nor was it the atrocities of the French; the French were only atrocious because the kings were going to war against 'em; they saw traitors everywhere (and with very good reason). But Wetwang was his friend and had armoured him against all such opinion. With heavy heart, we watched him go.

Well, as was widely foretold, the Duke made mud pies of that ridiculous campaign, but Alcuin stayed with the regiment; I stayed with the school; Tom Tutton (I fear) stayed with his irreconcilable ferocities of revolt. I might have done more to restrain him, I might have withheld him from his terrible end, but I did not. I did have a school to keep; but it shakes the very brain in my head to contemplate my negligence – some would say, my politic duplicity. For throughout the next five years, I scarce exchanged words with him save for medical need – and then we were correct together but with naught you could call warmth. As for Selina: I am not sure. I fancied she and he had something between them even yet; I thought it better not to pry. In those days she was so hot for all forms of liberty that to confide in her husband appeared to her a collusion with despotism. Ah, she was still young. Past thirty-five, 'tis true, but as fresh as the first primrose. She still is, despite all. And the pain I felt then, I still feel. When one whom you love, and whom you believe you know, is determined not to be known – of course there is abiding pain. You are fortunate if you do not (in unwitting retaliation) inflict it upon her.

"The day the blow fell." It was in fact a night. Toward the end of the month of May, 1798. A private room above a low public house in York. An extra-ordinary meeting of the East Yorkshire Corresponding Society, Dr Tutton in the chair, a Mr Brady from Dublin guest of honour. Mr Brady explained how the whole of Ireland was rising up in coordinated rebellion in order to achieve a republic. Dr Tutton called for a Republic of Great Britain, and demanded that members of the Society should immediately furnish their Irish preceptors with arms (if that were possible), with moneys to procure arms, and with every other shape of support within their power. There was, as it turned out, a government spy in the room – which might have been predicted, had there also been any common sense, but no: the excitement was too extreme. Long past midnight, the company having dispersed, Tom and the Irishman Brady were on their way up to bed in their inn. They were intercepted on the first-floor landing by a constable's posse, no less than six, it was later testified, armed with truncheons, pistols and broadswords. Brady pulled out a pistol of his own; Tom Tutton had a dagger (did he think he was a wandering bandit, good heavens?). They fought in the bedroom passages like demons. Brady was shot dead; Tom was wounded in the thigh and the forearm, was dragged away to gaol, and put upon his trial for high treason. Yorkshire gentlemen in flocks and herds, braying and quacking, crowded the courtroom; I made one of them, as sick as a dog at the vile charivari I was invited to observe.

It was worse than a charivari, it was a pretty little family party.

The government spy was one Hurn, sometime bailiff to Sir Reginald Wetwang and discharged for dishonesty. The prosecutor was Wetwang Croucher K.C., a cousin at some remove; while a Mr Justice Baker Fortescue, brother-in-law of the same Sir Reginald, sprawled upon the bench in draconian arrogance. Hurn, cross-examined, all but admitted that his dirty work for the attorney-general's office was found for him to keep him quiet as to disreputable passages in the past conduct of Major Jocelyn Wetwang, who had stood in some peril of forfeiting his commission. The judge at once put a stop to so tendentious a line of questioning, but –Good heavens, the friend of my son.

The major was not in court, my son was not in court and good heavens, I would have been so glad of it, had they been stationed with their regiment in any land but Ireland – aye, that's where Alcuin was – and what did he do in Ireland? Good heavens, we had had naught but rumour to depend on and the rumour was terrible. Barbarity of reprisal, devastation of the countryside, the gibbet and the flogging-triangle upon every village green – or so it was whispered, while Selina wrote letter after letter to Alcuin and Alcuin never replied – or scarcely ever and then not at all to the purpose – "My dearest Mama, I am in robust health, I am at length gazetted fully-fledged regimental surgeon, the weather is wet, the tour of duty excessively dull, next week we return to Dublin, my best wishes to Papa, etc." – such abbreviated blandness was surely contrived to deceive and we *knew* it was contrived to deceive. Was he defiant or did he despair? That we did *not* know – or, at any rate, not then.

There could be no doubt about the jury's verdict: a man who calls for a republic calls for the deposition or death of his king, and Tom Tutton in the dock stood and gloried in the crime. He asserted in short that it was *no* crime, it was the act of a patriot, and the jurymen could take it or leave it, he would not interfere with their consciences.

The court wasted little time with the others upon trial, a half-dozen of those who had listened to Tutton and Brady and were unlucky enough to be known to the man Hurn. The judge abruptly ordered 'em transported to New South Wales for their "attentive and sedulous sedition." But when he came to Tom Tutton (I am ashamed, as an Englishman, to write it), he took a lingering and ogreish delight in the agonizing sentence he pronounced, and then in its abominable sequel – genital parts to be sliced off, bowels to be dragged out, and all to be burnt under the eyes and nostrils of the half-hanged man (he being yet alive); carcase carved into quarters and parboiled, head to be cut off and parboiled; quarters to be thereafter distributed amongst the chief towns of the county, York, Wakefield, Ripon, Hull – and the head to Kirk Deerwood, for in that accursed place was the evil begotten and reared ... "This most ancient and respectable statutory provision for the division of the body of the traitor shall signify before man and under God that your horrid offence was to seek in like fashion to divide, tear asunder, dissect and dismember not only the living frame of the constitution of the realm but also the bowels, heart and patriarchal power of your Sovereign Lord the King. No detail of my sentence to be mitigated by foolish clemency or venality of the hangman; he shall carry it out to the letter. Mr Sheriff, you are charged so to oversee the execution as to make sure that he does. Thomas Tutton, you go trembling hence to meet your outraged Maker: may He lavish upon you the mercy that your fellow subjects in this kingdom must needs disdain to grant."

I was incapable of the magnanimity to visit a condemned man who had so roughly betrayed the sweetness of our previous ideals. I am aware that Selina, in the outburst of her grief, did compare me to Simon Peter, denial after denial under the echo of the crowing cock, but in the courthouse I had received a sufficiency of hell. I'd exhausted all my pleas through every lawyer of my acquaintance for means to a reprieve or reduction of penalty. I returned to Kirk Deerwood in a steaming crowded stage-coach like a derelict Faustus with a devil at each elbow, a gleeful farmer and a fat corn-factor talking endlessly across me, no less ogreish than the judge (and how quickly his vindictive message had sped through the populace!), they averred that this public extremity of pain would once-for-all get rid of any softness, so unEnglish, toward the cruelties of France – wasn't it proof, begod, that government was right up there in charge, and there'd be no more damn nonsense?

I had not wished to write too much about Selina. But this must be recorded. At the very beginning, when she heard of Tom's arrest, and the nature of the indictment, she had seemed to walk out of the world – which is to say, we led her to bed in a state of 'catatonia,' as ponderously diagnosed by the doctor we found for her from Hull, not at all another Tom, but a druidical pedant who leaked *babble* from every orifice ... So there she lay, neither speaking nor apparently hearing, week after week, and there she was lying when I shut down the school and went to York for the assizes: yet when I came home, she was gone. "Oh sir," exclaimed the housekeeper, "As soon as word was brought into town of that verdict, it wor like she'd already known it and she sprang out o' bed barefoot, running down to t'front door to cry her question, 'Will they hang him?', and when t'chaps i'street shouted back at her, 'Drawn and quartered baht mitigation!', why, she threw on her clothes all-anyroad and was straight off that minute for th'midnight coach to London and to see Mr Wilberforce, th'parliament man, tha knows, and she said, sir, she said, if she couldn't through him get to see Mr Pitt she was bound to see King George. And would you believe, she wore odd shoes, one black and one brown, and her hair all down her back."

I was confounded all at a blow with love and loss and terror for her: I should have gone to London after her: but how could I? I was beset by the parents of my boys – why was the school closed? what had I to do with the miscreant Tutton that I should flee from my duties? how far had his violence crept into my curriculum? It was a wonder there were any pupils left to me, but there were: I must reassemble them, I must teach. I put on the smoothest mask of pedagogical hypocrisy and told the children (a) that between permissible dissent and criminal insurrection lay a deep deterrent moat, precisely fixed by the law of the land, and (b) that if the law seemed less than human (as it often must, being contrived by human beings and therefore fallible), it could only be changed by rational, philosophical argument: an upsurge of violent passion must re-create the very crime that the law sought to remedy. Moreover, the judge's sentence (which had every boy in a buzz and twitter of unwholesome stimulation) was never in these modern times enforced – as they would see, as they would very soon see. Meanwhile, we would continue our studies. I was engaged, with the senior class, upon the masterly *Don Carlos* of Schiller, transposing his text into rough-and-ready English verse. I had proposed a private reading (assuming we finished the work), to the school in general, relatives and friends, for our regular half-term entertainment. I saw no reason to depart from this plan ... At the end of the following week a letter from Selina: –

Westminster, Tuesday.
Ah husband, sorrow and woe!
Mr William Wilberforce, our supposed friend, Member
of Parliament for Hull, has offered me naught better
than a spongeful of vinegar. To his shame and I shall
not forget it. I grant that in the past he has proven
himself a very Samson to attempt to pull down the
temple of slavery: but when he sees a goodly man,
sweet-natured, honest and good (of admittedly foolish
opinions) to be carved and cooked alive like a sacrifice
to bloodthirsty Baal, why, he walks at a full speed far,

*far from the spectacle. Mrs Hopkin thought me mad
that I said I would see King George. And yet I have
seen him. Toward which the abject Wilberforce did
indeed assist me. His Majesty was kind, I cannot deny
it, a dear old man in any other place or circumstance, he
lent me his own handkerchief against my tears, but no!
he could not, would not, give backword to his judges,
especially because our dear Tom (as he understood it)
had spoken for those "Irish Papists who would have me
contravene, what? what? the Protestant requirements of
my Coronation Oath." He was perfectly obstinate, and
yet he kissed me and praised my compassion. He is in
thrall to his fears and in thrall to his fearful ministers.
A sad prospect for the nation, but what can I do, save
pray to Our Lord & Saviour? – as, indeed, does Mr
Wilberforce – how should sincere religion find two such
opposed voices out of the one same Book?*

Your wretched S.

*PS: I shall be in London three more days, four, in the
hope that -   In the hope -   No but it is hopeless.*

It was in fact a full week before she came home, white-faced,
red-eyed, her sweet, soft mouth as taut as a ship's hawser – she
was startled, nay appalled, to find our evening with Schiller in
active preparation – how *could* we? she demanded, at so tragi-
cal a season? She then reviled me, as I have said, for my Simon
Peter cowardice. I ignored the accusation, but felt I must reply
to her first point, and truly I meant no idle smartness, but what
better for such times than a noble poetic tragedy? Whereat she
swung her hand and all but smote me, and then swung herself
away, her entire body, like a teetotum, such vitality of scorn. At
least it was not her erstwhile 'catatonia,' she was unimpeach-
ably alive, though in her grief she overlooked the very theme of
Don Carlos, its bugle-call for liberty.

All she said, after that, was, "Even Wilberforce concedes that
the delivery of severed limbs by special messenger across the
county is a practice most unjustified – 'barbarous, barbarous,'

he exclaimed, 'a gothical and morbid survival,' he will speak to the prime minister – ah no, I told him, no! for did *I* not speak to the *king* and yet received not one word of practical comfort?"

The execution was indeed carried out to the letter. It took place in York upon a very deliberate date, the 5th of November (public holiday for our nation's deliverance from the Gunpowder Plot). The scaffold was erected in front of the Redcap alehouse, where the Corresponding Society had held its fatal meeting. They say the hangman was all abroad and trembling; even the extreme Tories marked his clumsiness with the cutlery as beyond forgiveness – of course, he'd never done it before. They say Tom did *not* tremble: they say he was proud and derisive to the end, an heroic Roman out of the books, a Regulus who honoured his parole by taking ship to the torturers of Carthage, a Curtius who offered up his life to the dark gods of the underworld for the salvation of the city. I was incapable of the courage to return that day to York and to stand before the scaffold.

Nonetheless, upon the 5th of November, I went so far as to close the school for twenty-four hours, and damn the complaints; we hung black streamers from our balcony over the porch so that any person approaching the door would have to part them with his hands – maybe it would cause a pertinent flow of thought? Some young louts came running to throw stones and break our windows, for the good health (I suppose) of church and king. But when they saw Selina, how she sat there in the balcony, all in black and motionless, ominous and pale as a Sibyl, they were struck with such an awe that they scuttered away incontinent and did no more than cackle their rudeness from the far end of the street. I told her how brave she was; she ignored me; and that was that.

Not long before midnight, a galloper arrived from York with a pair of gruesome scarlet sacks tied across his saddle. One for us; the other for Hull, several miles down the road to the south. He routed out the mayor in the name of the king, he demanded and obtained an extraordinary torch-lit ritual in the market place, whereby Tom's severed head was stuck on a spike and lashed against the apex of one of the great stone urns that ornament the roof of our market cross. (Designed by Sir C. Wren, this grandly-proportioned edifice has been subjected to frequent squalor, strumpets plying their trade in its shelter, cattle befouling the pavement between its columns, but never before such disgrace as this, never.) The ceremony concluded with prayers – the vicar of the Minster refused to utter them, but the mayor and his cronies turned up an indigent chaplain from somewhere, gave him brandy and a prayer-book and told him to get on with it. A Gunpowder Treason bonfire was ablaze the other side of the square, with the cruel effigy of Guy Fawkes, that brave, deluded Yorkshireman, rearing up in midst of the flames like a damnable signpost (good heavens, he showed the road to the kingdom of Lucifer).

Despite a general disgust at this twofold exhibition, the town-crier's announcement of it drew more people out of their houses than an enlightened individual would care to contemplate.

So there the head remained, and was indefinitely to remain till it should disintegrate and fall of its own accord. Next morning I stared up at it for thirty minutes, no less: blackened with tar it was, eye-sockets black and empty, white teeth in a hideous grimace. I swore that never again, never, would I cast so much as a glance toward that market cross, and I have kept to my oath most firmly, even after the head was - I jump too far forward.

Within three days, *Don Carlos*: I had hired the town theatre, a tawdry little tea-caddie of a playhouse, twelve benches in the pit, five boxes in a semi-circle underneath a narrow gallery, the stage within its proscenium not much bigger than a four-poster bed. The reading was to be done by the half-dozen boys who'd made the translation; myself as King Philip; my usher, Mr Fly, as the Marquis Posa; two adult voices to give weight and balance to the whole. Of course, we were not to read the entire play – a selection of strong passages, that was all – I would summarize the plot as we went along. (I had hoped for Selina as the

Queen of Spain, but she refused me an answer; I press-ganged Mr Fly's sister, who readily complied.)

The audience attended by invitation only. Apart from the children of the school, it was for the most part our old circle from Tom Tutton's happier times, ah "sorrow and woe." But they did have a notion of the play and were anxious to hear it, if only to show their abhorrence of his trial and condemnation. There might have been two score of good people in the house when I led my little company onto the forestage; we quietly took our chairs and were about to begin, when all of a sudden Selina came upon us through the pit; she was calm, she was strenuous, as majestic as Mrs Siddons, in a sweeping wide gown of white satin. "Mr Fouracre," she declared, mounting the steps from the orchestra, "I apologize fervently for my procrastination, but I will, by your leave, read the part of the Queen. Miss Fly, I am sure, will be content with Princess Eboli?" Miss Fly very properly acceded, with some small disappointment; but the treacherous Eboli is a rich enough part, while the boy whom I had cast for it was also to read the Grand Inquisitor, so no great injustice either way ... My wife continued: "Mr Fouracre, all these days I have endured such an agony of spirit as to rob me of my good sense. And so wrong of me to imply that in our present tribulation the verses of Schiller have nothing to say to us. Let us read him, and digest."

Indeed I do not think Mrs Siddons could have interpreted the courageous Queen with more power, or charm, or pathetic sensibility. Her great speech to her stepson, Don Carlos, her affectionate rebuke for his erotic indiscretion, aroused not only applause but full-throated cheers, even though she delivered it from a spindly dressing-room chair, book in hand, no gesticulation, no pacing the stage –

> This gorgeous love is not for me, you have no right
> To aim it at one lady, nay but it needs
> An entire populace to fold it to their bosom.
> All of this Spain, all of the Netherlands,
> Must one day know your rule and you shall love them,

That is the duty of your amorous passion!
Learn to be king, and learn to be a king
Of godlike mercy, not of chastisement –

She was superb.

So we arrive at Act V and the assassination of the liberal-minded Posa by an unseen musketeer through the bars of a gate (a crime committed on behalf of repression and bigotry). Don Carlos denounces his father the King as initiator of the murder. Afterwards the King comes drifting "like a sleep-walker" amongst his grandees – it was not until I came to deliver his speech of conscience-stricken delirium that I understood how close the verses rode to my yearning for Tom Tutton –

I want my Posa's corpse, oh I must have
His bleeding corpse. I loved him but he scorned me
And he died. Where have you put him? O my lords,
I want him back. How sorely do I need
His good opinion –

There it was: I shudder even yet to recall it: right upon "good opinion," the very instant I declaimed the phrase: an interruption unimaginable, outlandish beyond all words. Before ladies, before children, it could not have been worse. My son Alcuin, bolt upright, chin lifted, at the edge of the forestage; he was framed within the left-hand proscenium doorway; he was roaring in his gullet with a noise like a watermill. He wore no uniform but was somehow hung about with a coachman's caped greatcoat, he was filthy, unshaven, blear-eyed as though thoroughly drunk. He was fumbling with what appeared to be a bundle of old blanket ... And then suddenly we saw he held the head of Dr Tutton, the strong fingers of his right hand hooked into it between tar-stiffened cheek and grinning teeth.

"Here you are," utterance uncertain, thick. "The *bleeding corpse*, or some of it, hey? no damned Spaniard but a right rascal Yorkshireman, and how dared they spike it up where it was? ... Hey, Papa, catch!"

He hurled it toward me, underarm at full stretch, like the bowling-man in an innings of cricket; but its weight must have unbalanced him; it flew awkwardly over my own head and up into the opposite stage-box (by a merciful providence, no-one was sitting there); he sat down plump upon the forestage and wept. As well he might indeed, for he'd placed us all in peril as accessories to the outrage – contempt of court at the very least, the head being brought to town by order of a judge – or sedition, or rebellion, who could say? Except that not one of us would go crawling to the law: we knew our own opinions and held fast. I broke off the reading and began to stammer to the company, they too had a difficulty in knowing how to comment, some of them hurried their children away, others would stay for some consensus of opinion – but I pled with them to go – I would deal with everything – my responsibility as headmaster of Newton House – the great Sir Isaac (from whom we take our name) was a philosopher before all, we must be no less serene – oh if we could, etcetera – if only we could.

Selina was apparently not struck with galvanic spasm by the irruption of our son. She was the only person present to appear unsurprised. I came to wonder, had she perhaps had an inkling of his arrival? I have asked her, in the aftermath, many times; she smiles like a mermaid, never tells. Nor speaks of her anguish when she knew the head and saw him hurl it. This she could not have expected. Her howl of grief astonished even herself and will live with me night and day.

We fetched Alcuin home, undressed him, put him under the pump, put him to bed. In the morning, to begin with, he said little; but then he sipped at a cup of coffee with a good spoon of brandy in it; item by item his story emerged.

First: he was out of the army, resigned from his post, having seen such deeds in Ireland as sickened him forever of the military life. He instanced just one, the least of them, he said. There were girls in the town of Newry who had wound the green ribbons into their hair. The soldiers laid hold of them, stripped them naked from waist to foot, muffled their heads in their own petticoats and chased them thus blindfold up the hill, whipping them all the way home. Whistling switches, gobbets of ugly laughter, *enough* ... "Hey!" cried my son, "those beastly lobsterbacks were approved by their own officers. And it wasn't my regiment. You do see, there was nowt I could do."

Second: he had been in Yorkshire for some time but had no heart to come direct to his father. (He did not allude to his mother; she kept her own counsel as he spoke.) He'd been working for an old friend, a veterinary out Bridlington way, "a coarse kind of job, but it soothed." And then, he said, he persuaded himself to hear our *Don Carlos*. "I don't know why," he said. "German poetry was never an accomplishment I could cling to. I was later into town than I'd meant, had a can or two to drink, was walking to the theatre through the market place, hey? – pitch-dark and sluicing with rain, not a soul on the street. That bandy-legged devil of a Jacobin cobbler, Simon Swayne, was propping up a ladder against a pillar of the cross, cursing and egging her on to -   Aye, *her,* his scrawny Janet, consumptive young wife, no better than she ever was, coughing blood at every gasp, she was perched up above and pulling and hauling at -   I saw her tangled hair all wet about her face, she was up there cursing down at him even wilder than he was and -   Right: the head came tumbling to the pavement, he gathered it into a knapsack, and then they saw me, both of 'em: there I was. I told 'em I could have them hanged for what they were up to. I told 'em they should give the head to me: I had a use for it. Their courage had brought them so far, so I told 'em, *I* was the man to take over. They were cold, they were wet, they were suddenly pisswater frightened, they agreed."

Third point and finally, and he said it with his head bent sideways, all abashed: if we'd not years ago turned our backs upon old Tutton, we'd either have kept him to a sensible good measure, or his so-called *enlightened cause* would have gained enough strength to stand firm against spies and mad judges. Which is why the head was hurled. Tom's loss of it was our loss and we needed to be told.

Major Wetwang was announced. Good heavens, we had no notion that *he* was in Yorkshire as well. A light-cavalry hard-rider, small stature, ginger whiskers, and a hair-queue hardened with wax after the crude Prussian fashion; why, it stuck out over his collar like a supernumerary pizzle – I was sure he had come with the constable behind him hotfoot upon a rumour of felony – but no. He kept his hat on his head with deliberate insolence, he jerked a bow to Selina, cut me dead and spoke to Alcuin: "Next time you get y'rself so damnably foxed that you can't keep off the theatrical boards, y'should just take a look, me boy, into the shadows of the gallery. Dammit, Alky, didn't you see him? my man Hurn, damn his eyes, up there all the evening with his bloody little notebook, entering his depositions of the treasonable foreign play ... So where's the traitor's head? where is it? you have it hid? you have it well hid? Never mind. I made a confiscation of Master Hurn's sordid testimony. I've had a word with the magistrates. I'd say you'll hear no more of it, supposing that that head don't resurrect. News is coming in that there's trouble enough with m'uncle Baker Fortescue and his comical sentence, not to have us augment it with more non-sense in our own town. Furthermore, you're an old chummy, though a blasted young fool. Furthermore, and furthermore, you were five years hard at work in the regiment: we do *not* want the regiment made ridiculous by publication of your dam-fool antics."

He spun upon his heel and strode out of the house. The huge plume in his cocked hat brushed the lintel of the front door, his scabbard clanged against the shoe-scraper. A horrid tyranni-cal creature, a sort of military hornet. I felt exceedingly lucky that none of us were stung. Mind you, my poor Alcuin had already been stung: his wretchedness at his Irish experience was palpable for many months, but at last he has grown out of it – though by no means so far as to embrace my liberal opinions, still less those of his mother, and never mind Tom Tutton's. But his strangely ingrained toryism has a nettle of good humour, a dandelion of expediency, blooming from its dirt (e.g. the care-less speed with which he saved the skins of Mrs Swayne and her man, a rashness that might well have cost him dear). Maybe this amiable quality will one day come to save his own lively spirit from political *catatonia*.

As for the head: the three of us will never forget how we wrapt all that we possessed of our beloved physician in a green and purple mantle, brocaded with silver thread, a treasured item of Selina's wedding trousseau (ah how even today that hurts my heart); we carried the melancholy bundle to the Minster churchyard after dark; we dug a hole for it over against a certain buttress of the choir; the good vicar whispered the burial prayers; Selina in due course planted a rose bush on the spot.

And as for the "trouble enough" that so vexed Major Wetwang: the authorities took care to suppress the dangerous news, but before long it became clear that the portions of cadaver (so inexpertly and hastily divided) had not been well received by most of those to whom they were sent. *Important I write it down, for I think no-one else has.* I do admit that Ripon, that notably loyal city, afforded great respect to Tom Tutton's right arm and some fragments of his chest and flank, as representative symbols of His Majesty's Sovereign Right. I am told they are still there, on a flagpole in front of the great church. But in Hull the sailors dragged a left leg, with buttock and rectum attached, from the gibbet where they used to hang the pirates; they sent a butcher's boy to hand it in at Mr Wilberforce's kitchen door. In Wakefield, the other arm, its shoulder and two-thirds of a ribcage, had been erected on a pinnacle of the bridge-chapel; they were pulled down by schoolboys and tossed into the River Calder. And in York, all was frenzy. After the public dismemberment, and after the wicked red sacks had been dispatched upon their travels, the volatile crowd broke the cordon of militiamen and surged across the scaffold. They snatched the right leg and what was left of the lower torso; flesh-and-bone together entirely disappeared amongst them; it has been said that certain citizens (huddled together by prior agreement, and far from volatile) tore it all into little pieces to carry away under their coats in the manner of ancient Christians with the relics of their martyrs. They would *venerate*, it has been said ... The hangman was overwhelmed and trampled very nearly to death.

*

I was never one to be visited by dreams, but since the day of his execution, Dr Tutton has come to me almost every night. He walks into my bedroom, quiet-footed, smiling; he sits down in my bedside chair, just as he did in the old days when I was sick and Selina had called for him. The difficulty is, that he wears no clothes, and is daubed all over with blood; his body being marked out in sections (like an engraving from one of Alcuin's anatomy books); they are sewn together, four quarters and his privities and the head, very roughly, great black stitches, and I cannot bear that he should lay his hands upon me.

But Selina sits near him, beyond him, almost out of my sight; she seems to huddle close to him. I can't see where she has placed her hands, but they are not where they ought to be.

Yorkshire Bluebeard

There was an ex-soldier in the fenland of Holderness, not far from Kirk Deerwood; he was called Chindit Hurn; he had been corporal in an infantry battalion. He came from a large and terrorized family, where he was the youngest child and the only son. His queer name was the choice of his father, a hard-nosed veteran of the Burma campaign in World War Two, a vindictive domestic martinet. As a boy Chindit had hated him, and would conspire with his embittered mother to outsmart the evil old ruffian: secret treats of cake and daring visits to the cinema. Only too often the ruffian would catch them at their tricks and knock them about and kick them till their blood was in spatters all over the kitchen lino.

In later years Chindit himself was to be vilified by the tabloid press in warily oblique terms: –

PURE EVIL? COPS' HORROR AT GARAGE OF DEATH

IS THIS MAN THE YORKSHIRE BLUEBEARD?

The headlines did not hit the mark dead-centre, but -   Indeed there was a strain of truth. Did he subconsciously give himself a bad name from the cruelties of his father? Did he believe such characteristics were inevitably congenital? At all events, there is no doubt that in the child's mind the father's behaviour gave a shocking bad name to the army. And yet, paradox: teenage Chindit was so overcome with uncontrollable visceral excitement at the TV images of the Falklands War that he could not wait to be part of such doings. As soon as he was old enough he hitched a lift into Kirk Deerwood and went straight to the barracks to enlist. His mother was dead and his sisters had taken flight, one after the other, to God only knew what sort of life in distant places (it is probable that more than one of them had been incestuously *ransacked*); while to "go for a soldier" was his own chosen route of escape. And not only escape: he felt a fierce subterranean craving for what his comic-books called "action," and he very soon got it, in almost unmanageable quantities. He fought hard in the north of Ireland against the IRA (he was taught to regard them as an assemblage of pure evil); he got himself into serious trouble during a riot in West Belfast and went to prison; on his release he served in the first Gulf War, fighting hard against the soldiers of Saddam Hussein (he was taught to regard him as evil incarnate.) He retired from the army in 1993, at the age of twenty-five, "psychologically unfit for further service," with bits and pieces of *friendly fire* lodged in his body. It is likely that these fragments contained depleted uranium and were hastening his death in all manner of unknown ways; this was denied by the Ministry of Defence, but one or two of his military doctors thought otherwise; he tried to sue someone, anyone, government, generals, colonels; every lawyer he approached told him he would get nowhere with it, better give over: he gave over.

His father, thank God, had died in the hospital of a malady of war, a long-standing tropical disease. Chindit inherited a cottage and a ramshackle garage (creosoted timber and corrugated iron) at a rural crossroads in the fen – a place called Hangman's Mere, no-one knew why. While he was in the army his elderly uncle George had looked after the garage business and kept it on a strong enough footing, maintaining trucks, tractors, ploughs, and so forth, for the local farmers, and supplying not only petrol and diesel but binding twine and linseed oil and paraffin and varnish or whatever else might be a nuisance to have to go into town for. George was a crafty mechanic, but he was also an eccentric with more time for his daft hobbies than straightforward work – for instance, he spent years fooling about with all shapes and sizes of scrap metal, chain-link, and coils of barbed wire, to put together a rusty, spiky attempt at what might be called a cottage at the door of the cottage – a huge trap or snare, with spring-loaded hatches, that would (he claimed to his ale-mates) catch fifty rats at a go, or rabbits, or foxes – "or lasses, like, for us to keep for us bed-an'-board, fat greasy lasses wi' big tits: 'Page Three,' tha knows, think on." He finally flattened his precarious construction (and broke three of his ribs into the bargain), tumbling across it while in drink ... So the strong enough footing was already much weakened when Chindit came home. Within three months the unhappy George, cursing and slobbering, was levered into a nursing home in a suburb of Hull; every evening Chindit handed over his petrol pumps to a dopey-looking lad, and sat alone at the kitchen table, puzzling over the ledgers and bank-books that the old soak had left behind him.

Sometimes he got up from the table, lifted from their hooks a shotgun and a powerful inspection-lamp, went out into the back yard, opened a narrow door in a brick-built windowless shed immediately opposite the kitchen and stood there in front of it, discharging cartridge after cartridge in rapid succession, a crash of gunfire that faded away unanswered into wide miles of fenland loneliness. The lad at the pumps would hear it, nobody else. He was startled, the first time; he left his post and began all a-gape to come creeping round the house. "Rabbits?" he called out cautiously. "Nay, Mr Hurn, I've not seen no rabbits."

Chindit jumped away from the shed door, flashed his lamp into the lad's face, dazzled him blind. "Rats," he barked abruptly. A practised parade-ground disdain. "And this yard's out of bounds after dark. D'you want to get shot? Your mum and your dad'd cauterize me bollocks. So fuck off quick sharp to them pumps." No more questions.

Chindit's gaol time in the 1980s needs a short explanation. The company had been sent to help intimidate an angry crowd who threw stones, iron bars and petrol bombs. The OC told the men that it was possible the IRA might use the ruction as a cover to open fire from surrounding buildings; but on no account must the soldiers open fire themselves unless they were shot at, or were in imminent danger of being shot at, or were given a direct order by an officer. "Remain watchful, your eyes not only at the crowd but *above* it. Roofs and balconies. Understood?" Thoroughly unnerved by this uncomfortable instruction, Chindit screeched out, "Terrorist!" and shot fifteen times at a young woman in an upstairs window. The young woman was killed; she turned out to be a naïve country schoolmistress from south of the Border, come to Belfast to stay with a cousin; she ought to have known better than to peer down at a furious riot as though it were a Corpus Christi procession.

Chindit's defence to a charge of murder was that the woman in the window held a rifle and was aiming it: every time he fired, she ducked below the sill, only to pop up again, holding her weapon in exactly the same posture, "why, a jack-in-a-box – like this, this, you're not bloody watching me, *this!*" and he jerked himself up and down in the dock, a crazy choreography of despair. He was found guilty of manslaughter – police evidence proved that the schoolmistress had no rifle in her hands or anything like a rifle; she was killed by Chindit's first or second bullet and all the other shots were at random and hysterical – the judge gave him five years and the army made an earthquake of a fuss – he was a very brave young soldier, he was only doing his duty, a prison sentence was most dreadfully detrimental to military morale – *The Daily Telegraph* launched a national petition. He was released after six months and the regiment took him back – after all, if the floozie he'd shot was *not* a terrorist, or at least an associate of terrorists, what the devil was she playing at in that part of town?

The garage did not do very good business and Chindit's hopes of rebuilding it and generally improving its facilities came to nothing. He had tried to borrow money from the bank, but could offer no security beyond the name of a distant relative, Sir Jacob Hurn of Kirk Deerwood, wealthy chairman of a chain of high-class butchery emporiums. But Sir Jacob had just sold out to Tesco upon advantageous terms and had bought himself a mansion in the Cotswolds; he had no desire to be entangled with some wretched little cowboy outfit in the most melancholy region of a county he preferred to forget. He had long regarded the Hangman's Mere branch of the family as an embarrassing excrescence.

Nonetheless, in the gaps between perennial financial worries, Chindit did contrive to find himself a life. He got rid of the young lad and ran the garage by himself; he was therefore able to shut it down for days at a time, and to drive off in his old banger of a van to Hull or to Leeds or even (upon occasion) to Newcastle, for some strenuous night-excitement in the pubs and clubs: booze, betting, fucking, fighting. He was short, strong and violent, with muscles like lengths of bullwhip, and he knew how to overcome a youngish woman – or a certain type of youngish woman, not so young, not so happy, not so beautiful, usually in transit and as lecherous as any of 'em. He did not employ force, nor did he flatter, he was just downright rude with such cocky and cheery effrontery that they really had to laugh, and once they started laughing – why, he *had* 'em. Brought 'em home despite all protest, rolled 'em in his scruffy bed, rolled 'em in the long grass in his bit of a paddock down the Hornsea road, rolled 'em on a pile of inner tubes in the dark of the garage, floundered about with 'em stripped-off in the secluded shallows of the mere – all according to the state of the weather, and always well-spiced with cigs and whisky and hash, and great plates of bacon and egg. They loved it; when he asked them to stay, they would surprisingly often agree.

And always, very soon, they'd had more than enough of it.

Those of them who went back to wherever they'd come from, and told their experiences to their friends, invariably said the same thing – Chindit Hurn was a mean, vicious, possessive little shit, whose only way of dealing with a woman (once the erotic fun-and-games had come to an end) was to order her here, order her there, keep his eye upon her everywhere, as pernickety as a social services clerk and as jealous as a dog with its basket. And the fun-and-games did come to an end in very short order. A few days of licentious highlife left him drained and depressed to an extent that his women were never prepared for. He turned his back on them, metaphorically and in physical fact;

he hunched over his ledgers and pocket calculator, revisiting his meagre resources again and again; he made sorties after dark with shotgun and lamp, as avid for dead rats as the Pied Piper of Hamelin (or so it seemed; he never let the women near him to see just what he was up to); he avoided conversation, communicating solely in angry imperative grunts and monosyllabic swear-words; when he wasn't understood he would launch into an extraordinary exhibition of paranoiac rage, jerking himself up and down like a jack-in-a-box and screaming, "like this, you pox-holed bitch, when I say scrub a frying-pan you do it like this, this, you're not bloody watching me, *this!*"

When he hit them, he hit them dreadfully hard, a trained soldier, an expert. Nor was it possible for them to accept the surge of violence as part and parcel of his love, or at any rate lust, to be enjoyed for its own sake. It was manifest hostility. They could not close their minds to it. They walked out on him then and there, or else he would drive them out. He hit them because he'd had enough of them, they were finished: he made it clear.

They did not all go back to their friends. There were certain bursts of anxiety here and there as to what might have happened to them. But nobody *did* anything. No question, for example, of *police*. These women all belonged to a quirky shifting milieu, some of them took quantities of drugs, none of them were known for the strength of their rational decisions. If they disappeared, it was (probably) their own choice.

Upon a spring evening in 2003, just after *Shock and Awe* had mendaciously been flung against Iraq, Chindit was in Kirk Deerwood, in a huge, crowded boozer that used to be The Jolly Postboys but was nowadays calling itself Flannery's Irish House – it was no more Irish than Chindit himself, save that Guinness was a speciality and hot mutton stew was always ready at the food bar. Chindit watched the war on a wide TV screen at one end of the saloon; at the other end there was an even wider screen with highlights of the week's football; but Chindit watched the war. He sweated as he watched, he felt his tool in his trousers growing large and hard and hot. He had ordered a plate of stew. It was brought by a small blonde waitress. She had poor enough English, but a perfectly delightful smile and a backside in her tight jeans like a pair of ribston pippins. Chindit surprised himself by turning away from the war. After all, why shouldn't he? the fucking war had turned *him* away; somebody else, this time round, was due to eat the shit and the sand and the oil and depleted uranium, and by Christ they were fucking welcome, this time round, why not? why not? – get rid of Saddam, evil bastard, once for all.

He grinned at the waitress and asked where she came from. She told him Bulgaria. She told him how long she'd been in England (six weeks). She told him what she earned (fuck-all or as near as). She told him that her papers were not all they might have been and she hoped he was not police. She was altogether foolish and he clasped her soft warm hand and they laughed like a pair of old friends. She was younger than Chindit's usual pickups, but as careless as any of them; when the bar-manager came and swore at her for neglecting her work, she turned on him and told him outright, "You are stupid fucker, no good: I finish here: take your clothes: I am not fucking thief, you know: good bye." She pulled off her apron and T-shirt (which had Flannery's shamrocky logo all over them) and threw them into his face. This left her in an undervest, bare-shouldered, almost bare-breasted, as she started for the door. It was a cold night outside but she didn't care. Chindit's tool was harder than ever; he ran after her, put his anorak around her, laughed with her to calm her down, and led her unresisting to his van.

Her name was Anna. Anna Protchichichev, or some such; maybe; she spoke it so fast. "Can't say it," scoffed Chindit. "All o'them snorts. Tell you what, we'll call you Prodgy." He wouldn't call her Anna. Nor would he tell her why... One of his long-gone sisters was an Annie: Too close to the bone.

She was a great laugher, perhaps because she had a difficulty saying things in English. She laughed in the van all the way to Hangman's Mere, she laughed at the overall chaos of Chindit's cottage, his deplorable bedstead laden with eiderdowns and old rugs and grubby blankets, she laughed at the state of his bathroom. Paradox: for his day-to-day existence he would do no more than provide himself with a small taut well-scrubbed working corner, table, chair, account books and computer (a regular get-fell-in *military* corner), in the midst of a wilderness of squalor. He ate off whatever shelf, chair or packing-case stood nearest to him; his cooking was confined to frying-pan and kettle; his sink was full of crockery and his fridge was green with mould. She laughed at this, and laughed. She made love like a houri in a Taliban Paradise.

Chindit told himself, "This one's for ever, oh she'll never do me dirt, oh by Christ I'm in fucking love."

In the morning he did his best to please her, washing and sweeping and throwing out the garbage. He gave himself a good wash and went so far as to Harpic the lavatory bowl. Everything about her pleased *him*, and no mistake. Oh, but perhaps there was one small mistake – no! he was in love with her, he would take no notice, except that -   No, but it was hard to take no notice of a girl who turned out in broad daylight to be not only careless and deliciously light-hearted but also most damnably curious. She was asking about everything. Christ, if she'd been in Belfast on that black day of riot, she'd surely have craned out of window and then some bloody squaddy might have -   No, he was in love and by Christ he was going to trust her.

He said, and it was something he'd never said to any other of his women, "Prodgy, pet: I ought to tell you. Me old mum, tha knows, she's dead, but afore she died she did me dirt; she used me to get at me dad. Fuck me, he was an evil bastard, but she'd no call to fix me into t'range of his fist and feet. And why did she do it? I trusted her, sitha, that's why. And why did them sisters play games with him, private? In his bedroom, dark and private, one at a time? Fuck me, they were complicit. I could never trust the likes o'them, not in this world, never. So if I'm to trust *you*, I'm to know you'll fix me nowhere. Hold this tool o' mine and promise." She was very happy to oblige him, if she did not quite understand the nature of her promise. But she did comprehend she was in some sort swearing fealty, and she loved the way he had her do it.

A little while afterwards, she strolled out into the yard. She looked at the brick shed and at all the shot-scars across it, wall and door. There was a hasp on the door and a heavy padlock, gleaming with oil. "Is big lock? What is in? You have secret? You have girls in there, you hide, that you think they are more sexy than Anna? Show me open, shall we see?" She was light-hearted, mischievous, brimful of careless laughter.

Chindit's brow darkened. This ought to be the time he should revile her and hit out at her and send her packing, quick sharp; for how dare she ask such questions? ... She came to caress him and to kiss. He moved away from her, no more than a step, but a straight, strong, definite step and suddenly her blue eyes were glistening, suddenly she was hurt – and he saw it. "Aye," he growled, slowly, endeavouring to improvise something more or less plausible. "I said that I'd trust you. Well I will. There's no girls in that shed, you know there's no girls, aye aye, it wor no more than your joke - except that -   It's not right a joke at all. There's stuff in that shed. Gear. Not mine, tha knows, no; I keep it for a mucker o'mine. And he don't tell me what it is, so I don't know and *cops* don't know, and *you* don't know, so shut it." She heard the word "cops," and realized he was serious. Heavy business, maybe criminal, maybe dangerous; this was not very surprising, but she'd have to take care; light-heartedness could bring trouble. Trouble for *her,* trouble (most importantly) for *him,* and she was very nearly sure that she loved him. Why, it was just like a movie. Had she not seen, not a year ago in Plovdiv, that old French thing with Belmondo, and June, Jane, Jean Seberg, was it not? only in black-and-white but how it *pierced.* And she'd wept into the soft neck of the boy that was with her, such tender emotion, and danger, and tremblings, and was not Belmondo shot down dead in the end?

So: her brand-new lover was telling her, importantly, that she was not to be curious about this very stupid shed? – so out of her mind it must go. And she said so; and he came back to her and they kissed and caressed for the rest of the morning. And for the rest of the week, and for all of two weeks after that – if she lasted a whole month, she'd be the longest in the cottage of any of his women – he warmed to the thought like a lazy desert serpent that lay sunning itself on an outcrop of rock. (Such as he'd seen in the war, in the hot, dusty, sun-glare of the war.) At about this time he so far weakened towards her as to tell her this and that about some of his previous women. Not so much boasting as assuring her that none of them were her equals in any possible way, body, mind or spirit. He told her that all of them had taken themselves off, out of plain incapability to adjust to a man who knew his onions and cooked accordingly.

For as long as Anna was with him he did not find it necessary to go shooting his gun in the yard, so she couldn't be curious about that. As for the shed, her curiosity was abated but certainly not quenched. The padlock, she reflected, was kept clean and oiled on a dirty old door where the paint had peeled away long since, and moreover it was of a type that would need a special sort of key – something like a Yale key, but heavier and more elaborately cut. At home in Bulgaria she had done a bit of thieving, at the time a popular sport for wayward schoolgirls such as herself: she was good at it, one of the best. She knew about locks and keys. Not that she intended anything – after all, she had promised – but of course she kept her eyes open. Only a complete fool would not keep her eyes open, however sweet the lovemaking, however hilarious the whole wild situation.

He was starting up his van one morning and she came out to him, full of merriment; he snapped at her unkindly. "Like I told you, I've to run into Hornsea. I'll not be there all day." He was crapulous and therefore crabby, though he may not have known he was crabby. "You can come if you want, but I'm only on business, a few words wi' Jack Heckstall, in his shop, not the pub, and then I'm done. He's a boring little bugger: you'll not find nowt to laugh at."

"Oh I know, I have met him. He is a tin can dried-up that when full it had creosote. Best I stay here. You have told me the petrol pumps; and you know I know the motor engines. If problems with customers, I suppose I can solve?"

"If you think you can, o'course you can. Question is, do *I* think it?" He was a good deal more begrudging than usual, and followed up his grouse with a fragment of jealousy: "Put your hand where you put it, so I know I can trust you." She reached into the cab to touch him fleetingly between the thighs, a squeeze and a pinch and a wink. "Right, then," he grunted. "I'm off."

She waited until the van was positively out of sight down the drear fenland road, then she slipped round the back into the yard. She stood looking at the shed, as a child may look at a sweetshop. Indeed, like a child, she sucked her thumb as she considered, and she yearned. She wore a light summer dress (the springtime weather was unusually warm); she had no underwear beneath it; her stance was strangely carnal, weight equally on both legs slightly astride, one hand to her mouth, the other on her hip, pelvis thrust forward, nipples scarcely screened by the fabric of the dress: one might have thought she was waiting for a lover, but the lover had just driven off. No, but this lover was other than human: his name alas was Mischief, and he had his swift fingers already in her cunt.

The previous night, while Chindit snored away, full of whisky and beer and wine from their evening's debauchery, Anna had stooped to his trousers where he'd cast them at random on the floor; with wily intrepidity she'd unhooked from his crowded key-chain the one key that might fit the lock of the mysterious shed. All morning, until he left, she was shivering with uneasy excitement lest he discover the loss; if he did, could she come up with a credible story? But he didn't, and she was safe – at least for the two hours that Jack Heckstall would surely take to come to any sort of financial decision. Two hours? More probably three ... But would she? Or wouldn't she?

True Love was defeated, False Mischief proved the conqueror. Anna made up her mind. She broke from her aphrodisiac posture and stepped briskly through the sunshine to the fatal padlock. She opened it, she opened the door, she peered inside.

It seemed to her afterward that she'd barely had time to catch her breath after her first scream of terror (absurdity of a scream, for who would have heard her?), when suddenly her ears were torn by the screech of the wheels of Chindit's van as he wrenched it off the road, around the cottage, into the wide-open yard gate. She knew at once what had happened: he had looked at his key-chain, even before he reached Hornsea, looked at it or *fingered* it, in his pocket next to that tool he was so proud of – whatever the precise antecedent of his rage, he was here at full speed to destroy her. She staggered away from the shed, trying instinctively to cram herself behind a row of farm-implements that were lined up for attention at the far end of the yard. She wouldn't be invisible there, and he could easily enough get at her, but it was the furthest spot away from him, except through the yard gate, and of course the gate was blocked because his van had stormed to a halt between gatepost and shed and he was scrambling out of it like a fox from a foxhole, all in one slick movement, *pouring* himself at her, never mind that he was so stocky and blunt and as little like a fox as a mastodon. He had a slash-hook in his hand – just the broad shining blade and nine inches of cut-off handle – she knew he always kept it on the floor of his cab, in case of hi-jackers, terrorists, vengeful ghosts, who could say what? – a trained soldier, he took precautions. Security.

But if he was a soldier, she was a guerrilla. She was lighter on her feet, quicker to twist her body, quicker to dodge and leap. She let him almost at her, and at once with a flick of her hips she was out and under his reach, clear away from the swing of the slash-hook, clear away from the muddle of harrows and ploughs, running back across the yard to the van. The engine was still running; and (as she'd said) she did know the motor engines. Her brother in Pazardzhik was a truck driver and she'd lived with him when their father died and she'd ridden with him all over the Balkans and she'd driven the truck when he was tired. She spun the van round in its own length, the driver's door flying out – she hadn't had time to shut it – and Chindit racing alongside, grabbing for the door-handle, roaring his curses, struggling at all costs to get in. A jerk on the wheel and the van spun again, this time across Chindit's course, right *into* him in fact, sending him a-sprawl through the cinders of his yard, the slash-hook lost from his hold two yards beyond him, his clothes befouled and ripped, his distorted face all bloody from the fall. The last she saw of him, as she furiously accelerated onto the road, was a glimpse in the side mirror of a species of jack-in-a-box, up-and-down up-and-down at the yard gate, pulling himself up upon one leg, the left leg, while the other leg, hurt (thank God) and useless, kept dropping him down again.

Anna had her reasons for avoiding police, but her discovery was so shocking that *someone* had to be told of it. She was on the road to Hornsea. Very well, she'd go to Hornsea, even though the only person she'd ever talked to in the little seaside town was Jack Heckstall, the ironmonger – creosote can, wasn't he? boring little bugger – but a sober solid citizen who might have a notion what to do. Moreover Anna had detected that Mr Heckstall did not much care for Chindit Hurn. He was always friendly enough, as shopkeepers had to be, but a studious young shopkeeper who'd been nowhere near an army barracks would not perhaps take kindly to a military loudmouth who bragged about women. Mr Heckstall had a wife, a careful, watchful girl with nice spectacles, who helped in the shop and cast a very bleak eye upon Chindit, turning her back and moving away whenever he began to boast. Anna had noticed, Chindit probably hadn't. And now she must test what she'd observed.

Would they believe her?

She rushed into the shop with her mouth wildly open, the dark dust of Chindit's yard in streaks on her skin and her clothing, her unstoppable tears running channels through the grime from eyelid to neck. "Please," she cried, "Help please. His girls. The dead girls. One two four six, I don't know, all against wall and in dresses, long dresses, gowns is it? O God, don't you hear what I tell you. O gracious God they are *bone*."

Mrs Heckstall led Anna to a chair behind the counter, sat her down and said, "Bone?"

They managed bit-by-bit to elicit vital details. It seemed that Hurn's shed was full to bursting with all manner of rubbish, but above and behind his piles of mechanical débris there was this line, rank, column, procession, of tottering cadavers; some of them complete, others only partial (legs or arms missing, half a set of ribs, etc.); some of them bare skeletons, upon others there was a substance, a thick sort of something, with the look of dark brown leather, that adhered to them in clumps. They were all draped fantastically in the multi-coloured rags of what had once been gorgeous garments; they were all shattered and blasted, it might have been by hailstorms or a virulent smallpox. If Hurn had not systematically been murdering his women, then what on earth had he been doing? And where in God's name was he now? Mr Heckstall rang the police.

A sergeant and two constables from Hornsea drove out in the squad car, under orders to take a look at Hangman's Mere in general and the shed in particular. There'd been rumours relating to Hurn; it would do no harm to check the fellow out. No doubt the girl's story would prove a bit of a mare's nest, though clearly she'd been badly scared. Bulgarian, was she? Right: that might require to be taken into consideration ... Hurn was not at home, and the padlock was fastened. The sergeant decided that a report involving multiple corpses, however improbable, could justify forcible entry, so he did some quick work with a crowbar, stared white-faced at what he saw, called up his superior, and ordered his subordinates (in a great fuss and flurry) to break out the official tape, cordon off the crime scene, divert all the traffic on the road – "They're fetching in the Serious Crime Squad from Hull: they'll need it properly sorted, and I tell you we're in trouble if we don't. So watch yourselves."

At that point ex-Corporal Hurn opened fire with his shotgun from the thicket of tall bulrushes that fringed the mere. He was an excellent marksman. The sergeant took a full load of buckshot in the face and fell down into the cinders with an unearthly, high-pitched cry. A condition ensued of total panic, the constables running behind walls, between the wheels of tractors, bawling from inside the shed into their two-way radios; while Hurn (as lame as a stark mad Vulcan) crashed and splashed among the rushes, from one point of vantage to another, reloading and pulling his trigger at every pause. Each time, they could hear him roar: "Up, down, up, down, you couldn't see the gun? – I saw the fucking gun – like this, this, you're not bloody watching me, this!" And then he was out of hearing, as he was already out of sight, no more shooting, not even the sound of his legs in the water – only the gulls from the nearby North Sea, whirling and screaming as though tracking his passage – a flock of helicopters on search-and-kill above the banks of the Euphrates.

The media got wind of things quite as soon as the Serious Crime people: within twenty-four hours the 'Bluebeard' stories were flooding the red-tops; even the broadsheets happily chorused 'Evil' – as though that explained everything that might frighten or repel the British public. All this gave the police some welcome publicity, burying folks' memories of recent corruption in the Kirk Deerwood CID (a nasty little scandal, with an inspector sent to gaol).

On the other hand they looked such fools when the human remains turned out to be at least two thousand years old.

An archaeologist from Hull University suggested that they might derive from a hitherto unknown cemetery of Iron Age fen-dwellers, preserved by a deposit of rich black peat as in certain bogs in Ireland and Scandinavia. Further investigation led into the depths of the old folks' home and cantankerous Uncle George. Interviewed with some difficulty, he eventually explained how he'd tripped over somebody's old skull while he was out after wildfowl on an island in the mere, how he spaded and trowelled and found every day more and more, "like that there owd Ezekiel, in his valley of dry bones, and there behold a great shaking, saith the Lord, an'all them bones to come together, like bone to his bone, an'where's there a chap to fettle it but owd daft George an'he could an'he did?" He spent a whole year re-assembling his discoveries, wiring them together from diagrams in a medical book which he lifted from his doctor's surgery.

Sometimes he must have been drunk and made mistakes: for instance, one of his specimens had feet on the ends of its arms, and on another the pelvis was upside down. But it seemed that the mistakes did not matter to Chindit; when he came across the skeletons, he happily used all of them as a grotesque troop of mannequins for garments left in wardrobes by his mother, his sisters, his periodic mistresses. Once he had dressed them up, he arranged them to suit his fancy, a sort of tableau as though they peered over his rusty old stockpiles, about to clamber across them to tear his head off – he'd seen something like it in a horror film on late-night TV. He would shine his great lamp at one of them (never more than one at a time, but each of them had her turn) and shoot toward her bang bang bang till she fell to pieces. And then he'd sit down in the light of his great lamp to meticulously rewire her and attend to her wounds with superglue and polyfilla. The rents in the dresses he left unmended. At one stage he typed out a statement on his office computer and tacked it up in the shed above the row of staring skulls.

WHEN I SHOOT I HIT. I'M WELL TRAINED.
BUT IF THEY JERK UP AND DOWN LIKE THAT TERRORIST
BITCH IN BELFAST
IT MIGHT WELL TAKE 15 SHOTS.
BUT I GOT HER IN THE END JUST LIKE I GET ALL THESE.
BEFORE I'M DONE, THEY'LL KNOW ABOUT ME, HERE
THERE EVERYWHERE
BEFORE I'M DONE, BEFORE I'M FINISHED, BEFORE I'M
FINISHED AND DONE.

And a scrawled PS in black felt-tip, obviously very recent.

<u>Memo for HQ Orderly Room.</u>
That Prodgy's a right little stunner.
Let me keep hold of her, just for a while. Please.

A heavy sea-fog rolled inland over the east coast of Yorkshire, about a week after the discoveries, cold, clammy, intensely penetrative. Chindit Hurn came out of the fog, a spectral apparition, bloodstained, mudstained, ragged, unshaven, famished; he still held his shotgun, his bag of cartridges hung from his shoulder; he was as dangerous as he ever was to 'Evil Incarnate,' whether in Belfast or in Basra or here on the outskirts of Bridlington. He lurched into a filling station, held up the staff and forced them to empty the till for him and put the money into a bag, also to put into the bag a batch of sandwiches and soft drinks from their snack counter, also to listen to him while he sang them a song. It was an ancient army ballad that had somehow survived into the 1980s to be chanted by a couple of tipsy old sweats in the canteen at Kirk Deerwood barracks. Hurn was no more than a pie-faced recruit when he heard it, and he'd forgotten nearly all the words. It went to an aggressive, trampling air, a sort of primitive 'Waltzing Matilda.'

> The drums they were roaring through the streets of Bridlington
> Who'll come a-fighting for Marlborough with me?
> Who'll come a-fighting,
> Who'll come a-fighting,
> Who'll come a-fighting – (etc.)

His memory dried up; he repeated "Who'll come a-fighting," over and over until the phrase was slipping sideways in his mouth. Then he swore at all the world in a burst of implacable fury, fired his gun into the shelves of bottles behind the snack counter and hurtled from the building. There was a car in the forecourt with keys in the dash – its owner stood petrified at a petrol pump – Hurn scrambled into it and was away out of town at insensate speed – one might have thought he had eyes that could see through the fog. But he hadn't. Fourteen miles to the south and a little to the east, he skidded smash into the rail of a bridge on a sharp bend. He went over into the Friarhouse Beck, seemingly little more than a land drain, but it carried the waters of the fen from Hangman's Mere to the North Sea and was deeper than one might think. When police and fire brigade were able to come up with him, they found him quite dead, battered and drowned all at once.

Someone in Serious Crime thought they ought to drag the mere and the neighbouring channels – just in case. They found what was left of two weighted bodies, probably female, which were certainly not prehistoric, but had been there for many months, or indeed years. They could not be identified and there was nothing to show how they'd died or who'd put them in the water or what had been done with their clothes. Nor was there anything to connect them with Hurn, except the location, and rumour.

And what about Anna? She stayed on in Hornsea and was given a job in Jack Heckstall's shop at the insistence of his kind-hearted wife, who did her best to help her to regularize her 'papers'. But when it appeared that Jack *fancied* his new assistant, indeed that he'd so far abandoned his intrinsic sense of propriety as to mount her from behind among the seed-sacks in his storeroom, Mrs Heckstall expelled her, quick sharp. The imprudent chit may then have gone back to Bulgaria, voluntarily or deported: certainly she was never seen again in Hornsea or Kirk Deerwood, or anywhere else in the region. Great pity, she was truly delightful, with not a jot of malice in her warm little body.

AFTERWORD

A few notes about the origins of these tales.

Part 1: Ireland.

Gallows came to me after I took part in a radio broadcast from RTE's Galway studio. There was something odd and out-of-this-world about the way I was expected to converse, from the isolation of an empty and windowless room, with an interviewer (whom I'd never met) in a similar room in Dublin, while our listeners would have had the impression that we were surely sitting across a table under the same roof looking into each other's faces. I felt nobody was altogether *in charge*. Supernatural possibilities seemed inherent in the situation.

I wrote *The Free Travel* after a perfectly dreadful experience with an ill-tempered bus driver in Limerick. I went so far as to complain to the Bus Éireann company: they said he was quite right to have tried to prevent waiting passengers getting onto the bus in a snowstorm; it was company policy. But he should not have been so rude and did I want them to take disciplinary action? I hastily told them, no; but I *would* like him notified of my complaint.

Molly Concannon & the Felonious Widow: two earlier stories about Ms Concannon were included in my previous collection, *The Stealing Steps* (Methuen, 2003). The ludicrous security and photo-opportunity brouhaha surrounding the arrival in Ireland of George W. Bush in 2004 seemed an open-and-shut occasion for Molly once again to obtrude herself. If the episode apparently echoes Ronald Reagan's Galway interlude* exactly twenty years earlier, that is because one unpopular visit did indeed echo the other. For some curious reason, the advisers of American presidents always seem to think that the Irish are a perennial soft touch and absurdly undiscriminating. This is a fallacy: the people have made very clear which transatlantic warlord they might wish to applaud, and why. Thus, Kennedy did well in Ireland, and so did Clinton: they showed what appeared to be a genuine concern for the sovereignty of the country and its future. Nor did they make it look as though they desired above all to see Ireland *warped* into their military labyrinth.

* as evoked in *Lizard Upon Two Legs*.

Part 2: London.

For the details of the Gunpowder Plot in *The Masque of Blackness* I relied upon Antonia Fraser's lively and sympathetic account of that horrid historical morass and of Ben Jonson's oblique involvement with it, a connection which had bothered me for at least thirty years. I vaguely but vividly remember how among some bookshelves somewhere in the mid-1970s I came across *Jonson's Romish Plot* by B. De Luna, a startling analysis of *Catiline* as a cloaked parallel to 1605. (Recent revelations from the Iraq war and from the north of Ireland may shed some modern light on the Jacobean mix of double-agents, provocative-agents, and 'helpful / unhelpful' intelligence.)

Dreadfully Attended. Browsing in a book about naval matters in the Galway public library, I read that John Masefield at the time of his death was making preparations to write an epic poem on the loss of HMS *Captain.* I have long been an admirer of Masefield's work, which I believe has been consistently underrated; I felt that if a tragic event had interested him so deeply, it would probably interest *me.* I had never heard of this disaster, so I made haste to look it up. I found that the *Captain,* an elaborately experimental man-of-war, proved so unstable that she sank on her maiden voyage. Nearly all of the crew were drowned, including the vessel's designer, Captain Cowper Coles RN, and the midshipman son of the First Sea Lord (appointed to the ship as an express demonstration of his father's faith in the designer's vision). The date was 1870. I had also been reading *The Dynamiter* by Robert Louis Stevenson and

Fanny de Grift Stevenson, which deals (in a fantastical fashion) with the Fenian bombing campaign of the 1880s in England. Again, I checked the history. Like the literary critic of *The Eatanswill Gazette*, I sought for a way to "combine my information."

Part 3: Yorkshire.

Lizard Upon Two Legs goes behind three of my stories in *The Stealing Steps,* to trace the beginnings of that "honest-to-goodness working journalist," Spike Oldroyd. And then I found that the equivocal Lee McStarna, having apparently survived his misadventure in Galway at the time of the Reagan visit, could not be kept out of *A Plot To Crack A Pisspot.* The latter tale might be seen as a semi-detached sort of sequel to *Lizard Upon Two Legs.* Spike Oldroyd gives way, as it were, to another honest-to-goodness Yorkshire entity, the Dryghtskerry Staithe Film Festival. I daresay some recollections of the stimulating (if occasionally envenomed) goings-on at the annual Galway Film Fleadh have contributed to my depiction of events beside the chill North Sea. Happily, I know of no Irish equivalent to Team Landmann and its enormities. (I should mention that *Secret Chats,* in *The Stealing Steps*, tells of a previous generation of the Pellinores of Dryghtskerry House.)

Yorkshire Pudding and *Yorkshire Sport* are recollections of my father's anecdotes of the East Riding, where he was born and reared, and where as a child I was often brought to stay. They are more or less true. By the same token, Kirk Deerwood is a bit like Beverley, but not quite. The other three 'Yorkshire-etc.' tales are my own invented fictions, although *Yorkshire Bluebeard* owes the notion of its titular personality to a letter by my partner Margaretta D'Arcy (on the far-from-fictional subject of violence against women) which appeared in *The Irish Times* in December 2006.

J.A., Galway, Ireland, 2009